The
A Life of Faith®
COLLECTION

What readers are saying...

Taylor, age 13

I have read all the Millie, Elsie, and the Violet books that have been released. I love to read and when I read these books it's like being in that time period. When I got the first Violet book I read it overnight! These books are so good, and when someone asks me what my favorite books are I say the *A Life of Faith* series!

Kelly, age 11

The Elsie books helped me get deeper in my faith, and helped me deal with everyday problems. I feel if I didn't have the books, I wouldn't be half as close to God.

Stephanie, age 14

It is very hard for me to have faith in God sometimes, but Millie's courage has helped me get through my bad times and turn them into good ones. She is definitely a role model for all girls, whether they be 4, 14, or 40! I can't wait to read the next book!

Ally, age 15

Violet is wonderful! I received books 1 & 2 for my birthday last week, and I can safely say that she is just as wonderful a heroine and role model as Elsie and Millie! She trusts God to take care of her and knows He's in control of every situation, no matter how complex.

Daizia, age 11

Laylie Colbert has touched my life in a way I cannot explain. A mixture of laughter and tears swept over me during her challenging yet exciting journey. I was not able to put this wonderful book down.

DEDICATION

This book is
dedicated to
the memory of
MARTHA FINLEY

*May the rich legacy of
pure and simple devotion to Christ
that she introduced through
Elsie Dinsmore in 1868
live on in our day and
in generations to come.*

Elsie's Endless Wait

BOOK ONE

of the
A Life of Faith:
Elsie Dinsmore
Series

Based on the beloved books by
Martha Finley

Mission City Press

Franklin, Tennessee

DINSMORE FAMILY TREE

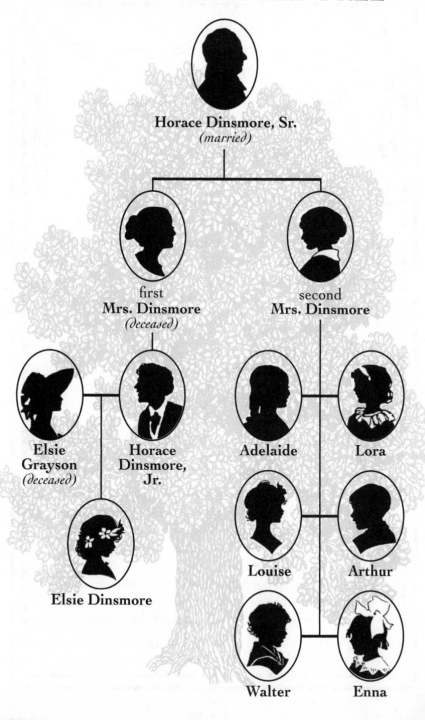

Horace Dinsmore, Sr.
(married)

first
Mrs. Dinsmore
(deceased)

second
Mrs. Dinsmore

Elsie
Grayson
(deceased)

Horace
Dinsmore,
Jr.

Adelaide

Lora

Elsie Dinsmore

Louise

Arthur

Walter

Enna

SETTING

$\mathscr{R}$oselands, a cotton plantation near a coastal city in the Old South during the early 1840s, some years prior to the American Civil War and the abolition of slavery.

CHARACTERS

∽ The Dinsmore Household ∽

Mr. Horace Dinsmore, Sr. — The owner and master of Roselands plantation; Elsie's grandfather.

Mrs. Dinsmore — Mr. Dinsmore's second wife and mother of six children:

Adelaide — Age 16	**Lora** — Age 14
Louise — Age 12	**Arthur** — Age 10
Walter — Age 8	**Enna** — Age 6

Mr. Horace Dinsmore, Jr. — Age 26: The only son of Horace Dinsmore, Sr., and his first wife, who died when Horace was a small boy. Once married to Elsie Grayson of New Orleans, Horace is a lawyer by training.

Elsie Dinsmore — Age 8: The daughter of Horace Dinsmore, Jr., and Elsie Grayson, who died shortly after Elsie's birth. Born in New Orleans, Elsie has lived at Roselands since she was four years old.

Miss Rose Allison — Age 17: Daughter of the Allisons of Philadelphia. She visits Roselands and becomes a close friend of Adelaide Dinsmore and Elsie.

Mrs. Murray — A Scots Presbyterian woman of deep Christian faith. Mrs. Murray was housekeeper to Elsie's guardian in New Orleans. She accompanied Elsie to Roselands but is now living in her native Scotland.

Miss Day — The children's teacher.

DINSMORE FAMILY TREE

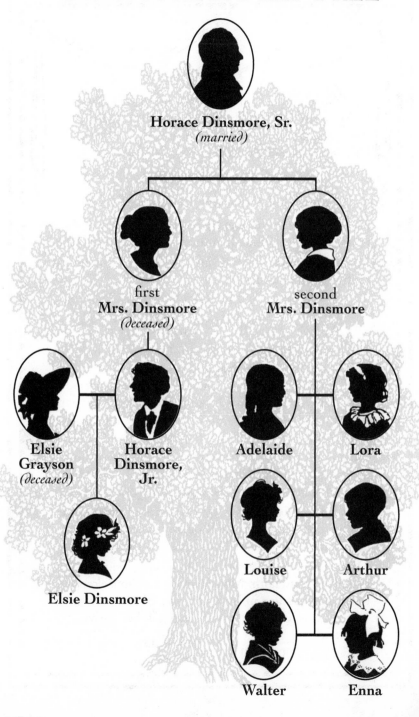

Horace Dinsmore, Sr.
(married)

first
Mrs. Dinsmore
(deceased)

second
Mrs. Dinsmore

Elsie
Grayson
(deceased)

Horace
Dinsmore,
Jr.

Adelaide

Lora

Elsie Dinsmore

Louise

Arthur

Walter

Enna

SETTING

*R*oselands, a cotton plantation near a coastal city in the Old South during the early 1840s, some years prior to the American Civil War and the abolition of slavery.

CHARACTERS

∽ The Dinsmore Household ∽

Mr. Horace Dinsmore, Sr. — The owner and master of Roselands plantation; Elsie's grandfather.

Mrs. Dinsmore — Mr. Dinsmore's second wife and mother of six children:

Adelaide — Age 16	**Lora** — Age 14
Louise — Age 12	**Arthur** — Age 10
Walter — Age 8	**Enna** — Age 6

Mr. Horace Dinsmore, Jr. — Age 26: The only son of Horace Dinsmore, Sr., and his first wife, who died when Horace was a small boy. Once married to Elsie Grayson of New Orleans, Horace is a lawyer by training.

Elsie Dinsmore — Age 8: The daughter of Horace Dinsmore, Jr., and Elsie Grayson, who died shortly after Elsie's birth. Born in New Orleans, Elsie has lived at Roselands since she was four years old.

Miss Rose Allison — Age 17: Daughter of the Allisons of Philadelphia. She visits Roselands and becomes a close friend of Adelaide Dinsmore and Elsie.

Mrs. Murray — A Scots Presbyterian woman of deep Christian faith. Mrs. Murray was housekeeper to Elsie's guardian in New Orleans. She accompanied Elsie to Roselands but is now living in her native Scotland.

Miss Day — The children's teacher.

Slaves of
Roselands Plantation

Aunt Chloe — The middle-aged nursemaid who has cared for Elsie since birth and taught her in the Christian faith.

Pompey — The chief house servant at Roselands and a special friend of Elsie's.

Jim — A young slave who works in the stables and frequently "babysits" the young Dinsmore children during their outings.

Aunt Phoebe — The Roselands cook and mother of Jim.

Ajax — An expert horseman and the Roselands carriage driver.

Fanny — A chambermaid.

The Travillas
of Ion Plantation

Edward Travilla — Owner of Ion and friend since boyhood of Horace Dinsmore, Jr.

Mrs. Travilla — Widowed mother of Edward, dedicated Christian, and caring friend to Elsie.

The Carringtons
of Ashlands Plantation

Mr. and Mrs. Carrington — Old friends of the Dinsmore family, owners of Ashlands plantation, and parents of five children including:

Lucy and Herbert — Age 8, twin sister and brother; Elsie's playmates.

— FOREWORD —

*I*n this book, the first of the *A Life of Faith: Elsie Dinsmore* Series, you are about to take a trip back in time and to revisit the enduring truths of Christian living. Your journey will begin more than 150 years ago in the American South, two decades before the War Between the States.

At the prosperous plantation of Roselands, you will meet a little girl named Elsie Dinsmore who has never known the love of a parent. You will share Elsie's trials as she deals with resentful and jealous family members, yearns to know and be loved by the father she has never seen, and struggles to find happiness in the face of rejection. From infancy, Elsie has been raised to follow the Bible in every way, including strict observation of the Sabbath, regular prayer and Bible studies, and willing obedience of Jesus' command to love and do good with no expectation of reward. But her unswerving dedication to her Christian principles often causes trouble in the Dinsmore household. With only her loving and faithful nursemaid to rely on, Elsie turns for comfort, guidance, and hope to her little Bible and to Jesus, her closest and truest friend.

Elsie is not perfect by any means, but once you know this extraordinary character, you will find it hard to forget her. So gentle in heart and spirit, yet so strong when the principles of her faith are challenged — Elsie is a nineteenth century child with the power to inspire and uplift people of any era.

7

Elsie's Endless Wait

Elsie Dinsmore made her first appearance in 1868, and her creator, Martha Finley (1828-1909), eventually wrote twenty-eight novels about the life and times of Elsie. For almost forty years, legions of dedicated readers eagerly welcomed each new Elsie book and treasured them for their enchanting central character and her pure and simple devotion to Christ. But with the arrival of the twentieth century, the popularity of the series faded, and Elsie was nearly forgotten. Now, almost a century after Miss Finley's death, interest in the adventures of her charming Christian heroine has been revived.

Mission City Press is very proud to continue Miss Finley's commitment to Christian faith and the Christian heart by re-introducing Elsie Dinsmore for a new generation and generations to come. It is our hope that you will not only enjoy every one of Elsie's adventures but will also find in them, as we have, a source of spiritual inspiration that is ageless.

This version is a careful adaptation of the *Elsie Dinsmore* series, faithful to the original yet rewritten for modern readers. Since every effort has been made to preserve the nineteenth century flavor of Miss Finley's original text, some terms and customs may require explanation and historical context. The following brief overview of some of the differences between Elsie's era and modern times will, it is hoped, add to the reader's appreciation of the story.

WELCOME TO ELSIE'S WORLD

In the 1830s, when Elsie was born, the family was the fundamental unit of society, just as it is now, but couples married at earlier ages and large families were common.

Foreword

Several generations often lived together, and members of a single household might include grandparents and great-grandparents, aunts, uncles, and cousins as well as immediate family. Children were expected to respect the full authority of their parents and to obey all their elders.

Life expectancy was much shorter than it is today. Because medical knowledge was limited and modern methods of treatment such as antibiotics had not been discovered, virtually every illness in a family was regarded as a serious threat. Childhood diseases that are easily prevented or cured today were especially feared by parents in the nineteenth century.

Apart from trains and steamboats, there were no motorized forms of transportation in Elsie's day, and few paved roads outside large cities. People depended on horses, carriages, and their own feet to take them from place to place. Schools were scarce in the rural South, and children were usually educated at home; wealthy families frequently employed live-in governesses to teach, although teenage boys were sometimes sent to boarding schools. Children learned many of their lessons by rote, or exact memorization, and perfection was expected in their oral recitations of these daily assignments. Even very young children memorized lengthy Biblical passages. This explains Elsie's ability to quote the Scriptures. The Bible was an important part of the total educational process in many families. It was used to teach spelling, grammar, and composition, as well as lessons in morality and proper conduct.

In the 1800s, people had no radios or televisions, no films or videos or audio recordings, no computers and no telephones. In this era, reading and letter-writing were the primary media for communicating news, entertainment, and learning. Letter-writing was considered an art,

newspapers flourished, and books were prized possessions even in the poorest homes. Visiting was also an
important means of bridging the great distances between
isolated farms and plantations. Wealthy homes were often
full of guests whose stays extended from overnight to
days, weeks, even months. In our story, friends and business associates join the Dinsmore family at mealtime, and
in the Old South (indeed, in many parts of the South
today), the main meal of the day, served at noon or one
o'clock, was called "dinner." The lighter evening meal was
"supper."

The Dinsmores are fortunate to live near a church
which they can attend each week. But in more remote
areas, Christian worship was observed at home, and families welcomed the occasional visit of clergymen, sometimes called "circuit riders," who traveled the countryside
on horseback. Plantation-owners were expected to attend
to the spiritual needs of their slaves and sometimes
employed clergy to conduct services.

At the time this book begins, slavery was an accepted
economic and social reality in the Antebellum South. Well-
to-do planters with large estates, such as the senior Mr.
Horace Dinsmore, "owned" many African-American slaves
who were regarded as private property. The workers who
plowed and planted and harvested the crops were the "field
slaves," while "house servants" tended to the needs of the
owner, his family, and the large plantation houses.

A master could do much as he pleased to discipline his
slaves and could sell his slaves at any time, often separating
families in the process. Although the planter's control was
nearly absolute, the law regulated the master-slave relationship to some extent. For example, it was illegal to teach

a slave to read and write, so the character of Aunt Chloe, who is Elsie's nursemaid, possesses a knowledge of Scripture learned by memorizing what she heard from Christian masters.

While many Southerners and Southern churches abhorred slavery and sought to abolish its practice, the right to own slaves was not officially ended in all the United States until the 1865 ratification of the Thirteenth Amendment to the Constitution.

Although Martha Finley wrote about the South, she never lived in the region or experienced slavery directly. She did, however, hold a firm belief in the importance of unity and equality among all people and all parts of her native land, and she wrote poignantly, in the preface to a later Elsie book, of "this great, grand, glorious old Union . . . . " She issued a plea to her readers and fellow countrymen to "forget all bitterness, and live henceforth in love, harmony, and mutual helpfulness."

CHAPTER

Trouble in the Schoolroom

*"It is better, if it is God's will,
to suffer for doing good
than for doing evil."*

1 PETER 3:17

Trouble in the Schoolroom

The schoolroom at Roselands was a very pleasant room. True, its ceiling was lower than in the rest of the large plantation house. But the schoolroom was in the wing built in the days before the Revolutionary War, while the main portion of the house was not more than thirty years old. The effect of the low ceiling was offset by tall windows that reached to the floor and opened onto a sunny veranda. The veranda overlooked a lovely flower garden, and the vista beyond offered shade trees, thick woods, and acre upon acre of farm fields. In this rich Southern earth, cotton was grown and picked to be shipped to mills in all parts of the world.

Roselands was the estate of Mr. Horace Dinsmore, Sr., and his house — surrounded by its many outbuildings, stables, gardens, orchards and, at a distance, the living quarters of the slaves — was the hub of all activity on the vast plantation.

On the warm, fall morning when this story begins, the activity in the Roselands schoolroom included lessons in history and geography, English literature and French grammar, arithmetic and penmanship. Six Dinsmore children of varying ages labored at their neat rosewood desks under the sharp eye and quick tongue of Miss Day, the governess.

Miss Day was giving a lesson to six-year-old Enna, the youngest of the group, and Miss Day's patience was wearing thin. The spoiled pet of both her father and her mother, Enna was a willful girl who often pushed her teacher to the limits.

Elsie's Endless Wait

"There!" exclaimed Miss Day as she shut the book and impatiently tossed it onto the desk. "I might as well try to teach old Bruno, for your dog would learn about as fast as you, Enna."

With a pout on her pretty face, Enna walked away, muttering under her breath that she would "tell Mamma."

Looking at her watch, Miss Day announced, "Young ladies and gentlemen, I will leave you to your studies for an hour. Then I will return to hear your recitations. Those of you who have done your work properly will be permitted to ride with me to the fair this afternoon."

"Oh, that will be jolly!" exclaimed Arthur, a bright ten-year-old with a love of mischief.

"Hush!" Miss Day said sternly. "I don't want to hear any more outbursts from you, Arthur. And remember, you won't go to the fair unless you have learned your lessons thoroughly."

Looking to Louise, who was twelve, and fourteen-year-old Lora, Miss Day instructed, "Girls, your French lessons must be perfect, and your English lessons as well."

Alone at a desk near one of the windows, a little girl of eight was bent over her slate and gave every appearance of industry. To her, Miss Day barked, "Elsie, every figure of that arithmetic problem must be correct, and your geography lesson must be recited perfectly, and you must write a page in your copybook without a single blot of ink."

"Yes, ma'am," the girl replied meekly. For an instant, Elsie raised her soft hazel eyes to her teacher, then immediately dropped her gaze back to the numbers chalked on her slate writing tablet.

Miss Day issued her final command to a shy boy of eight who was working quietly at his desk: "Walter, if you miss one word of your spelling, you will stay at home and learn the whole lesson again. And all of you are to remain in this room until I return."

"Unless Mamma interferes, as she's sure to do," Arthur said in a low voice as Miss Day's quick steps retreated down the hall.

For perhaps ten minutes, all was quiet in the schoolroom. Each child seemed absorbed in study until Arthur jumped up and threw his book across the room.

"I know my lessons," he exclaimed, "and even if I didn't, I wouldn't study another bit for old Day — or Night, either!"

"Do be quiet, Arthur," his sister Louise begged. "I can't study when you make so much racket."

Silenced, Arthur tiptoed across the room and crept up behind Elsie. Taking a feather from his pocket, he tickled it at the back of her neck. She jumped in surprise, then pleaded with Arthur to stop.

"But it pleases me to bother you," Arthur said, and he tickled her once more.

With all the persuasion she could muster, Elsie asked him again, "Please leave me alone, or I'll never get this problem done."

"All this time on one little problem?" Arthur replied with a sneering laugh. "You ought to be ashamed, Elsie Dinsmore. Why, I could have done it a half a dozen times before now."

"Well, I've been over it and over it," Elsie said sadly, "and there are still two numbers that won't come out right."

"How do you know they're not right, little miss?" Arthur asked, grabbing at her curls as he spoke.

Elsie's Endless Wait

"Please don't pull my hair!" she cried. Then she explained that she had the correct answer, so she knew that her answer was wrong.

"Then why not just write down the right numbers?" Arthur asked. "That's what I'd do."

"But that wouldn't be honest."

"Nonsense! Nobody will know if you cheat a little."

"It would be like telling a lie," Elsie said firmly, then sighed and put aside her slate. "But I'll never get it right with you bothering me."

Elsie tried to turn her attention to her geography book, but Arthur would not stop his persecutions. He tickled her, pulled at her hair, flipped the book out of her hands, and kept up his incessant chatter and questions. On the verge of tears, Elsie begged him once again to leave her to her lessons.

"Take your book out on the veranda, Elsie, and study there," said Louise. "I'll call you when Miss Day comes back."

But Elsie did not budge from her desk. "I can't go outside because Miss Day said we must stay in this room, so that would be disobeying," she explained with despair.

Giving up on the geography, she took her copybook and pen and ink from her desk. She dipped her pen into the ink and very carefully formed every letter on the clean, white paper. But Arthur stood over her as she wrote, criticizing every letter she made. At last, he jogged her elbow, and all the ink in her pen dropped onto the paper, making a large black blot.

It was too much, and Elsie burst into tears. "Now I won't get to ride to the fair! Miss Day will never let me go! And I wanted so much to see the beautiful flowers."

Trouble in the Schoolroom

Arthur, who was not always as hateful as he seemed, felt suddenly guilty about the mischief he had caused. "Never mind, Elsie. I can fix it," he said. "I'll just tear out this page with the ink stain, and you can start again on the next page. I won't bother you anymore, and I can help with your arithmetic problem, too."

Elsie smiled at him through her tears. "That's kind of you, Arthur, but I can't tear out the page or let you do my problem. That would be deceitful."

Arthur didn't expect his offer to be refused. He drew himself up and tossed his head. "Very well, little miss," he said with his usual smugness. "If you won't let me help, then it's your own fault if you have to stay home."

Louise was also astounded. "Elsie, I have no patience with you," the older girl exclaimed. "You always raise such ridiculous scruples. I won't pity you at all if you have to stay home."

Elsie said nothing. Brushing away her tears, she returned to her writing, and though she took great pains with every letter, she thought sadly, "It's no use. That ugly ink blot spoils it all."

When she finally finished the page, it looked very neat except for the blot. Then she returned to the arithmetic problem on her slate. Patiently, she went over every number, trying to find her mistake. But there was not enough time left, and she was so upset by Arthur's teasing that she couldn't concentrate on the work.

The hour was up, and Miss Day returned. Still, Elsie thought she might be able to complete her assignments, if only Miss Day would call on the other children first. Perhaps Arthur would explain about the ink blot, and everything would be alright after all.

Elsie's Endless Wait

As soon as the teacher had taken her seat, however, she called, "Elsie, come here. Bring your book and recite your geography lesson for me, and I want to see your copybook and your slate."

Although trembling with fear, Elsie recited quite well, for she had studied her geography before coming to the school-room that morning. But her recitation was not perfect, and with a frown, the teacher handed back the textbook. Miss Day was always more severe with Elsie than any of her other pupils — for reasons that will soon become clear.

Noting the two incorrect numbers in Elsie's arithmetic problem, Miss Day put down the girl's slate and opened the copybook. "You careless, disobedient child!" she shouted. "Didn't I tell you not to blot your book? There will be no ride for you today. You have failed in everything. Go back to your seat! Correct that problem and do the next one. Then write another page in your copybook. And mind, if there is a blot on the page, you will not get your dinner today!"

Arthur, who pretended to be studying at his desk, had watched Elsie throughout this scene, and his conscience clearly troubled him. But when Elsie looked at him imploringly as she returned to her desk, he turned his face away and whispered to himself, "It's her own fault. She wouldn't let me help, so it's her own fault."

Glancing up again, he saw that his sister Lora was staring at him, and her eyes blazed with scorn and contempt.

"Miss Day," Lora said indignantly, "since Arthur won't speak up, I have to tell you that it's all his fault that Elsie failed her lessons. She tried her very best, but he was teasing her constantly, and he also made her spill the ink on her copybook. She was too honorable to tear out the page or let him do her arithmetic, which he said he would do."

"Is this so, Arthur?" Miss Day demanded angrily.

The boy hung his head but didn't reply.

"Alright then," Miss Day said, "you will stay at home as well."

Lora was amazed. "Surely you won't punish Elsie now that I've told you it wasn't her fault."

Miss Day only turned her haughty gaze on Lora, and with ice in her voice, she said, "Understand this, Miss Lora. I will not be dictated to by any of my pupils."

Lora bit her lip, but she said nothing more.

As the other children recited their lessons, Elsie sat at her desk and struggled with the feelings of anger and indignation that were boiling inside her. Although she possessed a gentle and quiet spirit, Elsie was not perfect, and she often had to do fierce battle with her naturally quick temper. But because she seldom displayed her anger to others, it was commonly said within the family that Elsie had no spirit.

The other children had just finished their lessons when the door opened and a tall woman dressed in elegant riding clothes entered the schoolroom.

"Through yet, Miss Day?" Mrs. Dinsmore asked.

"Yes, madam, we are just done."

"Well, I hope your pupils have all done well and are ready to accompany us on the ride to the fair." Perhaps it was the sound of Elsie's sniffling that attracted Mrs. Dinsmore's attention at that moment. "What is the matter with Elsie?" she inquired of the teacher.

"She failed in all her lessons, and I've told her that she must stay home today," Miss Day replied, her anger rising again. "And since Miss Lora tells me that Arthur was partly to blame, I've forbidden him to come with us, too."

Elsie's Endless Wait

"Excuse me for correcting you," Lora said indignantly to her teacher. "I did not say 'partly,' because I'm sure it was *entirely* Arthur's fault."

Miss Day didn't have a chance to reply, as Mrs. Dinsmore addressed her daughter curtly, "Hush, Lora. How can you be sure of such a thing? Miss Day, I must beg you to excuse Arthur this time, for I have my heart set on his coming with us today. He's mischievous, I know, but he's just a child, and you shouldn't be too hard on him."

Miss Day's back stiffened, but she spoke with strained courtesy: "Very well, madam. You, of course, have the right to control your own children."

As Mrs. Dinsmore turned to leave, Lora spoke up again: "Mamma, won't Elsie be allowed to go?"

"Elsie is not my child, and I have nothing to say about it," Mrs. Dinsmore said with a condescending air. "Miss Day knows all the circumstances, and she is better able than I to decide whether Elsie deserves her punishment."

When her mother had gone, Lora turned to the teacher. "You will let Elsie go, won't you, Miss Day?"

Her anger now doubled by the insult from Mrs. Dinsmore, Miss Day replied, "I've already told you, Miss Lora, that I will not be dictated to. I've said that Elsie must stay at home, and I will not break my word."

"Why do you concern yourself with Elsie's troubles?" Louise whispered to her sister as Lora returned to her seat. "Elsie is so full of silly principles that I have no pity for her."

Meanwhile, Miss Day had crossed the room to stand over Elsie's desk. "Didn't I tell you to learn that lesson over?" the teacher asked. "Why are you sitting here doing nothing?"

Trouble in the Schoolroom

The little girl held her head in her hands as she fought to overcome her feelings. She didn't dare to speak because her anger might show in her words, so she brushed at her tears and opened her book. But Miss Day would not be satisfied. She was angry too, at Mrs. Dinsmore's interference and at the knowledge that she herself was acting unfairly. But Miss Day, unlike Elsie, could not keep her anger hidden. She was determined to vent her displeasure, and Elsie was, as usual, her innocent target.

"Why don't you speak?" Miss Day demanded, and she grabbed Elsie by the arm and shook the girl roughly. "Answer me this instant! Why have you been idling all morning, you lazy girl?"

"I haven't been idling," Elsie protested quickly. "I tried hard to do my work, and you're punishing me when I don't deserve it."

"How dare you? There!" Miss Day shouted, smacking Elsie hard on the ear. "Take that for your impertinence!"

Elsie wanted to shout her own harsh reply, but she restrained herself. Looking at her book, she tried to study, but her ear ached painfully and hot tears came so fast that she could not see the page.

It was at that moment that one of the house servants came to the door and announced that the carriage was ready, and Miss Day, followed by Lora, Louise, and the younger children, hurried from the schoolroom. Elsie, at last, was alone.

Putting aside her geography book, she opened her desk and took out her pocket Bible. The little book showed all the marks of frequent use. Elsie turned its pages deliberately and soon found the passage she sought. Fighting back her tears, she read to herself:

Elsie's Endless Wait

"'For it is commendable if a man bears up under the pain of unjust suffering because he is conscious of God. But how is it to your credit if you receive a beating for doing wrong and endure it? But if you suffer for doing good and you endure it, this is commendable before God. To this you were called, because Christ suffered for you, leaving you an example, that you should follow in His steps.'"

Now her tears came again. "I haven't done it," she sobbed, "I didn't endure it. I'm afraid I'm not following in His steps very well."

"My dear child, what is the matter?" asked a gentle voice, and a soft hand was laid on Elsie's shoulder.

The little girl looked up into the pleasant face of a young woman. "Miss Allison!" Elsie said in surprise. "I thought I was all alone."

"You were, my dear, till this moment," soothed Rose Allison, a recently arrived guest in the Dinsmore home. She drew up a chair and sat close beside Elsie. "I was on the veranda when I heard sobbing, and I came in to see if I could help. Won't you tell me the cause of your distress?"

The young woman's voice was full of kindness, but Elsie couldn't answer; her tears choked her and made speaking impossible.

So Rose went on, "I think I understand. Everyone has gone to the fair, and they've left you at home. Perhaps you have to memorize a lesson that you failed to recite."

The young woman's sweet voice and touch calmed Elsie a little, and she was able to answer, "Yes, ma'am, but being left is not the worst." Then her voice failed her again, and she could only point to the words she had been reading in her Bible.

With a fresh burst of tears, she sobbed out her misery. "I — I didn't do it! I didn't bear it patiently. They weren't fair, and I was punished when I wasn't to blame. Then I — I got angry. I'm afraid that I'll never be like Jesus. Never!"

Rose Allison, who had been at Roselands for just a few days, was extremely surprised by the child's great emotion. A devoted Christian herself, Rose was pained by the Dinsmore family's apparent disregard for the teachings of God's Word. She hadn't known the family before her visit, but her father was an old friend of Mr. Dinsmore's. As a kindness, Mr. Dinsmore had prevailed on Mr. Allison to allow Rose, who had been ill that year, to travel from her home in Philadelphia. She was spending the winter at Roselands where she could regain her strength in the warmth of the Southern climate. Although she was enjoying her visit and feeling much better, she had been struck by the family's lack of devotion. But until now, she had not spoken with Elsie.

Rose wrapped her arm around the child's waist. "My poor Elsie," she said. "That is your name, isn't it?"

"Yes, ma'am. Elsie Dinsmore."

"Well, Elsie, as you probably know, becoming like Jesus is the work of a lifetime, and we all stumble along the way. But Jesus understands, dear."

"Yes ma'am," Elsie said. "I know He does, but I'm so sorry that I've grieved Him and displeased Him. I do love Him, and I want so much to be like Him."

Rose stroked Elsie's hair and spoke tenderly, "But remember Elsie, God's love for us is *far* greater than we could ever imagine and it doesn't depend on our goodness, because none of us can be good enough on our own. It is

Elsie's Endless Wait

Jesus' righteousness that is credited to our account. You must have patience, little one. His Holy Spirit in you will bring about the purity of heart you desire."

Elsie was silent for a few moments as she thought about what the young woman had said. Then she brightened. "Thank you, Miss Allison," she said sincerely.

"And thank you, Elsie," Rose said with a little laugh, "for I'm very glad to find another person in this place who loves Jesus and is trying to do His will. I love Him too, so we will love each other."

Elsie was overjoyed. "Oh, I'm so glad," she said, "for no one loves me but my Aunt Chloe."

"Who is that?" Rose asked.

"My nursemaid," Elsie replied. "Aunt Chloe has always taken care of me. Have you seen her in the house?"

Rose considered. "Perhaps," she said thoughtfully. "I've met a number of nice servant women since I came here. But tell me, Elsie, who taught you about Jesus, and how long have you loved Him?"

"Ever since I can remember," Elsie said. "It was Aunt Chloe who told me how He suffered and died on the cross for us. She talked to me about Him just as soon as I was old enough to understand. Then she'd tell me about my own mother and how she loved Jesus and had gone to be with Him in heaven when I was just a week old. When my mother was dying, she put me into Chloe's arms and said, 'Take my dear baby and love her and care for her just as you did me. And be sure to teach her to love God.'"

Elsie drew from the bodice of her dress a gold chain from which hung a miniature portrait set in a golden locket. It was the picture of a beautiful young girl, no more than fifteen or sixteen years old. She had the same hazel eyes and brown curls that Elsie possessed, and the same regular features, fine complexion, and sweet smile.

"This is my mother," Elsie said softly as she placed the miniature in Rose's hand.

The young woman gazed at the portrait admiringly, then she turned to Elsie in puzzlement. "I don't understand," Rose said. "Are you not the sister of Enna and the other children? Is Mrs. Dinsmore not your mother?"

"She is their mother, but not mine," Elsie replied. "My father, Horace Dinsmore, Jr., is their brother, so all the other children are my aunts and uncles."

"Indeed," Rose mused. "And your father is away, isn't he?"

"Yes, ma'am. He's in Europe. He has been away since before I was born, and I've never seen him. Oh, I do wish he'd come home! I want to see him so much! Do you think he would love me, Miss Allison? Do you think he would put me on his knee and hug me the way Grandpa hugs Enna?"

"I'm sure he would, my dear. How could he help loving his own little girl?" said Rose, and she gently kissed Elsie's cheek.

Then she stood, picking up the little Bible and turning its pages. "I must go now and let you learn your lesson," she said. "But perhaps you'd like to come to my room in the mornings and evenings and read your Bible to me."

"Oh, yes, ma'am," Elsie exclaimed, and her eyes sparkled with delight. "I love reading the Bible best of anything! Aunt Chloe has always taught me that I must 'hide the Word in my heart.'"

"And have you memorized all of your verses by heart?" Rose inquired.

"Not all of them," Elsie said honestly. "But I've memorized many beautiful passages."

"Can you recite something for me?" Rose asked, for she could see that their discussion of God's Word greatly cheered the child.

Elsie thought for a few moments, then said: "Yes, ma'am. These verses from Colossians are some of my favorites." She quoted carefully: "'Therefore, as God's chosen people, holy and dearly loved, clothe yourselves with compassion, kindness, humility, gentleness and patience. Bear with each other and forgive whatever grievances you may have against one another. Forgive as the Lord forgave you. And over all these virtues put on love, which binds them all together in perfect unity.'"

"That is excellent, Elsie!" Rose said, smiling brightly. "And why do you like those verses?"

"Because they're so clear to me, Miss Allison. I sometimes have trouble understanding what I read in the Scriptures."

"Then perhaps I can help you. If you like, we can study God's Word together," Rose said.

"Oh, how kind you are," Elsie replied happily. "I would like that very much."

"Then please come and visit with me this evening," Rose said, and putting the little Bible into the child's hand, she kissed Elsie once again before she left.

Returning to her own room, Rose found Adelaide Dinsmore, the eldest of the Dinsmore daughters. Adelaide was nearly Rose's age, and the two young women had become friends. Now she was seated on the sofa and working busily on some embroidery.

"I'm glad to see that you're making yourself at home," Adelaide said as Rose entered. "Where have you been for so long?"

"I was in the schoolroom, talking with little Elsie. I thought she was your sister, but she tells me she is not."

"No, she's my brother Horace's child," Adelaide replied. "I thought you knew, but since you don't, I may as well tell you the whole story.

"Horace was a wild boy, pampered and spoiled and used to having his own way. When he was seventeen, he insisted on going to New Orleans to spend some time with a schoolmate. While he was there, he met a very beautiful girl and fell desperately in love with her. Her name was Elsie Grayson, and she was a year or two younger than he — an orphan and very wealthy. Horace knew that the families would object to their marrying because of their ages, so he persuaded the girl to elope and marry in secret. They had been married for several months before any of their friends suspected it."

Adelaide paused to thread a new strand of silk through her needle; then she continued her story: "When the news finally reached Papa, well, you can imagine how angry he was, and only in part because Horace and his bride were so young. You see, old Mr. Grayson was a tradesman and had made all his money in business, so my father didn't consider the daughter to be quite my brother's equal. Papa made Horace come home and then sent him away to college in the North. My brother studied law, and he's been traveling abroad ever since."

"But what about his wife?" Rose asked. "Elsie's mother?"

Elsie's Endless Wait

"I was just coming to her," said Adelaide. "Since her parents were dead, she had a guardian, and he was just as opposed to the marriage as Papa was. She was made to believe that Horace would never return to her. All his letters were intercepted, and finally she was told that he had died. As Aunt Chloe says, the girl 'grew thin and pale and weak and melancholy,' and she died when little Elsie wasn't quite a week old.

"We'd never met Horace's wife, and when she died, it seemed right that little Elsie stay on in the guardian's house. She was cared for by Aunt Chloe, who had been her mother's nursemaid, and by the housekeeper there, a Scotswoman named Mrs. Murray."

Adelaide looked up from her embroidery, and Rose could see that her face had become serious. "It was about four years ago that the guardian died," Adelaide continued, "and little Elsie, Aunt Chloe, and Mrs. Murray came to live with us. Horace never comes home, and he doesn't seem to care for his child. He never mentions her in his letters except in connection with business affairs. He's never even seen Elsie. Of course, I haven't spoken to my brother in many years, but I believe he must associate his child with the loss of his wife, for he did love Elsie's mother with all his heart. Perhaps that is the reason he has stayed away from his daughter."

"But she's such a dear little girl," Rose said. "I'm sure he'd love her if he could only meet her."

"Yes," Adelaide agreed, "she is dear enough, and I often feel sorry for her loneliness. When she came here, you see, she had never been around other children, and it has been difficult for her. I must admit that my brothers and sisters have not always been welcoming, but the truth is, I think we are all a little jealous of her. You've seen that she's very beautiful, and she is also heiress to an immense fortune. I have often heard Mamma fret that someday Elsie will quite eclipse my younger sisters."

Rose was confused by Adelaide's last statement. "Why would your mother feel jealous, " she asked, "when little Elsie is her own granddaughter?"

"But that's not the case," Adelaide explained, "for Horace is not my mother's son. His own mother died when he was quite young, and he was seven or eight when my mother married Papa, and" — she lowered her voice and her eyes — "I don't believe Mamma was ever very fond of him."

Both young women sat quietly for several minutes as Rose pondered this new information. "No wonder the little girl longs so for her father's love," she thought to herself, "and carries such grief for the mother she never knew." Adelaide's recounting of Elsie's lonely birth and her sad position among the Dinsmores perhaps explained, as well, the unusual maturity that Rose had sensed in the child. "God," Rose thought, "may be her only true friend."

At last Adelaide spoke again. "Elsie is an odd child, and I don't really understand her. She is so meek and patient that she will virtually allow the other children to trample her. Her meekness provokes my Papa, and he says she is no Dinsmore because she doesn't know how to stand up for herself. Yet Elsie does have a temper, I know. Ever so often it shows itself, but just for an instant. Then she grieves over it as if she had committed some crime, whereas the rest of us think nothing of getting angry a dozen times a day. And then she is always poring over that little Bible of hers, though what she finds so interesting I can't say. To me, it's the dullest of books."

"How strange," Rose said in surprise. "I'd rather give up all other books than the Bible. The Word of God is more precious to me than gold!"

Now it was Adelaide's turn to be astonished. "Do you *really* love the Bible so? Will you tell me why?"

"For its great and precious promises, Adelaide, and for its teachings about holy living. It offers inner peace and pardon from sin and eternal life," Rose said. "The Bible brings me the glad news of salvation offered as a free, unmerited gift. It tells me that Jesus died to save sinners such as me and that through Him, I am reconciled to God."

Adelaide could hear the deep emotion in her friend's voice as Rose went on, "I often find that my feelings and thoughts are not what they should be, and the blessed Bible tells me how my heart and mind can be renewed. When I find myself utterly unable to keep God's holy law, the Bible tells me of One who kept it for me, and who willingly suffered for my sins," Rose said with a solemn passion that made her seem much older than her seventeen years.

Both women sat silently for a time. Then Adelaide's face clouded, and she said a little sternly, "You talk as if you were a great sinner, Rose, but I don't believe it. It's only your humility that makes you think like that. Why, what have you ever done? If you were a thief or a murderer or guilty of some terrible crime, I could understand your saying such things about yourself. Excuse me for this, Rose, but your language seems absurd for a refined, intelligent, and amiable young lady."

Gently, Rose responded to her friend's complaint. "'Man looks at the outward appearance, but God looks at the heart,'" she quoted. Then she explained, "From my earliest existence, God has required the undivided love of my whole heart, soul, strength, and mind; yet until the last two years,

I was in rebellion against Him, not allowing Him to govern my life. For all my life, He has showered blessings on me. He has given me life and health, strength and friends — everything necessary for happiness. But I gave back nothing but ingratitude and rebellion. All that time I rejected His offers of pardon and reconciliation and resisted all the efforts of God's Holy Spirit to draw me to Him."

Rose's voice quivered, and her eyes brimmed with tears. "Can you not now see me as a sinner?"

Adelaide moved closer to her friend's side and put her arm around Rose's shoulders. "Don't think of these things, dear Rose," she gently admonished. "Religion is too gloomy for one as young as you."

"True religion is not gloomy at all," Rose answered, hugging Adelaide in return. "I never knew what true happiness was until I found Jesus. My sins often make me sad, but my faith in Him? Never."

CHAPTER

Someone To Talk To

"The purposes of a man's heart are deep waters, but a man of understanding draws them out."

PROVERBS 20:5

Someone To Talk To

When Rose Allison had left the schoolroom, Elsie got up from her desk and knelt down with her Bible before her. In her own simple words, she poured out her story to the dear Savior she loved so well, confessing that when she had done right and suffered for it, she had not endured the injustice. Earnestly, she prayed to be made like the meek and lowly Jesus, and as she prayed, her tears fell on the pages of her Bible. But when she stood again, Elsie's load of sorrow was gone, and as always, her heart was light with a sweet sense of peace and pardon.

She went back to her work with renewed diligence and faithfully completed all her assignments. When Miss Day returned from the fair, Elsie was able to recite her geography lesson without a single mistake. Her arithmetic problems were solved correctly, and the writing in her copybook was neat and careful.

But Miss Day, who had been in an ill-tempered mood all day, now seemed angry that Elsie did not give her another excuse for criticism. The governess handed the copybook back to the child and remarked sarcastically, "I see that you can do your duties well enough when you choose."

The injustice of Miss Day's words struck Elsie, and she wanted to protest that she had tried just as hard that morning. But she remembered her earlier, rash words and what they had cost her. Instead of defending herself, she meekly said, "I'm sorry I didn't do better this morning, though I really did try. I'm still more sorry for the disrespectful remark I made, and I ask your pardon."

"You ought to be sorry," replied Miss Day sharply, "and I hope you really are. You were very impertinent, and you deserved a more severe punishment than you received. Now go, and never let me hear anything like that from you again."

Elsie's eyes filled with tears again, but remembering how Jesus made no reply in the face of his accusers, she said nothing to Miss Day's hateful remarks. She simply put away her books and slate and left the schoolroom.

That evening, Rose was alone in her bedroom, thinking of her home and family so far away in the North, when she heard a gentle rapping at her door.

"Come in, darling," Rose greeted Elsie. "I'm so glad to see you."

Rose pointed to an ottoman, and Elsie, who had brought her little Bible, took her seat. "I may stay with you for half an hour; then Aunt Chloe is coming to put me to bed," she said.

Rose smiled. "It will be a pleasant half hour for us both."

Rose took her own Bible, and they read a chapter together, stopping now and then for Rose to give explanations. Then they knelt, and Rose offered a prayer for the teachings of the Spirit and for God's blessing on themselves and all their loved ones.

When they had risen, Rose folded the child in her arms and proclaimed gaily, "How I love you already, little Elsie. How glad I am that you love Jesus as I do and want to study His Word and pray."

"I'm not the only one," Elsie said with great seriousness. "Aunt Chloe loves Him too, very dearly."

"Then I must love her as well, for I have a special love for all who love my Savior."

With that, Rose sat down and put Elsie on her knee. Like old friends, they talked of the joys and challenges of Christian living and of the "race," as Paul the Apostle called it, that they were running and the "prize" they hoped to gain. They felt like pilgrims on the same path, and it was pleasant to walk awhile together.

A knock at the door interrupted their conversation, and a handsome, middle-aged black woman entered. She was extremely neat in her black dress, starched white apron, and turban-like headdress, and with a slight bow, she asked, "Is my little Elsie ready for bed now?"

"Yes, Aunt Chloe," said Elsie, running to her nursemaid's side, "but first I want to introduce you to Miss Allison."

Rose greeted her new guest warmly and took her hand. "How do you do, Aunt Chloe? I'm very glad to know you, since Elsie tells me you are a servant of the same Master I love and serve."

"Indeed I am, Miss Allison," Chloe said, grasping Rose's small hand in her two strong ones. "I love my precious Savior with all my heart."

"Then we are united through our faith in Him," Rose replied warmly. "For the Bible tells us that for all who love Him, there is neither Jew nor Greek, slave nor free, male nor female — we are all one in Christ."

Rose pressed Chloe's hands warmly, and between the two women — the one free and the other slave — the barriers of race and position melted away in the power of their shared faith.

Then reaching down, Chloe took Elsie's hand. "Good night now, Miss Allison. It's time I put this child to bed."

Elsie's Endless Wait

"Good night then, and please come again," Rose said. "And good night to you, little Elsie," she added, hugging the child again.

~~~

"What a blessed young lady," Chloe declared as she prepared Elsie for bedtime.

"Oh, Aunt Chloe, she's so good and kind, and she loves Jesus and loves to talk about Him," Elsie said happily.

"She reminds me of your mother, though she is not as beautiful. I think there never was a lady so beautiful as your mother."

Chloe brushed a tear from her eye as Elsie lifted the gold-framed miniature, which she wore day and night, and gave it a kiss. Then she slipped the chain inside her white nightdress. Chloe brushed back Elsie's hair and arranged the nightcap that protected Elsie's curls while she slept. "There now, darling," the nursemaid said, "you're ready for bed."

"Not quite yet, Aunt Chloe." Elsie knelt beside her bed and offered her evening prayer. Then she got her little Bible and began reading aloud from it as Chloe prepared herself for bed, removing her head scarf and replacing it with her own thick nightcap. Chloe, who was never willing to leave her charge for long, slept on a cot in one corner of the room.

When Elsie had finished her reading, she got into her bed, and Chloe tucked the covers securely around her.

"Please wake me early, Aunt Chloe, because I have a lesson to learn before breakfast."

"I will, darling," Chloe said as she snuffed out the light.

Someone To Talk To

Rose Allison was an early riser and always spent an hour or two reading before the family gathered for breakfast at eight o'clock. She had asked Elsie to join her at seven-thirty, and punctually at that time, she heard the child's gentle tap on her door.

Elsie, looking as bright as the morning, carried her Bible and a bouquet of fresh flowers, which she presented to Rose with a graceful curtsy.

"I gathered these for you because I know you love flowers," Elsie said.

"Thank you, darling. They're lovely," Rose said, rewarding Elsie with a hug. "Now we can have our time together before breakfast."

The half hour passed so quickly that both were surprised when the breakfast bell rang.

This was the first of many happy mornings for Elsie. Rose spent the fall and winter with the Dinsmores, and most mornings and evenings she and Elsie read and prayed together. Rose was often amazed at the depth of the little girl's faith in God and knowledge of divine things, but Elsie had received the best of teaching. Chloe, though not formally educated, was an earnest Christian, and she had, from the beginning, endeavored to teach Elsie about Jesus. For most of that time, Chloe had been assisted in her mission by Mrs. Murray, the Scottish Presbyterian woman who had accompanied them to Roselands. It had only been a few months before that Mrs. Murray had suddenly been summoned home to Scotland. An intelligent and pious woman, Mrs. Murray had carefully instructed Elsie, and her and

Elsie's Endless Wait

Chloe's efforts to bring Elsie to a saving knowledge of Christ had been blessed.

Young as Elsie was, she already had a well-developed Christian character. Though not remarkably precocious in other respects, she seemed to have very clear and correct views on her duty to God and her neighbor. She was truthful in both word and deed, very strict in her observation of the Sabbath — unlike the rest of the Dinsmore family — diligent in her studies, respectful to her elders, polite and kind to everyone. She was gentle, sweet-tempered, patient, and forgiving to a remarkable degree.

It was natural that Rose Allison should become strongly attached to Elsie and that the child would return this affection. Elsie felt deeply the lack of sympathy and love in the Dinsmore household, and before Rose came, she had only Chloe, who deeply loved the child.

True, Adelaide often treated Elsie affectionately, but they were far apart in age and Adelaide had little time to spend with her young niece. Lora, who had a strong sense of justice, occasionally intervened and took Elsie's side when she was unfairly accused. But none of the Dinsmores seemed to really care for her, and Elsie was often lonely and sad. Her grandfather, Horace Dinsmore, Sr., treated her with complete neglect and usually spoke of her as "old Grayson's grandchild." Mrs. Dinsmore genuinely disliked her, as the child of the stepson for whom she had no fondness and as a future rival to her own daughters. The younger children, following the example of their parents, usually neglected Elsie and sometimes mistreated her. Miss Day, knowing that there was no danger her employers would object, vented on Elsie the spite she dared not show her other pupils. Again and again, Elsie was made to give up her playthings to Enna, and sometimes to

Arthur and Walter. This treatment often caused Elsie to struggle with her temper; had she possessed less of a meek and gentle spirit, her life might have been wretched indeed.

But in spite of it all, Elsie was the happiest person in the family, for she had peace in her heart and felt the joy which the Savior gives to His own. She constantly took her sorrows and troubles to Him, and the coldness and neglect of the others only drove her closer to her Heavenly Friend. While she had His love, she could not be unhappy, and her trials seemed to make her naturally amiable character even more lovely.

Still, she thought constantly of her absent father, and she longed intensely for his return. Day and night, she dreamed that he had come home, had taken her to his heart and called her his "own precious child" and his "precious little Elsie," just as her grandfather often spoke to Enna. But from month to month, year to year, her father's return was delayed, and her heart grew weary with its almost hopeless waiting.

There were pleasant times, however, and on the morning of her first session with Rose, Elsie got an unexpected surprise. When she and Rose entered the breakfast room, Adelaide called them aside.

"Elsie," her aunt began, "the fair isn't over yet, you know, and Miss Allison and I plan to ride there this afternoon. If you are a good girl in school this morning, you may go with us."

Elsie eyes glowed with happiness, and she clapped her hands in delight. "Oh, thank you, Aunt Adelaide. How kind you are!"

Miss Day, who overheard Adelaide's promise, frowned. Her immediate instinct was to reprove Elsie for her noisy outburst, but the governess was somewhat awed by Adelaide, and so she said nothing.

Elsie's Endless Wait

At that moment Mrs. Dinsmore entered, and Elsie instantly fell silent. She could rarely utter a word in her step-grandmother's presence without being scolded and told that "children should be seen and not heard" — even though Mrs. Dinsmore's own children were always allowed to talk as much as they pleased. But the entire family was silent that morning. Miss Day seemed cross, and Mrs. Dinsmore, complaining of a headache, was moody and taciturn. Mr. Dinsmore retreated behind his newspaper and said nothing. So Elsie was relieved when the meal concluded. She hurried to the schoolroom and began her lessons before the other children arrived.

She had been working on her arithmetic problems for about a half hour when the door opened and, to Elsie's dismay, Arthur entered. The boy did not begin his usual teasing and tormenting, however. Instead, he sat at his desk and rested his head on his hand in a dejected manner. Naturally Elsie wondered what was bothering her uncle, and she stole glances at him every now and then. Finally, she asked, "What's the matter, Arthur?"

"Nothing," he said gruffly and then turned his back on her.

Elsie said no more and returned to her studies. By the time the school day began, Elsie was so thoroughly prepared that Miss Day had no excuse for finding fault. Elsie's lessons were all completed on schedule, and she joined Adelaide and Rose for the promised ride to the fair.

They returned to Roselands about an hour before supper, and with time to herself, Elsie decided to finish a drawing that she had left in her school desk. While she was getting it and hunting for a pencil, she heard voices coming from the veranda. She recognized them as Lora's and Arthur's, but she paid no attention to their conversation until her own name was mentioned.

"Elsie is the only person who can help you," Lora was saying.

"She has plenty of money, and you know that she is generous. But if I were you, I'd be ashamed to ask her, after the way you treated her yesterday."

"I wish I hadn't teased her," Arthur agreed, "but it's so much fun that I can't help myself."

"Well, I know that I wouldn't ask a favor of anybody whom I had treated so meanly," Lora said finally, and Elsie heard footsteps as the older girl walked away.

Elsie worked at her drawing, but her thoughts were of Arthur. What was it that he wanted? Was this an opportunity for her to return good for evil? She was hesitant to speak to him, but when she heard a deep sigh from the veranda, she left her drawing and went outside. Arthur was leaning against the railing; his head was bent and his eyes fixed on the ground. Without thinking, Elsie went to him, laid her hand on his shoulder, and asked if there was anything she could do to help.

"No — yes —" he answered haltingly. "I don't like to ask after — after —"

"Oh, never mind yesterday," Elsie said quickly. "I don't care about that now. I went to the fair today, and it was even better because I went with Aunt Adelaide and Miss Allison. So tell me what you want."

Encouraged, Arthur explained, "I saw a beautiful model of a ship when we were in the city yesterday, and I've set my heart on having it. It only costs five dollars, but my pocket money's all gone, and Papa won't give me a cent of allowance until next month. By that time, the ship will be gone because it's so beautiful someone is sure to buy it."

Elsie's Endless Wait

"Won't your mother buy it for you?" Elsie inquired.

"I asked, but she said she can't spare the money right now. It's so near the end of the month that we've all spent our allowances. Except Louise, but she says she won't lend money to a spendthrift like me."

Elsie took out her little purse and seemed ready to give it to Arthur. But she hesitated a moment, then returned it to her pocket. "Five dollars is a lot of money for a little girl like me," she said with a small smile. "I have to think about it, Arthur."

"I'm not asking you to *give* me money," Arthur contended. "I'll pay it back in two weeks."

Elsie only said, "Let me think about it until tomorrow morning," and she turned away from her disconsolate uncle. Arthur glanced at her retreating figure, and one angry word slipped from his lips: "Stingy."

But Elsie was still smiling as she ran down to the kitchen in search of Pompey, who was one of her special friends among the household servants. Finding him at last, she asked, "Pompey, are you going into the city tonight?"

"I am, Miss Elsie. I have some errands to do for Mrs. Dinsmore and the family, so I'll be leaving in about ten minutes. Is there something you want, eh?"

Elsie moved close and put her purse in Pompey's hand. Whispering, she told the old man about Arthur's wish and asked if he would take the money, and a half-dollar for his trouble, and purchase the coveted toy. And could he keep it secret from the others?

"I sure can do that," Pompey replied, a broad grin lighting his face. "I'll do this business just right for you."

When the supper bell rang, Elsie hurried to the dining room. Arthur sat across from her at the table, but when she smiled at him, he only averted his eyes, and his face darkened with an angry scowl.

When Elsie retired to her room after her evening hour with Rose, Chloe pointed to an item on the mantle. It was the model ship.

"Arthur was right," Elsie exclaimed with delight. "It's a beauty! He's going to be so pleased. Aunt Chloe, could you take it to the schoolroom and put it on Arthur's desk? And be sure no one sees you?"

"I can try, darling," Chloe said, carefully taking the beautifully crafted little boat into her hand.

"Wait a minute," Elsie said with excitement. She took a notecard from her table and wrote on it: "A present to Arthur, from his niece, Elsie."

"There," she said, placing the card on the deck of the little model. "Now please, Aunt Chloe, check the hallway to be sure no one is there."

Chloe opened the bedroom door, and with exaggerated caution, she looked up and down the empty hall. "Coast is clear," she said. "All the children are in bed, I expect." Then taking a candle in her other hand, she disappeared out the door. A few minutes later, she returned, assuring Elsie that the task had been completed and "nobody's the wiser."

Elsie went to bed very happy that night, anticipating Arthur's pleasure.

On her way to breakfast the next morning, she was surprised by two hands seizing her around the waist. It was Arthur, who had just run in from the garden.

"Thank you, Elsie! You really are a good girl," he said, a huge smile filling his face. "The ship sails so well. I've been trying her on the pond. But it mustn't be a present. You have to let me pay you back."

"No, that would spoil my fun," Elsie insisted. "It's a gift, and you're welcome to it. Besides, my allowance is so large that I usually have more money than I can spend."

"I wish that were my problem," Arthur laughed. Then his smile vanished, and he said gently, "I'm sorry I teased you, Elsie. I won't do it again soon."

Arthur kept his word, and for many weeks, Elsie was able to complete her lessons with no annoyance from him. Miss Day, however, was often unreasonable and demanding. Scarcely a day went by that Elsie wasn't expected to give up her toys or inconvenience herself just to please Enna or Walter or someone else in the family. But still, the entire winter was unusually happy; Rose Allison's love and constant kindness, and her ability to draw out the thoughts and feelings in Elsie's heart, warmed the little girl's life like sunshine. Besides, Elsie had learned how to yield readily to others, and when she experienced some unjust or unkind treatment, she would go to her Bible. Her communings with her beloved Savior made everything right again, and she would emerge as serenely happy as if nothing had happened. Her attitude bewildered the family. Her grandfather would sometimes contemplate her behavior when she graciously gave up her wishes to Enna. Then he'd shake his head and say to himself, "That girl's no Dinsmore, or she'd stand up for her rights better than that. She can't be Horace's child, for it never was easy to impose on him. He was a boy of spirit, not like this child."

Even Adelaide had remarked to Rose that Elsie was a "strange" child. "I'm often surprised to see how sweetly she gives in to all of us," Adelaide observed. "Really, she has a lovely temperament. I envy her, for it was always hard for me to give up my own way or forgive those who teased me."

"I don't think it has been easy for Elsie either," Rose said. "But the Bible tells us that it is to a person's glory to overlook an offense. I think her sweet disposition is the fruit of a work of grace in her heart. It is 'the unfading beauty of a gentle and quiet spirit' which God alone can bestow."

"I wish I had that," Adelaide sighed.

"You only have to go to the right source, dear Adelaide," Rose replied kindly.

"And yet," Adelaide went on, "I must say that sometimes I think, as Papa says, that there is something mean-spirited and cowardly in always giving up to others."

"It would be cowardly and wrong to give up *principle*," Rose said, "but surely it is noble and generous to give up our own wishes to another, when no principle is involved."

"Of course, you're right," Adelaide mused. "And now that I think of it, although Elsie gives in on her wishes readily enough, I've never known her to sacrifice principle. On the contrary, she has made Mamma very angry several times by refusing to play with Enna on the Sabbath or to lie to Papa about Arthur's misdeeds. Elsie is certainly very different from the rest of us, and if it's godliness that makes her what she is, then I think godliness is a lovely thing."

Elsie spent her mornings in the schoolroom, and in the afternoons, she walked or went riding, sometimes with her young aunts and uncles and sometimes with Jim, one of the younger slaves and an excellent horseman, who was assigned to watch over her on her rides. There was always company at Roselands in the evening, but she usually preferred sitting with Aunt Chloe by the fire in her bedroom to joining the guests in the parlor or playing with the other children in the sitting room or the playroom. When she had no lessons to learn, she often read aloud to Chloe, and the Bible was the book they both preferred. Sometimes Elsie would pull her little stool close by Chloe's side, put her head on the nursemaid's lap, and ask, "Please, Aunt Chloe, tell me about my mother."

Then, for the hundredth time or more, Chloe would recount the life and death of her "dear young mistress," as she called Elsie's mother. She would speak of the first Elsie's beauty, her goodness, and the sorrows she suffered during the last year of her short life. The story never lost its charms for little Elsie, and Chloe never tired of telling it. As Chloe spoke, Elsie would gaze at the miniature portrait of her mother, and when the story was finished, Elsie would say, "Now, tell me about Papa."

But about young Horace Dinsmore, Chloe had little information. She had known him only as a lively and handsome stranger whom she had seen occasionally during a few months and who had stolen the sunshine from her mistress, leaving her to die alone. Yet Chloe did not blame him when speaking to his child; her mistress had said that Horace did not desert her and their child of his own free choice. And even though Chloe could not believe him entirely blameless, she breathed no hint of her feeling to Elsie. Chloe was a sensible woman, and she knew that it would be hurtful to make her young charge think ill of her remaining parent.

Sometimes Elsie would ask if her Papa loved Jesus, and with a doubtful shake of her head, Chloe would say, "I don't know, darling, but I pray for him every day."

"So do I," Elsie would sigh. "How I wish he would come home."

Someone To Talk To

And thus the winter glided away, and spring came, and with it the time approached when Rose Allison was to return to her family in Philadelphia. Her departure was scheduled for the second of April, and it was now the last day of March. For a number of weeks, Elsie had devoted all her spare time to knitting a purse; she wanted to give Rose something made with her own hands because she knew Rose would prize such a gift more than something more costly.

Elsie was in her room with Chloe. She had been knitting, and suddenly she held up the purse. "See!" she exclaimed. "It's all done except for putting on the tassel. Isn't it pretty, Aunt Chloe? Do you think Miss Allison will be pleased?"

It was, Chloe agreed, a very pretty purse, beautifully knit in crimson and gold, and she was sure Miss Allison would be delighted. They were admiring the purse when Enna opened the door and came in. Although Elsie tried to conceal the purse in her pocket, it was too late. Enna had seen it, and she ran to Elsie, crying, "Just give that to me, Elsie!"

When Elsie refused, explaining that it was a gift for Miss Allison, Enna raised her voice even more and demanded, "Give it to me now, or I'll go and tell Mamma!"

"I'll let you hold it for a few moments, if you promise not to soil it," Elsie said gently. "And if you like, I'll get more silk and beads and make you a purse just like it. But I can't give it to you because then I wouldn't have time to make another one for Miss Allison."

But Enna was adamant: "I want that now, and I want it to keep!" She tried to snatch the purse from Elsie's hand, but Elsie held it up out of the screaming child's reach. Finally Enna gave up and ran crying from the room.

Elsie's Endless Wait

Chloe locked the door, remarking that it was a pity they had forgotten to lock it earlier. "I'm afraid Miss Enna will get her mother to make you give it up," she said sadly.

Elsie went back to her work, but her eyes were full of tears and her hands trembled with agitation.

Chloe's fears were well founded, of course, and it was not very long before they heard hasty steps in the hallway and the rattling of the doorknob. When the door refused to open, Mrs. Dinsmore's booming voice commanded, "Open this door immediately!"

Chloe looked at Elsie. Tearfully, the little girl slipped the purse into her pocket again and lifted her heart in a quick prayer for patience and meekness, for she knew she would need both.

Chloe slowly unlocked the door, and Mrs. Dinsmore entered, with a sobbing Enna hanging onto her hand. The woman's face was flushed a bright red, and she spoke angrily to Elsie. "What is the meaning of this, you little good-for-nothing? Why are you always tormenting my poor Enna? Where is the pitiful thing that this fuss is all about? Let me see it at once!"

Elsie took the purse from her pocket. Her voice trembled as she said, "It's the purse I was making for Miss Allison. I'll make one just like it for Enna, but I cannot give her this one."

"You *can* not? You *will* not is what you mean. But I say you *shall*, and I am mistress in this house. Give it to Enna this instant. I will not have her crying her eyes out just to humor you in your whims. There are plenty of more handsome purses in the city, and if you are too mean to give this one to Enna, then I will buy you another one tomorrow."

"But that wouldn't be my work," Elsie protested, still holding the purse to herself. "This is."

"Nonsense! What difference will it make to Rose anyway?" With those words, Mrs. Dinsmore grabbed the purse from Elsie and gave it to Enna. "There, my little one," she said in a cooing tone to her blubbering child. "It's yours now. Elsie is a naughty, mean, stingy girl, but she won't plague you when your mother is about."

Enna threw a look of spiteful triumph at Elsie and then ran from the room with her prize. Her mother followed, as Elsie collapsed on Chloe's lap and cried bitterly. Chloe had to call on all her faith in God to hold down the anger and indignation she felt. She let Elsie sob for a few minutes, soothing her only with silent caresses, and allowed her own fury to subside. Then she said, "Never mind, child. You just go into the city tomorrow and buy the prettiest purse you can find for Miss Allison."

But Elsie shook her head. "I wanted it to be my own work," she sobbed, "and now there's no time."

Chloe had a sudden thought. "I'll tell you what, pet. Remember the purse you were knitting for your father? The one Mrs. Dinsmore wouldn't send for you? Well, you can get that finished for Miss Allison, then knit another for your Papa before he comes home."

Elsie raised eyes full of relief, though they clouded almost at once. "But I don't have any beads to finish it, and Miss Rose leaves the day after tomorrow."

Chloe, however, would not be discouraged. "Pompey is going into the city this very afternoon," she said, "so we'll ask him to buy the beads. Then you can finish the purse by tomorrow evening and give it to Miss Allison before she leaves. It's going to be just fine."

Elsie's Endless Wait

"You're right, Aunt Chloe," Elsie said excitedly. "Thank you for thinking of it."

She went to her bureau and unlocked a drawer from which she carefully withdrew a purse of gold and blue beads — quite as handsome as the one taken from her — and she rolled it in a piece of tissue paper. She handed the small bundle to Chloe, who hurried away in search of Pompey. But Pompey informed her that with all his other errands, he wouldn't have time to attend to Elsie's needs. Chloe, who knew that Pompey was very fond of the child, believed him and didn't push the request. What could she do?

"I'll go myself, " she suddenly decided. "I'll ride with you, Pompey, and get the beads and silk myself."

She checked first that Elsie would not need her that afternoon, for Chloe was Elsie's servant only, with responsibilities for no one else in the family. Then she joined Pompey for the trip to the city. But it was late before they returned, and Elsie spent the evening alone in her room. She didn't even have her hour with Rose, who remained with the guests in the parlor that night.

At last, Chloe was back, with all the things Elsie needed. She wanted to begin her work immediately, but before she could start, a servant came to the door with a note. It was from Rose Allison.

"Dear Elsie," the note began. "I am very sorry that we cannot have our reading together this evening, but be sure to come early in the morning. It will be our last opportunity, for I have another disappointment for you. I had not expected to leave until the day after tomorrow, but I've just learned that the ship will sail a day sooner, and therefore I am obliged to begin my journey tomorrow. Your friend, Rose."

Elsie dropped the note on the floor and burst into tears. "Oh, no! Dear Miss Allison is going home tomorrow," she sobbed. But she soon stopped her crying, dried her tears, and gathered the items Chloe had brought from the city.

"I must finish the work tonight," she said firmly, and she set about her task. And though she did not sleep many hours that night, Elsie arrived at Rose's door at precisely seven-thirty the next morning.

Rose clasped the child in her arms as Elsie sobbed, "Dear, dear, Miss Rose, what shall I do without you?"

"You have a better Friend, Elsie, one who said 'I will never leave you nor forsake you,'" Rose whispered.

"And He is your friend, too," Elsie said as she wiped her tears. "Don't you think He will bring us together again some day?"

"I hope so indeed. And we must keep very close to Him, Elsie. We must commune with Him, and study His Word, and try always to do His will. If we have the assurance that our dear Friend is with us — that we have His presence and His love — we shall be supremely happy even though separated from our earthly friends. I know you have peculiar trials, little one, and you often feel the lack of sympathy and love here. But you will always find them in Jesus."

With this reassurance, Elsie and Rose shared their last morning of reading and prayer. Rose read the fourteenth chapter of John, a part of the Savior's touching farewell to His disciples. Then they knelt to pray, although Elsie's heart was so full that she could only listen.

"We will hope to meet again before very long," Rose said when her prayer was ended. "Who knows? Your father may come home and bring you to see me someday. He likes to travel, so it seems a good possibility."

Smiling now, Elsie said, "That would be wonderful!" Then she added, with a deep sigh, "But sometimes it seems that my Papa will never come home."

Cheerfully, Rose said, "Well, we can hope. And even though we must be separated for a time, we can still meet in spirit at the mercy-seat. Let's agree to do it every morning at this hour, shall we?"

The idea was a happy one for Elsie, and she eagerly assented.

"And I will write to you, dear," Rose continued. "I will write while I am traveling, if I can, so you will receive my letter a week from now. Then you must write to me. Will you?"

"If you won't care about my mistakes, Miss Rose," Elsie replied a little self-consciously. "I can't ask Miss Day to correct my letter because I don't want her to read it. But I will be so glad to get yours. I've never had a letter in my whole life."

"I won't care at all about mistakes," Rose assured, "and no one will see your letters except me. I don't want Miss Day reading them either."

Rose reached to hug Elsie once more, and the girl's hand went into her pocket, bringing out the finished gold and blue purse. "It's all my own work because I thought you would value it more," Elsie said shyly.

"And indeed I shall!" Rose said. "It's a beautiful purse in itself, but I will value it ten times more because it is your gift and the work of your hands." She hugged her little friend close, and Elsie, so unused to praise for her accomplishments, felt a kind of warmth she had hardly ever known.

They had only a few more minutes together, for immediately after breakfast, Rose's carriage arrived. The family,

who had all come to care for their visitor and would miss her presence in their house, gathered at the door to bid her farewell. One by one, they said their good-byes, and Elsie was the last. Rose kissed the child tenderly, and choking back her tears, she said, "God bless and keep you, my poor little darling, my dear little Elsie."

Elsie simply could not speak, and when the carriage had rolled out of sight, she ran to her room, locked the door, and cried out her grief. She had learned to love Rose completely and to depend on her new friend without reservation. Parting, with no certainty of ever meeting again, was one of the hardest trials the child had ever endured.

CHAPTER

3

An Unexpected Homecoming

"Hope deferred makes the heart sick, but a longing fulfilled is a tree of life."

Proverbs 13:12

An Unexpected Homecoming

It had been a week since Rose Allison's departure — a lonely week for Elsie — and at the breakfast table, Adelaide voiced the little girl's own thoughts. "I think we ought to hear from Rose soon," Adelaide said. "She promised to write during her journey."

Almost in answer to her words, Pompey entered the room, carrying the mail bag which he brought from the city every morning. He handed the bag to Mr. Dinsmore as Mrs. Dinsmore remarked, with some irritation, "You're late this morning, Pompey."

"Yes, ma'am," replied the old servant, smiling sweetly. "The horses were very lazy today. I expect they have spring fever."

"Do hurry, Papa," Adelaide said impatiently, "and see if there isn't something from Rose."

"Have patience, young lady," her father replied as he opened the bag and very deliberately adjusted his spectacles before sorting through the family's letters. "Yes, there is a letter here for you, and one for Elsie, too."

He tossed the letters across the table, and Elsie, being excused, eagerly grabbed hers and ran up to her room. It was like a feast for her — the first letter she had ever received — and from such a dear friend. For the moment at least, it gave her almost as much pleasure as Rose's presence would have.

Elsie had just finished reading the letter through and was beginning to read it again when she heard Adelaide calling. The next moment, her aunt entered the room.

"I suppose you've read your letter," Adelaide said, and a strange smile played on her mouth, "but now I have another piece of news for you. Can you guess it?"

Elsie's Endless Wait

"Is Miss Rose coming back?" Elsie ventured hopefully.

"What a silly guess," Adelaide said. "No, little Elsie, it's even more exciting. My brother — your Papa Horace — has actually sailed for America and is coming directly home."

Elsie jumped up, and her heart beat wildly. "Is it really true, Aunt Adelaide?" she asked. "Is he really coming? Will he be here soon?"

"He has really started at last," Adelaide assured, "but I don't know how soon he will be here." As she turned to leave, she added, "I've told you all that I know for the moment."

Elsie clapped her hands together and dropped down onto the sofa. The letter from Rose, so highly prized a few moments before, drifted unnoticed to the floor. The child's thoughts were now far away, imagining the father she didn't know as he crossed the ocean for home. She tried to picture how he would look, how he would speak, and how he would feel about her.

"Oh, will he love me?" she asked herself aloud. "Will he let me love him? Will he take me in his arms and call me his own darling child?"

But there was no one to answer her anxious questions. She would just have to wait and let the slow wheel of time turn until her father's longed-for, and somehow frightful, arrival.

In the schoolroom, Elsie recited her lessons indifferently until Miss Day sternly remarked that receiving letters did not seem to agree with her pupil. Elsie must do better, Miss Day said, if she wished to please her Papa when he came. For once, Miss Day's observation struck just the right chord; Elsie was extremely anxious to please her father and to gain his affection and approval. She turned her whole attention to her studies with such determination that Miss Day could find no more cause for complaint.

But what, indeed, did the father expect of his daughter? Horace Dinsmore, Jr., was, like his father, an upright and moral man who paid outward respect to the forms of religion but cared nothing for the vital power of godliness. Horace trusted his own morality entirely, and he regarded most Christians as hypocrites and deceivers. He had been told of his little Elsie's Christian devotion, and though he didn't acknowledge it even to himself, this information had prejudiced him against his child.

Also, like all the Dinsmores, he had a great deal of family pride. Although his wife's father, Mr. Grayson, had been a man of sterling worth — intelligent, honest, pious, and very wealthy at his death — he had begun life as a poor boy and made his fortune in business. For this reason, all the Dinsmores spoke of Horace's marriage to his beautiful heiress as a step down. Even Horace himself had come to regard his marriage as a boyish folly of which he was now ashamed. So often in his letters had Mr. Dinsmore referred to Elsie as "old Grayson's grandchild" that Horace had come to think of her as a kind of disgrace, especially because she was always described to him as disagreeable and troublesome.

Horace had loved his young wife with genuine passion and mourned her death bitterly. But distance and the passage of so much time had dimmed his memory of her, and he seldom thought of her now except in connection with the child, the child for whom, in his secret heart, he harbored a feeling of dislike.

At Roselands, scarcely anything was spoken or thought about outside of Horace's anticipated return, and for Elsie especially, the time crawled by. At last a letter came from Horace saying that he would arrive the next day.

"Oh, Aunt Chloe," said Elsie, jumping up and down and clapping her hands at the news. "Just think! Papa will be here tomorrow morning."

Then her wild delight turned sober, and concern clouded her face as the torturing question came again into her mind: *Will he love me?* She stood still now, as Chloe changed her from a riding outfit to a dress and smoothed her curls. Looking into the somber little face, Chloe couldn't resist hugging her little charge and pressing a gentle kiss on her brow.

It was at this moment that an unusual sense of activity seemed to fill the house. Elsie jumped, and the color rushed to her face as she listened intently. She heard the sound of running feet in the hall, and suddenly her door was flung open. "He's here!" Walter shouted as he grabbed her hand and pulled her from the room and down the stairs. But as they approached the parlor door, Elsie begged Walter to stop. She leaned against the wall, and her heart beat so fast she could scarcely breathe. This was the moment she had prayed for; yet she was unprepared and filled with fears she could not comprehend.

"Are you sick?" Walter asked, but not waiting for a reply, he pushed the door open and dragged her inside. Elsie was so overwrought that she almost fainted. The room seemed to spin, and for an instant, she hardly knew where she was.

Then a strange voice asked, "And who is this?" She looked up and saw a man — very handsome and youthful looking, in spite of his heavy, dark beard and mustache.

"Is this great girl *my* child?" Horace asked. "Why it's enough to make a man feel old." Then he took her hand, stooped, and kissed her coldly on the lips.

Elsie was shaking violently, and the power of her feelings made her incapable of speech. Her hand, still in his, was cold and clammy.

Horace searched her face, then dropped her hand. "I'm not an ogre," he said in a voice that betrayed his annoyance. "You need not be afraid of me. Alright, you may go. I won't keep you in terror any longer."

Dismissed, Elsie could only run back to her room where she fell onto the bed and wept as she never had before. For as long as she could remember, she had longed for this hour, yet the disappointment was so deep that it seemed her heart would break. Not even Chloe — who was in the kitchen, rejoicing in the assumption that her young charge was supremely happy at this moment — was there to offer comfort. Alone, Elsie wept as if she might weep her life away.

"Oh, Papa! Papa! You don't love me! Oh, Mamma, I wish I could be with you. There's no one here to love me, and I'm so lonely!"

This was how Chloe found her an hour later, still sobbing out her broken cries of anguish. Chloe understood at once how her child was suffering. She raised Elsie in her arms and cradled her feverish head, smoothing back the tear-sodden curls and bathing the child's swollen eyes and throbbing temples.

"My poor baby," she soothed. "You know your Aunt Chloe loves you better than life. And did you forget your Almighty Friend who loves you and says 'I will never leave you nor forsake you'? He sticks to us 'closer than a brother,' my precious child. Jesus' love is better than any other love, and I know you have His love."

"Then ask Him to take me to Himself, and to Mamma. I'm so lonely, and I want to die!"

"Hush, darling, hush now. I could never ask that. It would break my heart. You mean the world to me, and you know we must all wait for the Lord's time."

"Then ask Him to help me be patient," Elsie begged. "And ask Him to make my father love me."

"I will, darling, I will," Chloe said through her own tears. "And don't you be discouraged right away. I'm sure your Papa will love you once he comes to know you."

That evening, when the family gathered for supper, there was an empty chair at the table, and Adelaide sent one of the servants to find Elsie. When the woman returned, it was with the news that Elsie had a bad headache and didn't want to eat. Horace overheard the message, and he asked his sister, "Is she subject to such attacks? I hope she isn't a sickly child."

"Not really," Adelaide replied dryly. She had observed Horace's meeting with his child, and she felt really sorry for Elsie's evident disappointment. "I imagine that excessive crying has brought this on."

Horace flushed deeply, and in a caustic tone that betrayed his displeasure, he said, "So the return of a parent is a cause for grief, is it? I didn't expect my presence to be so distressing for my only child. I had no idea she disliked me so."

"She doesn't," Adelaide said, her own temper rising. "She has been looking forward to your return for as long as I've known her."

"That's hard to believe," Horace retorted, "given her conduct toward me today."

Adelaide could see that Horace was determined to misconstrue Elsie's behavior. She was afraid that any defense of the child would only increase his sour mood, so she said no more.

Upstairs in her bedroom, Elsie finally fell asleep, but not before she had turned in her sadness to Him who said, "I have loved you with an everlasting love." At least she had the sweet assurance of His love and favor.

The next morning Elsie came to breakfast in a state of hope and fear; she wanted, yet dreaded, meeting her father. But when she entered the dining room, he was not there.

"Your Papa isn't coming down this morning," Adelaide told her kindly. "He is very tired from his long journey. I'm sorry, but you may not see him at all today, for we expect a good deal of company this afternoon and tonight."

Disappointed once again, Elsie found it impossible to concentrate on her lessons. Every time the door opened, she jumped nervously and looked up, hoping it was her father. But Horace did not come to her, and that evening, the children were sent to dine in the playroom because there were so many guests for supper. Just as Adelaide had predicted, Elsie didn't see her father at all that day.

The next morning, however, the children were to breakfast with the adults because all the guests, except one gentleman, had departed. Elsie went early into the breakfast room, and to her surprise, she found her father alone, reading the morning newspaper.

He looked up, and she said in a trembling voice, "Good morning, Papa." The greeting made Horace start, for he had never before been addressed as "Papa," and it sounded strange to his ears. He regarded his child with curiosity and almost reached out to her. But instead of extending his hand, he simply said, "Good morning, Elsie," and returned to his paper.

Elsie remained in the middle of the room; she didn't dare to approach him, however much she wanted to. While she stood there, not knowing what to do, the door swung open, and Enna, looking rosy and happy, ran in and rushed to her brother. She climbed on his knee, put her chubby arms around his neck, and pleaded for a kiss.

"You shall have it, little pet," Horace laughed. Tossing down his paper, he hugged Enna warmly. "*You* are not afraid of me, are you?" he asked playfully, and added pointedly, "or sorry that I have come home?"

"No, indeed," Enna said.

Horace glanced at Elsie to see her reaction. Her eyes had filled with tears, and she could not stop herself thinking that Enna had taken her place and was receiving the love that should be hers. Horace read her reaction correctly, although he misunderstood its source. "She's jealous," he thought. "I cannot tolerate jealous people." He gave her a look that clearly displayed his displeasure, and Elsie, cut to the quick, had to leave the room to hide her tears.

"I am envious," she thought. "I'm jealous of Enna. Oh, how awful of me!" Silently she prayed, "Dear Savior, help me! Take away these terrible feelings."

An Unexpected Homecoming

Despite her youth, Elsie was beginning to learn how to control her own emotions, and in a few moments, she had recovered her composure so that she could return to the breakfast room and take her place at the table. Her sweet face was sad indeed and showed the traces of tears, but it was also calm and peaceful.

Her father took no notice of her, and she didn't trust herself to look at him. The servants filled her plate, and she ate in silence. To her great relief, the others were too busy talking and eating to pay attention to her, and she failed to see how often the visitor who was seated nearly opposite her fixed his eyes on her pale face.

When she had left the room, the visitor asked, "Is that one of your sisters, Horace?"

"No," said Horace, flushing slightly. "She is my daughter."

"Ah! I'd almost forgotten that you have a child," the man said. "Well, you have no reason to be ashamed of her. She is perfectly lovely. Sweetest little face I ever saw."

Anxious to change the subject, Horace suggested to his friend that they call for their horses and take a ride around the property. The subject of Elsie was dropped, and the two men left together.

Several hours later, Elsie was practicing at the piano in the music room when she felt suddenly that she was not alone. Turning around, she recognized her father's friend as Edward Travilla, the owner of a neighboring plantation.

"Excuse me for interrupting," he said and bowed politely. "I heard the sound of the piano. I am very fond of music, so I ventured in."

Elsie was timid with outsiders, but she was also very polite, so she welcomed the guest. "Won't you take a seat, sir? I'm afraid my music won't give you any pleasure. I'm only learning and cannot play very well yet."

Edward thanked her and took a seat near her side. "Will you do me a favor and repeat the song I heard you singing a few minutes ago?"

Though her cheeks were burning and her voice trembled at first, Elsie complied, and as she proceeded, her voice grew strong and steady. She had quite a nice voice for a girl her age, and she also had musical talent, which had been well cultivated by good teachers and diligent practice. Her music was simple, but her performance was very good.

Edward thanked her heartily and complimented both her playing and her singing. Then he asked for another song and another, and they chatted genially until Elsie lost all sense of embarrassment,

"I think your name is Elsie, isn't it?" Edward asked.

"Yes, sir. Elsie Dinsmore."

"And you are the daughter of my friend Horace Dinsmore?"

"Yes, sir."

"Your father has been gone for a long time, so I suppose you must have forgotten him."

"Oh, no, sir. I couldn't have forgotten him because I'd never seen him."

"Indeed," Edward remarked in surprise. "Then, since he is a stranger to you, I suppose you can't have much affection for him."

Elsie looked into his face, her hazel eyes very round, and said with astonishment, "Not love Papa? My own Papa who has no other child but me? Oh, Mr. Travilla, how could you think that?"

An Unexpected Homecoming

"I see I was mistaken," he said with a smile. "I see you care very much for your Papa. But do you think he loves you?"

To the gentleman's great dismay, Elsie dropped her face into her hands and burst into a torrent of tears. Trying to comfort her as best he could, Edward patted her quaking shoulder and said, "My poor child, forgive me. I am very, very sorry for my silly question. But trust me, dear girl, that whether your father loves you now or not, I know he will quite soon."

When Elsie had dried her tears and closed the piano, Edward invited her to take a little walk with him in the garden. He felt very sorry for the pain his thoughtless remark had inflicted, and the little girl interested him, so he did his best to entertain her as they walked. He talked to her about the plants and flowers. He told her about the foreign lands he had visited, and he related stories of his travels, deliberately choosing incidents in which her father had also played a part.

He discovered that Elsie was far from a dull companion. With a natural love of reading and ready access to her grandfather's well-stocked library, Elsie had read more books, and with more thought, than most children her age. The intelligence of her questions and conversation surprised and pleased Edward Travilla.

When the dinner bell rang, he escorted Elsie to the table and seated her at his side. Never was any great lady more carefully waited on than was Elsie at this meal. There were several more gentleman guests present who attended to the older women, so Edward felt at liberty to devote his attention to Elsie, talking to her — and making her talk.

Now and then, Elsie stole a glance at Mrs. Dinsmore, and to her great relief, the woman was too occupied to notice her. Once Elsie glanced at her father, and when their eyes met, his held an expression that was both curious and amused — a look she could not interpret. But since she saw no displeasure there, her heart grew light and her face glowed with happiness.

Later, in the drawing room, as Horace and his old friend talked alone, Edward said, "Really, Horace, your daughter is remarkably intelligent, as well as remarkably pretty. And I've discovered that she has a good deal of musical talent."

"Has she?" Horace replied. "Perhaps it's a pity she doesn't belong to you, my friend, instead of me, for you seem to appreciate her so much more highly."

"I wish she did," Edward said. "But seriously, Horace, you ought to love that child. She certainly loves you devotedly."

Surprised by his friend's assessment, Horace asked, "How do you know?"

"It was clear from what I saw and heard this morning. Horace, she would value a kind word from you more than the richest jewel."

"I doubt that," Horace said, but there was a hint of a question in his words. He turned to the window, and suddenly, without explanation to his friend, he left the room, for he had seen Elsie come out onto the portico. She was dressed in her riding clothes, and Jim, who usually accompanied her when she rode by herself, was bringing up her horse.

Horace approached his daughter and asked, "Are you going for a ride, Elsie?"

"Yes, Papa," she said and looked shyly into his face.

Horace leaned down and lifted her into his arms. Then he placed her in the saddle, saying to the boy, "Now, Jim, you must take good care of my little girl."

An Unexpected Homecoming

This time, the tears that came to Elsie's eyes were for joy. "He called me *his* little girl," she murmured to herself as she rode away, "and he told Jim to take good care of me. I'm sure he will love me soon, just as Mr. Travilla said he would."

From the portico, Horace watched his daughter as she rode down the long avenue that led from the house. He didn't notice Edward Travilla, who had come out to join him.

"How well she sits her horse," Edward said.

"Yes, she does," Horace replied in an absent way. He was thinking of a time some eight or nine years before when he had assisted another Elsie to mount her horse and had ridden for hours at her side. For the rest of that afternoon, memories came flooding into his mind, and in his heart, a feeling of tenderness began to grow for the child of the wife who had been so dear to him. When he saw little Elsie returning up the driveway, he hurried outside again, lifted her from the horse, and asked if she had enjoyed her ride.

"Oh, yes, Papa. It was very pleasant."

He looked into her beaming face, and without thinking, he kissed his child warmly. "I think I will ride with you one of these days," he said. "Would you like that?"

"Oh, very much, Papa. So very much."

Horace smiled at his daughter's earnestness and watched her as she raced away to her room to change her clothes and tell Chloe of her happiness.

Alas, the moment was like a transient gleam of sunshine that lighted her path briefly, then disappeared behind gathering clouds.

Elsie's Endless Wait

More company came to Roselands, and the drawing room was filled with guests that evening. Though Elsie was there, her father was too busy with his guests to give her even a glance. She sat alone and unnoticed in a corner and watched her father's every move. Her ears strained to catch his words. Then Edward Travilla, who had been talking with a group on the opposite side of the room, disengaged himself and came toward Elsie. Taking her hand, he led her to the center table where a pleasant-looking, elderly lady was examining some engravings that Horace had brought home from Europe.

"Mother," said Edward, "this is my friend Elsie."

"I am so glad to see you, my dear," the lady said, giving Elsie a kiss.

Edward set a chair for Elsie close to his mother, and he sat on the child's other side. He began to explain the engravings, and since he attached a clever anecdote to each, Elsie was thoroughly entertained and quite forgot to look for her father.

Suddenly, Edward laid down the engraving he was describing and said, "Miss Elsie, I want my mother to hear you play and sing. Will you do me the favor of repeating the song I admired so much this morning?"

Elsie blushed brightly and exclaimed, "I couldn't play or sing for so many people, Mr. Travilla. Please excuse me."

But from behind her, Horace's voice commanded, "Go immediately, and do as the gentleman requests."

His voice was stern, and Elsie saw that his face was even more so. Trembling, she rose to obey, but Edward, who could see her distress, said kindly, "Never mind, Miss Elsie. I withdraw my request."

"But I do not withdraw my command," her father said. "Go at once, Elsie, and do as I say."

She went, and Edward, silently scolding himself for causing her trouble, placed her sheet of music on the piano and whispered encouragingly in her ear, "Have confidence in yourself, Miss Elsie. That is all that is necessary for your success."

But Elsie was shattered by her father's attitude, and she could not control the tears that welled in her eyes. She could barely see the notes and words, and she blundered badly as she attempted to play the prelude. Her mistakes only increased her misery and embarrassment.

"Never mind the prelude," Edward said in an effort to help. "You can just begin the song."

But it was no use. Before she could get through the first verse, she broke into tears. Her father, looking mortified, came up behind her and spoke in low, hard tones, "Elsie, I am ashamed of you. Go to your room and to bed immediately."

Again she obeyed, and again, she cried herself to sleep.

The next morning, Elsie learned that Edward Travilla and his mother had returned to their home. Elsie was very sorry that she hadn't said good-bye to her new friends, and for the next few days, her sorrow increased, for her father's cold manner had returned. He scarcely ever spoke to her, and to make matters worse, her young aunts and uncles ridiculed her for the failed attempt to play at the party.

Even Miss Day, who seemed unusually cross, taunted her. Elsie tried to pay attention to her lessons, but she was so troubled and depressed that she failed repeatedly and was in constant disgrace with Miss Day, who threatened to go to her father. When Miss Day saw how this threat terrified Elsie, the governess used it all the more.

But what chiefly occupied Elsie's thoughts was how to gain her father's love. She tried every way she could to win his affection. She cheerfully obeyed his every order and tried to anticipate and fulfill his wishes. But he seldom seemed to notice her except for commands and rebukes, while he lavished attention on his sister Enna. Elsie could only watch them in silence until her feelings overwhelmed her and she rushed away to cry in secret and to pray for her father's love. She never complained, not even to Chloe, but the anxious nursemaid clearly saw that her beloved child was very unhappy.

"Maybe you should be more like Enna," Chloe suggested. "Be merry and run and jump on your Papa's knee. I think he'll like you better for it."

But the very thought terrified Elsie. "I can't do that," she said mournfully. "I don't dare."

So as Elsie grew increasingly pale and melancholy, Chloe's heart ached, and she, too, shed many secret tears.

CHAPTER

New Rules

*"Children, obey your parents
in everything, for this
pleases the Lord."*

COLOSSIANS 3:20

*S*o things went for about a week, until the morning when Elsie entered the breakfast room to be greeted by her father with an unusually pleasant "Good morning, Elsie." Then he took her hand and led her to the seat beside his at the table. Elsie, so used to being ignored, nearly glowed with pleasure.

There were several guests present, and Elsie waited patiently while they and the older members of the family were served. When her turn came, her grandfather asked, "Have some bacon, Elsie?"

But before she could answer, her father said, "None for Elsie. Once a day is often enough for a child to eat meat. She may have it for dinner at mid-day, but never at breakfast or supper."

Old Mr. Dinsmore laughed, "Really, Horace, where did you get such a notion? I always allowed you to eat whatever you pleased, and I never saw it hurt you. But, of course, you must manage your child in your own way."

When hot cakes were passed, Horace again said none for Elsie. Instead he placed a slice of bread on her plate and explained, "I don't approve of hot cakes and rolls and muffins for children, so you must eat only cold bread."

And as old Pompey was about to set a cup of coffee down for Elsie, Horace intervened again. "Take the coffee away, please," Horace said, "and bring Elsie a tumbler of milk. Or would you prefer water, Elsie?"

"Milk, please, Papa," the little girl replied with a small sigh. She was very fond of coffee, and it was not easy to give up.

Elsie's Endless Wait

Horace spooned a serving of stewed fruit onto her plate, and Pompey returned with her milk. "There," her father said. "You have your breakfast. In England, children are not allowed to eat butter until they are ten or twelve years old, and I think it's an excellent plan to make them grow rosy and healthy. I have neglected my little girl for too long," he added, smiling and laying his hand on her head for a moment. "But I intend to take good care of you now."

Whatever the cause for this change in him, his words and his manner were more than enough to reconcile Elsie to her meager meal, and she ate with relish. But the meager fare became a constant, and Elsie often looked longingly at the hot buttered rolls and cups of coffee enjoyed by the others. She tried to content herself with the assurance that her Papa was doing what was best for her and to remind herself that Jesus would be pleased with her obedience, but it was not so easy to understand these new rules.

One morning as he read in the drawing room, Horace overheard Arthur teasing Elsie as usual. "Isn't it great to have your Papa home?" the boy was saying snippily. "And how pleasant for you to live on bread and water, eh!"

"I don't live on bread and water," Elsie replied indignantly.

"Papa allows me as much milk and cream and fruit as I want. I can have eggs and cheese and honey and anything else except meat and hot cakes and butter and coffee. And I wouldn't trade any of those things for a father who loves me. Besides, Papa says I can have all the meat I want for dinner."

Arthur became even more scornful. "That's nothing," he mocked. "And I wouldn't give much for all the love *you* get from him."

The last Horace heard was what sounded like a sob, and he went to the window in time to catch a glimpse of Elsie running down the garden path.

Horace found Arthur just outside, leaning lazily against one of the pillars on the portico, "What do you mean, sir, teasing Elsie in that manner?" Horace demanded.

"I only wanted to have a little fun," Arthur replied sullenly.

"Well, I don't approve of that kind of fun, and you will leave the child alone in the future," Horace commanded.

Returning to the drawing room, Horace picked up his newspaper again, but it no longer held his interest. He kept hearing that little sob and seeing his child running from his brother's hateful taunts. When the ringing of the school bell broke into his thoughts, he tossed his paper down, took a card from his pocket, jotted a few words on it, and called a servant to take the note to Miss Day.

When the note was delivered, Miss Day looked at it and said to Elsie, "Your father wants you. You may go."

With some trepidation, Elsie left the schoolroom and hurried to find her father. Fanny, one of the housekeeping servants, directed her to the drawing room.

When Elsie entered, Horace smiled and held out his hand to her. "Come here, Daughter," he said, and her little heart thrilled, for he had never called her "Daughter" before. She stood at his side, and he took her hand in one of his, placed his other hand gently on her head, and looked deeply into her eyes.

"You've been crying" he said in a gently reproving tone. "I'm afraid you do a good deal more crying than is good for you. It is a very babyish habit, and you must try to break yourself of it."

She flushed, and in spite of herself, her eyes filled.

But Horace stroked her hair softly and said, "Don't begin it again. I have good news for you. I plan to drive over to Ion today, to see Mr. Travilla and his mother, and I would like you to go with me."

"Oh, thank you, Papa," she said eagerly.

"There are no little folks there, but I can see you want to go. Now run along and ask Aunt Chloe to get you ready, and tell her to dress you nicely. The carriage will be here for us in half an hour."

Elsie bounded away, and at the specified time, she came back, looking so pretty that her father gazed at her in proud delight and gave her a kiss as he lifted her into the carriage.

"Have you ever been to Ion?" he asked as the coachman guided the horses on their journey,

"No, sir, but I've heard Aunt Adelaide say it's a very lovely place."

"So it is, though not as pretty as Roselands," Horace said. "Edward Travilla and I have been friends since our boyhood, and I spent many happy days at Ion — long before I ever thought of you."

He smiled and patted her cheek.

"Tell me about those times, please, Papa," Elsie asked. "It seems so strange that you were ever a little boy, and I was nowhere."

Horace laughed and then said thoughtfully, "It seems just a short time ago, to me, that I was no older than you are now."

But instead of telling her more, Horace lapsed into silence. They drove on without speaking for some time, until Elsie spotted a squirrel darting up a tree, and she exclaimed, "Did you see that squirrel? Look, Papa, he's perched on that branch."

The coach moved on, and the squirrel was out of sight, but Elsie's outburst, far from annoying her father, reminded him of a day he had once spent hunting squirrels in those very woods. He gave Elsie a very animated account, including the moment when one of his companions accidentally fired his hunting rifle, and the bullet missed Horace by a hair's breadth.

"I felt like fainting when I realized how near I'd come to death," he concluded.

"Oh, Papa, how good God was to save you. If you'd been killed, I could never have had you for my father."

"Perhaps you would have had a better one, Elsie," he said.

Elsie was about to protest, but just then the carriage turned into a broad, tree-lined drive, and Horace cheerfully announced, "There it is, Elsie dear. There is Ion."

In another few minutes, they were alighting from the carriage, and Edward Travilla was greeting them. "Why, Horace, you've brought my little friend Elsie. This is really good of you," he said with genuine delight. The men shook hands enthusiastically, and Edward planted a little kiss on Elsie's cheek. Then he led them inside. "My mother will be so happy to see you both," he said, "and she seems to have taken a special fancy to Miss Elsie."

Mrs. Travilla's greeting was no less cordial, though somewhat less boisterous, than her son's, and she made Elsie feel at home immediately. When the men had left to tour the plantation, the woman and the girl spent an enjoyable morning together in Mrs. Travilla's room. They chatted, and Elsie helped Mrs. Travilla with some garments she was making for the field hands. Elsie soon learned that Mrs. Travilla was a devoted Christian — a tie that drew them closer. Mrs. Travilla was also a discerning woman; she had known Horace nearly all his life, and she already had some notion of the difficulties of Elsie's situation. Without alluding to anything specific, she nevertheless gave the little girl some excellent advice, for which Elsie was truly grateful.

Several hours had passed when Edward returned. "Come, Elsie. I want you to see my garden and hothouse. Will you come, Mother? We have just enough time before dinner."

"No, Edward, I have some things to attend to. So you do the honors," Mrs. Travilla replied.

"Where's Papa?" Elsie asked.

"In the library looking over some new books. Your father has always cared for books more than anything."

As they walked through the garden, Edward asked, "Well, what do you think of our flowers?"

"They're really beautiful," Elsie said. "And you have so many kinds. That's a lovely cape-jasmine, and look! There's a cactus I've never seen before. Mr. Travilla, I think you have more beautiful flowers than we have at Roselands," Elsie declared. Her admiration greatly pleased Edward, for he took intense pride in his garden.

At dinner, Elsie sat beside her father.

"I hope she hasn't given you any trouble," Horace said to Mrs. Travilla.

"On the contrary," the old lady laughed. "We have had a grand time together, and I hope you will bring her to see me again very soon."

After dinner, they all adjourned to the veranda where thick trees shaded the house from the day's heat and a small stone fountain bubbled gaily. But the adults' conversation soon bored Elsie, and she slipped away to the library. A book on the table caught her eye, and she settled on a comfortable sofa in the corner of the room. Soon she was lost to everything around her as she read.

"So here you are, Miss Elsie," came Edward's pleasant voice. "We've been wondering where you were these last two hours. I should have guessed you are a bookworm like your father."

He sat beside her and took the book from her hands. "You can finish that later. I want you to talk to me."

"But Papa will be leaving soon, and it's such a good book," she said.

"No, he won't come to take you away. I've made a bargain to keep you here," he said gravely. "You see, we think there are more than enough children at Roselands without you, and so your Papa has given you to me."

"You're only joking, Mr. Travilla."

"Not at all." he continued with great seriousness. "Can't you see I'm in earnest?"

Although Elsie was teased often enough by her aunts and uncles and should have recognized Travilla's jesting, her father's affection was too fragile and her fear of losing him too strong. At the thought of leaving him, she felt panic overtake her, and with a little cry of alarm, she ran to the veranda and into her father's arms. Clinging to him as if for dear life, she sobbed, "Oh, Papa! Please don't give me away. I'll be good! I'll do everything you say! I'll — "

"Why Elsie, what do you mean?" Horace asked in perplexity. Then he saw Edward standing in the doorway, a sheepish look on his face.

"Mr. Travilla says that you've given me to him," Elsie went on in great fright.

Elsie's Endless Wait

"Nonsense, Elsie," her father said. "How can you believe that I'd ever give you away? Why, I'd rather sacrifice everything I have than part with you."

Elsie looked up and searched his face. What she saw there brought reassurance, and sighing deeply, she laid her head on his shoulder and said, "I am so glad, Papa."

At this point, Edward came forward and patted her shoulder. "I must say, Miss Elsie, that I hardly feel complimented. I'm vain enough to think I'd be the better — or at least the more indulgent — father. Won't you try me for a month, if your Papa consents?"

Elsie shook her head.

"I'll let you have your own way in everything," Edward urged again.

"I don't want my own way, Mr. Travilla. I know that it isn't always the best," Elsie said decisively, making Horace laugh and run his hand over her curly head.

"And I thought you liked me," Edward said in mock disappointment.

"I do like you, Mr. Travilla. Very much. I'm sure you'd be kind, and I'd love you, but never as much as I love my Papa. You're not my Papa, and never could be, even if he did give me away."

Horace laughed again and said to his friend, "I think you'd better give up, Edward. It seems I have to keep her after all, for she clings to me like a morning glory vine."

"Well, Elsie, will you at least come play a little for me at the piano?" Edward asked. But Elsie still clutched her father, until he loosened her grip and said in his forceful way, "Go on now, Elsie, and do as you are requested."

She rose instantly to obey. (Later Edward would complain to his mother, "I wish that Horace didn't always second my

requests with his commands. The child should be allowed to comply of her own will.")

Elsie sang and played until supper time, and afterward she sat quietly while her elders talked.

On the drive home to Roselands, Horace asked if she had enjoyed the day.

"Yes Papa, very much, except . . . . "

"Except what?" he asked, smiling down at her.

"Except when Mr. Travilla frightened me so."

"And do you really love your own Papa best? Are you sure you wouldn't exchange me for another?"

"Oh, no, Papa. Not for anybody in the world."

Horace didn't reply, though a gratified smile settled on his face, and they rode the rest of the way in a comfortable silence.

When they reached Roselands, Elsie kissed her father good night, and ran up the stairs to tell Chloe about her day.

"What a very pleasant visit we had," she said excitedly. "Papa was so kind, and so were Mr. Travilla and his mother."

"I'm glad, darling, and I hope you're going to have many more such days," Chloe said. As she undressed the child and prepared her for bed, Elsie regaled her nursemaid with a minute-by-minute account of everything that had occurred at Ion, even the terrible fright Edward Travilla had given her and its happy resolution.

"Well, you are mighty happy yourself, little girl," Chloe said.

"I am," Elsie agreed, "because I think my Papa is beginning to love me a little, and I hope he will soon love me very much."

Elsie's Endless Wait

The next afternoon, Elsie was returning from her walk when she met her father coming down the driveway. But instead of greeting her, Horace said sternly, "Elsie, I've forbidden you to walk out alone. Are you disobeying?"

"No, sir," she answered meekly. "I was with Aunt Adelaide and Louise until about five minutes ago. They said I was so near home I could come alone. They were going to make a call on a friend and didn't want me along."

Horace was somewhat mollified and took her hand. "How far have you been?" he asked.

"We went down the river bank to the big spring. I think it's about a mile that way, but we took a shorter way back, across the fields and through the meadow."

"The meadow?" Horace said, and he tightened his hold on her hand. "You are never to go into the meadow again, Elsie, unless you have my express permission."

"Why, Papa?" Elsie asked in some surprise.

"Because I forbid it," he said, "and that's enough for you to know. All you have to do is obey. You need never again ask why when I give you an order."

Elsie's eyes filled and a big tear rolled down her cheek. "I didn't mean to be naughty," she said, "and I'll try never to ask why again."

"Another thing, Elsie, you cry too easily. It's entirely too babyish for a girl your age. You must quit it."

"I'll try," she promised. She wiped her eyes and made a great effort to control her feelings.

As they approached the house, a little girl about Elsie's age came rushing out to meet them. "Oh, Elsie," she said

excitedly. "I'm so glad you've come. We've been here a whole hour — Mamma and Herbert and I — and I've been looking for you all the time."

"How do you do, Miss Lucy Carrington?" Horace said. "I see you can talk as fast as ever." He laughed and held out his hand.

Lucy shook it and replied with a little pout, "To be sure, Mr. Dinsmore, it hasn't been more than two weeks since you were at our house, and I wouldn't forget how to talk in just that short time." Then she turned to Elsie, clasping her friend around the waist. "We've come to stay for a week," she chattered, "and won't we have a fine time together?"

Elsie finally had a chance to speak, "I am glad you've come," she said sincerely.

"Is your father here, Miss Lucy?" Horace asked.

"Yes, sir, but he's going home tonight, and then he'll come back for us next week."

"Then I must go in and see him. Elsie, will you entertain Lucy?"

As her father walked away, Elsie suggested that the girls go to her room to play.

"Oh, yes, but won't you speak to Mamma first?" Lucy asked. "And Herbert, too? You're such a favorite with both of them. They're still in the dressing room because Mamma is not very well, and she's feeling tired from the ride."

Lucy led the way to her mother's room, babbling all the time. When they entered, Mrs. Carrington rose from the sofa and hugged Elsie close. "Elsie dear, how are you? I'm so glad to see you. I suppose you are very happy now that your father has come home. I remember how you always looked forward to his return, constantly talking of it and longing for it."

Elsie wasn't sure what to say. Her father's return had not been as happy as she had always anticipated, but she didn't want to discuss it with Mrs. Carrington.

Luckily she didn't have to reply, because Herbert, Lucy's twin brother, came in at that moment and grabbed Elsie's hand. "I'm ever so glad to see you again, Elsie," he said, giving her hand a hearty squeeze. Elsie liked Herbert and felt sorry for him; he had suffered for several years from a hip condition that made him weak and sickly.

"Herbert always says that no one can tell such beautiful stories as Elsie," Mrs. Carrington chirped happily. "And no one except his mother and his nurse were so kind to him when he was bedridden here for so many weeks last year. Herbert has missed you very much, Elsie dear."

"How is your hip now, Herbert?" Elsie asked.

"Much better," the boy said cheerfully, though Elsie thought he looked very pale. "Sometimes I can take long walks now, but I can't run and leap like other boys. I still limp."

They all talked for awhile longer, then Elsie retreated to her room to dress for supper.

At the evening meal, Lucy, who was seated next to Elsie, took her third or fourth muffin and said, "These muffins are delicious! Don't you like them, Elsie?"

"Very much," Elsie said cheerfully.

"Then why are you eating cold bread? And you don't have any butter." Lucy turned to old Pompey and asked him to bring butter, but Elsie stopped him and then informed her friend, "I'm just fine, Lucy. And Papa doesn't allow me to eat hot breads or butter."

New Rules

At this, Lucy's eyes opened wide, and she drew in her breath sharply. "I'm glad my Papa doesn't try that on me," she said. "Why, I'd make such a fuss he'd have to let me eat what I want."

"Elsie knows better than that," said Horace, who had been listening to the girls' conversation. "She would be sent from the table and punished for her naughtiness."

"I wouldn't do it anyway," Elsie said.

In an unusually kind voice, Horace replied, "No, Daughter, I don't believe you would."

~⌒~

The days of the Carringtons' visit passed very pleasantly. Lucy attended classes with Elsie in the mornings, though Herbert stayed with his mother. But in the afternoons, they all went out together, walking or riding. And if the weather was too warm, they played together on the veranda and then took their ride after sundown.

One afternoon, all the children were taking a walk — Arthur and Walter running far ahead because they would not accommodate Herbert's slow pace — when Herbert asked to stop and rest for awhile. "I want to try out my new bow, and you girls can pick up my arrows."

"Thank you, sir," Lucy laughed. "Elsie can chase your arrows if she likes, but I plan to take a nap. This soft grass will make an elegant couch." And she dropped onto the ground and was soon slumbering soundly, or pretending to be. Herbert shot his arrows here and there, and Elsie ran to retrieve them until she was hot and breathless.

"I have to rest," she said, sitting down beside Herbert. "What if I tell you a story?"

"Please do," said Herbert, laying down his bow. "You know how much I like your stories."

When she had finished her tale, Herbert took his bow again and sent an arrow sailing into the meadow.

"See how far it went!" he shouted happily. "Will you get it for me, Elsie?"

"This is this last time," she said, getting up reluctantly. Then she ran to where the arrow lay in the meadow, forgetting entirely her father's prohibition. She didn't remember until she had given the arrow to Herbert, and then in agitation, she exclaimed, "Oh, Herbert, I have to go home as fast as I can! I've forgotten! How could I forget? Oh, what will Papa say?"

"What on earth's the matter?" Herbert demanded anxiously, for Elsie's obvious distress alarmed him.

"Never mind," Elsie said, although she was crying now. "Look, the boys are coming back. They'll take care of you, and I must go."

She ran as fast as she could back to the house, sobbing all the way, and when she saw one of the servants, she asked where her father could be found.

"He's in the house," the servant answered, "but I don't know exactly where."

Before another word could be said, Elsie rushed inside and hurried from room to room. But Horace was not in the drawing room or the library. He wasn't in his own rooms. Elsie was just asking Fanny, the chambermaid, for help when her father's voice came from the veranda. "I'm here, Elsie," he called. "What do you want?"

Running outside, Elsie stopped when she saw her father, then approached him timidly. "I have to tell you something," she said, unable to control the quiver in her voice.

Horace could see that her face was flushed and tear-streaked. He took her hand and asked again, "What is it, Elsie? Are you sick? Have you hurt yourself?"

"No, sir, but — oh, Papa! I've been very naughty. I disobeyed you and went into the meadow!" With that, she burst into tears.

"How is that possible? Would you dare do what I positively forbade the other day?" Horace asked in his most severe voice.

"I didn't mean to disobey, Papa. I forgot you had forbidden me to go into the meadow."

"That is no excuse, no excuse at all. If your memory is so poor, I must find a way to strengthen it," he said.

He paused for a moment, looking at his sobbing, trembling child, then slightly softening his tone, he asked for an explanation.

"Tell me the whole story," he said, "so I may understand how to punish you."

Elsie gave him all the details of what had happened, and when he perceived that she really had forgotten and that her confession had been entirely voluntary, he relented. "Well, Daughter, I won't be very hard on you this time," he said calmly. "You seem very penitent, and you've made a full confession. But you must obey me, or next time you won't escape so easily. I do not take forgetfulness as an excuse. Now, go to Aunt Chloe and tell her to put you to bed immediately."

"But it's only the middle of the afternoon," she said.

"And that is your punishment. You are to stay in bed till tomorrow morning."

"But what will Lucy and Herbert think when they return and I'm not here?"

"You should have thought of that before you disobeyed," he said, a bit of gravity coming back into his voice. "Tell Chloe that you may have bread or crackers for dinner, but nothing more."

Elsie looked into his face. She seemed to want to speak but was afraid.

"Do you have something else to say?" he asked encouragingly.

"Yes, Papa. I'm so sorry for what I did. Will you forgive me, Papa? I won't be able to sleep if you're still angry with me."

Her sadness touched him more than he expected, and Horace said gently, "I do forgive you, Elsie. I am not at all angry with you now, so you can sleep in peace. Now good night, my child." And he kissed her lightly on her brow.

"Good night, Papa," she said with a little smile, "and I hope I'll never be so naughty again."

With his forgiveness, she went to her punishment. But once again, she found comfort in the pages of her worn Bible. She searched for some time before finding the verse she wanted in the twelfth chapter of Hebrews: "No discipline seems pleasant at the time, but painful. Later on, however, it produces a harvest of righteousness and peace for those who have been trained by it." Elsie recited the verse over and over to herself until she felt her hope renewed.

She rose early the next day and had learned all her lessons before breakfast. When she came down the stairs, she could see through the open front door that her father and several of the field hands were standing outside, gathered around some object on the ground.

"Come here, Elsie," her father said when she walked out onto the portico steps. He held out his hand, and she ran to him. He led her a few steps forward and pointed down. A large rattlesnake lay almost at their feet. The snake didn't seem to move, but it was ferocious looking nonetheless.

Elsie immediately jumped back and screamed, "Oh, Papa!"

"It's dead," he said, "and can't hurt you now. The men killed it in the meadow. Do you understand now why I forbade you to go there?"

Squeezing his hand tightly as she realized the danger, Elsie almost whispered, "I do, Papa. I might have lost my life by disobeying. Oh, how good God was to protect me."

Gently, her father said, "After this, I hope you always know that I have good reasons for my commands, even though I may not explain them to you."

"Yes, sir, I think I will," she said, still staring at the dead snake and imagining the possible consequences of her misbehavior.

At breakfast, Lucy finally got her chance to whisper to Elsie, "Where were you last night? I couldn't find you, and your Papa wouldn't tell me where you were, though I'm sure he knew."

Elsie blushed deeply. "I'll tell you later," she said quickly.

When the meal was ended, Lucy grabbed Elsie's waist, pulled her toward the veranda, and then said impatiently, "Now, tell me what happened. You promised."

Elsie's blush returned, climbing to the roots of her hair. "I was in bed," she said meekly.

"Before five o'clock!" Lucy exclaimed. "Whatever for?"

"Papa sent me," Elsie said with an effort, "because I was naughty and disobeyed him."

Lucy, who was always more full of curiosity than sentiment, demanded brightly, "Tell me what you did."

Shamed to recall her behavior, Elsie slowly explained, "Papa had forbidden me to go into the meadow, and I forgot all about it. I ran there to get Herbert's arrow."

"That's all?" Lucy declared in astonishment. "My Papa wouldn't punish me for something like that. He might scold me if I did it on purpose, but if I told him I'd forgotten, he'd just look at me a little sternly and say, 'You must remember better next time, my girl.'"

"My Papa says that forgetting is no excuse. He says that I must remember his commands, and if I forget, he has to punish me so I will remember better," Elsie said.

"He must be very strict, and I'm glad he's not my father," Lucy replied in a voice full of self-satisfaction.

But before Elsie could respond, Adelaide came to the door and called, "Hurry, girls. We are starting out in half an hour."

The whole family and their guests were going up the river for a picnic. They had been planning this excursion for several days, and the children were all looking forward to it a great deal.

"Did Papa say I can go?" Elsie asked, for she was not sure her punishment was ended.

"I presume you can, Elsie," her aunt said good-naturedly. "He never said you couldn't. But you girls must hurry now and dress, or you'll be late."

Just then, the library door opened, and Horace came out.

"Horace," his sister inquired, "Elsie is to go on the picnic, of course?"

"I don't see why you assume so, Adelaide," he replied dryly. "No, Elsie is to stay at home and attend to her lessons as usual."

Elsie's disappointment was sharp and showed in her face, but she didn't say a word and turned to go upstairs. Lucy, throwing a look of angry indignation at Horace, ran after her friend, and once they were in Elsie's room, Lucy declared, "It's not fair, and if I were you, I'd go on the picnic just to spite him!"

"I wouldn't do that," Elsie protested. "I must obey my father. God says so. And I couldn't go even if I tried, for Papa would know it and he'd stop me."

"Then you have to coax him," Lucy went on. "I'll come with you, and we'll talk to him together."

Elsie shook her head. "My father never breaks his word. Nothing would convince him after he has said I can't go." She was trying hard not to cry, but the tears came to her eyes as she told Lucy, "You have to go dress now, or you'll be too late."

Turning, but hesitant to leave her friend, Lucy said, "Alright, I'll go, but I won't enjoy myself without you."

Downstairs, Adelaide was just as indignant as little Lucy. "Why can't the child go with us?" she demanded of her brother. "I can't conceive of a reason you might have for keeping her here, and she is terribly disappointed. Indeed, Horace, I sometimes think you take pleasure in thwarting that child."

"So you think I'm a tyrant," he said sharply. "But I beg you to let me manage my child in my own way. And I have no obligation to explain my reasons to you or anyone else."

Elsie's Endless Wait

But Adelaide could not let the matter rest. "Well, if you didn't intend to let her go, you should have said so and not let the child build up her hopes. It's cruel."

His face now red with anger, Horace said, "Until this morning, Adelaide, I did intend to let her go on the picnic, and I intended to go myself. But I've just learned that I must meet a gentleman on an important business matter. You know as well as I how often accidents occur during these pleasure parties, and I'm not willing to send Elsie unless I am there to watch over her. Believe it or not, it's concern for her safety, not cruelty, that leads me to keep her at home."

His explanation just made Adelaide more impatient. "Honestly, Horace, you have such strange notions about that child. The rest of us will take care of her."

"No," he said adamantly. "If there's an accident, you will have enough to do taking care of yourselves. I won't trust Elsie with the group since I can't be there myself."

Seeing that her brother was determined to have his way, Adelaide gave up her attempt to dissuade him and excused herself. Elsie's disappointment was, of course, enormous, and for a good while, rebellion boiled inside her. She tried to put the feeling away, but it was strong. She couldn't imagine why her father refused to let her go on the picnic, except for yesterday's disobedience. It was unjust, she thought, to punish her twice, especially as she had confessed freely to him. It was a pity she hadn't heard his explanation to her Aunt Adelaide, for then she could have been content. But Elsie, though she sincerely desired to do right, was not perfect, and she had already forgotten the lesson of the rattlesnake.

Sadly, she watched the picnickers depart, all in the highest spirits, but she was surprised to discover that her father wasn't going with them. In a way, this helped reconcile her to her own fate. She didn't expect to see him that day, but it comforted her to know that he wanted her at home because he was there himself. Perhaps it was a selfish love, but it was better than none. (These were not Elsie's exact thoughts, of course. She would never have thought of calling her father selfish. Her feelings were not so defined as she watched him help the ladies into their carriage and then return to the house. What she felt was a troubling mixture of anger, disappointment, and confusion about her father's actions.)

It was a terrible morning for Elsie. Miss Day was in a dreadful mood. The teacher was secretly mortified that she had not been invited on the picnic, and her private misery made her more difficult and unreasonable than ever. Her incessant fault-finding and scolding were almost more than Elsie could bear, but at last the lessons came to an end, and Elsie was excused from the schoolroom. At dinner, there were only Elsie, her father, and the gentleman who had come to do business. The guest was not the kind of man who cared to notice children, so he and Horace discussed politics and business and paid no attention to Elsie.

She was very glad when her father finally excused her, but as she was leaving the dining room, he called her back. He explained that he had planned to ride with her that afternoon but could not do so after all. Jim would accompany her instead. Her father spoke so kindly that Elsie regretted her rebellious feelings. If they had been alone, she would have asked his forgiveness.

When Chloe was dressing Elsie for her ride, the little girl suddenly asked, "Is Pompey going into the city today?"

"Yes, darling, he's leaving pretty soon now."

Elsie's Endless Wait

"Then please do a favor for me, Aunt Chloe. Take some money from my purse and ask him to buy me a pound of the nicest candy he can find. I haven't had any candy for a long time, and I saw what they had bought for the picnic, and it looked so good."

When the Dinsmores and the Carringtons returned from their outing just before supper time, Lucy rushed to Elsie's room to tell her all about their delightful day. She gave every detail of their sports and entertainments, interrupting herself now and then to lament Elsie's absence as the only dark cloud over her pleasure. She repeated her assertion that Elsie's father was very unkind, and as she chattered, Elsie felt her own resentments rising again. She said nothing but allowed her friend to accuse her father of cruelty and injustice without any protest.

Lucy continued her narrative during supper, in a slightly more subdued tone, and Elsie asked questions until her father turned to her and said in his stern way, "Be quiet, Elsie. You are talking entirely too much for a child your age. Don't let me hear another word from you until you've left the table."

Elsie flushed hotly under his rebuke, but she uttered not a sound.

When they were excused, Lucy grabbed her friend and said, "Let's go into the garden and finish our talk. Your father can't hear us there."

"Papa only stopped us because we were talking too much at the table," Elsie apologized. "I'm sure he doesn't mind your telling me about your day." Then she lowered her voice to almost a whisper, "But please, Lucy, don't say again that you think Papa was unkind. I'm sure he knows best, and I never should have listened to any unkind words about him."

"Never mind then," Lucy said with good humor, and they skipped together down the path. "I won't say another word. But I do think he's cross, and I wish you were my sister and had my kind, good Papa for your own."

Elsie sighed. "I'd like to be your sister, but I wouldn't like to give up my Papa, for I love him so much."

"That's funny, when he's so cross to you!" Lucy exclaimed.

Elsie put her hand over Lucy's mouth, and Lucy pushed it away. "Excuse me. I forgot. I won't say it again," she laughed.

While the girls were in the garden, Fanny, the chambermaid, came onto the veranda where Horace was sitting and smoking a cigar. The young woman, who carried a small bundle, inquired if he had seen Elsie.

"What do you want with her?" he asked.

"Only to give her this package that Pompey brought from the city."

"Well, you can leave it with me," Horace said.

Meanwhile Elsie and Lucy had returned to the house and finding Pompey in the hallway, Elsie asked if he had gotten the candy. He told her he had brought some very delicious treats and given them to Fanny to deliver. Fanny, who had just come their way, said that Elsie's father had the candy, and at this news, Elsie turned away in disappointment.

Lucy, who wanted to see her friend happy, as well as to enjoy a share of the sweets, said, "Go ask him for it, won't you?"

But Elsie just sighed, "I think I'd rather do without."

Lucy, however, was persistent, and she coaxed Elsie for some time. But when Elsie still refused to approach her father, Lucy volunteered to go herself.

Elsie's Endless Wait

Elsie agreed, and Lucy, trembling a little in spite of her boastful claim that she was not afraid, found Horace on the veranda. Putting on a great show of confidence, she said, "Mr. Dinsmore, sir, will you please give me Elsie's candy? She wants it."

"Did Elsie send you?" he asked coldly.

Somewhat frightened by his manner, Lucy said yes.

"Then, Miss Lucy, please tell Elsie to come directly to me."

Elsie received this message with fearful uncertainty. But as she had no other choice, she went immediately to her father.

"Did you want me, Papa?"

"Yes, Elsie. I wish to know why you sent another person for what you want instead of coming to me yourself. It displeases me very much, and you will never get anything you ask for in this way."

Elsie hung her head and said nothing.

"Are you going to answer me?" he demanded. "Why did you send Lucy instead of coming yourself?"

"I was afraid," she said in the softest whisper.

"Afraid? Afraid of what?" he asked, and she could hear the displeasure growing in his voice.

"Afraid of you, Papa," she replied in a voice so low he could barely understand the words.

His anger rose, and he exclaimed, "If I were a drunken brute, if I were in the habit of beating you, there might be some reason for your fear. But as it is, I can see no excuse for it at all, and I am hurt and disappointed."

"I'm sorry, Papa," she said. "I won't do it again."

Then after a moment's pause, she said in a hesitating way, "Papa, may I have my candy, if you please?"

"You may not. And understand that I forbid you to buy or eat anything of the kind again without my express permission."

102

New Rules

Elsie's eyes filled, and she choked down a sob as she slowly returned to Lucy. The two little girls sat close together on the steps of the portico.

"Have you got the candy?" Lucy asked eagerly.

Elsie shook her head.

Indignantly, Lucy raved, "It's a shame. He is just as cross as he can be! Why, he's a tyrant! That's what he is, a hateful, old tyrant! And I wouldn't care a cent for him, if I were you! I'm glad he's not my father!"

Elsie merely sighed and said, "I'm afraid he doesn't love me much. He hardly ever lets me have anything or go anywhere I want."

"Well, never you mind," Lucy said. "I'll send to the city tomorrow for *two* pounds of candy, and then we'll have a real feast!"

Sadder still, Elsie said, "Thank you, Lucy, but Papa has forbidden me to eat anything of the sort without his permission."

"He doesn't have to know about it," Lucy encouraged.

But Elsie shook her head again. "You're kind, but I can't disobey Papa, even if he never knows, because that would be disobeying God, and He would know."

Frustrated, Lucy could only lament, "You are very strange, Elsie."

To make matters worse, Horace approached the girls at that moment. From the doorway, he called, "Elsie, what are you doing out there? Haven't I told you not to go out in the night air?"

"I didn't know you meant the doorstep, Papa. I thought you meant the garden," she replied as she rose to go inside.

But Horace would not let her pass. "I see you intend to travel at the very edge of disobedience," he said harshly.

Elsie's Endless Wait

"Go straight to your room and have Chloe put you to bed."

Elsie silently obeyed, and Lucy started to follow, but Horace stopped her. "She is to go alone, if you please, Lucy," he said. And so the little girl, with a frown and a pout, turned on her heel and went to her mother in the drawing room.

Horace walked out onto the steps of the portico where he could watch the moon that was just rising above the tree-tops. But he was not to have this moment alone. From the shadow of a tree near the steps, Arthur sauntered forward and came to Horace's side.

"Elsie thinks you're a tyrant," Arthur began in a voice thick with snide conceit. "She says you never let her have anything or go anywhere and that you're always punishing her. She and Lucy had a fine time out here, talking about how badly you treat her and making plans to have candy behind your back."

"Arthur, I don't believe Elsie would deliberately plot to disobey me. And whatever faults she may have, I know she is above the meanness of telling tales," Horace replied. Then without a look at his younger brother, Horace turned and went into the house, leaving the crestfallen Arthur to creep away.

Chloe was not in the bedroom, for she hadn't expected to be needed so early and was down in the kitchen enjoying a chat. Elsie had to ring for her, and while the child waited, she reviewed in her mind the happenings of the day. She always did this before bed, but rarely was her retrospect so painful. Her tender conscience told her that she had more than once indulged in wrongful feelings toward her father. She had allowed Lucy to speak disrespectfully of him, and by her silence, she'd given the remarks her own tacit approval. Worse, she had complained about him herself.

Tearfully, she murmured to herself, "How soon I forgot the lesson Papa taught me this morning and my promise to trust him without knowing his reasons. How can he love me when I'm so rebellious?"

"What's the trouble, darling?" Chloe asked as she came in. She took Elsie on her lap, cradling the child's head as she said, "I can't bear seeing you so upset."

"I've been so bad today, Aunt Chloe. I'm afraid I'll never be as good as Papa wants me to be. I know he's disappointed with me because I disobeyed him today," Elsie said, as her tears rolled down her cheeks.

"Then you must go to the throne of grace and tell the Lord Jesus about your troubles," Chloe said. "Remember what the Bible tells us: 'If anybody does sin, we have one who speaks to the Father in our defense — Jesus Christ the Righteous One.' Speak to Jesus, darling, and ask Him to help you trust your Papa and obey him even when you don't understand his reasons."

"You're right, Aunt Chloe. Jesus will forgive me and give me right thoughts and feelings," Elsie proclaimed. Then she wrapped her arms around her nursemaid's neck for a loving embrace.

She told Chloe of her father's directions and began to prepare for bed. She had stopped crying, but her face was still sad and troubled. When she was in her nightdress, with her hair brushed and tucked in her nightcap, Elsie took her little Bible and in a trembling voice, read from the twelfth chapter of Proverbs: "Whoever loves discipline loves knowledge, but he who hates correction is stupid."

Elsie's Endless Wait

"I must learn to be grateful for Papa's correction," she told herself, "but Jesus will have to help me." Sighing, she knelt by her bed and prayed. Chloe, watching her little girl, was filled with compassion, and she gave the child every assurance of her own love before tucking her into bed.

But for the next half hour, Elsie shifted and tossed.

"What makes you so restless tonight?" Chloe finally inquired.

"Oh, Aunt Chloe, do you think Papa might come and see me? There's something I must tell him. Would you go and see if he is busy? Don't disturb him if he is, but if not, will you ask him to come see me for just one minute?"

Chloe was not gone long, and she returned with the news that Horace was indeed busy with the guests. "You just go on to sleep, darling," the nurse soothed, "and you can tell your father all about it in the morning."

There was nothing left to try, and Elsie finally cried herself to sleep.

The next morning Lucy was at Elsie's door bright and early. "I was in a hurry to see you, Elsie," she explained. "This is our final day here, you know. Wasn't it too bad your father sent you to bed so early last night?"

"Papa has a right to send me to bed whenever he pleases. I was naughty and deserved to be punished, and besides, it wasn't much earlier than my usual bedtime."

"You, naughty?" Lucy exclaimed. "Mamma often says she wishes I were half as good as you."

Elsie said nothing, for her thoughts were far away. She was thinking of what she had wanted to tell her father and gathering the courage to approach him this morning. "If I can get close to him when no one is near, and if he speaks kindly to me, then I can do it," she mumbled to herself.

"Can't you hurry, Aunt Chloe?" Lucy asked impatiently. "I want to run in the garden before breakfast."

Chloe, who had just re-tied Elsie's sash for the third time and smoothed the child's curls, laughed and said, "We're done now, but Elsie's Papa is very particular."

"He always wants me to look very nice and neat," Elsie explained. "When I go downstairs in the morning, he looks me over from head to toe. If anything is wrong, he's sure to notice and send me back to have it put right."

"You girls run along now and have a pleasant time before the bell rings," Chloe said as she tied the ribbon of Elsie's hat. "There, you look as sweet and fresh as a moss rosebud."

The girls skipped hand-in-hand out of the house and played in the garden until it was almost time for breakfast. Then Elsie went back to her room so Chloe could brush her hair smooth again. She had just rejoined Lucy in the front hall when they saw a carriage driving up to the front door.

"That's my Papa!" Lucy cried joyfully, and she ran straight to the arms of the gentleman who alighted from the carriage, receiving such hugs and kisses as Elsie had always longed for. Lucy was the Carringtons' only daughter and the apple of her father's eye, and Elsie watched this reunion with a strange ache in her heart.

But Mr. Carrington soon set Lucy down and turned to Elsie, taking her hand and giving her a warm kiss. "How are you this morning?" he asked her. "I'm afraid you can hardly welcome me, as I will be taking Lucy home. Have you two had a good time together?"

Elsie's Endless Wait

"Yes, sir, we have, and I hope you'll let Lucy come again soon."

"I certainly shall, but the visits mustn't be all on one side. I'll talk to your father and perhaps persuade him to let you return with us to Ashlands today."

"How wonderful!" Lucy said, clapping her hands. "Do you think he will let you, Elsie?"

"I don't know," Elsie said doubtfully. "I'm afraid not."

"Then you should coax him, as I coax my Papa."

Elsie simply shook her head, and they went to the breakfast room. Her father was there, but when she spoke to him, his reply was so cold and distant that she dared not say anything else. Horace hadn't intended to be influenced by Arthur's malicious tales, but unconsciously, he was. His attitude to his daughter this morning was colder than it had been in a long time.

After breakfast, Lucy reminded Elsie of her promise to show some beautiful shells her father had collected during his travels. The shells were kept in a curio cabinet in a small room off the library. Elsie knew that the items in this room, most of them belonging to her father, were rare and costly, and she was very careful of them.

But the girls were followed into the little room by Arthur, Walter, and Enna. Elsie, terrified of an accident, begged them to leave, but Arthur, declaring that he had as much right to be there as she, refused to budge. Instead, he gave Elsie a hard shove. Clutching at a small table to keep herself from falling, she dislodged a fine, old china vase that Horace prized dearly. It fell with a loud crash and shattered around their feet.

"Look what you've done!" Arthur shouted, and Horace, hearing the noise and the children's agitated voices, was soon on the scene.

"Who did this?" he demanded, looking from one child to the next.

"It was Elsie," Arthur said. "She threw it down and broke it."

Horace was angrier than Elsie had ever seen him. "You troublesome, careless child!" he yelled. "Go to your room immediately, and stay there till I send for you. And remember, if you ever come in here again without my permission, I promise you will regret it."

Elsie fairly flew from the room and up the stairs, and Horace rushed the other children out, slamming the door behind them.

In the hallway, Lucy turned angrily on Arthur. "How dare you blame it on Elsie? It was all your fault, and you know it, Arthur Dinsmore!"

"I didn't touch that old vase, and I'm not taking the blame, little miss," Arthur said threateningly. But coward that he was, he was all the while backing away from Lucy, with Walter and Enna close at his side.

For some time, Lucy was left to debate with herself: Did she have the courage to face Elsie's father and tell him what had really happened? At length, she resolved her dilemma in favor of her friend. Squaring her shoulders and holding her head high, she went back down the passage to the library. Horace was writing when she entered, and he looked up with an expression of surprise and not a little impatience.

"What do you want, Lucy?" he asked. "Speak up, for I am very busy."

"I just wanted to tell you," Lucy said boldly, "what really happened to the vase. Elsie was not at all to blame. It was Arthur. He pushed her hard and made her fall against the table, and that's how the vase fell."

"And why did he push her?"

"Because Elsie had asked him and Walter and Enna to leave. She was afraid they might do some mischief, and she was right."

Horace sat still for a moment, his pen suspended above his paper and his face clouded. But soon he turned to Lucy and said quite pleasantly, "Thank you very much, Miss Lucy, for your information. I would be very sorry to have punished Elsie unjustly. Will you do me the favor of telling her that her Papa says she need not stay in her room any longer?"

Lucy beamed with joy and relief, and she rushed away to her friend's room. Elsie was sobbing miserably when Lucy entered and delivered the good news. "So you don't have to cry or feel sorry for yourself now," Lucy concluded. "Dry your eyes, and we'll go down to the garden and enjoy ourselves."

Elsie was very grateful to Lucy and glad her father knew now that she wasn't to blame for breaking the vase. But his angry words had hurt her deeply, and though she tried to forget the incident and enter happily into Lucy's games, it would be a long time before the hurt was healed.

The girls played for much of the morning, then joined Mrs. Carrington in the drawing room. Herbert, who had not felt well enough to go outside, lay on the sofa with his head in his mother's lap. Horace and Mr. Carrington sat not far away, talking.

New Rules

Lucy ran to her father and sat on his knee. Elsie, stopping first to say something to Herbert, nervously approached her own Papa and, with her eyes down, said softly, "I'm sorry about the vase, Papa."

Taking her hand, he drew her close and leaned forward to whisper in her ear, "Never mind that, Daughter. We'll forget about the vase. And I am very sorry that I spoke to you so harshly, since Lucy tells me you were not at fault."

His words brought great relief, but before Elsie could respond, Mrs. Carrington called out, "Elsie, we want to take you home with us to spend a week. Will you go?"

"I'd like to very much, ma'am, if Papa agrees," said Elsie, and she looked a little wistfully at her father.

"What do you say, Mr. Dinsmore?" Mrs. Carrington inquired. "I hope you have no objection." Then Mr. Carrington added, "By all means, you must let her come, Dinsmore. You can surely spare her for a week, and with Lucy's governess — a superior teacher, by the way — she can keep up with her lessons."

Horace looked grave, and before he said anything, Elsie guessed from his expression what his answer would be. Horace had several times noticed Lucy's disrespectful looks at him, and remembering the conversation reported by Arthur, he had decided that the less Elsie saw of Lucy, the better.

"Thank you both for your kind courtesy to my daughter," he said politely, "but while I appreciate your invitation, I must beg to decline. Home, I think, is the best place for Elsie at present."

With good humor, Mrs. Carrington said, "I suppose we should hardly expect you to spare her so soon after your return, but I am sorry. Elsie is such a good child, and I am always glad to have Lucy and Herbert with her."

Elsie's Endless Wait

"Perhaps you think better of her than she deserves," Horace said. "I find that Elsie is sometimes naughty and needs correction, just as other children. I think it best to keep her under my eye," he concluded, casting a serious look at his daughter.

Elsie flushed hotly and struggled not to cry. Fortunately the dinner ball rang, and Horace led her to the table. But she couldn't help thinking to herself how naughty her father would judge her if he knew about her thoughts and feelings of the day before.

As the Carringtons prepared to depart, Lucy retired upstairs to put on her bonnet. Elsie was ready to follow, but Horace took her hand and held her back. "Lucy will be down in a minute," he said. He did not let go of her hand, even when Lucy came back, and he didn't leave her side as the girls said their good-byes.

But as Horace was talking to Mr. Carrington, Lucy ventured to say under her breath, "I think he's mean not to let you visit."

In equally low tones, Elsie protested, "I'm sure Papa knows best, and I have been naughty. But I'd dearly love to go with you."

Horace didn't loosen his hold on Elsie's hand until the Carringtons' carriage had disappeared down the drive. Then he told her to come to him in the library in a half-hour's time. Seeing that he had frightened her, he added, "Don't be afraid. I'm not going to hurt you."

Elsie tried not to be afraid, but she had to wonder what he wanted, and despite her best efforts, she trembled a bit when she approached the library. He was alone there, sitting at a table covered with papers and writing material. Elsie saw his account book, and beside it a pile of bank notes and gold and silver coins.

"Come here, Elsie," he said, motioning her to the table. "I have your month's allowance. Your grandfather paid it to you in the past, but of course, it is my responsibility now. You have been receiving eight dollars, but now it will be ten."

He counted the money carefully and laid it before her. "From now on, I will require a strict accounting of everything you spend," he continued. "I want you to learn to keep accounts, for someday you will have a great deal of money to take care of. I've prepared an account book for you, so you can do it easily. Every time you spend or give away money, write it here as soon as you can. Be particular about doing it, so you don't forget anything. At the end of each month, you must bring your account book to me and let me see how much you have spent and what your remaining balance is. If you can't make it square, then you will lose part or all of your next month's allowance, according to the delinquent amount. Do you understand?"

"Yes, sir."

"Very good. Now, let's see how much you can remember of your last month's expenditures. Take your book and write down everything you remember spending."

Elsie had a good memory, and she was able to recall almost every penny. She wrote each number down, then added all the numbers in the column correctly.

"That was very well done," her father said with approval as he looked over the figures. "Let's see. A half a dollar for candy. Remember that you are not to buy candy anymore, not as a matter of economy, but because I think it injurious. I want you to grow up strong and healthy."

Suddenly, he closed the account book and asked her, "Were you very anxious to go to Ashlands?"

"I would have liked to go, Papa, if you'd been willing," she said meekly.

"I'm afraid Lucy isn't a good companion for you. I think she puts bad notions in your head," he said seriously.

Elsie flushed, and she was about to make her confession when the door opened and her grandfather entered. She kept silent.

"Doesn't Lucy sometimes say naughty things to you?" Horace asked in a low voice, so his father would not overhear.

"Yes, sir," Elsie replied.

"I thought as much. I shall keep you two apart as often as possible, and I hope there will be no grumbling from you."

"No, sir."

Then he put the allowance money in her hand and dismissed her. After she left, he sat and quietly contemplated. The list of Elsie's expenditures had consisted almost entirely of gifts for others, especially the servants. There were some beads and sewing silks for making a purse and a few drawing things, but with the exception of the candy, she had bought nothing else for herself.

"What a dear, unselfish, generous little thing," Horace thought. But he had not yet rid himself entirely of his old prejudices against his child. "I must not leap to conclusions," he told himself. "I can't judge from one month alone. She seems submissive, but perhaps that is for effect. I overheard her speaking to Lucy, but she may have suspected that I was listening. Perhaps she really does think I am a tyrant, and she obeys out of fear, not love."

This last thought — which, had he known, expressed his own fears more than his child's — came strongly and drove away the tenderness that had been warming his feeling.

New Rules

When he next met Elsie, his manner was as cold and withdrawn as ever, and Elsie could not bring herself to tell him what was in her heart.

CHAPTER

Gold Watch Mischief

*"A wise man fears the Lord
and shuns evil, but a fool
is hotheaded and
reckless."*

PROVERBS 14:16

Gold Watch Mischief

One hot afternoon, in the week after the Carringtons' visit, Arthur, Elsie, Walter, and Enna had just set out for a walk when Elsie spotted an object that instantly sent a cold chill through her. Catching the light of the sun, the object glittered brilliantly — a gold chain dangling from the pocket of Arthur's jacket.

Elsie immediately recognized it, for there was only one such heavy gold chain within Roselands. Taking her young uncle by the elbow, she whispered urgently, "Arthur! How could you take Grandpa's gold pocket watch? Please, put it back now. You're sure to break it otherwise."

Arthur jerked his arm from her grasp. "Hold your tongue, Elsie," he hissed at her. "I can do exactly as I want."

"But Arthur, you know that Grandpa would never let you take his watch. He's told us all how very valuable it is. He paid a lot of money for it, and he says it's worth even more than he paid."

Arthur turned on her. "If this watch is such a prize, then Papa shouldn't leave it lying around on his table." The boy leered hatefully into her worried face. "I'll just teach the old man a lesson, I will. It's about time he learned to be more careful with his things."

Elsie pleaded once more, "Please, take it back now, Arthur. If anything happens to that watch. . . . You know how angry Grandpa will be. Then he'll ask us all what happened, and you know I can't lie to him. He'll ask me if you took the watch, and I can't say no."

"Oh, you're a great little tattletale, Elsie Dinsmore," Arthur snarled. "But if you ever tell on me, I'll make you pay. Believe me, Elsie. You *will* be sorry."

Elsie's Endless Wait

His threat issued, Arthur ran ahead, down the dusty drive, with Walter and Enna trying to keep pace. But Elsie lingered behind them. She walked slowly, but her mind was in a whirl. What should she do? Arthur would pay no attention to her, and all the adults in the household were away, so there was no authority to whom she could appeal for help. Perhaps she should just turn around and go back to the house then and there. If she were not present when the inevitable disaster happened, then she could not be a witness to it. But her father had firmly told her to stay with the other children that afternoon. Besides, she had already seen Grandpa's watch in Arthur's jacket. Even if nothing too terrible happened to the watch, she still knew that Arthur had taken it.

Unhappily she quickened her steps to catch up with the other children. Then another idea struck her. There was a faint hope that she could convince Arthur not to do anything that would endanger the watch. He might even let her take charge of it while he played. Ordinarily, Elsie would have been too afraid even to touch her grandfather's valuable possession, but if she could protect it from Arthur, then she would gladly be responsible.

Their play that afternoon was far from pleasant for Elsie. When the boys weren't running her breathless, then Arthur was up to some antic that made her tremble for the safety of the watch. Though she asked him to let her guard it while he romped and tumbled, Arthur merely answered back with jeers and taunts.

"I'll do just as I please," he laughed at her. "I will not be ruled by *you*, Elsie."

Then it happened. Arthur was scrambling up a tree when his jacket snagged on a limb. As Arthur tugged to release the cloth, his pocket was up-ended, and the precious watch fell, like a golden spark, to the hard ground. It hit with a thud and a sharp crack.

Elsie screamed, and Arthur, now pale with fear, clattered down from the tree and stumbled to where the watch lay.

Its crystal was shattered, and each broken bit of glass flashed at them in the sunlight. Gingerly, Arthur picked up the watch, and they all saw that its case was badly dented. They knew that it was damaged inside, too, for the delicate, little hands no longer moved.

Walter shouted at his brother, "Now see what you've done, Arthur!"

Enna whined, "What will Papa do?"

Elsie could only stare at the terrible mess that Arthur held in his shaking hand.

"All of you, hush!" the boy finally exclaimed. His voice quivered, but whether from fright or rage, it was impossible to say.

He glared at each of them in turn. "If any of you dares to tell about this," he said with defiance, "I'll make you sorry to the last day of your life. I promise I will. Do you understand?"

The smaller children cowered in silence, but Elsie spoke up. "Grandpa will know that *somebody* did it," she said. "He will blame somebody, and Arthur, you can't let an innocent person be punished for what you did."

"I don't care who gets punished!" Arthur exploded. "Just so Papa doesn't find out that I did it."

He turned on Elsie, narrowing his eyes to thin, dark slits. "Remember this," he said in a low and nasty voice. "If you dare to tell on me, little Elsie, I *will* make you pay."

Elsie stood firm. "I won't say anything, Arthur, unless an innocent person is blamed or I'm made to speak. But I won't lie for you then. I'll tell the truth."

Elsie's Endless Wait

Suddenly, Arthur put up his tight fists and lunged at the girl, but Elsie was too quick for him. She darted behind the tree, and before Arthur could grab for her again, she fled, running as fast as she could up the long, dusty driveway. The angry boy pursued, but before catching up to her, he apparently thought better of creating more trouble for himself. He quit the chase, and Elsie escaped into the safe haven of the house.

Careful not to be observed by any of the servants, Arthur managed to restore the pitifully damaged watch to its place on his father's table. Then he, Walter, and Enna gathered what courage they could to await their father's coming.

Arthur was not yet finished with his schemes. When he had calmed himself, he approached his little brother and took him aside. "I say, Wally," Arthur began in a voice as soft as butter. "You know my new riding whip?"

"Of course," said the smaller boy with interest.

"If I should give my new whip to you," Arthur asked, "what would you give to me in return?"

Walter's face lit up with his excitement. "Anything I've got," he almost shouted. Then his face fell. "You're just teasing me again. You'll never give me that whip."

"But I will give it to you," Arthur said agreeably, "if you'll be a good fellow and do what I tell you."

"What's that?"

"All you must do is to tell Papa that Jim broke the watch."

Astonished, Walter protested, "But Jim didn't do it! He wasn't even watching us. He was at the stables all afternoon."

"So what of it?" Arthur demanded with impatience. "Papa doesn't know where Jim was. He's just a slave anyhow. What do you care about him?"

"But I do care, and Jim will be punished," Walter said, "and I don't want to tell such a big lie."

"Then you won't get the whip. But if you don't do as I ask," Arthur went on, his voice becoming low and cold, "then I'm sure you will see a ghost one night very soon. There's one who comes to me sometimes, and I will send it to you."

The little boy cried out, "Oh, please don't do that, Arthur. I'm so afraid of ghosts." As he spoke, Walter looked nervously over his shoulder, half-expecting the dreaded haunt to appear at that very instant.

"If you don't do as I say, then I'll have the ghost come to your room tonight. Is that what you want me to do, Wally?" Arthur peered down at the terrified child, then he went on speaking even more softly, "You are a small boy yet, Wally. It would be easy for the ghost to carry you off. We'll probably never see you again."

Walter's eyes grew round, and his mouth fell open. Words tumbled out in a cascade of terror: "Don't, Arthur! Please don't send the ghost! I'll say anything you want me to say."

Arthur smiled. "That's a good boy, Wally. I knew I could trust you."

Arthur's terrible threat proved even more effective with little Enna, and she quickly promised to speak against Jim rather than face a ghostly visitor in the night.

Elsie's Endless Wait

Arthur could not try his tricks on Elsie. On returning to the house, she had gone directly to her room. For the remainder of the afternoon, she sat there in a state of terrible anticipation, waiting for the sound of footsteps that would signal a summons from her grandfather.

But the footsteps never came, and finally the dinner bell rang. When Elsie had nervously come downstairs and entered the dining room, she discovered, to her great relief, that her grandfather and Mrs. Dinsmore had still not arrived back at Roselands.

As Elsie slipped into the seat beside her father, Horace scrutinized his daughter's face. "You look pale," he said. "Are you well?"

"Yes, Papa, quite well."

Though Horace continued to study her with concern, he said no more, and when the evening meal was done, Elsie hurried back to her room.

It was not long before the elder Mr. Dinsmore and his wife returned. For once, they had brought no late-night visitors. They had not been in the house more than a few minutes when Mr. Dinsmore went to get his watch.

Grabbing up his shattered treasure, Mr. Dinsmore stormed into the drawing room. His suspicions had fallen immediately on Arthur, whose talent for mischief was well established at Roselands, and flushed with rage, the old man demanded, "Where is Arthur? Where is that young scoundrel?" Holding the battered watch out for all to see, he thundered, "This is some of *his* work, I've no doubt!"

In her smoothest tone, Mrs. Dinsmore said, "My dear, how can you say so? Do you have any proof? It's simply not fair to blame my poor boy for everything that goes wrong."

"He gets no more blame than he deserves," replied her furious husband. Bellowing, he called, "Arthur! Arthur, where are you?"

"He's in the garden, I think," said Horace. "I saw him walking there a few moments ago."

Mr. Dinsmore instantly sent one of the servants to bring Arthur inside. A second servant was dispatched to find the overseer of the plantation, and a third was ordered to assemble all the household and stables servants.

"I'll sift to the bottom of this," Mr. Dinsmore exclaimed, "and child or servant, the guilty person *will* suffer."

The old man was angrily walking the room when Arthur appeared. "How dare you meddle with my watch?" Mr. Dinsmore demanded of his son.

Arthur responded boldly. "I didn't, sir. I never touched it."

"There, my dear, I told you so," Mrs. Dinsmore declared in triumph.

"I don't believe him," said Mr. Dinsmore, then he turned his fiery eyes on his son. "Arthur, if you are guilty, as I strongly suspect, you had better confess at once, before I find the truth in some other way."

"I didn't do it, sir," Arthur lied. "It was Jim. Walter and Enna saw him, too. We all saw the watch fall from Jim's pocket when he was up a tree. He cried like anything when he found it broken, and said he didn't mean any harm. Jim said he only wanted to wear your watch for a little while and then put it back all safe. But now you'd find out and have him whipped."

"If what you say is true," the old man shouted, seeking out Jim's face among the servants gathered near the door, "I'll have him whipped and send him to work with the slaves in the fields. No such meddlers will stay in my house!"

Mr. Dinsmore looked at Enna. "What do you know about it?" he asked.

Glancing uneasily around the room, the little girl blushed and said, "It's true, Papa. I saw Jim do it."

"And you, Walter, did you see it, too?'

"Yes, Papa," the boy replied reluctantly. "But please don't punish Jim. I'm sure he didn't mean to break it."

"Hold your tongue!" the old man shouted with fury. "He *will* be punished!" Without asking any questions of Jim or hearing the young man's protests, Mr. Dinsmore pointed a shaking finger at the accused and ordered the overseer to "take him out now and give him a punishment that he will never forget!"

Alone in her bedroom, Elsie could hear nothing of the commotion below. She was trying to learn a lesson for the next day but found it very difficult to concentrate her thoughts. Suddenly, Aunt Chloe entered. She was clearly upset and held her apron to her weeping eyes.

"Oh, Aunt Chloe," Elsie said, "what's the matter?" In her alarm, Elsie dropped her book and ran to her nurse. "Has anything happened to you?"

"Not to me, little darling," Chloe sobbed. "It's Jim. He broke your Grandpa's gold watch, and now he's going to be whipped. Aunt Phoebe is crying fit to break her heart about her son, because —"

Elsie could hear no more. She ran into the hall, nearly colliding with her father. Bursting into tears, she exclaimed, "Papa! Oh, Papa! Don't let them whip poor Jim!"

"I cannot interfere," Horace said, trying to calm his distraught child. "Jim has done wrong and must be punished."

"But Jim didn't break the watch! I know he didn't because I saw it all!"

Much surprised, Horace asked, "Then who did break the watch, Elsie? It couldn't have been you, could it?"

"No, Papa! Not me. I never touched the watch. Please don't make me tell tales," she cried in great distress, "but it was not Jim! Please, Papa, stop them now, before he is whipped!"

Horace called out urgently to Aunt Chloe, "Go and tell my father to delay the punishment until I can speak to him. Tell him I will be down in a few minutes. Hurry!"

As the old nursemaid hastened down the stairs, Horace took Elsie's hand and led her back into her room. Drawing her to his side, he said, "If you want to save Jim, then Elsie, you must tell me all that you know."

The little girl pleaded again, "Don't make me tell tales, Papa. It's so mean. Isn't it enough for me to tell you that Jim didn't do it?"

"No, Elsie. It is necessary that you tell me all you know." He saw the tears flowing from her eyes, and he continued, speaking very kindly, "I would naturally be ashamed of you if, in ordinary circumstances, you were willing to tell tales on other people. But now it is the only way to save Jim. Unless you tell all you know, Jim will be severely punished and then sent away from this house. You understand how that will hurt his poor mother. Elsie, I think it would be wicked to let an innocent person suffer when you can prevent it. And as your father, I instruct you that you must obey me and tell the full truth now."

Elsie understood everything that her father was saying, and although reluctant, she did tell the whole story, her simple and straightforward words confirming her truthfulness for him.

The moment she finished, Horace took her hand and led her to the door. "You must repeat this story to your grand-father," he said.

Elsie's Endless Wait

Elsie pulled at his hand, wanting to retreat into her room. "Please, don't make me do it, Papa," she begged.

Sternly, Horace replied, "You must, my daughter," and he guided his child into the presence of her grandfather.

Except for Walter, the family were still gathered in the drawing room. Mr. Dinsmore, disturbed and angry, paced the room and cast occasional, mistrusting glances at Arthur. The boy, who had guessed the meaning of Aunt Chloe's message from Horace, was now the picture of guilt.

Walter had crept away from the scene. Crying over Jim's fate and his own lack of courage, the little boy told himself that he would make it up to Jim somehow — even if it cost a month's worth of allowance.

With Elsie's hand firmly in his own, Horace entered the drawing room and announced to his father, "I have another witness, sir. Elsie was there when your watch was broken."

"Then maybe I'll get the truth now," the old man exclaimed.

"It wasn't Jim, Grandpa. But please don't make me say who it was," Elsie cried.

Her father tightened his hold on her hand, and commanded, "Elsie! The whole truth now."

Elsie clung to his side and just caught a threatening look from Arthur. Horace, sensing her terror, also looked at Arthur and returned the boy's malicious gaze with his own hard stare.

Mr. Dinsmore addressed Elsie, "If you don't tell me what you know, child, then I can't let Jim off. Come now, Elsie. No one will hurt you for speaking the truth."

Sobbing, she blurted out, "I'll tell you, Grandpa, but please don't be angry with Arthur! Forgive him this time,

and he won't meddle anymore. I'm sure he didn't mean to break your watch."

Mr. Dinsmore was at his younger son's side in an instant. He seized the boy by the shoulder and raged, "I knew it had to be you!" Holding Arthur securely, he turned back to Elsie. "Let's have the rest of the story, little girl," he demanded.

When she had finished, Arthur began to plead for his father's forgiveness.

"Forgive you?" the old man spluttered. "I'll forgive you — after you have had a good spanking and a week of solitary confinement with nothing but bread and water!"

He was about to drag Arthur from the room when Elsie rushed to his side. "Please, don't punish him, Grandpa! He won't do it again, will you Arthur? And let me pay for the watch. I *want* to pay for it."

"I don't care about the money," her grandfather replied, a hint of contempt in his voice. "And where would you get that kind of money?"

"But I'm rich, aren't I?" she said softly. "Didn't my mother leave me a great deal of money?"

Her father gently took her to his chair. He sat down and held her before him. "No, Elsie," he explained. "Until you come of age many years from now, you have only what I choose to give you."

"Then please, give me the money for the watch, Papa."

"I can't do that, Elsie. Arthur must take the penalty for his own wrongdoing," Horace said firmly. "That is what your grandfather cares about, not the money."

At this point, the elder Mr. Dinsmore harshly dragged Arthur from the room — but not before the boy had shot a burning look of hatred and defiance at Elsie. She felt his intensity so deeply that she could hardly stand. Her father, seeing the exchange that had just taken place, steadied her and said soothingly, "Don't be afraid, Daughter. I will protect you."

It seemed to Elsie that her father was, at long last, about to lift her onto his knee, as he so often did with Enna, and to hug her close to him. But at that moment, a servant entered to announce the arrival of visitors, and Elsie was dismissed to her room.

As Elsie reluctantly left her father to his guests, she saw Mrs. Dinsmore, who plowed down the hallway like a massive ship in a storm; her face was grim and full of fury. Wanting to avoid any meeting with the woman, Elsie ran up the stairs to find solitude in her own quiet bedroom. But the room wasn't empty. Chloe awaited her. Aunt Phoebe was there too, and the woman's fervent expressions of gratitude made Elsie forget for the time that she wouldn't see her father again that night.

There was a knock at the door, and Jim put his head in. Elsie invited him inside and received his grateful thanks as well. Jim explained that he had been so astounded by the unexpected charges against him that he'd been unable to speak up in his own defense. Besides, Mr. Dinsmore had refused to listen to his protests of innocence. If it hadn't been for Elsie, well, no one wanted to contemplate what might have happened.

When Jim and his mother had gone and Chloe had settled down to her knitting, Elsie at last had time to think again of all that had happened. She remembered the understanding and kindness of her father that night, his loving words, and his protection and care. Bedtime came, and although she retired at precisely the time her father dictated, Elsie lay awake for some time, imagining — as she had done so often before — a future in which her father would truly love her as much as she loved him.

At breakfast the next morning, she greeted Horace with an eager yet shy, "Good morning, Papa."

His response was both serious and absent-minded. Immediately beginning a business conversation with his father, Horace paid no further heed to his child, except to supervise the food that she was allowed to eat. When the meal was done, Elsie lingered at the table, hoping for her father's attention. But beyond a brief glance in her direction, there was none. Horace informed his father that he would be riding to Ion, to see Mr. Travilla, and probably would not return before night. Sadly disappointed, Elsie returned to her room to prepare for her morning lessons.

For awhile, Elsie enjoyed complete freedom from Arthur's torments. Even when his punishment was ended, Arthur was much too afraid of his brother Horace to openly bother Elsie in any way. In secret, however, he nursed his desire for revenge.

Aunt Adelaide was always kind; Lora still stood up for Elsie when she saw an injustice; and Elsie's grandfather was nice enough in his gruff fashion. But the rest of the family did little to make her feel comfortable. Mrs. Dinsmore remained extremely angry with her because of Arthur's disgrace, and when Horace was not around, the woman treated Elsie most unpleasantly. The younger children were unusually cold and distant. Even her father, though careful to see that all her wants were met, seldom seemed to take much notice of her, unless to chide her for some fault. Nothing she did was too trifling to escape his eye.

One day, when Horace had sent Elsie to her room for some small thing, Adelaide said to him, "You seem to expect that child to be a great deal more perfect than any grown person I know. She is not even nine years old, yet you want her to understand all the rules of etiquette."

"If you please," he responded haughtily, "I would like to manage my own child as I see proper, without any interference."

Adelaide answered him calmly. "I had no intention of interfering. But really, Horace, you have no idea how eagle-eyed you are for any fault in Elsie, nor any idea how stern your tone is when you correct her. Remember that you have not been a father to her for more than a few months, and until you came home, she had never had a real parent before. But I've known Elsie for more than four years now; I've seen how sensitive she is and also how much she wants to do right and to please you. I'm sure that a gentle reproof would be just as effective and not hurt her feelings so."

"Enough!" Horace exclaimed impatiently. "Perhaps if I were ten years younger than you, instead of the other way round, you might be right to advise and direct me. But as it is, I regard your words as simply impertinent." With that, he angrily left the room.

Adelaide watched him depart and thought to herself, "I am glad you have no authority over me, dear brother."

All that Adelaide said was true; still, Elsie never complained or blamed her father. Indeed, in her heart she blamed herself for his cool aloofness. His many reproofs only made her more timid and sensitive, and she tended increasingly to distance herself from him. She seldom ventured to speak or even move in his presence, and she was far too young to understand that her behavior flowed naturally from his. As for Horace, he could plainly see that Elsie feared him. But prideful as he was, he was unable to admit the wisdom of Adelaide's words, so he attributed his daughter's reticence solely to her lack of love for him. And in this way, both father and daughter continued to walk their separate paths.

CHAPTER

6

Bird on the Wing

"Are not two sparrows sold for a penny?
Yet not one of them will fall to the ground
apart from the will of your Father.
And even the very hairs of your head
are all numbered.
So don't be afraid; you are worth
more than many sparrows."

MATTHEW 10:29 – 30

Bird on the Wing

It was the Sabbath morning, and Adelaide, Lora, and Enna were already in the carriage. Elsie stood on the portico steps, waiting for her father, and watched as the horses, two young steeds purchased by Horace only a few days before, stamped and tossed their heads.

As Horace came out, he remarked to Ajax, the coachman, "I didn't intend to harness that pair today. Where are the old bays?"

"Old Kate has a lame foot, sir, and your father said these youngsters have to be put to use sooner or later. I reckoned I might as well take them out today."

Horace, glancing first at the horses and then at Elsie, asked, "Are you sure you can hold them in?"

Smiling broadly with self-confidence, Ajax said, "I've driven these horses twice already, and they went splendidly. I reckon I can hold them in good as anything, sir."

Still uneasy, in spite of Ajax's assurance, Horace turned to his daughter. For a moment, he considered keeping her home from church that day, but he realized what disappointment this would cause her, so he lifted her into the carriage, and ordering Ajax to proceed with caution, Horace climbed in and sat beside his child.

"Change seats with me, Elsie," Enna said, sounding very much like her mother. "I want to sit next to my brother."

But Horace, putting his hand on Elsie's shoulder, said, "No, Enna. Elsie's place is beside me."

Enna started to pout. Horace, however, turned his attention to Adelaide who asked him a little anxiously, "Do you think there's any danger of the horses bolting?" She had seen Horace's concern, and she also realized that they were moving unusually fast.

"The horses are young, but Ajax is an excellent driver," Horace replied evasively. "Besides, I wouldn't have brought Elsie if I believed we were in any danger."

And in truth, their journey to church was uneventful. On the ride home, however, the horses took fright, and the carriage careered down a hillside at a frightful speed. Elsie thought they were going very fast, but she didn't suspect any danger until her father lifted her from her seat and placed her between his knees, holding her very tightly as if afraid that she might be snatched from his grasp. Elsie saw that his face was very pale and his eyes were fixed on her.

She whispered, "Don't worry, Papa. God will take care of us."

"I'd give all I'm worth to have you safe at home," he said hoarsely and held her even closer to him.

As their speed increased, the carriage bounced and shuddered and seemed ready to tip over at any second, an outcome they had little hope of surviving. Lora was leaning back in her seat, white with terror. Adelaide clutched Enna to her, and the little girl sobbed bitterly. But even in the face of death, Elsie remembered that they were in their Heavenly Father's hands. Her faith was strong, and she put her trust in Jesus.

As Ajax struggled to regain control over the charging horses, a large and powerful man, who happened to be walking down the road, heard a roaring, thudding sound behind him; he turned to see the galloping horses and imperiled carriage. Without a thought to his own danger, the man planted himself in the middle of the road, and as the horses neared, he reached out and grabbed their bridle — a sudden check that caused the horses to rear excitedly and then halt.

"Thank God, we're saved!" Horace exclaimed. He threw open the carriage door and leaped to the ground, lifting Elsie out first and then his sisters. They were near the entrance to Roselands, and they all preferred walking the rest of the way to returning to the carriage. As Adelaide led her sisters to the house, Horace, keeping Elsie at his side, remained some time, thanking and talking with the man who had, at the risk of his own life, saved theirs. Although Horace insisted the man accept a handsome reward, he knew it could never be enough for the courageous rescue.

Ajax guided the horses back to the stable as Horace and Elsie walked slowly up the drive. Neither spoke a word until they reached the house; then Horace bent and kissed his child and asked if she had recovered from her fright.

"Yes, Papa," she said softly. "I knew that God would take care of us."

"That He did," Horace replied, very seriously. "Now go upstairs and tell Chloe to get you ready for dinner."

Later that afternoon, Elsie was alone in her room when Lora surprised her by entering. It was seldom that the older girls chose to visit their young niece.

Lora still looked a little pale, and more thoughtful than Elsie could remember. Lora didn't say anything at first, then suddenly she burst out, "Oh, Elsie! I can't help thinking, what if we'd all been killed? Where would we all be now? Where would I be? I believe you would have gone straight to heaven, but I? I would be like the rich man the minister talked about this morning, lifting up my eyes in torment."

Elsie's Endless Wait

Lora covered her eyes and a shudder ran through her. Then she said, "We were all so afraid, but you, Elsie. What kept you from being afraid?"

"I was thinking of a Bible verse I know. 'Even though I walk through the valley of the shadow of death, I will fear no evil, for you are with me.' God said for us not to be afraid because He is with us. I knew that Jesus was there with me, and if I were killed, I'd wake up again in His arms. That's why I wasn't so afraid."

"I'd give anything to feel as you do," Lora sighed. "But didn't you feel afraid for the rest of us? I'm sure you must know that even though we go to church and study the Bible sometimes, we are not very good Christians and don't even pretend to be."

Elsie blushed and looked down. "It happened so quickly I only had time to think of Papa and myself. I've prayed so much for Papa, and I was sure God would spare him. It was selfish, I know, and I can't tell you how thankful I was that we were all spared."

"You did nothing wrong," Lora maintained. "And we haven't given you much reason to care what becomes of us. But Elsie, can you tell me how to be a true Christian? I want to try very hard and never rest until I am one."

Elsie was overjoyed, and she picked up her little Bible. "Let me show you Jesus' words," she said, finding the verse she wanted. "'For everyone who asks, receives; he who seeks, finds; and to him who knocks, the door will be opened.' That must encourage you.

"And see this verse: 'You will seek me and find me when you seek me with all your heart.' Oh, dear Lora, all you have to do is seek Him. The Bible promises that if you seek the Lord with all your heart, you will find Him."

"Yes," Lora said a little doubtfully, "but how do I seek Him, and what must I do to be saved?"

Elsie, who knew the Bible more thoroughly than most children her age, recalled the answer that Paul the Apostle gave to the jailer: "'Believe in the Lord Jesus Christ, and you will be saved.'" She turned to the tenth chapter of the book of Romans and read aloud: "'If you confess with your mouth, 'Jesus is Lord,' and believe in your heart that God raised Him from the dead, you will be saved.'

"You see, Lora," said Elsie, "you simply have to believe in Jesus. But you must believe with your heart — not just your mind."

"But how do I get rid of my sins? How do I make myself pleasing in the sight of God?" Lora asked eagerly.

Elsie turned to the book of First John. "See what it says here, Lora?" she asked. "'The blood of Jesus Christ, His Son, purifies us from all sin.' Jesus has already done all that is necessary. We have nothing to do but to believe in Him and accept His offer of forgiveness of sins and eternal life. Just accept them as free gifts, and then love and trust Him."

"But surely I must *do* something?" Lora asked.

Elsie thought carefully. "Well," she replied, "God says, 'Give me your heart.' You can do that. You can invite Him to come live in your heart. You can tell Him how much you need Him. And the Bible says, 'If we confess our sins, He is faithful and just and will forgive us our sins and purify us from all unrighteousness.' So you can tell Jesus your sins and ask Him to forgive them. You can ask Him to teach you to be sorry for your sins and give you a desire to be like Him — loving and kind and forgiving. Of course, we can't be like Him without the help of His Holy Spirit. But we can always get that help if we ask.

"Oh, Lora, don't be afraid to ask. Don't be afraid to come to Jesus. But you must come humbly, for the Bible says 'God opposes the proud, but gives grace to the humble.' He won't turn away anyone who comes to Him humbly, seeking to be saved."

For the rest of the afternoon, Lora stayed with Elsie, asking questions and reading from the Scriptures. Elsie explained that being a Christian meant having Jesus in your heart, not just attending church and reading the Bible. Then they sang a hymn together, and Elsie talked about her own peace and joy in believing in Jesus. "Oh, how good of God to make being saved so easy that anyone can do it — even children like us," she exclaimed.

When the supper bell rang, Elsie went to join the others with a new sense of happiness. Besides the joy of her conversation with Lora, she also remembered her father's deep concern for her during their perilous ride. "Surely he does love me," she murmured to herself.

When Horace met her at the table and asked with a smile, "How is my little daughter this evening?" her cheeks glowed, and she wanted to throw her arms around him and tell him how much she loved him. That was impossible for her, with all the family gathered around, so she simply returned his smile and said, "I'm very well, thank you, Papa."

But once again her joy was short-lived, and before the week was out, she was again in sad disgrace.

It was a bright afternoon several days later, and Elsie was walking alone in the garden when she heard a fluttering noise coming from a nearby arbor. Hurrying toward the source of the sound, she discovered an up-turned glass vase in which a beautiful hummingbird was imprisoned. Struggling to escape, the tiny bird fluttered and beat its fragile wings against the glass, causing the noise Elsie had heard.

Always tenderhearted, Elsie could never bare to see any living creature in distress. She knew that Arthur was often guilty of torturing insects and small birds — she'd several times endured his wrath to intervene on behalf of his small victims — so she instantly assumed that this was his handiwork. The desire to release the terrified bird overwhelmed her, and without a moment's hesitation or reflection, she lifted the glass, and the bird flew free.

Only then did she consider how angry Arthur would be, and the prospect caused a little shiver to pass through her. But it was too late now, and after all, she didn't really fear any consequences since she was sure her father would approve of her action. She'd often enough heard Horace reprove his brother for his cruel practices.

The day was very hot, and Elsie retreated to the veranda off the drawing room on the east side of the house, where a canopy of trees and vines provided cooling shade. Arthur, Walter, and Enna were just inside, enjoying a lively game of jacks, and Louise was stretched languidly on the couch, engrossed in her latest novel.

Elsie, taking up a book of her own, wondered why Arthur didn't go to check on his captive bird, but she soon forgot all about her uncle as she buried herself in the adventures of the Swiss Family Robinson.

The players were just finishing their jacks game when Horace suddenly burst into the room and demanded, in a voice full of rage, to know who had been in the garden and released the hummingbird he had taken such pains to capture. It was one of a rare species, he said, and an important addition to his collection.

Elsie was terribly frightened and would have been glad to sink through the floor at that moment. She dropped her book, and her face turned pale and flushed in turns as she struggled to choke out a confession, as her conscience told her she must.

Her father's attention was focused not on her, but on Arthur. "I presume it was you," Horace was saying angrily, "and if I'm right, you should prepare yourself for punishment as severe as your last."

"I didn't do any such thing," Arthur replied with fierce indignation.

"Of course, you'll deny it," Horace went on, "but we all know that your word is good for nothing."

At that moment, a small voice interrupted the brothers' angry exchange.

"Arthur didn't do it, Papa. It was I."

"You?" her father exclaimed, turning on her an expression that oddly mixed anger and astonishment. "You, Elsie? Can this be possible?"

Covering her face with her hands, Elsie burst into tears.

"Come here to me this instant," Horace commanded. He took a seat on the settee that Louise had abandoned. "Tell me what you mean by meddling in my affairs."

"Please, please, don't be so angry, Papa," she sobbed, moving to him. "I didn't know it was your bird. I didn't mean to be naughty."

"You never *mean* to be naughty," he said. "Your misbehavior always seems to be by accident. But I find you are a

very troublesome and mischievous child. Remember the valuable vase you broke the other day, and now you've caused the loss of a rare specimen that I spent a great deal of time to procure. Really, Elsie, I'm tempted to administer a very strong punishment. Tell me why you did it. Was it pure love of mischief?"

"No, sir," Elsie said in a whisper. "I was sorry for the little bird. I thought Arthur put it there to torture it, so I let it go. I didn't mean to do wrong, Papa, really I didn't," she pleaded, her tears falling faster than ever.

"You had no business to meddle, no matter who put it there," he said. "Now, show me which hand did it."

Elsie held out her right hand, and Horace took it in his. He could feel her trembling, and when he looked into her face, he saw her fear and pain. The evidence of her sorrow relaxed his anger, and the stern expression faded from his face. He was tempted at that instant to forgive her entirely. But the loss of the rare bird was extremely upsetting, and his anger flared again. She must be punished, he decided, but not with physical pain. He freed his hand from hers and began to reach into his pocket.

"Watch out, Elsie," Louise laughed maliciously. "He's reaching for his knife. I expect he wants to cut off your hand."

"Hush, Louise," her brother said sharply. "I'd as soon cut off my own hand as my child's. You should never speak anything but truth, especially to children."

"I think it's sometimes good to frighten them a little," Louise replied defensively. "And I thought that's what you intended to do."

"Never," Horace said firmly. "That is a very bad approach, and one I'll never adopt. Elsie will learn in time,

if she doesn't know now, that I never utter a threat which I do not intend to carry out. And I never break my word."

While remonstrating with his sister, Horace had taken a linen handkerchief from his pocket. Lifting Elsie's hand again, he said to her, "I shall wrap up this hand, for those who do not use their hands aright should be deprived of their use. There!" He finished knotting the handkerchief, making sure it was not too tight. "Now go to your room and stay there till supper." He gave her a little pat on the back and sent her off.

Elsie felt deeply humiliated, so Arthur's nasty laugh and Enna's smug little smirk added nothing to her suffering. Her father's punishment, which was indeed mild, had wounded her more than the most severe chastisement, because the mere knowledge of his displeasure was the worst pain she could endure.

Walter, whose heart was much kinder than his brother's or sister's, was touched by Elsie's distress, and he ran after her when she had left the room. "Never mind, Elsie," he said sincerely. "I'm so very sorry for you, and I don't think you were the least bit naughty."

She thanked him, for she was deeply grateful for his concern. Then she hurried to her room. Alone, she sat by the window, and through her tears, she tormented herself with questions. "Why am I so naughty? How can I be good so that Papa will love me?" And she raised an earnest prayer for help to do right and for the wisdom to understand how to gain her father's love.

When the supper bell rang an hour later, Elsie jumped up, but then she sat down again. Better to have no supper, she decided, than to show her handkerchief-bound hand and tear-swollen eyes at the table. It was not long, however, before a servant came to her door with a message from her father; she was to come down to the dining room immediately.

When she took her seat beside him at the table, Horace turned hard eyes on her. "Didn't you hear the bell?" he inquired.

"Yes, sir."

"Remember, Elsie, that you are to come as soon as you hear the bell, unless you are directed otherwise or you are sick. The next time you're late, I will send you away without your meal."

"But I don't want to eat," she said softly.

"Nevertheless, you will have your supper tonight, and there will be no pouting or sulking." His voice was low, but clearly irritated as he added, "Stop that crying at once." He spread some preserves on a slice of bread and laid it on her plate, and repeated, "Stop crying, or I'll take you from the table, and you will be very sorry."

Elsie was struggling valiantly to choke back her tears when her grandfather addressed her. "Why is your hand bandaged, little girl?" he asked. "Have you been hurt?"

Elsie's face flushed, but she said nothing.

"You must speak when you are spoken to," her father commanded. "Answer your grandfather's question now."

"Papa tied it because I was naughty," she said, a sob escaping with her words.

Horace made a move as if to take her away from the table, but Elsie begged him, "Please, don't, Papa. I'll be good."

"Then no more crying," he said. "This is shameful behavior for a girl of nearly nine. It would be bad enough for a child of Enna's age." He took a fresh handkerchief from his pocket and wiped her eyes. "Now eat your supper at once, and don't make me have to correct you again."

Elsie's Endless Wait

Elsie tried to eat her bread and jam, but it was almost impossible. Struggling as hard as she could to stifle her tears and sobs, she could not swallow and felt as if she might suffocate. She knew that her father was watching her closely, and she sensed that everyone else was looking at her. "If they would just forget about me," she thought.

It was at that moment that Adelaide, who had watched the whole scene, addressed a question to Horace and adroitly set the whole table talking about something else. How grateful Elsie was to her aunt for this time to regain her composure.

When they rose from the table, Elsie timidly asked if she might go to her room.

"No, child," her father said. Taking her left hand, he led her to the veranda. Horace settled in a comfortable chair and lit a cigar. He told Elsie to get his book from the drawing room; then he had her draw a stool close to his chair and sit beside him.

"Do not move from that stool. Let's see if I can keep you out of mischief for an hour or two," he said, and he began reading to himself.

"May I get a book to read, Papa?"

"You may not. Do just as I tell you, nothing more and nothing less."

Elsie took her seat on the stool and tried to amuse herself with her own thoughts. She watched her father's face as he read. "How handsome my Papa is," she thought. But her sadness came back to her again as she tried to decide how she could please him and win his love. More than anything, she wanted only to climb on his knee, hug him, and tell him how sorry she was about the bird. In her imagination, she could see him returning her affection with his own hugs and smiles.

A cry from Enna broke into her dream, and without thinking, Elsie jumped up from the stool. "Papa," she exclaimed, "there's a carriage coming up the drive. If it's visitors, please let me go to my room!"

"Why do you wish to go?" he asked coolly.

Elsie blushed and hung her head. "Because I don't want them to see me, Papa," she answered.

"You are not usually so afraid of strangers," he observed.

"But they will see that my hand is tied and ask me why. Oh, please let me go, Papa, before they get here," she pleaded desperately.

"No, you must stay, if only to punish you for leaving your seat without my permission. You must learn to obey me at all times, Elsie, and under all circumstances. Now sit down, and don't move again until I say you may."

Elsie sat quickly, but two hot tears dropped on her cheeks.

"You need not cry," her father said. "The visitor is only an old gentlemen here to see your grandfather on business. He never notices children, so he's not likely to ask you any questions. I really hope, Elsie, that you will learn to save your tears for an occasion that requires them."

Her father was right. The old gentleman paid no attention to her, and her relief was so great that, for once, she scarcely noticed Horace's rebuke. A half hour at least passed in silence, and Elsie grew so weary that without intending to, she laid her head on her father's knee and slept.

His voice seemed to come to her from far away. "You may go to bed now, Elsie, if you like."

She stood up slowly and was turning to go, but she hesitated.

"Do you have something else to say?" Horace asked.

Elsie's Endless Wait

"Yes, Papa. I'm sorry I was naughty today. Will you forgive me?" Her words were spoken softly, but she managed not to cry again.

Horace responded sternly, "In the future, will you try not to meddle in the affairs of others and not to sulk and pout when you are punished?"

"I will try to be a good girl always," she promised.

"Then I forgive you," he said, and he carefully untied the handkerchief and removed it from her hand.

But she still lingered, hoping for some token of his forgiveness. Sensing what she wanted, Horace considered what to do. With a hint of impatience, he said at last, "No, Elsie, I will not kiss you good night. You have been entirely too naughty. Now go straight to your room at once."

Could she *ever* win her father's love? The wait seemed endless at times. In her bed that night, Elsie searched her little Bible for words of hope. And she found them in the promise of God's eternal love: "For I am convinced that neither death nor life, neither angels nor demons, neither the present nor the future, nor any powers, neither height nor depth, nor anything else in all creation, will be able to separate us from the love of God that is in Christ Jesus our Lord." Whatever else happened to her, God's love would be with her always.

CHAPTER

A Terrible
Injustice

*"Consider it pure joy, my brothers, whenever you
face trials of many kinds, because you
know that the testing of your faith
develops perseverance.
Perseverance must finish its work
so that you may be mature
and complete, not lacking
anything."*

James 1:2 – 4

A Terrible Injustice

*E*ach month, Miss Day presented the parents with reports on the conduct and recitations of her pupils. Horace Dinsmore had received one such report since his return to Roselands. It had been most satisfactory, as Elsie was usually a diligent scholar who tried to carry her religious principles into her studies as in everything else. As much as Miss Day looked for faults, Elsie's work rarely gave her good excuses.

Horace had pronounced the first report quite good. "I'm glad to see that my daughter is industrious and well-behaved," he had told Miss Day, "for I want her to grow into an intelligent and amiable woman."

Now the time for the second report arrived, and Elsie knew it would not be as the first. The warm weather of the last month had distracted her, and more seriously, she had often been too depressed and anxious to concentrate fully on her lessons. Arthur had become more annoying than ever; in the schoolroom he was forever shaking Elsie's chair and jogging her elbow when she was writing. Her copybook was very messy as a result, and Miss Day's report on her work had never been so bad. With secret satisfaction, the governess presented the report to Horace, together with a long list of complaints about the child's idleness and inattention.

"Send her to my room immediately," Horace said angrily.

Elsie was still in the schoolroom, putting her desk in order, when Miss Day brought the message. With a hateful smile, she said, "Elsie, your father wishes to see you this moment. He is waiting in his room."

Elsie's Endless Wait

The look on Miss Day's face told Elsie what to expect, and for several moments, the little girl was quite unable to move.

"I advise you to go quickly," said Miss Day, "for the longer you wait, the worse it will be, I have no doubt."

As the teacher spoke, Elsie heard her father's voice calling her name; struggling to control her fear and trembling, she hurried to obey.

The door to Horace's room was open, and Elsie walked slowly in. "Did you call me, Papa?" she asked.

"Come here to me," he said. He was sitting with her copybook and the report in hand, and she could both see and hear his reproachful attitude. But Horace could see as well, and the terror in Elsie's face touched him. Less sternly he asked, "Can you tell me how it happens that your teacher has brought me so bad a report of your conduct and lessons? She says you have been very idle, and this report tells the same story. Your copybook is really shameful."

Elsie could answer only with tears, which seemed to irritate him. "When I ask a question," he said, "I require an answer at once."

"Oh, Papa. I — I *couldn't* study! I'm very sorry. I'll do better. Please don't be angry with me, Papa!"

"I am angry with you. Very angry, indeed. And strongly inclined to punish you. You couldn't study, eh? For what reason? Were you not well?"

"I don't know, sir."

"You don't know? Well, you could not have been very ill without knowing it, and you seem to have no other excuse. However, I will not punish you this time, as you seem to be truly sorry and have promised to do better. But do not let me see this kind of report again or hear such reports of your idleness, unless you wish to be severely punished. I warn you, Elsie, that unless your next copybook is much improved, I will certainly punish you."

As he spoke, he leafed through the pages of her writing book. "There are a number of pages here that look quite well done," he noted in a slightly milder tone. "They show what you can do, if you choose. There is an old saying, 'A bird that *can* sing and *won't* sing must be *made* to sing.'"

Elsie started to speak, but he commanded her to be quiet. "Not a word. Just go now." Then he leaned back in his easy chair and began to read his newspaper.

But Elsie, though dismissed, lingered in his room. This was the first time she had ever entered his room, and it should have been a happy occasion. She felt she couldn't leave without some word of kindness from her Papa. But when Horace finally saw her standing there, he only said, "I gave you permission to go, Elsie. Go at once."

So she sought solitude in her own room, and again and again she reproached herself for her failures during the last month. Then she had a thought which added greatly to her misery. Arthur! He was sure to continue his persecutions, and how could she possibly make her copybook more presentable if he would not let her alone? Miss Day usually left the schoolroom during the writing hour, and the older girls were often absent, too. With no one around but the little children, Arthur had ample opportunities to torment her and ruin her work. Elsie didn't tell tales; besides, she could never have sought help from the adults. Arthur was his mother's great favorite, and telling on him would have brought a great deal of trouble to Elsie herself. She wondered if she might persuade her uncle to give her some peace, but that course seemed hopeless.

Elsie's Endless Wait

In desperation, she took her trouble to her Heavenly Father and asked for His help. She was still on her knees when someone knocked on the door. Elsie opened it to find her Aunt Adelaide.

"I'm writing to Rose," Adelaide said cheerfully. "Would you like to write a little note to her? I can enclose it in my letter." But as she spoke, she saw Elsie's tear-stained face and worried expression. "Whatever is the matter, child?" she asked, taking Elsie's hand and drawing her close.

With a great many tears, Elsie sobbed out the whole story, including her father's threat and her fear that she could not, because of Arthur's endless teasing, do well enough to avoid the punishment.

Adelaide's sympathies were fully enlisted, and wiping the child's tears away, she said reassuringly, "Never mind about Arthur, dear. From now on, I will take my book or needlework to the schoolroom every day, and I'll sit there through the writing hour. That will take care of Arthur. But why didn't you tell all this to your father?"

"I don't want to tattle, Aunt Adelaide, and it would make your mother so angry with me. Besides, I can't tell Papa anything."

"I understand," Adelaide comforted, and to herself, she said, "It's no wonder the child can't talk to him. Horace is strangely stern with her, and I mean to give him a good talking to!"

Leaving Elsie with a warm kiss, Adelaide had every intention of finding her brother and carrying out her mission. But he had gone out, and when he returned, brought several gentlemen with him. It was some time before she had the opportunity to get Horace alone, and by then, her resolve had disappeared.

A Terrible Injustice

Still, Adelaide's promise had come like an answer to Elsie's prayer, and when her aunt left her room, Elsie's heart was greatly lifted. Locking her door against any surprise intrusion by Enna, Elsie went to her bureau, unlocked a drawer, and removed the purse she was knitting for her father, to replace the one she'd given to Rose Allison. Elsie had started this project even before Horace's return, and now it was nearly finished. How many of her hopes and fears were woven into its bright gold and blue beads!

With her aunt's kind promise fresh in her mind, Elsie settled into her sewing chair and began to work. Her little fingers moved briskly, and the bright, shining needles glanced in and out. As she knitted, her thoughts moved equally swiftly: "No wonder Papa is vexed with me. I've never had such a bad report. What's come over me? It seems I can't study. Maybe I need a holiday. Could it be laziness? If it is, I should be punished. I *will* try harder next month. It's only a month, after all, and then June will be over. Miss Day will go North, and she won't return till August or maybe September, and we'll have a long summer holiday. And this month won't be so hard. No classes on Saturday. That means no class tomorrow, so I can finish this purse. I wonder if Papa will be pleased." She sighed deeply. "I've disappointed him twice this week — the bird and now my bad report. But I will do better next month, especially with Aunt Adelaide's help."

Her thoughts ran on in this way. "I wonder how we will spend our vacation? I went to Ashlands last summer, and then the Carringtons came here, and poor Herbert had such a dreadful time with his hip. How thankful I am not to be lame and always to be so healthy. But Papa probably won't let me go to Ashlands this year, or ask them here. He thinks Lucy isn't a suitable companion, and I was very naughty when she was here. Have I been more naughty than I ever was before he came home? I wonder if he will punish me severely? I wonder what that means?"

At that, a new and horrible thought struck her, and she dropped her work. "He can't mean *that*! He wouldn't send me away! It would break my heart! I must be very, very good, so that I never deserve a severe punishment; then it makes no difference what he means."

Elsie had heard vague stories about naughty children who were sent away by their parents. She had heard of schools where children actually lived, separated from their families and their homes. In her imagination, this was the most terrible thing that could happen to a child. What if this were the severe punishment her Papa had threatened? The thought of it made her tremble with fear. For all her troubles, she could not bear to be separated from her dear father when she had so recently found him. At the thought of losing him again, she became more determined than ever to do her best to please her Papa and to win his love.

The next day, when she had put the final touches on the beaded purse, she asked Aunt Chloe if her father was at home.

"No, darling," the nurse replied. "He rode out earlier with some gentlemen."

Elsie neatly put away her knitting things and took a piece of notepaper from her desk. Then she wrote, in her very best hand: "A present for my dear Papa, from his little daughter, Elsie." Carefully she pinned the note to the purse and carried it to her father's room. Fearing that he might have returned, she rapped gently at the door, but as there was no answer, she went in. She was about to place the gift on her father's dressing table when his voice startled her.

"What are you doing in my room without my permission?" he demanded.

Elsie quaked and tried to hold back tears as she silently put the purse in his hand. He looked at the present, then at his daughter.

"I made it for you, Papa," she said softly. "Please take it."

"It is really very pretty, " he said, examining the beaded purse closely. "Is this possibly your work? Of course it is. I had no idea you have so much taste and skill. Thank you, Daughter. I'll be happy to take it, and I will use it with great pleasure."

He had taken her hand as he spoke, and now he lifted her onto his knee and asked, "Elsie, my child, why do you always seem so afraid of me? I don't like it."

With a sudden impulse, she threw her arms around his neck and kissed his cheek. Dropping her head onto his shoulder, she sobbed, "Oh, Papa, I love you so very dearly! Won't you love me? I know I've been naughty, but I will try to be good."

For the first time since they had met, Horace folded his child in his arms and kissed her with all the tenderness of a loving parent.

"But I do love you, my little Daughter," he said softly.

So great was Elsie's happiness that she did not try to stop her tears.

"Why are you crying, dear?" Horace asked.

"Because I'm so very happy!"

"Then if you care so much for my love, you mustn't tremble and turn pale whenever I speak to you. I'm not a cruel tyrant, you know."

"It's only because you look so stern. I can't bear to have you so angry with me," she said and added, "but I'm not afraid of you now."

He hugged her again, and as they sat there together, they heard the supper bell. "Now go into my dressing room and wash your face," Horace instructed, "and we'll go down together."

There were several visitors at the table that evening, and the conversation centered on the adults, but every now and then, Horace bestowed a loving look on his daughter, and he carefully attended to all her needs. She was happier than she had ever been.

Things proceeded this way for some time. Elsie did not see as much of her father as she wished, because he was often away on business and he frequently brought guests home on his return. But whenever he saw her, he showed great kindness, and she gradually began to overcome her fear of him. She looked forward to the time when he would have more leisure for her, but she was genuinely happy even so. With her mind now at ease, she could concentrate on her lessons. Adelaide faithfully kept her promise, coming to the schoolroom every day. With Arthur unable to annoy her, Elsie progressed well with her writing; her copybook showed marked improvement in her penmanship. There was not a single blot on any page, and she was actually anticipating with pleasure the next report to her father.

But there came a morning when Miss Day was in her very worst humor — peevish, fretful, irritable, and unreasonable to the extreme. As usual, Elsie took the brunt of her bad temper. Miss Day found fault with everything Elsie did; she scolded and shook the little girl, refused to explain the method of solving a very difficult arithmetic problem, and wouldn't allow the girl to ask help of anyone else. Then she punished Elsie when the problem was done incorrectly. Elsie struggled to hold back her tears but at last she began to cry, and Miss Day derided her as a baby for shedding tears and a dunce for not understanding the arithmetic.

Elsie bore it all without answering back, but her patience only provoked Miss Day all the more. Finally, when Elsie came up to recite her last lesson, Miss Day deliberately put her questions in the most perplexing way and then didn't allow the child to answer. Throwing down the textbook, Miss Day angrily scolded Elsie and marked down the lesson as a complete failure.

Poor Elsie could take no more. She protested, "I *did* know my lesson Miss Day, every word of it. But you didn't ask your questions as usual or give me time to answer."

"I say you did not know it, and you failed," Miss Day angrily replied. "Now sit down and learn every word of it over again."

But Elsie did not sit down. "I do know it if you will hear me right," she cried indignantly, "and it is unjust of you to mark it a failure."

Miss Day was furious. "Impudent girl!" she screamed. "How dare you contradict me? I'm taking you to your father right now!"

Seizing Elsie by the arm, the teacher dragged her from the room and into the hallway.

"Please don't tell Papa!" Elsie begged, but Miss Day only pushed her to Horace's door. It was open, and he was inside working at his writing desk.

"What is all this?" he asked as they entered.

"Elsie has been very impertinent, sir," Miss Day said. "She accused me of being unjust, and she contradicted me."

Elsie's Endless Wait

Horace was frowning darkly now. "Is this true, Elsie? Did you contradict your teacher?"

"Yes, sir," she said softly.

"Then I certainly must punish you." He picked up a small ruler from his desk and took Elsie's hand as if he meant to strike it.

"Oh, no, Papa!" she cried in alarm. But he put the ruler down and said, "I shall punish you by depriving you of your play today and giving you only bread and water for your dinner." He pointed to a stool in the corner of his large room. "Sit down there and do not move."

Then with a dismissive wave of his hand at Miss Day, he said, "I think she will never do the like again."

Soon after, the dinner bell rang, and Horace left, and after a little time had passed, old Pompey came up the stairs carrying a tray with a tumbler of water and a slice of bread on a plate.

"This isn't much of a meal, Miss Elsie," he said as he put the tray down beside her. "Mr. Dinsmore says it's all you can have, but if you say so, I'll ask Phoebe to send up something more for you before your father comes back."

"That's kind of you, Pompey, but I can't disobey Papa," Elsie said, "and I'm really not hungry at all."

Pompey lingered a bit, hesitant to leave her alone, but Elsie told him to go back to the dining room where he might be needed.

When her father returned, the glass of water and piece of bread lay uneaten on the tray.

"What is the meaning of this?" he demanded. "Why haven't you eaten what I sent to you?"

"I'm not hungry, Papa."

"That's nothing but stubbornness, Elsie, and temper. Take that bread and eat it now. You will eat every crumb and drink every drop of your water."

She obeyed instantly. As he watched, she took a bite of bread, but hard as she tried, she simply could not swallow it. "I can't," she said. "It chokes me."

"You will obey me," he said coldly. "Take some water to wash it down."

She saw that it was no use to protest, and at length every crumb of bread and every drop of water was gone.

His severity in no way diminished, Horace said, "Never dare show me such temper again, Elsie. You won't escape so easily next time. You are to obey me always. Do you understand?"

She knew that his words were unfair — it had not been temper — but Elsie was too fearful now to speak in her own defense. As the tears gathered in her eyes, Horace told her that she was to stay in his room until he returned.

Timidly she asked, "May I have my lesson books, Papa?"

"You may. I'll have them brought to you."

"And my Bible?"

"Yes, yes," he said impatiently as he left the room and shut the door on her.

When he returned to the drawing room, Adelaide asked him what troubled Elsie.

"She has been impertinent to the governess, and I've confined her to my room for the rest of the day," he said with impatience.

"Are you so sure, Horace, that Elsie was to blame?" Adelaide asked as gently as she could. "From what Lora has told me, I believe that Miss Day is often cruelly unfair to your daughter — more than to any of the others."

Horace looked at his sister in surprise. "Are you certain of that?"

"I am. And it is a fact that Miss Day sometimes mistreats her."

Horace colored deeply. "I will not allow that," he said heatedly. But after a moment's thought, he added, "I think you are wrong in this instance, however. Elsie herself acknowledged that she had been impertinent. However severe you think I am, I didn't condemn her without a hearing."

"Believe me, Horace, if she was impertinent, it was after serious provocation. Her acknowledgment is no proof at all, to my mind, for Elsie is so sensitive she'd think herself impertinent simply because Miss Day said so."

"Surely not," he said incredulously. "Elsie does not lack sense."

But Adelaide's words troubled him, and he was half-inclined to go back upstairs and question his child more closely. He considered this, then gave up the idea, telling himself, "If she refuses to be frank with me and speak up for herself, she deserves her punishment. And there was that stubbornness about eating." Horace was very proud, and he did not like to admit, especially to himself, that he may have punished his child unjustly.

It was almost supper time when Horace finally returned to his room, but Elsie didn't hear him enter. He saw that she had not moved from the stool and sat bent over her little Bible. When he came close, she looked up with a start. "Papa," she said, "will you forgive me?"

"Certainly I will, if you are really sorry." He leaned over and kissed her, a cold and dutiful kiss. "Now go let Aunt Chloe dress you for supper."

A Terrible Injustice

But Elsie's punishment was not truly over, for she continued to struggle with herself. She was particularly distressed about her bad mark that day and how it would appear on her monthly report. Yet it had not been her fault, and again and again she determined to tell her father what had really happened. Again and again, however, she failed to summon the courage to approach him, and the days passed without her speaking to her father — until it was too late.

CHAPTER

8

Arthur's Scheme

*"For God will bring every deed
into judgment, including
every hidden thing,
whether it is good
or evil."*

ECCLESIASTES 12:14

Arthur's Scheme

*I*t was Friday, and Miss Day's reports were to be presented on the next morning. School was over, but Elsie remained alone in the classroom to arrange her books and her writing and drawing materials. When she had finished, she took her report book from the desk and looked over her marks for the last month. As her eye stopped on the one bad mark, she lamented yet again that she had never told her father the whole story of what had occurred. Her copybook, however, gave her complete satisfaction, for every page showed painstaking care and clear improvement. And not a single ink blot marred any of its pages.

"This will surely please Papa," she said to herself. "How good Aunt Adelaide was to come sit with me!"

Then she replaced the copybook and locked her desk securely. She went to her room and placed her desk key in its habitual place on the mantel.

That afternoon, when Elsie and the others had gone out for their walk, Arthur found himself alone in the house with nothing to do. Having gorged himself on candies a few days before, he still felt too sick for his usual activities and lounged lazily in the children's playroom. Although Arthur was not generally fond of reading, he decided to amuse himself with a book he had seen Elsie reading that morning. It was her book, of course, and she was not there to give it to him. But Arthur had very little respect for property rights, except his own.

With Elsie out and Chloe in the kitchen, Arthur felt certain no one would stop him from taking the book, and he went to Elsie's room. It was lying on the mantel, beside Elsie's desk key. Catching sight of the key, Arthur couldn't suppress a squeal of delight, for he knew exactly which lock the key fit. In an instant, he conceived a plan for the revenge he'd been seeking ever since the affair of his father's gold watch.

His hand reached for the key, but he hesitated. He had to think this through to avoid any chance of detection.

He wanted to deface Elsie's copybook, but Adelaide would testify to the girl's neatness, for his eldest sister had been in the schoolroom every day at writing hour. Adelaide, however, had just left to visit a friend and would be gone from Roselands for several weeks, so she posed no danger. Miss Day, to be sure, well knew the appearance of Elsie's book, but she was even less likely to interfere, and Arthur knew of no one else who could speak up for Elsie.

He decided to run the risk, and he grabbed the key. Checking the hallway to be sure no servants might see him, he hurried to the schoolroom. Almost giddy with glee, he unlocked Elsie's desk and took out her copybook. Using her own pen and ink, he proceeded to blot nearly every page. Some pages got big, black ink drops; others, two or three splatters. He also scribbled between the lines and in the margins so Elsie's work would appear as ugly as possible.

He knew that Horace was sure to be very angry with Elsie, and that thought pleased him mightily, but bad as Arthur was, it must be said that he was unaware of Horace's threatened punishment. The mischief did not take long to accomplish, though Arthur was frightened several times by the sounds of footsteps outside the schoolroom door. No one came in, however, and when the book was thoroughly ruined, he carefully replaced it, wiped the pen and replaced it too, and locked Elsie's desk. Then he rushed back to Elsie's room, put the key in its place on the mantel, and took the book that had been his original objective.

In all this, he had been seen by no one, and back in the playroom, he settled on a couch to read. But he could think of nothing except his vengeful act and its probable consequences. Now that it was too late, he experienced some doubts; yet he never for a single moment considered confessing and saving Elsie from blame. Then another thought struck him: he had Elsie's book, so it was obvious he had been into her room. That would raise suspicions. He jumped up, intending to take the book back, but at that moment, he heard Elsie's voice from the hall. "Well," he thought to himself, "I'll just bluff it out."

Elsie didn't notice the guilty look on his face when she entered. "I'm looking for the book I was reading. I thought it was in my room," she said, searching likely places. Then she saw it in Arthur's hands. "Oh, you have it! You can keep it, Arthur," she said, "and I'll finish it another time."

But Arthur tossed the book to her. "Take it back," he said roughly. "I don't like it. 'Tisn't any fun."

"I think it's very interesting, and you're welcome to read it," Elsie said politely. "But if you don't want to, I will take it."

The next morning was the last day of the school term, and the writing hour was omitted, so Elsie had no reason to open her copybook. As soon as the children had finished their brief exercises, Miss Day announced, "Young ladies and gentlemen, this is the regular day for your reports, and they are all prepared. Elsie, here is yours. Now take it and your copybook directly to your father."

Elsie obeyed. She was very conscious of the one bad mark in her report, but her copybook had been written with such care and effort that she hoped her father would not be seriously displeased. Neither she nor anyone else except Arthur knew what had been done to her careful penmanship.

She found her father in his room and handed him the report. With a slight frown, he remarked, "There is one very bad mark here for recitation. But as all the other marks are remarkably good, I will excuse it."

Then he took the copybook. He opened to the first page, and to Elsie's surprise, he threw her a look of great displeasure. His face darkened as he leafed through the rest of the pages. Finally, he said, his voice low and edged with anger, "I see I shall have to keep my promise, Elsie."

"What, Papa?" she asked, turning pale with fear.

"What!" he shouted. "You ask what! Didn't I tell you positively that I would punish you if your copybook did not present a better appearance this month?"

"But it does, Papa! I tried so hard, and there are no blots in it."

"No blots?" He thrust the book under her face. "What do you call these?"

Elsie gazed at the pages of her book in unfeigned astonishment. At first, she could hardly believe the book was really hers. Then she turned to her father and said earnestly, "I didn't do that, Papa."

"Then who did?"

"I don't know, Papa."

"I must get to the bottom of this business," he declared, "and if it isn't your fault, you won't be punished. But if you

are telling a falsehood, Elsie, you shall be punished more severely than if you'd admitted your fault."

Taking her hand, he led her to the classroom where the other children were waiting to meet with their parents. Horace pushed the open copybook at the teacher and asked, "Elsie says these blots are not her work. Can you tell me whose they are?"

"Elsie *generally* tells the truth," Miss Day said smoothly, "but I must say that in this instance, I think she has not. Her desk has a good lock, and she keeps the key, so no one else could have gotten at her copybook."

Horace turned back to his daughter. "Have you ever left your desk unlocked," he asked "or left your key lying about?"

"No, sir, I'm sure I haven't," she answered quickly, though her voice trembled and her face had grown very pale.

"Then I am certain you have told me a falsehood, for the evidence is clear that this must be your work. Come with me." His face was almost as pale as hers, from rage rather than fear, and grabbing her hand again, he dragged her from the room. "I'll teach you to tell the truth to me at least."

Lora, who was just coming back to the schoolroom, heard Horace's angry words. She knew Elsie would never tell a falsehood, and as she looked around the room, her eyes fell on Arthur's guilty face. She hastily crossed to his desk and whispered, "I know that you had a hand in this, Arthur. You'd better confess it quickly, or Horace will half-kill Elsie."

"You don't know anything," Arthur replied.

"Oh, yes, I do," Lora persisted, "and if you don't speak up at once, I will save Elsie myself and find proof of your guilt later. It would be better for you to confess."

Elsie's Endless Wait

Arthur shoved his sister and shouted angrily, "Go away! I have nothing to confess."

Seeing that Arthur could not be moved, Lora rushed to Horace's room and banged the door open without a thought of knocking. She was just in time, for Horace's hand was raised, and he was just about to administer the first spanking of poor Elsie's life. The look he cast at his sister burned with fury, but she took no notice. Instead, Lora cried urgently, "Don't punish Elsie, for I'm sure she's innocent!"

Horace stayed his hand and demanded, "How do you know? What is your proof? Tell me, for I want to be convinced."

Elsie stood rigid at his side, too terrified even to cry.

"In the first place," Lora began, "there is Elsie's established character for truthfulness. In all the time she has been with us, she has always been perfectly truthful in word and deed. And what motive would she have for spoiling her own book? She knew that your punishment was certain to be very severe. Horace, I'm sure Arthur is at the bottom of this. He won't confess, but he doesn't deny it. And I saw Elsie's book just yesterday. It was neat and well written and had absolutely no blots."

Horace's expression changed dramatically as Lora spoke, and he found himself trembling at the thought of what he might have done if his sister had not intervened. "Thank you," he said softly when she finished. "Thank you, dear Lora, for stopping me before I punished Elsie unfairly. I need no more than your word to establish her innocence."

Lora, deeply relieved that she had prevented an injustice, quietly left the room as Horace was taking Elsie into his arms. "My poor child," he said. "My poor little Daughter, I have been terribly unjust to you."

Elsie hardly knew what to reply. "You thought I deserved it, Papa."

"And you have every reason to be angry with me," he continued, his voice strained with emotion. "I love you very much, Elsie, even when I seem cold and stern. And I am more thankful than words can express that I haven't punished you wrongly. I could never forgive myself if I had done that, and I think you have reason now to hate me for what I have done."

This idea struck Elsie like a bolt, and she sobbed, "Oh, Papa, I could never hate you. Never! Never!"

"There, there. Don't cry anymore, dear Daughter," he said, attempting to soothe both her and himself. "Adelaide tells me that perhaps you were not to blame for being impertinent to Miss Day the other day. I want you to tell me all the circumstances now. I won't encourage you to find faults with your teacher, but I also have no intention of allowing you to be mistreated."

"Aunt Lora was there, and she can tell you what happened."

"I want the story from *you*, Elsie. I want to know exactly what passed between you and Miss Day, as best you can remember."

For all her desire to defend herself, Elsie was extremely reluctant to speak against another. She was careful to tell the truth without casting blame on Miss Day, but as she spoke, her father grew increasingly incensed.

"Elsie," he said at last, "if I'd known all this at the time, I would not have punished you. Why didn't you tell me that you were ill treated?"

"But you didn't ask, Papa."

"I asked if it was true that you contradicted Miss Day."

Elsie's Endless Wait

"Yes, sir, and that was true."

"But you should have told me the whole story, though I understand now that I frightened you with my sternness. Well, Daughter," he said gently, "I will endeavor to be less stern in the future, and you must try to be less timid with me."

"I will try, Papa, but I can't help being afraid when you are so angry with me."

Elsie and Horace sat together for a long time, and Elsie talked with him more freely than she had ever done. She spoke about her sorrows and her joys. She told him about Rose Allison and the many happy hours they had spent together in Bible study and prayer. She described how sad she felt when her dear friend went away, and she told him about the wonderful letters she received from Rose. Horace was both pleased by and interested in his child's conversation, and he encouraged her with occasional questions and words of approval. While she was talking, he noticed the gold chain around her neck. "What is this?" he asked.

Gently, Elsie took out the miniature, and Horace needed no explanation to recognize the beautiful face in the portrait. The sight took him back many years, to the few short months he had shared with his wife. Looking from the portrait to his child, he said, as if addressing someone else in the room, "Yes, she is very much like — the same features, the same expression, complexion, hair, and all. She'll be the very counterpart someday."

Elsie caught part of his words, "Am I like Mamma?" she asked him.

"Yes, you are, darling, very much indeed."

"And you loved Mamma?"

"Very dearly."

"Then tell me about her, please," she begged.

"But I haven't much to tell," he sighed. "We knew each other such a short time before we were torn apart. And now we can never meet again on this earth."

"But we may meet her again in heaven, Papa," Elsie said with certainty, "for she loved Jesus, and if we love Him, we will go to heaven when we die. Do you love Jesus, Papa?"

This question greatly concerned Elsie, but instead of answering her, Horace asked, "Do you, Elsie?"

"Oh, yes, sir! Very much. I love Him even better than I love you, my own dear father."

He searched her little face. "How do you know that?" he wondered.

"Just as I know I love you," she responded with evident surprise. "I love to talk of Jesus. I love to tell Him all my troubles, and ask Him to forgive my sins and make me holy. It means so much to know that He loves me and always will, even if no one else does."

Horace set her down from his lap and said, "It's almost dinner time. Go now, and get ready, dear Daughter."

"Are you displeased, Papa?" she asked a little anxiously.

"Not at all, dear," he replied with a gentle laugh. "I thought we might ride together this afternoon. What do you say?"

At her eager response, he again told her to prepare for dinner, but before she could leave, he asked one question more: "Do you remember where you put your desk key yesterday? Did you take it when you went riding?"

"No, sir. I left it on the mantel in my room and —"

She stopped suddenly, but her father instructed her to continue. "I don't want you to express any suspicions," he assured her, "but I must have all the facts you can furnish. Was Aunt Chloe in your room while you were out?"

"No, sir. She was in the kitchen with Aunt Phoebe until I came back."

"Do you know if anyone else entered your room?"

"I don't *know*, sir, but I think Arthur must have been there, because when I came home, he was reading a book I'd left on the mantel."

"Ah, ha!" her father said, and nodded with satisfaction. "Now I see. Elsie, go on to your dinner, and I'll join you shortly."

But Elsie, who did not fully understand the implications of her father's questions, lingered a moment, and when her father looked at her inquiringly, she said, "Please don't be too angry with him, Papa. I don't think Arthur meant to take my book without permission."

"Don't worry, Daughter, I won't hurt him."

It so happened that the elder Mr. Dinsmore and his wife were visiting some friends in the city, and Horace was acting as head of the household in his father's absence. Though Arthur's father was expected back that evening, his mother would be away for several days, and Arthur was beginning to worry very much about the consequences of his actions — not without reason. His brother's wrath was fully aroused, and Horace was determined that this time, his younger brother would not escape punishment for his misdeeds.

Arthur was seated at the table when Horace entered the dining room.

"Step into the library a moment," Horace said to the boy. "I have something to say to you."

Arthur's Scheme

Arthur didn't move, but answered back, "I don't want to hear it."

Without raising his voice even a fraction, Horace said, "I'm sure you don't, sir, but that makes no difference. Walk into the library at once."

Under his breath Arthur muttered something about doing as he pleased, but he was too intimidated by Horace's determined look and forceful manner to disobey. Reluctantly he stood up and slowly followed his brother.

In the library, with the door closed, Horace said evenly, "Now tell me how you came to meddle with Elsie's copybook."

Arthur's denial was hot with false indignation, but Horace simply went on, "It's useless for you to deny it, Arthur, for I know it all. You went to Elsie's room yesterday, when she was out and Aunt Chloe was in the kitchen. You took her desk key from the mantel and went to the schoolroom and did your mischief, hoping to get her in trouble. When you had returned the key, you thought you had escaped detection. And I very nearly gave my innocent child the spanking you deserve."

Arthur looked up in amazement. "Who told you?" he demanded. "No one saw me!" Then catching himself, he said quickly, "I tell you I didn't do it. I don't know anything about it."

Suddenly, Horace revealed his anger, taking Arthur by the collar and shaking him. "How dare you repeat your falsehood?"

"Let me go," Arthur whined. "I want my dinner."

"You will get no dinner, sir," Horace replied. "I am locking you in your room until our father returns. And if he doesn't punish you as you deserve, I will. I intend that you receive your just deserts at least once in your miserable life. I know you did this in revenge for the watch business, but I give you fair warning — if you even attempt to harm my child in any way, you will regret it."

Arthur seemed to want to protest, but the look in Horace's eyes told him it was useless. He fell into a sullen whimpering: "You wouldn't treat me like this if Mamma were here."

"But she is not here, and even if she were, she could not save you this time," Horace answered. He had by now hauled Arthur up the stairs and to his bedroom. Horace pushed the boy inside, locked the door, and pocketed the key.

If Arthur expected sympathy from his father, he was sadly disappointed. Mr. Dinsmore took great pride in Horace and trusted his judgment in almost everything. Besides, the older man had a strong sense of justice, and he hated any mean and underhanded behavior. So when the older man returned and Horace had reported on his brother's latest activities, Arthur received a punishment which he truly never forgot.

CHAPTER

9

A Matter of Conscience

*"Judge for yourselves whether
it is right in God's sight
to obey you rather
than God."*

ACTS 4:19

A Matter of Conscience

*H*appy days had come for little Elsie. Her father treated her with the most loving affection and kept her with him as much as possible. He took her wherever he went — riding, walking, on visits to the neighboring plantations. She was much admired for her beauty and sweet disposition, but even with this new attention, she lost none of her natural modesty. She felt grateful for all the kindness she received from others, but her happiest hours were spent at home with her father. She could sit for hours with him, talking or reading. He helped with her studies and taught her some botany and geology on their walks. He helped with her drawing. He sang with her when she played piano, bought her stacks of new sheet music, and hired the best music masters to instruct her. In short, Horace took a lively interest in all she did and gave her the most tender care. He was extremely proud of her, and flattered by the praise of others.

Everyone could see the change in Elsie herself. Her eyes became bright with happiness, and her face lost its pensive expression, becoming as rosy and merry as Enna's.

During their summer holiday, Horace took his daughter traveling, and they stayed at several fashionable resorts. Elsie, who had not traveled anywhere since arriving at Roselands, enjoyed every minute of their trip. They were gone from July until September, and Elsie was rested and ready to resume her studies. But she was not sorry to learn that Miss Day had been delayed in the North for a few weeks and the start of school was to be postponed.

Elsie's Endless Wait

Adelaide was delighted by the changes she saw in Elsie on the day that the child and her father returned home. The family was gathered in the drawing room, and Elsie was entertaining her younger aunts and uncles with stories of her holiday.

"It's good to see how entirely she seems to have overcome her fear of her father," Lora agreed, watching as Elsie ran confidently to Horace and appeared to be asking him for something. With his permission, she displayed a richly bound book of engravings acquired on the journey.

She had, indeed, lost her fear and could now talk to Horace as freely as Enna ever did. And during all their time together, he had never had occasion to scold her or use a single harsh word.

On the first Sabbath afternoon after their return, Elsie was alone in her room. She had asked not to accompany her father on his ride; instead, she spent the time with her favorite books — the Bible, her hymnbook, and *Pilgrim's Progress* — and in self-reflection. She had just opened the Bible to the story of Elijah, which she promised to read to Chloe later, when she heard a rattling at her locked door.

"Open this door right now, Elsie Dinsmore!" Enna shouted imperiously. "I want in!"

Elsie sighed, realizing that this was the end of her nice afternoon, but she opened the door and asked pleasantly, "What do you want, Enna?"

"I want to come in," Enna declared in a saucy little voice, "and I want you to tell me a story. Mamma says you must, because I have a cold and can't go out."

A Matter of Conscience

"Well, I'm going to read a beautiful story to Aunt Chloe when she comes back, and you're welcome to stay and listen."

"No!" Enna cried. "I don't want it read." She flounced across the room and took her seat in a delicate rosewood rocking chair that Horace had recently given to his daughter. With her sharp little thumbnail, she began to scratch on the arm of the chair "Please don't do that to my new chair," Elsie said in alarm. "It's a gift from Papa, and I don't want it spoiled."

"Who cares for your old chair," Enna said scornfully and dug another gouge into the wood. "You're a little old maid — so particular about your things. That's what Mamma says. Now, tell me a story."

"If you stop scratching the chair," Elsie said with remarkable patience, "I can tell you about Elijah on Mount Carmel, or Belshazzar's feast, or the children in the fiery furnace. . . . "

"No! None of your old Bible stories. I want to hear the pretty fairy tale that Herbert Carrington likes so much."

"But I can't tell that one today," Elsie said firmly. "I can tell any story that's suitable for the Sabbath and honors God, but not fairy tales. I can tell it to you tomorrow if you wait."

"I want it now!" Enna shouted. "If you don't do what I want, I'll tell Mamma on you!"

With that, the little girl jumped from the chair and dashed out of the room, and it was not many minutes later when a servant came to summon Elsie.

Mrs. Dinsmore began chiding Elsie the moment she walked into her room: "Aren't you ashamed of yourself, Elsie? Why do you refuse Enna so small a favor, especially when the poor child isn't well? I believe you are the most selfish girl I've ever seen."

Elsie's Endless Wait

Elsie tried to explain: "I offered to tell a Bible story or anything suitable for the Sabbath. But it would be wrong to tell a fairy tale today, for the Bible tells us to 'observe the Sabbath day by keeping it holy.'"

"Nonsense! A fairy tale is no more harmful today than any other day," Mrs. Dinsmore said angrily.

At her side, Enna sobbed and whined, "I want a pretty fairy tale. Make her tell me the fairy tale, Mamma!"

Enna's wailing and her mother's scolding had apparently disturbed the elder Mr. Dinsmore, who came charging in from the adjoining room. From his puffy red eyes and tousled hair, Elsie thought he must have been napping, and he was in no mood to listen to a quarrel.

"What's all this fuss?" he roared.

"Nothing," said his wife, whose voice had suddenly grown sweet, "except that Enna is not well enough to go out and wants a fairy tale to help pass the time. And your granddaughter" — she stared pointedly at Elsie — "is too lazy or willful to tell it."

Mr. Dinsmore turned on Elsie. "Is that so? Well, there's an old saying, little girl. 'A bird that *can* sing and *won't* sing must be *made* to sing.'"

Elsie, who knew the meaning of the saying all too well, started to speak, but Mrs. Dinsmore cut her off. "The child pretends it is all on account of conscientious scruples. She says it isn't fit for the Sabbath. I don't care what that Mrs. Murray taught her. *I* say it is a great impertinence for a child of Elsie's age to set her opinion against yours and mine. I know very well it's just an excuse because she doesn't choose to oblige."

"Of course, it's an excuse," Mr. Dinsmore said hotly. Though by nature a just man, he also had a quick and often unreasonable temper, like all the Dinsmores.

186

Elsie spoke up, "No, Grandpa. It's not an excuse — "

"How dare you contradict me, you impudent little girl!" Catching her by the arm, he set her down hard on a chair. "Now, little miss," he shouted, "don't move from that chair till your father comes home. Then we'll see what he thinks of such impertinence. If he doesn't give you the punishment you deserve, I miss my guess."

"Please, Grandpa, I — "

Again he stopped her. "Hold your tongue, girl!" he bellowed. "And not another word until your father comes."

For the next half hour — and a very long one it seemed — Elsie sat in silence, wishing for, yet dreading, her father's return. Would he punish her as her grandfather seemed to wish? Or would he listen patiently to her side of the story? Might she be punished in either case? A few months before, she would have been certain of serious chastisement. And even now, though she trusted her father's love beyond a doubt, she also knew that Horace was a strict disciplinarian who never excused her faults.

At last she heard the sound of his steps in the hall, and her heart beat faster as he entered the room and addressed his father, "You wanted to see me, sir?"

"I want you to attend to this girl," Mr. Dinsmore said gruffly, nodding his head toward Elsie. "She has been very impertinent to me."

Horace's expression was of complete amazement, and he turned to her with such grave eyes that her tears immediately began to flow.

"It is hard to believe," Horace said, "that my little Elsie could be guilty of such conduct. If she has been, she must be punished, for I cannot allow this kind of behavior. Elsie, go to my dressing room and stay there until I come to you."

Elsie's Endless Wait

"Papa, I — "

"Hush!" he commanded with some of the old sternness. Sobbing, Elsie instantly obeyed.

Horace took a seat and turned to his father. "Now, sir, if you please, I'd like to hear the whole story," he said calmly. "Precisely what has Elsie done and said? What was the provocation, for that must be taken into account if I am to do her justice."

"If you do her justice, you'll spank her well," Mr. Dinsmore grumbled.

Horace colored deeply, for he strongly resented interference in his management of his child. But he calmed himself and asked again for the details. Mr. Dinsmore deferred to his wife, and she painted as bleak a picture as she could against Elsie. She was, however, obliged to state that it was Elsie's refusal to humor Enna and to tell a fairy story on the Sabbath that started the whole upset. This admission vexed Horace immensely, and he informed his stepmother that, while he did not always approve of Elsie's strict notions on such matters, his daughter was not to be made a slave to Enna's whims. If Elsie chose to tell Enna a story — or do anything for her — he had no objection. But never was Elsie to be forced, and Enna must understand that she had no right to Elsie's favors.

His father, hearing the whole story for the first time, agreed.

"You are right there, Horace," he said, "but that doesn't excuse Elsie's impertinence to me. I have to agree with my wife that it is a great piece of impudence to set her opinions against ours. Besides, she contradicted me flatly."

He then related the exact words of his exchange with Elsie. But he changed the tone of her words, and omitted the fact that he had interrupted her before she could complete a

sentence. From this recounting, Horace received the erro-
neous impression that Elsie had been very disrespectful, and
he left the room with every intention of giving her a severe
punishment indeed. But as he walked slowly to his room, his
anger began to cool, and he determined that, to be fair, he
must hear her side of the story before he condemned her.

When he entered his room, Elsie could see that his face
was sad and serious, but there was little sternness in it. He
sat beside her on the couch and hugged her gently. Finally,
he said, "I am very sorry to hear so bad an account of your
behavior. I don't want to punish you."

Elsie didn't say anything, but he could feel her shaking as
she cried.

"I won't condemn you unheard," he said gently. "Now tell
me how you came to be impertinent to your grandfather."

"I didn't mean to be saucy," she managed to say.

"Then stop crying and tell me everything that happened.
I want to know what words passed between you and Enna,
as well as Mrs. Dinsmore and your grandfather. I know I
can trust you to tell the truth and not to use a falsehood to
save yourself from punishment."

"Thank you for saying that, Papa," Elsie said, smiling up
at him. "I will try to tell you just what happened."

Carefully, she repeated everything that had occurred,
word-for-word when she could. Her account sounded very
different from her grandfather's, and she added that she had
tried to explain to Mr. Dinsmore that it was not unwilling-
ness to oblige Enna, but fear of doing wrong that led her to
refuse to tell the fairy story.

"Was I very naughty?" she asked when she had finished.

"So much depends on the tone," her father said honestly.
"If you spoke to your grandfather as you did in repeating

your words just now, then no, I don't think you were impertinent. But you must always treat your grandfather with respect. And understand that to him there is something quite unseemly about a little girl setting her opinion against that of her elders. You must never do that with me."

Elsie hung her head and asked, "Are you going to punish me, Papa?"

"Yes," he said, "but first I'm going to take you downstairs to ask your grandfather's pardon. I know you don't want to do it, but you must."

"I'll do whatever you want, Papa, but please tell me what to say."

"You must say 'Grandpa, I did not intend to be disrespectful, and I'm very sorry for whatever seemed impertinent in my words or tones. Will you please forgive me, and I will try always to be respectful in the future.' You can say all of that with truth, can't you?"

"Yes sir, because I am sorry and I do intend to be respectful to Grandpa always."

When they went to his father's room, Horace said, "Elsie has come to beg your pardon, sir."

Mr. Dinsmore, casting a triumphant look at his wife, said, "That's as it should be. I told the girl you wouldn't support any such impertinence."

"I will never support her in wrongdoing," Horace replied, a marked tone of displeasure in his voice, "but neither will I allow her to be imposed upon. Now speak, Elsie, what I told you to say."

When Elsie had sobbed out her apology, Mr. Dinsmore said coldly, "Yes, I must forgive you, girl, but I hope your father won't let you off without a proper punishment."

A Matter of Conscience

"I will attend to that," Horace replied in a tone as frosty as his father's. "I certainly intend to punish her *as she deserves*."

He had laid special stress on those final words, and Elsie totally misunderstood his meaning. She trembled so with fear that he had to carry her back to his room. When they were out of anyone's hearing, he wiped her tears away and said with a smile, "Don't be so afraid, Elsie. I'm not going to be severe."

She looked at him in glad surprise.

"I said I would punish you as you deserve, so I intend to keep you here with me until your bedtime. You can't go down to supper, and I'm going to give you a long lesson that you must be able to recite perfectly before you go to bed."

Elsie worried for a moment that the lesson might be something inappropriate for the Sabbath, but she relaxed when her father took his Bible and pointed to the thirteenth and fourteenth chapters of John.

"But that won't be a real punishment, Papa," she laughed. "I love these chapters, and I've read them so often I almost know all the words already."

Pretending to be very stern, Horace said, "Hush! Don't tell me my punishments are *no* punishments. Now take your book to that seat by the window and learn what I tell you."

Horace took up a newspaper, but in fact he spent most of his time looking at his child as she diligently studied the holy book. It struck him with great force how important she was to him, and he wondered how he could ever have been harsh with her.

When the supper bell rang, Horace got up to leave. "I'll send some supper up to you, and I want you to eat it," he said at the door.

Elsie's Endless Wait

"Will it be bread and water, Papa?" she asked with a smile.

"Wait and see," he laughed.

The tray of food that Pompey soon brought to Elsie was a far cry from the fare provided during her last imprisonment. Elsie was truly astonished when she saw a plate of hot, buttered muffins, a large piece of broiled chicken, a cup of jelly, and another cup filled to the brim with steaming coffee.

"I reckon you have been a very nice girl today," Pompey said as he set the tray down, "or else your Papa thinks you're a little sick."

As Elsie put away her book and began to eat, Pompey told her, "Just ring the bell if you want something more, and I'll fetch it for you. Your father told me so himself."

Elsie certainly enjoyed every crumb of her supper, and when Horace returned, she thanked him graciously. "But I thought you didn't allow me such things," she commented.

Playfully, he said, "Don't you know, Daughter, that I am absolute monarch of this small kingdom and you are not to question my decrees?"

His tone then became more serious, "I do not allow it as a rule, because I do not think it for your good. But this once, I don't think it will hurt. I know that you don't presume on favors, Elsie, and I wanted to indulge you a bit. I think you were made to suffer more than you deserved this afternoon."

His words were very tender, and before he went on, he kissed her gently on the forehead.

A Matter of Conscience

"Don't think, though, that I'm excusing you for impertinence. I am not. But what you had to endure from Enna's insolence — it will stop, for I will not have it."

"I don't mind it much, Papa," Elsie responded. "I'm used to it, for Enna has always treated me that way."

"And why did I never hear this before?" he asked, his temper rising. "It's abominable! Not to be endured! And I shall see that Miss Enna is made to understand that *my* daughter is fully her equal in every respect and to be treated as such."

Elsie, who was somewhat frightened at his vehemence, made no reply, and her father continued in a somewhat softer tone, "I have no doubt your grandfather and his wife would have liked me to force you to give in to Enna's whim. But you are to use your own judgment wherever Enna is concerned. If I had bidden you to tell her that story, well, that would have been a different matter. You are never to set your will, or your opinion of right and wrong, against mine, Elsie, for I won't allow it. I don't altogether like some of these strict notions of yours, and I give you fair warning — should they ever come into conflict with my wishes and commands, you are to give them up.

"But don't look so alarmed, Elsie," he added very kindly. "I hope that will never happen."

Her face was very serious as she lay her hand on his shoulder and said, "Oh, Papa! Please don't ever ask me to do anything wrong. It would break my heart."

"Elsie dear, I never want you to do wrong. On the contrary, I want you always to do right. But *I* must be the judge of what is right and wrong for you. Remember that you are only a little girl and not yet capable of judging for yourself. As long as you obey your father without hesitation, there will be no problem."

His tone was kind but firm, and Elsie had a strange sense as he spoke, as if she were in the shadow of some great, impending trouble. But with some effort, she managed to banish this feeling of foreboding and enjoy her present blessings. She knew that her father loved her dearly, and he was not requiring her to do anything against her conscience. Perhaps he never would. God could incline his heart to respect her principles. Or if the dreaded trial should happen, He would give her His wisdom and strength to bear it, for she remembered His promise, "And God is faithful; He will not let you be tempted beyond what you can bear. But when you are tempted, He will also provide a way out so that you can stand up under it."

"What are you thinking about?" Horace asked her at length.

"A good many things, Papa. I was thinking of what you said and how glad I am to know that you truly love me. And I was asking God to help us both to do His will. And I thought that I might be able to always do what you bid, without disobeying Him. May I say my lesson now? I think I know it perfectly."

"Of course," he said in an abstracted way.

Elsie brought the Bible to him and drew up a stool for herself beside his chair. With her arm over his knee, she began to repeat with great feeling the chapters she had learned — the touching description of the Last Supper and Jesus' farewell to His sorrowing disciples.

"Isn't it beautiful, Papa?" she asked when she had finished her recitation. "'Having loved His own who were in the world, he now showed them the full extent of His love,'" she quoted again.

"It seems so strange that Jesus could be so thoughtful of them when all the time He knew the dreadful death He was going to die. And He knew they were all going to run away and leave Him to His enemies. It's so sweet to know that Jesus is so loving and that He loves me and will love me forever."

"But do you think you are good enough for Jesus to love you?" Horace asked.

"I know I'm not at all good, Papa," she said with grave seriousness. "My thoughts and feelings are often wrong, and Jesus knows all about it. But that doesn't keep Him from loving me because it was sinners He died to save. How good and kind He is. And who could help loving Him?"

She looked up into her father's eyes, and Horace was surprised to see sadness there as she went on, "I used to feel so lonely sometimes, Papa, that I thought my heart would really break. I think I would have died if I had not had Jesus to love me."

Her words moved Horace deeply, and he asked, "When were you so lonely and sad, darling?"

"Sometimes when you were away and I'd never seen you, I used to think of you and my heart would ache to see you and have you hold me and call me Daughter, as you do now." She paused and had to struggle to keep back her tears. Then she said, "But when you came home, Papa, and I saw you didn't love me — oh, that was the worst. I just wanted to die and go to Jesus and to Mamma."

She broke into tears, and Horace lifted her to his lap, hugging her close. "It was very, very cruel of me," he said, his own voice choking with emotion. "I don't know how I could close my heart like that. But I had been much prejudiced and led to believe that you feared and disliked me as a cruel tyrant."

Elsie's Endless Wait

Elsie was amazed at this admission. "How could you think that, Papa? I've *always* loved you, ever since I can remember."

Later, in her own room, Elsie thought seriously of everything that had happened that day and everything her father had said. In her prayers, she expressed many thanks to the Lord that her father had learned to love her. Then she added a fervent petition that her father would come to love Jesus and would never bid her to break any of God's commands. But the gray shadow of foreboding had not vanished entirely, and storm clouds were already gathering in the distance.

CHAPTER

10

Elsie's Sabbath Day Choice

*"If you keep your feet from breaking the Sabbath
and from doing as you please on my holy day,
if you call the Sabbath a delight and the
Lord's holy day honorable, and if you
honor it by not going your own way
and not doing as you please or
speaking idle words, then you will
find your joy in the Lord...."*

ISAIAH 58:13–14

Elsie's Sabbath Day Choice

*O*n a Sabbath day some weeks later, quite a few guests had dined at Roselands and were gathered in the drawing room. The gentlemen were laughing and joking, talking of politics, and conversing with the ladies, and everyone was in high spirits.

Adelaide, noticing that one of the men was glancing about the room in an attitude of disappointment, said, "May I ask what you are searching for, Mr. Eversham?"

"Yes, Miss Adelaide. I was looking for little Elsie. Edward Travilla has given me such a glowing account of her musical talent that I hoped to hear her sing and play."

"And so you shall, Eversham," said Horace, who had overheard his guest's request. He crossed the room to summon a servant, but he was stopped by a hand on his arm.

"You'd better not send for her," Mrs. Dinsmore whispered.

"May I ask why not?" he inquired in a tone of annoyance.

"Because she will not sing," his stepmother replied coolly.

"Pardon me, madam, but I think she will, if I bid it."

Though Horace was becoming heated at the woman's words, Mrs. Dinsmore maintained her cool, haughty manner as she said, "No, she will not. She will tell you she is wiser than her father and that it will be a sin to obey you. Believe me, Horace, she will defy your authority. You had better take my advice and leave her alone. Save yourself from the embarrassment."

Horace, biting his lip to control his anger, replied, "Thank you, madam, but I believe this lies solely in your imagination. I'm at a loss to understand you, for Elsie has never shown the slightest resistance to my authority."

With a slight arch of her eyebrow, Mrs. Dinsmore left him, and Horace gave the bell rope a hard pull. A servant appeared and was sent to summon Elsie. Horace joined a group around the piano, where Adelaide had just begun to play.

Though outwardly calm, Horace was already having doubts about his action. He had never understood the full depth of his child's convictions, and in his desire to display Elsie's talents, he had forgotten her conscientious scruples about the observance of the Sabbath. But he saw clearly that there would be a struggle, for on a point of principle, Elsie would be as unyielding as he. Though he felt sure Elsie would obey him in the end, he might have avoided the conflict but for his pride. He had gone too far to retreat, and perhaps, he told himself, it was just as well that this inevitable struggle should take place here and now.

When the servant came to her room with her father's message, Elsie immediately sensed what was about to occur. Elsie had been taught since her earliest days that the Sabbath is a day to rest and honor God by focusing on Him. With alarm now, she said to herself, "Papa wants me to do something that is not right on the Sabbath." Though she hoped that she was wrong, she nevertheless knelt quickly and prayed to the Lord for the strength to do right.

Elsie's Sabbath Day Choice

When she entered the drawing room, her father greeted her affectionately, but Elsie turned pale as he led her to the piano where Adelaide had just finished playing. He selected a piece of music that Elsie had learned during their holiday and handed it to her. "My friends are anxious to hear you play and sing," he said, "and I think this song will be perfect."

In almost a whisper, she said, "Won't tomorrow do, Papa?"

From the corner of his eye, Horace caught the smug expression of Mrs. Dinsmore as he replied to Elsie, "Certainly not, Daughter. You know this piece very well without more practice."

"That's not the reason," the little girl said. "But you know today is the holy Sabbath."

"What of it, child?" he asked, struggling to keep his voice mild. "I consider this song perfectly proper to be sung today. That should satisfy you that you are not doing wrong. Remember what I told you a few weeks ago. Now, sit down and sing."

"Oh, Papa, I can't sing it today! Please let me wait until tomorrow!"

But in his most stern manner, Horace commanded Elsie to sit and perform. She complied to the extent of taking the stool, but with her eyes full of tears, she again refused to sing. "I can't, Papa! I can't break the Sabbath," she cried in heartfelt agony.

"You must," he said as he placed the music before her. "I've told you it will not be breaking the Sabbath, and you must let me be the judge."

At this point, several of the guests urged Horace to let the matter go. Adelaide good-naturedly said, "Let me play it, Horace. I think I can do it almost as well as Elsie."

201

Elsie's Endless Wait

Horace could not be swayed. "I have given my child a command, and it must be obeyed," he said sternly. "She may not set her opinion of right and wrong against mine."

But Elsie, tears streaming down her face, made no move to obey her father. An uncomfortable silence settled on everyone for a few moments, until Horace finally said, "You shall sit here until you obey me, Elsie, no matter how long it takes."

"Yes, Papa," she replied, her words barely audible, and with relief, the guests drifted away from the scene.

Horace went to join a group of the men when Mrs. Dinsmore halted him with a remark. "I told you," she said in a low, self-satisfied tone, "how it would end."

"But it hasn't ended," Horace snapped, "and before it does, Elsie will know who has the stronger will."

Though none of the guests talked to her, Elsie felt that they were all looking at her, and the embarrassment was hard to bear. She was deeply troubled, too, by the thought that her father's displeasure would lead to the withdrawal of his affection entirely. As the time passed, she became extremely uncomfortable on the little seat of the music stool. It was an unusually warm fall afternoon, and the sultry heat of the drawing room caused her head to throb. Feeling that she might faint, she leaned forward and rested her head on the piano.

She had sat this way for almost two hours, when Edward Travilla came to her side. "I'm so sorry for you, my little friend," he said gently, "but I advise you to submit to your father. You can never conquer him, for I've never known a more determined man. Won't you sing the song? It will only take a few minutes, and your trouble will be over."

Elsie raised her tear-stained face. "But, Mr. Travilla, I don't want to conquer my father," she said earnestly. "I want to obey him in everything and honor him as the Bible tells me. But I can't disobey God, even to please my Papa."

"But, Elsie, would it really be disobeying God? Is there any verse in the Bible that says you must not sing songs on Sunday?"

"The Bible says to keep the Sabbath *holy*. It says that we are not to do as we please or go our own way or speak idle words. We're to rest from our work and honor God by giving all our attention to Him. We're to study the Bible, or worship and praise Him. But, Mr. Travilla, there's not a word of praise in that song. Not one word about God or heaven. I wish it were a song of praise; then I could obey my father."

Seeing that he could not convince the child, in spite of her obvious desire to please her father, Edward approached his friend. "Horace," he said, "I'm convinced that Elsie is entirely conscientious. Won't you give in to her in this instance?"

"Never!" Horace replied with some consternation. "This is the first time she has rebelled against my authority, and if she succeeds, she will expect to have her way always. I must subdue her now, whatever the cost."

The elder Mr. Dinsmore added his hearty agreement. "Quite right," he said. "Let her know from the start that you are the master."

"But I have to question a parent's right to coerce a child to act against her conscience," Edward contended, then added in a lowered voice. "You know, my friend, that this is no rebellion against you but entirely a matter of faith."

"Nonsense!" Horace replied harshly, but in truth this battle of wills with his daughter was wearing him down

almost as much as his poor child. "Elsie must learn to let me be the judge in these matters for many years to come."

Edward Travilla was not the only guest discomforted by Horace's strong discipline. At the moment, Mr. Eversham, who was feeling regret and responsibility for what had happened, was asking Adelaide if she might tell him how to repair the situation. But Adelaide could only shake her head sadly. "There's no moving my brother," she said, "and as for Elsie, I doubt any power on earth can make her do what she considers wrong."

"But where did she get such odd notions?" Eversham asked.

"Partly from the Scottish lady who cared for her for many years," Adelaide explained, "and partly from her Bible study. She is forever reading her Bible. I think it would break the child's heart to do anything that she sincerely believes would betray her faith."

"Then I can do nothing," Mr. Eversham said with a sigh.

Another hour dragged by, and when the supper bell rang, Horace went to his daughter and asked her once more to sing the song. She again refused.

"Very well," he said in a voice that no longer held any anger. "You know I cannot break my word. You must stay here until you obey, and you cannot eat until you do. Your obstinacy is causing great pain for us both."

After supper, the guests moved to the veranda where the breeze was cool, and Elsie was left alone in the darkening drawing room. The air inside the room seemed to draw close around her, and at times she could barely get her breath. Her whole body ached, and the pain pounded in her head. Her thoughts began to wander, and she forgot where she was. Her head seemed to spin, and everything swirled in confusion until she finally lost all consciousness.

Horace, Edward, and several others were talking just outside the drawing room when a sudden noise as of something falling startled them. Edward rushed inside, and seeing a small bundle by the piano, he rushed to Elsie.

"A light, quick!" he shouted as he raised the child. "She's fainted."

One of the men found a lamp and brought it close. In the light, they could see Elsie's deathly pale face and a stream of blood from a gash on her temple. She was a pitiable sight — her hair, face, and neat white dress covered with blood.

"Horace, you're a brute!" Edward said as he gently laid the child on a sofa. Horace bent over his little girl, but he was too anguished to make a reply.

Fortunately, there was a physician among the guests, and he hurried to treat Elsie's wound and give her restoring medication. But it was some time before she returned to consciousness, and her father was all this while terrified that she might die. But when her eyes at last opened, she gazed at Horace and asked, "Are you angry with me, Papa?"

"No, no, my darling child," he murmured. "Not at all."

"But what happened?" she asked in bewilderment. "What did I do?"

"Not a thing," he assured. "You were ill, but you are better now, so don't think any more about it."

The doctor said Elsie should be put to bed at once, and Horace tenderly cradled her in his arms and carried her upstairs.

"There's blood on my dress, Papa," Elsie said weakly.

"You fell and hurt your head, but you will be fine now."

"Oh! I remember," she moaned.

Elsie's Endless Wait

Horace helped Chloe, who was steady as a rock even at the sight of so much blood, and they prepared Elsie for bed.

"Are you hungry, darling?" Horace asked.

"No, Papa, I just want to sleep."

So Horace carried her to the bed and was about to tuck her in when Elsie suddenly cried, "My prayers, Papa!"

"Not tonight, dear. You're too weak."

"Please, Papa. I can't sleep otherwise."

So he helped her to her knees and listened as she spoke. To his surprise, he heard his own name mentioned more than once, coupled with a request that he should come to love Jesus.

When Elsie was at last wrapped in her covers, he asked, "Why did you pray that I might love Jesus?"

"Because I want you to be happy, and I want you to go to heaven, Papa."

"And what makes you think I don't love Him?"

"Don't be angry, Papa, but you know what Jesus says: 'Whoever has my commands and obeys them, he is the one who loves me.'" As Horace leaned down to kiss her good night, Elsie threw her arms around his neck and whispered, "I love you very, very much."

"Better than anyone else?" he asked with a smile.

"I love Jesus best, and you next."

When she woke the next morning, Elsie felt nearly as good as ever. After her bath, Chloe carefully brushed her hair so the curls concealed the bandage on her temple, and except for a slight paleness, there was nothing about Elsie's appearance to betray the accident.

Elsie's Sabbath Day Choice

She was reading her morning Bible chapter when her father came in and sat down beside her. "You look very pretty this morning," he said, winning a sweet smile. "How do you feel?"

"Fine, Papa."

"Do you know that you came very near dying last night?"

Elsie's face showed obvious disbelief, and Horace explained, in a voice that trembled with emotion, "The doctor says that if the wound had been half an inch nearer your eye. . . . Well, I might have lost my little girl."

Elsie said nothing for a few moments, then she asked, very softly, "Would you have been very sorry?"

"Oh, Elsie," he said, almost overcome by her question. "You are more precious to me than all my wealth, all my friends, and all my family. I would rather part with everything else than lose you."

She lapsed into silence again until he inquired what was on her mind now.

"I was just wondering whether I was ready to go to heaven, Papa. I think I was. I know I love Jesus, and I know Mamma would be glad to see me. Don't you think she would?"

"I can't spare you yet," he said, trying to keep his emotions under control, "and I think she loves me too well to wish it, dearest child."

Elsie continued to consider these things solemnly that morning, and as there was no school and her father was called into a business discussion, she retreated to the garden to read her Bible. She had been alone there for some time when she heard someone approaching. It was Edward Travilla.

He saw how intent she looked, and sitting beside her, he glanced at the book she held.

"What can you be reading that affects you so?" he asked.

"Oh, Mr. Travilla, doesn't it make your heart ache to read how our dear Savior was so abused, and then to know it was all because of our sins. Isn't it wonderful to know that we can be saved from the penalty for our sins, and be His friend now, and someday go to heaven?"

Her ideas intrigued him. "Really, Elsie," he said, "you are quite right, but aren't such ideas very serious for a young girl like you?"

"Mr. Travilla," she exclaimed. "These ideas bring me such peace and joy. When I read my Bible like this, I sometimes feel as if Jesus were sitting here beside me, just as you are."

"Can a person really be that close to God?" he asked half-jokingly.

"Oh yes, sir. Our dear Savior wants all His children to draw near to Him. You only have to *want* to spend time with Him, for He is always ready and waiting with His love," she replied.

"And how did you come to have such a close relationship with Jesus?"

"Aunt Chloe and Mrs. Murray taught me from the Bible, Mr. Travilla, that everyone who calls on the name of the Lord will be saved. I was just a little girl when I asked Him to forgive my sins and come into my heart."

"Then perhaps you know these words," he said and quoted, "'For God so loved the world that He gave His one and only Son, that whoever believes in Him shall not perish but have eternal life. For God did not send His Son into the world to condemn the world, but to save the world through Him.'"

Elsie nodded, for she knew the verses well.

Elsie's Sabbath Day Choice

Edward, who found himself curious about the depth of the child's faith, went on, "Do you think it is necessary for a person to ask in order to be saved, my little friend? What of a person who simply leads an honest, upright, and moral life? Cannot that person be saved?"

Elsie thought for several moments, then said slowly, "I know that the Bible teaches that there is not a person on earth who always does right and never sins. The Bible says it is by *grace* that we are saved, through our faith in Jesus — not by our good deeds. I don't think we could ever be perfect enough to win God's love and forgiveness. But we don't have to be perfect, because God gives us His gifts freely. The Bible says that we only have to believe with our hearts and confess with our mouths that Jesus Christ is Lord, that He died for our sins and rose from the dead. Do you remember, Mr. Travilla, that the Bible tells us that to enter the Kingdom of God we must be 'born again'?"

"And do you know what is meant by being born again?"

"It means that when we accept Jesus' death on the cross as payment for our sins," Elsie explained as carefully as she could, "then God's Holy Spirit comes to live in us and changes our hearts. We are born into a new life. That's the life of the Spirit, Mr. Travilla. And our change of heart makes us want to honor Jesus and be like Him and please Him in every way — not because we have to, but because we love Him and *want* to do it."

As Edward looked into Elsie's solemn little face, he suddenly remembered something else Jesus had said: "I praise you, Father, Lord of heaven and earth, because you have hidden these things from the wise and learned, and revealed them to little children." It was now obvious to Edward that the child had been very well taught, but he marveled that her acceptance of these great Bible truths was so natural. "No wonder," he thought to himself, "that Jesus spoke of the need to have 'faith as a little child.'"

Suddenly Edward saw tears welling in Elsie's bright eyes, and in an attempt to jolly her out of this serious mood, he said teasingly, "Well, my little friend, let us hope that everyone will repent and believe before they die."

But Elsie heard nothing humorous in his comment. She looked at him and asked, "Do you know how near I came to death last night? Then you know there can never be time enough, Mr. Travilla."

Edward, still wondering at this child's unusual spiritual maturity, quoted, more to himself than his little companion, "Blessed are the pure in heart for they shall see God."

Realizing that the morning was almost over and they would soon be expected for dinner, Edward hurriedly walked Elsie back to the house where the guests were gathered in the drawing room. When Horace saw his daughter enter the room, he asked her to sing, and Elsie obliged with enthusiasm. Her performance made her father very proud indeed.

For all his outward reserve, the events of the previous day had greatly deepened Horace's tender feelings for his daughter. His one desire now was to protect her from all dangers and to save her from the unhappiness of so many children who were raised without discipline. His own brother Arthur, not yet in his teens, was already a liar and a sneak. Horace would never let such a fate befall his beloved child. In their short time together, she had become more important to him than his own life.

Looking into Elsie's lovely face, so much like his lost wife's, he wondered how he could ever have been prejudiced against her or doubted her love for him. One thing he would never forget, and that was how close he had been to losing his precious little Elsie forever.

As Elsie began to sing another cheerful song for her father, Edward, standing somewhat apart from the group around the piano, regarded his old friend closely. Although he often disagreed with Horace's stern methods, he knew that Horace only wanted what was best for the child and had come to love Elsie as much as she loved him.

"But his love may not be enough," Edward thought, "for I fear Horace still does not share the deeper love that is Elsie's first loyalty. Can he ever understand how God's love sustained her through all those lonely years when her earthly father was absent? I wonder what their future will be. Can their happiness survive another clash between Horace's pride and Elsie's faith?"

Edward was so deep in his musings that he failed to notice when Adelaide came to stand at his side.

"Why, Mr. Travilla," she said brightly, "what makes you look so gloomy on this happy day?"

Quickly recalling himself to the present, Edward replied with a smile, "Not gloomy at all, Miss Dinsmore. It is only that the sight of your brother and your niece reminded me of some words of Scripture I learned many years ago."

Adelaide followed Edward's gaze to Elsie's shining face. "And will you share those words with me, Mr. Travilla?" she asked.

Edward began to speak with an intensity that surprised Adelaide. "'Let the little children come to me,'" he quoted, "'and do not hinder them, for the Kingdom of God belongs to such as these.'"

Are Elsie's troubles *really* over?
Will her father *ever* understand her and the deep faith that guides her?
Can she find love at Roselands?

Elsie's story continues in:

ELSIE'S IMPOSSIBLE CHOICE

Book Two of the
*A Life of Faith:
Elsie Dinsmore* Series

Available at your local bookstore

Collect all of our Elsie Dinsmore books and companion products!

* Now Available as a Dramatized Audiobook!

Millie's Unsettled Season

BOOK ONE

of the
*A Life of Faith:
Millie Keith*
Series

Based on the beloved books by
Martha Finley

MCP
Mission City Press
Franklin, Tennessee

KEITH FAMILY TREE

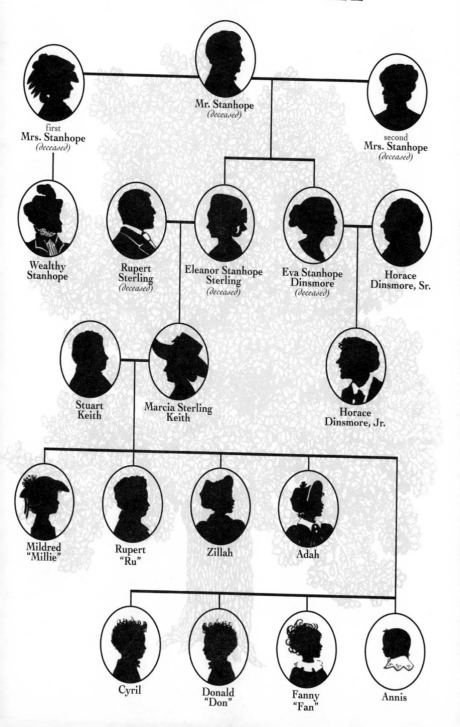

SETTING

Our story begins in the 1830s in Lansdale, Ohio, a charming town, bustling with commerce and activity. Lansdale is home to the Keith family and was the birthplace of Millie Keith.

CHARACTERS

THE KEITH HOUSEHOLD

Stuart Keith — the father of the Keith family; a respected attorney-at-law.

Marcia Keith — the mother of the Keith family and the step-niece of Wealthy Stanhope.

The Keith children:

> **Mildred Eleanor ("Millie")** — age 12
>
> **Rupert ("Ru")** — age 11
>
> **Zillah** — age 9
>
> **Adah** — age 8
>
> **Cyril** and **Donald ("Don")** — age 7, twin boys
>
> **Fanny ("Fan")** — age 5
>
> **Annis** — an infant girl

Wealthy Stanhope — a woman in her mid-50s; Marcia's step-aunt who raised her from infancy; step-aunt to Horace Dinsmore, Jr.

FRIENDS IN LANSDALE, OHIO

Annabeth Jordan, Beatrice Hartley and **Camilla Stone**—Millie's best girlfriends since childhood, known affectionately as "A, B, and C."

Frank Osborne—a childhood friend of Millie's, age 14.

Mrs. Hall—the matriarch of the wealthiest family in Lansdale, age 72.

Mr. Martin— a local schoolteacher.

Mr. and Mrs. Wiggles— friends of the Keith family.

Mr. Garlin— a friend of the family.

FRIENDS IN PLEASANT PLAINS, INDIANA

Mr. and Mrs. George Ward—old friends of Stuart Keith who live out on the prairie.

Mrs. Prior—the landlady of the Union Hotel.

Mrs. Lightcap—a widow who works as a laundress.
> **Gordon**—age 16, a blacksmith
> **Rhoda Jane**—age 14
> **Emmaretta**—age 8
> **Minerva**—age 7

Dr. and Mrs. Chetwood—the town physician and his wife.
> **William ("Bill")**—age 14
> **Claudina**—age 13

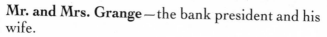

Mr. and Mrs. Grange — the bank president and his wife.

        Lucilla — age 14

        Teddy — age 9

Mrs. Gilligut — a widow.

Mr. and Mrs. Monocker — the owner of the local mercantile store and his wife.

        York — age 16

        Helen — age 15

Mr. and Mrs. Ormsby — a local businessman and his wife.

        Wallace — age 15

        Sally — age 5

Mr. and Mrs. Roe — local farmers.

        Beth — 14

        Joseph ("Joe") — 15

Celestia Ann Huntsinger — live-in housekeeper to the Keith family, age 17.

Reverend Matthew Lord — the new minister.

Damaris Drybread — a local teacher.

Mrs. Prescott — a widowed neighbor.

        Effie — age 7

Red Dog — an Indian man, member of the Potawatami tribe.

— FOREWORD —

*I*n this book, the first of the *A Life of Faith: Millie Keith* Series, you are about to take a journey into the past. Your trip will begin in 1833, in the midwestern United States of America. As you will see, many things were different back then, but one central fact remains unchanged — the importance of family.

Our story begins in Lansdale, Ohio, a thriving town of its day. Lansdale is home to the Keiths — a large and happy family — and their oldest daughter, Millie. Millie is a bright twelve-year-old girl who is full of energy and good intentions. As the eldest child of eight boisterous brothers and sisters, Millie tries to be a big help to her loving, Christian parents. Together the family will travel west to start a new life in a young and undeveloped prairie town called Pleasant Plains, Indiana. There Millie will live among people, cultures, and traditions very foreign to her early childhood days and she will learn many lessons about living a life of faith.

The stories of Millie Keith, known formerly as the *Mildred Keith* novels, were published in 1876, eight years after the well-known *Elsie Dinsmore* books were introduced. Martha Finley, the creator of both characters, was a fascinating woman whose own life was the basis for part of the story of Millie Keith. Miss Finley was born in Ohio and moved to the Indiana Territory as a young girl — just like Millie.

This book is a careful adaptation of the original Mildred Keith story. In rewriting the books for modern readers, the

Christian message has been strengthened, the plot enhanced, and a number of new features have been added. Also included is a section on the history and social customs of the time period and a helpful family tree.

Millie's story is a portrait of courage and conviction, love of family and country, and a strong determination to live a life worthy of the Christian calling. We are confident that you will not only love Millie, but also find in her a model of the timeless virtues of Christian living.

Mission City Press is very proud to carry on Miss Finley's commitment to Biblical values by re-introducing Millie Keith to a new generation of readers. It is our sincere hope that you will gain many insights into your own life of faith as you follow Millie's exciting adventures.

✎ WELCOME TO MILLIE'S WORLD ✎

The westward expansion of the United States in the nineteenth century is one of the most thrilling chapters in our American history. Settlers who ventured out to find a better life in undeveloped territories faced challenges and hardships we can hardly imagine today. Obstacles, distresses, suffering, and miserable conditions met them constantly. It took great courage and vision to leave the comforts of home with established ways of living to plot uncharted paths to lands unknown.

During this time of the early 1800s, our young nation experienced the most rapid migration it would ever see, with Americans settling in large numbers in what is now called the Old Northwest Territory. The Northwest Ordinance of 1787 had provided for the governance of public lands there, establishing the process by which U.S. territories would qualify for statehood. The Constitution of the United States went into effect in 1789 and gave Congress the power to regulate these territories, as the first lands surveyed under the Land Ordinance Act of 1785 were made available for sale. The settlements west of the Appalachian Mountains and east of the Mississippi River at the beginning of the 1800s were made by pioneers who felt the lure of the Northwest Territory, with its thick oak forests, rich farmland, rivers that made transporting goods and families possible, and land that was cheap—$1.25 for about half a hectare.

The Land Ordinance Act surveys changed the way towns, cities, and states were formed. To mark off property boundaries, people had previously used waterways, ridge tops, or tree lines, but over time trees died and streams dried up or shifted off course, making boundary lines difficult to determine. Recognizing that clear land titles were essential to the stability of our fast developing country, Congress ordered that a rectangular survey of all land be performed before it could be sold. Today, it is a source of amazement to fly over the vast lands west of the Appalachians and see the straight roads and rectangular fields that remain as a result of the Land Ordinance surveys.

In 1833, when our story begins, there were only twenty-four states in the United States. Ohio, where Millie lives at the outset of our story, became a state in 1803. Indiana, where the Keiths will be heading, was the nineteenth state admitted to the Union, achieving statehood in 1816. More than half the states that make up the United States today had not become states at this time. Andrew Jackson was sworn in on March 4, 1833, for his second term in office as the seventh President of the United States.

Millie's Unsettled Season

The day-to-day world in 1833 was very different from ours in many ways. For instance, without modern communication—radio, television, telephones, and the Internet—Millie and her family had to rely on letters to send and receive messages across town or across country. The mail, which was primarily delivered by stagecoach, was not reliable or quick in those days because scheduled stage routes in the unsettled territories and the Pony Express mail delivery would not start for almost thirty more years. A handwritten letter was a highly prized possession and would be read again and again as a treasure. People thought carefully about what they would say and how they would say it. An envelope could contain pages of local and family news accompanied by deeply felt prayers and Scripture references—all included for the reader's benefit and comfort.

Travel and transportation in Millie's time were also very different from today. Journeys of any great distance could take weeks and months. They were normally difficult and uncomfortable, and often unsafe. Walking was by far the primary means of transportation for short distances, but you will also read about travel on horses, carriages, stagecoaches, and wagons over long distances.

Riding on a stagecoach was not as romantic as old Western movies portray it to be. It was not smooth travel in roomy comfort. As many as eighteen to twenty passengers could be crammed together with mailbags and passenger luggage, with everything getting jostled by every bump, choked with dust, and all at the mercy of the natural elements. Before way stations (buildings set up every twenty miles or so that housed both stables and an eating room for stage passengers) were created in the 1860s, stagecoaches went for long distances without stopping. If the stage suffered a breakdown, passengers and cargo had to be unloaded while repairs were made. If the driver decided too much weight was to blame, mailbags were the first things to be overthrown—left abandoned by the wayside, never to reach their destination.

There were no national freeways like the ones we enjoy today. Pioneer Indiana was served by only two roads, and a large network of wagon paths. The federal government financed the building of the National Road that ran from Maryland to Illinois, with the Indiana portion (now U.S. Highway 40) completed in 1834. This horizontal road ran east to west through the center of the state, and the north-south Michigan Road ran from Madison, Indiana, in the south (on the Ohio River), straight up through Indianapolis to South Bend (on the St. Joseph River) near the northern state line. Thus Indiana became known as the "Crossroads of America" in the early 1800s.

Water travel was fast becoming the link from one place to another, with steamers, keelboats, packet boats, and sloops providing different forms of navigation. Man-made canals linked key rivers such as the Ohio to the Great Lakes, making commerce possible for inland states. The Ohio and Erie Canal, built between 1825 and 1832, brought prosperity to Ohio by making it possible for the farmers to market their goods in Cleveland, Chicago, and other larger cities. Packet boats were pulled up and down the canals by teams of mules or horses that walked along towpaths. Although they were slow, they were one of the safest ways to travel. Steamers had only been on the scene since around 1819, and journeys on them were still quite dangerous. Rivers were unpredictable at best, and high water periods brought even more dangers—uprooted trees and floating logs could drive a boat off course. Steamer wrecks were not uncommon, and anyone journeying on one had to face the risks.

Keelboats were graceful, bow-bottomed freighters that used three means of locomotion to ensure passengers and cargo reached their destinations. About seventy feet long and eighteen feet wide, they contained a roofed cabin in the center, with a narrow walkway on each side, where six to twelve oarsmen would use bowed oars or long, straight poles to push the boat through the water. In addition, they contained a mast with a sail, and a "cordelle" (a long rope attached to the mast crossbar) for dragging the keelboat when water obstructions or weather conditions made it impossible to row, pole, or sail. Sloops were smaller and used for milder waters (like lakes) and shorter distances (frequent ports).

Providing for schools was a challenge for Indiana pioneer communities. The state constitution of 1816 directed the government to establish and maintain tax-supported schools free of charge, but the few tax dollars collected were spent for building roads and draining marshlands. School in the undeveloped land was, at best, held in a local one-room building, often times built by farming families who pitched in to help. More fortunate children were given the choice of attending the local school or learning at home under the guidance of their parents and other adults. Much like today, families who schooled their children at home would set up special rooms in which to teach, and multiple-aged children would all be taught together. This type of homeschooling required even more creativity than it does today, however, for there were no printed curriculum materials available, and the success of the education often depended upon the knowledge of the person teaching.

Foreword

The changing face of a free and growing society mirrored the growing pains that Millie felt as an adolescent girl. Unlike the Southern states, slavery had never been a common practice in the Northwest Territory, and was not tolerated in the unsettled prairie towns of Millie's world. These courageous men and women worked their land and built their towns and settlements without the aid of slaves. They were not, however, immune to their own prejudices. Exaggerated tales of savage Indian tribes spread like wildfire, causing the Native Americans to be disdained and feared by these settlers. Prior Indian wars provided some justification for their fears. For example, in the Black Hawk War of 1832, the last Indian war in the Northwest Territory, Chief Black Hawk and five hundred warriors, along with their families, came back across the Mississippi to take back their lands in Illinois. They were defeated in Wisconsin, and Black Hawk was returned to his people in Iowa after a year in prison.

The federal government had been making treaties with the Indians and moving them off their lands since the late 1700s, and in 1830 Congress had passed the Indian Removal Act that provided for the creation of an "Indian Country" and funds to transport eastern tribes across the Mississippi River for resettlement. By 1834 this land, known as the Indian Territory, was established in what is now Oklahoma, and most of the tribes native to Indiana had been forced from their land by the hostile removal efforts of the federal government. The Indian chiefs from various tribes further west who would become key players in the wars against white settlement—Sitting Bull, Geronimo, and Crazy Horse — were just being born during the early 1800s. It would be another twenty to thirty years before they would rise to power and try to prevent the federal government from buying or taking their lands.

Overall, however, it was a love of freedom, fresh opportunity, and a desire for a better life that drew most people westward. Though the risks were great, the possible rewards seemed even greater. Hard work, good humor, and a strong faith were essential to survival. Somehow all the obstacles did not dissuade these pioneers who had a fortitude we can only admire in retrospect. It was hopes and dreams that propelled these brave people onward.

CHAPTER 1

Surprising News

*Do not boast about tomorrow,
for you do not know what
a day may bring forth.*

PROVERBS 27:1

Surprising News

*A*s the winter of 1833 melted away, the woods and gardens around Lansdale traded their blankets of snow for the glad rags of spring—a tinge of yellow-green spread over the woods, violets and anemones showed their pretty faces, rivulets danced and sang under apple, peach, and cherry trees in full bloom. Creation seemed to whisper, "Rejoice! He is risen!" And with the next breeze, "He is risen indeed!"

The girlish figure who slipped out the back door of the stately brick home in the center of town didn't seem to notice the whisper. She clutched a large, well-worn book to her chest, closed her eyes and leaned her head against the door.

Trust in the Lord...

"Millie!" A child's voice called, "Millie? Where are you?"

"Oh, not now!" Millie protested and ran across the garden to a fragrant cave beneath the arching lilacs. When she was sure that no one could see her behind the curtain of purple blooms, she sat down and opened the book.

"You know I am trying to acknowledge You, Lord," she prayed out loud. "But has there been a mistake? Something has gone wrong this time. I'm sure it has. Remember the verse Mamma gave me just yesterday? You must remember it, it's in *Your* book!" She flipped the Bible open. "Proverbs 3:5—"

Something cold touched her neck just as her finger found the place. Millie jumped, and whirled to find a little brown and white terrier looking up at her. He pressed his cold nose against her hand.

"What are you doing here, Wannago Stanhope?" Millie asked, scooping the pup into her arms. "I'm sure Aunty doesn't know you have escaped!" The dog whined and wagged his stub of a tail.

"Come on, I'll take you home." She tucked her Bible under one arm, the dog under the other, and walked across the garden to a wrought-iron gate; through the gate and another smaller garden to a tall brick house with vine-covered porches.

Windows opened to the wide porch across the back of the house, and a sweet voice was drifting from one of them.

"A mighty fortress is our God...," sang the voice.

"Aunt Wealthy?" Millie called.

"...a bulwark never failing!"

"Aunt Wealthy?" Millie called again.

"In here, dear," the voice sang from the parlor window. "Don't bother running around to the door. Step right in the window!"

Millie put her Bible on the sill, gathered up her skirts and petticoats and, after glancing around to make sure no one was watching, swung her legs up and over the window. Wannago bounced to the floor and started to bark up at a tiny, middle-aged lady who was perched like an ornamental vase on the large mantel above the fireplace. Her chintz gown was of her own peculiar design, and a scandalous flash of ankle showed each time she swung her little boot. She was fanning herself with a letter.

"Aunt Wealthy!" Millie exclaimed. "Whatever are you doing up there?"

"Spring cleaning," Wealthy said. "I was dusting the top of the mirror. Getting *down* is quite a different matter than getting up, isn't it? The stool tipped when I tried to step on it."

"How long have you been up there?" Millie asked, setting the stool upright.

"For one long letter and half a hymn," Wealthy said. "It is fortunate that I found a misplaced epistle from my nephew Horace Jr. on the mantel. It kept me good company for a half hour, but even accounts of the young Dinsmore's college life could not stretch much longer on the printed page. Wannago fled when I started to sing, and now here you are!"

Millie pushed the stool closer to the mantel and held up a hand to help her aunt down.

"Oh, Aunt Wealthy," Millie cried, as Wealthy's boot touched solid ground. "It's decided!"

"My child, what is it?" asked the older lady, dropping the letter to take the girl's hand and draw her to a seat on the sofa. "What is decided?"

Millie spoke with a determined effort to be calm.

"This morning at breakfast, Pappa told us—us children, I mean—he and Mamma had talked it over last night, and you know they have been praying about it, and…"

"And?" Wealthy clasped Millie's hand to her heart.

"We are going to move … to … to … Pleasant Plains, Indiana."

"The frontier!" Wealthy gasped, sinking back on the couch.

"Just as soon as we can get ready. Isn't it marvelous?" Millie said, and burst into tears.

For a moment her listener was dumb with surprise, but it was not in Wealthy Stanhope's nature to witness distress without an effort to comfort and relieve.

"Now, now, Millie dear," the older woman said, drawing her niece close. She stroked the hand she held. "There will be, perhaps, some adventures on the journey. I thought you yearned for adventure."

"I do! But I already know my adventure is completing my studies with Mr. Martin, and then Camilla and I will become the first female students to attend Tristan College. And then we're going to do something grand, something no woman has ever done before, something amazing! We will be doctors, or missionaries to some uncharted place on a faraway continent. We have it all planned! Aunty, I've been praying so hard about this, and I was sure God would find a way for me to stay in Lansdale. I don't want to leave my friends yet. Mamma even gave me a verse: 'Trust in the Lord with all your heart and lean not on your own understanding. In all your ways acknowledge him, and he will make your paths straight.'" She recited the words aloud, speaking earnestly as if she would carve the words into her heart. " 'He will make your paths straight.' Proverbs 3:6. I thought that meant if I trusted Him I could stay!"

Wealthy patted her hand in silence for a moment, then said, "You mustn't ignore verse 5, dear. 'Lean not on your own understanding.' Why, I remember," the tiny lady said, "when God changed my adventure. I was having a wonderful time living in a small room in Boston, helping servants just out of their indentures to find work, and teaching them to read the Scriptures. I was sure I would spend my whole life working with the Ladies Aid Society. Then I received word that my beloved sister's husband had died, and she herself was ill. I hurried home to care for her and her two-year-old daughter, but she was taken home to the Lord. As you can imagine, I was heartbroken and confused. My whole life had to change. I found myself with a child to raise—your mother. And look at what the Lord has done!

A spinster like me, with a niece as dear as a daughter and eight just-as-good-as grandchildren. God had a very special plan."

"Well, I *thought* He had one for me," Millie said. "Maybe I did something wrong and He changed His mind!"

"Nonsense," Aunt Wealthy said. "He isn't just sending the Keith clan. He is sending His very own Millie Keith, the bravest, most outspoken girl I know. There must be something very special He wants you to do in Pleasant Plains. Come along." She led the way into Millie's favorite place in the world, her well-stocked library. On any other day, Millie would have paused as she entered, breathing in the smell of leather bindings, book paste, and paper. If it were quiet, she would imagine that she could hear the voices of the books, a thousand adventures waiting to be discovered. But today, she followed Aunt Wealthy straight to the atlas that lay open on a table. Wealthy flipped to the new state of Indiana and traced an overland route with her finger.

"What roads there are will be very bad this time of year. Heavy wagons would get bogged down in the mud."

"Pappa said that, too. He said the best route would be up the Ohio and Erie Canal to Lake Erie, and around Michigan by ship."

"Very sensible," Wealthy agreed. Millie examined the maps while Aunt Wealthy pulled another book from the shelf.

"Tsk!" Wealthy said, flipping a page quickly. "Tsk, tsk!"

"What are you reading, Aunty?"

"Hmmmmm? Oh, just a little book written by a friend of mine. He spent some time in the territory that became the state of Indiana not too long ago. Oh dear!"

"What is it?" Millie asked. "What does it say?"

"Never mind," Wealthy said, replacing it on the shelf. "Perhaps I'll read it later. Would you like to take the maps to school with you today, to show your friends?"

"Oh, Aunty," Millie's eyes filled with tears again. "That's the worst part, the part I can't bear—no more school for me. There's too much sewing and packing to do between now and when we leave. But what's worse is that out on the frontier, there won't be school for me either—at least not like I have with Mr. Martin."

"No school?" Aunt Wealthy was speechless for a full minute. She brushed a tear from Millie's face. "You will still have books, and your father and mother—both educated people—will help you, and who knows but what you may end up with a better education than school can provide. I've found that the knowledge I've gained by my own efforts is often the most useful. Your skill with a needle and thread wasn't learned in school. You are a great help and comfort to your mother because of it."

"You're only saying that to cheer me up," Millie said.

"Nonsense," Aunt Wealthy said. "Since your mother had to let the servants go, you have been a great help to her. You not only help with the mending, you watch the little ones and—"

A blood-curdling scream brought Wealthy up from her seat, and they both raced to the window. A little girl with golden ringlets flying and wide blue eyes burst from the hydrangea bushes and raced to the porch, two seven-year-old red-headed boys right behind her.

Aunt Wealthy reached through the window and scooped the child into her arms.

"Fan! Cyril! Don!" Wealthy said, "Whatever are you doing?"

"Playin'," Cyril said, quickly hiding something behind his back.

"We're going to the wild frontier!" Don yelled. "Wahoooo! I'm going to be a longhunter like Davy Crockett!"

"Me too," said Fan, not to be outdone. "I'm going to hunt bears and wildcats!"

"I'm not going to wear any clothes!" bellowed Don.

"Donald Keith!" scolded Millie. "You most certainly will wear clothes! And Cyril, what are you hiding behind your back?"

"His tomahawk," said Fan, wiggling out of Aunt Wealthy's arms. "He was going to scalp me!"

Millie held out her hand. Cyril reluctantly produced a twisted root that looked a bit like a hatchet.

"Cyril, you know better than to play with things like that," Millie said.

"You're not mother," Cyril replied.

"Now, I'm sure your mother would want you to obey Millie," Aunt Wealthy chided.

"Maybe," said Don, handing over the pretend tomahawk. "But I asked Mamma not to let her tell us what to do." He leaned close to Aunt Wealthy and whispered, "Millie pinches."

"Yeah," Cyril agreed. "She pinches *hard*."

"Only when you are very wicked," Millie said, flushing red, "and won't pick up your toys, or when you shout and wake the baby…or…or…try to scalp your little sister!"

Cyril skipped out of reach, and Don peeked around Aunt Wealthy's skirts.

"That's quite enough," Aunt Wealthy said firmly. "There will be no scalping today. It is a nasty habit, and quite unnatural."

"Indians scalp people," Don said.

"They did not until some wicked soldiers from France taught them to," Aunt Wealthy said. "A brave longhunter would never scalp his sister. He would lay down his life to protect her, because he would be a Christian gentleman and do just as Jesus would do."

"Was Jesus brave?"

"Very brave," Aunt Wealthy assured him. "He laid down His life for the world. It was the bravest thing anyone ever did. Now, did your Mamma say you could play in the back garden?"

"Yes," Cyril said.

"But first we had to find Millie," Don explained. "Mamma wants her. Rupert went with Pappa to the mercantile, and she needs someone to mind Zillah, Adah, and the baby."

"Zillah and Adah are playing dolls," Fan volunteered. "Yuck!"

"Why didn't you say Mamma needed me straightaway?" Millie asked, exasperated. Cyril poked out his tongue at her from the safety of Aunt Wealthy's skirt-tails. Millie's fingers itched to pinch him, but Aunt Wealthy's words were still echoing in her head: Christian gentlemen do just as Jesus would do. Of course Christian ladies should do the same. *Jesus, You didn't pinch Your younger brothers and sisters, did You?* Millie prayed. *Didn't they ever deserve it? I know James must have at least once, so You must know how I feel. I do want to be like You, but it's so hard! Please help me!* She shoved the offending fingers deep in the pockets of her apron.

"I think I'll take a walk around town," Aunt Wealthy said. "I always pray best when I'm walking, and I want to talk to my Lord. Come along." Millie followed her aunt but kept a safe distance from her brothers, just in case.

A few moments later, they said good-bye to Aunt Wealthy at her own gate. Millie stood for a moment and watched as her aunt, armed with a large cotton umbrella, marched briskly towards the business part of town. Could Aunt Wealthy be right? Did Jesus have something for her, Mildred Eleanor Keith, to do in Pleasant Plains? What possible difference could a twelve-year-old make in a frontier town?

2

Preparing the Way

The Lord said… "Now then, you and all these people, get ready to cross the Jordan River into the land I am about to give to them."

JOSHUA 1:1-2

Preparing the Way

Millie tucked baby Annis into her bassinet and pulled the blanket up to her chin. Adah and Zillah had decided to go shopping with Pappa and Rupert. Don, Cyril, and Fan were playing explorers in the garden. Millie found her mother in the room off the kitchen where the washing was done. She stood for just one moment, watching her. Millie thought she was beautiful, even in her housedress with her sleeves rolled up and her arms deep in the big washtub of soapy water. Before Pappa had lost his money, the washer woman would have done the laundry; now the family had only the help of a cook. Once upon a time, Millie and her Mamma would have had time to read books and take walks with the children. But now, Millie watched the little ones while Mamma kept house. Washing alone for eight children took half the day! The clothes had to be boiled and scrubbed in the big wash bucket, wrung by hand and hung on the line. When they were dry, Millie would take them down and Mamma would iron them.

"Mamma?"

Marcia looked up with a smile. "Yes, Millie?"

"Mamma, did you know that we were going to move when you gave me that Bible verse?"

Marcia paused for a moment, wiping a stray hair from her face, and then said, "I suspected we might."

"How do you learn to trust the Lord?"

Marcia wiped her wet, soapy arms on her apron, then walked over to the table and pulled out a chair. "Sit down, Millie," she said.

Millie sat in the chair.

Millie's Unsettled Season

"Now, daughter, what is keeping you from tumbling to the floor?"

Millie looked surprised. "The chair!"

"Aren't you afraid it will let you fall?"

"Of course not. It's never let me fall before."

Marcia went back to the washtub. "I can trust in God because He has never let me fall. But everyone has a first time for trusting Him. Everyone has to learn for themselves that He loves them and won't let them fall. This is a good time to learn, my love."

"But it doesn't make sense! Didn't He know that Mr. Arnold would embezzle Pappa's money? That we would be poor and have to move?"

"It is hard. And a little scary. But you know, daughter, you are not the only one who has memory verses. Do you want to hear mine?"

Millie nodded.

"It's Hebrews 13:5: 'Make sure that your character is free from the love of money, being content with what you have; for he himself has said, "I will never desert you, nor will I ever forsake you," so that we confidently can say, "the Lord is my helper, I will not be afraid. What will man do to me?"' If Jesus was everything to me when I had servants and wore silks, Millie mine, how could He not be everything still, even if I am a servant and wear...suds?" She blew a bubble from the tips of her fingers. "Good heavens, what is that?"

Millie followed her gaze out the window. Wannago Stanhope was marching down the walk at the head of a comical caravan. Aunt Wealthy was right behind him, umbrella held high. Three small mountains of brown paper parcels followed her. Over the top of each parcel could be seen just a bonnet, and beneath them, boots skipping and hopping to avoid the puddles left by the recent rain.

"She's brought Annabeth, Bea, and Camilla!" Millie cried. "A, B, and C!"

"Run and open the gate," Marcia said, "while I clean up."

Millie flew down the steps and opened the gate, then led the way into the parlor. The girls laid the packages on the table.

"She wouldn't say a word," Annabeth said. "Not one word. But when Miss Wealthy Stanhope buys every fabric remnant in Lansdale, then you know that something is amiss."

"And so we came to find out what," Bea said practically.

"It isn't what we fear, is it, Millie?" Annabeth said. "It can't be. We've all been praying and praying…"

Millie's eyes stung, but she blinked hard. "My father and mother have been praying too, and they decided…the opportunities are just so good in Indiana…"

"Indiana!" Camilla collapsed in a heap on the ottoman. "Not possible. You can't! There should be a law against it!"

"A law against the Keiths moving to Indiana?" Bea shook her head.

"Of course not," Camilla said. "A law against the Keiths leaving Lansdale at all. I think we should sign a petition!"

"Annabeth, dear, are you quite all right?" Wealthy was looking at the tall, quiet girl.

Bea and Camilla stopped their chatter.

"We've always been together," Annabeth said. "How can you leave?"

Millie's throat felt tight. Even if she could have spoken, there was no word to express all the feelings jumbled inside. Not one word.

"Rump," Aunt Wealthy said, as if to sum up the situation. The girls glanced at one another.

"Pardon?" Bea said. "I'm afraid I didn't hear correctly."

"I mean this reminds me of my dear friend Hildegard Rump," Wealthy said. "Hilly and I have been friends forever. When the Lord called me to Boston to work with the Ladies Aid, we became even better friends. Somehow, we could share more of our hearts in letters than we could speaking face to face. And it was so wonderful to receive that letter every week. Dear Miss Hienden."

"Excuse me, Miss Stanhope, but who is Miss Hienden?" Camilla asked. "Weren't you speaking of a Miss Rump?"

"My goodness!" Wealthy said, flushing red. "Of course I meant Hienden! Hildegard Hienden. What was I thinking?"

The girls managed to contain their giggles until a squeak escaped Camilla; and then they all, including Aunt Wealthy, dissolved into laughter and tears.

"Aunt Wealthy!" Marcia said, entering the room. "You've come at last! And it looks like you have brought sunshine with you, as always." The girls burst into giggles again. "Hello, girls. You've been out shopping?"

"Yes, at every store in town," Aunt Wealthy replied. "So you're going to leave Lansdale, Marcia?"

"Yes, Aunty, and you. That's the worst of it."

"Not so fast. Who says that I'm to be left behind?"

"Aunt Wealthy! Do you mean it? Is it possible you could think of such a sacrifice?" cried Marcia.

"Pish-tosh," Aunt Wealthy said. "I have been sedentary for quite long enough. I can't give up the Stanhope homestead, as you very well know. But I have found a tenant for it. The young minister and his wife will be very happy to set up housekeeping, and they will take good care of my furniture and belongings for a year. I intend to see you all safely settled in Hoosier land before I return. It will be quite an importation of Buckeyes, won't it — all of us coming in one lot? Now to business," said Aunt Wealthy, attacking the parcels. "I'm going to help you, Marcia, in getting your tribe ready for their exodus out of this land of plenty into that Western Wilderness. Here are two or three dress patterns apiece for the little girls to travel in. I think they had better be made long-necked and high-sleeved, don't you?"

Millie had visions of her little sisters waddling like geese, their long necks stretched before them and arms held high.

Even Marcia looked slightly puzzled; then a light broke over her face. She was used to her aunt's odd way with words.

"I don't know," she said. "Wouldn't it make them look a little old-womanish? Low necks and short sleeves are prettier for children, I think, and they're used to it. Summer's coming on, too, and we must expect warm weather."

"It will be cool on the water."

"Yes, that's true," Marcia said. "I'll take your advice after all."

"Good. They'll be less likely to catch cold from any little exposure, and their necks and arms will be protected from the sun."

Before the Keiths' troubles had begun, Marcia would have engaged a seamstress or two, but now, her carefully managed household funds were just enough to pay the bills and the cook. It would take some weeks of very diligent work by three or four pairs of hands to accomplish what the mother deemed necessary in the way of preparing their wardrobe for the journey.

Millie's Unsettled Season

"Let me help with your sewing," Annabeth said.

"I'll help too," said Bea. "I know Mother will let me!" Annabeth and Bea were clever with their needles, and for the last two years the girls had worked together when they needed special gowns for parties or balls. Bea was especially clever at designing skirts that twirled when one danced, and Annabeth was simply the best at sewing lace.

"I think that would be wonderful," Marcia said. "You can keep Millie company."

Camilla looked down at her shoes. Everyone knew she was a disaster with a needle, and nothing less than frightening with a pair of scissors. Her mother ordered her gowns from Chicago, and Camilla was perfectly happy with that arrangement, as it left her free to pursue her studies.

Millie took her friend's hand. "I think we will need some help with baby Annis, too," she said.

"Really?" Camilla looked hopefully at Marcia.

"I know we will," Marcia said.

The girls agreed that they would be over after school the next day and then they said their good-byes.

Millie helped sort the fabric as Aunt Wealthy and Marcia discussed plans for the trip. Suddenly, the door burst open, letting in two little girls and a boy who was just a year younger than Millie. The girls were almost in tears, but the boy's blue eyes danced with mischief and fun.

"Softly, softly, children." Marcia said, looking up with a smile as they came in. "The baby is sleeping. Rupert, eleven is quite old enough to begin to act in a more gentlemanly way, don't you think?"

"Yes, Mamma, I beg your pardon. Yours too, Aunt Wealthy. I didn't know till this moment that you were here."

Preparing the Way

"Now, Adah, Zillah, what is this about?"

"Ru says we'll have to live in wigwams like the Indians and eat raw fish with their eyeballs still in," Zillah said. Adah, who hated fish, started to cry.

"I'm sure we will have bread and butter," Millie said, hugging her little sister, and glaring at her brother.

"Rupert, my son, was it quite truthful to tell your sisters such things?"

"I was only making fun," he answered, trying to turn it off with a laugh, but blushing as he spoke.

"I never object to innocent fun. But amusement is too dearly bought at the sacrifice of truth," Marcia said.

Zillah and Adah caught sight of the dress fabric and instantly forgot wigwams and fish. "Are we getting new dresses, Mamma? Can mine be blue? Will you sew lace on my collar? Will we be beautiful?"

"Beautiful? Why, I have the most beautiful girls in the world! And my wife is the most beautiful of all!" said Stuart Keith, who stood in the doorway, Fan tucked under his left arm and Cyril and Don dangling by their suspenders from his right hand. "Look what I found lurking in the bushes. A pack of wild children. May I keep them, dear?"

"If you promise to wash them and teach them their manners," Marcia said, rising to kiss her husband.

"On my word, I will." He sent the boys and Fan to wash up, then tossed his hat onto the hat rack. "Hello, Aunt Wealthy. Have you heard the news?"

"That you are going to Indiana, Stuart? Yes, I've heard something about it," Wealthy said with a twinkle in her eye. "Not content to live in this civilized and cultured town, are you?"

Millie's Unsettled Season

"Lawyers are not so plentiful there, and as more folks move in, legal services will be in great demand. I plan to open my own practice. And land is cheap. I'll invest in a portion of it and hope to see it increase in value as the town grows. However," his voice grew solemn, "it will mean the sundering of some very dear ties here."

"Do you know," Marcia asked, smiling at Wealthy, "that since you left us this morning something has happened that takes away more than half the pain of leaving Lansdale? Aunt Wealthy is coming along!"

"Truly?" Stuart pulled Wealthy from her seat and waltzed her across the floor. "The Lord has blessed us!"

They were interrupted by a summons from Mary, the cook. She was always prim and very discreet, and she would have disapproved of the display, if it had been proper to notice it at all.

"Thank you, Mary," Marcia said. "Will you set an extra place for Aunt Wealthy?"

Millie loved suppertime. She could pretend that nothing had happened and that life was just the same as it had always been. The family gathered at the table in the soft glow of oil lamps. Mary served them quietly and then left.

Stuart bowed his head and led the family in a prayer. Then the meal began with the sweet ting of silver on china.

"So what has my family been up to today?" Stuart asked.

"We told Mr. and Mrs. Wiggles that we were moving to Indiana," Fan said. "She said she would pray for us."

"Mr. Wiggles said he would pray for the Indians," Don volunteered.

"Very kind of him, I'm sure," Stuart said dryly. "But most of the tribes have been removed. They have gone to live west of the Mississippi, where there is more land and fewer white men. There is just one tribe left in Indiana."

"The Wotapotamies?" Wealthy asked.

"The Potawatamies, yes."

"A fascinating people," Aunt Wealthy said, without pausing to correct herself. "The Potawatamies fought very fiercely against the British. They were allied with the French. Then they fought as allies with the British against the Americans."

"Did the bad soldiers teach them to scalp peoples?" Fan asked, eyes as big as saucers.

"Well...yes," Aunt Wealthy said. "During the French and English war. But that was a long time ago, child."

"Pappa," Rupert asked, "what about Black Hawk? They say he is out of prison. Couldn't the Indians come back?"

Millie put her fork down. She remembered the talk in school about Black Hawk, a fierce Sauk warrior. He believed that the Indians had been cheated out of their land and tricked into signing contracts they did not understand. He gathered a band of five hundred Sauk and Fox warriors. Along with their women and children, they came back across the Mississippi to the lands that had once been their home and fought with soldiers of the United States government. When Black Hawk was finally defeated, it was a terrible massacre. Soldiers shot down women and children, killing even tiny babies. Black Hawk's followers were wiped out. Millie remembered Mamma crying when she read the accounts in the paper.

"Black Hawk has lost his followers," Stuart said. "The Sauk tribe looks to Keokuk now, a reasonable man who wants peace. Mr. Wiggles was right. We should pray for the Indians."

CHAPTER

3

A Big Decision

*If any of you lacks wisdom, he should
ask God, who gives generously
to all without finding fault,
and it will be given to him.*

JAMES 1:5

A Big Decision

As the weeks passed, Millie was grateful for her friends' company in the afternoons as they sewed. Their conversation almost took the sting out of leaving Mr. Martin's class. Millie had begun to think, under Mr. Martin's tutelage, that she might want to be a teacher herself one day. His classroom was a botanical and zoological wonder, with specimens and samples of all kinds. When Bea complained that girls should not be expected to learn mathematics, history, Latin, and Greek as the boys were, Mr. Martin had removed his spectacles, polished them carefully, then perched them once again on his beak-like nose.

"I suppose you adhere to the wisdom of young ladies studying only music, drawing, embroidery, and French, Miss Hartley?"

"Why, yes," Bea answered. "Although truthfully, I would rather dispense with the French altogether."

Mr. Martin shook his bald head, then picked up the flower they had been sketching. "The lily is a work of art, don't you agree?"

"Of course," Bea said. "It's beautiful."

"And beautifully and thoughtfully made. Do you realize that each and every part of this flower has a purpose?"

"Yes," Bea agreed. "We have been studying the lily."

"You are beautifully and thoughtfully made also," Mr. Martin said. "And every part of you has a purpose. As God saw fit to give you a good brain, I expect you to use it. There is room in that lovely head for embroidery and mathematics, Miss Hartley!"

Camilla thrived in the classroom setting, and after school each day as the girls sewed, she described the lessons to

Millie's Unsettled Season

Millie, pouring over her notes until Bea and Annabeth begged her to stop. The conversations and company were very dear to Millie, since she wanted to spend every minute possible with her friends, but the long hours beside Mamma and Aunt Wealthy while they were alone proved more useful in getting the work done.

The Keith house began to look less and less like home, as trunks were packed and belongings sorted into those that would travel with the family, and those that would be shipped ahead. Wagons were loaded and sent away, leaving the house with empty corners and echoes in the halls.

"Have you any cord, Marcia?" asked Aunt Wealthy one morning while they worked together in the sewing room.

"Yes," Marcia answered, turning to her work basket. "Why, what has become of it? I had two or three pieces here. And that paper of needles has disappeared. Millie, did you use them?"

"The children were here half an hour ago," Millie said. "I remember seeing Donald looking into your basket."

"Run out and see what they have done with the cord," Marcia said. "Ask after the needles too. We don't want them turning up in the wrong place."

Millie hesitated in the empty hall, listening for sounds to tell her where the children were. Little voices were prattling in the garden near at hand. Stepping to the door she saw Cyril and Don seated on the grass, busy with a kite Rupert had made for them.

"What are you doing?" she asked, going nearer.

"Making a longer tail."

"Where did you get that piece of string?"

The only answer was a guilty look on the two grubby faces.

A Big Decision

"Oh, I know! You took it from Mamma's work basket. And now Aunt Wealthy needs it, but you've spoiled it entirely. Don't take things without leave. Did you take a paper of needles too?"

"No, we didn't," Don said. "You always think we are the ones causing trouble."

"So you didn't see the paper of needles?"

"We *saw* it," said Don, "but Fan took it."

"Yeah, she was bothering us," added Cyril.

I will not pinch. No matter how much they deserve it, Millie said to herself. She shoved her hands in her pockets and went in search of her little sister. She found Fan sitting in her little garden, the empty needle paper lying near. Fan was sitting cross-legged, her chin resting on her fist, staring at the ground.

"Fan," said Millie as she picked the paper up, "what have you done with the needles?"

"Sowed them in the ground," said Fan, smoothing the dirt with her little rake. "When they grow into baby porkypies, we'll have lots of needles! I have to watch careful, or the porkypies will get away."

"Porcupines," Millie corrected her.

"Will you help me pluck them, Millie?" Fan asked, holding up her chubby hands. "They'll prick me!"

"No they won't. Needles do not grow into porcupines. Who told you that story, silly little puss? Never mind, I can guess. Show me where you put them."

"I put them in the ground, round and round."

Millie picked up a stick and poked about in the fresh earth for a minute or two.

Millie's Unsettled Season

"This is as hopeless as looking for needles in a haystack," she said. "Come on, I'm sure you can play with Zillah. She is making a dress for her doll."

She went back into the house with the report of the hapless fate of the missing needles, but the boys were there before her. They'd washed their faces and their hands up to the wrists and slicked down their hair. Millie was sure she could smell just a hint of rose water.

"We didn't think, Mamma," pleaded Donald, penitently holding out the ruined cord. "We're very sorry."

"Very, very sorry," Cyril said earnestly.

Marcia leaned over and gave him a kiss. "My boys must learn to think. And they must not take mother's things without asking. Now run along and try to be good children."

"Mother, I do think you're a little too easy with them," Millie said with frustration. "They've been telling Fan terrible tales to keep her out of their way, and they do know better than to take your cord."

"Perhaps," Marcia said, "but if I make a mistake, it is far better to do so on the side of mercy than of severity. And they did apologize."

"That's true," Aunt Wealthy said. "What have they told Fan this time?" she asked.

Millie related the story of Fan's baby porcupines, and she couldn't help laughing along with her mother and aunt.

"We can't do without needles, I'm afraid," said Marcia when Millie was finished. "Will you run to the store and get a new paper, Millie?"

Millie put on her bonnet. She felt almost guilty escaping into the beautiful day. If it hadn't been for the fact that she would miss her afternoon reading, she would have been perfectly happy.

A Big Decision

News had traveled, and everyone in town knew that the Keiths were moving. People greeted Millie as she walked along the street and asked her about her family and their preparations. Millie gave each an answer and a smile. As she turned a corner onto Main Street, she almost ran into Frank Osborne, the boy who sat in front of her in class.

"Millie, what a surprise!" he said, jumping aside. He recovered his balance and took her hand in a friendly greeting. Millie felt her cheeks grow warm. Frank was the smartest boy in school, and a year ahead of Millie. She greatly enjoyed talking about books and history with him. Bea, Camilla, and Annabeth had started to tease her about the amount of time Frank spent sitting under the tree in the schoolyard, reading with Millie.

"The news of your moving has come as a great shock to the whole class," Frank said, dropping her hand. "Can it really be true? You are going to Indiana?"

"Yes, to the land of the Hoosier, wild Indians, and wolves," Millie said gaily. "Don't you envy me?"

"I envy those that go with you," he answered. "And I wonder who will challenge me in the spelling bee now. You won't forget old friends, Miss Millie?"

"No, no indeed, Frank," she said heartily. "I won't forget. But good-bye. I must purchase my supplies and hurry home," and with a nod and smile she left him. Millie didn't look back, but she caught a reflection in the glass door of the shop as it swung open—a ghostly picture of Frank standing on the walk where she had left him, his hands in his pockets.

Millie had just finished paying for the needles when a woman called her name.

"Mildred Keith!"

259

Millie's Unsettled Season

"Good morning, Mrs. Hall," Millie said politely. The Halls were the wealthiest family in town, good Christians, and always ready to help anyone in need.

"I am so glad I ran into you," Mrs. Hall said. "I have been meaning to speak to your mother, but I have been too busy to get by. Will you walk with me to my carriage?"

"Of course," Millie said, taking Mrs. Hall's package, and walking beside her.

"Millie," the elderly lady said, "I have been speaking to your teacher, Mr. Martin. He has told me how much you value your education, and how sorry he is to lose you as a pupil. He thinks very highly of you, and of your possibilities, my dear. I've heard of the difficulties your father had. I have had some difficulties of my own lately—Dr. Brent has said that I must not strain my heart. I was thinking I could get a girl to stay with me, to help with the light lifting and accompany me on walks." Millie's heart skipped a beat.

"Perhaps it would be too great a sacrifice for your dear parents. But you could continue your education, and they would know you were in a good Christian home. What do you think?"

"I…I truly don't know what to think, Mrs. Hall. It's such a kind offer! But…"

"Oh, I know the decision will be up to your parents," Mrs. Hall said with a smile. "I simply thought you might put in a good word for me."

"Thank you, Mrs. Hall. I will speak to Mamma about it." Millie watched the carriage roll away.

Stay in Lansdale! Was it possible? She started to walk toward home, but suddenly stopped, tucked the paper of needles into her sash, and ducked into the hedge beside the road. She ran until her breath was coming in gasps, up the

hill to the old oak that grew on top. She pulled herself up until she was standing on the lowest branch, petticoats and all, and hugged the trunk of the tree. She hadn't climbed the oak since she was Zillah's age. Somehow the rough bark against her face was comforting.

Lansdale stretched across the valley before her, lovely brick homes, tree-shaded streets, white church steeples pointing at the sky. Lansdale where everyone knew her, where her friends lived. Where she could finish her studies with Mr. Martin, and then attend college.

"Could this be Your plan?" Millie prayed out loud. "Could You want me to stay after all? But what about Mamma and Pappa? I don't know what to do!" Millie sighed. "I am willing to trust in You. But please, show me what I should do!"

CHAPTER

4

A Double Rescue

*Turn your ear to me, come quickly
to my rescue; be my rock of refuge,
a strong fortress
to save me.*

PSALM 31:2

A Double Rescue

*M*illie's steps were a little slower as she made her way home. Lansdale had looked dear and bright on her walk to the store, when she had known that she would be leaving. Now the future was not as certain. How could she stay with her friends and continue her education while her dear Mamma and Pappa traveled to a strange place? And the children!

She delivered the needles and cord, and set to pulling out a seam that had gone wrong.

"Mamma, how does God answer you when you pray?"

"Well," Marcia replied, snipping the end of her thread. "Sometimes He talks to me as I am reading my Bible—a verse just stands out. At other times, He brings a Scripture that I have memorized to mind. Sometimes He speaks to me through your father, who is a very wise and godly man. Sometimes it takes a long time, and sometimes," she exchanged a knowing look with Wealthy, "it doesn't. He seems to have answered Pappa's prayer about the house already."

"He has?" Millie set her sewing down.

"Pappa just sent word. Mr. Garlin's nephew is willing to buy our house! But we have to be out by the first of June—in just two more weeks!"

Millie looked at the pile of fabric waiting to be turned into dresses, pants, and shirts. "Couldn't God have taken a little longer, Mamma? How can we possibly finish in time?"

"When you ask God for help, sometimes you get a surprise," Aunt Wealthy said. "Just think about the children of Israel, when they left Egypt. The Red Sea before them and Pharaoh's army behind them. When they cried out for

God to save them, I'm sure they didn't expect Him to tell them to march right through the sea! When God has a plan, He makes a way!" She stood and gestured, as if by a wave of her hand she would part the calico and chintz and they would sort themselves into neatly sewn garments.

"The Israelites still had to do the marching," Marcia said practically. "And we still have to do the sewing. But I know He will help us get this done. I am determined to finish Adah's dress today."

The words had scarcely left her lips when there came a loud crash and scream from the hall, and the sound of tumbling and rolling.

Scissors, thimbles, and fabric flew in every direction as Marcia, Millie, and Aunt Wealthy sprang up all at once.

Millie rushed into the hall and almost tripped over Cyril, who was lying at the foot of the stairs, amidst the fragments of a large pitcher.

"You kilt him, Fan!" Don cried, looking down from the landing. "He's dead!" Fan, sitting halfway up the stairs and completely drenched with water, started sobbing hysterically.

"Cyril's dead!"

"No, he ain't," said Cyril, sitting up. "Mamma, I didn't mean to. Ow!" The hand he raised to his head came away bloody. A stream of blood poured down the side of his face. "Oh, I can't stop it!"

"Shhhh. We'll take care of it," said his mother, taking his head in her hands and holding the lips of the wound together. "A basin of cold water, Millie, quick! And be careful not to step on any sharp shards. Aunty, there is sticking plaster in the worktable drawer. Hush, Don. Don't cry anymore, Fan; Cyril isn't hurt too badly. Mother will soon make it all right."

A Double Rescue

Millie brought the basin, water, and a clean cloth, and Aunt Wealthy the plaster. Marcia cleaned the wound and then pressed hard on it to stop the bleeding.

"Come along, Fan," Millie said, as her mother commenced bandaging Cyril's head. "Let's get you into a dry frock."

Cyril was still sniffling when they returned. His head was wrapped in a clean white bandage.

"Now, Cyril," Aunt Wealthy said, taking off her brooch. "That's enough of that." She pinned her brooch on the front of his bandage. "There! You look just like a Sheik of Araby."

Don eyed the headband enviously.

"Don't even think of throwing yourself down the stairs, Don," Millie said. "Aunty hasn't any more brooches on her."

"Now, how did this happen?" Marcia asked.

"Why—why," said Cyril, "Fan wanted to wash her hands cause she'd been digging in the garden."

"Yeah, digging in the garden," Don echoed. Millie made a mental note to check the garden for buried valuables.

"Her hands was all dirty and there wasn't any water in the pitcher, so we brung it down and got it full and I was carrying it up and my foot tripped and… and I fell down with it and knocked Fan over 'cause she was behind me. And I couldn't help it. Could I, Don?"

"You couldn't," Don agreed. "Fan couldn't neither."

"And he's got a bad hurt on his head," put in Fan pityingly. "Poor Cyril!"

"Yes, he's punished enough, I think," said Marcia, adjusting his bandage. "His intentions seem to have been good; but next time you want water, dears, come tell

Mother or sister Millie. And now you must play quietly for a time, for Mother has lots and lots of work to do."

"Well, the morning's gone," said Millie, "and half the afternoon, too—wasted by the pranks of those children. I hope they've finished up their business for today." When Annabeth, Camilla and Bea knocked on the door a few moments later, Millie felt as if reinforcements had arrived just in time.

Camilla took the younger children in hand, promising to read to them from Millie's new copy of *Ivanhoe* as she led them upstairs, while Bea and Annabeth set about cutting fabric to Aunt Wealthy's patterns. Bea chattered happily about the boys at school and the plans for a summer dance in the town square. She had three months to convince her mother to let her stay up late for the moonlight dance. Millie shook her head at her friend's plans.

"I'll be thirteen by the dance," Bea said. "I'm sure Mother will let me stay up. That's practically grown!" The grand ballrooms and gowns Bea spun in the air certainly made the time pass quickly, and it didn't seem to hinder their sewing at all. Even Annabeth joined the fun, helping Bea imagine the colors and fabrics of the gowns, until Bea looked up from her stitches. "Oh, Millie," she said, "do they ever have dances in Indiana?"

"I'm sure they must," Millie said. But she wasn't sure at all. *It's not as civilized*, Pappa had said. *And we may have to do without a few comforts we are used to. But we will be a part of something grand—building a town!* "Though they may not be as grand as the dances in Lansdale."

"I'm sure they're not. Honestly, Millie, you are as brave as King David, or at least one of his mighty men," Bea said.

"Leaving everything you know and hold dear, traveling to a distant land fraught with peril."

"I'm sure that's making her feel much better, Bea," Annabeth said with a touch of sarcasm. "Knowing that Indiana is not only fraught with peril, but is devoid of dances."

"Oh, I'm sorry, Millie," Bea said. "Perhaps…perhaps you can dance with the savages. They wear dresses made of deerskin, don't they? I wonder how you sew that. It seems to me that it would itch."

"Honestly, Bea, you should pay more attention in class," Annabeth said. "Mr. Martin taught us all about Indians last fall. Cured doeskin is soft enough for babies' clothes. And they make it beautiful by sewing on beads and dyed porcupine quills. Weren't you paying the least bit of attention?" Bea shook her brown curls.

"I don't think your velvet gown will itch," Millie said, changing the subject before her friends started to bicker. The girls discussed Lansdale activities for the rest of the afternoon, and somehow managed to accomplish more in two hours than even Marcia had thought possible.

When Millie showed her friends to the door and said good-bye, her heart ached. She wanted to tell them all about Mrs. Hall's offer, to ask what they would do. Or simply to say, I will need a gown for the ball too, Bea! I'm not going to Indiana after all! But she knew she should talk to her Mamma and Pappa first. She shut the door behind her friends and went back to the parlor. Mamma had started hemming Adah's dress, and the needle fairly flew in her quick fingers. Millie picked up her own sewing. How could she tell Mamma? What could she say? Suddenly shrieks and wails once again brought the three to their feet.

"What now?" Marcia exclaimed. They followed the squeals to a door on the second floor.

"Tsk," said Aunt Wealthy when the door was opened, "what a dreadful mess!"

Every chair was out of place and turned on its side, the bed-clothes were all tumbled, and bits of paper littered the carpet.

Howls and grunts were coming from a large oak bureau that was tipped forward, leaning precariously against a chair. Four skinny little legs stuck out of the lowest drawer. Don's boots were kicking and he was grunting like a penned bull. Cyril's one visible foot was still, but the banshee-like howl had to be coming from his throat.

"Ouch," someone yelled, "you kicked me!" and then, "Shhhh."

The grunts stopped.

"I think someone's out there," Cyril said. "You're gonna be in really big trouble. Ouch!"

"I'm not going to be in trouble. You are!" said Don. "You're the one that wanted to take the coach. I told you we shoulda taken the horses."

"Shhhh," Cyril said again. "Hello? Is anybody there?"

Marcia and Aunt Wealthy answered by lifting the bureau upright. Millie pulled the boys out of the drawer.

"Thank you, Mamma," Cyril said.

"What were you doing in the drawer?" Aunt Wealthy asked.

"We were on our way to rescue Rowena," said Cyril, straightening his shirt. "I told him we shoulda taken the horses instead."

"Horses?" Aunt Wealthy asked, looking around.

"Aw, he means the chairs," Don motioned to the upside-down chairs. "We're tired of ridin' them."

"And where is Rowena?" Marcia asked, checking the upper drawers.

"Locked up in the tower." Cyril motioned to the wardrobe with his thumb. "Safe and sound."

Millie unlocked the wardrobe. Fan was sitting quietly in the back corner, chin on her hand.

"Oh, Fan," Millie said. "How long have you been in there?"

"Since Camilla left," the little girl said. "Cyril and Don said I had to wait for them to rescue me. I was getting tired of waiting."

"The naughty boys!" cried Millie. "Mother, I do think they ought to be punished."

"We didn't hurt her," Don muttered, hanging his head. "It was just a game. And we didn't mean to tumble the bureau over. Did we, Cyril?"

"You might have been hurt very badly yourselves if the chair had not been where it was," his mother said gravely. "I am very thankful for your escape, and you must never do such things again. Especially never lock each other into a wardrobe or closet," she added, sitting down and drawing Fan to her lap. Aunt Wealthy and Millie restored the contents of the bureau drawers, which the boys had unceremoniously tossed upon the carpet.

"Why, Mamma?"

"Because it is very dangerous. Your little sister might have died for lack of air."

"Died dead?"

Marcia nodded gravely. Don's eyes filled with tears.

"I won't ever, ever do it again," he said tremulously.

"Of course not. I don't believe my boys would be so mean and cowardly as to hurt anyone smaller or weaker than themselves," Marcia said.

Millie's Unsettled Season

"But we didn't hurt her, Mamma," Cyril said.

"I think you hurt her feelings very much."

Fan nodded. "I think I need a bandage," she said, pointing to her heart. "Right there."

"Oh," Marcia said. "Bandages won't help there. But kisses will." She drew Fan into her ams and kissed her.

Cyril considered the scene with folded arms.

"I'm sorry, Fan," he said at last. "Here," he said as he pulled the brooch from his headband and pinned it over her heart. "Now don't be a cry-baby."

"Now, I want you to pick up this room, children, and keep out of mischief for the rest of the day. Millie will watch over you while you set it right. And I expect you to do a good job."

"Yes, Mamma," Don said.

Cyril nodded.

"I must go back to my work," Marcia said, following her aunt, who had already left the room.

Millie was congratulating herself on the fact that she had not pinched Cyril or Don even once since her conversation with Aunt Wealthy weeks ago, and was rarely even tempted to anymore, when she came upon her treasured copy of *Ivanhoe*, tumbled in a blanket. The pages were folded and creased, and one, a picture of Rebecca at the stake, was torn down the middle.

"You naughty boys!" Millie said. "Look what you have done to my book! I think you should get spankings all around."

"We wanted to know what happened next," Cyril said. "I tried to read it to Don and Fan, but the words were too hard."

"Well, you're not going to find out now," Millie said, closing the book carefully, and pressing the covers together

to straighten the pages, and gripping it hard to keep her fingers busy. "I'm putting it away."

"You can't just put it away," Cyril said. "What happens to Ivanhoe? Does he get his castle back?" His freckles were standing out against his white face.

"I most certainly can put it away, Cyril Keith," Millie said adamantly. "It is my book, and you have mistreated it! You didn't even say you were sorry! I'm putting it away for good."

Fan crept close to Millie and slipped her arms around her.

"I'm sorry, Millie," she whispered.

"Me, too," Don said.

"Well, I'm not," Cyril said, wiping a tear from his cheek. "I'm not sorry at all. You are the meanest ol' sister in the whole world!"

"Pride goeth before a fall," Millie quoted.

"What's that s'posed to mean?" Cyril asked.

"Nothing to you," Millie said, and pinched him.

It was evening. Two candles burned on the sitting room table, and beside it sat Millie and her mother, still busy with their needles. The rest of the family were in bed and Aunt Wealthy had gone to her own home long ago.

"What are you thinking, daughter?"

Millie realized that her hands were resting in her lap.

"I am wondering how you put up with so much trouble from the children," Millie said.

Marcia smiled. "I had a lot of practice with their older sister," she laughed. "You were just as mischievous as they are, Millie mine. As soon as you could crawl, you spent your days pulling tablecloths down, breaking, tearing, climbing fences and trees, and even getting out of windows onto roofs. And you had a perfect mania for tasting everything that could possibly be put in your mouth—soap, candles, camphor, lye, medicines, whatever you could lay your hands on. I was in constant fear for your life."

"Poor, dear mother," Millie said. "How can I ever hope to repay you for your patient love and care?"

"You have been well worth all the trouble. I cannot tell you how much I enjoy the company and confidence of my eldest daughter. However, it is time to put up your work for tonight. You've had a long day."

Millie set her work aside and started to leave the room, but turned back.

"Mamma, I am so disgusted with myself. I know I couldn't sleep!"

"Why, Millie, what's wrong?"

Millie explained about the torn book and her harsh words with Cyril.

"I'm sorry about your book," Marcia said. "I didn't know they had caused such destruction."

"It was easy to forgive Don and Fan because they said they were sorry, and I know they meant it," Millie said. "But I haven't forgiven Cyril yet. It wasn't wrong to be angry, I know. But I haven't forgiven him, and that is a sin. The Bible says, 'Be angry, but do not sin. Do not let the sun go down while you are still angry.' The sun has been down a long time, and I am still so angry! I don't know what to do!" Millie knelt and laid her head in her mother's lap.

Marcia stroked her daughter's hair for a moment before she spoke. "You were angry because Cyril tore a book that was very precious to you," she said.

Millie nodded.

"I think you need to give your book away," said Marcia.

"Not to Cyril!" Millie sat up.

"No," said her mother smiling. "Not to Cyril. Give it to Jesus. Then ask yourself if He would forgive Cyril for tearing His book. If you give Him the things that are precious to you, you will be surprised what He can do with them."

"Mamma, that's not all." Millie's voice didn't want to work, but she forced herself to explain how she had pinched her brother.

"You have taken the first step, Millie mine," said Marcia. "Sins have a hold on you if you keep them hidden inside. The Bible tells us to confess our sins to each other and pray for each other so that we may be healed. I am glad you confessed to me. Now would you like me to pray for you?"

"Yes, Mamma."

"Dear Heavenly Father," her mother prayed, "I thank You that Millie's heart is tender toward You. And I ask You to help her control her temper, and not to pinch anymore."

"I'm sorry, Jesus," Millie said. "I'm sorry I wasn't like You, and I'm sorry I was prideful, and I'm sorry I hurt Cyril."

"You know He forgives us as soon as we ask, don't you, dear?" Marcia whispered.

"Yes, Mamma. And I will apologize to Cyril in the morning."

"Goodnight, Millie."

Millie lit a stub of a candle and kissed her mother goodnight. When she reached her room, she took the copy of

Millie's Unsettled Season

Ivanhoe from the top shelf and found a fresh quill on her desk. She uncorked the inkwell, dipped the nib, and marked out her own name from the bookplate. Then carefully, with her best penmanship, she wrote in "Jesus" instead. She blotted the letters carefully and left the book open for the ink to dry as she knelt beside her bed.

"Jesus," she prayed, "Mamma said that You could do amazing things if I give You the things that are precious to me. So…I want You to have this book. You can do anything You want with it. And…and I want to give You my hopes and dreams, too. I want You to have my future, Jesus. Please, please do something amazing with it!"

Millie crawled into her bed and pulled the blankets up to her chin. *So that's what answered prayers are like*, she thought. Because she knew, just as certainly as if someone had whispered it in her ear, that Jesus wanted her to go to Indiana—even though it would tear her heart as surely as Cyril had torn her book.

CHAPTER

5

The Journey Begins

This calls for patient endurance and faithfulness on the part of the saints.

REVELATION 13:10

The Journey Begins

The mood of the small group of family and friends gathered on Aunt Wealthy's vine-covered front porch on the last day of May was an odd mixture of excitement and tears. Millie was sure she knew exactly how the children of Israel had felt when they faced the Red Sea. She swallowed hard, and tried to smile at her friends.

"The girls do look sweet, Millie," said Bea as she adjusted the bow on Zillah's bonnet. Millie had to agree. Adah and Zillah were neat and clean in their new travel outfits. Millie had sewn Adah's herself, and Bea and Annabeth had finished Zillah's. "Do you suppose there will be shops in Pleasant Plains? I expect the fashions will be a bit backward—"

"Who cares about the fashions?" Camilla said. "What are you going to do about your studies? And are you taking books to read on the way?"

"I expect there will be shops," Millie said. "And I have packed my own books to read, though who knows how much time I will have, as I am minding the children." Millie bit her lip. Even if there were no shops, no parties, and not the slightest hint of fashion, she knew she could get by. But her friends! What would she do without them? Without Bea to help with dresses, without Annabeth to understand her heart before she even spoke, without Camilla to read sonnets?

"I wish I were taking you all with me!" Millie said. Annabeth took her hand and squeezed it.

"Is the stage late, Pappa?" Rupert asked.

"Just a little. Don, get down off that trellis."

"But Pappa, I want to be the first one to see it!"

"I think we can arrange that without pulling down Aunty's vines." He swung Don up onto his shoulders. "Let's take a little walk down the street."

He strode off with Zillah and Adah on each side, and Cyril and Fan dancing along behind.

"You have nappies for the baby?" Aunt Wealthy asked, for the third time.

"Yes, Aunty dear. I have everything we will need."

"I can't believe you are really going," Annabeth said to Millie. "Remember, you promised to write us every week."

"And send the letters to you by turns," Millie nodded, "so that you can read them together. The first will go to Camilla." Camilla just nodded. There were tears in her sweet blue eyes, and Millie knew she was fighting to keep them from falling.

"It's coming!" Ru was the first one to run back up the street. "The coach is coming!"

Millie turned to look one last time at the beautiful brick home she was leaving. That window with the morning glory vine was Mamma's room—and that's where Millie had been born. The nursery, the kitchen that was filled with gingerbread smells at Christmas, the dining room where Pappa always led the prayers...Millie felt an arm slip around her waist.

"It was a beautiful home," her mother whispered. "God blessed me with eight children there. And the same God that blessed me there will be with us wherever He leads us." Millie and her mother turned back together, just as four prancing steeds swept around the corner, and swaying and rolling, the coach dashed up to the gate.

The driver drew in rein, and the guard sprang from his lofty perch, threw open the door, and let down the steps.

The Journey Begins

Wannago stood on his hind legs and spun in place, afraid he would be left behind, but Aunt Wealthy opened her carpetbag and he jumped in. She zipped it almost shut with just his nose peeking out.

There were hurried embraces and farewells, a hasty stowing away of bags, bundles, and passengers large and small in the inside, and of more bulky baggage in the boot.

The inside of the coach was so crowded with Keiths that Stuart gave Ru permission to ride on the seat with the driver.

Aunt Wealthy handed in Wannago's bag and then exclaimed, "Wait! Oh, wait!" and rushed past the well-wishers and the young pastor and his wife into her home. She returned with an embroidered pillow from the settee in her library.

"I never travel without this," she said, hugging the pillow close. "Mother filled it with her own feathers!"

"Was great-grandmother a bird?" Fan asked, looking puzzled.

"No," Adah said. "The feathers came from her geese, silly."

The steps were replaced, the coach door slammed, the guard's horn tooted a warning to traffic on the street, the coachman's whip cracked, and they were off. Millie watched through the back window, until they had turned the corner and she couldn't see her friends anymore. *Jesus*, she prayed silently, *it's more than I can bear. Will I ever see them again?* The familiar town scenes outside the coach window slowly changed to countryside, then long low hills. When Millie could no longer recognize the hills and trees of Lansdale, she laid her head on her arms and tried not to weep.

The few hours' drive it took for the travelers to reach the town where they were to exchange the stage for a canal

boat were quite enough to convince Millie that she did not enjoy adventures. The coach was stuffy and became stuffier as the day grew warm.

The rocking stage soon lulled baby Annis to sleep, but the other children had a hard time keeping still. Wannago wiggled and squirmed until Aunt Wealthy was forced to let him out. He settled himself on Don's lap and gazed out the window.

Marcia produced a catalogue and after reading several stories aloud, used scissors from her basket to clip out figures that Adah and Zillah and Fan made into paper dolls.

When the coachman finally opened the door, the young Keiths practically exploded down the step, Cyril and Don tumbling over one another.

"Is this Pleasant Plains?" Fan asked, looking wide-eyed at the new town.

"No," Stuart laughed. "This is where we get aboard the canal boat. But I think we should stretch our legs and have some dinner first."

Stuart let the young ones run until they had used up some of their energy, then sat the family down to a good meal at a hotel nearby. After they had dined, they boarded the packet *Pauline*, which was docked at the wharf. Millie was fascinated by the little boat. It was really nothing more than a floating box; one cabin that housed all of the passengers below, and the deck, which was simply the roof of the cabin. The passengers seated themselves on a cushioned bench that ran around the inside of the cabin, while the hands stowed baggage on the deck. The quarters were only a little less confined than those of the stage. The *Pauline's* interior was so narrow that when the table was to be set for a meal, most of the passengers had to go on deck to be out of the way.

The Journey Begins

When all of the passengers and luggage were aboard, a two-mule team was hitched to the front of the packet. With a shout from the mule driver, the mules started plodding along the towpath. The ropes grew taut, and the packet started to move slowly up the canal. The mules were changed every fifteen or twenty miles, day or night, and a fresh driver and team pulled the packet on.

New passengers arrived at almost every dock and old ones departed, so there was a constant panorama of humanity. When the *Pauline* came to a lock, some of the passengers would get off and walk along the towpath, catching the boat again past the lock. The young Keiths took several such walks with Aunt Wealthy and Wannago as the afternoon wore on.

Finally, the captain announced that it was time to prepare for supper. The passengers climbed the short steps up to the deck. The Ohio countryside, hills green with early summer, dragged by at a slow mule's pace. The passengers found seats on their chests and crates, and children ran amongst them playing tag and making new friends.

Millie sat between Aunt Wealthy and a very large, nervous young woman who introduced herself as Ann Leah.

"I do hope there are no bridges," Ann Leah said, her fingers fluttering to her throat. "I shouldn't want to spoil my dress lying on the deck."

Pappa had explained that when they came to a bridge, anyone on deck would have to get down on their hands and knees, or be swept off the deck into the murky waters of the canal.

"Now, dear, I'm sure the captain would not have sent us all up here if there were any bridges looming," Aunt Wealthy said, scratching Wannago's ears.

Millie's Unsettled Season

Ann Leah still craned her neck, watching the front of the boat fearfully until they were summoned below.

Supper was a simple meal of cold meat and bread. Afterwards the passengers were sent aloft again as the cabin was prepared for the night. The bench they had been sitting on all day was used as a lower bunk, and other shelves hung above it. Blankets were produced, and the passengers settled into their narrow, uncomfortable berths.

Millie helped her mother put the children to bed, all in a group along one wall. Rupert and Fan had the uppermost berth, though Ru had to be careful not to bump his head when he sat up. Adah and Zillah were below him, and then Cyril and Don, left together only when they promised not to talk and to go right to sleep.

Stuart said prayers with each of the children, listened as they whispered their Bible verses in his ear, then went up on deck, leaving Aunt Wealthy, Marcia, and Millie to tuck them in.

"The blankets are all damp," Zillah said. "I don't like it."

"That's because we are on the water," Marcia said. "But they will keep you perfectly warm."

The passengers around them settled into place with complaints and groans. Some were soon fast asleep, while others talked quietly.

"Tell me a story, Millie," Adah said.

"Not tonight," Millie said. "It would disturb the others." She rubbed the little girl's back, feeling her muscles relax into sleep.

Suddenly a rumbling growl filled the cabin. Adah jerked upright. The rumble came again, more terrible than before.

"I heard a bear, Mamma," she said. "I'm afraid!"

284

"No, dearest. That is just a gentleman snoring." The snorer grunted suddenly, as if he had received an elbow in the ribs. His growls subsided into gargles and whistles, and Adah lay back down.

"I don't like sleeping with all these people," Zillah said. "I want my own bed. I want my own room!"

"Shhhh," Marcia said. "My children must be considerate of others."

Babies cried; older children fretted; some grown people indulged in loud complaints. Ann Leah was much too large to fit on the narrow bench-beds, and so had to spend the night sitting up. All together the cabin was a scene of confusion, and the young Keiths felt very forlorn.

But mother, aunt, and older sister were very patient. They soothed, comforted, and at length succeeded in getting them all to sleep.

Ann Leah, saying that she couldn't possibly sleep, and probably wouldn't sleep all night, offered to watch over the children if Wealthy, Millie, and Marcia wanted to go up on deck for an hour to enjoy the moonlight. Grateful for the offer, the three climbed up the short flight of steps that led from the stern to the deck. Stuart found them seats on some of their own trunks.

There were a number of other passengers sitting about or pacing to and fro. Among the former was a portly gentleman who sat on a crate at the stern end of the boat, his elbow on his knee and his bearded chin in his hand, gazing idly over the moonlit landscape.

After a pleasant half hour, Stuart and Marcia excused themselves, saying that they would watch over the children, leaving Millie, Wannago, and Wealthy on the deck. The *Pauline* glided onward with easy, pleasant motion. All had

285

grown quiet in the cabin below, and the song of the bull-frogs, the dull thud of the mule's hoofs, and the gentle lap of the water against the sides of the boat, were the only sounds that broke the stillness.

"So how do you like travel?" Aunt Wealthy asked. "Is it as exciting as you expected?"

"I don't like it at all so far," Millie confessed. "It is cramped and uncomfortable, and I don't know how the children are going to stand days of this. I thought it would be more... well, exciting."

"But it is exciting!" exclaimed Aunt Wealthy. "The breeze is so refreshing, the moonlight so beautiful."

"Yes, the moonlight is enchanting," said Millie, "and one gets a good view of it here."

"Low bridge!" sang out the steersman suddenly.

"Low bridge, everybody down!" The cry was repeated in louder, more emphatic tones.

Millie dropped to her hands and knees beside Aunt Wealthy, and looked towards the helmsman. The boat was already sweeping under the bridge. She glanced around. The passengers were all hugging the deck, ladies in fine dresses, and dock workers alike — all but one. The gentleman seated on the back of the ship was a lone silhouette against the sky.

"Get down," someone called, but the thinker didn't move. "Get down, I say!"

Suddenly there was a rustling of skirts beside her, as Aunt Wealthy stood up. And then Wealthy was racing down the deck just ahead of the advancing bridge, Wannago at her heels. Millie saw her leap over a small chest, petticoats flying. Then the shadow of the bridge swallowed them, and Millie saw no more.

286

CHAPTER

A Hard Lesson

*You shall not covet . . . anything
that belongs to your
neighbor.*

Exodus 20:17

A Hard Lesson

illie heard the thud of something heavy hitting the deck, a muffled exclamation, and then silence. The air beneath the bridge was chill and damp with a mist that was rising from the water. It was as if they had stepped though a veil into colder, darker night.

Then the bridge was past, and the moonlight revealed Wealthy Stanhope, sprawled atop the portly gentleman, while Wannago sat — head quizzically cocked to one side — on the box the gentleman had previously occupied.

"I say!" the gentleman freed himself as quickly as possible and helped Wealthy to her feet. "I believe you've saved my life! I was completely absorbed in my thoughts. Can't swim a lick, and I'm sure to have been knocked unconscious by the bridge! I say, Madam! You could have been killed yourself!"

"Nonsense," said Wealthy, straightening her hair and brushing off her skirt. "I am a strong swimmer. I'm sure I would have been fine. A Christian lady does not stand idly by while others are in peril, sir. She does what Jesus would do."

"Incredible," the gentleman said, removing his spectacles and polishing them. "You have just saved the life of Percival Fox, M.D. I am completely at your service, and that of your family." He bowed.

Dr. Fox insisted on helping Wealthy down the steps. It was with some difficulty that she persuaded him to allow her to cross the cabin alone, pleading that his deep voice might wake the children. Wealthy hurried to Marcia and Stuart.

289

Millie's Unsettled Season

"Who was that gentleman?" Marcia asked.

"A Dr. Hound," Wealthy said.

"I think it may have been Fox," Millie whispered.

"Yes," Wealthy said, "yes, that's right, Dr. Fox." She explained what had happened on the deck in hurried whispers. In the dim light, Millie could just see her mother's hand cover her mouth, and she knew she was trying not to laugh out loud.

"Really, Marcia, it isn't the least bit funny," said Wealthy.

The next day, when they awoke and the passengers went on the deck as the crew prepared for breakfast, Aunt Wealthy looked around quickly. Millie tugged her sleeve and pointed. Dr. Fox was sitting on the same crate that had almost been his downfall the night before.

"Hmmm," Aunt Wealthy said. "This way, children!" She led them to the bow of the ship—and away from Dr. Fox.

It was a beautiful morning, the air sweet with the smell of honeysuckle. Bees buzzed past the packet, and the birds were creating a riotously joyful noise in the tree tops. The passengers who had been most vociferous about their discomfort the night before, greeted one another almost jovially, the light of the sun seeming to make all the difference in their personalities. *Am I like that, Jesus?* Millie had never thought of it before. Her own Mamma and Pappa and Aunt Wealthy had seemed just as pleasant and polite in the damp crowded dark of the night as they were in the cheerful light of day. It was as if what was inside them could not be changed by the world outside of them. *I want to be like them, Jesus,* Millie prayed. *I want to be constant in Your ways and in Your love.*

"Hey, lookit that!" Cyril exclaimed. The mule team had been changed during the night, and a boy no older than Ru

was driving the team. His baggy pants, which were held up by suspenders over his bare shoulders, ended just below his knees. The boots on his feet looked two sizes too big, and his skinny bare legs were spattered with mud. But the most striking of all was the skunk-skin cap perched jauntily on his head, its long tail hanging down his back.

"Pardon me," a deep voice said.

They turned to find Dr. Fox standing behind them. His hair was parted neatly down the middle and curled on each side of his forehead, and he was holding a freshly picked bouquet of wild flowers. He lifted his hat and started a bow, then froze in place, hat suspended over his head, flowers held before him—a chivalrous, but comical, statue.

"Good morning," Aunt Wealthy said, waving away a bee that strayed too close to the flowers. Dr. Fox didn't move.

"Are you quite all right?" Wealthy asked.

The gentleman's lips moved.

"I said, 'are you quite all right?'" Wealthy spoke more loudly.

Dr. Fox blinked twice and his lips moved again. Ru leaned in close, and then nodded.

"He's deathly allergic to bee stings," he explained.

"Well, that's simply solved." Wealthy snatched the flowers from his hands and tossed them overboard. "There!"

"I believe you have saved me again," the gentleman declared. "But you've lost your bouquet..."

"Oh, was that for me?" Wealthy asked. Adah and Zillah giggled.

"Well, er, yes," the doctor stuttered. "I gathered them myself along the path this morning. They were lovely, and smelled so good."

"Bee bush always does," Wealthy said. "You don't travel much, do you, doctor?"

"No, my health is delicate—"

"I thought that might be the case," Wealthy said. "Good day!"

At the first available lock, Aunt Wealthy volunteered to take the children for a walk along the towpath. The steersman was describing the workings of the lock to Ru, but the little ones were all eager to go, and Wannago was beside himself with excitement at the chance to chase squirrels and stick his nose down gopher holes.

Cyril and Don wasted no time at all in seeking out the mule boy, while Aunt Wealthy and the girls spent their time chasing Wannago along the path.

"Now where have they gotten to?" Aunt Wealthy asked, as they returned to the boat. Zillah pointed to the *Pauline*, where Don and Cyril could be seen listening to the steersman with Ru.

When the ladies boarded the packet, Dr. Fox was waiting with a cool drink for Wealthy, a tasty treat for Wannago, and a smile for the little girls.

Millie saw Cyril and Don nudging one another and grinning, and gave them a stern look.

"Would you allow me to find you a comfortable seat?" Dr. Fox asked. Wealthy sighed, looked longingly at the shore, and then accepted.

Millie spent the rest of the morning composing a letter to her friends and addressing it to Camilla. She set it aside to post at the next town. When she went on deck after the noonday meal, the mule team was being changed, and the boy turned to wave at the deck where the Keiths were standing. Cyril waved back.

A Hard Lesson

"Do you know that young man?" Stuart asked, surprised.

"Sure. His name's George," Don said. "He's really nice."

"I wonder what happened to that dreadful hat?" Marcia said.

Cyril flushed. "It wasn't dreadful, Mamma," he said. "It was a real, authentic polecat hide. He got it from a mountain man named Augustus Melodious Malone, who wore it while he fought Indians!"

"I wonder why he would part with such a treasure," Stuart said.

"He sure didn't want to," Don said. "Cyril had to trade him my pocketknife and his slingshot for it. It belongs to both of us now."

"Bring it here at once," said Marcia.

Cyril fetched the hat from beneath the deck, and Marcia examined it closely, checking it inside and out.

"Oh, no," she said, as she examined the inside of the hat. "Did you put this on your head?"

Cyril admitted that they both had, but that they hadn't let Fan touch it.

"That is a mercy, at least," Marcia said. "It is infested with lice." Don's hand went to his head and he started scratching. Cyril smacked it away when he saw Millie looking. Stuart picked the skunk-skin up gingerly by the tail and dropped it over the side of the boat. It hit the water with a plop, and sank instantly out of sight.

"What are we going to do, dear?"

"There's only one thing to do," he said. The boys were made to sit together on a crate until they reached the next town; and then Stuart took them each by the hand and they went to see the barber.

293

Millie's Unsettled Season

Marcia cried when she saw them coming back, bald as new eggs. The boys had been shaved, and their heads scrubbed and rinsed with turpentine and water.

There was no hiding the smell of the turpentine, or what it meant. Several mothers pulled their children away, and Millie heard them whispering about people with lice. Don and Cyril pretended not to care, but Millie could tell that they were hurt when they overheard several people asking the captain to move them away from the Keiths at the table.

"I can't imagine the impression we will make in Pleasant Plains," Marcia said, putting her head in her hands.

"Now, dear," Stuart said, "It can happen to anyone."

"I am sorry, Marcia," said Aunt Wealthy. "I should have watched them more closely." Dr. Fox, who was hovering behind her, wrung his hands.

"I'm sure you were perfectly vigilant, dear lady," he said.

"Nonsense," Aunt Wealthy said. "I should have watched more closely. Look at them! The poor things are miserable."

Cyril and Don had found seats for themselves behind the steersman. If they stood and walked around the deck, mothers pulled their children out of the way, so the two boys sat close together, ignoring the children who pointed and stared. At every dock, someone new came aboard, saw the boys, shook their heads and moved away.

Finally, Millie couldn't stand watching anymore. "Do you want to play cat's cradle, Cyril?" she asked, pulling a ball of yarn from her pocket. Don looked up hopefully, but Cyril just snorted.

"That's a girls' game. Leave us alone, Millie, or they'll shave your head, too." He put his head down on his arms.

"Itchy head, bugs in bed!" a girl called, scratching her head and laughing. "Bet you're gonna wish you're dead!"

"That's very bad grammar," Millie said, starting toward the girl. How dare she tease that way! Cyril hadn't done anything wrong. He just didn't think about what he was doing.

The little girl ran to the back of the boat where her mother was sitting, and Millie stopped where she was. She turned and almost ran down the steps to the cabin. She rooted through her carpetbag until she found *Ivanhoe*, opened it to the picture of Rebecca, and ran her finger down the tear. *Cyril just didn't think.*

She took the book up onto the deck, and settled into the shade by her brothers.

"Don't yell at us anymore, please, Millie," Don said. "We can't stand it. We're sorry about the picture."

"I wasn't going to yell," Millie said. "I was going to read to you." Soon Adah, Zillah, and Fan were listening too.

Ivanhoe was read and acted out by the young Keiths at the front of the ship. Aunt Wealthy found scarves to be made into ladies' hats, and Stuart made the boys swords from fence pickets he purchased from a lumber barge going the other way. Dr. Fox surprised everyone by offering to read and then doing so brilliantly, almost like an actor on stage. His deep voice was such fun to listen to as it boomed out over the deck, that other youngsters gathered as close as they dared, and looked enviously at the Keiths.

Millie was sitting beside him when he reached the torn page, and she saw the look of disapproval on his face.

"I know, it's terrible," she said, "but Jesus seems to be able to use the book anyway."

"Say what? I don't quite understand. This is not a Bible, young lady. Why would the Lord care about *Ivanhoe*?" He looked so puzzled that she explained the story of the torn page, and how she had struggled to forgive her brother.

"And the most brilliant part," she finished, "is that of course Jesus not only forgave Cyril for tearing His book, He did something wonderful with the book I gave Him. He used it to help Cyril and Don!"

"Hmmmm," Dr. Fox said, polishing his glasses. "Hmmmm." When he started reading again, there was just the tiniest catch in his voice.

Fair Rowena and godly Rebecca were saved, and the Saxon knights defeated and King Richard returned, before the packet docked in Cleveland.

Dr. Fox said his farewells at the wharf, and Millie was surprised to be sorry to see him go. Even Wealthy blushed when he took her hand to say farewell.

"What a beautiful city!" exclaimed Millie as they stepped ashore. "Do let us walk to the hotel, Pappa, if it is not too far."

"Do just as Aunt Wealthy and your mother say," he replied. "I am told it is but a short distance, Marcia. I will have our heavy baggage carried directly to the steamer which leaves this afternoon, and Rupert and the girls can take charge of the satchels and small packages."

"I don't wanna walk," Don said. "Can't we get a hack or take an omnibus? People are looking at us funny."

"Will you walk with me?" Stuart said. "I would be proud for all of the people of Cleveland to know that you are my sons." He took the boys by the hand and the Keiths rallied around them. Wannago and Aunt Wealthy with her purple umbrella brought up the rear.

Millie was thrilled by the sights and sounds of the city. Omnibuses and carriages filled the streets, and pedestrians — elegant in suits, silk top hats, or gowns of pale summer splendor — decorated the sidewalks. Newsboys stood on corners

shouting headlines, and a man on the corner offered to shine Stuart's shoes for a penny. The houses were tall and elegant, and Millie wished that Bea could see the gowns and parasols, boots and buckle shoes in the windows of the large, handsome stores. Wannago made the acquaintance of a very fine poodle outside of Roe & Watson, Booksellers. Millie asked her Pappa for two bits to buy a copy of William Lloyd Garrison's paper *The Liberator* at the bookstore. Mr. Martin had brought a copy to school once, and explained that Mr. Garrison was an abolitionist—a person who believed that slaves should be freed. When Millie heard of the horrible conditions of the slaves in the southern states, she decided that she was an abolitionist, too. Millie had never seen a copy of the paper aside from the one her teacher had. The bookseller hesitated to sell her a copy until Pappa intervened, and then he cautioned them about carrying the paper too openly in the street. Abolitionists were considered to be troublemakers, and many people shunned them.

Millie carried the paper folded under her arm until they reached the hotel, and then she read it cover to cover in the privacy of their rooms. There was a wonderful article about Prudence Crandall, a Connecticut woman whose home was burned to the ground because she dared to run a school for Negro children there. There was a very good article about the conditions of the slaves on sugar cane plantations. The writer ended with a plea to give up sugar, as it was a slave product.

"Are you ready for dinner?" Marcia asked, as Millie put down the paper. Stuart led them to the hotel dining room, and Marcia ordered for the children.

"Excuse me," Millie said to the waitress after Marcia ordered lemonade all around. "Is your lemonade sweetened with sugar?"

"Yes, miss," the waitress said.

"I think I would prefer water."

"What's wrong with the lemonade?" Ru asked. Millie explained about the men, women, and children being worked to death on the sugar cane plantations. She had almost finished the story when the tall, cool glasses of lemonade arrived.

Ru pushed his away. "I think I would like water, too," he said.

A man at the next table who had obviously been listening to Millie's impassioned descriptions of the plantations made a loud comment about "slave lovers" as he stood to leave.

Marcia gave him a cool look. "I believe our Millie is right, Pappa," she said. "People should be willing to make sacrifices for what they believe. And I believe slavery is wrong. There are other ways we can sweeten our meals that don't contribute to the misery of others. I'm proud of you, Millie."

No one touched the lemonade, although Stuart said that they should pay for it because they ordered it. When the meal arrived, Don poked dismally at his vegetables. "Are green beans grown on plantations?" he asked hopefully.

"Oh, no sir," the waitress said. "Those are grown in the glorious state of Ohio!"

"Figures," Don said.

After dinner, Stuart, his wife and children went out for another stroll about the city.

When they returned to the hotel, they were surprised by packages addressed to Cyril, Don, and Millie, and a large bouquet with a card for Wealthy.

"'My dear lady,'" Wealthy read aloud, "'Please accept these flowers as a token of my thanks. I am sure I have never met

a family quite like the incredible Keiths. It was a pleasure traveling with you all.' Signed, Percival Fox, M.D."

"Can we open the boxes, Mamma?" the boys asked. "Can we?"

Marcia looked at Stuart.

He nodded.

Paper and string flew, and Don and Cyril pulled out two brand new coonskin caps.

"Pappa! Can we keep them?"

"Of course," Stuart smiled. "You will be the envy of Pleasant Plains!"

"What have you got, Millie?" Ru asked.

"A book," Millie said. "*The Last of the Mohicans*, by James Fennimore Cooper, and a letter."

My dear Miss Keith,

I hope you and your family will enjoy reading this book together—and I wanted you to know how much your story and your copy of Ivanhoe—I mean, of course, Jesus' copy of Ivanhoe—have meant to me. You see, when your glorious aunt saved my life, I was lost in thought about what I had done with my life, and what I should do with my future. I had a successful practice, and all of the money a single gentleman could want. I had respect and honor from my friends, but something was missing. I think I have found out what it was. I, too, have given my future to Jesus. If He can do so much with a tattered book, what do you suppose He might do with a portly, allergy-prone doctor?

When Millie looked up from reading the letter, there were tears in Aunt Wealthy's eyes. "I just love adventures," Wealthy said.

CHAPTER

7

A Dark Day

A wise son brings joy to his father,
but a foolish son grief
to his mother.

PROVERBS 10:1

A Dark Day

There were three vessels in port that could take them on the next leg of their journey— a steamboat and two sloops. Stuart let Millie and Rupert decide which they would book passage on. They walked to the docks and looked over their choices. Millie was taken at once by the tall sailing ships. They looked elegant and almost poetic, their masts and lines stark against the blue sky.

"Look at that wheel," Rupert said, pointing to the steamboat. "I'd love to see the boiler rooms fired up!" The steamer was large, and would have more room to carry more passengers, but Millie's eyes kept going back to the larger of the sloops, the *Queen Charlotte*.

Although she (Pappa had explained that boats and ships are always called "she") sat at anchor with her one tall mast bare, Millie could imagine her skipping across the waves, her crisp, white sails fat with wind.

"How about the sloop, Ru?" Millie said.

"She's nice," Ru said without looking at her once. "I wonder what that wheel weighs? Can we really choose her, Pappa?"

Stuart glanced at Millie and winked.

"Of course. But I have been wondering…"

"Wondering what?" Ru looked up.

"Oh, just wondering what it would have been like to sail with John Paul Jones," Stuart said, "in one of the very first ships of the American Navy!"

Stuart had Ru's attention now.

"I thought John Paul Jones's ship was a clipper called the *Ranger*," Ru said.

303

"Before the *Ranger* was built, Jones was the captain of a sloop, the *Providence*, very much like the *Charlotte* there. She carried 12 guns."

"12 cannon?" Ru was looking at the sloop now.

Stuart nodded.

"And Jones fought more than three dozen sea battles in her, many against larger, better-armed ships. He captured over forty vessels, and sent thirteen more to the bottom of the sea!"

The sloop had Ru's full attention now.

"Captured forty! She must have been fast!"

Stuart nodded.

"I think I would like to sail on her," Ru said, still staring at the *Charlotte*.

Stuart winked at Millie again before he made the arrangements for their trunks to be moved aboard. Once it was settled, it took very little time to stow their belongings.

Millie helped her mother and aunt arrange their belongings below deck, while Wannago inspected their work from a post on Wealthy's berth. The cabins were small, but tidy and private, and Millie felt that she might sleep again at last. No one was more delighted, it seemed, than Wannago, who believed himself to be the instant friend of the ship's cat, Mr. Whiskers. Whiskers, an elegant gray puss with white boots and a snowy bib, did not agree. He leapt to Millie's shoulder and glared down at Wannago with fire in his green eyes. Millie had to usher Wannago from her cabin and shut the door before she could untangle the cat from her bonnet strings.

With the door shut, the cabin was just large enough to turn around in. Millie deposited the cat and bonnet on the

berth. There was a small bedside table, a closet just large enough to hang a few outfits, and a small round window. It was a perfect dollhouse room. Millie closed her eyes and spread her arms wide. It was the first time in weeks she had been really, truly alone, with walls and doors between her and any other human soul; it was blissful. She stood for a moment, just enjoying the aloneness, before she hung her travel dresses in the closet. Last of all she set her Bible on the bedside table and smiled. Now it was home.

When everything was in good order, Millie hurried on deck again where Rupert had been left in charge of the younger children. She found him in earnest conversation with a boy not much older than herself. His brown hair was pulled back in a club, sailor-fashion, and held together by tar, like the hair of other sailors on the ship.

"Why do you have that awful stuff in your hair?" Zillah asked.

"Zillah, don't be rude," Millie reprimanded.

"It's a good question," the boy said. "And I don't mind answering. While we are aboard ship there is no time to have our hair cut. This keeps the hair out of our faces while we work. And," he leaned down close to the little girl, "if we should have to fire the cannon, I would use little bits of tar to plug my ears. That way the cannon's roar won't make me deaf." He pretended to clean out his ear with his little finger. "If pirates attack and we have to roll out our cannon, I'll loan you some."

Zillah looked at him doubtfully, and edged closer to Millie.

"Now you are frightening her," Millie said, taking the little girl's hand. "There are no pirates on Lake Erie these days," she said reassuringly.

"That's true enough," the young sailor laughed. "I didn't mean to offend."

"My sister, Miss Millie Keith, Mr. Edward Wells," Ru said formally.

"Edward is the Captain's son," Adah said, a little in awe.

"Happy to make your acquaintance," said the boy gallantly, lifting his cap and bowing low. "Hope you'll enjoy your voyage on the *Queen Charlotte*. We shall do all we can to make the trip pleasant for you and your brothers and sisters."

"Thank you, sir."

"Oh, I hope you will call me Edward," he said, his gray eyes crinkled at the corners. "Your family already does. They remind me of my own young sisters back home in London town. Are you ready to set sail?"

"I don't see how we can," Millie said. "There is no breeze. And the sails are still furled."

"Ah-ha! You would make a good sailor," Edward laughed, taking Millie's arm and pulling her aside just as a yellow blur that must have been Mr. Whiskers went by, followed by Wannago. "But look." He pointed to the steamer that lay along the port side. Sailors were lashing the ships together with fat hemp ropes. "We don't want to miss the tide, so the steamboat will give us a lift until we reach the lake. There is almost always wind enough there to fill our sails. The steamer will give the old *Milwaukee*, the sloop on the other side, a lift too."

"I'd still like to see her boilers," Ru said wistfully, "as she hauls us all."

"She won't even complain," Edward said. "She's that powerful. But when we catch the wind—ah, then the *Charlotte* will outdistance her."

A Dark Day

Millie stood for a moment watching the frantic activity aboard all three ships. Sailors swarmed like ants, carrying loads and tying lines.

"I'm glad we chose the *Charlotte*," Millie said. "She is the most beautiful ship. I can't wait to see her sails unfurled and full of wind. It will be just like the pictures in my books. But don't you think *Queen Charlotte* is an odd name for an American ship?"

"Yes," Edward said, turning quickly away. "Yes, it is odd. Why don't we go aft? The steamer's wheel is about to start turning if I am not mistaken."

Rupert caught Millie's arm and pulled her back as the little ones followed their new friend. "Be a little circumspect, Millie," Rupert said. "Edward is English, after all. The *Charlotte* is quite old you know — older than dear Aunt Wealthy in fact. This sloop was captured — taken from the British during the Revolutionary War. Edward seems a little tense about it still, so try not to tweak him."

"The War for Independence was fifty years ago!" Millie said. "It's ancient history, before our parents were born. How can it trouble him now?"

Rupert shrugged.

"Well, I won't twit him, unless he says something mean or exasperating about Washington or America," Millie said.

"If he does, then twit him as hard as you like, and I'll lend a hand," Ru said. "But he doesn't seem the type. His head is stuffed full of history books, ships, and sea battles."

"Our heads are stuffed full of history books, too," Millie pointed out.

"True. But his books were written by Brits. Who knows what they say about the war." They caught up with their company at the stern of the ship.

Millie's Unsettled Season

The steamer's wheel began to turn, the ropes creaked, timbers groaned, and the three ships started to move. The Keiths watched in fascination as the *Queen Charlotte* and her consorts slowly cleared the harbor.

"That part of the show is over," Edward said. "Come on, let's find some seats in the shade." He led them to a spot sheltered by the forecastle, and they seated themselves on giant coils of rope.

"Aren't you needed to sail the ship?" Zillah asked.

Edward laughed. "I would be, if the ship were sailing. But since she is being towed, there's not much for me to do. When we hoist sail, I'll be needed up there." He pointed to the ropes attached to the mast and jib.

"What's that?" Don asked, pointing to a platform three quarters of the way up the mast.

"That's the crow's nest," Edward said.

"I want to see a crow," Fan said.

"You're looking at one, matey." Edward tucked his fingers into his armpits, and flapping his elbows said, "Caw!"

"You mean you get to climb up there?" Cyril said.

"Not only do I get to, I have to. I keep watch from the crow's nest. I can see other ships, or storms on the horizon, long before the people down below could see them."

"Pirate ships?" Zillah asked, obviously still worried.

"Well, not recently," Edward admitted. "But you never know."

Millie frowned.

"It's really rather boring most of the time. I often carry a book up with me. Father doesn't mind, so long as I don't drop it on anyone's head."

The travelers now had a good view of the Canadian and Michigan shores. Millie thought it was strange to see two

A Dark Day

countries at once, and how much stranger still it must be for neighbors who lived on opposite sides of the border where the countries were not divided by a river, or any real boundary at all. If, by chance, your pappa owned land on one side, you were an American; on the other, a Canadian. She wondered if God saw the invisible lines between countries that separated families, neighbors, and friends; and if angels were flying over them right now, did they know when they passed from one country to another?

When they had passed through the Detroit River and so far out into Lake St. Clair that little could be seen but water and sky, Edward offered to show them over the vessel. They started with the Captain's quarters and the galley, a tiny kitchen where the food was cooked. They had already seen the comfortable passengers' cabins. Edward gave them the grand tour, leading them down companionways and through hatches, showing them the crew's quarters, which were even more cramped than the berths on the *Pauline* had been, and ending up in the dark hold where the cargo was stored.

"We're underwater here," he said.

Millie touched the wooden wall imagining the deep water beyond. "It's nice knowing the Captain's son," she whispered to Ru. "I can't imagine we'd get the grand tour otherwise."

"Is there anything below us?" Ru asked, stomping on the floor.

"The bilge, full of water," Edward said.

"I expect it's full of rats, too," Ru said.

"Maybe a few," Edward said. "They do climb up the ropes when we are docked. But it's Mr. Whiskers' job to see them off, though he seems a bit preoccupied at the moment."

"I want to go up," Fan said.

"And a very good idea, too," Edward agreed. "It's time for dinner."

Millie was seated at the Captain's table between Rupert and Edward. There were many more passengers of both sexes, several nationalities, and a variety of ages, from infants in arms to hoary-headed grandparents. Cyril and Don had already made friends with a cheerful, mischievous boy named Billy Kress who invited them to sit with him and his mother.

The company was polite and genial, the food was excellent, and every one present seemed content and in good humor. The elder Mr. Wells enjoyed children, and laughed a good deal, making the meal more pleasant still.

"Look," Aunt Wealthy whispered, motioning to the table. "Don't you think that's what the feast of the Lamb will look like? All sorts of people mixed together, laughing and having fun?"

Millie smiled. It was possible Aunt Wealthy hadn't seen Billy Kress slip a bone into his napkin and onto his lap. From there it made its way to Don, who managed to toss it to Wannago, who was hiding under Fan's chair. Wannago collapsed in a happy heap and chewed on it for the rest of the meal.

Millie awoke in the gray of the morning and crept quietly out of her berth. She slipped into her clothes, picked up her Bible, and made her way up to the deck.

"Good morning, Jesus," she whispered. "Thank You for letting me come on this trip. Maybe I do like adventures after all."

A Dark Day

She leaned against the bulwark and watched as the sun came up like a fiery ball out of the lake. There was still no breath of wind. She had a few precious moments to read. She had been in the habit of reading her Bible at least once a day since she had become a Christian two years before. Pappa had knelt with her when she prayed to accept Jesus as her Lord, and then he had given her his own Bible. It had been worn then, but it was positively tattered now. Millie had carried the book with her not only to church and to school, but up trees and under hedges—all of her favorite reading places. Now, it showed the wear and tear of this trip, too, but Millie didn't care. She was so absorbed in her reading that she hardly noticed when the passengers began coming on deck, calling hello and good morning back and forth between the ships. Marcia appeared with little Annis wrapped in a blanket and the other children in tow. The baby was fussing and restless.

"She's getting a new tooth," Marcia said.

"Let me hold her," Millie offered, setting her Bible aside and taking her little sister on her lap. "You can sleep a little longer, Mamma. You look so tired."

"Do take your daughter's advice," Edward said, strolling over to the family. "I'll watch over the rest of the children."

Marcia gratefully accepted. The baby had fussed and fretted most of the night, falling asleep just before dawn, then waking with the sun.

The children explored the ship once again with Edward, and then Zillah arranged a game of tag with the mast as base and barrels and coils of rope as safe islands, and so they played through the morning.

It was almost noon, and Annis was fussing again when Millie looked up to see Cyril and Don atop the railing, looking intently at the deck of the steamer. Edward caught Cyril by the suspenders and pulled him back aboard the ship.

"What are you fellows up to?" he asked.

"Billy said he jumped from the *Queen Charlotte* to the steamer and back again," Cyril said excitedly. "I think I could do that. Can I try?"

"No," Edward said, hauling him back aboard. "It's against the Captain's rules."

"I think you might let a fellow try," Cyril grumbled. "I know I could do it."

"No, you couldn't," said Don, peeping over the ship's side. "It's a big, big place."

"Could too," Cyril insisted.

"Could not."

"Let's go below deck for a bit," Millie suggested. "The baby is fussing and needs Mamma."

Edward gave the children into Millie's care, saying he had to check in with his father, and they followed her as she carried the baby on one arm with Fan holding the other hand. They had almost reached the cabins when Millie remembered her Bible.

"I'll get it for you," Cyril said. "Just tell me where you put it."

"Promise to come right back," Millie said.

Cyril nodded. "I promise."

Millie was trying to quiet Annis by rubbing her gums, when she heard the sound of something heavy plunging into the water.

"What was that?" Don asked. "Are they throwing something in?"

At the same instant a startled cry came from the deck of the *Milwaukee*. "Man overboard!"

A Dark Day

"Man overboard!" The fearful cry was taken up and repeated on all sides.

"Oh, no!" Millie cried. "Please, Lord, don't let it be Cyril!" She ran back the way they had come, the children following behind her. Her heart was in her throat when she saw Cyril standing by the rail with her Bible in his hand. Edward appeared and pulled him away again.

"Billy!" Cyril yelled. "Where'd you go?"

"You fellows sit down and don't move," Edward pushed Don and Cyril to the deck, then jumped to the lines and scrambled up the ropes to get a better view.

"Can you see anyone?" Millie called.

Edward shook his head. "They'll lower a boat," he said.

Almost instantly strong arms were pulling a small rowboat for the spot, already left far behind, where the splash of the falling body had been heard. The crews and passengers of the three vessels crowded the decks, following the boat's movements. The boat's crew pulled backward and forward, calling out to the drowning one that help was near.

"I see him!" cried Edward. "His head's above the water, I see his hat. And they see him too, and are pulling toward him with all their might! They're up with him! They have him now!" A wild cheer rose from hundreds of throats on the ships, but Edward dropped to the deck with a groan.

"What's wrong?" Millie hugged the baby to her.

"It was his hat—only his hat. They've given it up and are coming back without him."

"But they can't give up!"

"It's no use, Millie," Edward said. "He's gone down, and there is no finding him. He's… gone."

Every face wore a look of sadness for the few moments of silent waiting as the rowers returned.

Millie's Unsettled Season

They gained the deck of the *Queen Charlotte*, and one of them—a rough, hardy sailor—came forward with tears in his eyes.

"Mrs. Kress," he said, in a choked voice, "we did our best but we couldn't find him." He held out a blue hat.

"No! Not Billy! No! My little one!" she shrieked. The sailor caught her as she tried to leap the rail herself. Then she fell weeping to the deck.

Aunt Wealthy pushed her way through the crowd, knelt by the weeping woman, and put her arms around her. The woman buried her head in Wealthy's shoulder, and allowed herself to be led below.

Millie wiped her face with her hand. She hadn't realized that she was weeping. Captain Wells did not bother to hide his tears as he ordered the sailors back to work. The sad story spread in hushed tones to the passengers who had not been on deck, and grief for the mother and lost child spread over the ship.

"But how did it happen?" Marcia asked.

"He was jumping back and forth from one vessel to another," said the young sailor who had retrieved his hat. "He missed his footing, and fell in between the *Milwaukee* and the steamer. He must have been struck by the wheel, as he never came up."

"Oh, Stuart! It might have been one of ours," sobbed Marcia, pulling Cyril and Don into her arms. "That poor mother. I was so frightened when I heard the cry. I don't know how I got up the cabin steps! I thought…" Tears choked her voice.

Stuart wrapped all three of them in his arms and held them close.

A Dark Day

The sad event of the morning had a subduing influence on all the passengers. Parents kept their children below decks or by their sides. It was a very quiet day on board. Even Wannago gave up looking for Mr. Whiskers and lay with his tail between his legs and his nose on his paws.

When the sun dipped into the lake, the passengers said their goodnights. A breeze sprang up in the night while they were sleeping, and the vessels parted company.

CHAPTER

8

A Brief Adventure

They told them, "Go, explore the land."

JUDGES 18:2

A Brief Adventure

$\mathcal{B}$y daylight the breeze had stiffened into a wind, and the waves rose and fell in mighty hills and troughs. A slashing rain was falling, and the gray lake met the gray sky so that no one could tell where one ended and the other began. The ship tossed about on the waves with a motion that turned the landlubbers in both cabins and steerage pale and a little green.

Millie tried to get up for breakfast, but the floor wouldn't stay still. Each time she tried to take a step, it seemed to move again, and she staggered and stumbled until she gave up and crawled back into bed. Everything in the cabin that was not nailed to the floor or walls was moving, sliding back and forth with the rocking of the ship, until it made her nauseous to open her eyes.

"Millie?" Rupert knocked on the door. "Do you want any breakfast?"

"No," Millie groaned. "I don't ever want to see or smell food again!" She pulled the covers up over her head. She had read about seasickness in her books, but it hadn't seemed as horrible as this. She longed for fresh air, but the rain was falling heavily and great waves swept across the deck. Rupert stopped by to offer her some tea, but Millie couldn't swallow it. "Try to keep your mind off it," Rupert said. "Think of something else. Try thinking about—oh, I know—Edward. He must be up in the rigging now, fighting to keep the sails from being destroyed by the storm. Just imagine the ship rocking below him as the mast sways back and forth, back and forth, like a metronome…"

"Uhhhhhh," Millie groaned reaching for her bucket. "Go away, Ru."

Millie's Unsettled Season

By the next day the storm had passed, and they were able to open the hatch and let in some fresh air. All the Keiths had suffered from seasickness, but Millie was the last to recover. It was not until towards sunset of the third day that she could leave her berth. Stuart helped her up the cabin stairs to the deck, where Marcia and Aunt Wealthy had prepared a couch for her.

"Now, dear, the fresh air will help," Aunt Wealthy said, as Marcia tucked a blanket around her.

The little Keiths gathered near their sister.

"You look bad, Millie," Zillah said.

"Real bad," said Don. "Kinda blotchy and pale."

"Run and play, children," Marcia said. "And keep a close watch over them, Ru."

"I'll keep them safe, ma'am." Edward Wells had come up behind her. "I have a surprise for them."

"What?" Cyril asked.

"I found Mr. Whiskers this morning."

"He didn't get drowned?" Fan asked, clasping her hands.

"No. We thought he was lost in the storm, washed away by a wave," Edward explained to Millie. "But I found him this morning. Mr. Whiskers had kittens. I think I may need some help naming them all."

The children laughed with delight as he led them away. Marcia's eyes followed them for a moment before they came back to Millie.

"If I didn't know better, I would think that young man was an angel," Aunt Wealthy said, "sent just to watch over the Keiths! Here's some tea, Millie, dear. It will calm your digestion."

By the time Captain Wells came up to offer his congratulations on her recovery, Millie was almost herself again.

A Brief Adventure

"I am very much afraid my children impose upon the good nature of your son," Marcia said.

"Don't let that trouble you, ma'am. Edward is able to take care of himself. Besides, it's quite evident that he enjoys their society as much as they do his," said Captain Wells, taking a seat near Millie's couch. He remained chatting with her and the other ladies until it was time for them to retire to their cabins.

Fair weather and favorable winds made the remaining days of the voyage a pleasure till one bright June morning they entered the Straits of Mackinac and reached the island of the same name. A fort situated on the 150-foot cliff above them watched over the straits. Millie could see huge cannon barrels protruding from the walls.

"We will lay here a day or two," Captains Wells said, "to take on cargo. In the meantime, would anyone like to feel *terra firma* beneath their feet once again?"

Nearly everybody eagerly accepted. The boats put off from the ship, each with a full complement of passengers, and landed just under the white walls of the fortress. The passengers climbed up a long flight of stone steps. At the top, they entered the parade ground, which was paved with stones and clean as a well-swept floor. On one side of the parade ground were the officers' quarters and the barracks of the men. Three great cannons stood by the wall, giant pyramids of cannon balls by each. Millie followed her parents up another flight of stairs, and they walked along the top of the fort wall.

"I can't imagine anyone ever storming this fortress," Aunt Wealthy said, pointing out how the cannons watched over the harbor and the village of Mackinac.

After they had toured the fort, the Keiths visited the town. Stuart bought them moccasins made by Indians and maple sugar candy. "It's made with sap from maple trees, not sugar from sugar cane," Millie explained when Zillah looked worried.

"Thank you, Lord," Cyril said prayerfully and sincerely as he sucked the hard candy. "I'm glad you had the afore-thought to make sugar trees."

Wannago escaped from Wealthy long enough to charm the butcher into giving him a sausage by lying on his back, legs stiff in the air. Millie and Fan found him just as he was demonstrating his trick, hoping for another treat.

"Now where did he learn that?" Millie laughed.

"I teached him!" Fan said proudly, lying on the ground to demonstrate. The butcher offered her a sausage too, but Millie politely declined as she picked Fan up and dusted her off. They returned to the ship tired but full of content.

Millie was on the deck early the next morning, as usual, but this time she had not managed to slip away. Her sisters and Ru were with her, Cyril and Don being detained by a lecture from Aunt Wealthy regarding the wisdom of keeping buttons and other small objects out of their ears.

Cyril bellowed once, and Millie saw the other passen-gers, who had no idea what was happening, glance at one another. The sound wasn't repeated, so she assumed that the button had been successfully retrieved, and turned back to the sunrise.

"How very still it is! Hardly a breath of air stirring," Millie was saying to her father as Edward Wells drew near the little group.

"We are becalmed," said Stuart.

"And very possibly may be detained here for several days," said Edward, greeting them cheerfully. "And we will have a chance to explore the island. That is, if you will allow it?"

"Oh, Pappa, may we? May we?" chorused the children.

"We will see," he said. "Now watch or you'll miss the sight we left our beds so early for."

The matter was discussed at the breakfast table by Stuart, Marcia, and Wealthy, and it was decided that it would be good for the children to go ashore.

They spent the morning exploring the beaches, catching sand crabs and looking for birds' nests along the rocky cliffs. As they were eating the sandwiches and cheese that their mother had ordered for them, Ru pointed out a cave on a hill above them, and it was decided that they would try to find it by hiking inland, then doubling back. Edward and Ru carried Adah and Fan piggy back, while Millie, holding Zillah's hand, led the way. Cyril and Don were in back.

The trees soon closed around the path, hiding the fort from sight and hushing the sounds of the town and harbor. It was so quiet and still that Millie could almost imagine they were the first people to set foot on this part of God's creation. Even Cyril and Don were quiet, in awe of the hush around them.

They climbed a small hill so that they could see over the trees, and Edward got his bearings. Following his lead, they left the well-worn trail and took a smaller, less traveled way. It turned out that his sense of direction was good, because they soon came out on a ledge beneath a rocky outcrop, and the cave opened up before them.

"Someone's been here, perhaps even lived here," Ru said, pointing to the top of the cave. It was blackened by soot.

Millie's Unsettled Season

"No, not lived here," Edward said and pointed to three white crosses scratched into the rock. "I remember the story now. Three American trappers stopped on this island to trade with the Indians. They had been here before, but there was a different tribe this time, a tribe that didn't know them—a tribe that was allied with the French. When the trappers realized their mistake, they ran for their lives. It was too late to make it back to the boat, and they were cut off. They made the cave, and took their ammunition with them. The Indians were armed with bows and knives and couldn't get to them, but they wanted their scalps for the bounty the French army would pay. The trappers held them off for three days before the Indians built a fire at the mouth of the cave. The trapped men couldn't come out, or they would be shot full of arrows, so they stayed in the cave and suffocated in the thick smoke."

"That's horrible," Millie said.

Edward nodded. "There were French missionaries traveling with the French army. When the Indians told the story and traded their scalps for the bounty of knives and beads, the missionaries insisted that a detail of soldiers be sent to bury the bodies, and they scratched the crosses in the wall themselves."

"Why did the Indians do such a bad thing?" Zillah asked, tracing a cross with her finger.

"It was war," Ru said. "They were fighting to keep the settlers from taking over their land. I expect this island belonged to them, in those days."

Millie thought of Black Hawk and the women and children of his band who died trying to return to their land, and shuddered. Surely God had a plan for America. But men had brought evil with them, and found evil here as well.

Suddenly, there was a snapping of twigs, and a doe broke from the bushes fleeing something below. When she saw the children, she spun on her hooves and raced off in a new direction.

Adah shrieked and clutched Millie's skirt.

"Shhhh!" Millie said, though her own heart was in her throat. "Shhhh. It was only a deer."

"I want to go home," Zillah said.

"We can go back to the ship right now," Millie assured her.

"No!" the little girl sobbed. "I don't want the ship. I want my own house in Lansdale. I want my home!"

"I am so sorry," Edward said, looking at Millie over Zillah's head. "I should never have told that story."

"I expect we'll hear worse where we're going," Ru said.

"Ru!" Millie gave him a stern look, and he shrugged and picked up Fan.

"Let's go back," he said, "unless somebody else wants to explore the cave."

Cyril and Don were all for exploring the cave, but they followed the little band back to the *Queen Charlotte*.

Adah reached the ship looking heated, weary, and troubled. "Oh, Mamma," she cried, with tears in her eyes. "We saw a cave where some trappers were hiding from the Indians and got smoked to death. Oh, I'm so afraid of the savages. Do persuade Pappa to take us all back to Ohio again!"

The mother soothed and comforted the frightened child with caresses and assurances of the Lord's help and care, banishing her fears so that she was willing to proceed upon her journey.

However, with the calm continuing, nearly a week passed and many excursions had been made to the island before they could quit its harbor.

Millie's Unsettled Season

At length one day directly after dinner, a favorable wind having sprung up, the good ship weighed anchor and pursued her westward course out of the straits into Lake Michigan. All night and the next day, she flew before the wind. Then, finally, she rode safely at anchor in the harbor of Chicago. This was the port of the *Queen Charlotte,* where her passengers must be landed and her cargo discharged.

"Now, if you ever decide to become a sailor, Millie," Edward joked, as he handed her from the gangway to the dock, "remember the *Queen Charlotte* has first claim on you."

"I don't think there is a fear of that," Millie said, remembering the nights and days of seasickness during the storm. "I think God must have some other plan for me!"

"I might be seeing you again, though," Ru said, clasping Edward's hand.

"If you do, I'll put you to work," Edward assured him. "No more of this passenger business. I'll have you in the rigging, and on the lines. We'll teach you to be a real sailor!"

He gave each of the little ones a piece of maple sugar in the shape of a leaf that he had bought on Mackinac Island. Cyril and Don received a book on tying sailors' knots and a length of rope to practice on. Finally, he shook hands with the boys and Stuart, bowed to the ladies, and went back aboard to help his father. Millie felt as though she'd said good-bye to a dear brother.

"Isn't it strange how quickly you can become close to someone, Mamma?" she asked.

"Not when they have merry, kind hearts," Marcia said.

"I've often wished I could take them all with me," Aunt Wealthy said, "all of my dear friends. But that would make travel a bit difficult, I suppose."

A Brief Adventure

St. Joseph, on the opposite side of the lake, was the next port to which the Keiths were bound. A much smaller vessel carried them across. They had a rough passage, wind and rain compelling them to keep closely housed in a little confined cabin, and were glad to reach the town of St. Joseph. It was a dreary place without grass or trees. The hotel was a large two-story building. The hot summer sun streamed in through windows, dimmed only slightly by a thick layer of dirt on the panes of glass. The boys fought almost the entire three days that the family was detained waiting for their household goods to catch up.

"Can't we leave sooner?" Cyril asked, after being scolded once again for tweaking Don's nose. "We could take the train or the stage."

"We are past the furthest tracks now," Stuart explained. "There is not even a stage road from this point on, no steamers on the river. The only way to get to Pleasant Plains is by keelboat."

Millie used her time wisely, writing to A, B, and C of her adventures on the *Queen Charlotte* and Mackinac Island. Washing was hard on board ship, so Millie and Marcia now spent some hours with a borrowed laundry tub. When the clothes were dry, Millie pulled them from the line and Aunt Wealthy attacked them with a flat iron heated on the wood stove. Millie folded them, making sure each member of the family had at least one clean outfit for their arrival at their new home. It was hard to believe that after all of these days, their journey was almost done.

Finally, the morning arrived when they started on the St. Joseph River, for the last leg of the journey to Pleasant

Plains. The sun shone brightly on the rippling, dancing waters of the lake and river, as they went on board the keelboat *Mary Ann*.

The boatsmen pulled at their oars and the *Mary Ann* moved slowly upriver against the current, more slowly even than the canal packet. They slid past green miles of unbroken forest. Sometimes one or another would point out a finger of smoke in the distance, rising from the forested hills, but whether it was from an Indian village or a settler's home there was no telling. Sometimes they passed a solitary clearing with a lonely log cabin, and sometimes a little village.

Ragged children ran to watch the boat in either case, mouths open in surprise at seeing strange children on the river. The Keiths waved and smiled, and some of the children waved back, calling greetings across the water.

The river flowed swiftly along, clear and sparkling, between banks now low, now high, and green to the water's edge. A few more buildings began to appear, and then a wagon track beside the river. The sun was nearing the western horizon as, at last, the boat was run in close to shore.

"Here we are, folks," one of the boatsmen said. "This here's the town of Pleasant Plains."

CHAPTER

9

Disappointments

*Their hearts sank and they turned to
each other trembling and said,
"What is this that God
has done to us?"*

GENESIS 42:28

Disappointments

"Oh, let's not stop here, Mamma," Adah said. "I don't like this ugly place. Tell them to keep going to the pretty part."

Millie took her sister's hand. "Now, Adah, there is no other place for the boat to land. I expect we shall have to walk from here." She wanted to say "walk to the pretty part," but something heavy in her heart told her that if this was the best face Pleasant Plains could show to a new arrival, the pretty part might be harder to find than she hoped. A feeling of dread settled over her, but Millie shook it off. Surely the rest of town would be an improvement over the riverfront.

As the keel of the *Mary Ann* grated on the gravelly shore, a tall figure in rough farmer attire came springing down the bank, calling out, "Hello, Stuart! Come at last with wife and children, and all, eh? I'm glad to see ya! Never was more delighted in my life."

"Hello, George," Stuart exclaimed, shaking his hand. "May I present my wife, Marcia Keith? George Ward." Stuart introduced each one of them as he handed them from the boat.

"I declare, I wish the missus and I lived in town," George said, "but we're three miles out on the prairie. I brought my team along, though, and if you'd like to pile into the wagon, all of you, I'll take you home with me."

"There are quite too many of us to crowd into your home, I'm sure, Mr. Ward," Marcia said, smiling. "We would be grateful if you would take us to the best hotel."

"That would be the Union," George said. "It's not just the best hotel, it's the only hotel. Mrs. Prior runs a clean establishment. I thought you might prefer staying in town, so she's expecting you. Here, let me carry you, bub," he said, picking Don up. "The soil's real sandy here and makes heavy walking."

The sand was difficult to walk in, just as the beaches of Mackinac Island had been, only without the pleasant dampness by the water's edge. Millie struggled along until she reached the wagon. The boys scrambled into the wagon's bed, while Stuart and Mr. Ward handed up first Marcia and Wealthy, and then the girls. They seated themselves on bales of hay. Millie took off both of her shoes and poured a handful of sand out of each.

Mr. Ward took the driver's seat, yelled to his mules, and they were off. Millie was glad for her bonnet, as there were no trees shading the wide street, only huge stumps where majestic trees had once stood. The wood from the trees had evidently been milled and turned into the buildings they were passing—rough frame structures, many without paint, the wood already weathered to a dull gray. Wannago was the only one who seemed excited by his new home, running beside the wagon, and barking happily up at Wealthy.

"That's the tanner's," Mr. Ward said proudly as they passed yet another shabby, gray building. "And this here's the bakery. You can get fresh bread most days." The shop windows were bare and unadorned, and even the signs were rough and plain. Millie was dismayed to see that the sand did not end by the river's side, but continued up into the town, piling up here and there against fences and walls. The wagon pulled up in front of a two-story building painted bright white. "Here we are," Mr. Ward said. "The Union!"

Disappointments

Mrs. Prior, a pleasant-faced, middle-aged woman, met them at the door with a welcome nearly as hearty as that of Mr. Ward.

"I'm glad to see you," she said, bustling about to wait upon them. "We've plenty o' room here in town for new folks, and especially ladies o' refinement!"

She showed them into her parlor, the only one the house afforded. The furniture was plain—a rag carpet, green paper blinds, a table with a red and black cover, Windsor chairs, two of them rocking chairs with chintz-covered cushions and the rest straight-backed and hard. On the high wooden mantel shelf were an old-fashioned looking glass, a few shells, and two brass candlesticks as bright as scouring could make them. Not one speck of dust could be seen. The window panes glistened, and the rough boards of the floor were neatly swept.

"What a wonderful place," Marcia sighed.

"Ha! I'm afraid it must seem a poor place to you, ladies," the landlady said, pushing forward a rocking chair for each. "And you're dreadful tired, ain't you, with your long journey. Do sit down and rest yourselves."

"You are very kind, and it looks like heaven after that keelboat!" Marcia answered, as she accepted the offered seat and began untying Annis's bonnet strings.

"I didn't expect to find accommodations half so good in these western wilds," Aunt Wealthy admitted, glancing round the room. "I thought you had no floors to your carpets, nor glass to your panes!"

"Well, some houses here in town still have the hard-packed dirt. And carpenters here don't make the best of work—I think sometimes I could a'most plane a board better myself. But to get the carpets is the rub. We mostly make 'em ourselves from rags, but they don't last hardly at all. No use puttin' anything fine on the floor here. Soil's sandy, you see, and it wears the carpets right out."

"They say this country's hard on women and mules," put in Mr. Ward, "and I'm afraid it's true."

Millie saw Rupert's brow furrow at the mention of his mother and a mule in the same sentence, but Mrs. Prior cut in before Ru could speak.

"Now don't be frightening them first thing, Mr. Ward," laughed the landlady. "We don't want them gettin' right back on the boat. Take off your things and the children's, ladies, and make yourselves to home. Here, just let me lay 'em in here." She opened an inner door, revealing a bed covered with a patchwork quilt.

"You can have this room if you like, Mrs. Keith; I s'pose you'd prefer a downstairs one with the baby and t'other little ones? There is a trundle bed underneath that'll do for them. And the rest of you can take the two rooms right over these. They're all ready and you can go right up to 'em whenever you like. Is there anything more I can do for you now?"

"No, thank you," Marcia said. "And these rooms will be fine."

"Then I'll just excuse myself," she said, "for I must go and see to the supper." She passed out through another door, leaving it ajar.

"That's the dining room, 'cause I see two big tables set," whispered Cyril peeping in, "and there's not a bit of carpet on the floor."

"Well, darling," Stuart said, putting his arms around his wife, "the Lord has brought us all safely here. I'll go and see to the landing of our goods, and hope they have fared as well. Will you come along, George?"

Disappointments

Marcia kissed her husband and smiled, but Millie thought her mother's shoulders slumped just a little when he left the room.

"May I take the children to see their rooms?" Millie asked.

"Yes, and help them tidy up for the supper table while you're at it," Marcia said.

Millie found bare floors everywhere, of boards none too well-planed either, making walking without shoes a hazard for toes. The beds were covered with homemade quilts, and everything was scrupulously clean. She poured water from a pitcher into a porcelain basin and helped the children wash their faces and hands.

"Stop it, Millie," Don said, when she checked behind his ears. "It's just sand, see!" He rubbed his hands vigorously through his hair, and a shower of sand fell to the floor.

"How did you get sand in your hair? You haven't been rolling on the ground."

"Wind, I guess," he shrugged. "But sand ain't dirt, it don't stick to you. I expect I'll never have to take a bath again, living here."

"I expect you will," Millie said.

"Yes," said Fan. "We can take dust baths like sparrows!"

"Not before supper, you're not," Millie said, catching Cyril and slicking down his cowlick with a little water. Millie inspected the children, then ushered them downstairs.

The gentlemen returned and the guests were summoned to the table by the ringing of a bell on top of the house.

"Mamma, these cups sound funny," Zillah said, tapping the side of a metal cup with a blue and white glaze, "and the plates do too!"

"Delftware might not be elegant, like china, miss," said Mrs. Prior, "but it suits us here. China cups and plates are hard to replace when they break. Now this," she tapped the side of a pitcher with her two-pronged fork, causing it to ring like a cowbell, "you can pack with you wherever you need to go. You could clobber a bobcat with one of these, and it wouldn't more than dent it."

"Why would one want to dent a bobcat?" Aunt Wealthy asked. Every eye at the table turned on Wealthy. Millie wished she had a napkin to hide her smile, and Ru couldn't hold in his laugh, but covered it by pretending to sneeze.

"What?" Aunt Wealthy looked around at them all. "Oh! I see! You meant dent the pitcher!"

Stuart bowed his head, and the children followed suit. "Dear Lord," he prayed, "we thank You for bringing us safely to our journey's end, and ask that You bless this town, and let us be a blessing to it."

"Amen," Mrs. Prior agreed heartily, and the meal began. After supper, Marcia produced her own bag of maple sugar to sweeten the tea. As she explained about the sugar boycott, Mrs. Prior shook her head.

"I don't believe in slave-holding myself," she said. "But I don't believe I could go as far as you folk. Good for you, though there are some folk in this town who won't hold your opine."

"What about the goods, Stuart?" asked Marcia on their return to the parlor.

"I have had them carted directly to the house; that is, I believe the men are at it now."

"The house?" Marcia said, surprised. "We have a house?"

"It was a 'Hobson's choice', my dear, or you would have seen it first."

"When can we see it?"

"Now if you like. It won't be dark yet for an hour. If you ladies will put on your bonnets, I'll take you round."

"Adah and me, too, Pappa?" cried Zillah eagerly.

"I'm goin'," said Cyril. "Me and Fan and Don."

"You couldn't think of going without your eldest son," said Rupert, looking about for his hat.

Marcia turned an inquiring eye upon her husband.

"Is it far?"

"No, it's on the very edge of town, but we are almost on the edge here. Even Fan can easily walk it. Let them come. You, too, Millie," he said, taking Annis from her arms. "I'll carry the baby."

"We'll make quite a procession," Millie said. "Won't the people stare?"

"Who could help but stare at such an attractive family?" Stuart laughed.

"This way!" cried Rupert, stepping back from the doorway with a commanding wave of the hand. "Procession will please move forward. Mr. Keith and wife taking the lead, Miss Stanhope and Miss Keith next in order, Zillah and Adah following close upon their heels, the three inseparables after them, while Marshal Rupert brings up the rear to see that all are in line."

Everybody laughed and promptly fell into line as directed. They passed a few substantial brick homes, but most of the houses were rough-hewn wood or log cabins. Few had yards of any kind, and one had a pig sitting on the porch, enjoying the shade. People did stare from open doors and windows. Millie tried not to stare back, but Cyril and Don, splendid in their coonskin caps, moccasins, and gaping grins, waved and bowed at the onlookers until Stuart put a stop to it. It was not difficult at all to walk from one end of the town to the other. Soon the houses and buildings were farther apart, and they started up a hill.

Millie's Unsettled Season

"Do you see that yellow frame yonder, my dear?" Stuart asked, pointing to a large building on the side of the hill.

"Oh, my," Marcia said.

"I don't see it," Wealthy squinted. "Is it behind that barn?"

"That's not a barn, it's a house," said Stuart. "Our house."

"No, I mean the barn with the gable-end to the street and two doors in it, one above and one below," Wealthy said. "That's the one I'm looking at."

"I'm looking at the same," said Stuart.

"It looks like a warehouse, Pappa," Ru said in dismay.

"Well, it was a warehouse until recently...but it is the only building large enough to accommodate a family of our size." He looked at the building. "It has several rooms inside, and I'm sure we can make something of it."

"A warehouse." Marcia stood for a moment. Millie stood close, and put her arm around her mother's waist. She could feel the tension in Mamma's muscles, but not a sign of it showed on her face.

"It is a poor place to take you to, my dear." Stuart said, "but it was a 'Hobson's choice,' as I said. There really is no other."

Marcia looked at the building for just one moment more, then stood on tiptoe to kiss her husband's cheek.

"Can't you just imagine Joseph saying that to Mary?" She made her voice deep. "'It's a "Hobson's choice," my dear. This was the only stable available in Bethlehem.' God had a plan for them, Stuart. And he has a plan for us, too."

"We'll soon have our things, everything you need to make it a home," Stuart said, relief obvious in his voice.

"I have everything I need to make it home right here with me," Marcia said, taking his arm. He put his hand over hers and they started on together.

Disappointments

Millie hung back. The feeling of dread she had experienced upon arriving in Pleasant Plains was not only sinking in, it was taking root in her soul. Stables were perfectly all right for Bible stories. It was nice to think about the baby and the sweet-smelling hay at Christmas time. But this wasn't a Bible story. It was real life. She tried to hold her feelings inside, but they boiled up.

"It's horrid!" The words were out of Millie's mouth before she could stop them. "How can Pappa expect our Mamma to live there? It isn't a house at all. It fronts on the street and the door opens right out onto a sand bank."

"There's a big yard at the side and behind," said Zillah.

"Something green in it, too," added Adah.

"Those are weeds!" The blur of tears in Millie's eyes made the weedy yard swim, looking almost like a garden. If she cried hard enough, this horrible thing might look a little like the home they had left with its large garden and endless flower beds. The June roses and the woodbine must be out by now—the air sweet with their delicious perfume—but they and those who had planted and tended them were far away from this desolate spot. How could she write to her friends that she was living in a warehouse?

"Not a tree, a shrub, a flower, or a blade of grass!" Zillah said.

"Never mind, we'll have lots of flowers next year," said Rupert.

The front door was wide open, as the last load of their household goods had just been brought up from the river, so the Keiths walked right in. The men were carrying in the heavy boxes and setting them down upon the floor of the large room.

"Where's the entry hall?" asked Cyril.

Millie's Unsettled Season

"There isn't any," Zillah said. "No cupboards or closets at all. Just bare walls and windows."

"Don't forget the floor and ceilings," Rupert said. "They are important, too."

"And a door on the other side," said Ada, running across the room and opening it.

"Not a mantelpiece to set anything on, nor any chimney at all! How on earth are we going to keep warm in the wintertime?" Millie asked despairingly.

"With a stove, miss. Pipes run up through the floor into the room above," said one of the men, wiping the perspiration from his forehead with the sleeve of his shirt.

Stuart stopped to settle with the men for their work, and the family walked on into the next room. It was as bare as and darker than the first, though somewhat larger. It had only one window, and an outside door, opening directly upon the side street. Behind the two rooms was a small kitchen with a chimney and fireplace, and a small closet under a flight of steep and crooked stairs that led from the kitchen to the story above.

"Look at this!" Don said, dragging something huge and hairy out of the closet. Wannago threw himself on it with a savage growl.

Adah screamed, but Stuart laughed.

"It's a buffalo robe," he said. "I wonder how it got here? It could have been left by a mountain man, or perhaps it once belonged to an Indian."

"Can we keep it?" Cyril asked.

"I don't see why you shouldn't," Stuart said. "The owner seems to have left it for you." After examining the robe and running their fingers through the coarse brown hair, the children climbed the crooked stairs, followed by Aunt Wealthy and Marcia.

Disappointments

The upper floor consisted of two rooms, the first extending over the kitchen and sitting room. There was a door on one side; Wealthy opened it and peered out at the thin air beyond.

"Oh, my, that's quite a first step!" she said, looking at the sheer plunge to the street below. "What an odd place for a door. Do you think they ever planned to put stairs outside? But the sky is so beautiful, it's almost like a doorway to heaven!"

"You might get to heaven more quickly than you would like if you stepped out!" exclaimed Marcia.

On the other side of the room was another door, which opened into a front room of exactly the same size. There was no way to reach it without passing through the first room.

"Not much privacy," Ru said.

"Millie's right," Zillah said. "This isn't a house! How'll we ever live in it? I want my own room!"

Marcia stood in the first upper room, turning from side to side, a look of bewilderment on her face.

Aunt Wealthy, who had pulled the door to heaven shut, saw it and came to the rescue. "Never mind, dear; it will look very different when we have unpacked and arranged your furniture. Do you know that in China they make walls out of paper? With the help of curtains, several rooms can be made out of this, and we'll do nicely."

"No doubt," Marcia answered. "This front room shall be yours."

"No, no! You and Stuart must take this one."

"I'm quite set on having my own way," Marcia said. "It is the best room, and you must take it. Besides, I should be afraid to have the little ones in there with that outside door opening onto nothing."

"We'll nail it shut," Wealthy said, "just in case."

"Well, wife, what do you think?" asked Stuart, coming up the stairs.

"I think it will keep the rain off and the children in," Marcia said. "And it's a great deal nicer than a tent. What more could we ask?"

"I think we could ask for a lot more!" Millie said. "It's a great big dirty barn with plaster all over the floor and spattered on the windows too."

"I hope it can be cleaned," her father said, laughing at her rueful face. "Mrs. Prior can probably tell us where to find a woman to help with it."

Stuart and Marcia seemed determined to discuss plans for the arrangement of the inside of the dwelling, so Millie went back downstairs and stepped outside. The scene had not improved. In one direction she saw only a wall of rough weatherboarding with one window in the second story. In the other direction, a heap of sand and a wilderness of weeds. Behind the house was a small stand of willows and a cow shed. Beyond that, a grassy hillside.

"Could You show me the reason for bringing us here, Lord," Millie said out loud, "because I ... I'm dumb with despair!"

"Can dumb folks talk?" Cyril asked, coming up behind her. The family was pouring out the door, like ants from a nest.

"We'll cover it with vines," said Aunt Wealthy, seeing Millie's look.

"And I'll clear the yard and sod it," added Rupert, seizing a great mullein stalk and pulling it up by the roots as he spoke. "Won't be nearly as hard as the clearing the early pioneers of Ohio had to do, our grandfathers among them."

Disappointments

"We will be pioneers ourselves," responded Stuart, who had followed them outside. "Almost pioneers! Let's walk down the hill and around the other side." They followed the road past the yellow house and down the hill. Their nearest neighbor on the hillside lived in a shabby, one-and-a-half-story frame house with a blacksmith shop attached. The sign over the door read "G. Lightcap", but there was no smoke from the stovepipe nor anyone in the yard. The road curved sharply back down the hill to the center of town, and the Keiths made their way back to the Union.

Mrs. Prior joined her guests in the parlor that evening. "Well, how did you like the house?" she asked.

"I am sure we will be able to make ourselves comfortable there," Marcia said.

Mrs. Prior nodded approvingly. "You can get possession right away, I suppose."

"Yes, but there is some cleaning to be done first, and we'll need help."

Mrs. Prior recommended a woman for that without waiting to be asked, and offered to "send round" at once and see if she could be engaged for the next day. The offer was accepted with thanks and the messenger brought back word that Mrs. Rood would be at the house by six o'clock in the morning.

"But," suggested Aunt Wealthy in dismay, "she'll need hot water, soap, cloths, and scrubbing brushes."

"I'll lend a big iron kettle to heat the water," said the landlady. "A fire can be made in that kitchen fireplace, you know, or outdoors with the brushwood."

"And brushes and soap can be had at the store, I presume," suggested Stuart.

"Yes, and if they ain't open in time, I'll lend mine for her to start on."

"Thank you very much," said Marcia. "But, Stuart, we may as well unpack our own. I can tell you just which box to open."

"You amaze me, Marcia," he said. "Can we be up in time to be on hand at half past five?"

"We can try. Mrs. Prior, where is your market? I have not seen it yet."

"We haven't got *that* civilized yet, ma'am," replied the landlady, laughing and shaking her head.

"No market? How do you manage?"

"There's a butcher shop where we can buy fresh meat once or twice a week—beef, veal, mutton, lamb, just whatever they happen to kill—and we put up our own salt pork, hams, dried beef, and so forth, and keep codfish and mackerel on hand. Most folks have their own chickens, and the country people bring 'em in, too, and butter and eggs and vegetables, though a good many town folks have gardens of their own, and keep a cow for milk and butter."

"Then I think we must have a little brown cow, with big brown eyes," Stuart said, "for my children must have milk."

"We get a cow!" Fan said, clapping her hands in delight.

"But who will milk it for us, Pappa?" Zillah asked.

"We're on the frontier now," Ru said sagely. "I expect folks here have to milk their own cows."

"Oh, and afore I forget," said Mrs. Prior as she produced a packet of mail, "Mr. Ward dropped these off for you. Had 'em under the wagon seat the whole time." Stuart took the mail and everyone waited as he sorted it—two letters for Wealthy from the Dinsmores, her southern relatives; several for Marcia from friends and neighbors in Lansdale; and one envelope for Millie, fat with pages from A, B, and C.

Disappointments

Aunt Wealthy read the family news from the Dinsmores aloud. Everyone at the Roselands Plantation was well, but Horace Dinsmore Jr. was still away at college and had not been heard from in some time.

Millie carried her own letters up to her room and lit the lamp. She crawled into bed and pulled the covers up around her before she opened the envelope.

Dear Millie, Camilla wrote. *How I envy you the marvelous adventures you write about.* Suddenly, the handwriting changed, and Bea's flowery script continued, *Do tell all about Dr. Fox! Is he terribly handsome?? Are Aunt Wealthy and Dr. Fox corresponding?* An ink blot, and then in Camilla's precise blocky letters again, *How I envy you the solitude you must occasionally experience. Bea is driving me absolutely insane. If I hear one more word about the summer dance...* Bea seemed to have wrested the quill from Camilla's fingers once again. *I am getting to stay up late! I convinced Aunt Alicia — my mother's great aunt — to petition Mother, who petitioned Father, who said he would Think About It! I spent hours, simply hours in prayer. And Father said yes! He said yes!* The rest of the page was filled with Bea's plans for the party. She was plotting to dance with Frank Osborne and at least three other boys. She told every detail of her gown, slippers, and hair combs. Camilla had given up and used her own page to continue, filling Millie in on the goings-on at school. Frank had taken first place in the exams and was planning to avoid Bea at the dance.

Annabeth, too quiet to fight with the other two, had added her own special page with a pressed flower and illustrations of her own design along the borders.

The room seemed to fill with their voices as Millie read. She pressed the flower to her face and could just smell the faintest hint of Lansdale, of gardens and summer breezes. "This isn't Pleasant Plains, it's unPleasant Plains," she cried. The tears flowed freely, and Millie buried her head in her pillow and sobbed. "Why, Lord? Why have You brought us to this terrible place? I'm sure I can't bear it. I can't bear it!"

When the tears subsided, Millie picked up her Bible and opened it, intending to read from the book of Psalms, where she often found comfort. The book fell open to the forty-fifth chapter of Isaiah, and as she glanced down, her attention was distinctly drawn to some words on the page. "I will give you the treasures of darkness, riches stored in secret places, so that you may know that I am the Lord, the God of Israel, who summons you by name," read verse 3.

Millie read the words again slowly. They seemed alive somehow, like they were speaking right to her. Millie's heartbeat quickened. *Could this be what Mamma was talking about when she said that sometimes a Scripture just jumps out at her?* Sweet comfort spread through her. *Treasures of darkness? Riches stored in secret places? Why do I suddenly feel such an odd sense of peace?*

Millie studied the page in silence.

Lord, this passage is about someone named Cyrus, but are You trying to tell ME something? Millie waited for a reply, but heard none. Still, she wondered, could God have something special for them in this gloomy place? Could there be treasure she couldn't yet see?

I'm sorry I was so disappointed in our new house, God. I'm sorry I let my words spill out and make the children disappointed, too. Show me what Your plans are, Lord. Help me be strong. Help me trust You.

CHAPTER

Visitors

*Mary was greatly troubled at
his words and wondered
what kind of greeting
this might be.*

LUKE 1:29

Visitors

The next morning, Marcia left the children with Millie and Aunt Wealthy, and met the cleaning woman at what they had begun calling the Big Yellow House. Millie was determined to follow her Mamma's lead and keep a cheerful heart, no matter what happened. As she put A, B, and C's letter in the pocket of her apron, she promised herself that she would not cry, not shed one tear the whole day, no matter what. Had Rebekah cried when she left her family to travel to a distant land and marry Isaac? No. Had Joshua cried when God sent him to take the Promised Land? No. Would Millie Keith shed any more tears for her friends and home? Never! Millie washed her face carefully, and pressed a cool cloth to her still-swollen eyes.

Mrs. Prior served a good breakfast, and after making sure the children were all dressed and the baby clean and changed, the group set out for the house. Women and children came to the windows of their houses to stare, just as they had the night before.

"I hate this," Millie said. "I feel like a carnival parade!"

"Now, dear," Aunt Wealthy said. "They don't have a newspaper or a telegraph. Newcomers in town must be a source of entertainment."

Millie found out how entertaining after she dropped the children at the Big Yellow House and went to the butcher shop for ham and the baker's for bread. The butcher shop door was ajar so it opened quietly, and she found herself standing behind two ladies of the town, and with them was a girl in a red gingham dress, with dark braids and a plain red bonnet. It was the first girl of her own age Millie had seen, and she wanted desperately to say hello, but suddenly felt very shy. She was glad they hadn't seen her, as it gave her a moment to compose herself.

"You won't believe it," the tall thin woman was saying. "My husband helped cart the goods in, so he should know. He said they've got a real store carpet for that front room, and a sofy and chairs covered with horsehair cloth, and white curtains for the windows and pictures for hanging up onto the walls."

A tingle spread over Millie as she realized they were talking about the Keiths.

"In a warehouse?" the other woman snorted. "That's puttin' on airs. At least the Lightcaps is honest about their poverty. No airs for them!"

"And the little girls wears white pantalets—calico ones such as our youngsters wear isn't good enough for them."

"Ahem," the butcher said, standing up behind the counter and motioning towards Millie with his chin.

The thin lady glanced over her shoulder, then flushed red beneath her fan. "I'll be goin' then," she said, brushing past Millie without saying hello. The short woman followed her out, but threw a brief, apologetic smile in Millie's direction as she went, and the girl gave Millie an open, curious stare.

"Now don't mind Mrs. Gilligut and Mrs. Roe," the butcher said. "This town is friendly like, but the ladies don't have much to talk about. You folks have caused quite a stir. I'm sure we are all pleased to have you."

Millie thanked him, gave him Mamma's list, and asked that the meat be delivered, then hurried home. She found her mother with a broom, preparing to lay down a carpet.

"Will you watch the children, Millie?" she asked. "They are playing behind the house. Ru is with them, but I would feel better if you watched over them all."

Just behind the house was a grove of saplings. Millie found Rupert bending down the smaller trees and tying their tops together to make a green, leafy house. The buffalo robe was spread inside it, and baby Annis sat happily in the middle.

"What's wrong, Millie?" Ru said, when he saw her face. "You look like a storm cloud."

"I am not wearing calico pantalets, that's what," Millie said, flopping down by the baby. "And I am never going to make friends in this town."

"Huh?"

"Oh, never mind. Where are the children?"

"Gathering flowers for the house," he said. "Cyril's watching over Fan."

Millie could hear the girls in the distance, prattling to each other, and now and then uttering a joyous shout as they came upon some new floral treasure. In a little while they came running back with full hands.

"See, see!" they said. "So many and such pretty ones — blue and white and purple and yellow."

"Here, Millie," Zillah said. "You take these and we'll pick some more for Mamma and Aunt Wealthy. We'll make a big bunch for each of them."

"Mamma hasn't any vases unpacked yet," Millie said. "Let's make garlands for your hair."

"I don't want no dumb flowers on my head," Don said, coming into the leafy house. "Why do girls do that?"

"To make them smell better," Cyril said.

The girls began sorting the flowers with eager interest, little Annis pulling at them too, cooing and chattering.

Suddenly Zillah gave a start and laid a trembling hand on Millie's arm. There was a look of terror in her large blue eyes. Millie turned quickly to see what had caused it.

"Ru," she said, trying to stay calm. "I think we have company." A tall Indian with rifle in hand stood at the edge of their clearing. He had a tomahawk and a large knife in his belt. He wore moccasins and leggings, and he had a blanket about his shoulders; feathers on his head, too, but no paint on his face, and he stared at them curiously. Behind him was a young woman in deerskin dress with a great bark basket slung on her back.

The Indian man said something in a language Millie didn't understand. She shook her head, and he took a step closer.

Ru's face was very white. "If he touches that tomahawk, I'll charge him," he said, picking up a branch, "while you pick up the baby and run home."

The Indian spoke again, in a different language this time, pointing.

"That's not Indian talk," Millie said. "He's speaking French!"

"He must be a Potawatami," Ru said. "They were allies of the French."

"And the French soldiers taught them to scalp people," Zillah cried, clapping both hands on top of her head. The man turned his black eyes on her for a moment, then repeated, "Ne manger pas bon."

"Please speak slowly," Millie said in her best French. "I don't understand."

The man squatted on his heels by the leafy door, and pointed to Annis.

"Ne manger pas bon," he said again.

Millie glanced at Annis. Petals, leaves and stem of a flower were hanging out of her mouth.

"Oh! 'Don't eat good!' Not good to eat!" Millie said, grabbing up the baby and prying the vegetation out of her mouth. "Thank you! Vous remercier!"

The man's hand flashed down, and he grabbed at a fat black beetle.

"Manger bon," he said, holding it out to Zillah. She cowered back against Adah, who clung to her.

"Cat's sake," Cyril said. "He's just being friendly. Here, I'll eat it." He reached for the beetle.

"Don't you dare, Cyril Keith!" Millie cried, but Cyril snatched the beetle from the man's hand and started to pop it in his mouth.

Just before Cyril got the wiggling bug to his lips, the Indian slapped it away.

"Hey!" Cyril said. "That wasn't friendly!"

"Pas bon, pas bon!" The warrior laughed as the beetle escaped into the grass.

"Not good, not good!" Millie translated.

"It was a joke," Ru said in amazement. "Do savages make jokes?"

"I didn't think so," Millie said thoughtfully. "I don't think savages act this way at all." The Indian motioned for his wife, speaking to her in their own language. She brought her basket close, and poured a pile of berries onto the robe.

"Blackberries!" Zillah squealed, forgetting to hold her scalp. "Can we eat them, Millie?"

"Bon manger." He winked. "Bon."

"Yes," Millie said, "I'm sure Mamma wouldn't mind." She looked at the young woman and said, "Vous remercier."

The woman smiled, restored her basket to its place, and the two Indians walked leisurely away.

"Wait!" Millie called after them. "Please come back some time. Come to our house and meet our parents! I know they would like to meet you."

The little girls gazed at each other in astonishment.

"Oh, weren't you frightened?" Zillah said with a mouthful of berries. "I thought he was going to kill us!"

"Why, they were practically friends and relations!" Cyril said, wiping berry juice from his chin. "I wonder if they live around here."

"I hope not," returned Adah with a wise shake of her head. "I'd rather not see 'em even with their berries."

The feast had hardly ended when they saw a gentleman walking along the road beyond the grove. He wore a long black coat and a tall black hat, and his clean but shabby pants were a bit too wide and a bit too short for his tall, lanky frame. He stopped suddenly on seeing them, then turned and came toward them with a hurried stride, his loose clothing flapping in the breeze. When he removed his hat and smiled, his eyebrows went up, giving him the appearance of a pleasantly surprised scarecrow.

"Good morning," he said, and his large Adam's apple bobbed up and down. "You are the Keith children, I believe?"

"Yes, sir," answered Zillah.

"I'm glad to see you here safe at last," he said, shaking hands with them, "and I should like to make the acquaintance of your parents. Are they at home, in the house yonder?"

"Mother is, sir, but I saw Father go away a little while ago."

"Do you think your mother could see me for a moment? My name is Lord."

Don's eyes opened very wide, and he gazed up into the gentleman's face with an expression of mingled curiosity and astonishment.

"But you know Mamma and Pappa already," he said. "Don't you?"

"I am afraid I have been remiss in my visitations," the gentleman stuttered. "But I would like to speak to them now."

Don stared at him slack-jawed.

"Donald, don't be rude," Millie whispered. "Let me show you the way, sir. They're just cleaning the house." She picked up Annis. "If you will follow me, I will announce you."

"Oh, I'll just chat with the children for a bit, while you announce me," Reverend Lord said. Don trotted along beside Millie all the way to the house. Marcia and Aunt Wealthy were busy overseeing the opening of boxes and the unpacking of the household gear.

"Mamma," Don cried breathlessly, before Millie could utter a word, "the Lord's out yonder and he wants to see you! Can he come in? Shall I bring him?"

"Who?" Marcia asked with a bewildered look.

"The Lord! What does the child mean?" asked Aunt Wealthy.

"It's a gentleman, Mamma," Millie said. Suddenly, Marcia smiled.

"Yes, bring him in," she said, and turning to her aunt as Don sped on his errand, "It must be the minister, Aunty. I remember now that Stuart told me his name was Lord. Millie, don't put the baby down. There are tacks and scraps everywhere, and we will need to clean them up before we set her free in here."

"Lord—that's an odd name for a minister, don't you think?" Wealthy said. "I'm sure I won't forget it!"

Millie explained briefly to her mother about the Indians, saying she was sure they were friendly. Marcia agreed, and Aunt Wealthy beamed when she heard that Millie had spoken to them in French; she had no time to elaborate on the story, because at that moment Reverend Lord came in apologizing for his "neglect in not calling sooner" because he had been engaged with his sermon and the matter had completely slipped his mind.

"I think you are blaming yourself undeservedly, sir," Marcia said, giving him her hand with a cordial smile. "We arrived in town only yesterday. Let me introduce you to my aunt, Miss Stanhope."

The two shook hands.

"Pleased to meet you, Mr. Almighty," Wealthy said.

"Lord," the minister corrected, blushing.

"Oh, my, yes, Lord. That's what I meant. Won't you have a seat?" Wealthy waved at a chair.

Reverend Lord, still blushing, fumbled with his hat, and then seated himself not on the offered chair, but on a box next to it, which was completely covered with paper tacks waiting to be used.

"My word!" he sprang to his feet, brushing frantically at the seat of his britches to dislodge the tacks that were imbedded there. He apologized for this impromptu jig, and his mistake, blushing even redder.

"Never mind," Marcia said kindly. "I apologize to you. We are in such disorder!"

Wealthy gathered the scattered tacks from the floor as Marcia offered the chair again. "You will find this a more comfortable seat," she said.

The young man examined the seat carefully, then sat gingerly down.

"I trust you are church-going folk?" he asked.

"Oh, yes," Wealthy said.

"My husband is a Christian man," Marcia said. "And from the very first day of our marriage we have been determined that our household will follow the Lord."

"Excellent," the young minister said, and began telling them about the church he had recently organized.

Annis grew heavy in Millie's arms, and she realized the baby was asleep. She waited politely for a break in the conversation, but Reverend Lord was excited about every detail of his church, and didn't seem to feel the need to breathe between one sentence and the next. Finally, there was a pause long enough for Millie to break in.

"Pardon me, Mamma," she said. "Annis has fallen asleep."

"Asleep?" The young minister looked abashed. "I am afraid I sometimes have that effect on people. I don't mean to be long-winded."

"Nonsense." Marcia had just a touch of a smile on her face. "The baby is tired and much too young to be interested in church."

"May I carry her back to the clearing?" Millie asked. "I want to be on hand for the other children."

"Yes," her mother said. "I will send Don along with food directly."

Millie said good-bye to Reverend Lord, carried the sleeping baby back to Rupert's house of trees and laid her in the shade. Cyril and Fan were riding saplings that Ru had pulled over for them, pretending they were horses, while Zillah and Adah finished their garlands of flowers. Millie cautioned them to be quiet while the baby slept, then leaned back against a nearby tree.

"What kind of a place have You brought us to, Lord?" she asked. "This doesn't seem much like the promised land at all! Public gossips, savages that want to be friends, and I know, Lord, that You call Your ministers, and I know You choose them. But this one," Millie glanced around to make sure no one was listening, and lowered her voice anyway, "this one looks like Ichabod Crane! This place is never, never going to feel like home!"

Home. Suddenly she realized that the same ghost moon that was looking down on her from the bright afternoon sky was looking over Lansdale, too. Bea and Annabeth and Camilla might be gazing up at it right now, wondering about her. She took the letter from her pocket and pressed it against her heart. Could they ever imagine what a strange and horrible place she had come to?

"They wear calico pantalets, Bea," Millie whispered. "And you would hate it, Annabeth. Camilla, I haven't seen a single book since I arrived, and I'm sure they haven't any!"

CHAPTER

11

Home At Last

Enlarge the place of your tent, stretch your tent curtains wide, do not hold back; lengthen your cords, strengthen your stakes.

ISAIAH 54:2

*M*illie's eyes misted with emotion. *I am not going to start that again!* She pulled her knees up and rested her chin on them.

"Trust in the Lord with all your heart and lean not on your own understanding. In all your ways acknowledge him, and he will make your paths straight." Could it have been only months since her mother had given her that verse? That trusty chair in the washroom seemed a hundred years in the past. It hadn't let her fall. *But I feel like I'm falling, God. I feel like I'm tumbling, tumbling down, and I just haven't hit the ground yet.* That was just it. She hadn't hit the ground. Maybe she wasn't falling at all.

Mamma has lost a lot more than I have, and she is still trusting God. Jesus, I want to trust You like that. I want to know You like that. But I don't know how yet. Millie sat up and straightened her shoulders. *I'm going to try to be like Mamma while I learn.*

Suddenly the Scripture from the night in the hotel came back into her mind, sharp and clear: *"I will give you the treasures of darkness, riches stored in secret places, so that you may know that I am the Lord, the God of Israel, who summons you by name."*

"Jesus," Millie prayed, "are You going to show me the treasures hidden in Pleasant Plains?"

Just then, Don came running from the house, carrying a covered basket. All the little Keiths gathered around the door to their leafy playhouse.

"He wasn't the Lord at all," he announced, setting the basket down, "and he didn't talk long. Well, not long for a preacher," he corrected himself. "I guess 'cause he was uncomfortable on account of sitting on a bunch of tacks.

Millie's Unsettled Season

Mr. Hendrix at home never sat on tacks, and he always talked longer. But Mamma sent us a picnic, anyways."

"I'm not too hungry," said Adah. "Did you tell Mamma about the Indians and the berries?"

"Yes, Millie told her most everything already," he glared at Millie, "but I told her about the beetle. And she says we needn't be a single bit afraid; they sound like nice folks. And she said to tell Cyril not to try eatin' any more beetles."

"Well, I'm as hungry as a bear," Ru said. "Let's eat."

"Wait," Millie said. "We need to say a blessing first."

"I'll do it," said Cyril, "That way it'll be quick." He closed his eyes and folded his hands. "Dear Lord, we thank You for the gingerbread and turnovers and—and all good things, like berries, beetles, and snakes."

Millie's eyes flew open, and she looked around quickly, but Cyril's hands were still folded, and his head bowed. He looked almost angelic with the sunlight illuminating the fuzz on his head.

"Amen. Now gimme mine, Millie." He held out both hands.

"What snakes?" Millie asked.

"It got away," Cyril said.

"Snakes don't like pockets, I guess." Don reached for the basket.

Millie glanced at Ru. He just shook his head.

"Ladies first," Millie said, gently pushing Don's hand away. "Now spread your handkerchiefs in your laps to keep the greasy crumbs from your clothes. Adah, Zillah, and Fan may help themselves."

"Go ahead, Millie," Ru said, when the little girls had chosen a sandwich. "You're a lady."

"No, I'll serve myself last, the way Mamma does."

Home At Last

There was more than enough for them all. Millie made sure the remains of the meal were put carefully back in the basket, then hung it up on a branch near at hand. As she did so, Adah squealed, "Mamma's coming!" Annis woke at the commotion and started to cry.

"May I come in?" Mamma asked at the door.

"Yes," Zillah said.

Marcia wiped her feet neatly on the grass, then stooped to enter their little house. She sat down on the robe and took Annis in her arms.

"Did you have enough to eat?" she asked.

"Yes," Ru said. "Thank you, Mamma."

"You quite deserved it, taking care of yourselves and Annis all morning, and not giving any trouble to anybody."

Fan covered her with sticky kisses, and she laughed. She had to hear the story of the Indians all over again, with each one adding a new detail, and Don and Cyril acting out the parts of the Indians, complete with leaves in their hair instead of feathers.

"Are you getting done fast, Mamma?" Zillah asked. "Can we sleep in the Big Yellow House tonight?"

"Not tonight. We've scrubbed the wood floors and I want them to dry thoroughly before we move in. We will go back to the Union for our supper and to sleep tonight. But tomorrow..."

"We will be in our own house!" Fan yelled.

"Not the nice house we used to have, though," sighed Zillah.

"What!" Marcia said. "You are not telling me you don't like our new home! Did Indians ever visit at our old house? Just think of it! They were the first of our new neighbors to greet us! And we had no buffalo robes, or houses made of saplings to play in. It is not the same, but I am sure God has a very good plan for the Keiths!"

Annis had returned to her nap in her mother's arms. Marcia laid her down gently on the robe and pulled a light covering over her, then motioning them to follow her, she crept from the little house and brushed off her apron. From its pocket she drew out a book of stories for Millie to read to the younger ones.

"Now mind the baby," she said quietly. "I have to go back and help Aunty."

"Read a story, Millie," Cyril said, and then as an afterthought, "Please?"

"I'll read 'Androcles and the Lion'." Millie flipped through the book. "You always like that."

"An' then the one 'bout the girl that had a silk dress and couldn't run and play 'cause her shoes pinched," begged Fan.

"Look!" exclaimed Adah in an undertone. "Those girls haven't got silk dresses or shoes to pinch their toes. Don't they look odd?"

Two little girls—one about Adah's size, the other a trifle smaller—were standing just at the edge of the Keiths' clearing, looking longingly toward the spot where the Keith children were seated.

They had sunburnt faces, and dark braids fell over their shoulders. Their thin little forms were scarcely covered by their faded, worn, calico dresses. Pantalets of the same material but different color, showed below their skirts. Their feet were bare, and very brown, and on their heads were sunbonnets of pasteboard covered with still another pattern of faded calico.

"Can we ask them to come and join us?" queried Zillah. "Please, Millie! They could be company in our house!"

"You may be the hostess," Millie said to her.

"Good afternoon, little girls," said Zillah, though they must have been close to her age. "Will you come and sit with us?"

They shook their heads, and the younger one put her thumb in her mouth. Zillah looked at Millie.

"Perhaps they are shy," Millie whispered. "Let's just start to read and see what happens. Don't stare at them, now." She began the story, glancing up after a few paragraphs. The little strangers had edged closer. Millie lowered her voice, as the story was getting exciting. The next thing she knew, the little girls were sitting on the edge of the robe, just as intent as the other children.

Zillah and Adah were clearly more interested in the new-comers than in the story. When she finished, Millie closed the book and smiled.

"Hello," she said. "My name is Millie Keith. What's yours?"

"Emmaretta Josetta Lightcap," said the bigger girl, "and this is Minerva Louisa Lightcap. She's my sister. We call her Min."

Min nodded without taking her thumb from her mouth.

"My name is Zillah, and this is Adah, and Ru and Don and Cyril and Fan, and our baby Annis is sleeping," Zillah said, and then, remembering that she was the hostess, "May I offer you some tea?" She leaned toward Emmaretta and whispered, "I don't really have any tea. But we have some good things in our basket."

"Thrilled and delighted," said Emmaretta.

Ru handed the basket down from the branch, and Zillah opened it up, spread a napkin for a tablecloth, and set out the remains of the feast. Emmaretta and Minerva helped themselves. Every time they finished one delicacy, Zillah produced another.

Millie settled back to reading, while the girls concentrated on finishing every crumb left in the basket. They had completed the job when they were summoned by a woman's voice from the direction of the smithy.

"That's our mother," Emmaretta explained.

Min nodded, licked a smear of jelly from her finger, then put her thumb back in her mouth.

"You must come calling," Emmaretta said, wiping her hands on her skirt. "I don't have any tea, either, but Gordon found a bee tree last week, and we've got honeycomb!" Then they turned and ran for home.

Millie helped Marcia and Aunt Wealthy put the finishing touches on the house the next day. By mid-afternoon, everything was in order.

"Ahhhhh," Stuart said, sinking into his chair, when he returned from arranging his office in town. "There is nothing like your own castle!"

"There is no castle, Pappa," Adah said. "Just our house."

"Are the floors clean?" Stuart asked.

"Yes," Zillah said.

"And we all have rooms, and beds?"

"Our walls are made out of curtains," Zillah said.

"Do we have chintz-covered and cushioned lounges, and pretty, dainty tables?"

"They are made of packing crates, Pappa," Adah laughed. "Mamma just covered them with fabric!"

"See?" Stuart said. "A castle. Too bad the moat has filled up with sand. I would like to go for a swim."

"It's time for supper, your majesty," Marcia said, appearing at the door. The family gathered about a neatly appointed table set out in the center of one of the three lower rooms. They all bowed their heads as Stuart prayed, blessing the meal, their new home, and his family.

"We are going to have a new addition to our family," Stuart announced as the meal began. Millie looked at her mother, but she looked just as puzzled as the rest of the gathering at the table.

"Her name is Belle. She has sad eyes, and I expect all of you will be kind to her until she gets used to her new home." He winked at his wife, then said, "Would you pass the bread, Millie?"

"A new girl, Pappa?" Fan said. "Will she sleep in my bed?"

"Oh, no," he said. "I don't expect she would fit in your room. And she might have some trouble with the stairs. I think she'll have to stay in the shed by the willow trees."

"I'll stay there with her then," Fan said, "so she won't be afraid."

"She's not going to be afraid, you goose," Ru said. "Pappa would never make a real girl sleep in the shed. He's bought a cow! Isn't that right, Pappa?"

"A cow!" There was a great deal of excited talk among the children over who would feed it and milk it.

"When will we get her?" Aunt Wealthy asked. "I'll show the children how to milk."

"If there is light after supper, Ru can fetch her. I bought her from Mr. Rinwald, who lives across town. She will sleep in the shed. We will feed her sweet hay and let her graze in the field on the other side of the hill. I think walking her to the field will be a job for Cyril."

Cyril sat up taller. "Mebbe you can help," he said to Don. "Sometimes, anyway."

Ru left as soon as the meal was finished to get the cow. Aunt Wealthy and Stuart and Marcia sat on the porch enjoying the evening, while Millie and the younger children cleared the table, washed the dishes, and made the kitchen all neat.

"Ru's comin' back!" Don yelled. "He's got the cow!"

The entire family assembled in the yard as Ru walked the little brown cow into the yard.

"She's beautiful!" Millie said, and everyone had to agree. She had a sweet face, and long black lashes over her big brown eyes. The family followed Ru to the cow shed, where he tied her halter to the rail.

"She's full of milk, too," Aunt Wealthy said. She called for a stool and a bucket, and gave the family their first lesson in milking. The little cow looked around quizzically as Aunt Wealthy settled the stool and bucket in place, but soon returned to chewing her cud placidly, as Aunt Wealthy began to milk.

"You grab a teat like this," she said, demonstrating. "Pinch it between your thumb and finger, just so…and squeeze!" A stream of milk shot into the bucket. Wannago watched in fascination until Wealthy directed a stream of warm milk at his face. He jumped back, then licked his chops and sat on his hind legs begging for more. He caught the next stream in his mouth, and everyone laughed.

"You are amazing, Aunty," Marcia said, when Belle's udder was empty and the bucket full. "I didn't know you knew how to milk!"

Home At Last

"Tsk, Marcia," said Wealthy. "You can't live to my ripe age without learning a thing or two!"

Stuart put some fresh hay in the cow's trough, and shut the shed for the night.

This done they returned to the sitting room. The great family Bible lay open on the table before Stuart, a pile of hymn books beside it. Rupert passed out the hymnals while Stuart read a few verses of Scripture, then led them in a hymn. Marcia's sweet voice sang harmony, and the others joined in as a full chorus of praise filled the Big Yellow House.

When it died away, Stuart prayed for each of the children before he sent them up to bed. Each little one came to claim a goodnight kiss from Mamma, Pappa, and Aunt Wealthy, then cheerfully followed Millie up the steep, crooked stairway to the large room above, to sleep and dream their first dreams in the Big Yellow House.

CHAPTER 12

First Impressions

What I feared has come upon me;
what I dreaded has happened
to me.

JOB 3:25

First Impressions

illie awoke the next morning to the feel of her own pillow, the smell of Mamma's lavender soap—and someone shaking her shoulder.

"Wake up, Millie," Fan said. "I want to ride the cow."

"Don't be a goose," Millie said sleepily. "People don't ride cows. Where are Mamma and Pappa?"

"They went to see about Pappa's new office, and they took Ru. And Aunt Wealthy is walking all over town, talking to God. She said to let you sleep, but I want to ride the cow, too!"

Millie was suddenly wide awake. "What do you mean, *too*?"

"Don said he was going to ride it," Fan said. "He said I was too little!"

Millie jumped out of bed and rushed downstairs in her nightgown and bare feet. She made it out the back door just in time to see Don launch himself from the fence onto poor Belle's back. Belle turned her head placidly to look at him, then started to walk.

"Wahooo!" Don yelled. Cyril shouted encouragement from the fence, where he was perched holding one end of a rope he'd tied to Belle's halter. Belle reached the end of the rope, gave one jerk, and the rope came off the halter. Wannago raced ahead of her, yapping happily.

"What kinda knot was that?" Cyril said, jumping off the fence.

"Slip knot, I'd guess," Don said, kicking his heels against Belle's sides.

373

"Bring her back here, Don! I wanna get on, too!" Cyril yelled. Belle had her own ideas, it seemed, and they had something to do with the wide-open prairie beyond the hill.

"Don! Get off that cow this instant!" Millie called.

"I can't," Don yelled back. "She's too high. I'll bust a leg!"

"Where are you going?" Cyril demanded, starting after them.

"Wherever she wants, I guess," Don replied.

Belle was trotting now, Don bouncing like an India rubber ball on her back.

She changed her mind about the prairie, and turned and started down the street toward the center of town.

"This is not happening!" Millie cried. "What will people say? We will be the family who lives in a warehouse and rides cows!" She picked up her long cotton nightgown and ran, catching Belle by the halter just as they passed the blacksmith's shop.

"Aw, Millie," Don said. "Just when she was goin' good, too!"

"That's a pretty dress."

Millie glanced around quickly. The two little girls from the willow grove were standing in the front yard.

"Real pretty," Emmaretta said. Minerva nodded agreement, thumb firmly in her mouth. Behind them stood an older girl. She smiled, but Millie ducked her head in embarrassment, and pulled on Belle's halter.

"No more riding the cow," she said firmly as she tied Belle up. "Pappa will be very upset when he learns how you have treated her." She made sure the cow had water and alfalfa, then stopped at the well to pull up a bucket of water to wash her dusty feet. The foot washing was a success, but the hem of her nightgown was all muddy when she was through. She sighed as she went back up the stairs to the kitchen.

"Millie, is that you?" Marcia called.

"Yes," Millie said, stomping into the dining room, "And you won't believe what Don has done now—"

Marcia was standing with a finely dressed woman and two girls about Millie's age. They wore bright, pretty bonnets and carried a basket of freshly baked bread, jars of homemade jam, and just-picked daisies.

Marcia blinked at Millie's muddy nightgown and unbrushed hair, took a deep breath and said, "And this is Mildred, my eldest daughter, the one I was telling you about, Mrs. Chetwood."

Millie self-consciously smoothed her nightgown, torn between the desire to strangle Don and the wish to sink into the floor. Both girls' eyes traveled from Millie's muddy hem to the furniture made of crates and covered with fabric.

Millie had never felt poor before, never in Lansdale, even after Pappa's money was gone, and not even when Pappa had shown them the Big Yellow House. But suddenly she saw the Big Yellow House not as Pappa's pretend castle, but as her home, made of broken parts and pieces and leftover goods.

"Oh, never mind your nightgown, dear girl," Mrs. Chetwood said, sensing her embarrassment. "I know you weren't expecting us—we met your mother at the door. We just wanted to stop by and say 'Welcome to Pleasant Plains.' My, you look so much like your mother! This is my daughter Claudina Chetwood. She's thirteen and her good friend here, Lucilla Grange, is nearly fourteen." Mrs. Chetwood smiled graciously.

Millie's Unsettled Season

The two girls curtsied. Millie returned their gesture. She heard a nervous giggle, and to her horror realized the sound was coming from her own throat.

"I was chasing a cow," she started to explain, but gave up. "Mamma, will you excuse me for a moment?"

"Of course," Marcia said, and Millie practically flew out of the sitting room, through the kitchen and up the stairs. She pulled on her petticoats and skirt, and ran a brush through her hair.

"Give me courage, Lord," she prayed as she started back down the stairs.

"So, my husband and yours will no doubt meet, if not today then very soon," Mrs. Chetwood was saying when Millie entered. Aunt Wealthy had returned from her walk, and was listening attentively as well. "Dr. Chetwood is the local physician and his office is only a few doors down from the one your husband has taken. And Mr. Grange runs the bank, so I'm certain they'll meet, if they haven't already. Mrs. Grange, Lucilla's mother, would have come with us but she is feeling poorly, I'm afraid. Sends her warmest regards."

"I hope it is nothing serious," Aunt Wealthy said to the girl. "Let us know if there is anything at all we can do for her."

"Thank you, ma'am. I will tell her of your concern." Then she turned to Millie. "Do they call you Mildred," she asked, "or do you have a nickname?"

"Most people back in Lansdale called me Millie."

"I hope you will allow us to call you that, also?" Lucilla said properly, and then, smiling, "You can call me Lu."

The ladies said their good-byes, promising future visits. Marcia offered her great thanks for the visitors' courtesy and the lovely basket.

376

"Not at all, Mrs. Keith. I suspect you would have done the same. So very nice to meet you too, Miss Stanhope. I do hope we all become friends," Mrs. Chetwood said, clasping first Marcia's hand and then Aunt Wealthy's.

Millie thanked the girls for stopping by.

"You must return the visit," Claudina said.

"Yes, you must," Lu said.

"I am never going out in public again," Millie said, smiling through clenched teeth, as she stood at the door waving good-bye. "Never."

"Nonsense," Aunt Wealthy said. "I think you will be great friends with those girls."

Millie watched as they made their way down the street, past the piles of sand and weeds. Then she ran up to her room, threw herself on her bed, and covered her head with a pillow. *Great friends? After the way they looked at me?* She sat up and threw her pillow across the small room. She didn't need any friends. She had her books, and books never judged you because of the clothes you wore, or the house you lived in. But they didn't talk much, either. Millie picked up her pillow, splashed water on her face, and went downstairs to help Mamma and Aunt Wealthy with the day's chores.

The next few days were a whirlwind of constant activity and hard work for Millie and the whole Keith family. Marcia and Aunt Wealthy had done a great deal of work on the Big Yellow House, but there was still much to be done.

In addition to his new responsibility for Belle, Rupert discovered gardening and carpentry, and Cyril and Don and

Millie's Unsettled Season

Fan were under his feet all day trying to help as he worked on the house, or broke ground for a garden. Millie and the older girls helped Marcia and Aunt Wealthy about the house, or tended to Annis.

Stuart bought a churn, and Aunt Wealthy showed Millie how to skim the cream off the top of the buckets of frothy milk and churn it into butter. When the butter was formed, she poured it out on a slab, mixed salt in, and then formed it into blocks that were stored in the cool well with the milk. All of the young Keiths thought that Belle's butter was the best they had ever tasted.

Even Mrs. Prior agreed, when she stopped by for a visit on Saturday evening.

"Are the neighbors making friendly yet?" she inquired after she had finished her buttered scone.

"Mrs. Chetwood brought her daughter and Lucilla by," Wealthy said. "They seemed very friendly."

"The others will come along, I'm sure," she said. "I expect they are set back by Stuart being a lawyer. Oh, and if you are looking for a girl to help around the house, I hear Celestia Ann Huntsinger is looking for a place. Her pa has a lot of mouths to feed. She's seventeen years old, and a real hard worker. I must be going. Now don't you be formal with me, but run in whenever you can. I'll always be glad to see you."

Stuart stood to walk her home, as it was already dark outside.

"No, never mind your hat, Mr. Keith. I don't want a beau, and I'm not the least mite afraid of walking alone. Goodnight to you all."

The candle flared in the draft from the open door. Aunt Wealthy hastened to snuff it. "These are miserable candles. If you will get me some tallow tomorrow, Stuart, I'll make a better variety. We have the molds and the wick; all we need is the tallow."

"Cow milking and candle making. You do amaze me, Miss Stanhope!" Stuart said.

"We are lucky to have you," Marcia agreed. "There is so much to do, I would be lost without you, Aunty." Stuart looked thoughtfully from one to the other.

"What do you think, wife?" he asked. "Should we hire the girl Mrs. Prior mentioned?"

"If she is a hard worker, she would be of some help," Marcia said. "And if she needs a place, we could be of some help to her."

"Then it sounds like a match," he agreed. "I'll have Mrs. Prior send her around."

The Keiths were up and dressed early the next morning, for it was the Sabbath. Millie took special care as she chose the little girls' dresses and bonnets, and Stuart inspected each of the boys from head to foot before they set out along the narrow foot path that led past the grove of saplings to the little church.

The tall grass on each side of the trail was still wet with dew, and Millie showed Zillah and Adah how to lift their skirts and jump the puddles so as not to soil their shoes. Cyril kept wandering from the path anyway, following Wannago on his adventures, and his britches were soaked to the knee by the time they reached the church.

Reverend Lord was standing on the steps, greeting each family as they arrived. His Sunday suit was long enough in the arms, and even the pants fit well.

"Good morning," he said, shaking Stuart's hand. "I am glad to meet you at last! I think your family will double my Sunday school enrollment!"

Millie's Unsettled Season

Wealthy spoke firmly to Wannago, and he lay down to wait on the steps.

Most of the families attending were townsfolk who arrived walking like the Keiths, but a few families had come in from the surrounding country in wagons. There was little display of fashion or style in dress. Most of the women and girls wore calico.

Claudina Chetwood and Lucilla Grange smiled at Millie as she entered. The inside of the church was very different from any the Keiths had been in before. The windows were plain glass, and the seats rough wooden benches without a back. There was no organ or even piano.

"This doesn't look like a church at all," Zillah whispered as they took their seats.

"Shhhh," Millie said. "The sermon is about to begin."

The last member having arrived and been duly greeted, the Reverend Lord shut the door and strode up the center aisle. He stood for a moment behind his rough pulpit, and then he asked the people to join him in prayer and bowed his head.

As he spoke, his awkwardness fell away. Millie could almost hear the water lapping at the sides of the boats as he spoke of Jesus in Galilee. People young and old sat transfixed by his words. How could she ever have thought he looked like Ichabod Crane? For the first time in weeks, Millie felt truly at peace.

When the sermon was over, they stood for a hymn.

"Pappa, where are the hymnals?" Zillah whispered. "I can't find one!"

"Just listen," Stuart said.

Reverend Lord began the hymn by calling out the first line of a familiar hymn, then the congregation sang that verse together. Just as they finished, he called out the first

line of the second verse, and so it continued until they had finished the hymn.

People lingered after church, complimenting Reverend Lord on his sermon and text, discussing the happenings of the week. The Keiths were warmly welcomed, and assured of intentions to call. Many people expressed hopes that they would "like the place," the country people adding, "Come out and see us whenever you can."

Millie had almost forgotten her embarrassment of the day before when Claudina Chetwood approached her and smiled, her deep dimples peeking out.

"I'm hosting a young ladies' Bible study at my house on Wednesday," she said. "Would you be interested in coming? Many of the girls from church will be there, and Mother will serve us a light meal."

"I would love to attend," Millie said. "But I'll have to ask Mamma first." They found Marcia just as a tall, gaunt woman approached her.

"Oh, dread," Claudina whispered. "I'll wait for your answer, Millie. I think my mother wants me just now." Millie watched in surprise as the girl walked quickly away.

The woman who had approached Marcia was of uncertain age. She had yellow hair and pale, blue eyes. Her dress was almost austere in its simplicity: a dove-colored calico, cotton gloves of a darker shade, a white muslin handkerchief crossed on her bosom, a close straw bonnet with no trimming but a piece of white ribbon put straight across the top, brought down over the ears and tied under the chin.

"My name is Drybread," she announced with a slight, stiff curtsy. "Damaris Drybread."

"Mrs. or Miss?" queried Marcia pleasantly.

"Miss. And yours?"

"Mrs. Keith. Allow me to introduce my aunt, Miss Stanhope, and my daughter, Mildred. These little people also belong to me."

"Do you go to school, my little lass?" asked the visitor, unbending slightly in the stiffness of her manner as she addressed Fan.

"She's not little!" Don said protectively, putting his arm around his sister. "And she's not your lass, neither. She's our lass."

"She's too young for school," Cyril added. "Pappa won't let her go."

"Don! Cyril! My boys must not be rude," reproved Marcia.

The boys apologized, and then Marcia sent them to run and play.

"They're pretty children," remarked Miss Drybread as the boys disappeared.

"Very frank in the expression of their sentiments and wishes, sometimes," Wealthy said.

"How do you like Pleasant Plains?" Miss Drybread asked.

The question was addressed more particularly to Wealthy, and it was she who replied.

"We are quite disposed to like the place, Miss Stalebread. The streets are widely pleasant and would be quite beautiful if the forest trees had been left."

"Drybread!" the woman corrected. "A good, honest name; if not quite so aristocratic and fine sounding as Keith."

"Pardon me!" said Wealthy. "I have an unfortunate memory for names and had no intention of miscalling yours."

"Oh. Then it's all right." She smiled, and her face was almost pretty. "Mrs. Keith, I'm a teacher; I take young girls of all ages. Perhaps you might entrust me with some of yours? I see you have quite a flock."

"I will take it into consideration." Marcia returned her smile. "What subjects do you teach?"

"Art and music, embroidery, manners…everything that is proper for a young lady to learn. The school is not far from here, and within easy walking distance of your home."

"You don't feel girls could benefit from lessons in history, mathematics, and science?" Millie asked.

"Whatever for?" Miss Drybread seemed surprised.

"To make use of the brains God gave them," Millie said, remembering the fun she'd had in Mr. Martin's class. She was all set to continue, reproducing one of his famous speeches, but Marcia gave her a look.

"I will certainly consider your school," Marcia said. "But I should speak to my husband first."

As the Keiths walked home, they discussed the service and the pleasant people they had met. Zillah and Adah were eager to go to school to make new friends, but Stuart was not easily convinced.

"These years are very important to your future education," he said. "I want you to learn arithmetic, history, botany, and every subject your heads can hold!"

"But there is no other school here, Pappa," Zillah reasoned.

"And we will meet all of the girls!" Adah pleaded. "Please, Pappa!"

Stuart finally agreed that he would make arrangements for Zillah and Adah to start with Miss Drybread the very next morning. Fan was too young for school, and Millie too advanced for any classes Miss Drybread offered.

After the children had been changed from their Sunday best, the family had a cold dinner of sandwiches and pickles. "My dear," Stuart said as they were finishing the meal, "several days ago, I asked you to take a walk with me. Will you take another now?"

"Of course," said Marcia.

"And us, too?" asked Don.

"I wouldn't leave without you," Stuart said.

Once more Rupert became the marshal of the family. This time as their walk took them through the town, people they had met in church smiled and waved. Millie smiled back and called hello to several girls. Stuart stopped on a hill high above the town overlooking the valley and the river. There were several ancient oaks standing guard on the hill, grand old trees that had seen the storms of centuries.

"What a beautiful spot, Stuart!" Marcia exclaimed. "What views! I haven't seen the whole area at once like this."

"It gives you a feeling of grandeur," Millie said, "to look out over the land from here, doesn't it?" In one direction, she could see the river, rippling in the sun; in the other the growing town stretched out before them. If she were a princess, this is where her castle would sit, high above the town, almost touching the clouds, with the gnarled old trees standing like sentinels day and night.

"Do you really like it?" Stuart asked, drawing Marcia close.

"I do," Marcia replied.

"I believe you've said that to me before, my dear," he teased.

"And I meant every word!" she laughed.

"Then I will build you a house right here."

"Really, Stuart?" Marcia spun around, taking in the view.

"I mean every word," Stuart said. "I am confident enough to spend some of the funds we received from our old house on the purchase of this land. We can't afford to start building just yet, but when the house is finished, we'll be able to see the Kankakee Marsh from the second story windows."

"Marsh?" Wealthy asked in a tone of alarm. "How far off is it?"

"We're about two miles from this end; it is two hundred miles long, you know, extending far over into Illinois. Why?"

"Ague!"

"Bless you," Millie said, coming out of her castle daydream.

"Ague is not a sneeze," Marcia explained. "It's a terrible sickness. A fever. It comes off the marshes and swamps in the air. We never had it in Lansdale, as there were no swamps."

"We'll cross that bridge when we come to it," Stuart said. "This is a beautiful spot. I think we can make it more lovely than our gardens in Lansdale."

"I think so, too, if we can keep these fine old oaks," said Marcia.

"We'll manage our building in a way not to interfere with them," Stuart assured her. "Our grandchildren will climb them."

"How soon can the house be done?" Millie asked, a little alarmed at the talk of grandchildren. Surely they would not have to wait that long!

Millie's Unsettled Season

"Better to ask how soon it will be begun," laughed her father. "If we get into it by next spring we may consider ourselves fortunate."

"Oh," groaned Cyril, Don, and Fan with one accord.

"The time will slip around before you know it, dears," said Aunt Wealthy cheerily.

"And we'll get this ground fenced in. You can spend your time digging and planting and planning," said Stuart.

"May I help plan the house?" asked Ru.

Stuart smiled. "You may," he said. "It will be the Keith house — not the parents' only, but the children's too."

"Then I want to plan the gardens," Millie said. "I think a swing would be perfect under that giant of a tree."

"That is a wonderful idea," Stuart said. "Millie's swing will be the first thing we build!"

Stuart bought rope and a sturdy board for a seat the very next morning. Millie and Ru were excused from watching the children. Rupert made holes in the board, and together they walked through town and up the hill. Ru shimmied up into the tree, and Millie threw him both ropes. While he tied the ropes to the branches, Millie threaded them through the holes in the board seat and tied a fat knot so that they couldn't pull out. When it was finished, Millie had the first turn, pumping her legs and leaning until the swing rose high above the branch, pausing for a breathless moment before it rushed back down. She could see the swamp in the distance, and houses and fields, all of Pleasant Plains at a glance, and then it was gone. Millie sat on the swing long after Ru had lost interest and wandered away. It was the first thing in Pleasant Plains that was really, truly hers.

CHAPTER

A Bible Study

Have I now become your enemy
by telling you the truth?

GALATIANS 4:16

A Bible Study

"Mamma, what do you think?" Millie twirled to show off her fresh skirt and apron. Aunt Wealthy had plaited her golden hair in two braids along her head, and Millie had chosen a pretty hat that set off her blue eyes.

"I think my daughter looks every inch the lady," Marcia said. "And I am proud to have her represent the Keiths at a Bible study."

"All that's lacking is the Bible," Millie laughed. She ran upstairs to her bedside table and picked up her Bible. The pages showed the wear and tear of constant use, but Aunt Wealthy had made a clever slipcover for the book out of boards, fabric, and paste to keep it together a little longer. Millie slipped it into her black satin reticule.

"Lord," Millie prayed, "I know it takes time to become friends. But let me start to find a friend today!"

Claudina Chetwood met her at the door of a lovely brick home, and ushered her inside. The house smelled of wax and wood polish, and every rail and table top gleamed. The fluted curtains that hung over large windows were stiff with starch, each fold perfect. Millie smiled. It felt like home — like the lovely homes of her friends in Lansdale. Claudina led the way into a pleasant room full of girls ranging in age from twelve to sixteen. Millie was instantly the center of attention as Claudina introduced her.

"How nice to have a new girl in town," said Helen Monocker, the oldest girl present. "And we hear your father has purchased a lovely piece of land on which to build."

"Yes," Millie said, "though it seems a little far from the center of town."

Millie's Unsettled Season

"Not everyone can live in the original neighborhoods," Helen said. "But you must admit, it will be an improvement over a warehouse."

Millie blinked, but before she could reply, Claudina cut in.

"We were just discussing the new fashion in skirts," she said. "We are so far behind times here. Were you very current in Lansdale?"

Millie was uncomfortable with all the attention, but she thought of Bea and smiled. "Some of us were more current than others, I suppose," she said. "But you don't seem at all backward to me."

"I should hope not," Helen smoothed her skirt. "Mother orders the latest from Chicago. But more petticoats are needed to achieve the new look."

"Alice Winston certainly achieved a look at her party last month," Lucilla said, laughing. "I don't know what she was thinking!"

The attention of the group turned suddenly away from Millie, but this new train of conversation made her more uncomfortable than the last.

"Well, I do!" Helen said. "Emma says Alice has been sweet on him forever. She said Mrs. Gilligut told her that Alice writes him letters every day."

Several of the girls giggled.

Millie began to feel very uncomfortable, and Lucilla noticed at once.

"Oh, Millie," she said. "I apologize! How rude of us. You weren't at the party, and know nothing of these people!"

"I'm sure Millie enjoys an intrigue as much as the rest of us," Helen said. "I love Emma's tales!"

Millie bit her lip. If she were in Lansdale, she would have quoted Pappa: "Repeating second-hand knowledge is hearsay

in the courts of man, and gossip in the courts of heaven. I don't want to be guilty of either!" She wasn't in Lansdale with her friends, though. She was an invited guest in a new place. But wasn't right right and wrong wrong no matter where you were? And God's Word was very clear about gossip.

"I think…" Millie began, but at that moment Mrs. Chetwood came out to offer the sandwiches and lemonade she had prepared. She encouraged the girls to start on the verse at hand as soon as they were finished eating. Millie was relieved, but a little ashamed of herself for not finishing her sentence. She gratefully accepted a sandwich, but left her lemonade untouched.

When the dishes were removed, Claudina cleared her throat and tapped her glass with a spoon. The other girls giggled at her, but it was time to begin, and it did seem that several girls were actually ready to study.

Claudina began with prayer, remembering each of their families, and particularly the Keiths.

"We will be studying the sixteenth chapter of First Samuel today, starting at the seventh verse," she said.

Millie opened her reticule and pulled out her Bible.

"How… quaint," Helen said. "I've never seen a Bible quite like that before."

"Oh," Millie knew she was blushing, but couldn't help it. "My Aunt made this cover for me. The Bible is worn, you see." She slipped off the cover and showed the tattered cover.

Several of the girls looked at each other.

"It must be very old," Helen said, "to look like that. Won't your father buy you a new one?"

"Oh, no. I mean, of course Pappa would, if I asked him." Millie tried to smile. "I like this one, even if it is well used."

"I've never heard of anyone wearing out a Bible before," Helen said. "My grandmother has gone to church every single Sabbath of her life, and her Bible looks like new!"

"I'm sure she's very careful with it," Millie said, flushing even redder.

"Could you read the verse for us, Millie?" Claudina asked.

Millie smiled her thanks, and flipped quickly to the verse.

"'The Lord does not look at things the way man does,'" she read. "'Man looks at the outward appearance, but the Lord looks at the heart.' And thank goodness for that!" Millie added.

"Actually, I find that verse confusing," Lucilla said. "I'm sure the Lord can look at a heart. But why did God put it in the Bible if we can't look at hearts? We only see the outside of people. How else are we to choose our friends if not by how they dress and behave? I mean, rules of behavior and appearance are so important, don't you think?"

"I completely agree with you, Lu. This verse is talking about what God does, not what we should do," Helen said. "Appearance is important. I would no more wear something inappropriate to church or to a social than I would quack like a duck!"

"Aren't we supposed to do just as Jesus would do?" Millie asked.

"Of course," several voices agreed.

"Didn't Jesus say He did what He saw His Father doing? Right here in John 10:37." Millie flipped to the verse and read, "'Do not believe me unless I do what my Father does.' Doesn't that imply that we should try to look at things the way God does?"

"Are you saying we should not dress well and do our hair?" Lu asked.

"That's begging the point," Claudina said. "This verse isn't saying we mustn't wash our faces and brush our hair one hundred strokes. I think it implies that we must not think less of people who do things differently."

"Shouldn't our motivation always be to bring honor to our Lord? In our dress, our manner, our actions and words...in all we do, shouldn't we strive to please God?" Millie asked. The girls were clearly listening to her intently, or she would have stopped right there. "Of course I want my outward appearance to be neat and clean. But I want God to look at my heart, and to see something beautiful there. My mother is the most beautiful woman I have ever known, even when she is tired and her hair is messy. She has taught me what inner beauty is—the kind of beauty that will last a lifetime. That matters so much more than where you live or what you wear."

"It's understandable that you should feel that way," Helen asked.

"What do you mean?" Millie asked, but a hush fell over the group as Mrs. Chetwood entered the sunporch carrying a tray with more lemonade and tea cakes for dessert. She quickly retreated, smiling at the girls as she went.

"I think our outward appearance, the appearance of a lady, is very important," Helen said, when she was gone. "Of course, it is most likely different for those who are not in our social circle. The lower classes, for example...the less educated...well, you know, it must be simply dreadful for them, but that is just how it is. Perhaps God was looking at their hearts when he gave them their humble circumstances. Perhaps they don't deserve any more. After all, everybody has their place, even if they long to leave it. Or do people in Ohio have a differing opinion?"

Millie felt her face growing hot again.

"Really, Helen, you can be such a snob," said Lu. "Not all servants are in dire straits. I imagine it's possible they are quite content in their world. Take Rhoda Jane Lightcap, for example. She is the most stubborn-headed girl I have ever known. I doubt she misses a minute of our parties and socials."

"Do you mean that she isn't invited or that she chooses not to attend?" Millie asked.

Claudina blushed this time. "You've not met Rhoda Jane, Millie. Her family lives just up the street from you. I'm sure you've noticed their shop. Mr. Lightcap was a blacksmith in our little town until he fell ill and died."

"Their house is not nearly as...big as yours, Millie," Lu said. "Their house is hardly more than a shack. And their mother doesn't have time for the church because she's so busy taking in washing to keep the wolf from the door. It's a shame really, because Gordon is so handsome. I wish he were a gentleman!"

Helen laughed and said, "Gordon Lightcap as a gentleman? It's too funny!"

"I'm afraid I don't understand," said Millie. "The mother works hard to feed her family. And the son, Gordon? If he is of good character, then isn't he a gentleman already?"

"People from Ohio seem to have very progressive ideas," Helen said. "But they may find they have progressed in the wrong direction!"

Claudina stood up, barely hiding her embarrassment. "Girls, I have to say that today's Bible study was of little value. At the very least, we should stay focused on the

Scripture at hand, which was, as I recall, about the important difference between outward appearances and what's in one's heart!"

Lu and Helen stared first at Claudina and then at Millie.

"What did I say?" Lu asked. "I am sorry if I spoke out of turn or offended anyone here. Though I do think I have a right to my opinion." She and Helen both stood to leave. Everyone said their good-byes, but Millie could barely speak. Her tears were too near falling.

When the other girls had left, she turned to Claudina.

"I am so sorry," she said. "It was a perfectly lovely afternoon and I spoiled it."

"I will admit we have never had a Bible study quite like that before," Claudina said. "But I don't think you said anything wrong. How can you study the Bible and not speak the truth? Besides, I know Helen and Lu. They will have forgotten about it by tomorrow." She walked Millie to the door.

"I want to apologize to you, Millie," she said. "I knew you were right, and I didn't stand up for you. I am so envious of your courage!"

"I was afraid to truly speak my mind," Millie confessed. "If my temper hadn't flared, I might not have. My friends in Lansdale would have chided me for that."

"Do you miss your friends?" Claudina asked.

"More than I can say."

Claudina linked arms with Millie as they walked down the steps. "How about this? I will pray for you, Millie Keith, to make new friends who will chide you daily about your temper. And you pray for me to have more courage to speak to my old friends."

"Oh, is it over already?" Mrs. Chetwood said, coming out onto the porch. "How was the study?"

Millie's Unsettled Season

"Terribly wonderful," said Millie.

"Wonderfully terrible," said Claudina, and they both burst out laughing.

As she walked home in the warm, clear sunshine, Millie paused when she saw the hand-lettered sign over the Lightcaps' shop and house. She couldn't help but wonder about Rhoda Jane and Gordon. She was sure they hadn't been at church. She didn't remember seeing the little girls at church, either. In Lansdale all of her friends had lived in neat brick homes in tree-lined neighborhoods. Had she known any poor people? What would she have thought if a girl who lived in a warehouse had come to her Bible study? Her thoughts were interrupted by a shout.

"Hello! Is this here the Keith house?" The girl's face was sun-browned, and she was hardly taller than Zillah. She wore a man's hat on her head. Her dress was shabby, but clean, and she appeared to be wearing a pair of men's overalls underneath instead of pantalets or petticoats.

"Yes," Millie said, extending her hand to the girl, "this is the Keith house. I'm Millie Keith."

"Yes'm," the girl replied, as she grasped Millie's offered hand in a firm grip and jerked it up and down like a pump handle. "My name is Celestia Ann Huntsinger and I come to work for your ma. Don't mistake me for my size. I can heft a cow, if I need to."

"We do have a cow," Millie said. "But I don't think she needs hefting. Won't you come in?"

Celestia Ann pulled off her hat at the doorstep, and Millie almost gasped. Her red hair was short, and as tangled as a

396

bird's nest. The girl saw Millie's look, and ran her hands over it.

"Too tangled to brush out," she said. "I guess I should have the barber chop it off, but I'm that picky about my head. Don't like anyone touching it. I'm a Christian, ma'am, and I thank the Lord for my red hair every day. Thank You!" she said, waving her hat at the sky, "In case I fergot!" And then in a whisper to Millie, "But it seems He could have made it less tangly."

Millie could only nod.

"When Mrs. Prior over to the Union told me you folks wanted a girl, I knew it was the good Lord's doin'," Celestia Ann said, squinting. "She said you was real Christian folk, and I can see it on you."

Millie almost laughed. Did the Lord have a sense of humor? Meeting Celestia Ann on the doorstep right after that prayer meeting...

"Celestia Ann, how old are you?" Millie asked as she opened the front door.

"Jes' turned seventeen years, ma'am. Why?"

"Because I have not yet turned thirteen years of age and since you are older, I think you ought to call me Millie, not 'ma'am'."

"Yes, ma'am, I'll do that. Thank you kindly, ma'am." Millie smiled and shook her head as Celestia Ann crossed the threshold of the Keiths' home.

If Marcia and Aunt Wealthy were taken aback by Celestia Ann's appearance, they showed no sign of it. Marcia interviewed the girl, asking about her previous experience and references before she hired her.

Aunt Wealthy showed her the small room they had curtained off in the back of the kitchen for her. Celestia Ann

ran her hands over the goose-down pillow and touched the oil lamp by her bed.

"It's as good as a palace," she declared, "and I'm glad to have it."

Millie had liked Celestia Ann from the moment she saw her. She was not surprised to hear that Mamma and Aunt Wealthy were of the same opinion. The very first day Celestia Ann proved herself a hard worker and a good cook. Cyril, Don, and Fan were mesmerized by the stories of Indians and wild animals that she spun effortlessly as she cooked. When Millie told her about the Indians they had met, Celestia Ann explained that they weren't permanent neighbors at all, just resting a few weeks as they passed through. The U.S. government was moving them all away. Celestia Ann, in turn, listened open-mouthed while Millie explained the reason the Keiths used only honey or maple sugar to sweeten their food. "You seen this all in print?" Celestia Ann asked. Millie produced the paper and read the article aloud. "I never knowed it. I will never touch a drop of sugar myself again. Never! To treat human be-uns like they was animals! That's wrong before God!"

After the table was set, Marcia invited Celestia Ann to sit with them during supper, but she was up and down the whole time bringing dishes from the kitchen and taking plates away.

"You are very quiet this evening," Stuart said, patting Zillah's head after dessert. "How were your studies today?"

Adah looked at Zillah, and Zillah looked at her plate. "I'm at the head of the class in spelling," she said.

"That's wonderful!" Aunt Wealthy said. "And how about you, Adah?"

Adah paused for a moment before she answered. "I like the girls," she said at last.

"You two look exhausted," Aunt Wealthy said. "Studying and playing must be hard work."

"Yes," said Adah. "I am very tired."

"And how were my boys today?" Stuart asked. "The climate was certainly amenable to outdoor activities."

Celestia Ann's fork paused in mid air.

"He means we're having nice weather," Millie explained.

"Powerful nice," Celestia Ann agreed. "When the good Lord sends us a sweet cool spell in summer, like this un here, a body ain't even got a fightin' chance of breakin' a sweat! We all oughta thank Him good."

"Amen, Miss Huntsinger," Stuart said. "Amen!"

CHAPTER

New Experiences

*Do not forget to entertain strangers,
for by so doing, some people have
entertained angels without
knowing it.*

HEBREWS 13:2

New Experiences

*I*n a little over a week, Celestia Ann Huntsinger was well on her way to becoming a full-fledged member of the Keith family. Marcia cut down one of Millie's old dresses for her, and Aunt Wealthy found one of hers that would just fit the girl. Millie even persuaded the girl to let her tease the knots out of her hair. Celestia Ann would only sit still for this in the evenings, while the family gathered to hear Stuart or Marcia read, so the project took almost the full week, but the result was amazing: an elf-like sprite with a halo of red curls to match her freckles.

Not only was Celestia Ann a very diligent worker, but proud of her talents, too. She loved to show Millie how things were 'done on the frontier,' but if she found that Marcia, Wealthy, or Millie had done some small chore that she considered part of her job, her feelings were hurt.

Marcia had more time to spend with the younger children, and Millie had more time to spend with friends. One day, Millie found herself lying flat on a quilt in the fading summer twilight. She and Claudina had spent the afternoon together on the Keiths' hilltop, swinging and twining flowers in their hair. The early evening was alive with the noise of crickets and a lonely frog by the well. The scent of grass and flowers mingled with the delicious smell of Celestia Ann's blackberry cobbler cooling on the kitchen windowsill.

The girls were exhausted but happy. Millie's twin braids were now fastened with blue ribbons and cheerful daisies; Claudina's long dark curls wore a wreath of delicate lavender blossoms.

Millie's Unsettled Season

"Do you know that this spot is lovely in the gloaming?" Millie asked.

"I might agree with you, if I knew what a 'gloaming' was," Claudina said.

Millie smiled, but it was a sad smile. Camilla would have known what the gloaming was. Claudina was fast becoming a friend, but Millie still missed discussing books and ideas and dreams for the future more than she could say. And though she wrote letters to her friends faithfully each week, the ones she received in reply were few and far between.

"The gloaming is the twilight just before dark," Millie said. "When the shadows all turn purple."

"Oh, why didn't you just say that? Of course it's lovely then."

"In the gloaming," Millie said dreamily. "It's lovely in the gloaming."

"If you keep filling your head with words from books, Millie Keith, you will have no time for fun. Have your parents decided if you can go to Beth's party?"

Millie had received the invitation two days before. Beth Roe was holding a rag-rolling party and all of the young ladies in the neighborhood were invited. They would work all afternoon making rag balls to be used for making rugs, and of course Mamma and Pappa would have no objection to that; but after the work was done, the young men were invited for games and dessert.

"Pappa said he was sure that the Roes are respectable," Millie said. "And he was sure that my behavior would be impeccable."

"Are you serious!" Claudina said. "You can come?"

Millie nodded. "I must confess, I am a little nervous. The last time I appeared in public it was a disaster."

New Experiences

Claudina threw a daisy at her, and Millie smiled.

"Honestly," Millie said, "I haven't seen Helen or Lu since your ill-fated Bible study, except at church."

"Oh," Claudina lay back down, "you should have no fear then. You won't see Helen or Lu at a rag-rolling party. The Roes are not cultivated people, or very refined, but they're good folks and kind neighbors. If there is trouble or sickness they are the first ones to offer help. I'm so glad your parents are letting you go. The Roes would be dreadfully hurt if you should decline their invitation."

"What time does one arrive for a rag party?" Millie asked, as the girls rose and began walking home.

"We are invited to work, you know," said Claudina, laughing, "so we will be expected early, no later than one o'clock, I think. And it's not very nice work—carpet rags are apt to be dusty—so you shouldn't wear anything that will not wash. I'm wearing a calico dress and carrying a big work apron with me, and bringing my own sewing basket."

"Then I'll do the same. And I'm sure Celestia Ann will come. She's invited too, you know."

The girls arrived at the Big Yellow House and sat outside near the shed, admiring Belle and chatting gaily until it was time for Claudina to leave.

Suddenly, Zillah called from the back door, "Millie! The Indians are coming!"

Millie and Claudina hurried to the back door and in through the kitchen.

"The Indians ain't comin'," Celestia Ann said, as they passed through the kitchen. "The Indians are here!"

And they were indeed, standing in the dining room, and the sitting room, filling the open door, spilling out into the front yard and the street. Tall men with still faces, women with little children, and tiny babies with dark, solemn eyes.

Wealthy was speaking French with the man who appeared to be their leader.

"He's the one that gave us the berries," Zillah said. "And there's his wife!"

Millie looked through the front window and gasped. The street in front of their house was full of Indians, some on horseback, some on foot.

"His name is Pe-pe-ne-way," Wealthy said. "The government agent told them they have to leave. He said Millie invited him to meet her parents."

Millie stepped forward and spoke in her best French, "Welcome to our house."

He nodded, then spoke too quickly for her to understand. She looked despairingly at Wealthy.

"He said good-bye, and that you will not see them again. The U.S. government says they must go west, west of the Mississippi, where there are fewer white people."

"They're walkin' the whole way? The poor things! They look tuckered already!" said Celestia Ann. She was past Millie in a flash and out on the porch. She made her way through the Potawatami people to the well and started cranking.

"Can we get cups, Mamma?" Millie asked.

"Good thinking," Marcia said. "Hurry now."

The young Keiths rushed to the kitchen for the cups, and by the time Celestia Ann had pulled the bucket of water up, they were waiting.

She filled the cups from the dipper, and the children carried them to the waiting people, offering cool well water in fine china cups to everyone who was thirsty.

The Indians were of all ages, from ancient warriors to babies tied into little wooden troughs that the mothers

stood up on end on the ground. The babies were very quiet, and all you could see of them were their little round faces and dark eyes. They were wrapped in cloth that pinned their arms and legs, with nothing to amuse them but a string of tiny bells across the trough in front of their faces.

The horses dragged travois behind them, full of bundles wrapped in hides and blankets. One travois was the bed of an ancient warrior. Millie stopped to offer him a drink, but he turned his face away from her and closed his eyes. A tiny old woman spoke to him sternly, but still he wouldn't accept the drink.

Aunt Wealthy was standing on the front porch, watching, and as the people drank, she started to speak. Her French was smooth and beautiful, but Millie couldn't follow it all.

"What is she saying, Mamma?" Millie whispered when she went back to the porch.

"She's telling them about Jesus," her mother said quietly.

The Indians listened politely until she was done, and then Pe-pe-ne-way spoke.

"He says that he's heard of this Jesus before, and believes he is a powerful God. He says that if we are friends of Jesus, we should ask Him to help the Potawatami. Their own friends have left them, and their life is leaving them, too. He is asking us to pray for them."

Wealthy bowed her head and prayed, and there were tears running down her cheeks. Then Pe-pe-ne-way nodded his head, turned, and walked away. His people followed him down the street. The Keiths watched until they disappeared.

Millie could hardly touch her supper that night.

"Where are the babies going to sleep, Pappa?" Zillah asked. "Will they have houses west of the Mississippi? What will they eat?"

Millie's Unsettled Season

"They will have to make houses," Stuart said. "And they will eat deer and fish and berries."

"At least there won't be white people there, puttin' up fences and kicking them from one place to the next," Celestia Ann said.

"Not yet," said Stuart. "Not yet."

That night at bedtime, they prayed for the Indians again.

The next day, Millie dressed for the rag party in her oldest calico dress and a huge work apron.

"Oh, you're beautiful," Celestia Ann exclaimed when she saw her. "Girl, you could dress in a feed sack and still look like an angel!"

Millie thanked her for the compliment, yet she couldn't help but wonder what her old friends would think of this party dress, or of her leaving home with the maid to attend the same party.

"Don't worry, Millie," Celestia Ann said as they walked down the path. "I'll show you just what to do."

A dozen young ladies, mostly under twenty years of age, were collected in "the front room" at the Roe's house. Millie knew most of them from church, except one pretty girl perhaps a year older than herself, wearing a thin, worn dress. She knew she had seen her before, but couldn't place her until Celestia Ann shouted, "Rhoda Jane! I'm glad as that to see you up and about!"

It was Emmaretta and Minerva's sister, and Millie had seen her the day the cow ran away. She remembered Rhoda Jane's shy smile, and was ashamed that she had been thinking so much of her own embarrassment that she hadn't smiled back. She smiled now, but Rhoda Jane merely nodded.

New Experiences

A large basket filled with many colored rags, torn or cut into strips of various lengths, was set in the middle of the floor. A number of girls were grouped about it, armed with needles and thread, scissors and thimbles. Millie watched for a moment as they picked out the strips, sewed the ends together, and wound the long strips into balls. Some girls had filled their aprons with rags and seated themselves here and there about the room. They seemed a very merry company, laughing and chatting as they worked.

"Oh, how d'ye do?" said Beth, catching sight of Millie. "Thought you wasn't comin' at all." She leaned close to Millie and whispered, "Sorry about that at the butcher's. Ma didn't know you were regular folk, but Mrs. Prior said you was." And then more loudly, "Let me take your hat. Here's a seat for you 'long side of Miss Chetwood. Guess you're better acquainted with her than anybody else."

"Ladies, this is Miss Keith and Celestia Ann."

"I don't need no introduction," laughed Celestia Ann. "'Ope you're well, Miss Beth."

The others looked up with a nod and a murmured word or two, as Beth named each in turn. Then they seemed to take up their conversation where it had been dropped, while Millie tied on her apron and took the chair assigned her. She threaded a needle and helping herself, by invitation, from Claudina's lap, began her first ball.

"Are we all here now?" asked someone.

"All but Damaris Drybread. She's oldish for the rest of us, but she's the schoolmarm, you know, and likes to be invited. She works dreadful fast when she does get at it."

"Pshaw! I wish she hadn't been asked. She spoils everything. She's as solemn as a funeral and 'pears to think it's a sin to laugh."

"Yes," added another voice, "that's so and she never forgets that she's a schoolmarm, but takes it upon herself to tell you your duty without waiting to be invited to."

"Hush!" Beth said. "That's her now."

"Good afternoon," Damaris Drybread said in solemn tone, addressing the company in general. She made a stiff little bow, then giving her sunbonnet to Beth, she seated herself in a bolt upright manner and fell to work.

The laughter went out of the room like the light of a lantern that was turned down. Millie studied Damaris's face. How could her mere presence be such a damper? Perhaps if they gave her a chance, she would join the fun.

"I wonder," Millie said loudly, "if any of you know which territory is mentioned in the Bible?"

"There weren't no territories then, nor states neither," Beth laughed, "so none could be mentioned."

"Oh!" Millie said, feigning surprise. "I must have misread it. I thought it said, "Noah looked out of the ark and saw...""

"Arkansas!" they yelled.

"Who's the shortest man in the Bible?"

"Zacchaeus?" someone guessed.

"Bildad. He was just a Shu-hite."

"I thought it was Nee-high-miah," Claudina said, and everyone laughed.

She glanced at Damaris again. The schoolmarm's face had become even more grave. But the smiles were returned and everyone giggled as Claudina and one or two others began telling jokes, too.

"I declare I haven't laughed so hard since hens grew teeth!" Celestia Ann said at last.

The laughter died again as Miss Drybread spoke. "Permit me to observe to you all that life is too serious and

solemn to be spent in laughing and joking. Allow me to say, Miss Keith, that I am astonished that you, a church member, should indulge in such frivolity."

"Do you think a Christian should always wear a long face?" asked Millie.

"I think that folks who claim to be religious ought to be grave and sober, and let the world see that they don't belong to it."

"But surely there is no harm in laughter," Millie said, "and if anybody in the world has a right to be happy, wouldn't it be the ones who know that Jesus loves them?"

"There is a season for all things," Damaris Drybread said, drawing herself up. "And I believe it is unseemly to laugh and joke when people are suffering and dying."

"People are getting married and being born too," Rhoda Jane said, almost defiantly. "Flowers are bursting into bloom, and breezes are whispering."

"You are hardly an expert on religion," Damaris countered.

"That is true," Rhoda Jane said. "I, for one, want none of your long-faced, sour-looking religion!"

"But," Millie said, "the Bible is full of commands to God's people to rejoice, to be glad, to sing for joy, and the best Christians I know are the happiest people on earth."

"You're rather young to set yourself up as the judge of who's the best Christian," returned Damaris condescendingly. "Don't you think?"

"No, I don't think so at all," Millie replied. "Jesus said, 'By their fruits you will know them.' When I see people serving God with gladness, walking in His ways, rejoicing in His love, and making the Bible always their rule of faith and practice, I think I can be safe in saying they are Christians."

Millie's Unsettled Season

"I think so, too!" said Claudina emphatically. She looked startled, then a little pleased.

"So do I." "And I," chimed in several other voices.

"And you know these people?" Damaris asked. "I'm sure we would all like to meet them."

"Of course," Millie said. "I'm talking about my father and mother. And dear Aunt Wealthy, too."

"That's a fact," spoke up Celestia Ann. "You 'ave to live with folks to find 'em out, and I've lived there and I never seen better Christians. They don't keep their religion for Sundays, but Mr. Keith 'e reads in the good book every night and mornin' and prays just like a minister — only not so long — and they sing 'ymns. And I never 'eard a cross word pass between Mr. and Mrs. or Miss Stanhope neither, and they never threaten the children that they'll do something awful like breakin' their bones or skinnin' 'em alive, as some folks do; but just speaks to 'em quiet-like, sayin' exactly what they mean. And they're always minded, too."

"There had better be less talk and more work if these rags are all to be sewed today," remarked Miss Drybread, taking a fresh supply from the basket, then straightening herself till she was, if possible, more erect than before.

"I can talk and work too; my needle haint stopped because my tongue was runnin'," said Celestia Ann, "and it strikes me you've been doin' your share of gabbin' as well's the rest."

CHAPTER 15

A Special Gift

See how the lilies of the field grow. They do not labor or spin, yet I tell you that not even Solomon in all his splendor was dressed like one of these.

MATTHEW 6:28-29

A Special Gift

y second ball's done," said Claudina, tossing it up.

"A good one too, and wound tight," said Beth, giving it a squeeze, then rolling it into a corner where quite a pile had collected.

"How can you roll so quickly, Claudina?" Millie asked, hoping to change the mood.

"I've been at it quite a while. But some here can make two to my one." She glanced toward Miss Drybread, who was just beginning to wind her second.

"I suggest a contest," Millie said, "and the prize will be my silver thimble!"

The young ladies began to stitch and wind with determination. Millie focused on stitching her fabric into long strips. She had quite a pile of them tangled on her lap when she looked up.

"I'd begin to wind if I were you, Millie," Claudina laughed, "or your thimble is lost!"

"That's three!" Damaris Drybread said, tossing a ball into the corner.

"Four," Rhoda Jane said, throwing one right after it.

Damaris gave her a grim look, and her fingers flew.

Rhoda Jane smiled and stretched, then picked up another rag. She looked relaxed, but her fingers were moving just as fast as Miss Drybread's, if not faster.

"I think my thimble is already lost," Millie whispered, leaning close to Claudina.

They worked in silence, each intent on her own ball.

"Supper's ready," announced Mrs. Roe, opening the kitchen door.

"Put down your rags, ladies," said Beth.

"Five!" Damaris said triumphantly, holding up her final ball of rags.

"Six." Everyone turned to look at Rhoda Jane, who was also holding up her last ball.

"I believe you have won," Damaris said sourly.

"I believe I have." Rhoda Jane smiled.

"Celestia Ann, why haven't you been throwin' your rags in the corner?" Beth asked. "You have a pile!"

"Din't want to waste time countin' till the rollin' was done," the girl said with a mischievous smile. There were rag balls scattered in her lap and at her feet. "It appears it's done now." She picked up a ball and tossed it in the corner.

"One," she said. By the time she reached four, the whole room was counting with her. "Five…," Damaris and Rhoda Jane exchanged a look. " Six. Seven. Eight!"

"All nice-sized and tightly-wrapped too," Beth announced.

The girls cheered as Millie gave Celestia Ann her thimble and a hug.

"Now it's time for supper," Beth said.

"It seems that I, for one, need some preparation," said Millie, looking at her hands.

"Oh, yes, we'll wash out here," said Beth, leading the way.

A tin bucket full of water, a dipper and washbasin, all bright from a recent scouring, stood on a bench in the shed at the outer kitchen door. A piece of brown soap lay there also, and a clean wash towel hung on a nail on the wall close by. The girls used these in turn, laughing and chatting merrily all the while.

When they gathered about the table, they found it bountifully spread with good plain country fare — chicken, ham,

dried beef, pickles, tomatoes, cucumbers and radishes, cheese, eggs, pie, cake and preserves in several varieties, hot cakes and cold bread, tea and coffee.

None of the family partook with their guests except Beth. Claudina explained to Millie that they would eat afterwards, when the guests had all had their fill. Mrs. Roe busied herself waiting upon the table, filling the tea and coffee cups in the shed where the cooking stove stood during the months of the year when its heat was objectionable in the house.

"I don't know as we've earned our supper, Miz' Roe," remarked Celestia Ann, stirring her tea. "We hain't begun to git all them rags sewed up yet."

"Well, then, I'll just set you to work again as soon as you're done eating. Folks don't always pay in advance, you know."

"And if we don't finish before the boys come, we'll make them help," said Rhoda Jane.

"Boys don't use needles," Damaris said. Some of the girls giggled.

"I don't see why not," Rhoda Jane said. "They've got fingers. And I think some of them are pretty old to be called boys."

"Yes, that's true," said a girl. "Rod Stuefield must be thirty at least."

"And Nick Ransquate's twenty-five if he's a day," remarked another.

"Well, the rest's young enough," said Mrs. Roe. "Pass that cake there, Rhoda Jane. There's Gordon Lightcap who just turned sixteen, and York Monocker, Wallace Ormsby, my own Joe, and Claudina's brother Bill, are all younger than him."

Millie's Unsettled Season

The meal concluded, the work went on quite briskly again. Millie caught now and then a whispered word or two about getting through with it in time to have some fun. She rose to help Beth and Mrs. Roe carry the dishes to the kitchen. Everyone else was so much quicker at winding the rag balls, she felt she could be of better help there.

"Look!" said Beth, as they deposited a load on the sideboard. "There's Gordon and Joe." Millie followed her gaze. Two young men in rough work clothes were standing outside the window, looking up intently at something above them.

"Joe's the one with the hat," Beth said. "And Gordon's the handsome one!"

Joe glanced in the window, as if he sensed they were talking about him. He made a face at Beth, and tipped his cap to Millie; then lifted one muddy workboot and put it into the stirrup Gordon Lightcap had made out of his hands. Gordon lifted, and Joe practically sailed up out of sight. There was a brief scraping on the wall and a thud above their heads.

"What on earth are they doing?" Millie asked, as Gordon reached up, took hold of something, and walked up the wall like a mountain climber.

"Goin' up to Joe's room to change. Claudina's here," Beth giggled, "and Joe's plum sweet on her. He wants to slick up afore she sees him. Oh!" Beth clapped her hand over her mouth. "I wasn't s'posed to tell nobody that."

"Don't worry," Millie said. "I can keep a secret."

Joe and Gordon appeared in less than half an hour, dropping out of the sky the same way they had gone, quite "slicked up," as Beth elegantly expressed it, though their preparations had been made under difficulty. Their hair

was neatly combed, and their shirts and pants clean and pressed.

Joe tapped on the window.

"My land!" Beth exclaimed, opening the window, "what a time you've been up there. I never knowed you to take half as long to dress before."

"My fingers are all thumbs," Joe said, a hot flush spreading over his sunburnt face when he realized Millie was still in the room. "I can't tie this tie decent noway at all. Pardon, Miss."

"Well, just wait till I can wipe my hands, and I'll do it." Beth wiped her hands then leaned out the window. "There, that'll do. The girls aren't going to look real hard at that bit o' black ribbon."

"Maybe not, but I'm obliged to you all the same for fixin' it right."

The boys decided to wait in the yard until more of the fellows arrived. Millie and Beth went back to their work, finished the dishes and retired to the sitting room. When the young men finally entered, there were three together — Joe, Gordon, and Nicholas Ransquate.

Nicholas was short and thick-set, had scarcely any hair, and moved like a man made of wood. He carried his head thrown back on his shoulders. Even his face was stiff, with large features and a stolid expression. But he was not bashful in the least, and seemed to have no fear that his society would be less than acceptable to anyone he might meet.

"Good evening, ladies. I'm happy to see you all," he said, making a sweeping bow to the company, hat in hand. "And I hope I see you well."

"Well, you seen us," someone quipped, and the girls giggled.

"Good evening," responded several voices more politely.

"Good evenin', Mr. Lightcap." Millie was surprised to hear Celestia Ann's voice.

Gordon glanced at her and smiled.

"Find yourselves seats and we'll give you employment threading our needles for us," Rhoda Jane said, "for I hear your species cannot sew."

Beth introduced Nicholas to Millie, and then managed to seat him on the far side of the room next to Damaris Drybread, upon whom Nicholas bestowed a smile.

"Ah, the charming schoolmarm. May I untangle your rags as you wind?"

"As you wish," Damaris said stoically.

Gordon took an empty chair by his sister's side, and Joe sat by him.

"I guess you never sewed carpet rags before," Joe said to Millie.

"Is it my awkwardness that makes you think so?" Millie asked with a smile.

"No," he said, "you do it...beautiful!" His eyes were fixed on Claudina, whose dark tresses reflected the candlelight as she picked up more rags. "I mean...I...what did you say?"

"Let me give you some work," Millie said, taking pity on his embarrassment. "Will you thread this needle for me?"

"And then mine, please," put in Claudina, who had seated herself on Millie's other side.

Joe struggled with Millie's needle, and then reached for Claudina's. When he returned it she smiled, and to his apparent delight launched into a reminiscence of a candy-pulling they had both attended the year before. Millie was able to sew without saying a word.

A Special Gift

By twos and threes the other "boys" came flocking in. The room was getting crowded, and there was some tossing back and forth of the balls, amid rather loud laughter. But some of them unwound and became entangled, and so that sport was given up and the work put away. The girls washed their hands as they had before supper.

Damaris Drybread situated herself in a corner while the group cleared the floor for Blindman's Bluff. Millie found herself laughing out loud as Nicholas allowed himself to be blindfolded, spun in place, then staggered around the room trying to tag the others as if he were no more than Rupert's age. It was ridiculous and hilarious at the same time, and by the end of the game, the only one not laughing was Damaris Drybread, who had situated herself in a corner and refused all offers to play.

Other games were suggested and played with as much zest as if the revelers had been a group of children. Then refreshments followed, served up in the kitchen.

There was more laughter and stories of other parties as huckleberries with cream and sugar, watermelons, muskmelons, doughnuts, and cupcakes were devoured.

At ten o'clock the party broke up. Nicholas offered to see Celestia Ann and Millie safely home, but Celestia Ann just laughed.

"It's not more than a hop, skip, and a jump," she said. "I don't expect we need mindin'."

As they walked home through the moonlight, Celestia Ann talked about the party and the games, but Millie was thinking about Damaris sitting, stiff and aloof, as everyone played.

Lord, Millie prayed. *Show her Your joy!*

Millie's Unsettled Season

"That was the strangest party I have ever been to," Millie confessed the next morning as she helped Mamma with Annis. "Not like a Lansdale party at all."

"Do you miss the gowns and the dances?" her mother asked, with a twinkle in her eye.

"Yes," Millie admitted. "It's not vanity to love dressing up, is it, Mamma?"

"No, not unless you become prideful, or consider others less than yourself."

Millie sighed. "It's too bad there is nothing in Pleasant Plains to dress up for," she said.

"Really?" Marcia asked. "Then I suppose you haven't heard of the Christmas social."

"A social?"

"That's what I hear. In mid-December the whole town is invited to a grand ball. It's three months away, but girls are ordering their dresses already, and fabric is flying off the shelves at the store."

"Mamma, are we going? I could alter the yellow gown I wore last year to Bea's party. It still fits."

"That's true, you haven't grown an inch. But that dress just doesn't suit you anymore."

"What do you mean?"

"I mean," said Marcia, "that you are becoming a young lady. That yellow dress is much too young for you." She pointed to a crate chair. "You might find a package under there, if you were to look."

Millie lifted the crate top and saw a brown paper package. She tore it open to find yards of emerald green silk.

A Special Gift

"Oh, Mamma! Where did this come from? I'm sure there is nothing like it in the store!"

"I'm sure there is not. Did you think I would forget that my daughter was turning thirteen in December? I bought it in Lansdale, and have carried it along. And in three months time, we are going to make the most beautiful dress Pleasant Plains has ever seen!"

For the next week they poured over patterns and catalogues that Aunt Wealthy pulled out of nowhere. She also produced a beautiful length of French lace for collar and cuffs. Every detail was planned before scissors ever touched the silk. Marcia measured carefully, suggesting that if Millie wore heels they could leave the skirt long. Then she would be assured of wearing the dress more than once, even if she decided to grow. If she did not, it could always be hemmed. Finally, Aunt Wealthy laid out the pattern and the fabric was cut.

Aunt Wealthy was working on a gown of wine-colored velvet for Celestia Ann, who protested that she would not wear it, but loved to feel the fabric, even so.

It wasn't the same without Bea and Annabeth, but Millie loved sitting up late with Mamma and Aunt Wealthy, with needles busy, talking about everything under the sun.

CHAPTER

16

Another Rescue

*Rescue the weak and needy;
deliver them from the hand
of the wicked.*

PSALM 82:4

Another Rescue

The leaves on the maples, oaks and sycamores began to turn slowly from every shade of green to gold and russet, orange and scarlet. The air, which had been heavy and hot, gradually grew cooler, and the mornings were quite brisk. Millie's gingham-checked dresses and white pantalets were put away for heavier, darker-colored frocks, and cotton stockings. The carefree, rough and tumble days of summer were seemingly gone overnight, and autumn was upon them.

Rupert spent almost as much of his time at the office with his father as he did working around the house. Adah and Zillah had settled into school, and Cyril, Don, and Fan spent their days exploring with Wannago or pretending to be Indians, and their evenings listening to Bible stories at Pappa's side.

The routine of the Keith household had been restored, even in the Big Yellow House. Marcia had somehow worked the pieces of her life, as a Christian woman, wife, mother of eight, mistress of a growing household, and volunteer to charitable causes, into a beautiful quilt that kept her family warm and safe.

"Make sure the boys and Fan eat something," she told Millie one day as she and Wealthy left for a meeting of the ladies society. "We will be back before the girls return from school."

Millie curled on a cushion in a beam of sunlight, her Bible open on her lap, gazing out the window. She could see Fan sitting with her back to the tree in the yard, and her head on her knees. She looked so much like Zillah. Millie shook her head. Her little sister had become so solemn in the last few weeks since Zillah and Adah had begun school with Damaris Drybread.

Millie remembered Damaris in the corner of the room at the rag party, a look of disapproval on her face. How could she possibly show God's joy and love to the children in her classroom if she did not have it herself? Or was it possible that God expected such solemnity of a teacher?

Millie read the verse before her. "Not many of you should presume to be teachers, my brothers, because you know that we who teach will be judged more strictly," said James 3:1. Perhaps Miss Drybread was so rigid and solemn because she feared being judged. But surely she knew that God was a loving Father! The very next verse, James 3:2, said, "We all stumble in many ways. If anyone is never at fault in what he says, he is a perfect man, able to keep his whole body in check." God knew that no one was perfect, not even a teacher. If He had grace for His children, how much more must He have for those who loved His children and wanted to teach them? Millie was sure God loved Mr. Martin, her beloved teacher in Lansdale, because Mr. Martin obviously loved Him and all of His children.

She shut her Bible and put it on the table by her bed, then gazed once again out the window. Fan was still sitting against the tree, her head on her knees. Was she sad, or missing Zillah and Adah?

Millie walked downstairs and out across the yard. Fan didn't lift her head up.

"Are you sad, kitten?" Millie asked, gathering her skirts and sitting down beside her.

"Yes," Fan said. "I'm mad, too."

"Why are you mad?" Millie asked, surprised.

"Because they tied me to the tree," Fan said.

"Tied!" Millie leaned over. Don's rope was around Fan's waist, hidden by her apron. The knot was behind the tree where the little girl couldn't reach it.

"The wicked rascals!" Millie said, working at the knot. "Why did they tie you up?" Don's knots were getting better. He'd pulled the cords tight, and Millie had to work hard to loosen them.

"Because they went on the warpath, that's why," Fan said, as Millie worked to free her. "They always leave me!"

"On the warpath?"

"Yep," Fan said. "They're gonna rescue Zillah and Adah from the witch."

"Miss Drybread is not a witch. She's just a…a…"

"Adah said she was a witch."

"She did?"

Fan nodded. "And Cyril, he said that he was gonna save Zillah and Adah, cause that's what Jesus would do. And Jesus was brave, and He wouldn't be afraid, even if He wasn't an Indian."

The knots finally came loose, and Fan jumped up. "I'm gonna catch 'em," she said, starting for the path that led over the hill to the schoolhouse.

"Oh, no, you are not." Millie caught her by her apron strings and pulled her back. "I think you need to come talk to Celestia Ann, while I go find Cyril and Don before they get into trouble."

"I want to go, too!"

"Celestia Ann is baking gingerbread," Millie said, "and she might let you lick the bowl. Let's go ask her."

Millie explained the situation briefly to Celestia Ann.

"Good for them," Celestia Ann said, brandishing a wooden spoon. "It warn't my place to say, but if'n I had two

little ones like Zillah and Adah, I wouldn't send them to Drybones to learn nothin'!"

"I'm sure Mamma and Pappa wouldn't want us to call her that," Millie said.

"I expect you're right," Celestia Ann said, "but it fits. You want to lick the whole bowl yourself?" she asked Fan.

Fan considered this a moment.

"Can I wear war paint while I lick it?"

"Why not?" asked Celestia Ann. She dabbed a finger in the soot along the rim of the coal bucket, then traced a black line down Fan's nose, and another across her cheeks.

Millie left Fan chattering happily. She walked briskly up the path toward the top of the hill, praying under her breath as she went. What could Adah have meant, calling the teacher such a name? It wasn't like her at all.

She reached the top of the hill, and she could see the schoolhouse across the valley. Smoke curled out of the chimney in the cool of the morning. Millie could just imagine the little scholars inside, safe and sound, not suspecting in the least the excitement that was about to ensue. In fact, it was upon them now, for Cyril and Don had almost reached the school, coonskin caps bobbing as they ran from one bush or rock to another, and ducked for cover.

"Cyriiiil! Don!" Millie called, but she was sure they couldn't hear her. The boys had reached the woodpile beside the school. Cyril climbed up the stack of wood as if it were a staircase, stepped across on the roof and reached down for something Don handed up to him. When Cyril stood up, Millie could see he had a large shake shingle and a rock. He started across the roof, placing his moccasin-clad feet carefully, like a cat.

Millie didn't realize what he was doing until he reached the chimney. He laid the shingle over the smoking hole and put the rock on top of it to keep it in place, then started back the way he had come.

Millie reached the schoolyard just as they jumped off the woodpile.

"Cyril and Don Keith!" They both whirled. Their faces were striped with berry juice.

"Shhhh!" Cyril said. "They'll hear you."

"I don't care if they do," Millie said. "You go right back up there and take that shingle off the chimney. The whole school will fill with smoke!"

Cyril smiled his gap-toothed smile and nodded. At that moment, the schoolhouse door burst open, and children exploded into the schoolyard, choking and coughing. Smoke poured out of the door behind them.

"What on earth!" Miss Drybread came out last of all, craning her neck to look up at the roof.

"Run, Zillah, Adah!" Don yelled. "Now's your chance!"

Zillah and Adah caught sight of Millie, and did indeed run toward her. Miss Drybread followed.

"Is this your doing?" she demanded. "We will have that shingle off the chimney this instant, and all of my scholars back in school!" She reached for Zillah's hand.

"No, Millie, don't let her take them," Cyril cried. "She's a bad old witch! She said she's gonna burn 'em up in the stove!"

Zillah backed up against Millie's side.

"Is this true?" Millie asked the little girl.

Zillah hid her head in Millie's apron, but Adah said, "Yes."

Miss Drybread's face went very white, and she took a step forward.

Cyril and Don, losing their courage, jumped behind Millie, and now all of the little Keiths peeked around her at the woman. What should she do? Surely the teacher was an authority over her sisters. But something was clearly wrong. *Jesus, help me know what to do!* she prayed silently, then squatted and put her arm around her sister.

"What did she say, Zillah?" Millie asked.

"She said she was going to roast to death any child who talks too much," Adah whispered. "She said she was going to build up the fire hot and put them in the stove and cook them!"

"Surely you didn't believe her," Millie said.

"Yes," Zillah said. She was trembling, and Millie could tell she was frightened. "I wasn't afraid for me, Millie, really I wasn't. But Adah is too little to know not to talk!"

"This is nonsense," Miss Drybread said. "I merely said that to keep them quiet in class. Now as soon as that board is removed, we will all return to our studies."

"The board will be removed," Millie said, standing up, "but no Keith is going to return to this classroom."

"Aren't you taking a bit much on yourself again?" Miss Drybread said. "That decision will be made by your parents, I think."

"I am sure that I speak for my parents, for they are very strict about telling lies," Millie said, pulling her sisters close. "Cyril, get back on the roof and remove that shingle."

For once in his life, Cyril ran to obey her. He scrambled back up the woodpile and jumped to the roof, pulled the shingle off, and smoke began to pour out of the chimney once more. Millie gathered her brothers and sisters and started for home, leaving Miss Drybread and her class standing in the schoolyard.

Another Rescue

When Marcia came home that afternoon, she found all of her children waiting for her. The story started spilling out of them before she even removed her hat. Fan and Celestia Ann, who had heard it told at least once already, crowded around to hear it again. When the children finished their tale, she gave them all hugs and put her hat right back on.

"I think I need to have a talk with your Pappa," she said.

"We're in really big trouble," Cyril said. "Ain't we?" His face still had red stripes where the berry juice war paint had stained it, and the rest of it was red from trying to scrub it off.

"Boys who take matters into their own hands instead of consulting their pappa can expect to be disciplined," she said. Cyril's face fell, and Don gulped. "But your Pappa is a fair man, and you were trying to save your sister. I don't think you have too much to fear."

It was a solemn afternoon at the Keith house as the children waited for their parents to arrive. It became more solemn still when Stuart and Marcia came home and explained that they had been to see Miss Drybread, and while Adah and Zillah were not going back, Cyril and Don were expected to write letters of apology for calling her such a terrible name.

Stuart took each of the boys aside and spoke to them privately, and then gathered the children together. "It would break my heart if you did not tell me when you have trouble," he said.

If Stuart noticed that when Celestia Ann served the gingerbread for dessert, Cyril and Don not only had the biggest pieces, they had the only pieces with whipped cream and maple sugar, he didn't say a word.

Later that evening, after prayers had been said and children tucked in, Millie sat with her Bible and her oil lamp's warm glow.

"He who desires to be a teacher desires a good thing," she read.

Lord, she prayed silently. *I know I can't do this without You. But You know the desire of my heart. And wouldn't this be a good time to start?* She prayed for a few moments longer, and then went downstairs to the room where her parents and Aunt Wealthy were sitting by the fire.

"Millie!" Stuart said, "I thought you were in bed."

"I was, Pappa." She sat on the couch beside him, pulled up her feet and tucked them into her nightgown. "But I wanted to talk to you and Mamma about what happened today."

He set his reading down.

"I am afraid I did not treat Miss Drybread in a very Christian manner. But I didn't know what to do."

"I think you did very well," Marcia said, sighing. "Miss Drybread has a great deal of knowledge, but…"

" 'Knowledge puffs up, but love builds up'," Wealthy quoted, and sniffed.

"Perhaps she will learn," Marcia said gently. "And one day she will be an excellent teacher."

"That's what I wanted to speak to you about, Mamma," Millie said. "Zillah and Adah shouldn't neglect their studies. I was wondering if…"

"Yes?"

"I want to be their teacher. I know I can teach them reading and sums. And with your help, and Aunt Wealthy's…"

"That's quite a responsibility," Stuart said. "Some people would even say these are the most important years of their education. If they don't learn to love learning…"

"That's just it, Pappa," Millie said earnestly. "I may not have all of the knowledge I need. But I love my sisters. And I love to learn. I think I might make a good teacher."

Another Rescue

"I'm very proud of you for asking," Stuart said, wrapping her in a hug. "But your mother and I will have to discuss it and pray about it. We will let you know in the morning."

"Yes, Pappa." Millie gave her father a kiss, and then gave one to Mamma and Aunt Wealthy before she went to bed. She could hear their voices in earnest conversation as she climbed the stairs, but she tried hard not to listen.

⌒

When Millie sat down to breakfast the next morning, she found a cowbell by her plate.

"What's this, Pappa?" she asked.

"Why, I thought you might like it. You will need something to call your scholars to class."

"Really?" she jumped from her chair and gave him a hug.

Before a week had passed, Millie had established a routine. Her daily teaching job began with a time of private prayer and Scripture reading in a corner of her room. After breakfast, she gathered her students in the sitting room for prayer. Reading, penmanship, and sums were finished by noon, with Millie grading papers as her scholars worked.

Marcia or Aunt Wealthy often looked in with a kiss and an encouraging word, and sometimes sat to help with corrections. Ru, who was more advanced in his studies, worked alone in his room and recited his lessons for Pappa, when they met for the noon meal. After they were done, and the little ones were released to play, Ru worked in the yard, or went to Pappa's office, or met his friends. Bill Chetwood, York Monocker, and Wallace Ormsby had incorporated Ru into their circle, though at eleven he was the youngest of the group.

Millie's Unsettled Season

Millie was also becoming friends with more of the girls in Pleasant Plains, even Helen Monocker, who rarely agreed with Millie but never seemed to remember their disagreements for very long.

Millie's favorite time of the day was when she could walk to Keiths' hill to read her Bible or just to talk to Jesus. She found that she had much more patience with her students if she prayed for them, spending time talking to Jesus about their needs. At the swing one day, Millie realized that she hadn't even thought of pinching Cyril or Don in the longest time. It was strange, she couldn't remember when the impulse had stopped troubling her. Mamma's prayer had worked—Jesus was making her more patient! And the strangest thing was how it had happened. She hadn't tried to stop pinching at all. She had just tried to be like Jesus. He was changing her heart a little bit at a time. Millie made the swing fly that day, almost touching heaven with her toes.

CHAPTER

17

Answered
Prayers

The entire law is summed up
in a single command:
"Love your neighbor
as yourself."

GALATIANS 5:14

Answered Prayers

*O*h, do you think it's come at last?" Lu was clearly focusing on the tiny snowflakes falling outside the window, rather than the Bible lesson this Sabbath morning. Even inside the church, the morning air was cold enough to make clouds when they breathed, but the ground outside was still brown and bare.

"Winter has a way of arriving every year," said Wealthy, who was teaching the class.

"Oh, but Miss Stanhope, you don't understand," Helen explained. "It's not winter we want, it's snow!" She threw her arms wide and spun around. "White, beautiful snow."

"Enough for a sleigh ride," Lu said, as if that explained everything.

"It's the Christmas social," Millie said, a little annoyed with herself for being as excited as Helen and Lu. Her friends had been talking about nothing but the social for weeks, the splendid dinner, formal dance, carolling, and sleigh ride. Bill Chetwood had been describing the delights of the huge potluck to Ru. The girls talked of almost nothing but new dresses and dancing, and Millie couldn't wait to wear her new, grown-up gown.

"The social," Aunt Wealthy said, setting her Bible down. "I see," she said with a twinkle in her eye. "And is the Christmas social more important than Joshua and the battle of Jericho?"

The young people looked at her a bit dismayed.

"It's just…" Bill began.

"The Bible all happened so long ago," Helen finished. The rest of the class looked relieved that someone had said it, and it hadn't been them.

Millie waited. She had seen that twinkle in Aunt Wealthy's eye before.

"It did happen long ago," Aunt Wealthy agreed. "But it happened to people just like you. Did you ever think of that? And most of the stories that were written down were the big, important battles. But don't you think God cared about Joshua on the days when he wasn't marching around Jericho?"

"Well, I suppose He did," Bill ventured. "Doesn't the Bible say God loves us?"

" 'For God so loved the world that He gave His one and only Son,' " Wealthy quoted. "And if you love someone, do you care what happens to them only on certain days?"

"No," said Celestia Ann. "You care every day, and night, too. Jes' like it says in Psalm 23, 'The Lord is my shepherd'... He is always watching out for you!"

"I'll tell you a secret," Wealthy said, lowering her voice. "God cares about the Christmas social. He cares about fun."

Helen looked at her doubtfully. "Damaris Drybread says that we should be solemn all of the time. I know she won't dance a step at the social. And she knows her Bible. She was our Bible teacher before you came."

"Hmmmmph," Wealthy said. "Do you know what I am going to do when I get to heaven?"

The class shook their heads.

"I'm going to a wedding feast. See—it says so right here." She flipped her Bible open to Revelations 19:6 and read, " 'Then I heard what sounded like a great multitude, like the roar of rushing waters and like loud peals of thunder, shouting: "Hallelujah! For our Lord God Almighty reigns. Let us rejoice and be glad and give him glory! For the wedding of the Lamb has come." ' " Have you ever been to a wedding?"

"When my sister Annabelle married Joel Husker, we had us a feast," Celestia Ann said. "And a fiddler, too, and folks danced all night!"

"That's right!" Wealthy said. "A wedding feast is a party, like a social. And Jesus Himself is going to be there! Now why were you worried about snow?"

"We always have a sleigh ride," Lu explained. "And sing carols. But we usually have plenty of snow by now. And there haven't been but a few flakes this year."

"Well," said Wealthy, folding her hands. "Let's just talk to Him about that." By the time class was over, they had talked to the Lord about snow, dresses, and shoes. Bill had put in a special request for someone to be inspired to bring a rhubarb pie. Everyone was laughing, and it was almost as much fun as the social itself.

Millie walked home with Claudina that afternoon, Lu and Helen by their side. Even though it was a month until Christmas, the Chetwoods' house was bright with holiday decorations. Wreaths of evergreen made bright with holly berries filled the whole house with a delicious Christmas smell. The Chetwoods were always the first family to decorate for the season, Claudina explained. Once Mrs. Chetwood hung the greens, the whole town began to break out in holiday cheer. She served the girls hot cider and ham sandwiches to eat.

"Have you started your gown?" Claudina asked.

"It's almost done," Millie said. "I'm just sewing on the French lace."

"Emerald green silk and French lace?" Claudina said. "Why, Millie Keith, with your angel eyes and golden hair, you will be the belle of the ball!"

Millie's Unsettled Season

"I'm sure that is not true," Millie said. "Besides, I have a dreadful feeling I will catch cold, and my nose will be bright red!"

"Oh, me too!" Claudina said. "I am so nervous. I know I am going to trip on my gown. Or spill punch on the sleeve of a stranger."

"A handsome stranger," giggled Lu.

Finally, the young ladies took their leave. Bill and Claudina offered to walk them home, as it was growing dark, and still talking about the details of the party, the girls accepted. They dropped Lu at her home first, then turned up the bluff toward the Big Yellow House. The sun had not yet set, but heavy gray clouds darkened the sky.

"I believe Someone was listening as Aunty prayed," Millie said as a harsh gust of cold wind nearly knocked her over.

"Let it snow!" Bill yelled, raising his arms to the sky. The wind seemed to answer, pushing them along.

"Brrrrr. It's getting cold," Claudina said.

"You have only a thin jacket," Millie said. "I can almost see my house from here. Run home, and I'll see you on Sunday!"

They said their good-byes and Millie hurried toward home. As she neared the blacksmith's shop, she saw two figures coming up the street, huddled together. The taller one seemed to be protecting the smaller one, sheltering her from the wind.

"It's Rhoda Jane," Millie said to herself as they drew closer. "And little Min. It looks like they forgot their coats, too. Good thing they're almost home."

"Hi, Rhoda Jane!" Millie began as she caught up with them, but the look on Rhoda Jane's face took her breath away. There was something fierce in Rhoda Jane's eyes. She opened her mouth to say something, but suddenly gripped Min's shoulder instead. She swayed for a moment, and collapsed.

"Rhoda Jane!" Min cried, squatting beside her. "Get up!"

"What's wrong?" Millie cried, kneeling beside the fallen girl.

"I told her to eat her potato," Min said. "But she said I could eat it. I was so hungry! I'm sorry, Rhoda Jane. Please get up!"

Millie suddenly felt as if something large and dark had walked by, touching them with its shadow. There was something here, something terrible, that she did not understand yet, but she knew she had to act quickly. "Lord," she prayed aloud. "Help us!" She stripped off her coat and wrapped it around the girl laying on the ground.

"Run and get your mother, Min," she said. "Run!"

"Ma's gone to work," Min whimpered. "Only Gordon's home."

"Get Gordon, then!" Millie said.

The little girl ran for home, and Millie cradled Rhoda Jane's head in her lap, trying to block the wind as huge, fat snowflakes started falling.

It seemed like an eternity before Gordon came running through the darkness.

"Rhoda Jane?" he called, kneeling beside her and shaking her shoulder. She groaned. "She's going to be all right. Soon as we get some food in her. She's got weak blood, that's all," his voice sounded choked, "That's all."

"I do not have weak blood," Rhoda Jane said. "I just got dizzy."

Millie's Unsettled Season

Millie had never been so relieved to hear anyone's voice.

"Let's keep the coat on her while you take her home," Millie said.

"I do not need a coat!" Rhoda Jane said.

"Hush," Gordon said, scooping her up in his arms.

Millie followed along behind Gordon as he carried his sister, and held the door open for him when he reached the smithy. It was bitterly cold and almost completely dark inside. "Where are the matches and lamp?" Millie asked. Gordon nodded in the direction of a wooden box on a nearby table. Fumbling in the dark, Millie found a stone and the matches. She struck the match, found the lamp, lit it quickly, and the room began to come to light—bare wooden walls with knots missing where the wind could come in, and a bare wooden floor. The only furnishings were two chairs, a table, and a small wood stove. A shelf of books against the back wall was the only thing in the room that spoke of anything but poverty. She remembered how embarrassed she had felt when Claudina and Lu had come to the Big Yellow House to welcome her to town, and her heart suddenly ached for Rhoda Jane.

"Run and get some blankets, Minerva," Gordon said. "I want to put Sister in here until she is warm." He settled Rhoda Jane in a chair by the wood stove and set to work building a fire. The little girl ran into the next room and came back with a thin blanket, and Gordon tucked it around his sister. "I told you to eat your own potato," he said. "Now look what's happened!"

"Hush," Rhoda Jane said, glancing at Millie. "I'm fine. Can we offer you some tea?"

Millie wanted to say no and run from this place, but she couldn't. "Yes," she said, as if it were the Chetwoods' sitting room. "I would love a cup of tea."

Gordon put a kettle on the wood stove, and Millie edged closer to the warmth as it started to steam. He dropped the leaves in the teapot, poured the hot water over them, and set them to steep while he peeled three potatoes. He set a skillet on the stovetop to heat while he poured the tea.

"Would you like some sugar?" Rhoda Jane asked.

"We can't have sugar," Min said. "It's only for company or Christmas!"

"Hush, now," Gordon said, putting a scant spoonful in Millie's cup. "One spoon or two?" he asked.

"Two," Millie said, sure that he would be insulted if she turned down the sweet, or even if she asked for just one. *Lord, forgive me!* Millie prayed as Gordon put two heaping spoonfuls in Millie's tea, and then the same in Rhoda Jane's.

"Gord…" Rhoda Jane began, but he interrupted her. "Drink it," he said. "I'll put the potatoes on."

Millie drank her weak, too sweet tea, thinking of the buckets of milk and cream in the shed at the Big Yellow House. How could she ever have felt poor? Her eyes went back to the books.

"You like to read?" Rhoda Jane asked, surprised. "I thought you were like Claudina, with a head full of fluff."

"I love reading," Millie said, flushing a little for her friend's sake. "My Aunt Wealthy has the most wonderful library back home. I think I miss it almost as much as I miss my friends!"

"Father used to read to us every night," Rhoda Jane said. "I miss his voice."

"Rhoda Jane reads to us now," Min said. "She says you don't need friends if you have books."

Books never judge you because of your clothes. They don't mind if you don't have money. And…and they will still sit with you, even

if your house is cold. Millie had not felt more kindness or hospitality in any home in Pleasant Plains. When the others offered her tea, she knew they had plenty for themselves. The Lightcaps were giving her their best, all they had. *I will give you the treasures of darkness, riches stored in secret places...* Millie drew in her breath as she remembered. *Could the Lightcaps be the riches God promised? They certainly are hidden in darkness!*

The front door opened with a sharp gust of wind, and Mrs. Lightcap and Emmaretta blew in. "Good heavens!" she said, dropping her heavy load of laundry and stooping to unwrap Emmaretta, who looked like a mummy bundled in a blanket. "I didn't realize we had company!"

"Rhoda Jane wasn't feeling well," Millie said. "Would you like me to send for Dr. Chetwood?"

"No," Mrs. Lightcap said quickly. "I think we will be fine. Won't you stay for supper?"

Millie tried hard not to look at the one skillet of potatoes.

"No, thank you," she said politely. "My mother is probably worried about me already."

"It's dark out," Mrs. Lightcap said. "And the wind would take a candle. How about you carry the lamp for her, Gordon?"

Gordon carried their only lamp, leaving his family waiting in the dark until he returned, and he and Millie hurried up the hill toward the bright lights of her home. She left her coat, and he hadn't any, so they walked quickly with their shoulders hunched against the wind. When she reached the step, Millie turned.

"Thank you for the tea," she said. "It was delicious."

Gordon Lightcap had a beautiful smile.

CHAPTER

18

Broken Hearts

*He who despises his neighbor
sins, but blessed is he who
is kind to the needy.*

PROVERBS 14:21

"*M*illie!" Stuart said when she came in the door. "I was just setting out to look for you! The snow is starting to pile up. I think it is safe to say there will be sleigh rides this winter!"

"Oh, Pappa, I don't care about sleigh rides at all!" Millie poured out her story of the Lightcap home.

"I thought you knew the Lightcaps was poor," Celestia Ann said. "They kinda wandered into Pleasant Plains on accident two years ago. But their Pap got sick, and when he died, they just stuck. Gordy shoes horses and can put a rim on a wheel, using the tools that used to be his pa's. Mrs. Lightcap takes in wash."

The Keiths were subdued as they sat down to supper. As soon as the younger ones had all been tucked in their warm beds, Millie went to the parlor with Pappa and Mamma and Aunt Wealthy. Celestia Ann brought in a tray of tea, and Stuart invited her to stay.

"I don't understand, Pappa," Millie said. "If God cares about little things, doesn't He care about the Lightcaps?"

"Of course He does," Stuart said. "Sometimes He uses His children here on earth to reach out to people. Perhaps He can use your hands, Millie, to help them."

"Mine?" Millie was embarrassed to realize that she had never reached out to Rhoda Jane. "But how? Should we go over there tonight with money and food?"

"You'd shame 'em to death if you took them a thing," Celestia Ann said. "All that fam'ly has left is guts and pride. And if you go givin' 'em charity, you take that away, too."

"I think she's right," Aunt Wealthy said. "But what can we do?"

"I'm sure I can send some work Gordon's way, if I speak a few words to my clients," Stuart said.

"Emmaretta's big enough to milk a cow," Celestia Ann suggested. "An' churn butter too. And Belle's always givin' more than we need. I could ask her if she wants a job milkin' and churnin' and tell her to keep the extry."

"Good idea," Stuart said.

"But I want to do more," Millie said. Her mother kissed her on the forehead.

"You've already begun, Millie mine. Tonight you allowed them into your heart. And your broken, compassionate heart is a prayer rising up to heaven."

Marcia wrapped her in a hug. "We will all watch and pray. I know the Lord uses people who are willing, and I for one am willing to do anything at all to help our neighbors."

That night as Millie lay in her bed, her heart was broken, and the only way to ease the pain was to lift it up to her Heavenly Father. *Rhoda Jane doesn't have much food, Lord. And maybe she wouldn't take it if it were offered. And she doesn't have any friends…show me what to do!* Pictures of the cold, bare room ran through her mind, but she always came back to the shelf of books.

When Millie woke the next morning, the snow had covered the earth in a soft, white blanket, and the frost had left lace on the windowpanes. She dressed quickly and spent a quiet half hour with her Bible before she went downstairs.

"Do you mind if I visit Rhoda Jane this morning, Mamma?" Millie asked. "I want to see how she is."

"Of course you may." Her mother smiled.

Millie took her copy of *Ivanhoe*, tucked it under her arm, wrapped up in her warmest cloak, and started down the hill. The air cut like a knife, but the ice crystals made rainbows, a million tiny promises, caught in every tree. Millie stopped for a quick prayer before she reached the Lightcaps' door.

"Give me courage, Lord," she said, then lifted her hand and knocked.

Rhoda Jane answered the door, looking a little pale. "Why, Millie! I wasn't expecting you so soon! The coat's in the other room. Just let me get it…"

"Thank you," Millie said. "But I didn't come for the coat. I was wondering if you might let me borrow a book."

"Borrow a book?" Rhoda Jane looked blank.

"I couldn't help but notice your library," Millie said. "And I have been so starved for good books. I finished this one," she held out her precious copy of *Ivanhoe*, "and I thought…perhaps we might trade. Only for a little while."

Rhoda Jane reached out slowly and took the book, but her eyes were searching Millie's face.

"That's all you want, to borrow one of my books?"

"Yes," Millie said. "I mean no! I do want something more, Rhoda Jane. I want someone to talk to. I haven't had anyone to talk to…I mean, really talk to…in months."

"Come in," Rhoda Jane said.

Millie stomped the powdered snow off her boots and followed Rhoda Jane into the kitchen. The stove was warm, and the kitchen smelled of fried potatoes. Emmaretta and Minerva sat at the table, with a book open before them. There was a piece of slate with chalk letters on the table.

"You're teaching them yourself!" Millie exclaimed.

Millie's Unsettled Season

"We don't have enough money to send them to school," Rhoda Jane said. "And I wouldn't send them to Miss Drybones even if we did."

"I wouldn't either," Millie said. "I'm teaching Zillah and Adah, too." She explained briefly about Cyril and Don's raid on the schoolhouse.

Rhoda Jane smiled. "I heard about that," she said. "Help yourself to a book."

Millie took her time examining the books on the shelf, and finally chose a book of poetry by William Blake.

"Thank you," she managed, and ran out of things to say.

"You are welcome," said Rhoda Jane as she led her to the door. "Stop by when you have finished it. That's one of my favorites."

Millie split her time between devouring poems, working on her green gown, and dreaming about the social. Stuart had found some people with work for Gordon, and the ring of the hammer on the anvil in the distance made her smile. When she had finished the book of poetry, she took it and her copy of *The Last of the Mohicans* and walked down the hill again.

"Hello, Millie," Rhoda Jane said, opening the door. "Won't you come in? The girls are playing house right now, so we can talk." She offered Millie a seat, and heated water for tea, which she served with cream and biscuits.

"How did you like the book?" Rhoda Jane asked when she placed a steaming cup in front of Millie.

"I loved it." Millie smiled, and quoted:

Tyger! Tyger! burning bright
  In the forests of the night,
  What immortal hand or eye
  Could frame thy fearful symmetry?

Rhoda Jane nodded and joined her for the second verse:

In what distant deeps or skies
  Burnt the fire of thine eyes?
  On what wings dare he aspire?
  What the hand dare seize the fire?

They finished the poem together, while Emmaretta looked on, open-mouthed.

"Blake's words are like thunder!" Millie said. "What about you? Did you enjoy *Ivanhoe*?"

"I fear I am in love with him, and woe is me." Rhoda Jane put her hand to her forehead, her wrist limp. "Woe is me, for he loves fair Rowena well!"

This time, both girls laughed. "I do have a question, though." She pulled the book from the shelf and opened the cover to Millie's bookplate.

"This book belongs to Jesus?"

Millie looked down at her own writing. It seemed so long ago now, a hundred years at least. Millie began with the story of the book, but as it spilled out, she found that it was all mixed up with how hard it had been to leave her friends in Lansdale. She was surprised to realize that she hadn't told anyone the story of her trip since she arrived.

As Millie described Aunt Wealthy's saving Dr. Percival Fox, Rhoda Jane was laughing so hard that tears ran down her face. But when she described Dr. Fox's decision to live for Jesus, Rhoda Jane grew solemn again.

"I'm sure that it is very comforting for you, Millie," she said. "I almost wish I had faith in something like that."

"Why, Rhoda Jane, do you mean you don't believe in God? Surely you can't read the Bible without knowing, just knowing that He loves you!"

"That is one book I have never read," Rhoda Jane said. "When my father was sick, Drybones brought me a Bible. She said that my father would not be sick if we were not sinners, and that perhaps if we read the Bible we would mend our ways, and he would get well. My father died that night," Rhoda Jane said matter of factly. "If anyone else had given me that book, even Reverend Lord, I might have read it. But it was Damaris Drybread. I burned it."

Millie was horrified, and her heart was breaking all at once. How could anyone, anyone burn God's Word? But how could someone say something so horrible? What if her own dear Pappa lay dying?

"It's not like that, Rhoda Jane," Millie said. "I'm sure God didn't kill your father to punish you! It must have broken His heart…"

"I don't want to talk about it, really," Rhoda Jane said. "Do you want to borrow another book?"

"Yes," Millie said, bringing out her copy of *The Last of the Mohicans*. "And I have another for you."

Millie selected Shakespeare's *Much Ado about Nothing*, said her good-byes and hurried up the hill.

Cyril and Don had built a snow fort in front of the Big Yellow House.

"Who goes there," Cyril bellowed as Millie approached.

"Be ye friend or foe?" Don asked.

"I be your sister," Millie said. "And I want to get inside."

"No," said Don lobbing a snowball at her. "No one passes!"

Millie ducked her head and charged through the hail of snowballs to the front door. She slammed it behind her, and was taking off her cloak when someone knocked. She opened the door to find Claudina and Helen standing on the step. Claudina held a package in her arms. There were no snowball marks on her cloak or the paper of her package, and she had a beautiful smile on her face.

"How did you get past the fort?" Millie asked.

"Simple," Claudina said. "I told them I would kiss them once for each snowball they threw. They didn't throw even one! Millie, my gown has arrived. And the slippers. I just had to show you! But you were just coming in! Where have you been? I haven't seen you for ages!"

"I was visiting with Rhoda Jane," Millie said.

A look of dismay came over Helen's face. "Millie, you must be careful. Everyone knows that this," she motioned to the make-do furnishings around her, "is temporary and that the Keiths will be building a fine new home. But Mrs. Lightcap...Why, she does our laundry, Millie. Charity is one thing, but friendship is quite another."

Millie was trying to think of a reply, but Claudina continued as if there had been no interruption.

"Look at this." She pulled a pale blue velvet gown from the bag. "Made in Chicago by my mother's seamstress," she said, holding it up and waltzing around the room. "Isn't it beautiful! And Mother says I may wear my hair up with silk roses. What do you think?"

"I think you will be beautiful," Millie said. "And quite grown up."

Millie's Unsettled Season

"Now you must let us see your gown," Helen said.

"Oh, no." Millie didn't feel like talking to them at all. "I don't want anyone to see it until it's finished."

The girls stayed and chatted for an hour, though Millie's mind was clearly elsewhere.

"Isn't that your father coming home?" Claudina asked at last. "I didn't realize it was so late. It's time to be going, Helen."

Millie was glad to see them to the door, but gladder still to see her own dear Pappa coming up the hill. They passed the fort unmolested under his watchful eye, then turned and waved to Millie before they started home.

Millie could scarcely keep her mind on her sewing that night, as she told her parents about her day, and what Damaris Drybread had done when Mr. Lightcap lay dying.

"Ouch," she said, laying her seamwork aside and sucking a bead of blood from the finger her needle had pierced. "How could anyone be so horrible?"

"Damaris Drybones," Stuart said, "might be a fitting name after all."

"Now, Stuart," said Marcia. "You know that Jesus loves her."

"That's true, my dear," he said. "And I ask your pardon and His forgiveness. But I do think she has done a great deal of harm where she should have done good."

CHAPTER

Christmas Wonders

Do not merely listen to the word,
and so deceive yourselves.
Do what it says.

JAMES 1:22

illie found teaching more and more difficult as her students' attention turned to the excitement of the season. The Lord had answered Aunt Wealthy's prayers with an abundance of snow. Rupert and his friends built a sledding hill, packing the snow into heaps and piles to make their sleds leap. Gordon joined them when work allowed.

"You should see his sled fly!" Rupert reported. "He made the runners himself, and no one is faster!"

Since the snow was too deep to climb to her swing, Millie sometimes joined Ru in his sledding after lessons, but more often than not she would walk down the hill to the Lightcaps. She understood now why Aunt Wealthy liked to walk as she prayed. For every trip to the neighboring house, Millie prayed the whole way, asking God to help her show her new friend His love.

Rhoda Jane normally kept her students seated at the table well past their noon meal. Three days before the social, Millie arrived just as Min finished wiping soup from her slate.

"I spilt my soup on it," she explained matter of factly. "Because I was writing down the in. . . in. . . ."

"Ingredients," Rhoda Jane said.

"Yeah," Min said. "That's what's in here!"

"You run your schoolroom so efficiently," Millie giggled. "Really Rhoda Jane, Em and Min are reading very well. And I am sure you are better at teaching sums than I am. Wait a minute!" Millie sank into a chair. "I have just had the most wonderful idea!"

"If it is anything like your last idea, I think you should forget about it right now, before any damage is done," Rhoda Jane said.

"Teaching subtraction and addition using gumdrops would have worked very well if Cyril hadn't eaten them all, and you know it," Millie said, smiling.

"At least he understood the subtraction part," Rhoda Jane laughed.

"It was a good idea," Millie insisted. "But this one's better. What if we put our school rooms together tomorrow? It will be too hard to concentrate on anything with just one day left before the social. We could make it a party. I could teach reading, and you could teach sums. I'm sure the girls would love it. We could meet in my sitting room, where there are more chairs…"

"Please, Rhoda Jane!" Min said, clapping her hands. "It would be a real school!"

Marcia and Aunt Wealthy quickly approved the plan, and the next morning attendance in Millie's school had doubled. Emmaretta and Minerva brought their own meals of cornbread and boiled eggs in pails, and Zillah and Adah insisted on having their food in pails, too. Snowflakes were falling once again, so Millie spread a tablecloth on the floor and they had a picnic while Rhoda Jane read aloud.

After the picnic, Zillah invited Emmaretta and Minerva to participate in a Christmas play; they would have costumes and lines to memorize. The boys would join them.

"You can be an angel," Zillah told Cyril. "And Don will be a shepherd."

"Wahooo!" Don said, twirling his rope like a sling. "Wannago's gonna be the sheep!"

Cyril scratched his head and considered. "I don't wanna be a Christmas angel," he said. "I like the smiting kind, the ones that marched in the treetops when David went to war, or the ones with chariots and horses on the hills around the town where Elijah and his servant stayed. Now those are angels!"

"They were the same angels," Millie said.

Cyril scratched his head and considered. "Are you sure they were the very same ones? Christmas angels seem kind of like sissies. All they did was sing."

"God has lots of angels, so they might not have been exactly the same ones. But they were singing praises to God," Millie said, "just like we do in church, or in the evening when Pappa leads us. Does Pappa sound like a sissy?"

"No," Cyril had to admit. "He sounds happy."

"Do you think that the shepherds were sissies?"

"No!" Don yelled. "Shepherds had to stay out all night alone, fighting wolves and bears and robbers!" He punched an imaginary robber. "Pow!"

"I want to be a shepherd," Fan said.

"You can't." Don patted her head. "You're a girl. Girls can't fight wolves and bears."

"Can too!" Fan yelled.

"Can not!" Don yelled back.

"What is all of this yelling about?" Aunt Wealthy asked, coming into the room.

"Don says I can't be a shepherd," the little girl said, throwing herself against Aunt Wealthy in despair.

"Well, that is true," Aunt Wealthy said. "You cannot be a shepherd. You will have to be a shepherdess. You will have to be strong and brave and beautiful. Like Rachel. She was a shepherdess, so she had to be brave. And she was so beautiful that Jacob was willing to work for seven years so she would be his bride."

"He said girls can't fight wolves and bears," Fan said, still not certain.

"Of course they can't," Aunt Wealthy agreed. "Not by themselves. But neither can boys. Do you think David fought lions and bears all by himself?"

"No," Ru said. "David said the Lord delivered him from the paw of the lion and the bear."

"It's God's job to help us fight the lions and bears," Aunt Wealthy said. "Whether we are boys or girls, it's our job to trust Him."

"I still think the Christmas angels were sissies," said Cyril, folding his arms.

"If the shepherds were brave, then the angels were not sissies." Millie opened her Bible to Luke 2:9. " 'An angel of the Lord appeared to them, and the glory of the Lord shown around them, and they were terrified.' "

"You mean they hafta be terrified of me?" Cyril asked. "Well, that ain't too bad!"

The dispute over angels and shepherds resolved, the children ran to Zillah's room to work on their parts and costumes.

"The Keiths are definitely the most peculiar people I have ever met," Rhoda Jane said, as Aunt Wealthy ushered the last of the little ones out of the room. "All of that is in this book?" she asked as she flipped through the pages of Millie's Bible.

"Oh, yes," Millie said, "and lots more." She wanted so desperately to tell Rhoda Jane about Jesus, and how He had died for the world. That was the real reason for Christmas. She said a quick prayer and waited for the right words to come to her.

Celestia Ann arrived instead.

"Lookit who blew in," she said, ushering Helen, Lu, and Claudina into the room, and helping them out of their coats.

Millie's heart sank, but she greeted her visitors cordially. The afternoon was immediately focused on the Christmas social, Helen and Lu giggling over who would ask them to dance, their hairstyles and what, if any, jewelry their mothers would allow them to wear.

"Oh," Claudina said, suddenly seeming to realize that Rhoda Jane was not joining the chatter, "are you going to the social, Rhoda Jane?"

Rhoda Jane flushed, as all eyes turned to her.

"And is Gordon going?" Now all eyes shifted to Claudina, who turned pink in turn. Helen's eyebrows went up just a hair.

"Gordon plans to attend," Rhoda Jane said. "He loves to dance."

Claudina turned even pinker, and Lu giggled.

"I did not know that any of the Lightcaps danced," Helen said. "I have never seen either of you at a social before."

"Perhaps our social circles have simply not collided until now," Rhoda Jane said dryly.

"Then I will be pleasantly surprised, I'm sure," Helen said. "After all, everyone is invited," she said, glancing at Millie.

"I'm sure we will enjoy the company," Rhoda Jane replied.

"Would anyone like some hot cider?" Millie asked, desperate to change the subject.

"I would," Claudina said quickly.

Millie's Unsettled Season

"I'll help you prepare it," Rhoda Jane said, standing up. She followed Millie into the kitchen. Once there, Rhoda Jane gripped the edge of the table and leaned against it.

"I shouldn't have said that," she said. "I can't go. But Gordon is going, and he does love to dance."

"Why can't you?" Millie asked, pulling out a chair for her friend.

Rhoda Jane just laughed. "Shall I wear this?" She smoothed her faded calico. "Or my other dancing gown?"

"Oh. Oh." Millie said, sitting down beside her. How could she not have thought of it? Of course, Rhoda Jane had no dress to wear. And with one day until the social, there was no time to sew one, even if she had fabric.

"In Lansdale I traded gowns with my friends all of the time," Millie said. "We are about the same size. You could borrow one of mine. I know we could make it work."

"I couldn't do that."

"Why not?" Millie said. "I would. I wore a borrowed gown to a dance last year. Besides, you said you were going! Don't you want to see Helen's face when you and Gordon arrive?"

"You really think we can make one of your gowns work?"

"I know we can," said Millie. "You just come over a few hours before the social tomorrow. Promise?"

"I will," Rhoda Jane said and lifted her chin.

"Good," Millie squeezed her hand. "Now, let's get that cider."

After the girls had left, Millie climbed the stairs to her bedroom and opened her trunk. She pulled the yellow gown from the bottom and smoothed it on her bed. The puffed sleeves and sash with a bow were hopelessly out of style, and it did look

childish. She fingered the ink stain that Zillah had left on the hem when she borrowed it to play dress-up. Then she hung it on the wall next to her new green gown.

Marcia asked Millie to join them in the parlor for tea as Stuart put the children to bed. Millie was glad to have a moment to speak to her parents. She dropped down on the sofa with a sigh.

"You seem pensive tonight," Marcia said, putting an arm around her. "I thought you would be excited about the social and the sleigh ride."

Millie told her about the day, starting with the shared lessons, and the interruption just as Millie was prepared to talk to Rhoda Jane about God's Word, and finishing with her plan to loan Rhoda Jane a dress.

"What do you think, Mamma?" Millie asked.

When she had finished, Marcia stroked her hair. "I am so proud of you," she said. "Will you let me say a short prayer?"

Millie nodded and laid her head on her mother's shoulder.

"Please give Millie courage and wisdom and strength," Marcia prayed. "And give her Your special joy. Lord, I pray for Rhoda Jane to learn of Your love and care. Let her see how much You love her. Shine Your light through my precious Millie. In Jesus' name. Amen."

Lessons were cancelled the next morning as Millie, Aunt Wealthy, and Marcia attacked the yellow gown with scissors and needles and thread. The bow was removed, the puff on the sleeves tucked and sewed. By raising the hem just a hair, they were almost able to hide the ink stain. It was finished by noon, and Millie stood back to look at their work.

"Well," she said, "it's not horrible."

"It's not horrible at all," said Marcia, gathering Millie in her arms. "It will be lovely."

Rhoda Jane arrived at three, still uncertain.

"I don't see how a gown of yours will fit me," she said. "I'm two inches taller!"

"Well, let's try it and see." Millie led the way up the stairs to her room. Rhoda Jane looked at the two dresses hanging side by side in Millie's room. It was clear from the stain on the hem which one was used. Rhoda Jane took the yellow dress off its hanger and held it up in front of her. "It is pretty," she said.

Millie swallowed hard. She wasn't sure until this moment that she could get through this without tears, but suddenly she knew she could.

"Oh, that's not your gown," she said. "The green one is for you. The yellow one would be too short, don't you think?"

Rhoda Jane sucked in her breath. "The green one? Millie, are you sure?"

"Of course, I'm sure," Millie said. "It's too long for me, and we don't have time to hem it now." It wasn't lying not to mention that she had planned to wear heels. "So you will have to wear that one."

Aunt Wealthy helped Rhoda Jane with her gown and hair, while Marcia helped Millie. Celestia Ann insisted on doing everything herself, and her wild curls and mischievous grin were just the same when she came upstairs to show off her gown and the shawl Wealthy had loaned her.

"How are you gettin' on? You look mighty nice, Millie."

Millie spun in front of the mirror and sighed. They had done wonders for the yellow dress, but the style was still too young, and if her dancing slippers had had the least hint of a heel, the skirt would have been too short. Her hair did shine like a river of gold where it fell over her shoulders, and Millie looked very much the princess.

Celestia Ann gasped as Wealthy led Rhoda Jane into the room.

"It's Rowena!" Zillah declared, clapping her hands. "Just like in *Ivanhoe*, Millie!"

"You're so pretty!" Adah cried.

Wealthy had swept the girl's hair up and fastened it with combs. Her brown eyes were huge in her heart-shaped face.

Wealthy turned Rhoda Jane toward the mirror, and in that instant, when Rhoda Jane caught sight of her reflection, Millie was sure she had done the right thing. Rhoda Jane's mouth opened, then shut again, as she touched the French lace at her throat. She shook her head, and burst out in tears.

"No, no, no!" Wealthy said, producing a handkerchief. "No crying! You don't want your eyes all red for the party! No crying!"

"Of course not," Rhoda Jane said between sobs, crying even harder.

Wealthy had managed to dry the tears by the time Rhoda Jane left to help Gordon get ready.

"We'll meet you there, Millie," she said, giving her a hug.

Millie finished her own preparations, and stood with Celestia Ann, Ru, and Stuart and Marcia, as Aunt Wealthy inspected them.

"Oh, you all look so beautiful!" she said. "I am sure you will have the time of my life!"

"We will try," Stuart said seriously.

"And don't you worry about the little ones. Wannago and I are perfectly capable of caring for the lot."

"Of course you are," said Marcia.

"We really should be going," Stuart said, looking at his pocketwatch.

"Aren't you forgetting something?" Marcia asked.

"I don't think so," Stuart said.

"Stuart!"

"Oh, you must mean this!" He pulled a slender velvet box out of his pocket.

"Miss Mildred Keith, you will no doubt be the loveliest girl at the social tonight. And I humbly ask you to hold one dance for me. But until then, I want you to have a token of my great esteem for you. Will you do me the honor of accepting this little gift?" Stuart opened the box for Millie to see inside. Resting on the black velvet was a golden chain with a single pearl.

Millie was speechless as her father laid the necklace around her throat and her mother checked the clasp to be sure it was secure.

"This is a Christmas and early birthday present," her mother said, kissing her forehead.

Millie was absolutely glowing as she picked up her cloak and muff, and kissed Aunt Wealthy good night.

The Pleasant Plains Pavilion was used for everything from livestock auctions to town meetings, Sunday afternoon meals, and hymn sing-alongs after church. But one

night each year, in mid-December, the simple place was transformed. The rafters were draped with evergreen garlands, a holiday feast laid out, and tables lit with cozy lanterns and candles.

Millie heard the music growing stronger as they approached the pavilion. The lively sounds of fiddle, guitar, and piano floated on the evening air and greeted them in full force as they entered.

Everyone was dressed in their very finest, and laughter rippled from groups of people already gathered in the hall. Stuart soon joined a group of men discussing business matters and politics, and Marcia wandered over to a group of ladies giving finishing touches to the tables and offered to help.

Millie, Rupert, and their friends clustered together. The young men were smiling and joking, the young ladies looking beautiful in their much-worried-over gowns. Claudina wore her pale blue velvet gown with matching cape. Her long dark curls were held together with a mother-of-pearl comb. Lucilla and Helen's dresses were cut in very different styles but made from similar shades of deep crimson satin. All the girls admired Millie's new pearl necklace.

"A Christmas surprise from your parents? How lovely!" Lucilla said.

"Yes…lovely," Helen said, giving Millie's gown a puzzled glance, and Millie saw her eyes travel down to the hint of a stain on the hem.

Celestia Ann saw the look and smiled. "That's the rage in Paree," she said.

Millie blushed.

At that moment a handsome couple stepped in the door. Gordon Lightcap stood tall, holding the arm of his sister.

Millie's Unsettled Season

Rhoda Jane had been beautiful at Millie's house; in the soft light of the ballroom she was breathtaking.

The girls rushed to greet her. They made her turn around in dizzying circles so they could admire her lovely dress.

"Why, Rhoda Jane, that lace is just the perfect trimming for your gown!" Helen said "Where on earth did you get it?"

Millie's eyes met Rhoda Jane's, and she prayed that her friend would be spared any sort of embarrassment.

As if on cue, Mr. Grange announced that the dancing was to begin, and York Monocker stepped forward. He bowed ever so slightly and offered his hand to Rhoda Jane. "Miss Lightcap, you outshine the stars tonight. Would you do me the honor of granting me the first dance?" Rhoda Jane took his hand, and he led her to the floor. All eyes in the room were fixed on the couple as they swirled about the pavilion.

"Well!" Claudina said. "Rhoda Jane was certainly telling the truth when she said Lightcaps could dance!"

"My sister is a very truthful girl," Gordon said, bowing. "Would you care to dance with a Lightcap, Miss Chetwood?"

Claudina pinkened to the tip of her nose, but she took his hand and they stepped onto the dance floor.

"Rhoda Jane is the most beautiful girl here tonight," Millie said.

"The second most beautiful for sure," Celestia Ann said. "Somethin' in you sure does shine, Millie!"

Marcia and Stuart Keith made their way through the crowds to their daughter and son.

"Are you ready for your dance?" Stuart asked, offering his arm to Millie. She stepped onto the floor and followed her father's lead. As she twirled, she had flashes of Rupert trying valiantly to waltz with his mother.

Finally, Stuart leaned over and whispered in Millie's ear, "I must abandon you to save your mother's toes." Millie smiled and returned to her friends.

The hour grew late, the food was nearly gone, and even though she would never have admitted it, Millie was exhausted long before time for the midnight sleigh ride home.

The large omnibus sleigh drawn by four horses with jingling bells on their harnesses waited outside, under the light of a full golden moon. The sleigh was piled high with buffalo robes and blankets for keeping the cold at bay.

"I don't think I can move," Claudina said, after taking her seat. She was bundled in a cloak and scarf, cap and gloves, with a buffalo robe piled on her.

"You don't have to move," Celestia Ann said, snuggling in beside her. "Just sing."

The Reverend Lord and Miss Drybread sat in their midst keeping a sharp eye on them, just in case the moonlight got the best of anyone. The girls began to giggle and glance at the young men. Millie rolled her eyes.

The driver shook the reins, and with a jingle of bells, the sleigh was off, runners hissing almost silently over the snow. They sang Christmas carols and laughed until they were hoarse. Bill Chetwood and Ru, who had pretended not to be interested in the ride, ambushed them as the sleigh reached the center of town, pelting them with snowballs, then running after them and swinging up into the sleigh.

When every possible carol had been sung, and some twice, the sleigh began to drop people at their doorsteps. Shouts of good night and Merry Christmas were heard, and if any young man was bold enough to walk a young lady to her door, everyone cheered or hooted.

Millie's Unsettled Season

The sleigh was more than half empty when it started up the hill toward the Big Yellow House. Rhoda Jane leaned close to Millie.

"I know what you did, Millie," she whispered. "I just wanted to say…thank you." She slipped an envelope into Millie's muff.

Millie felt in her bag for the gift she had wrapped for Rhoda Jane. "Here."

"It's a book!" Rhoda Jane said, feeling through the paper. She tore the wrapping paper off.

"The Holy Bible," she read, holding it up to the bright moonlight. Her face went very still.

Millie held her breath as Rhoda Jane opened the book and read the inscription.

For my dear friend Rhoda Jane Lightcap.
From Mildred Eleanor Keith, Christmas of 1833.
My prayer for you is found in the Gospel of John,
Chapter 3, Verse 16.

Millie waited for her to say something, anything, but Rhoda Jane did not even look at her. Her eyes lifted to the grim face of Damaris Drybread instead.

"Smithy," the driver called, and the sleigh stopped.

"Merry Christmas," Millie called, as Rhoda Jane stepped down. Suddenly, the robes and blankets rustled, and York leapt out.

"May I walk you to your door, Miss Lightcap?" The sleigh exploded with hoots and catcalls, but York just waved.

Rhoda Jane took his arm, and he walked her to the door, Gordon following a polite distance behind. They said good-

bye at the door, and Rhoda Jane and Gordon disappeared. York returned to the sleigh, and they were off. Millie retrieved the envelope Rhoda Jane had slipped in her muff, tearing it open with impatient fingers. The moonlight was more than bright enough to make out the words:

Dear Millie,

I wanted to give you something fine for Christmas, but all I have to offer is my friendship. I don't give it lightly, but you have been a true friend to me. And I will be yours forever.

Rhoda Jane Lightcap

The next stop the sleigh made was the Big Yellow House. Millie, Ru, and Celestia Ann jumped down and waved as their friends sped away. Millie stopped on the doorstep and looked back down the hill. There was a glow in the Lightcaps' window and sparks rising from the stovepipe.

Don't burn it up, Rhoda Jane. There is a Friend who will love you much more than I ever could. Please don't burn it up.

Millie turned the doorknob and stepped inside. She pulled off her hat and tossed her muff on the table before she realized that something was very, very wrong. Marcia stood beside the couch, one hand over her mouth. Stuart knelt beside it, with a little golden head cradled in his arms. Fan's face was pale, almost blue in the lamplight, and her eyes were closed.

"Oh, Lord, help us," Aunt Wealthy cried. "I only turned my back for an instant!"

What troubles are ahead, and will Millie's faith see her through?

When a Southern relative comes to visit, what family secrets will be revealed?

Find out in:

MILLIE'S COURAGEOUS DAYS

Book Two
of the
*A Life of Faith:
Millie Keith* Series

Available at your local bookstore

Violet's Hidden Doubts

BOOK ONE
of the
*A Life of Faith:
Violet Travilla*
Series

Based on the characters by
Martha Finley

Mission City Press

Franklin, Tennessee

TRAVILLA/DINSMORE FAMILY TREE

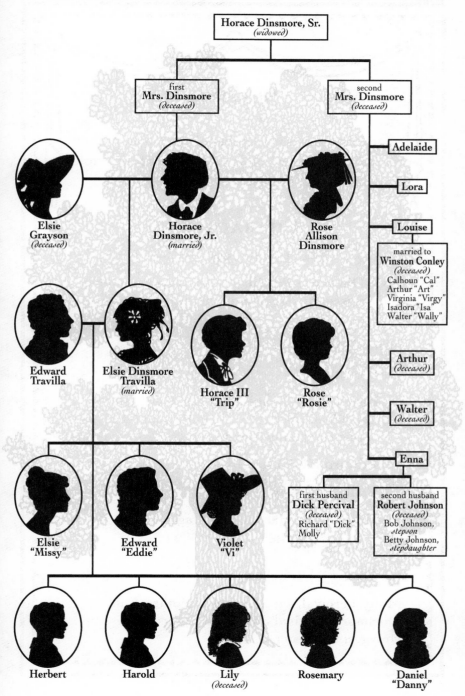

Horace Dinsmore, Sr.
(widowed)

first
Mrs. Dinsmore
(deceased)

second
Mrs. Dinsmore
(deceased)

Elsie
Grayson
(deceased)

Horace
Dinsmore, Jr.
(married)

Rose
Allison
Dinsmore

Adelaide

Lora

Louise

married to
Winston Conley
(deceased)
Calhoun "Cal"
Arthur "Art"
Virginia "Virgy"
Isadora "Isa"
Walter "Wally"

Edward
Travilla

Elsie Dinsmore
Travilla
(married)

Horace III
"Trip"

Rose
"Rosie"

Arthur
(deceased)

Walter
(deceased)

Enna

first husband
Dick Percival
(deceased)
Richard "Dick"
Molly

second husband
Robert Johnson
(deceased)
Bob Johnson,
stepson
Betty Johnson,
stepdaughter

Elsie
"Missy"

Edward
"Eddie"

Violet
"Vi"

Herbert

Harold

Lily
(deceased)

Rosemary

Daniel
"Danny"

SETTING

*T*he story begins in October of 1877 at a Southern plantation known as Ion, the home of Violet Travilla and her family.

CHARACTERS

∞ ION PLANTATION ∞

Elsie Dinsmore Travilla, Violet Travilla's mother and the wealthy daughter of Horace Dinsmore, Jr.

Edward Travilla, Violet's father and owner of Ion plantation

Their children:

> **Elsie** ("Missy"), age 20; engaged to Lester Leland, an artist studying in Italy and the nephew of family friends
>
> **Edward** ("Ed"), age 18
>
> **Violet** ("Vi"), age 14
>
> **Herbert** and **Harold**, twins, age 11
>
> **Rosemary**, age 7
>
> **Daniel** ("Danny"), age 3 ½

Molly Percival, age 21, and her mother, **Enna Dinsmore Percival Johnson** (Horace, Jr.'s youngest half-sister)

Aunt Chloe — Elsie's faithful maid and companion, and **Joe**, her elderly husband

Ben — Edward's valet and lifelong friend, and his wife, **Crystal**, the head housekeeper at Ion

Christine — nursemaid to Rosemary and Danny

Enoch — a farm worker

∽ THE OAKS PLANTATION ∽

Horace Dinsmore, Jr. — Violet's grandfather, owner of The Oaks plantation

Rose Allison Dinsmore — second wife of Horace Dinsmore, Jr. and mother of Horace ("Trip") Dinsmore III and Rosie Dinsmore

∽ ROSELANDS PLANTATION ∽

Horace Dinsmore, Sr. — Violet's great-grandfather, a widower; owner of Roselands plantation

Louise Dinsmore Conley — widowed daughter of Horace Dinsmore, Sr., and mother of:

Cal, age 29, manager of Roselands

Art, age 25, a physician

Virginia, age 23

Isa, age 21

Walter, age 20, a cadet at West Point

∽ VIAMEDE PLANTATION ∽

(Elsie Travilla's plantation in Louisiana)

Mr. and Mrs. Mason — Viamede's chaplain and his wife

Mr. Spriggs — the plantation manager

Aunt Mamie — longtime housekeeper at Viamede

Mrs. Maureen O'Flaherty — a new employee

∽ OTHERS ∽

Dr. Barton — retired family doctor and close friend of the Travillas and Dinsmores

Dr. and Mrs. Silas Lansing — an eminent surgeon and his wife

Dinah Carpenter — granddaughter of Chloe and Joe; now living in New Orleans with her husband and young children

Mr. and Mrs. Mayhew — a New Orleans lawyer and his wife

Mrs. Duke — a mission volunteer

Richard ("Dick") **Percival** — Molly's brother; a recent graduate of medical school in Philadelphia

James Keith — a young minister from the Midwest

Louis Embury — owner of Magnolia Hall, a plantation near Viamede; a widower with two daughters, Corinne and Maddie

Dr. Bayliss — a physician who serves the people of Viamede plantation

— FOREWORD —

*M*ore than a century-and-a-half ago, Miss Martha Finley (1828-1909) — a former schoolteacher who became a best-selling author of Bible-centered fiction for children and adults — penned a novel about the life of Elsie Dinsmore, a young girl growing up in the pre-Civil War South. Miss Finley intended to write just one book about her heroine. But the response to her first Elsie story, published in 1868, was so overwhelming that she eventually wrote twenty-eight more, plus a companion series about Elsie's cousin Millie Keith.

Although Miss Finley never had children of her own, she possessed a remarkable understanding of the hearts and minds of young people and their struggles to live their Christian faith in a world filled with challenges and temptations. During her life, Miss Finley's works provided inspiration, hope, and guidance to millions of readers throughout the United States and abroad. When her final Elsie novel was published in 1905, however, tastes in reading had changed, and her wonderful stories of faith and courage were almost lost to new generations. Then in the 1990s, Mission City Press undertook the adaptation of Miss Finley's stories for modern readers, launching *A Life of Faith* books with *Elsie's Endless Wait* in 1999. Since then, eight Elsie Dinsmore novels and eight Millie Keith books have been published by Mission City Press.

Now the tradition continues with the first of a new *A Life of Faith* series focused on Elsie's middle daughter, Violet Travilla. *Violet's Hidden Doubts* begins in 1877 and picks up the story of Elsie and her family several months after the conclusion of *Elsie's Great Hope* (the eighth book in the *A Life of Faith: Elsie Dinsmore* series.) For readers who haven't yet met Violet Travilla and her family, the following background should be very helpful.

∾ VIOLET TRAVILLA: A NEW HEROINE ∾

Violet was born in London, England—the third child of Elsie Dinsmore Travilla and her husband Edward. Her arrival was especially joyful because the family was enduring, as were all their fellow Americans, the tragic consequences of the Civil War. Family members were fighting on both sides in the war, and letters from home brought heartache upon heartache to the family. From Shiloh to Gettysburg, beloved brothers, uncles, cousins, and friends were dying in battle. Vi's birth on a sunny June day in 1863 was like a pledge of renewal to the troubled family.

The Travillas were wealthy Southern plantation owners. They opposed slavery and supported the cause of a united nation, but they also loved the South. When the Civil War began, the Travillas and Vi's grandparents were visiting in England. Their first impulse was to return to their homeland, but their families in the United States urged them to stay in England until the War's end. So Vi, as she's called, was two years old before she first set foot on American soil.

After the War, the Travillas went home to Ion—Vi's father's plantation located near a Southern seaport city on the Atlantic coast. Violet's grandfather, Horace Dinsmore, Jr., and step-grandmother, Rose, live at The Oaks, a plantation close to Ion. Vi's great-grandfather, Horace Dinsmore, Sr., lives at nearby Roselands plantation with his widowed daughter Louise Conley and her children. The

Foreword

Travillas have a large circle of family and friends in their rural community and are highly respected for their Christian faith, kindness, and the ethical treatment of their employees, many of whom are former slaves. Edward Travilla is a hero to many for his battle to rid the region of the racist Ku Klux Klan during the Reconstruction period (*Elsie's Tender Mercies*).

Vi has six sisters and brothers. Missy is the eldest — age 20 at the time this novel opens and recently engaged to marry. Vi's elder brother, Ed, is 18. Vi (age 14) is next, followed by twin brothers, Herbert and Harold, who are 11. The two youngest Travillas are Rosemary (7) and Danny (3 1/2). Another sister, Lily, died after a long illness, when Vi was 11 years old.

In 1869, when Vi was almost 6, the Travillas became the guardians of Elsie's cousins, Molly and Dick Percival. The young Percivals had experienced a number of personal tragedies, including a terrible accident that cost Molly the use of her legs. Molly has now become a successful writer of stories, and despite seven years' difference in their ages, Vi and Molly are very close friends.

As *Violet's Hidden Doubts* opens, life at Ion is very busy for the Travillas. Though they have many servants, the children are expected to help with chores; they make their beds, clean their bedrooms and their classroom, and assist their mother and their nursemaid, Aunt Chloe, with other household tasks. Missy, Ed, and Vi also care for their younger siblings when an extra hand is needed.

The children are schooled at home by their parents. Vi studies languages and literature, mathematics, history, and science. Like most girls of her time, she is also learning to sew and embroider. She and her sisters take lessons in piano and in drawing and painting. Though not musically gifted like her mother, Vi is artistic and loves to sketch the beautiful scenery around her home. The Travilla children enjoy plenty of outdoor activities — riding horses, playing games, and exploring the countryside. Vi gets to travel more than most children of her time — trips to her mother's plantation in Louisiana, summer holidays at the seashore, and visits to New York and Philadelphia.

No matter where the Travillas are, Bible study and prayer are regular parts of their daily life. Vi's parents, both devout Christians, have raised their children to love the Lord and honor His commandments. God is a living presence in all their lives, and they rely on Him to guide them through each day.

As a little girl, Vi was a lively and sometimes unpredictable child. When she was a toddler, she had the habit of sleepwalking, but to everyone's relief, she grew out of it. She has always been an imaginative girl, curious to learn about the world and dedicated to her studies. She is very close to her father — in part because they share the same sense of humor and independent spirit — and it is he who helped her through her darkest time, when her sister Lily died. Vi is normally very forthright, but there are occasions when she tries to hide her emotions in order to protect others. Now a teenager, she is sometimes unsure of herself and uncertain about her future. Her faith in the love of her Heavenly Father is unshakable, but her belief in herself is not so secure and can cause her to feel… hidden doubts.

And now, Mission City Press takes pride in carrying on Martha Finley's legacy and welcoming readers to Violet Travilla's exciting life of faith.

CHAPTER

1

Bruised Feelings

Then Jesus said to her,
"Your sins are
forgiven."

Luke 7:48

Bruised Feelings

*V*iolet Travilla sat at her bedroom window, looking down onto the circular driveway and gazing at her Papa. Edward had just returned from his early morning ride and was drawing his horse to a halt near the entrance to Ion. As Vi watched, he dismounted and handed the reins to a stableman. Edward patted the young man on the back and said something that brought a broad smile to the stableman's face.

Papa is so handsome, Violet thought, *even at his age, and Eddie looks more like him every day. Oh, dear, I must stop thinking of my big brother as "Eddie." He gets so annoyed by that name now. He is Ed Travilla, and I must remember to call him what he wishes. It's a good thing that Missy doesn't ask me to forget her nickname, too, though my darling big sister will be changing her name soon enough. Mrs. Lester Leland—Elsie Eugenia Travilla Leland—that will be our dear sister's name when Lester returns from Italy and they are wed. So many changes in our lives.*

Vi sighed and rose languidly from her seat. *Too many changes*, she thought as she went to her dressing table and took up her brush to give her dark, shining hair one last smoothing. She caught her reflection in the mirror and stared at herself. This was not an act of conceit. Quite the opposite. Violet, at fourteen, considered herself the ugly duckling of her family. The face that looked back at her seemed to hold none of the beauty of her mother's and elder sister's. Even her little sister, Rosemary, though only seven, was clearly blessed with their mother's ringleted hair, delicate complexion, perfect features, and clear hazel eyes. Despite the passing years, her mother, Elsie Dinsmore

Violet's Hidden Doubts

Travilla, was still regarded by all as a great beauty (although, as Vi well knew, her mother cared very little about such things).

Vi contemplated her hair. *It curled when I was little*, she thought, *and now it is as straight as an old stick. How did that happen? And how did I grow so tall? Oh, I'm not sure I want all these changes. Why can't I look like Mamma and my sisters? Why do I always have to be so different?*

In the mirror, her deep-brown eyes flashed back at her with self-reproach. "You have no reason to envy anyone," she told herself firmly. "Hasn't our Heavenly Father commanded us not to covet and warned us against the sin of envy?"

She turned away from her image and resolutely squared her slim shoulders. She strode to her desk and made a neat pile of the books and papers she would need for her studies. She was especially careful to include the neatly penned French lesson that she was to recite to her mother that day. Then she moved to her bed, took up the small Bible she had been studying earlier, marked her place with a ribbon, and gently set the book on her bedside table. Closing her eyes, she raised a brief but earnest prayer, asking the Lord to help her accept herself as she was and to resist all jealous thoughts. Refreshed by the understanding that He would give her strength, Vi hurried from her room.

Her family was already gathered at the table when she entered the dining room. Her father had just seated her mother and was now helping young Danny into the high chair that all the Travilla children had used when they were toddlers. Danny sat on one side of his mother and Rosemary at the other. Missy was seated at the center on the far side of the long table, with the twins, Harold and

Herbert, like bookends on either side of her. Vi's own place was on the near side of the table, between her brother Ed, who held her chair and complained in a joking tone that his eggs were growing cold, and Molly Percival, the dear cousin who had come to live with the Travillas nearly eight years earlier, after the accident that crippled her. (Molly's mother, Enna, now also resided at Ion with the Travillas, but she usually had breakfast in her room.)

Vi slipped into her seat quickly. Her father, having settled Danny in the high chair, took his own place at the end of the table opposite his wife. Immediately all heads were bowed and Edward said the blessing over the meal.

Breakfast began and everyone was soon eating and conversing about their plans for the day. As the hands on the mantel clock moved to the half hour, Ben—Edward Travilla's valet and trusted friend—entered the room. He carried a large stack of letters on a small tray. Ben said "Good morning" to the family and was warmly greeted in return, as Edward began to sort through the mail—a ritual followed every day for as long as anyone could remember.

There were a number of letters for Elsie and Edward. Two envelopes were passed to Ed—one an invitation and the other from a school friend. Molly was handed several envelopes—all, it appeared, from the publishers of her stories and translations. Rosemary, the twins, and even little Danny each got a note from their grandmother, Rose Dinsmore, who saw them almost daily but understood the joy that receiving letters brings to young children. At the bottom of the stack was a fat envelope addressed to Missy.

As he passed the letter to his eldest child, Edward said with a twinkle in his eye, "This seems to carry the scent of salt air and sea water. Perhaps it has journeyed across an ocean to find you, Missy dear."

The young woman blushed prettily and smiled as she took the envelope. "I hope it had a pleasant voyage," she said, gazing at the bold handwriting of the address—the same artistic hand that had signed a large still-life painting which hung above the sideboard in the dining room.

"Since you seem to have eaten your fill," Edward said, "I think your mother will agree to excuse you now, Missy. You may wish to read Lester's letter in privacy."

Missy turned to her mother with a question in her expression, and Elsie nodded with a smile. Missy stood and hurried from the room with the light and lively steps of one who thrives on love.

Edward returned to the mail. After a minute more of shuffling through the letters, he looked at Violet. Those who did not know him might have thought his face was marked by grave disappointment as he said to his middle daughter, "It seems that you and I have been left out, Vi."

"But you have lots of letters, Papa," Vi protested.

"Ah, there you are mistaken, my pet. I have lots of bills to be paid and business queries to answer," he said, "but not a single line from friend or relative to gladden my heart."

"Nor do I, Papa," Vi snapped. "But I would rather you not announce it to everyone. They don't have to know that I've been left out," she added sharply.

Vi hung her head, but not before Edward saw tears glistening in her eyes. Surprised, he looked to his wife at the other end of the table. Elsie seemed as bewildered as he, but she did not comment. Preoccupied with their own letters, no one else noticed Vi's little outburst or the look of concern that passed between her parents.

Recovering himself quickly, Edward said in his light-hearted style, "I think we are all done now, so everyone may be excused. I have a little business to attend to, and I'm sure that the rest of you could use a few extra minutes to review your lessons before your classes with Mamma. We shall all return here at nine for morning devotion."

There was a general rustling of chairs as the Travilla children stood—remembering to thank their parents before scattering to their rooms. Ed, who at eighteen was as tall and nearly as strong as his father, lifted Molly from her seat and carried her easily to her wheeled chair; he pushed the chair, accompanying his cousin out to the veranda for a breath of the clean autumn air. At the sound of feet exiting the dining room, Danny's nursemaid, Christine, entered to take her young charge away to have his hands and face thoroughly washed.

Alone, Edward and Elsie expressed their mutual astonishment at Vi's behavior.

"Her remark to you was rude, as was her tone," said Elsie, "but I do not believe she intended any disrespect."

"Nor do I," Edward agreed. "In fact, the disrespect was mine. I teased her in front of her brothers and sisters, and I should have known better. Vi's resilience and genial humor have always hidden a deep well of sensitive feelings. I must admit that I cannot get used to the fact that she is growing up and that I must be more thoughtful."

Elsie said, "I, too, have difficulty realizing that our Vi is becoming a young lady."

"No longer our little fairy," Edward replied with a gentle smile. "But I must make amends to her and cultivate the habit of biting my tongue when I am tempted to tease."

Then an idea struck him. "Would you allow her to miss school this morning?" he asked.

Violet's Hidden Doubts

"At your request, I would," his wife said, putting her hand lovingly upon his arm. "But what do you have in mind?"

"I was thinking that she might enjoy a father-and-daughter day. I have to go to the west field where the men are clearing that old oak grove. It's a good ride there and back, and the day is clear and warm. Vi might enjoy an outing and a picnic."

"And some concerted attention from her adored papa," Elsie smiled.

"I hope she will like that, too," Edward said. "I shall enjoy some time alone with her even more."

Elsie squeezed his arm and looked into his handsome face. "You are so much alike, you and Vi," she said. "I realized many years ago that should there ever be conflict between the two of you, it would come from likeness rather than differences. And like you, Vi cannot stay angry for very long. By all means, ask her to join you today. An outing will be good for you both."

Vi had gone straight to her room after breakfast. She sat on her bed and dabbed at her eyes with her handkerchief.

"What a silly goose you are, Violet Travilla," she said sternly to herself. "Papa meant no hurt to you. He was only teasing, and you were dreadfully rude."

Just the thought of her father brought a fresh rush of tears, and her face burned with shame. She wiped at the tears, struggling to banish them.

"You must apologize," she said with determination. "That's all there is to it. You must not let Papa leave the house until you have said that you are sorry and asked for his forgiveness."

Bruised Feelings

She went to her mirror, as she had done earlier that morning, but this time she saw only her red-rimmed eyes and flushed cheeks. She found a fresh handkerchief and was wiping away the last traces of tears when she heard a soft knock at her door.

She hesitated for a moment, hating to see anyone until all signs of her distress had been erased, but then she said, "Come in."

She was still looking into the mirror when she saw the door open behind her and her father reflected in the silvery glass. Instantly, she turned around and ran into his open arms.

"I'm so sorry, Papa," she sobbed, "for what I said and how rude I was. I don't know why I acted that way. I never meant to hurt your feelings."

Edward hugged her close and began softly, "I accept your apology, pet, and I hope you will accept mine. I was wrong to tease you, and especially wrong to tease in front of others. I had no right to embarrass you. The truth, dearest, is that I spoke before I thought."

He pulled a handkerchief from his pocket, and raising Vi's face, he patted the soft cloth against her cheeks.

Vi looked into his eyes and saw that they were full of love. She struggled to control her crying, taking in several large gulps of air to steady her voice and calm the trembling sensation in her stomach.

"But, Papa," she said at last, "I like your teasing, for you are never cruel or thoughtless. I don't know why I got upset this morning. I had no reason to feel embarrassed or to talk back the way I did."

Edward slipped one arm around her shoulder and guided her to the narrow bench that stood in front of her window. Together, they sat down, and he kept his arm about her.

Violet's Hidden Doubts

"You're becoming a young lady," he said. "You will be fifteen on your next birthday. At your age, we all have new feelings, and our emotions sometimes rule our heads. It's a natural part of growing up. Perhaps you might have phrased your complaint more politely, but I should have realized that my casually spoken words could cause you pain. I am not so old yet that I should forget how I felt at your age."

Vi looked sideways up at her father, and a little smile tugged at the corners of her mouth. Her rich brown eyes, now dry of tears, sparkled. "You're not old, Papa," she said. "At least, not *so* very old."

Edward sat back, as if in surprise. "Why, Vi," he exclaimed, "I am but a spring chicken! A mere pup! Whatever do you mean—not so very old?"

"Well, not as old as Grandpapa, though he is your best friend," she replied with mock seriousness, "but older than Mamma, and much, *much* older than I."

He laughed, and at the sound of it, Vi felt a weight of guilt lift from her heart. Edward's laughter was to her among the sweetest, most reassuring sounds in life.

"I don't think that I want to grow up, Papa," she said. "Everything seems so complicated now, and I worry about things that never bothered me before—silly things like not getting a letter this morning. The older I become, the more mistakes I seem to make, like being rude to you because I didn't get a letter."

"Again, dearest, that's natural. The secret is to see each mistake we make as an opportunity to grow in wisdom and to learn from all that we experience. Things do get more complicated as we grow older, but when we are wise, we can recognize our errors and ask for the forgiveness of our

Heavenly Father and of those we may offend. And with wisdom, we can forgive others as our Lord forgives us."

"Then you really forgive me, Papa?" she asked.

"Of course, I do," he answered. "And will you forgive me?"

"I do," she said, adding, "though my impertinence was the worse fault."

"Then all is settled between us, and we will both ask our Father for His forgiveness. Now we must make amends. I shall try to be more thoughtful and understanding if you try to be less quick to take offense," he said, squeezing her shoulder as she nodded her head in agreement.

"So let us speak no more of it," he went on. "I have what I hope will be a happy suggestion. I must go out to the west field, and as it is such a beautiful fall day, I thought you might accompany me. If you change to your riding habit now, we can leave right after devotion and prayers. Your mother has agreed that you may have a holiday from your studies, if you like."

"Oh, dear," Vi said in confusion.

"If you have a more important engagement..."

"Oh, no, Papa. Not an engagement. It's just that I have a French lesson with Mamma today, and I have worked very hard on my pronunciation. I'm not sure if..."

"Don't worry yourself, pet," Edward said cheerfully, though in truth he felt a twinge of disappointment. "We can go tomorrow. The clearing of that field has been slow and will continue for several days more. Today, I'll work with the men, but tomorrow I promise to be your attentive escort. If we ask her politely, I'm sure that Crystal will prepare a delicious meal for us, and we can enjoy a ride and a picnic. What do you say?"

Violet's Hidden Doubts

"That would be perfect, Papa," she agreed with enthusiasm.

"Then tomorrow it will be—unless you receive a better offer," he said.

"You're teasing me again, Papa," Vi giggled. "What better offer could there be?"

Edward hugged her to his side. "You must allow me a little teasing, dear girl, for it is a habit of mine that I cannot break easily. We shall keep it just between us."

Vi reached up and grasped the strong hand on her shoulder. "Please, Papa, don't ever change. Promise me that you won't," she said in a near-whisper. Edward, who was closely attuned to the natures of each of his children, caught the genuine seriousness that now infused her tone.

"I shan't, pet," he said. "I will always love you from the fullness of my heart and be here for you until the end of my days."

They sat for a minute more in silence—father and daughter bathed in the golden light of the autumn morning—and Vi drew confidence, as she had since she was an infant, from the strength of her Papa's love. Then Edward took his watch from his pocket, and he saw that the time was but a few minutes before nine.

"May I escort my lovely daughter to the dining room for our devotion?" he asked with exaggerated formality.

"You may, kind sir," Vi replied in the same manner. They rose, and Edward took her hand and put it upon his arm. As if she were the most regal princess of Europe, he led his daughter from the room.

CHAPTER 2

Lessons in Love

*The entire law is summed up
in a single command: "Love
your neighbor as
yourself."*

GALATIANS 5:14

Lessons in Love

As soon as the morning's devotion—which included all the members of the household staff—was concluded, each person went to his or her daily duties. Edward, with Ben at his side, rode out to the fields, while Elsie and the younger children gathered in the schoolroom. Molly went to her room where she would spend the morning at her writing. Young Danny was having a romp in the garden, under Christine's watchful eye.

From the youngest to the eldest, each person in the large, well-run household felt the comfort of the familiar—knowing that work was being done, chores were attended to, and life was proceeding according to their expectations.

Ed, who was entering one of the great Eastern universities in just a few months, was taking advanced studies with a tutor in the city. He left the house shortly after his father and would not return until the afternoon. Missy usually assisted her mother in the schoolroom, but the receipt of her fiancé's letter excused her on this day.

In the kitchen, Crystal and her helpers were busy preparing the midday meal. Aunt Chloe, still spry in her seventies, was making her morning visit to the servants' quarters, checking on the health and well-being of every employee and putting together a mental list of their needs. Old Joe—far less mobile than his wife but no less sharp in mind—directed the housemaids about their work. Beds were made, dishes washed, laundry gathered, furniture dusted and polished, ashes raked, and logs laid in all the fireplaces. The jobs that kept the house and plantation humming and productive were being tended to as usual on

Violet's Hidden Doubts

this altogether ordinary Tuesday morning. Not in their wildest imaginings could anyone have guessed what the rest of the day would bring.

In the schoolroom, Vi was focused entirely on her French recitation. She had, as she told her father, been working very hard on her pronunciation. As she waited her turn for Elsie's attention, she silently mouthed each word in the lengthy recitation, forming her lips and tongue to shape the foreign sounds with precision. Nothing that was happening around her penetrated her concentration. Vi herself often marveled at this ability to concentrate so intensely on her studies, when her thoughts seemed so confused at other times.

Finally Elsie called Vi forward, and the girl declaimed the entire passage—selected from the work of a French philosopher—to near perfection. Elsie was more than pleased. She offered several suggestions to enhance Vi's pronunciation, but on the whole could do little more than offer praise. Elsie's pride increased as they discussed the contents of the difficult passage. Vi had not only learned the words correctly but had also delved into their meaning, and her comments were remarkably astute for one of her age. Vi glowed with satisfaction at her mother's praise.

Brought into the schoolroom by Christine, Danny crawled happily onto Elsie's lap and asked for the story of Goldilocks and "the twee bears." All the children, including Vi, gathered round to listen.

"So what do you think of Goldilocks, Danny?" Elsie asked when she finished the story.

"She's a wude girl," Danny said with great conviction. "She ate the bears' bweakfast and slept in their beds and didn't even ask!"

"Maybe she doesn't have a mamma and papa as good as ours," Rosemary said, "to teach her the right way to treat others."

"Not that we're so perfect," Vi responded, thinking of her own rudeness that morning and again feeling regret.

"Vi is right. None of us is perfect," Elsie said, "and that's why we are so grateful that the one who is perfect, our Lord Jesus, taught us the ways to show love and respect for our fellow men. Would you like to hear a story that Jesus told us about love for others?"

"Yes, please," Danny replied, snuggling against his mother.

"It's from the tenth chapter of Luke," Elsie began. "One day, a man asked Jesus about the command to love our neighbors as we love ourselves. The man wanted to know who his neighbor was. So Jesus told him about another man who was traveling from Jerusalem to Jericho when he was attacked by thieves. The thieves took away everything he had, beat him, and left him lying half-dead beside the road. Soon a priest came down the road, but seeing the beaten man, the priest crossed to the other side and walked on. Then another man, a Levite, happened down the same road. And he saw the beaten man, but he also crossed to the other side and walked past."

Two red circles had appeared on Danny's chubby cheeks. He said forcefully, "That's so bad!"

Elsie said, "The man must have looked terrible — like a beggar or even a thief. Would anyone have the love to help him?"

Violet's Hidden Doubts

"I don't know," Danny said in a small whisper.

"Well, a man from Samaria came by. We don't know his business there, but Jesus tells us that the Samaritan had a donkey and money. Surely he had no need to stop, but the Samaritan took pity. He cleaned the man's wounds and took him to an inn. The Samaritan stayed with the man until the next day. When he left, he gave money to the innkeeper so that the man would be cared for until the Samaritan returned. Now who is the real neighbor?"

"The man with the donkey!" Daniel exclaimed.

They laughed, and Elsie patted her little boy's head. "That's right, Danny. The Good Samaritan didn't think of himself. He showed mercy to someone in need, and Jesus tells us, 'go, and do likewise.'"

Vi said nothing, but she closed her eyes and tried to imagine what she would have done. *Would I have been afraid and run away? Would I have thought only of myself?* She pictured the Samaritan hurrying to the wounded man. *The Samaritan did not think about himself. Oh, dear Lord, help me to be like the Samaritan! Help me to put the needs of others before my own selfish wishes. Help me to be a loving and merciful person.*

When Vi opened her eyes, the other children were discussing the parable. Rosemary commented thoughtfully, "If Goldilocks was a Good Samaritan, she wouldn't go into the bears' house and sleep in their beds and eat their food."

Elsie smiled as she listened to the children's spirited conversation, and Vi understood why. Elsie and Edward had taught their children to see the Lord's teachings as the great blueprint for their earthly lives.

In joy and in sorrow, Vi thought, *as Mamma says, the answers to life's questions are all in God's Holy Word.*

~~~~~

As the morning came to an end, the young Travillas began to tidy their desks. They were almost done when Missy entered. She went to her mother and said, "Molly and her mamma have already eaten, for Aunt Enna seemed quite hungry after her walk. But Papa hasn't returned yet, and Crystal asks if you wish to delay lunch until he arrives."

Elsie considered for a moment, then replied, "No, I think we will begin at the usual time. Your father said that he might eat with the men." She looked at the little watch pinned to her blouse. "Please tell Crystal that we'll be down in fifteen minutes, Missy dear. And take Rosemary to wash her hands."

Missy got her little sister; Herbert and Harold, too, went to prepare themselves. Danny was playing with a slate and some chalk, and Elsie was putting the lesson books back on the shelf when Vi came to her side.

"Mamma, I want to apologize for my behavior at breakfast," Vi said softly. "I was rude to Papa and no less so to you, for my remark showed disrespect."

"Did you apologize to your father?" Elsie asked.

"Yes, ma'am, and we talked before he left. He was so understanding," Vi said.

Elsie smiled. "Yes, he is. He has an uncanny ability to put himself in the shoes of another and understand not just the behavior but its causes as well. You and your brothers and sisters are most fortunate to have a father like Edward. And I also accept your apology, dearest."

Vi put her arm around her mother's waist and hugged her. "Thank you, Mamma. I try so hard to keep my feelings to myself, but it is as though they escape me no matter what I do."

"But, Vi, we do not expect you to hide your feelings," Elsie said. "Papa and I are here to listen to you and help you in every way we can. And no matter what you feel, you can always take it to your Heavenly Father."

"I know that, Mamma, but my feelings seem so small and petty sometimes. It seems wrong to take them to God when others have so many terrible problems."

Elsie stepped back and put her hands on her daughter's shoulders, which were level with her own now. She looked straight into Vi's beautiful, troubled eyes and said, "God bears all our burdens and relieves our suffering. Nothing is too small for Him, and you should never hesitate to speak to Him. Do you remember these verses from Matthew 10? 'Are not two sparrows sold for a penny? Yet not one of them will fall to the ground apart from the will of your Father. And even the very hairs of your head are all numbered.' Vi, not even the hairs on your head are too small for the Lord's attention. He wants to hear all your thoughts and troubles and to help you at all times."

Vi dropped her gaze. "I often think my worries are too unimportant for Him."

"Well, child, I can tell you that you are incorrect. Nothing is too trivial for Him. Take all your worries and concerns to God, and He will give you His love and strength and guidance. He may not help or answer you in the way you hope or expect, for His wisdom is beyond our comprehension, but He will always do what's best for you. Trust Him always."

Vi raised her eyes again and replied, "Love and trust are inseparable, aren't they, Mamma? I know that I love God

and He loves me, so I must trust in His love no matter what—even when it is difficult."

Elsie smiled warmly. "Knowing that is a sign of great wisdom, Vi. Keep the promise of Psalm 32 with you, that the Lord's unfailing love surrounds those who trust in Him. Keep faith with Him, my dearest girl, for He always keeps faith with you."

"Thank you, Mamma," Vi said simply, though many thoughts suddenly filled her mind. A new understanding of the meaning of trust seemed to have burst upon her, and she realized that she had much to talk over with her Heavenly Father and Friend.

At that moment, however, small hands tugged at both Elsie's and Vi's skirts, and mother and daughter looked down into a bright, chalk-covered face.

"I'm hung-wee," Danny said.

"Of course you are, my darling," Elsie laughed, sweeping him up in her arms. "But first we must find a damp cloth and wipe the chalk from your nose and cheeks. Vi, you go ahead, and my dusty boy and I will join you in a few minutes. We can talk more this evening if you like."

"I would like that very much, Mamma," Vi replied.

Luncheon was served though Edward had not arrived. As they ate, the children talked about their activities for the afternoon. Herbert and Harold were to have a riding lesson. Missy requested permission to take the buggy and go into the city to do a few errands (chief among them, though she didn't say so, to mail her return letter to Lester), and she asked if Rosemary and Vi might accompany her. Rosemary's face lit up at the idea of an excursion, but Vi declined, saying that she wanted to do some pencil sketching outdoors. Elsie herself announced that she would be going to The Oaks and that Danny would go with her—Molly and Aunt Enna, too, if they wished.

Vi did want to sketch that afternoon. She loved the colors of early autumn and was planning to do a series of watercolor paintings of locations about the plantation—works that she hoped would be good enough to present to her parents for Christmas—and her sketches would be her starting point. But she also had a lot of thinking to do. Her earlier conversation with her mother had stirred new ideas about the nature of trust, and she wanted to talk with both her parents. She hoped that she might be able to have some time with her father when he returned.

In fact, she expected him to come into the dining room at any minute, for she had not heard Elsie say that he might stay in the field all day. The meal went on, and when he had not appeared as dessert was being served, Vi began to feel a little anxious. *Perhaps he will work till day's end*, she thought. *He sometimes does. Then he'll be tired, and I may not be able to talk to him until tomorrow.* If there was a hint of selfishness in her concern, it was not intentional. Vi was sensitive to her father's well-being. She had teased him that morning about his age; in truth, however, she'd become increasingly aware of how much Edward worked, and she sometimes worried that he pushed himself far too much. He was always so willing to take on tasks that might easily be assigned to others.

Despite his youthful looks, Edward was in his late fifties, and to Vi, this was an age when her father should begin to rest from hard labor. But Edward often said that to be able to work was one of God's gifts, and he reveled in days like

this, when he shared the physical labor of farming with his employees. But Vi, always the most sensitive of the Travilla children, never failed to notice when her father seemed fatigued or his endless supply of good humor was a trifle low. As the others ate their desserts and chatted on about their activities, she raised a quick, silent prayer — *Thank You, Lord, for my Papa, and please watch over him and help him in all his hard work* — before turning her attention back to the apple custard that had been placed before her without her even noticing.

Everyone had just been excused and Vi was about to leave the dining room when her mother called her back.

"You seemed unusually quiet during lunch," Elsie said. "I hope you're not still worried about the matter of this morning."

"I was just thinking of different things. I've been hoping that Papa would be back this afternoon."

"Ah, I see," Elsie smiled. "There are times when a girl just needs to talk to her father. When I was your age, my own Papa was the world to me. Even now, there are times when I simply need to talk things over with him. That's one of the reasons I'm going to The Oaks this afternoon. Are you sure you won't join us for the ride?"

"No, ma'am, unless you desire me to," Vi said. "I really want to sketch today. The light is so clear, and I want to work on some drawings of the boathouse and landing at the lake."

"The day is most definitely a brilliant one for those with an artist's eye," Elsie agreed. "I will give your grandparents your

love. But don't stay out too late. The weather turns chilly rather early now, and I don't want you to catch a cold."

Elsie kissed Vi and went to the rear of the house to invite Molly and Enna on the ride to The Oaks. Everyone else had scattered, so Vi left to get her drawing supplies from her room. The prospect of an afternoon of drawing cheered her. *The sun will chase away my dark thoughts*, she told herself as she climbed the stairs in the main hall—taking them two at a time as she used to when she was a little girl.

No one was near the front door when a horse and rider charged up the driveway at full gallop. The rider pulled the horse to a rearing halt and, dropping the reins to the ground, dismounted even before the horse had stopped.

Breathing rapidly, Ben dashed inside and looked about. Seeing no one, he ran down the entrance hall and into the dining room. Crystal, his wife, was there, checking that the table was clear of all the dinner things. She looked up at her husband and instantly recognized the import of his dreadful expression.

"What's happened?" she asked.

"Got to find Miss Elsie," he gasped. "Mr. Edward's been hurt, and they're bringing him back now, in the big cart. Got to find her."

Crystal grabbed his shoulders. His face was covered with dust but she saw two tracks—the mark of tears—that ran from his eyes across his checks. She put her hand gently to his face.

"I'll get Miss Elsie," she said. "She was planning a ride to The Oaks this afternoon, but I don't think she's left yet.

You stay here and catch your breath. Whatever the news, you got to have your wits about you when you tell her."

"Then go quickly," he said, waving her hand away. "Just don't let the children hear you."

"How bad is it?" Crystal asked even as she crossed to the door.

"Don't know exactly," he answered in a breaking voice. "I sent one of the boys to fetch Dr. Arthur at Roselands. But I could see it was bad. Real bad."

Crystal was gone before the last words left his mouth.

CHAPTER

3

Trouble in the Field

*In this world you will have
trouble. But take heart!
I have overcome
the world.*

JOHN 16:33

Trouble in the Field

*A*t about the time Violet and her siblings were sitting down to their meal, the men in the west field of Ion were just returning to their work. They had stopped for food — cold, roasted meat and corn cakes brought from the quarters that morning, hot coffee brewed over a campfire in the field, and water from barrels hauled to the site in a large farm cart, which had also carried the saws, axes, and other tools required for the work of clearing.

Edward ate with his men, and they talked about the work underway; then Edward asked each man about his family, especially the children. Edward Travilla was their employer, but to many of the men he was also a friend. Some, like Ben, had known Edward all their lives; most of the workers, however, had come to the plantation after the Civil War and emancipation. Among the former slaves of the region, it had become known that the owner of Ion was a just and fair man who paid good wages and wasn't afraid to get his own hands dirty when there was hard work to be done. Edward's reputation had gained as well from what was still called the "Battle of Ion" — the brief but tumultuous conflict that had rid the area of the Ku Klux Klan a decade earlier. In the years since, Ion had attracted a highly capable and loyal workforce, and Edward always repaid the loyalty of his employees in kind.

Their task that afternoon was felling an enormous oak tree that would have to be cut into parts before it could be hauled away. The tree was old and large, and the undergrowth was dense with bushes and thick vines. There was always the danger of accidents, but the men were both cautious and experienced. Edward joined his men as they assembled at the oak tree. The line of its eventual fall had been calculated, and the tree was rigged with a network of ropes that would be used to pull it down into a clear space.

His shirt sleeves rolled up tight around his strong, tanned upper arms and his face streaked with dirt and sweat, Edward grabbed one side of the saw. A man named Enoch, a match to Edward in size and strength, grasped the opposite handle in his large, gloved hands. Back and forth they drew the saw, ripping into the wood until the blade neared the mid-way point. Another pair of men stood by, but Edward and Enoch carried on, the rhythm of their movements in perfect unity. It appeared they might attempt to finish the job.

Suddenly, there was a low sound almost like a moan that seemed to come from the earth itself. The moaning quickly rose to a high-pitched scream. Edward and Enoch appeared not to hear, but the other men recognized the noise. The weakened old tree was splitting at some point inside. As the tree's groaning and shrieking increased, the shouts of human voices joined the chorus, and several men rushed forward to pull Edward and Enoch away from the saw. They all had to run, for there was now no way to know how the great tree would fall.

Edward, backing away from the tree, shouted an order to the workers manning the guide ropes. He hoped they might be able to pull the tree to the right position. He looked around to locate the other men, seeing that all were headed for safe areas.

Watching from some distance, Ben yelled frantically, "Get outta there, Mr. Edward! She's coming down!" The huge oak was beginning to sway and buckle under its own weight, and Ben could see that it would crash not in the direction the men expected, but in the area where Edward now stood.

Hearing Ben's voice, Edward at last turned. Behind him, he heard a roaring crack like a cannon blast, and he knew that he must run for his life. He did run, praying as he did that all the men were clear. But then he encountered a stretch of rough undergrowth, thick with snake-like vines that grabbed at his feet and threatened to drag him down. The cracking and splintering noises were now like a barrage of gunfire, and as he forced his way forward, Edward felt, rather than heard, the shifting of earth as if the ground itself were heaving under his feet. Then the air was sucked from his lungs. With a horrible *whoosh*, the tree toppled.

Ben saw it happen. Edward running; the tree falling as if in pursuit of him; then Edward vanishing in a cloud of green and gold and brown as the tree hit the ground with a terrible, awesome thud. The ground shuddered with the blow. Then, except for the gentle quivering of the tree's dry leaves, there was silence.

In seconds, Ben, followed by other workers, reached the place where he had last seen Edward—though Ben always said later that time seemed to stand still in those moments. But the tree's mighty limbs and the dust raised by its fall obscured their vision. The men began searching, and someone called for handsaws to cut away the larger branches. Someone else yelled for quiet so they might listen for a voice, but no call for help was heard.

"Where are you, Mr. Edward?" Ben cried out in desperation as he tore at the branches and leaves. Seconds later a deep voice called, "Here! He's here!"

Ben raised his gaze and saw the powerful figure of Enoch standing not many feet away. Enoch was waving an

axe above his head as if it were a flag, and the searching men scrambled toward him.

Edward lay still, his face to the ground. He was trapped at the fork in a large branch, and its two thick fingers pinned down his legs and torso. Ben moved swiftly but with great gentleness to lift Edward's head and clear his mouth of dirt. Putting his own face close to his fallen friend's, Ben felt a soft, unsteady flow of air. Edward was breathing but unconscious.

Instantly, saws and axes were put to work to remove the huge limb. When it was severed from the tree, Enoch and several others bent to lift it. With strength that seemed beyond human capabilities, Enoch held the limb above the ground, enabling the others to free Edward's limp form. With great care, the men moved Edward away from the spot, and only when Enoch saw that all were beyond danger did he release the limb. It fell with a crash that eerily echoed the thundering collapse of the giant oak.

Two of the men had removed one side from the farm cart and brought it to where Edward now lay. A rough blanket was spread atop the long, flat, wood rectangle, and steady arms lifted his body again, placing him on the makeshift stretcher. Ben could see that Edward's leg was broken, and he called for someone to bring straight branches for a splint. Another man tore his own shirt off and ripped it into strips to bind the splint. They worked hurriedly. No one said anything, but all the men shared an understanding that Edward's injuries were likely to be much graver than a broken leg.

The splint completed, the men lifted the stretcher and bore it back to the cart. The mules had been hitched, and the driver was in his seat, ready to depart at Ben's signal.

Trouble in the Field

Ben climbed into the cart and knelt beside his friend just as Edward opened his dazed eyes. Ben offered words of comfort as Edward slowly came to awareness.

"You'll be all right, Mr. Edward," Ben said. "We're takin' you up to the house, and I already sent young Gus to Roselands for Dr. Conley. You'll be fine, I just know it."

Edward's mouth moved as he attempted to speak, and Ben tried to quiet him.

"Don't say nothing, sir. Save your strength now."

But in a harsh whisper, Edward forced the words out— "Tell...Elsie. Go...tell...Elsie."

Ben understood immediately. "I will," he said. "I'll go straight to the house."

Ben looked up and motioned to someone standing nearby. Enoch climbed into the cart and came to Ben's side.

"Now, Enoch's going to sit with you while I ride on up to the house," Ben said to Edward. "Enoch's going to make sure you have an easy journey back home. Don't you worry, Mr. Edward."

Edward looked into his old friend's eyes and tried to smile. But even that small effort contorted his ashen face with pain, and his eyes fell shut once more.

Enoch took Ben's place beside the stretcher, and Ben quickly got down from the cart. He went to the front and consulted with the driver, warning the man to proceed slowly lest the bumping of the vehicle cause further injury to its passenger. Tears began to stream from Ben's eyes as he hurried to mount Solomon—Edward's horse—and spur the animal to a gallop.

Violet's Hidden Doubts

By a stroke of good fortune, both Dr. Arthur Conley and his brother Cal were at Roselands when Gus rode up. Without dismounting, the young Ion worker called out to see them, and so apparent was the urgency of his demand that an old servant standing on the portico steps rushed inside without asking a question.

Arthur and Cal appeared just moments later, and Gus told them what had occurred. Cal asked for more details of the accident while Arthur ran back into the house to get his medical bag. He summoned one of the housemaids and dispatched her to the stable. Within five minutes, Arthur's and Cal's saddled horses were being led to the house.

Arthur then instructed the stableman who had brought the horses to take the fastest steed available, ride for Dr. Barton, and escort the old physician to Ion. The little housemaid had joined the anxious group, and Cal told her to take Gus inside and inform old Mr. Dinsmore of the accident. To Gus, Cal said, "Try not to alarm our grandfather too much. He has not been well, so there is no need to speculate about Edward's injuries." Cal then instructed Gus to ride to The Oaks to inform Horace, Jr. of the events.

The maid spoke up: "I'll take care of your grandpa, Mr. Cal. I'll see that he isn't too much disturbed."

"Thank you," Cal said. "You will have to speak to my mother as well. Tell her that she is to stay here with Grandpa until we have more news."

"You can trust me, sir," the young woman said. "I'll handle Miss Louise. We'll all be praying for Mr. Edward as hard as we can."

Gus arrived at The Oaks about a half hour later, and much the same events were repeated. As soon as Horace Dinsmore heard the report, he ordered that his horse be

brought, then hurried to tell his wife of the accident. They decided that Rose should follow him to Ion as quickly as possible, bringing what they would need for an extended stay.

"God willing, Edward's injuries are not serious, and we shall not be required there for long," Horace said. He clasped Rose's hands to his chest and closed his eyes. "Let us pray, love. Whatever has happened, Dear Lord, give us the strength to support Edward and our daughter and grandchildren through this time of trial."

"And the wisdom to accept Your will, Dear Father, whatever it may be," Rose added in a voice that trembled poignantly.

When Horace, with Gus at his side, galloped up the drive to Ion, they were greeted by the incongruous sight of the large, weathered farm cart standing before the gracious entrance to the plantation house. Coming closer, they saw many men, including Ben and Cal Conley, gathered near the cart. Horace's daughter was in the wagon, bent low over her husband as Arthur Conley ministered to the inert figure lying on a panel of rough boards.

Is he dead? Horace thought desperately as he left his horse and pushed through the men to a place beside Cal near the rear of the cart.

As if in answer to his question, he heard Arthur saying, "We're going to take you inside now, Edward. We will try to cause you as little pain as possible."

"All is ready for you, my dearest," Elsie crooned to her husband. "You will soon be off this hard board and in bed."

Violet's Hidden Doubts

Then she stood, and her cousin Cal reached out, put his hands around her waist, and lifted her from the wagon to the ground. Seeing her father there, Elsie swayed slightly, and he took her in his arms. Horace could feel her shaking, as she had when she was a child and afraid, but her spine was straight and she showed no sign of fainting. Instead, she grasped his hand and held it tightly as she watched her husband being moved.

The men, Enoch in the lead, took over—sliding Edward's pallet from the cart and hoisting it down in one swift, sure movement. Five of them, two on each side and one at the foot of the wooden stretcher, bore it up the front steps and into the house.

CHAPTER

4

Whose Fault?

My heart is in anguish within me; the terrors of death assail me.

PSALM 55:4

Whose Fault?

*V*i had watched everything from her bedroom window. The mules, held tightly in check by one of the field workers, pulling the farm cart ever so slowly toward the house. The farm hands walking in silence behind the cart. Her mother and Ben running to meet the cart and then walking alongside it until it came to a stop at the entrance to the house. A powerful man in the cart lifting her mother up, and then her mother down on both knees, bending over the still figure that lay there. Arthur and Cal Conley riding at full gallop up the drive.

With a rising sense of dread, Vi watched and listened to the voices below her. Cousin Arthur's voice, her mother's — snatches of their low talk: "unconscious…" "clean break…" "don't want to move him yet…" "my darling…" Vi could see her father's body and Arthur's hands touching it. She could see her mother's back and, when Elsie turned her head, the drawn look of her face in profile, but not her father's face.

Vi leaned as far out of the window as she could. But still her father's face eluded her. *Oh, to see his face for a second! To see his face and to know that he is alive. If I could just be sure he was alive, I could move from this spot and do as I was told. It's like a nightmare! Maybe that's all it is,* Vi thought frantically, *just a horrible nightmare that I will wake from at any moment.*

When Ben had broken the news to Elsie, she'd immediately asked Crystal to find Vi, Missy, and the other children right away and send them to the nursery. Catching Vi as she was about to leave the house, Crystal had said only, "Your Papa's been hurt, and your Mamma wants you to keep the little ones in the nursery. Now don't you worry. It'll be all right. Just go on up and wait till your Mamma can get to you. It'll be just fine." And Vi had dutifully gone back upstairs, but not to the nursery.

Despite Crystal's assurance, Vi knew instinctively that something was terribly wrong. So she ran to her room, drawn back to the same window from which she had watched her father ride up the driveway that very morning, laughing and sharing a joke with the stableman. Edward's expression from that morning floated before her eyes — his face so alive with the simple pleasure of his ride. She could see again the motion of his hand as he patted the stableman's shoulder in comradeship.

Oh, God, at least let me see him move! her mind cried out. *Let me see some sign that he is alive!*

Directly below her window, Old Joe had come out on the veranda, and one of the workers had joined him. Vi could not see the men but she could hear them clearly.

Joe asked what happened, and the other man replied, "That big, old oak fell while Mr. Edward was cutting it. Came down like thunder and caught him before he could get clear. Broke his leg, I know, but..."

"But what?"

"But it's worse than that, Joe. I've seen men hurt before, and this is bad."

"We don't know that," Joe said forcefully. "We can't know nothing like that till Dr. Conley tells us. You and the men — don't you be spreading any stories before we get the truth from Dr. Conley."

"We ain't, Joe," the other man protested. "But you oughta know that it could be bad."

"I'll believe it when I hear it from the doctor or Miss Elsie — and not before."

Then they stopped talking. But the words tore at Vi's mind and heart—*could be bad.*

She wanted to scream at the invisible men below her: *How bad? Please just tell me how bad!*

With her eyes glued to the wagon, she struggled to hear more. All the while, the most dreadful thoughts hammered at her. *If he dies...my fault...if I'd only gone...if only...it's my fault. God, save him! It's all my fault!*

Then she saw her father's hand move. Or did it? Yes, her father's hand had moved, and her mother had taken it in her own.

A voice spoke behind her, and Vi jumped at the sound.

"You come away from that window, Violet," Aunt Chloe was saying. "I need you in the nursery now, like your mamma said."

Grabbing the old nursemaid tightly, Vi exclaimed, "Papa's alive! I saw his hand move!"

"Sure he's alive," Chloe replied, keeping her own fear out of her voice. "And if you wanna help him, you come along with me and stay with your brothers and sisters and just wait for your mamma."

Taking the girl's trembling hand, Chloe led her across the room. Vi didn't resist. In truth, she had little sense of what she was doing. Her body seemed to move without her being conscious of it. All she could think of were the words she had uttered—*Papa's alive!*

Under Arthur's supervision, the men had taken Edward inside and gently moved him onto the bed in one of the back

rooms. Arthur slipped a pillow under Edward's head, and Crystal drew the covers up.

The men watched for a few moments, and then, without a word, they stood back as Elsie entered, followed by her father. Still in silence, the workers raised the empty stretcher and departed.

Elsie took her husband's hand but sought Arthur's eyes. Reading her unspoken question, Arthur said, "He has lost consciousness again, but his breathing is more regular. From my examination and what Ben tells me of the accident, I'm sure Edward has not suffered any head or spinal injury. His leg is broken, but it is a clean break and I've set it. I also believe several ribs are broken, yet his lungs sound clear, so I will bind his chest. But…" He hesitated.

"But there may be injuries you cannot see," Elsie said, completing his thought in a voice so firm and strong that it surprised everyone in the room.

"Yes," Arthur said simply. "I sent for Dr. Barton, and he should be here soon to consult."

"Is there anything we should be doing?" Elsie asked.

"I must bind his ribs, and I can use Crystal's assistance. Then we must keep him still. The risk is that any movement may cause a damaged rib to puncture a lung."

Elsie turned to Horace, "You will stay here, won't you, Papa? I must go to the children, but I will not be long. Then we will keep watch together."

"Of course," Horace replied. "And yes, you must hurry to the children. They are surely terrified for their father and only you can give them the comfort they need. But Rose will arrive shortly, to care for them. She and I will stay as long as you and Edward and the children need us."

He went to her and placed his arm around her shoulder. Elsie stood very still, holding her husband's hand, and she was calmed by her father's embrace. A part of her longed to break down and let her tears flow and wash the overwhelming fear from her body. Yet the stronger part of her knew that now was not the time for weeping. As Edward had always been her rock in times of trial, so she must be doubly strong for him and their children. Until Edward was restored to them all, she must be both mother and father.

Rose Dinsmore's carriage had pulled up to the portico not long after Edward was taken inside. When she entered the house, Rose found Old Joe sitting in a chair in the hallway. The old servant struggled to rise, but Rose bade him to remain seated.

"Stay where you are, Joe," she said kindly. "Where is Mr. Edward now?"

"They took him into the back bedroom, the one next to Miss Molly's room," Joe replied. "Miss Elsie is with him, and Mr. Horace and Dr. Arthur."

"And the children?"

"They was all about to go off when Ben brought the news, so they know what's happening—that their papa's been hurt. Miss Elsie told everybody to go up to the nursery and wait for her. Chloe's there, too. But Mr. Ed, he's not home from the city. I expect him right soon, and I thought maybe I best stay here in case he needs me."

"Yes, do wait for him, Joe. And when you see my husband, please tell him that I have arrived and gone to the children."

"I'll surely do as you ask, Miss Rose," Joe said. "I'll keep a lookout, and while I'm sittin', I'll pray with all my heart for Mr. Edward to get well. I can't think what we'd do without him, Miss Rose. I just can't bear to think of it."

Rose tried to reply, but the words caught in her throat. So she lay her hand on the old man's arm in a reassuring gesture that she hoped might comfort them both.

If Rose had expected tears when she entered the nursery, she was surprised. The young Travillas were quiet and solemn but dry-eyed. Herbert and Harold sat at the play table, for which they were both too large now, with Rosemary between them. The three were working a picture puzzle — the boys encouraging their little sister to find the pieces and guiding her progress. Near the fireplace at the end of the room, Missy sat in a high-backed armchair with Danny on her lap. In soft tones, Missy was reading her baby brother a story, and Danny curled against her and sucked his thumb. Nearby, Chloe was in a rocking chair. Her two hands clasped an old black Bible to her breast, and she seemed to be drawing strength from the mere touch of the book. The last to catch Rose's attention was Vi, who sat in the window seat, her feet drawn up and her arms clasped around her knees. Her face was pale and expressionless as she stared out the window.

At Rose's entrance, the children looked to her for news of their father, and Rose felt a hot wave of helplessness pass over her. She could not give them the answers they longed to hear.

An uneasy moment went by before Harold spoke, "Is Papa all right?"

"Can we see him?" Herbert added.

Moving to the little table, Rose said, "Your Cousin Arthur is with him now, and Dr. Barton is on the way. I

wish I had more news, but I haven't seen your Papa. Yet I know that Arthur and your mamma and grandpapa are taking very good care of him."

Rosemary suddenly jumped up from her seat, her chair tumbling over behind her.

"Is he dead?" she screamed, running to Rose and burying her face in her grandmother's skirt. "Is my Papa dead?" she sobbed.

Rose bent to cradle the child. "Oh, no, Rosemary darling. Your papa is not dead. Believe me." She lifted the girl up in her arms. Stroking Rosemary's curls, she gently began to sway as if she were soothing an infant. "Your Papa is alive, and your Mamma is taking good care of him, just as she cares for you when you are sick. God is watching over your papa. God loves your papa, and He will do what is best for him. God loves you, Rosemary, and all of us."

Rosemary's sobbing seemed to subside a bit, and in a small, choked voice, she said against her grandmother's shoulder, "I want my Mamma. I want Mamma."

Still rocking the child in her arms, Rose said to them all, "Your mamma will be here soon. And we must be very strong for her. Your papa and mamma need your strength and your courage, children. Can you be very brave and wait until she is able to come here to us?"

"Yes, Grandmamma," Herbert and Harold replied.

"I'll be brave, too," Rosemary said in a whisper, though she clung to her grandmother more tightly than before.

Chloe had risen from her chair, and she motioned for Rose to take her place. Gratefully, Rose settled herself and Rosemary in the sturdy old rocker. Herbert and Harold followed and sat on the floor beside Missy's chair, huddling close to her as if to protect themselves against cold winter winds.

Only Vi remained apart from the group. From the window seat, she gazed upon her loved ones, but she felt incapable of moving. Her legs seemed to be made of lead, her arms and shoulders of solid stone. Inside this body of metal and stone, her heart raced. She wanted to cry—to sob as Rosemary had done—but her eyes were dry, so dry they burned. She knew that Papa was alive, but what did that mean? Over and over, she heard the words of the farm worker: *Could be bad. Could be bad.*

Vi listened as Missy began to pray aloud, followed by Rose and the twins and even Rosemary, and Vi wanted desperately to add her own words. She wanted to join her family in their expressions of hope, to share their fears and be warmed by their embraces. But this body of stone and lead would not allow her to move. She was like a prisoner held back by impenetrable walls and bars. *How can I take comfort from my family when I am the reason for their sorrow? How can I ever tell them that what happened was my fault—that I could have prevented it?* Each guilty thought hammered at her brain, and her head throbbed. But far worse was the pain that gripped her heart with its icy fingers.

Vi's head dropped forward until her forehead touched her knees, and she began her own soundless, solitary prayer: *Lord, please, please,* she begged. *Please make Papa well and strong again. Please don't let him die like this. Have mercy on my family and do not take him away from us. Oh, please, Heavenly Father, save our Papa!*

CHAPTER

5

The Vigil Begins

*Even though I walk through
the valley of the shadow of
death, I will fear no evil,
for you are with me.*

PSALM 23:4

The Vigil Begins

*N*ot long after Rose's arrival, Elsie made her way to the nursery, and even Vi roused herself to find shelter at her mother's side. Elsie gathered her children close and explained what had happened. She told them what Ben had said, that their father had refused to run until he saw that all the other men were safe. She explained his broken leg and ribs. She did not, however, speculate about other injuries, for there was no need to raise fears without reason.

Missy asked about Dr. Barton, and Elsie said that the doctor had reached the house just as she was coming upstairs.

"But why does Papa need two doctors?" Vi asked, for this news fueled her growing fear that her father's condition was worse than anyone dared say.

"Well, Dr. Barton is one of our oldest and dearest friends, and he was our family doctor for many, many years before he retired. He would want to be called," Elsie replied. "Dr. Barton has a great deal of experience, and we all value his knowledge and his judgment."

"Can Papa talk to us?" Herbert inquired.

"He's sleeping now, and sleep is good for him," Elsie said. "But I did speak to him when he was first brought to the house, and he wanted me to tell all of you how much he loves you. He is counting on you to be very strong."

"I want to see my Papa," Rosemary said softly. "Can I, Mamma?"

Elsie touched her daughter's soft, warm cheek and smiled: "Not right now. We do not want to wake him, no matter how much we wish to hear his voice. I cannot tell you exactly when you may see him, for we must do as Cousin Arthur and Dr. Barton think best. But you can help Papa if you will."

"How, Mamma?" Harold asked.

"Well, I want you and Herbert to help Grandmother Rose and Aunt Chloe and take charge of the nursery," Elsie said.

"Of course, Mamma," Harold agreed.

"But is there nothing else for us to do?" Herbert asked in a plaintive tone.

"For the time being, that is what I need of you boys," Elsie said. "Missy, I'd like you to come downstairs and keep watch for Ed."

"Yes, ma'am," Missy said, glad of this task. She had been worrying about her brother, and she wanted to be with him when he received the news of their father's accident.

Looking to her middle daughter, Elsie said, "Will you come too, Vi? I'd like you to sit with Cousin Molly and Aunt Enna. They know what has occurred, but I am afraid Enna may become upset. Enna always enjoys your company, and you may be able to assist Molly as well."

Vi nodded her agreement. She felt better, somehow, because her mother expected her to help someone else. Her own emotions were in such a frightening tangle. If she was with Molly and Aunt Enna and if together, they all prayed very, very hard for her Papa—then maybe her secret feelings of guilt and shame would fade away.

"And me, Mamma?" Rosemary was asking.

Rose spoke up, "I'm counting on you to watch over Danny, dearest."

And so the young Travillas were given their assignments—in part because Elsie knew how much they wanted to help and that it was important for them to feel

that they were doing something for their father. She also genuinely needed their assistance, especially that of the older children.

"The most important thing we can do," Elsie said, "is to pray for Papa. When we are together and when you are alone, lift your prayers to our Heavenly Father. Speak from your hearts, my children, and He will hear you and give you comfort. Shall we all pray now?"

"You say the words, please, Mamma," Rosemary begged.

Elsie led them in a prayer of hope. Edward was the focus of her tender words, but she asked God's guidance as well for Arthur and Dr. Barton. She offered thanks for Ben and Enoch and the rest of the men who had rescued Edward. She prayed for God's mercy: "We are afraid, Heavenly Father," she said, "and we seek Your grace and strength to help us and our beloved father and husband and friend through this crisis. You, Lord, are our song and our salvation, an ever-present help in times of trouble. We cry out to You to hold us all in Your strong arms as we pass through this dark valley. Please, blessed God, fortify our faith. Comfort us so that we may comfort one another. Restore Edward to health and to our loving arms."

Then she recited the familiar words of Psalm 23, and everyone joined in. Elsie's eyes were closed, but she felt the warmth of her children, her stepmother, and her devoted Chloe surrounding her as if a great blanket of love enfolded them all. She heard the quality of their love and faith in their voices. So revived was she by the prayer and the closeness of her family, Elsie did not notice the absence of one voice—nor did she recognize the strange quality of pain and fear in Vi's dark eyes.

Violet's Hidden Doubts

Ed arrived at Ion, and Missy informed him of their father's accident. Together, they went to the nursery to comfort their siblings. Meanwhile, Vi was sitting beside Enna on a comfortable settee in Molly's room. Vi's head rested on Enna's shoulder, and the woman gently patted the girl's dark, silken hair.

Vi, of course, knew only a little of her great-aunt's past. Enna had been severely injured—and her mind impaired—in an accident when Vi was young, so to Vi, her Aunt Enna had always been Molly's strange, childlike mother. Then, less than a year ago, Enna had almost drowned in Ion's small lake, and she had lain in a coma for more than a week. When she at last "came back," as Molly always said, Enna was changed. While still childishly simple in many ways, she was almost always rational now and kind and thoughtful to everyone. What's more, Enna had become a Christian, opening her heart in love and gratitude to the One who had restored her to life and to her family.

Vi dearly loved her great-aunt and her Cousin Molly, and she often sought out their companionship. Her affection for Molly was owed in part to respect for the fact that Molly, despite her physical handicap, had thrown off self-pity and was determinedly making a life for herself and her mother. Molly was a published writer of growing repute. She loved all the Travillas but had a special affinity for Vi. She admired the girl's spirit and intelligence, and she understood Vi's frustrations as well.

"Mamma wanted me to comfort you," Vi was saying. "But it is you who give me comfort."

"That's what family is for," Molly said.

Tears began to trickle from Vi's eyes. "I don't know what we'll do if... Papa..."

"I think it is never wise to anticipate outcomes over which we have no control," Molly said thoughtfully. "You know that Cousin Arthur is doing his best for Edward right this minute."

"And Dr. Barton," Vi said.

"Dr. Barton is a fine man," Enna remarked in a dreamy kind of tone. "He helped to save my life, you know. Saved me twice."

Enna continued to hold Vi close and caress her hair, but Molly could see that her mother had drifted back to another time and place—a time when Enna had been the patient and her life hung in the balance.

Molly rolled her wheeled chair forward, took Vi's hand, and spoke softly: "I know that you're afraid, but you must not let yourself be overwhelmed by your fears. Neither you nor I nor anyone can know what will come to pass, for only God can see the future."

In halting phrases, Vi tried to say what her heart longed to reveal. "But I should have...if I'd...but I didn't..."

"What did you fail to do, dear girl?" Molly asked. "You didn't prevent your father's accident? But you had no way to do so. Even had you been there on the spot, you could not have changed what occurred. You musn't blame yourself, Vi. No one understands better than I the harm that guilty feelings can do."

Vi looked up suddenly, and her eyes were full of questions. *Does she know? Does Molly know what I did?*

Molly continued gently, "For a very long time after the accident that took away the use of my legs, I lived in a land of resentment and fed myself on thoughts of 'might have' and 'should have.' I blamed myself, and I blamed Mamma. I spent so much time blaming that there was nothing left over for healing. I was so full of fear and anger and guilt that I made everyone miserable, most of all myself."

Vi had not heard this before, and she couldn't imagine her cousin ever being the bitter person Molly was describing. As she listened to Molly, Vi forgot her own secret sorrow. She asked what had changed Molly's heart.

"After Mamma's first accident, your father and mother brought me into this house to live. They loved me and let me have my grief. But most important, they introduced me to Jesus. With His love and your parents' help, I began to see that I could not reclaim the past. I will never forget one remarkable night—I was reading the Bible with your mother, and we came to a passage in the Book of Isaiah. The words almost leapt from the page at me: 'Forget the former things; do not dwell on the past. See, I am doing a new thing! Now it springs up; do you not perceive it?'"

Molly paused, and then continued tenderly, "At that moment, I understood somewhere deep inside myself that God wanted me to stop thinking about what might have been and let Him do something new. I had no notion of what it was, but I knew that I could do nothing if I kept myself chained to blame and regret."

Molly squeezed Vi's hand lovingly and then shifted her position so that her back rested more comfortably against her chair. "My situation was not the same as yours, Vi, but I do know that we cannot move forward if we are endlessly looking back. We may lament the past, but we cannot undo what has been done, for that is not in our power."

The Vigil Begins

"I know," whispered Vi. "I must think only of Papa now. But...but I'm so afraid. I want him to be well again, but what can I do?"

Enna had been listening to their conversation more closely than either Molly or Vi suspected. "Hope and pray," she said suddenly. "We must pray together."

"Yes, Mamma, we must," Molly said. Leaning forward again, she reached toward Vi with one hand and her mother with the other, and they were linked in a small circle. Molly began to speak, and as the sweet words of hope flowed from her, Vi opened her heart to the source of all consolation. For those minutes, the dark shadow was lifted. But it did not disappear — not yet.

As afternoon wore into evening and evening into night, a strange quiet settled upon all of Ion. If anyone had wandered into the star-sprinkled darkness, going from the plantation house to the workers' quarters and on to the tenant houses that lay scattered far and wide, he would have heard few of the sounds of normal life. Dogs barked, horses neighed and stamped in their stalls, and cattle lowed in the pastures. But the usual sounds of human activity — the laughter and quarreling of children, the chatter of adults as they completed the tasks of the day, the whistling of night visitors returning to their homes — were absent. Sharp ears, however, might have picked up a low hum of prayers coming from house after house. Sharp eyes would have seen that the lights burned late into the night in the church in the quarters. Here and there, voices were joined in soft and solemn hymns.

Violet's Hidden Doubts

The stillness that affected all the residents of Ion was repeated at Roselands, The Oaks, and beyond. News of Edward Travilla's grave injuries had spread rapidly throughout the countryside, and there was no gaiety among his friends and neighbors that night. A man who had earned the respect of all and the friendship of many was in danger of being taken away from this close community, and few could bring themselves to contemplate such a loss. But where there is life, it is said, there is hope. Prayers of hope for Edward Travilla were raised by rich and poor alike, and even some who had lost the habit of praying found themselves in conversation with the Lord, asking for His mercy on the good man of Ion and all who loved him.

CHAPTER

6

Fears and Prayers

Out of the depths I cry to you,
O LORD; O LORD, hear
my voice.

PSALM 130:1-2

*D*r. Barton's consultation with Arthur was lengthy and troubling. They thoroughly examined Edward, concluding that their friend and patient had suffered severe injuries to several vital organs. Dr. Barton recommended that they get a specialist's opinion, and Arthur readily agreed. So just before ten o'clock, Dr. Barton took his leave, but instead of heading for the comfort of his home, the elderly physician turned his buggy toward the city. There he would seek out Dr. Silas Lansing, an eminent surgeon of his acquaintance. He was determined to bring Dr. Lansing back to Ion with all speed.

It was left to Arthur to explain to Elsie and Horace. This he did with honesty and compassion. He also told them that Dr. Barton had gone to find Dr. Silas Lansing and would return as quickly as possible. Until Dr. Lansing could examine Edward, Arthur did not want to offer any prognosis.

"I am a country doctor," the young man said modestly, "and I'm aware of my limitations. As you may know, Dr. Lansing distinguished himself as a battlefield surgeon in the Civil War, and he is widely respected for his innovative surgical techniques. We are fortunate that he lives so close to us."

As she listened, Elsie's face grew pale, but she remained clear-eyed and attentive to her cousin's every word. Horace began pacing the floor, trying to absorb the implications of Arthur's words.

"I know that Lansing is a good man, and his professional reputation is excellent," he said when Arthur finished, "but are there others we should call upon? I think I ought to send one of the men to the rail station with a telegraph message for Dick Percival."

"What can Dick do, Papa?" Elsie asked.

"I do not intend for him to come here, dearest," Horace replied, "but his former teachers in Philadelphia are among the best doctors and surgeons in all the country. They might suggest others who specialize in such injuries."

"That's a good idea, Uncle Horace," Arthur agreed. "I doubt we can find better than Dr. Lansing, but every avenue should be explored."

Arthur turned back to Elsie and said, "I wish that I could give you more definite news, but you must not lose hope. Edward is strong in both body and spirit. I know of no man with a more intense love of life, and his dedication to you and his children is powerful. Even in my short career, I have seen how the will to live can work wonders."

"Thank you, Arthur," Elsie responded with a tiny smile. "Be assured that I have not given up hope. But may I return to Edward now?"

"Of course," Arthur said.

When she had gone, Horace had another question for Arthur. "Is there anything more I should hear?" he asked.

"No, sir," Arthur said. "I have told you and Cousin Elsie all that I know. I will keep nothing secret from either of you, or from Edward when he asks."

"As he surely will when he is awake," Horace said with a sad shake of his head. "Edward is my oldest and closest friend, and I cannot begin to adjust my mind to the possibility of losing him. But if that is God's will, we must accept it, and Edward will want the truth. I am absolutely confident that you will know what to say."

Fears and Prayers

Arthur was gratified by his uncle's words, for he was all too conscious of his own lack of experience. "Thank you, sir," he said. "Now, shall we write your telegram to Dick?"

Dr. Barton had found Dr. Lansing at home and retired for the night. Dr. Barton made clear to the sleepy-eyed butler who answered the door that the situation was of great urgency. With a little prodding, the butler went to summon his employer.

After speaking briefly with Dr. Barton, Dr. Lansing hastened back to his bedroom to dress and gather his medical equipment. He also called upon his wife to locate a nurse whose skills the doctor valued highly and send a carriage to transport this nurse to the patient's plantation.

It was after midnight when Dr. Lansing and Dr. Barton arrived at Ion, only to learn that Edward's condition was worsening. He had been slipping in and out of consciousness, and his fever was rising, indicating infection. After Dr. Lansing had examined the patient, it became impossible to escape the conclusion that Edward's chances of survival were slim. His internal injuries were extensive, and the best the medical men could do was to keep him as free of pain as possible. It would soon be necessary, they agreed, to inform the family of the gravity of the situation.

Seeing the pain in Arthur's face, Dr. Lansing said, "I feel sure Edward will come through this night, so we need not speak to Mrs. Travilla yet. Let us tend to our duties and see how Edward progresses. We will know better in the morning. I do not believe in giving false hope, but neither do I wish to draw too hasty a conclusion."

Violet's Hidden Doubts

Dr. Barton put a firm hand on Arthur's shoulder. "We will tell Elsie all that we know, for she deserves our honesty. But as Silas says, we cannot predict the outcome of Edward's illness. God alone possesses that knowledge."

It was nearing dawn when Edward awoke. Elsie saw his eyelids flutter open and leaned over to kiss his damp brow. His fever, which had risen during the night, seemed to have reached a plateau.

Dr. Lansing took Edward's wrist. The doctor counted the beats and after a few moments, he said to Elsie, "His pulse is steadier now. Let me lift his head, so you can give him water."

Elsie took a glass and gently held it to her husband's lips. With great effort, Edward managed one sip, then another. As the cool liquid entered his parched mouth, he tried to smile, but his eyes closed and he seemed to drift away again.

The doctor lowered his patient back onto the pillow, thinking the injured man had lost consciousness. But Edward's eyes opened once more, wide this time, and sought Elsie's face. She could see the fever that seemed to burn like a fire in his eyes, but Elsie realized that he was focusing on her.

"Oh, my darling!" she exclaimed in a voice breaking with emotion.

"I'm here," he answered in a slow, rasping tone that signaled the great effort each word required.

"Don't speak, my love," Elsie implored. "Save every ounce of your strength."

"I must," he said, his voice no stronger than a whisper. "I'll be going home soon. I'm ready, Elsie. Ready to meet" — he stopped and struggled to draw in breath — "my Savior."

She bent closer so that her cheek touched his. "If that is His will," she said softly, "but I pray it is not. I need you so much, my darling, my dearest love. Let me give you my strength so we can fight this infection together."

Faintly and with great effort, he said, "I want to live but I'm ready to die. Know that I love you and always will. Tell the children that I love them. Tell them to be happy because I will be happy. We will all be together again."

His eyes fell shut, and he seemed to sink deeper into the pillow.

Elsie instantly raised her panicked gaze to Dr. Lansing.

"He's only sleeping," the doctor assured her.

Elsie looked into her husband's beloved face — the face whose every line she knew as well as her own. She wanted to take him in her arms and enfold him in her own strength. *Oh, Dear Father in Heaven*, she prayed desperately to herself, *do not take him from us now. Help my beloved Edward fight for his life. Show me how to fight with him and for him — for without him, I do not know how to go on. Show me the way, Lord. Show me the way.*

Edward continued to sleep for several hours, and his sleep was almost peaceful compared to the restless, fevered unconsciousness of the night. As dawn broke and light began to seep into the room, his fever seemed to abate a bit under the constant, cooling ministrations of Elsie and the physicians.

Violet's Hidden Doubts

Despite the urgings of the others that she rest, Elsie refused to leave Edward's side. And she was not the only one who kept a waking vigil. Rose and Chloe had gotten the younger children to bed and soothed them to sleep, but Missy, Ed, and Vi had refused all coaxing. They had gathered in Missy's little sitting room and talked and prayed throughout the night. With her sister and brother, Vi realized, she was better able to battle against the fear that threatened her.

Since her prayers with Molly and Enna, Vi had put aside the agonizing guilt that seized her when she first saw her father lying in the wagon beneath her window. As she prayed with Missy and Ed, Vi thought only of her Papa, and she began to believe that their hope was not in vain and that he would be restored to them. He would live through the night, she decided, and the new day would renew his strength. *Maybe it's not so bad as everyone says.* In her mind, she could see her Papa sitting up in bed, weak but getting better. She would be there with him, reading to him from one of their favorite books and helping her mother nurse him back to health. *If only I can pray hard enough...*

It was almost seven in the morning when Arthur came to Missy's room. He told his cousins that Edward's fever had leveled off and he was sleeping more easily. Getting through the night, Arthur said, was a good sign. But he wanted them to understand that their father was by no means out of danger and that it was impossible to say what would happen in the next hours.

"How is Mamma?" Vi asked.

Fears and Prayers

"She won't leave your father," Arthur said, "but she's resting at the moment. Dr. Lansing's nurse arrived from the city and is tending Edward now."

Ed wanted to know when they could see their father.

"Perhaps when he wakes again," Arthur replied. "I know that your mother will want you there. But we're giving Edward potent medicine to help him sleep, for it is in sleep that the body can best heal itself."

He went on to explain Edward's internal injuries and Dr. Lansing's diagnosis. It was the most difficult discussion Arthur had ever had, but he knew that his cousins needed the truth. When he had finished, Vi asked the question that he so dreaded.

"Will Papa live?" she said softly, and the hope in her dark eyes nearly broke the young doctor's heart.

"I do not know," Arthur replied at last. "I respect you too much to give you false expectations. Your father's injuries are severe, and no surgeon alive has the skill to repair them. The infection is the worst danger. Edward is very strong, and his love for all of you is a powerful incentive to live. Dr. Lansing is probably the best physician in the country for this kind of situation. But truly, it is all in God's hands now. You must hold on to your faith, just as your father does."

As he spoke, the brother and sisters drew closer to one another. Missy's tears flowed freely, and Ed wrapped her in his arms as their father would have done. But Vi did not cry. Her face wore a blank look, but the light of hope in her eyes, which had shined so brightly just moments before, flickered out, and Arthur thought he had never seen such depths of pain before.

Violet's Hidden Doubts

He took her hand. It was cold as ice. Arthur reached for a woolen shawl that lay on the couch and draped it around her. He knew Vi was in shock; all these dear young people were. He stood to leave, saying that he would have hot tea and toast brought up to them. A little sternly, he instructed them to eat and drink what he prescribed, for they must stay strong in body. Missy and Ed nodded in promise, but Vi didn't move. She was like stone, and Arthur resolved to return within the hour to check on her. With one last look at Vi's devastated face, he departed.

How many prayers were said that day is not possible to calculate. What had to be done on the plantation was done, but most of the work that normally occupied the people of Ion was suspended, and the church in the quarters became a gathering place for the workers and their families. The main house itself was eerily quiet as the servants went about their tasks. The children kept to their rooms and the nursery, as their mother requested—the younger ones huddling close to their grandmother and Aunt Chloe, while Missy, Ed, and Vi sheltered together and waited for more news of their father. Food was brought, and at Arthur's insistence, even Vi ate a little. The suggestion that they try to sleep was politely received and then ignored.

Just after midday, a rider arrived with a telegram from Dick Percival. Dick had sought advice from the best of his medical professors in Philadelphia, and they had all agreed that the most prominent physician available was Dr. Silas Lansing. Dick also stated that he himself was preparing to leave for Ion on the first train he could get.

Horace was truly grateful for Dick's efforts, though he had already settled his mind as to Dr. Lansing's skill. Horace conveyed the message of Dick's impending arrival to Molly and Enna, and he could not help smiling at the happiness in Enna's eyes when she heard that her son would soon be at her side.

Horace found himself almost envying Enna's gentle simplicity. He wished that he could know the peace of accepting whatever might come without question. But the thought of losing his dearest friend and of Elsie's and his grandchildren's grief and sorrow tore at his heart. *Strengthen me, Heavenly Father, for what lies ahead,* he prayed as he walked slowly back to the room where Edward lay. *Lift this frustration from me and let me feel the contentment that comes from accepting Your will. If You must take my friend now, help me to feel joy for him and for Your saving grace that will someday reunite us all in Heaven.*

CHAPTER

7

The Journey Home

*For to me, to live is Christ
and to die is gain.*

PHILIPPIANS 1:21

It had passed noon when Missy, Ed, and Vi heard steps in the hallway.

"It's Grandpapa," Ed said, recognizing Horace's familiar tread. He jumped from his chair and rushed to open the door.

Horace's face showed the strain of worry and lack of sleep, but his words were a balm to the young Travillas. "Your father is awake, and he wants to see you," he announced.

"Oh, is he well now, Grandpapa?" Vi cried out.

Horace hesitated a second before saying, "No, he is still very ill. But he is conscious, and he has asked for all of you. Go down now, while I get Rose and the little ones. Your mamma is waiting for you."

He started to leave but turned back. His expression was softened with emotion. "You must be strong, children. Your papa's fever has risen again, but he wants to see you before he takes more medication. Do not be dismayed by his weak appearance. Just remember that he is fighting very hard to recover. Be strong for him now as he has always been for you."

Horace's voice broke as he concluded, "Go to your papa, my dears, and…"

But he could not finish. He held his arms open wide, and his three grandchildren fell into his embrace.

There were a number of people in the bedroom when the young Travillas entered, but they saw no one except their father and mother. The room was dim, for the curtains had been drawn and light came only from the oil lamps. But the windows must have been opened, for the room was cool and the air was fresh.

Edward lay absolutely still upon his bed, his arms extended above the light cover and his head raised slightly on a pillow. His face was pale and drawn, yet also spotted with the flush of fever. Elsie was gently pressing a cool cloth to his brow and temples and whispering to him.

When she sensed her children's presence, she looked up at them with a gentle smile that bid them to come forward. What fear they might have felt melted away in love and compassion.

"Missy and Ed and Vi are here, dearest," Elsie said to Edward. Then she rose so that her children might take her place beside the bed.

At the sight of them, Edward's face seemed to lighten. "My precious gifts," he said hoarsely. "My greatest blessings."

Vi longed to put her arms around him and cling to him as she had always done in times of trial. Instead, she laid her hand softly upon his, feeling his fever under her fingers. In the cool of the room, the heat of his skin shocked her, like touching a burning coal. But she didn't draw back. She would have braved a roaring fire just to feel his gentle touch once more.

"We're here for you, Papa," Ed said.

"We love you so much, Papa," Missy added.

"Pray for me?" Edward asked.

"Oh, yes, Papa, every minute since you were hurt," Missy replied.

With enormous effort, Edward focused his eyes on Ed. His mouth moved but he seemed unable to speak. The

nurse, who stood at the opposite side of the bed, put a damp cloth to his dry lips, and after a few moments, he was able to form the words.

"Ion will need you," Edward said to his son, "but not yet. Go on to school, Eddie. Learn and be wise for your brothers and sisters. You will be as father to them and right arm for your mother."

His speech faltered, and the nurse put the soothing dampness to his mouth again.

The full import of his father's words struck Ed with a sudden force that seemed to draw the breath from his chest. *He is saying good-bye*, the young man thought, and he wanted to shout in protest. Instead, he said, "I love you, Papa. I will do as you say."

"I love you, Eddie. I trust your good heart to do what is right always."

Edward's gaze shifted to his eldest daughter. "My first-born. So like your mother in beauty of spirit. Begin your life with Lester in joy and happiness, dearest Missy. I want you to be happy as Mamma and I have been. Walk always with our Lord. I love you, my daughter, and always will."

"And I will always love you, Papa," Missy said through her tears. "Always, always, you will be the finest part of me."

Edward's eyes closed. Vi, who stood nearest to him, her hand still covering his, did not dare breathe as she looked on her father. A single, frantic thought battered at her brain—*Don't go, Papa! Don't go!*

Edward lay motionless for several minutes. The nurse applied the damp cloth to his face and neck, and Dr. Lansing came forward to check his pulse. Otherwise, no one moved.

Violet's Hidden Doubts

Then Edward's eyelids opened. He looked straight at Vi.

"Child of her father," he said. "We are alike, you know. You must follow your dreams, my pet, and listen to your heart. Do not be afraid of the world. God has a plan for you, and it may not be what you expect. Remember what our Lord said — 'Do not fear, for I am with you.'"

His lids fluttered, but with enormous strength of will, Edward kept his eyes open and upon his daughter. "I love you, pet. Remember that."

Vi didn't understand the full meaning of all her father's words, but she knew, just as Ed and Missy did, that he was taking leave of them. If a heart could truly break, hers would have split apart at that moment. There was so much she wanted to say, but where were the words? In all the world, there were no words that could make him well again. He was slipping away before her eyes, and no words could pull him back. Then she saw his mouth move ever so slightly. And she knew he was trying to smile at her. Her throat was choked with pain, but suddenly the words came: "I love you, Papa, and I will never forget. I promise."

Elsie touched each of the three gently, and without wanting to, they stepped back from the bedside as Harold, Herbert, and Rosemary came to take their places. As he had with the eldest, Edward now conveyed a special message of love to each of the younger children.

Last was Danny, held in his mother's arms. Elsie bent forward, holding Danny so that he might give his father a kiss. Even so young, Danny must have sensed the solemn moment, for he kissed and patted Edward's face with heartrending tenderness.

With all his children standing around his bed now, Edward drank in their presence, and a look of peace

seemed to radiate from him. Then he closed his eyes and said in the softest whisper, "You are the sunshine of my days."

Time seemed to stop for them all until Dr. Lansing said, "He is sleeping."

Without being told, the children knew that it was time to leave. Elsie handed Danny to Horace, and Rose took Rosemary's small, trembling hand. Reluctantly but with no hint of protest, the young Travillas left the bedside and were guided from the room by their grandparents and Arthur.

The children begged to remain in the hallway outside the door, but the adults prevailed, and everyone proceeded to the sitting room not far away. Chloe was waiting for them, and she took Danny onto her lap. Molly and Enna were there too, and Molly beckoned to Vi and Missy. Vi took her place next to Enna and was instantly enfolded in her great-aunt's arms. Missy sat beside Molly, and the two young women clasped hands. Horace and Rose retired to a couch, Rose cradling Rosemary and Horace sitting between the twins with one strong arm around each of the boys. Ed took a seat but soon rose and began to pace the floor—his hands clasped behind his back and his handsome head bowed in despondency.

No one spoke. Tears fell from many eyes, but there was no whimpering or sobbing. From the youngest to the eldest, everyone knew that they had entered a time of waiting... and of ending.

Violet's Hidden Doubts

What was said between Edward and Elsie during that next hour was never fully known. The doctors and the nurse, who tended their patient closely, were too professional to listen and too respectful to reveal what they may have overheard. As for Elsie, though she would tell much, there was more that she would hold in her heart forever. The final words and prayers spoken between husband and wife were for them alone.

The end came near twilight. Edward had fallen into unconsciousness, and Elsie knew without being told that this time, he would not return to her. She sat beside him, holding his hand, and asked Dr. Lansing to summon her family.

They were all with him — wife, children, friends of his lifetime — when Edward Travilla made the journey to his Heavenly home.

Few words were spoken. In a voice strangled with emotion, Dr. Lansing pronounced, "He is gone." And Elsie, still holding the hand of her beloved, quoted softly but clearly Jesus' words from the sixteenth chapter of the book of John: " 'Now is your time of grief, but I will see you again and you will rejoice, and no one will take away your joy.... I came from the Father and entered the world; now I am leaving the world and going back to the Father.' "

In a room grown suddenly dark with sorrow and loss, these words of the Savior shone like a beacon in the storm. Edward Travilla had gone home, to their Heavenly Father, but in time, they would all be reunited. God's promise to His faithful would be fulfilled. Edward was with God now; of that, no one doubted.

For those left behind, the time of grieving had come.

CHAPTER

8

Going On

*The LORD is close to the
brokenhearted and saves
those who are crushed
in spirit.*

PSALM 34:18

Going On

*I*n the days that followed Edward's funeral, Elsie came to wonder how anyone could bear such loss without faith. Elsie had known the depths of sorrow before, and now, in this time of her greatest loss, she turned instinctively to her Savior. In her Bible and through endless hours of prayer, she found solace and understanding. God wanted her to live, and Christ's own life, death, and resurrection showed her the way. She suffered, yet never did her faith waver. Her faith was genuine, and she would go on, with her Lord and Friend always beside her.

As days turned to weeks, Elsie's terrible pain began to give way to hope and determination. She was able to attend to the tasks of mourning—responding to the outpouring of condolences she and the family had received from so many friends near and far. It moved her deeply to read the expressions of others—people of every age and social position—whose lives Edward had touched and bettered in ways that she often had not known about.

Elsie also resumed many of her domestic duties, including daily lessons with the children. At first, going back to the schoolroom seemed awkward for all of them, and they often put aside their assignments simply to talk and pray and sometimes to cry together. Missy and Ed would join them frequently, and most mornings were passed with sweet reminiscences of the man who had been the linchpin of all their lives.

Violet's Hidden Doubts

It was during these times, however, that Elsie began to sense that Vi was not dealing with the loss as might have been expected. Vi would listen to her brothers and sisters with seeming attention. She would sometimes cry with the others, but she rarely participated in their conversations. On those few occasions when she did talk about her papa, it was always some story that did not involve herself. Asked to share a memory, Vi would relate some anecdote about how Edward had helped this person or that person. But Vi's shared memories were impersonal—almost, her mother thought, like newspaper accounts of some event in a distant place.

In the beginning, Elsie credited her daughter's reticence to Vi's innate sensitivity and the normal diffidence of a girl her age. But as time passed and Vi still did not respond, Elsie tried a different approach. She began turning the children back to their schoolwork, hoping that Vi's love of learning might revive her spirits. Elsie continued to talk of Edward with the others, but in a casual way—giving them more individual time outside the schoolroom.

It was not that Vi was difficult. On the contrary, her everyday behavior was almost *too* good. She resumed her studies with diligence. She completed all her chores without complaining. She never squabbled with her siblings—not even when the twins sorely tried her temper with their teasing. And she undertook a new activity that seemed to bode well for her recovery. With her mother's permission, Vi began to accompany Chloe on her daily rounds of the workers' quarters.

"Is she helpful to you?" Elsie asked Chloe about a week after this new routine was initiated.

"A big help," Chloe affirmed. "She carries that heavy basket of medicine for me, and she visits with the old people. You oughta see how she keeps the children entertained, so I can talk to their mothers. Vi's got a real good way with the little ones, Miss Elsie. They just naturally trust her. But I'll tell you something. I'm worried about our girl."

"How so?" Elsie asked. She had not as yet discussed her own concerns about Vi with anyone else, and she wanted to hear Chloe's observations.

"It's hard to put in words, but she's just not like herself anymore," Chloe said. "She told me the other day that she didn't want any presents for Christmas. When I said that I know how hard it's gonna be this year without Mr. Edward, she said no presents for her ever again. 'I have too much already,' she said. Then she said she don't deserve what she has now—never mind anythin' new. That's not like our Vi. Not that she values presents all that much, but she's always been our Christmas girl and more generous to others than people are to her."

Chloe paused and scratched her head. Then she said, "It's like all the joy just drained outta Vi when Mr. Edward passed. One of the little boys was cuttin' up down at the quarters today, being funny, and I saw Vi smiling at him. But as soon as the child went his way, Vi's smile just vanished. Just vanished, Miss Elsie, quick as a wink. I thought to myself that she's not lettin' herself have even that little pleasure. It's like she's punishin' herself for somethin'."

Elsie agreed with Chloe that Vi was acting oddly and then confided her own worries to her old nursemaid.

"Have you tried to talk to her?" Chloe asked.

"I have," Elsie said, "and I cannot complain of her responses. She is polite and she answers my questions honestly. But she is not—" Elsie paused, trying to find the right word. "She isn't *forthcoming*. Our old Vi could sometimes keep her feelings to herself, but I never knew her to hold back like this."

Violet's Hidden Doubts

"You're right that she's never been one to keep her secrets for long," Chloe concurred. "But Mr. Edward's dying, it's taken a toll on all the children. I'd be wrong to expect each of them to act just alike. Maybe Vi just needs more time than the others to begin the healin'. But I'm gonna keep my eye on her all the same."

"Please do," Elsie said. "Something is troubling her, Chloe, but I hardly know how to help her. I have an idea that she is carrying a burden that goes beyond the loss of her father; yet how can I help if I don't know what it is?"

Elsie knew from sad experience that grief is easier to bear when shared. And whenever her own pain threatened to overwhelm her, she turned to her parents. To Horace and Rose, Elsie could unhesitatingly confide her fears—that she was insufficient to be both mother and father to her children, that she did not have the skills to take Edward's place as the head of Ion, that she lacked the strength to support those who now depended on her alone.

So Elsie naturally sought out her father and stepmother and told them what Chloe had said. They, too, had noticed signs of change in Vi.

Rose asked a difficult question that Elsie had also pondered: "Do you think Vi is suffering from some crisis of faith? I mean, is it possible that she may be having doubts that Edward is in a better place? She is of a vulnerable age, and Edward's death was so sudden and unexpected."

Elsie said, "I have considered that, but I do not think so. When I can get her to talk of Edward, she seems sincerely to believe that he is with our Heavenly Father now. No, I

do not believe that her faith has been shaken. In fact, I think her trust in God is the one comfort she allows herself. It is something else."

"Perhaps she needs more time," Horace suggested.

"That's what Chloe says," Elsie relied. "And you are probably right. If only Edward were here," she added wistfully. "He would know what to do."

One evening a few days before Christmas, Vi and the older children retired to the parlor with Elsie, Rose, and Horace after supper. Missy sat at the piano and began to play. She chose a rustic tune that had been a favorite of her father's, and soon Ed and the twins were blending their voices in the familiar song. When they finished, Elsie asked for another song, naming one that had been popular when she and Edward were newlyweds. The young Travillas were not sure of the words, so Elsie, Horace, and Rose taught them a verse and then led them through the chorus.

The songs seemed to open the floodgates of memory, and Horace related to his grandchildren the tale of an amusing adventure that he and Edward had had when they were young men traveling in Europe. It was a story the children had not heard before, and they asked their grandpapa for more tales of their father's youth. Horace happily obliged, and the parlor was soon ringing with the sounds of laughter and happy conversation.

The evening wore on, and no one noticed the passage of time until Elsie saw that Harold's eyelids were growing heavy and Herbert was stifling a yawn.

Violet's Hidden Doubts

"Oh, my dears," she said, "the clock is about to strike ten, and it is time to prepare for bed. It has been so pleasant an evening, but I must bring it to an end."

"It has been pleasant, Mamma," Missy agreed.

"The kind of night Papa always enjoyed," Ed added.

Horace happened to be looking at Vi, and he saw a dark look pass over her face. Sensing that she and the others were surprised by their good moods, he said, "I feel sure that your father would be happy tonight to hear music and laughter in this house once more."

"But is it right of us?" Vi burst out. "How can we enjoy ourselves when Papa is not here!"

Elsie reached out to Vi and drew her close. "Your Papa is *here*," she said, laying her hand over Vi's heart. "His memory lives in all our hearts. We have shed tears for him, but our laughter honors him as well, for there was never a man who took more delight in the laughter of his children. Trust me, dearest. When we find joy in our memories of the times we had with Papa, we are honoring him more than any monument carved of the finest marble in the world ever could."

"If he were standing right here, I bet he'd be making a joke with us right now," Harold said.

"And then chasing us up to bed," Herbert added.

Vi still looked doubtful, but Ed teased her gently. "Smile for us, little sister, for when you smile, you look just like Papa. Your eyes sparkle, and you get that little dimple at the corner of your mouth."

"What dimple?" Vi asked in amazement.

"Do you not know?" Missy replied. "Why, Violet, you have always been the image of Papa. If you smile at yourself in the mirror, you'll see it. And you are the only one of us who has it. It's Papa's special legacy to you."

Going On

This statement was a kind of revelation for Vi, and quite beyond her control, her face brightened.

"There it is," Ed exclaimed jovially, "the famous Travilla dimple!"

"Good!" said Harold in a rush of relief. "Vi's smiling, and I'm awfully sleepy."

"May we be excused, Mamma?" Herbert asked for himself and his brother.

"Of course, boys," Elsie said, keeping Vi at her side. "Go up now, and I will join you soon for prayers."

As the twins bounded from the room, Ed and Missy were bidding good night to their grandparents. Vi looked into her mother's face and said in a whisper, "I'm sorry if I said something wrong, Mamma. I don't want to make you sad."

"You didn't say anything wrong, Vi darling," Elsie said reassuringly. "Not at all. I do not expect you to keep your feelings hidden. I would be sad if I thought you could not express yourself within your family. Come, now, and let us say good night to Grandmamma and Grandpapa. Then I'll accompany you upstairs, and perhaps we may talk a bit more, if you like."

Later, in her room, Vi did open her heart a little way to her mother. For the first time since Edward's death, Vi shared some of her personal memories of him.

"Do you remember when I got lost in the middle of the night and Papa found me?" Vi asked.

"I remember all too well," Elsie said. "You were sleep-walking, and somehow you got out through a parlor window and wandered all the way down the drive to the road. When Missy found your bed empty, she raised the alarm, and everyone began searching high and low. Your father found a torn piece of your nightgown on the window, and he followed your trail until he finally found you huddled under a tree not far from the road."

"I don't remember much," Vi said softly, "except that I was very scared and I thought I saw monsters."

"They weren't monsters," Elsie said, "but you did see something awful. We didn't realize until later that you had witnessed a brutal attack by several Ku Klux Klan members on one of our neighbors."

Vi lay her head against her mother's shoulder and said softly, "I do remember praying for Jesus to let Papa find me, and He did. And I remember feeling safe because Papa was carrying me and telling me that there are no monsters. I've always wondered how Papa knew where to look for me."

"Perhaps he knew because he had also been a sleepwalker when he was a child," Elsie replied, "and he once became lost just as you did. You and your Papa share so many qualities, and sleepwalking was just one of them. I am very thankful that you both outgrew it."

"Me too," Vi said with a deep yawn.

"It's time for you to sleep, dearest," Elsie said. She kissed her daughter's forehead and bade her good night. When she left Vi's room, Elsie thought to herself that something important had just happened—that this sharing of memories might be the beginning of a breakthrough.

With a hopeful heart, Elsie silently prayed: *Dear Heavenly Father, thank You for giving me this glimpse into my child's true heart. Bless her, dear Lord, with the healing grace of Your endless love. Please guide me, as You always guided Edward, to calm Vi's fears and help her through her time of grief and sadness.*

CHAPTER

9

A Brother's Departure

*If we confess our sins, he is faithful
and just and will forgive us our
sins and purify us from
all unrighteousness.*

1 JOHN 1:9

A Brother's Departure

*W*inter turned unusually cold and bitter that year, and it seemed to Vi that even nature was grieving the loss of one who had always greeted each new season in the spirit of hope and renewal. There were several heavy snows in December and January, but without her father, Vi found no joy in the fluffy blankets of white that cloaked the hard ground and enticed the younger children out to play. She had a new worry on her mind.

Ed would soon be leaving for the University, and she could hardly bear to think of Ion without him. She knew that he must go — that he would honor his promise to his father so that he could someday take over the running of Ion. She didn't want to hold her brother back, for their father's wish was Ed's as well. But just the thought of being separated from her beloved big brother sent chills through her that had nothing to do with snow and ice.

She often thought about unburdening herself to Ed and telling him the truth of what she'd done. He would understand better than anyone, she was sure. But each time she started to speak, something held her back. She would tell herself that it was not the right time, that she would talk to him another day. But the days passed, and still she guarded her secret.

Then the days dwindled to hours, and Ed would be leaving the next morning. One last time, Vi would try to find the words to unlock her troubled heart.

Violet's Hidden Doubts

Ed was tucking the last of his traveling clothes into his case when he heard a knock at his bedroom door. "Come in," he called and looked up to see Vi enter.

"Here to bid your big brother a fond farewell?" he asked playfully as he went back to his packing.

But Vi didn't reply. She walked to Ed's bookcase, now half-empty because his favorite volumes and his other things had already been shipped ahead. She ran her fingers along the spines of the books that remained — mostly adventure tales that he had loved when he was a boy.

Wondering what was on her mind, Ed said, "You can have those if you like, Vi. They're ripping good stories."

"I've read most of them," she said in a flat tone.

"Well, I haven't much else to give you, little sister, unless you'd like a piece of my mind before I go," he joked.

Vi, who had always been quick to answer her brother's jesting with her own, said nothing, and Ed let the matter go. *She has something on her mind*, he thought. *Give her time. That's what Papa would do.*

Several minutes passed, and Ed was about to close his case when Vi said, "Don't forget your Bible. It's on your table."

Ed hadn't forgotten; he planned to pack the Bible in his small valise so it would be at hand on his journey. But he said only, "Thanks, Vi. I'll remember."

She had turned her back, appearing to look at the books again, when she said, "Do you remember your accident, Ed? When you were little and you — ah — hurt Papa?"

"As clear as yesterday," he replied evenly.

"What did you do when it happened? I mean, did you tell what you had done?"

Ed was staring at her back now. He had no idea why she was asking him these questions, but he knew that she had no desire to cause him pain, so he answered as truthfully as he could. "No, I didn't tell at first. After the gun went off and I knew that Papa was injured, I just fell on the ground crying, and poor Archie Leland stayed with me. We were in that little grove down by the bend in the driveway. No one could see us, and no one knew that I had done the shooting. I guess I knew that I had to tell, but I was so stunned with guilt and fear for Papa that I couldn't move. It was Crystal who found us there, a long time later as I remember it. It wasn't till the next morning that I was able to see Papa and confess that I'd fired the shot that wounded him."

"Did you feel better...after you confessed?"

"Yes, in a way. I never planned to lie. And Papa forgave me immediately. I was punished, of course, but not harshly. I asked God to forgive me, and I knew that He did. But do you know the worst part, Vi?"

She turned now and looked at him at last.

Seeing the anxiety in her face, he said, "The worst part was forgiving myself. I wasn't even eight years old, yet I knew that I had almost caused the death of one of the two people I loved most in all the world. And I knew that if I had killed Papa, that it would almost be like killing Mamma as well. But why do you want to know about all that?"

Vi kept her gaze steadily on him as she said, "Because I was too little to realize what was going on, and I've never asked how you felt. And you're leaving tomorrow morning, and I just thought I should know. I mean, Missy says that what happened changed you, and I just wanted to know..." She hesitated, unsure how to say what was in her heart.

575

Violet's Hidden Doubts

Sensing her uncertainty, Ed smiled and motioned to her to come and sit beside him on the bed.

"I hope it changed me for the better," he said. "As young as I was, I knew that the whole thing was my fault; it was my hotheadedness and my pride. My cousins had that gun, and they were teasing me, saying that I was a baby because I wouldn't touch it. I let them get my goat, and I did something I knew not to do. Even as I grabbed the gun and pulled the trigger, I knew it was wrong. Papa helped me so much, Vi. He didn't make excuses for me like some parents do, but he didn't blame me either. I guess he understood that my conscience was punishing me more than he ever could. But he talked with me a lot, and he helped me begin to understand what it means to be responsible."

"What did Papa say it means?" she asked.

"Well, that being responsible means taking the blame when we do something wrong. But it also means thinking before we do something that might be wrong and considering the possible results of our actions."

She looked at him. "But what if you did something that most people wouldn't think was wrong. What if you didn't even know if what you did was really wrong?"

He gazed at her earnest face for several moments before he said, "Do you mean something that troubles your own heart even though it might not trouble others?"

She nodded.

He thought again and then said, "I'd talk to our Lord. When I feel guilty about anything, I take it to Him and ask Him to forgive me and to wash me clean again. And then I try to make amends as best I can. If I think I've wronged someone, I talk to the person and tell him what I did."

A Brother's Departure

Vi dropped her eyes and said softly, "But we can't always make amends, Ed. We just can't."

Very gently he asked, "Won't you tell me what's troubling you, Vi? I'm nowhere near as good at this as Papa, but I'm a pretty good listener."

She shrugged and forced a smile as she replied, "I'm fine, really I am. It's just that you're leaving and Papa is gone, and I'm going to miss you so much!"

Tears suddenly streamed from her eyes, and Ed quickly put his arm around her shoulders to comfort her. "Not half as much as I'll miss you," he said. "If there's something bothering you and you can't figure it out for yourself, promise me that you will talk to Mamma or Grandpapa or Grandmamma. Will you do that for me, pretty Violet?"

When she didn't answer, he lightened his tone and joked, "If you try to keep everything inside, you'll pop, and that would not be pretty at all."

Vi looked into his face. Though her cheeks were wet with tears, she smiled, and Ed saw the dimple appear. He took that as her answer.

The next morning was cold but clear—one of those early February mornings when the hard and frost-covered ground twinkles like a carpet of diamonds in the sun. Some tears were shed as Ed prepared to leave, but there was also much cheerful jesting as his family bade him Godspeed. Horace reminded him to telegraph home as soon as he reached his destination. Crystal and Chloe made sure he had the package of sandwiches and cakes they'd prepared, and Ben checked the carriage one last time, assuring himself that there were blankets inside to warm Ed's journey.

Bundled against the cold, the family stood around the carriage, and everyone had one last good wish to bestow upon Ed, one final hug and hearty handshake. Ed paid special attention to Vi, but she seemed to be all right again—a little withdrawn, but that had been her way of late. When he hugged her, she whispered, "Thanks for the advice, Eddie. I'm very glad you're my big brother."

Teasingly, he responded, "That's *Ed*, little sister, and don't you forget it."

No one wanted to let him go, but Elsie stepped forward, took her son's arm, and turned him to the open carriage door. She kissed his cheek and said, "The Spanish have an expression, 'Vaya con Dios.' It means, 'Go with God.' I will miss you, my darling, but I know that God is your constant companion and watches over you always. Now go, Ed, with my love. The world is waiting for you."

He stepped up into the carriage, and Elsie signaled to the driver. The horses pulled away; the carriage rolled down the drive, picking up speed, and was soon out of sight. The others quickly sought the warmth of the house, but Vi still stood in the drive, her eyes on the bend in the road where the carriage had turned and disappeared from view. She hardly noticed the cold and might have remained standing there for a long time. But her mother called her inside, and Vi put her lonely thoughts into hiding—as she was now in the habit of doing. She went into the house to begin another day of pretending to be happy.

CHAPTER

10

Searching for Answers

I sought the LORD, and he answered me; he delivered me from all my fears.

PSALM 34:4

*E*d had been at school for six weeks, and from poring over his letters home, everyone could tell that he'd made the correct choice. Horace and Rose had returned to The Oaks, though Horace managed to find some reason to ride to Ion almost every day. And the Travillas were not without other company. Isa Conley, their cousin who was now twenty-one, appeared almost as often as Horace, sometimes bringing her older sister, Virginia. Cal and Arthur Conley came whenever their busy schedules permitted. Other friends and relatives stopped by, and their company proved to be of great solace to Elsie and the children.

The Travillas also made the short trip to Roselands at least twice each week, for old Mr. Horace Dinsmore, Sr.— Elsie's grandfather—was mostly housebound. Edward Travilla had been much more than a grandson-in-law to the elderly head of the Dinsmore family. He had been a close friend, and the senior Mr. Dinsmore felt the loss keenly. But the frequent visits of his granddaughter and great-grandchildren never failed to lift his spirits. Even his daughter Louise Conley, who cared for her father at Roselands, allowed her frosty façade to slip a bit when Elsie came to call. Louise, embittered by the death of her husband in the War, had never hidden her jealousy of Elsie's happiness. But perhaps now that Elsie, too, was a widow, Louise sensed the bond that they shared.

As the first signs of the season's turning appeared—the bright yellows of forsythia and crocuses and early daffodils that always foretold the return of the warming sunlight of spring—Elsie felt a growing confidence in her ability to guide Ion and its operations.

"Edward would be most pleased with the way you are managing, my dear," Horace said one morning as he and Elsie enjoyed coffee together before going about their separate tasks.

"Do you really think so, Papa?" Elsie asked. "I feel his absence so acutely at times, especially when a major decision must be made."

"And what decision do you face today?" he inquired.

"I received word from Viamede some days ago that our plantation manager, Mr. Spriggs, wishes to leave his post as soon as I can find a replacement. In the same letter, he informed me that Dr. Bayliss, who has for so long tended to the health of our workers, is planning to retire. But worst of all is the news that came yesterday. Our dear chaplain, Mr. Mason, writes that he has been offered a teaching position at a seminary in St. Louis. He says that he will gladly stay with his congregations if no replacement can be found. But I can tell that this appointment means the world to him, and I would do nothing to hold him back.

"With so many changes at once, I think I should go to Louisiana. Yet how can I leave the children, Papa? This just is not the right time for me to be away. The loss of their father is still so fresh, and Ed is no longer at home. I don't think they need another separation, especially when I may be required at Viamede for two months or more."

"I agree," Horace said thoughtfully. "This is not the time for a lengthy separation. Yet with such important jobs falling vacant at Viamede, you are needed there as well. I could go in your place, but it's important that you make such hiring decisions."

"I thought of taking the entire family," Elsie remarked tentatively.

"And what do you think Edward would have said to that idea?" Horace asked.

Elsie smiled. "You know exactly what he would say. 'Pack them up, Elsie my dear. Pack each in a trunk—a valise will do for Danny—and ship them off on the next steamer to New Orleans.'"

Horace laughed at her imitation. "I can almost hear him speaking those very words."

Suddenly Horace slapped his knee and jumped up from his chair with the spring of a boy of sixteen. "He would be right, too!" he declared. "Let's pack up and go to Viamede. Your mother and I would be delighted to accompany you. And Molly, of course. And Enna and her nurse. And Christine for the little ones."

"It seems there will be no one left at Ion," Elsie said, laughing as she caught her father's enthusiasm. He was pacing the room now, and Elsie saw something very like a little hop in his step.

"Ion will be perfectly safe in the competent hands of your manager and Ben and Crystal," he said.

"And Aunt Chloe and Joe," Elsie added, "though I shall miss their company."

"I know," Horace said, his face clouding for a moment, "but Joe cannot make a long trip, and Chloe would never leave him behind. Still," he brightened, "it will be good for the rest of us. We can leave in two weeks and miss the worst of the fever season. I shall book our boat passages this very day. Oh, my dear, I fully expect this visit to bring the apples back to all my grandchildren's cheeks— Vi particularly."

Violet's Hidden Doubts

"I thought she was improving," Elsie sighed, "but now I'm not sure."

"Vi is still trying very hard not to show her sorrow," Horace observed, "but she does seem to be taking more interest in activities."

Elsie shook her head and said, "I cannot explain myself well, but I still see signs of some hidden doubt or fear or guilt—whatever it is. I don't think I'm being overly protective, Papa. Something weighs on our Violet, and she cannot go on like this, bearing it alone." Her voice broke as she said, "If she would only share it with me, I know that I could help her."

"She will," Horace said gently, "when she's ready. Our Heavenly Friend is her comfort and guide, and He will lead her to you in time. Her path may be arduous, but He will not let her fall. We must trust Him and have faith in His ways."

Then he added, "Perhaps this trip will do her good. A change of scene may be what Vi needs. At Viamede, she may begin to see things differently."

So it was decided, and everyone was soon engaged in preparations for their journey to Viamede—the Louisiana bayou plantation where Elsie had been born. It was at Viamede that Elsie always felt closest to the mother she had never known.

When she'd told her children about the plans, they'd all been excited, and even Vi seemed to look forward to the trip. Maybe Horace was right, and what Vi needed was a change of scene.

As the day of their departure approached, Elsie was often engaged with business matters, so Missy and Chloe supervised the packing. "Our Miss Rosemary got herself in a twist yesterday when we said she couldn't take a whole trunk load of her dolls and toys," Chloe chuckled one day as she made her progress report to Elsie.

"Oh, dear," Elsie said, "I hope she didn't have a temper tantrum."

"Well, Miss Elsie, she's got Dinsmore blood in her veins, and she can be mulish like her grandpa and great-grandpa," Chloe replied with a grin. "But when I told her about all those toys in the nursery down at Viamede and how they were the things you played with and her Grandmother Elsie, too—well, she calmed down right quick."

Elsie relaxed. "I can always trust you to find a solution, Chloe," she said. "I will miss you terribly while we're away."

"You know I'm gonna be missing you and the children every minute," Chloe said, the smile fading from her still handsome face. "I'd have liked to visit Dinah and her family down in New Orleans, but I'll get there in God's good time."

"You must be so proud of Dinah and Reverend Carpenter and their new mission," Elsie replied, referring to the New Orleans ministry founded by Chloe's granddaughter and her husband. "I just wish Dinah could continue teaching. She is so gifted."

"But she has," Chloe said. "Dinah's got herself a school started right there in the mission, doin' God's work by teaching readin' and writin' to every poor child who walks through her door. You think you might see Dinah while you're down in Louisiana?"

"Yes, I will," Elsie said. "I certainly will."

Violet's Hidden Doubts

"Then you give her and my great-grandbabies lots of hugs and kisses from their Chloe and Joe."

"I will," Elsie promised. Then another thought struck her. "Perhaps it will do Vi good to see Dinah and visit the mission," she mused almost to herself.

"That's a fine idea," Chloe said. "Just fine. It just might do our Vi a world of good. Somethin' different might be what she needs to get out of them doldrums."

"Mamma, have you seen Vi anywhere?" Missy asked. It was the afternoon of the day before the family would leave for Viamede.

"No, dear, but she will turn up," Elsie answered.

"I want to tell her about Cousin Isa coming with us now that Aunt Louise has finally given her permission. But I have been searching for an hour, and Vi is nowhere to be found."

"Did you try the kitchen?"

"I did."

"Molly's room?"

"Molly hasn't seen her since breakfast. I even went down to the stables."

Elsie thought for a moment then said, "The lake. You know how she loves to sketch in the afternoon light."

"Of course," Missy sighed. "Where is my head? I should have looked there first."

"I imagine that at least a part of your mind lingers on a certain handsome artist on foreign shores, my dear, and not the banks of our little lake," Elsie said with a smile. "When you find your sister, tell her to come in now, for twilight is approaching."

After brushing her mother's cheek with a quick kiss, Missy hurried from the sitting room, and Elsie returned her full attention to some important correspondence she was completing.

Some twenty minutes passed before Missy returned—without Vi.

"She was not at her favorite place by the lake, and there's no sign of her drawing things," Missy said breathlessly. "I looked all around the lake, and I checked upstairs again, too. Mamma, I'm getting worried. Where can she be?"

Missy's words and anxious expression caused a prickling sensation to lift the hairs on the back of Elsie's neck, but smiling, she rose from her little desk and went to Missy, taking her hand.

"Don't fret now, darling. In your diligent search, you have probably crossed paths with her unknowingly—you going up the front stairs while she came down the back way. I'm finished with my letters and could do with some exercise. I will take up the search while you help Christine with the little ones."

Elsie looked down at the little watch pinned to her blouse. "My goodness," she said. "Supper will be ready in less than an hour. You run along and see that everyone is neat and tidy. And remind the twins to wash behind their ears."

Her mother's casual air reassured Missy, and she left to find her brothers. But Elsie was not as lighthearted as she appeared. It wasn't like Vi to disappear and tell no one where she would be.

Do not panic, she told herself. *Vi is here, and you will find her. Now, think. Where might she go? She probably wanted to be alone, and she usually goes to the lake when she is in a solitary mood. But I can depend on Missy to have made a thorough search there.*

587

Violet's Hidden Doubts

From deep in Elsie's memory, a small idea began to emerge, like a shadowy form seen through a fog. Her brow furrowed as she struggled to lift the haze. *Concentrate!* she commanded herself. *Oh, Lord, help me remember!*

And there it was—a picture clear in every detail. But was it the right picture?

Elsie dashed from the library to the back stairs of the house. Gathering her skirts about her like a little girl at play, she climbed the steps. At the rear of the house was a kind of half-floor, some four feet above the second floor, where two uninhabited rooms and the entrance to the attic were located. Elsie went up the short flight of wooden steps, but at the landing, she paused. Taking deep breaths, she calmed her rapidly beating heart and relaxed her shoulders. Quietly, she walked to the door at the right side of the narrow, roughly plastered hallway and carefully turned the knob. *Dear Jesus, I felt You guide me here. Please let me be right.*

"Violet?" she asked of the still, damply chill air in the luggage room. Light, what little there was of it, came from a small oil lamp on the floor in one far corner. "Are you here, pet? Are you all right?"

"Yes, Mamma," came a faint voice from the opposite corner of the room. "I'm here."

CHAPTER

11

Released from Darkness

Then your light will break forth
like the dawn, and your healing
will quickly appear....

ISAIAH 58:8

e've been looking for you," Elsie said as she approached a pile of old trunks atop the largest of which her daughter was sitting. "Missy has been searching high and low. She wanted to tell you that Cousin Isa will be traveling to Viamede with us."

"That's very nice, Mamma," Vi replied flatly. "I've just been here. I went to the cemetery first, to Papa's grave. Then I came up here."

Elsie drew near and sat down on the lowest trunk in the stack. Her instinct had been to put her arms around her child and lead her by the hand from this stuffy, cold room back to the warmth of the family. But a voice seemed to speak deep inside her, saying, *Not yet.*

"It took me some time to remember this place," Elsie said, trying to keep her voice even. "You used to play here by yourself. Your father would say that this was your 'special place,' but I'd almost forgotten about it." Then without skipping a beat, she added, "What were you thinking about when I came in?"

"Papa. I was…" Vi stopped herself, for she had almost said something she intended to keep to herself.

"Ah," Elsie sighed. She was going to ask another question, but the inner voice that was guiding her said, *Be silent, and wait.*

There was no clock in the room to tick away the minutes. To Elsie it seemed that a very long time passed before Vi finally said in that strange, flat tone, "I was trying to talk to Papa. It's silly, but I just thought that if I was here, he might hear me. I wanted—I want—I have to tell him that I'm sorry."

With enormous self-control, Elsie remained silent. She had no idea what Vi wanted to say, and she could not risk putting the wrong words in her daughter's mouth. Then she heard a little noise almost, she thought, like a baby's burp. The noise was repeated and magnified—not a burp but a sob.

Then came a gasp of pure anguish as Vi cried, "I can't hold it inside any longer, and it won't go away!"

There was another wrenching gasp as Vi at last released the secret she had been struggling for so long to bury: "It's my fault he's dead, Mamma! It was my fault, and I can't ask him to forgive me! He's dead because of me, Mamma, and sometimes I wish I were dead with him!"

A thundering of sobs echoed in the small room, and Elsie's instincts took over. She leapt up, grabbed Vi, and pulled the girl from the high trunk and into her embrace. She held Vi as tightly as if they both were caught in a buffeting storm, cradling the girl's head against her shoulder.

The sobbing shook Vi's thin body with such force that Elsie began to fear her child was suffering a seizure of some sort. But she did not release her hold, and after some terrifying minutes, the sobs and shaking seemed to lessen in intensity. Still Elsie held Vi, and at last she spoke in a soft, crooning manner.

"You did not kill your father. You did not. It was an accident caused by no one. It was an accident like Enna's accident when she fell into the lake. You did nothing to harm your Papa. You must believe that."

Vi's sobbing gradually subsided into little, wet hiccups, and through her tears, she managed to say, "But I could

have stopped him that day. If I hadn't been so—so—so selfish, he wouldn't have been in the field. He'd be alive right
now, but for me."

"Why do you think that, dearest child?" Elsie asked.

"Because he wanted me to go with him and have a picnic," Vi replied, "and I said"—she gulped for air—"I said
'no' because I wanted to show off my French to you. If I'd
gone with him, I know that he wouldn't have been cutting
that tree. He'd have been with me. We might have ridden
somewhere together, and he wouldn't have been anywhere
near that tree when it fell. But I just thought about myself
and my perfect French lesson. And I'd spoken so rudely to
him at breakfast."

"But he had forgiven you for that," Elsie said, caressing
Vi's hair. "He told me so. He told me that he had asked your
forgiveness as well."

"He told you?"

"Just before he left the house that morning. He said that
you two had made your plans for the next day, and that he
was very proud of you for being responsible and tending to
your studies."

"He did?"

"I would not tell you a falsehood," Elsie said. "And I can
tell you that you could not have prevented the accident had
you been standing at his side. Your father wanted to work
with the men that day. He looked forward to the work. And
he was struck because he stood his ground until all the men
were out of danger. Ben has told us everything that happened. When your father ran, he became entangled in the
undergrowth and could not reach safety. Do you hold yourself responsible for the falling of the tree or the twisting of
the vines?"

Violet's Hidden Doubts

Hesitantly, Vi answered, "N—no, Mamma. But I remember the story about the time when Papa and Grandpapa were boys, and Grandpapa was nearly shot by one of their friends. That was an accident, but Papa always said he was as guilty as if he'd fired the rifle himself. And I talked to Ed about what he did to Papa. That was an accident, too, but Ed was responsible because he could have prevented it. But they were able to ask forgiveness and make amends. I can't do that, Mamma, because Papa is gone," she sighed.

"Your father felt guilty because he had allowed others to be careless. Ed was responsible because he let his temper get the best of him. It is not the same. Papa's accident was not caused by carelessness or thoughtlessness—neither yours nor anyone else's."

Elsie finally released her grip on her daughter. She seated the girl on the low trunk and then fetched the oil lamp from the far corner of the room and placed it nearby. Sitting down, Elsie drew Vi to her and said gently, "You've been carrying a heavy burden of guilt, my child, but it is time to lay it down. Think now. When you decided not to go with your father that day, did you act from anger or the desire to hurt him in some way? Did you know that he was in danger yet do nothing to prevent it?"

Vi looked into her mother's eyes, and even in the pale light, Elsie could read the shock in her daughter's face. "Oh, no, Mamma!" Vi exclaimed. "I really wanted to go with him. But I wanted more to recite my lesson to you. I'd worked very hard on it, and I was afraid I might forget the passage if I put it off. I just thought Papa would be there the next day, and we'd have our picnic and ride then. But he wasn't there, and he never will be there again!"

"Am I responsible because I didn't ask him to stay at the house that day?"

"Never, Mamma! You couldn't have known."

"Nor could you," Elsie said with some firmness. She slid her arm around Vi and drew her closer. "Don't you see, darling, that we cannot take responsibility for what might have been? Remember what is said in Proverbs: 'Do not boast about tomorrow, for you do not know what a day may bring forth.' Only God knows what each day, or even the smallest part of the next second, may bring. We're responsible for our actions and must carefully consider the possible consequences of what we do, but God does not expect us to see into the future or feel guilt for that which is beyond our power to control.

"Consider this, too. When your father asked you to accompany him to the field that day, he offered you — from his own free will — a choice, and he respected your decision. It was very important to him that you and your brothers and sisters learn to make good choices and to feel confident in your decisions. That day you chose — for reasons your father approved wholeheartedly — to stay at home and attend to your lessons. He chose to go to the fields and work. There is no more guilt attached to your choice than to your Papa's."

Vi sniffled and then said, "I never thought of that, Mamma. Papa's dying was so horrible, and I miss him so much. It hurts worse than anything I've ever felt — even worse than when Lily died."

"And you wanted to blame someone for your pain, so you blamed yourself," Elsie said. "We humans tend to do that when we cannot understand the reasons for our suffering. But there is much that we are not meant to understand —

things beyond our comprehension. God alone has infinite knowledge and wisdom, and He wants us to open our hearts and trust in Him even when we are suffering."

"The lesson of Job?" Vi said.

"Yes, dearest child. Suffering is part of God's great plan for us — as is joy. It's not for us to question His reasons but to trust that He does what is right for us. Never forget or doubt that God is in control and is working out His perfect plan in the lives of all His children. Hold fast to the truth that God is good and all He does is good."

Elsie paused to allow her words to sink in. Then she continued. "As we choose to trust Him, we will find moment by moment the help and strength we need. The Bible promises that 'the Lord is close to the brokenhearted.' He will never fail you, Vi. And what's more, He gives us the comfort of one another." She hugged Vi affectionately, and then said, "I am glad you have confided in me, darling, though I wish we had spoken of this earlier. Have you taken all your feelings to Jesus? Have you poured out your heart to Him?"

"Yes, Mamma, but I think that I wasn't truly listening for His answer," Vi replied, shaking her head from side to side as if she were trying to dislodge some thought.

"Ever since Papa died, I've felt like I've been going around in a circle. I pray, and I feel so much better. Then I start thinking about what happened, and I come right back to the beginning — to feeling so guilty and so terribly sad. I thought if I punished myself, that would make the feelings go away. But no matter what I did, they just came back, worse than ever...."

Vi paused, and Elsie knew that her child needed to gather her thoughts. After a minute or two, Vi resumed: "I'm beginning to see that I've been too deep in my own

sadness. It's as if I've been locked away in one of these dusty old trunks with nothing but my guilty feelings all around me. God has been answering my prayers all along, but my ears and eyes have been closed to everything but my sorrow."

"God was answering my prayers, wasn't He?" said Vi, and her voice was lighter than Elsie had heard in many months. "He gave me you and everyone who loves me and wants to listen to me. Only I couldn't see that He wanted me to tell you how I felt."

Then Vi flung her arms about her mother and exclaimed, "I'm so happy that our Lord led you to find me here, Mamma. I know He helped you remember this place because He's been watching over me all along and He directed you to come to me. Don't you think that, Mamma? Don't you think that the Lord is truly the greatest and most loving Friend?"

"I do, darling," Elsie said from the bottom of her heart. "I do."

"Mamma," Vi said, her tone serious once again, "does it seem to you that I am very different from your other children? I never seem to feel things the way Missy and Ed and the rest do. I've wanted so much to be like them—to be sad but also glad for Papa, that he's with God now. But I just kept thinking how disappointed God must be by my selfishness. I thought He couldn't forgive me and Papa couldn't forgive me. And you, Mamma—how could I make your suffering worse by telling you my feelings?"

Gently, Elsie said, "There is much of your father in you, you know. But I see myself there, too. When I was a girl, I often tried to hold my feelings inside, lest I cause pain to those I loved. I didn't understand that keeping fear and

Violet's Hidden Doubts

doubt hidden in the dark gives them the power to torment us. But I learned through trial and error—and with much help from your Papa—that the Lord wants us to bring our feelings into the light and share our troubles with those who care about us. God doesn't want us to suffer alone, and His abiding love for us includes the gift of other people to help us in our misery and grief."

"I wanted to tell you, Mamma, so many times. I wanted to tell Ed before he left. But whenever I tried, I couldn't get the words out of my mouth. I was so ashamed," Vi said, her voice trembling as she recalled her terrible loneliness over the last months. "I was so confused and frightened."

"I know that, pet," Elsie said. "But even when we think that our worries are completely hidden, the people who really love us can sense our feelings. They might not know the cause of our sorrow, but nonetheless our pain is painful for them."

"Did you know?" Vi asked.

"I knew that you were suffering, and I grieved at your grief," Elsie answered honestly. "I knew that I would do anything in my power to help you, if you would let me."

Elsie hugged her daughter gently and said, "I trust your good and loving heart and the healing power of the Lord. But I have worried a great deal about you. I wanted to help, Vi, and now you have allowed me to. That makes me feel very good. From the time you were a small girl, you were always able to turn to your Papa when you were troubled. I can never take his place, but I am here for you, my darling. No one can protect you from all the troubles of life, but believe me, Vi, troubles are easier to bear when they are shared."

"Would it be all right…" Vi began. Then she hesitated. After a moment, she resumed, "Would it be all right to keep

this between us, Mamma? I mean, should I share what I told you with the others?"

"Only if you want to," Elsie replied. "What is most important for you is to learn the lesson of opening yourself completely to our Heavenly Father and holding nothing back from Him. I know that it's hard for you, because you think you are imposing your troubles on Him. But that is what the Lord wants—to share our troubles and to bear them for us. The Bible says, 'Cast all your anxiety on him because he cares for you.' And the Lord also gives us people who love us to help us through our pain. When we allow ourselves to be helped, then we are better able to help others in their times of need."

Vi smiled, and Elsie continued. "You said that you felt as if you were going around in a circle, and I understand now that you must have been very frightened because you thought that you were in that circle alone and you could not see your way out. But God was with you all the time, and He always will be. That is what it means to open our hearts to Him. When we invite Him into our hearts, then we are never alone. Instead of a circle of pain, His is a circle of love—love that is without beginning and without end."

In the near-dark of that small, cold room, Vi leaned against her mother and felt the love—pure and warm—surrounding her. For the first time in so many months, she was free of the shadows of her guilt and regret.

Softly, she said, "That is what everyone has been trying to tell me—Molly and Ed and you, Mamma, and God most of all. And now I can hear you. Oh, thank You, God, for answering my prayers by bringing my Mamma here to me tonight."

Violet's Hidden Doubts

Elsie added her own words: "Yes, thank You, Heavenly Father, for bringing us together and showing us Your way."

And for some minutes, mother and daughter simply sat together, embracing each other and warming themselves in the embrace of the greatest love of all.

But at last Elsie became aware of the time, and she said, "I want to talk more of this with you, for I believe we both have many lessons to learn together. For the moment, however, I think our family will best be served by our appearance in the dining room. They are surely wondering where we are. Are you hungry, my pet?"

The wick in the lamp had burned so low that Elsie couldn't see her daughter's face, but she heard the amazement in Vi's response.

"I am, Mamma. I don't know why, for I have hardly wanted to eat anything lately. But all of a sudden, I'm starving! Isn't that strange, Mamma?"

And Elsie could not control the smile that came to her lips on hearing those words. *Thank You, dear Lord*, she thought, *for bringing Vi home to us again!*

"I'm strangely hungry myself," Elsie said as she took her daughter's hand and they departed the luggage room together. "I can't wait to see what Crystal has prepared for us."

They returned to the main part of the house—to the warm, clean air and the sounds of voices at work and play. And all around her, Vi felt something she had almost forgotten: the excited bustle of her family preparing for their trip to Viamede. Laughter spilled from the dining room where her sisters and brothers were already gathered.

As they approached the room, Vi squeezed her mother's hand and said, "Papa would be very happy for us tonight,

wouldn't he, Mamma? He was always so full of joy whenever we were about to leave on a journey."

"He would be happy for us," Elsie agreed. Then she added, "He would be happy for *you*, my darling."

CHAPTER

12

A New Face
at Viamede

*But as for me and my
household, we will
serve the LORD.*

JOSHUA 24:15

A New Face at Viamede

*S*everal days later, the travelers from Ion landed in the bustling port of New Orleans and were met by Mr. Mason, the chaplain at Viamede, and Mr. Mayhew, a lawyer who was Elsie's chief business representative in Louisiana. Elsie had decided not to stop in the Crescent City, where Mr. Mayhew lived, but to proceed immediately to Viamede. So their luggage was soon unloaded and transferred to another, smaller steamboat which would take the party back into the Gulf waters and up the Bayou Teche to Viamede. This final leg of the trip could be lengthy, but the weather was calm, and on the afternoon of the following day, the riverboat reached its destination.

From the plantation's dock, a wide gravel driveway led up a gentle, grassy slope to the house. The drive was lined with massive live oak trees whose branches trailed wispy fingers of moss and formed a canopied frame for the antebellum plantation house in the distance. The splendid white mansion with its broad balconies and verandas had not changed much in appearance since Elsie had lived there as a small child. In the afternoon sun, Viamede seemed to vibrate with light, beckoning the family forward.

An open carriage stood waiting at the dock for Molly, her mother, and Christine, who carried Danny. But the rest of the group chose to walk to the house. The twins and Rosemary ran ahead, bounding over the soft lawn and playing hide-and-seek around the old trees.

Watching them romp, Vi was reminded of her first visit to the plantation, when she was about five. She smiled at her memories of chasing over this same lawn with her father; she could almost hear him laughing like a boy when he played tag with her, Missy, and Ed. And she realized for the first time that whenever it had been her turn to be "it," Papa would always let her catch him. It was a wonderful memory — one that just a few days ago would have been like a stab of pain to her troubled heart. For what must have been the hundredth time since the night in the luggage room with her mother, Vi said a silent prayer of thanks to the Lord for releasing her from the darkness of her guilt and doubt.

As they walked, Elsie and her parents chatted with Mr. Mason about the state of the plantation's many workers. When Elsie inquired about Aunt Mamie, the head house-keeper, Mr. Mason smacked his forehead in frustration and exclaimed, "How could I have forgotten? Mamie has been afflicted with circulation problems in her legs. Dr. Bayliss says that it is not too serious but could become worse if she does not rest. Between us, the doctor and I finally convinced her to give up her more taxing duties. We had to be quite firm, I can tell you. She wouldn't agree to curtail her activities until we found a temporary house-keeper of whom she approved. I say 'temporary' because we did not want to make a final decision without your approval, Mrs. Travilla."

"I do appreciate your concern," Elsie said, "but you say the person you hired meets Mamie's standards?"

"I was somewhat surprised at first," Mr. Mason continued. "We interviewed a number of highly qualified ladies, but Mamie found none to be wholly satisfactory. Then we interviewed Mrs. O'Flaherty, and Mamie took her on a tour of the house and kitchen as she did with all the applicants. When the

two returned to me, Mamie declared in no uncertain terms that Mrs. O'Flaherty was the one."

Rose asked the obvious question: "But why did Mamie's judgment surprise you, Mr. Mason?"

The chaplain's round face turned beet-red. "I am ashamed to say, ma'am, that I had not been impressed. But Mamie saw what I did not. If I had doubts, they were over-ridden first by Mamie and then by my good wife, who took to Mrs. O'Flaherty as quickly as Mamie did."

Mr. Mason came to a halt and shook his head in confusion. "Is it possible that women see one another differently than we men do? A most interesting idea. I must make a study of the subject," he said to himself. Then he picked up his pace and caught up to the others.

"How would you describe the new housekeeper, Mr. Mason?" inquired Horace, who had overheard the chaplain's short soliloquy and was struggling to suppress a chuckle.

"As a diamond in the rough, sir," said Mr. Mason. "I had appraised her more rough than diamond, but since she has taken up her duties here, I believe she is a gem. But you must judge for yourselves."

Their first view of Mrs. O'Flaherty came moments later as the woman emerged from the house and waved to the approaching crowd. *She does look a bit rough*, Elsie caught herself thinking.

Mrs. O'Flaherty hurried down the entrance steps, raising her calico skirts to ease her steps and in the process revealing a pair of highly polished, men's work boots and brightly patterned stockings. Elsie quickly raised her gaze up Mrs. O'Flaherty's tall frame (almost as tall as Horace) and broad shoulders to her head, which was as eccentric as

Violet's Hidden Doubts

her feet. In the sunlight, her black hair, braided and coiled like a snake atop her head, seemed almost metallic blue. A brilliant smile showed an abundance of white teeth that sparkled in the light; on coming closer, Elsie realized that the sparkle came from one tooth in particular—a gold one in the center of the smile. Mrs. O'Flaherty's face was ruddy and furrowed about the eyes and mouth. But what really arrested Elsie's attention were the woman's eyes; they were large and clear and fringed with fine, black lashes, and the irises—made large in the daylight—were the pure blue of sapphires.

On reaching the large group, Mrs. O'Flaherty looked to Mr. Mason, and he responded with an introduction.

"Mrs. Travilla, I'd like you to meet Mrs. Maureen O'Flaherty, who has so kindly come to us as the temporary housekeeper of Viamede," he said with grave formality. "Mrs. O'Flaherty, this is Mrs. Travilla."

Elsie looked into the extraordinary face, and although she could not have explained her reaction, the mistress of Viamede instantly understood what Mamie and Mrs. Mason had seen there. Elsie extended her hand and received the grasp of a hand larger than her own and as firm as a man's. Even through her gloves, Elsie could feel the hardness of Mrs. O'Flaherty's palm—hardness that came from the calluses of labor.

But when Mrs. O'Flaherty spoke, Elsie experienced a new shock. The voice said only, "So glad to meet you, ma'am. Welcome home." But the sound of it was like music—rich, deep, and accented with Irish charm. Elsie, who had spent many years in the British Isles, recognized the accent instantly as that of a person raised in circumstances far more genteel than the life of a housemaid.

A New Face at Viamede

"Thank you, Mrs. O'Flaherty," Elsie replied courteously. Then she proceeded to make introductions to her father and mother and the rest. Each time Mrs. O'Flaherty replied to one or another of the party, they all felt a kind of thrill at the sound of her voice.

At last the housekeeper turned back to Elsie. "I've seen Miss Percival and her mother to the downstairs suite, ma'am. And your nursemaid to the little one's room. All the other rooms are ready, and the maids will unpack when your luggage is brought up. I can show you to your rooms now, but perhaps you would prefer the parlor. We have tea prepared—and cold lemonade for those who enjoy it."

At this last remark, she darted a look at the twins and Rosemary and winked.

"I think we would all like some refreshment," Elsie replied.

"We certainly shall," Horace agreed. He felt a tug on his jacket pocket and looked down. Rosemary stood beside him, and in the best whisper she could manage, she said, "I'm hungry, Grandpapa."

Mrs. O'Flaherty said, "I believe we can find a little something to satisfy you, Miss Rosemary. Perhaps you and your brothers would like to come with me."

Rosemary looked to her Mamma, who smiled and nodded. The child slipped her small hand into Mrs. O'Flaherty's large one. With a little curtsey to Elsie, Mrs. O'Flaherty departed, Rosemary at her side and Harold and Herbert close at her heels. As they entered the house, Elsie heard one of her sons ask the housekeeper, "Are you a pirate, Mrs. O'Flaherty?"

Violet's Hidden Doubts

Mrs. O'Flaherty's "little something" turned out to be a luxurious spread for all the new arrivals. A variety of tasty sandwiches, cakes, and fresh fruits soon sated the appetites of all the travelers, and by the time they were shown to their rooms, their baggage had been delivered and the contents unpacked.

Vi was pleased to find that she would be sharing the suite of ground-floor rooms with Missy and her cousin Isa Conley. Molly and Aunt Enna occupied the other bedroom, which adjoined their common sitting room.

"Well, what do you think of Viamede?" Vi asked Isa, who was lounging on the couch in the sitting room.

"It's magnificent," Isa replied. "I never imagined a mansion this beautiful. Did you know that every bedroom in the house opens onto a porch or a balcony?"

"They're called 'galleries'," Missy explained, "and the doors open so the breezes can cool the whole house."

"And what do you both think of Mrs. O'Flaherty?" Vi asked mischievously. "Could she be a pirate, as Harold guessed?"

"One gold tooth does not a pirate make," Missy laughed. "She seems very kind and incredibly organized. She has a remarkably handsome face, too. I'm sure Lester would want to paint her."

"And her voice," Isa added. "I wouldn't be the least surprised to learn that she sings grand opera."

Vi dropped her eyes as she said, "I want to know more about her. How old is she? Where is she from? Her name and her accent speak of Ireland. I wonder if she has family there? Oh, is it very rude of me to be so curious?"

"Not at all," said Molly, who at that moment was wheeling her chair into the room. "Curiosity is a positive virtue in

my profession. What is rude is to let curiosity be satisfied with gossip and hasty conclusions. I, too, am very curious about Mrs. O'Flaherty, but I'm sure we will learn more about her as time goes on."

"Well, I'm curious about this gorgeous house," Isa said, flopping back against a pile of soft pillows. "It seems strange to have so beautiful a place without a family in residence."

"I think our Mamma is quite sentimental about Viamede," Missy commented. "It was the home of her mother, bought and renovated by her grandparents. Mamma and Papa spent their honeymoon here, and Papa loved the place as much as she. I often heard Papa lament the fact that so many of the great houses on the Teche have been abandoned or fallen into disrepair since the War. He wanted Viamede preserved, and he and Mamma felt they were in the best position to do that."

"Do Mr. and Mrs. Mason live in the house?" Molly wondered.

"They have their own house not far from here," Missy said.

"Oh, when may we have a tour of everything?" Isa asked eagerly.

"Tomorrow morning," Missy said. "We will see the whole house and the gardens. We can take a horseback ride, if you like. Mamma says there is a wonderful small cart, Molly, and she will have a driver ready if you want to accompany us."

"We could have a picnic in the orange grove. And then we can visit the little cemetery," Vi proposed. "It's not at all gloomy, but like a small park with monuments and benches and beautiful lawn and flowers. Mamma used to play there, before she moved to Roselands. I played there too, when I was little."

The girls indeed got their full tour on the following day, from top to bottom of the grand old house and around the grounds. Molly and the twins joined them for their picnic. Their last stop, the tree-shaded cemetery where Elsie's mother and grandparents lay, proved to be just as Vi described. It was a lovely place to talk together and contemplate the splendor of a perfect April day—and what promised to be a perfect holiday for them all.

CHAPTER 13

New Friends and Complications

Blessed is he who comes in the name of the LORD!

MARK 11:9

New Friends and Complications

*T*hough the Travillas' state of mourning meant that there were no social events at Viamede, the young family members found plenty to occupy their time and were more than happy in one another's company. If boredom did threaten, they discovered that the remarkable Mrs. O'Flaherty always had a good idea for activities.

Elsie and her father spent their days primarily in discussions with the Viamede manager, Mr. Spriggs, and with Mr. Mason. She and Horace also made several business trips to New Orleans to meet with Mr. Mayhew and other lawyers and bankers there. But Elsie's primary concern was the hiring of a new manager and a new chaplain for Viamede. It seemed a daunting task: How could she hope to find employees of the uncommon character and loyalty of the two very different men who had served Viamede for so many years?

A new manager was the first priority. But the search for Mr. Spriggs's replacement proved surprisingly easy. A neighbor suggested they speak to a certain Mr. McFee. The name was immediately recognized, for had not a Mr. McFee and his wife taken over the running of Viamede during the War? The neighbor explained that this Mr. McFee was the nephew of the former manager. After several interviews, Elsie and Horace were fully satisfied with the young man's credentials and capabilities. He was offered the post and accepted immediately.

As for Mr. Mason and his good wife — was it possible that anyone could take their places? Were ever shepherds more attentive to their flock? Mr. Mason had seen to the spiritual needs of the people of Viamede for more than twenty years now, and he still went about his duties with the gleeful enthusiasm he brought to the post when he was a fresh-faced theology student. Some years previously, Mr. Mason had taken on the additional responsibility of ministering to a local Protestant congregation, so that church was also losing its much-loved pastor.

Elsie wrote letters of inquiry to several schools of theology, and responses began to come in. She also conducted interviews with candidates recruited by Mr. Mayhew's associates, but none of these efforts produced candidates who seemed right to her.

The local congregation was conducting its own search, and from time to time, they engaged a visiting minister to conduct services. Just such a guest was in the pulpit on the first two Sundays that the family attended church. He seemed, to Elsie, a righteous man but too bound by the law to remember the compassion of grace and faith. Others of the congregation must have had similar feelings, for when the minister's visit was ended, he was not invited to stay on.

"We have another guest pastor coming on the second Sunday in May," Mr. Mason informed Elsie one day in late April. The expression on his face revealed such a confusion of hopefulness and anxiety that Elsie almost laughed. "I don't know his name," Mr. Mason said, "but he comes highly recommended."

Still, Elsie's experience thus far did not raise her hopes on that second Sabbath in May. She tried to keep an open mind, but as she settled into the family pew in the country church, her expectations were not high.

A neighbor—the same neighbor who had brought Mr. McFee to her attention—rose to introduce the visiting

minister. His name meant nothing to Elsie, but when it was said, Horace Dinsmore, who was seated beside her, gasped. She looked at her father and saw that an uncharacteristic flush had suffused his face. But before she could ask if he was well, Horace waved his hand to signal that he was fine.

The guest in the pulpit began to speak. His voice was strong, carrying to the farthest corner of the church, but melodious and full of warmth. His explication of the text for the day — Matthew 4:18-22, Jesus' calling of the first disciples to be "fishers of men" — was both intelligent and plainly stated, so that not even the youngest of the congregation were excluded from his message. So engaging was his sermon and so conversational his tone that Elsie hardly noticed his appearance until he finished speaking. But when the churchgoers rose for a final hymn and the benediction, given by Mr. Mason, she looked more closely and saw that the guest was younger than she had supposed — perhaps no more than twenty-seven or twenty-eight. He was handsome in a way that was not showy, with eyes the dark blue of the sea and hair a reddish-brown that caught the light through the church windows.

When the service ended, Elsie intended to hurry and catch the minister, for she hoped that he might join her family for luncheon that day. But a hand held her back.

"Let the others go first," Horace said in a low whisper.

So Elsie hung back with her father while Rose guided the rest of the family outside to meet the young pastor. Certainly there was a buzz in the church, and as people passed by her, Elsie listened.

"Most impressive" — "made me think" — "felt like he was talking straight to me" — "nearly as good as Mr. Mason, I'd say." The snatches of conversation that came to Elsie's ears told her that her own response to the sermon was not unique. Even old Mrs. Caulkin was overheard to say, "A mite young but better than any other we've heard of late," which was high praise indeed from a woman who rarely had a good word for anyone or anything.

It was some time before the church was cleared out, but Horace finally nudged Elsie, and they made their way to the porch where the guest and Mr. Mason were standing.

Horace stepped forward and said, "Elsie dear, I would like you to meet the Reverend James Keith who is, if I am correct, a cousin of ours."

Elsie was dumbfounded. She looked first at her father, whose face wore an odd smile, then to the minister, who appeared no less surprised than herself. The younger man found his voice before she did and replied, "I believe I am, sir. I know that I am James Keith. If you are Horace Dinsmore, Jr., and this is Mrs. Travilla, then we are surely kin and there is no mistake."

Horace, forgetting protocol, took the young man's hand and began shaking it heartily. "You are Marcia's grandson and Cyril's son," he said. "Aunt Wealthy has written to me of the new preacher in the family."

"And she and my grandmother have told me of the Dinsmores," Mr. Keith responded. "I knew that you had property in this area, but I hardly expected—"

"Nor did we, Mr. Keith," Elsie said, for her father's mention of Aunt Wealthy Stanhope clarified something of this extraordinary meeting. "I'd planned to ask the visiting pastor to join us for lunch today. How much more exciting to invite a member of the family."

"Exciting indeed. Overwhelming," he said with obvious pleasure, but then his brow furrowed slightly. "But I must

decline, Mrs. Travilla, for I am dining with my host, Mr. Embury, and his family."

"I would not be the barrier to a happy family reunion," came a deep voice from the foot of the porch stairs. Mr. Louis Embury, the neighbor who had brought Mr. McFee to Elsie's attention, climbed the steps. "Please, Mrs. Travilla," he said, "take my delightful houseguest with you. He will be staying with us for several weeks, and I believe we can share his company."

"Then you must join us too, Mr. Embury," Elsie said. "This reunion is apparently due to you, and I would not have you miss its outcome."

Mr. Embury, a widower in his early thirties, agreed. Elsie, suddenly remembering that Mr. Embury had young children, quickly included them in her invitation. But Mr. Embury declined on their behalf, for both his daughters were abed with spring colds.

"Perhaps Mr. and Mrs. Mason will ride with us," Mr. Embury said.

They all turned to the chaplain, whose normal river of words had literally ceased to flow (perhaps because his mind had been bubbling with ideas as he observed this chance encounter). He opened his mouth, but nothing came out. He gulped, tried again, and managed a "yes"—as high and shrill as a baby chick's peep.

He looked into the face of each person standing there, and a smile as joyful as a cherub's broke over his round face. "Thank You, dear Father and Savior," he proclaimed, "for what You have delivered to us this day! Thank You for family and friends and for this glorious morning and all the new opportunities it brings!"

Violet's Hidden Doubts

Needless to say, luncheon at Viamede was not so quiet as on a normal Sabbath. The young people were only a little surprised to hear that the pastor and Mr. Embury would be at their table. But imagine their amazement on learning that the Reverend Keith was kindred — cousin to all the Travillas and their grandfather and great-grandfather.

"What should we call you?" Harold asked with some concern.

"I guess I should be 'Reverend Keith' or 'Mr. Keith' when we are at church," the newfound family member said with only slightly exaggerated seriousness. "But I prefer 'Cousin James' among family, if that suits you fellows."

"But what of us who are not related?" Molly asked.

"If it is not too forward, I would like to be cousin to all, for blood is not the only measure of family."

So Cousin James was welcomed to Viamede and into the hearts of everyone there. He became a frequent visitor — often accompanied by Mr. Embury. Both men were sincerely respectful of the family's mourning, yet James sensed that their visits were no burden at Viamede. And the contacts with so many sociable and interesting ladies and gentlemen were good for Louis Embury, who had lost his wife only two years previously.

Besides, James was an instant favorite with Mr. and Mrs. Mason, who showed him every aspect of Viamede, with special emphasis on its spiritual life. By the time he delivered his next sermon in the local church, James was well aware that Mr. Mason's interest was not without its hidden motives. The church needed a new pastor; the plantation needed a new chaplain; and Mr. Mason clearly needed to know that he would be leaving his Viamede congregation and the church in good hands.

When James realized that he was in the running for both positions, he began thinking seriously about the prospect of making his home in Louisiana. A Midwesterner by birth, educated in the East, he had never contemplated a ministry in the South. He'd come to the region only as a tourist, accepting an invitation from Louis Embury, whom he had met through one of his seminary instructors.

On the afternoon following his second Sunday sermon, James was sitting with Molly, Missy, Vi, and Isa on the veranda of Viamede. The young women were telling him about the informal Bible study group they had started and received his promise to attend their next gathering.

"Might we meet tomorrow?" Vi asked.

Molly and Isa quickly agreed, but Missy interrupted them, saying, "I have nearly forgotten. Oh, where is my head?"

"In Italy, I suspect," Isa laughed. "But what have you forgotten?"

"Mamma plans to go to New Orleans tomorrow and stay for a few days. She will visit Mr. and Mrs. Carpenter at their mission, and she wants to know if we would like to accompany her. We will return on Friday."

"Where will we stay?" Vi asked.

"With Mr. and Mrs. Mayhew," Missy said. "Mrs. Mayhew has volunteered to give us a tour of the city."

"Is there some other reason for this visit?" Vi inquired, for she thought her mother's business in New Orleans had been completed.

"I don't know," Missy replied. "Yesterday, Mamma received letters from Dinah and Mrs. Mayhew. And that's when she decided to make the trip."

Vi said only, "Oh," but she sensed that there was something more in this hurried journey.

"Is this Mrs. Carpenter an old friend of yours?" James inquired.

"Yes, and more," Vi said. "She is the granddaughter of our Aunt Chloe."

"Another family member?" James asked.

A faint blush touched Missy's face. "Chloe was a slave, and she cared for our mother from the moment she was born," Missy explained in a soft tone. "She cared for me and Vi and the rest when we were small. She is not kin, though I wish she were, for we love her—and her husband—with all our hearts."

"But surely the affection you have is good?" James said, for he had observed the downcast eyes of the other girls as Missy spoke.

"Oh, I guess we are all embarrassed to admit that our Aunt Chloe was ever a slave," Vi responded. "You see, Cousin James, our parents never believed in slavery, and they did their best to fight it. They broke the law by educating their workers, and Papa even supported the fugitive slave movement before the War. But they couldn't put an end to the system by themselves, so they owned slaves until the War abolished the system."

"Please do not think me impertinent," James said hesitantly, "but may I ask why slaveowners who believed slavery wrong did not free their slaves? Would that not have set the example for others to follow?"

"It would not have been as easy as it sounds," Vi said. "Even in the North, freed slaves were subject to capture and being brought back to the South and sold into bondage again. Before the War, white people who espoused abolition here

were also in grave danger. Even after the War, our papa was the special target of violent men who wanted the old system restored. They tried to kill Papa and burn our house."

"I didn't know," James said. "I regret reviving memories that are so painful."

"You have nothing to regret," Isa said. There was a quaver in her voice that betrayed her strong emotion. "I, for one, do not want to forget those times. We must never forget the pain or the injustice of treating our fellow human beings as slaves. Never! For what we forget, we are more likely to repeat."

James stared at Isa, seeing for the first time beneath her lovely appearance. *There is steel in this girl*, he thought.

"We're glad to discuss this subject with you, Cousin James," Missy said. "Some people think it's not proper for ladies and girls to talk of politics and the problems that plague our society, but we are more advanced than that."

Molly then added, "I wish you could have known Missy and Vi's father, for Cousin Edward was an extraordinary man. He believed without reservation in the equality of all, and he taught each of us to respect our minds and use them."

James said, "I would like to continue the discussion. There is a great deal I must learn about the South and its unhappy history. My attitudes have been shaped from afar, yet I begin to understand that my thinking has been too simple."

Elsie, who had come onto the veranda in time to hear the last part of this conversation, walked forward. Catching sight of her, James rose and offered his seat.

"Thank you, Cousin James," she said, taking her place in the group. "Missy, have you told everyone about our plans for tomorrow?"

Violet's Hidden Doubts

"Yes, Mamma," Missy replied.

"Well, I'm hoping our Cousin James might join us if his schedule permits," Elsie said, smiling graciously at James. "I think you would be interested in the work that Reverend and Mrs. Carpenter are doing. Like you, they have chosen to devote their lives to the ministry."

"Oh, please come with us," Vi begged excitedly.

The others joined her in encouraging their cousin to accept, though in truth James required little persuading. "I should like very much to join you," he said. "But will it be an imposition on your friends, the Mayhews? I can easily stay at a hotel."

Elsie assured him, "I am sure they can find a room for another of the Dinsmore clan."

"Or a large wardrobe if there is no room," Vi giggled.

~~~

As it turned out, one of the group was missing the next morning when they boarded the riverboat for the voyage to New Orleans. Molly had decided not to make the trip, for the weather had turned very warm and she feared becoming fatigued by travel. So she chose to stay at Viamede with her mother and Horace and Rose.

"Do you think Molly is feeling sick?" Vi asked as she and Isa stood on the deck of the boat, watching the Viamede dock disappear around the turn in the river.

"Not in the way you mean," Isa replied with a knowing smile. "I'm not worried about her health."

At Vi's quizzical look, Isa said, "Did you know that Aunt Rose has invited Mr. Embury and his daughters to dine at Viamede today?"

624

"But what has that to do with Molly?" Vi asked.

"Perhaps nothing," Isa said. "Perhaps everything. Oh, I'm sorry. I do not mean to sound like an old gossip, but I have noticed that Mr. Embury seems to take a special interest in our Molly's company."

"Um," was Vi's only response, for this was an observation she had missed.

The lush bayou landscape flowed past, its panoply of cypress, palmetto, thick vines, and water flowers interrupted occasionally by stretches of pasture and low-lying rice paddies. Isa said, "I had not realized there were so many shades of green in nature."

"I think you may be right," Vi said, still pondering Isa's observation about Mr. Embury and Molly.

"God has truly painted this country with a magnificent palette," Isa commented.

"He has," Vi said, "but I was talking about Mr. Embury. I think you may be right. Now that you mention it, he is very attentive to Molly when he visits. I often see them deep in conversation, and Molly told me that she has read some of her poems to him. You know how reserved she is about her poetry. She won't even hear suggestions that she publish it."

Isa laughed, "So I am not the only gossip."

"This isn't gossip," Vi protested. "We are merely comparing notes. Don't we have a responsibility to guard our cousin's happiness?"

"We do," Isa agreed, "but we must not rush into judgments based on speculation. That's my mother's specialty, and I know what harm it can do. I want to think that Molly can find love. I want to think we all can—as Missy has—find loving helpmates to share our days. But I believe Molly has convinced herself that marriage is denied to her because of her handicap."

"Maybe she needs to make a study of these greens," Vi said.

Now it was Isa's turn to be confused. At her questioning look, Vi said, "I've learned about color from trying to paint it. Look around, and you'll see green everywhere, because that's what you expect to see. But scrunch up your eyes like this"—she demonstrated by contorting her face—"and you can see yellows and blues, purples and reds, browns and black. The green is really made up of lots of colors and of light and shadow. That's what people are like. God makes us in endless variations. If we look only for green—for a single quality in others—then we miss the real beauty of each variation God has made."

"That's a lovely metaphor," Isa said. She squinted her eyes and stared into the thick vegetation along the river's bank. In this way, she saw what Vi was talking about—a kaleidoscope of colors wheeling and dancing before her. She held her gaze until her eyes began to hurt and she blinked.

"It's like magic, isn't it?" Vi said. "But it isn't magic because God has made all this color for us to see, if we will only use our eyes. 'Man looks at the outward appearance, but the Lord looks at the heart,'" she said, quoting a familiar verse of Scripture.

Turning back to her younger cousin, Isa said, "Perhaps Mr. Embury is the type of man who looks beneath the surface to see all the colors hidden in the green. But whatever his feelings, I pray that our Molly can look beyond her crippled legs and see the wealth of beauty and intelligence and love she has to give."

⌒

That afternoon, as the riverboat plowed its way toward the Gulf, a most pleasant outing was underway back at Viamede. Under the watchful eyes of Horace and Rose, four children—Rosemary, Danny, and the two energetic Embury girls, whose names were Corinne and Madeline ("Maddie" for short)—played in the shade of the orange grove. Not too far away, the girls' father carefully pushed a wheeled chair and its occupant along a hard dirt path to a small glade formed by a semicircle of crepe myrtle trees.

Stopping to rest, Mr. Embury sat on the grass, and he and Molly talked of many things, for he was a man of excellent education and shared many of Molly's interests in literature and art and music. By chance, the subject of his marriage was raised when he mentioned his late wife's passion for opera.

Molly asked, in total innocence, "Would you ever consider marrying again, Mr. Embury, for your children?"

He paused, and Molly was suddenly and painfully aware of the impertinence of so personal a question. But Mr. Embury took no offense.

"Until recently, I would have said no," he replied slowly. "And I should still say the same if you mean would I marry only to give my youngsters the benefit of a mother. I believe that true love between husband and wife is among the greatest gifts that God gives us. The love of two parents for one another serves as the model of marriage when their children grow up and choose their own life partners."

Molly, her cheeks burning in a reaction that had nothing to do with the temperature, stammered, "I—I'm so sorry, Mr. Embury. I had no right to ask..."

Violet's Hidden Doubts

"You have every right, Miss Percival, as my friend. I do count you as a friend, and I value your forthrightness."

"Still…"

"My answer to your question is yes, I would marry again."

"What has changed your mind, Mr. Embury?"

He looked off to some distant point and said, "Time, perhaps. They say it is the great healer. Time and…" He hesitated.

Turning back to look into Molly's eyes, he smiled. "But let's just leave it at that, Miss Percival. For now."

CHAPTER

14

Seeing
New Orleans

*Through the blessing of the
upright a city is
exalted....*

PROVERBS 11:11

*V*i tugged her thin bathrobe close and rapped lightly on the door of Elsie's sleeping cabin.

At the sound of her mother's questioning "Yes?" Vi entered.

Vi approached the small berth and sat down. Seeing the open Bible on Elsie's lap, she said, "Did I interrupt your prayers, Mamma?"

"No, dear. I was just searching for some inspiration. But tell me what brings you to my side at so late an hour. Couldn't you sleep?"

"No, ma'am," Vi replied in a voice so sweet it sounded like a child's. "I've been thinking about you. You've been working so hard since we got to Viamede. And tonight, for the first time, I saw that you looked tired, and I'm worried about you."

Elsie extended her arm and drew Vi close. "I admit it," she said. "This visit has been tiring. But I promise you, darling, that I am just fine. A person can be tired without being ill, so there's no cause for you to worry."

Vi snuggled close. "I don't want you to be sick, Mamma. I just can't bear the thought of your being sick or—or..."

"Or of my dying?"

Soft tears began to trickle from Vi's eyes as she said, "Or that. To think of a world without Papa and you. It's horrible. Just too horrible."

"Oh, my darling, you must trust that I would not jeopardize my health any more than yours," Elsie said. "I'd sell Viamede tomorrow if doing its business were too much for me."

Violet's Hidden Doubts

She put her hand under Vi's chin and lifted her daughter's face. With a smile, she went on, "I'm a very sensible woman, you know. And besides, I'm not planning to leave you for a long time unless the Lord has need of me. I'm always prepared to answer His call, but being ready is not the same as being silly enough to ignore common sense."

Vi brushed away her tears. "Sometimes I think that I think too much," she sniffled.

This drew a warm laugh from her mother. "Not too much by any means," she said. "I want you to be thoughtful, but it is wise not to anticipate the worst before you have contemplated other possibilities. I am tired because I've been working hard, but I also feel satisfied with what has been accomplished. Viamede's business is in excellent shape, just as your father left it. We have employed Mr. McFee, and I have a feeling we may soon have a new chaplain."

Vi had already guessed her mother's choice. "Then you've asked Cousin James to stay at Viamede?" she asked.

Elsie's eyes opened wide in amused surprise. "No, I haven't spoken to Cousin James yet, and don't you breathe a word of this to him. I still must consult with the congregation at Viamede. If that goes well, I will offer the post to James. But I do not want him to feel pressured. He never planned to come to the South to live, and this will be a difficult decision for him, I'm sure. He must feel free to choose what is best for him. So let's keep this matter strictly between the two of us for now."

"Of course, Mamma," Vi pledged, feeling quite mature enough to share an important confidence with her mother.

"Are you ready for sleep?" Elsie asked. "If we both look tired at breakfast, the others are sure to notice, and one worrier is all I really need."

632

"May I ask one more question?"

"A quick one."

"This trip was so sudden. Is something wrong with Dinah?"

Elsie settled back against her pillow, still holding her daughter close. "Dinah and her family are all well," she said. "But I do have plans beyond seeing the sights of New Orleans. I want us to spend some time at the mission, so I asked Dinah if we could visit for a day or two. I think it's important for you girls to see the work that the Carpenters are doing."

"And Cousin James, too?" Vi asked.

Elsie smiled and said, "Yes, Cousin James, too. He should meet the Carpenters, for they can provide a perspective on the South that is very different from mine. But this visit is for the benefit of us all, dear. I've been giving a lot of thought to the mission and what we can do to help Dinah and Mr. Carpenter with their work."

"You gave money, didn't you?" Vi asked.

"Yes, dear. Your Papa and I gave funds to start the mission and acquire the property where it is located, but there are needs that money alone cannot meet," Elsie said. "The point is to do what will genuinely benefit the Carpenters and all the people who are served at the mission. Your Papa always said that the best way to know another person is to walk in his shoes for awhile, and that's what I hope we will all try to do."

Vi thought for a few moments, then she said, "I understand, Mamma. To serve others, a person has to do more than just talk about it. We have to *live* God's commandment—truly live it every day. Jesus told us to love our neighbors as ourselves, and loving others means understanding and respecting them, doesn't it? Because that's how we want to be treated."

"I believe it does," Elsie said. "To love others, we have to care about them. And when we really care about someone, we try to understand that person's heart. That's what your Papa meant about walking in another person's shoes. We can't *be* another person, but we can try to look beyond appearances and better understand what is inside."

Elsie hugged her daughter close and added, "I am very glad you decided to visit with me tonight. Your father and I so often talked like this after you and your sisters and brothers were tucked in bed at night. You have reminded me of how helpful it is to open my heart to a kindred spirit."

"Thank you, Mamma, for asking me on this trip," Vi said as she kissed Elsie's cheek and stood to go back to her own cabin. "It's a very grown-up kind of trip, isn't it?"

"I knew you were ready for it," Elsie said. "But go to your bed now. We both need our sleep, for we have several very busy days ahead."

When Vi was snugly back in her own berth, she had a thought just before she fell asleep: *Maybe growing up won't be so bad after all, if I can be like Mamma and always find ways to help others.*

~⌒⌒⌒

The boat trip was delayed by many stops to pick up cargo along the way. So Elsie and her young companions arrived in the port city later than expected the next afternoon. They were met by Mr. Mayhew and driven directly to his home in one of the most beautiful residential sections of the city.

Seeing New Orleans

Mrs. Mayhew—a small, stout woman with a personality as outgoing as her husband's was staid—greeted them with hugs, a delicious meal, and plans for the next day. Elsie would accompany Mr. Mayhew to a final meeting with her business managers, and the others would be entirely in Mrs. Mayhew's hands. During supper, Mrs. Mayhew previewed her sightseeing itinerary, and all her young houseguests were excited by this opportunity to see the city, even Vi and Missy. Though they'd both visited New Orleans on a number of occasions, they'd never had a full-fledged tour with so jovial a guide as Mrs. Mayhew.

"I will run you young people ragged tomorrow," Mrs. Mayhew promised as she bid them good night. "Now, be sure to wear your coolest frocks, girls, and don't forget your parasols. The carriage will be open so you can have the best views, but our New Orleans sun will bake you like muffins if you don't have your parasols."

The tour began bright and early, and the visitors quickly discovered that their hostess was as well informed as she was affable. Mrs. Mayhew was a native Orleanian, and she regaled them with the kind of stories that made the city's history come alive. She told them about the first French settlers and how French rule had given way to Spanish. As they reached the French Quarter, the streets narrowed, and Mrs. Mayhew explained that this was the oldest residential part of the city. The houses seemed small compared to those in the Mayhews' neighborhood; "but don't be deceived," the good lady warned. "These houses extend far back, with magnificent gardens in the rear. When the French developed this crescent of land formed by the Mississippi River, they adopted the style of their homeland, building on long, narrow lots and erecting gated walls in front. Where the gates are open, look through and you will see the open courtyards."

"Some of the houses look almost Spanish," Missy observed.

"You have a good eye," Mrs. Mayhew said. "Have you heard the term 'Creole'? It's a French word that refers to the people of European origin who settled in the New World and to their descendants. Here in New Orleans, Creole means a person of both French and Spanish descent. It also applies to architecture and foods—oh, so many things where the two cultures have mixed and blended over a century and a half."

"Are you a Creole, Mrs. Mayhew?" Vi asked.

"No, I'm an American," the lady replied. "You may think it odd I say that, because we are all Americans. But when Napolean Bonaparte secretly sold the Louisiana Territory to the United States in 1803, the Creole citizens were none too happy to learn about it. Many of them regarded the Americans who flooded into the city as barbarians and would not associate with the newcomers except by necessity. And that sense of division is still with us, though it is softening with each new generation. I have many Creole friends, but there are a few old-timers who still long to see the French flag flying over our city hall in place of the Stars and Stripes."

She then told them about the other waves of immigrants—German, Irish, Caribbean, Chinese, Italian—who had made New Orleans the most international city in all the United States, by her reckoning. "When Mr. Mayhew and I first traveled to Paris many years ago," she chuckled, "I wondered why we had bothered, for it seemed just like home. I was quite young," she added as explanation, "but

I soon realized that New Orleans is not Paris nor Madrid nor any other place, but a unique blend of all the influences that its people brought from their native lands."

Their first stop was Jackson Square, where the statue of Andrew Jackson overlooked the tourists as they walked about. Posed on the back of a rearing horse, the hero of the Battle of New Orleans in the War of 1812 seemed to be raising his hat in salute to the three towers of the St. Louis Cathedral. Mrs. Mayhew told them that the congregation had been active since the early 1700s, though the church had been destroyed twice—first by a hurricane, then by fire—and that the current structure had been extensively remodeled before the Civil War.

They proceeded next to the Ursuline convent not far away, and Mrs. Mayhew told how the nuns of the Ursuline Order had arrived in the 1720s after the most harrowing ocean voyage, bringing medical care and education to the settlement. "I doubt there would be a New Orleans without the Sisters of Ursula," Mrs. Mayhew said. "There is no counting the number of lives those good women have saved. And no words can convey their bravery in the face of every kind of disaster."

The carriage was halted before the convent building, which was one of the oldest in the United States, and Mrs. Mayhew's expression became serious. Her voice deepened as she said, "Our city is often characterized as a place devoted to worldly pleasures. But it was founded on faith, and the love of the Lord is strong here. You will see churches of every religion today, and the people who worship in them are strong in faith. It's not easy to live in a city that was built on a swamp and protected from the waters of the Mississippi only by earthen levees. The people of New

Violet's Hidden Doubts

Orleans have endured unimaginable suffering—hurricanes from the Gulf that have swept away everything in their paths, fires that have consumed entire areas of the city, and worst of all, the epidemics of yellow fever, typhoid, and other raging plagues that can take hundreds of thousands of lives in just a few weeks. But with each trial, our Heavenly Father has strengthened the people and supported them as they rebuilt and recovered. Today, New Orleans is a prosperous city, yet the dangers of epidemics and natural disaster are always with us. It is not worldly pleasure that enables the people to endure. It is faith, my dears, the shield and helmet of faith."

They were all silent for some moments. Looking again at the low buildings that had housed the religious women who served God by caring for the sick and the poor and the abandoned, Vi thought of her conversation with her mother on the riverboat. With no regard for their own safety or comfort, those women had *lived* their faith through service to others.

As she marveled at the steadfast courage of the Sisters of Ursula, Vi heard Mrs. Mayhew giving instructions to the carriage driver. She turned to her companions and saw that a cheery smile again reigned on Mrs. Mayhew's face. "Our next stop is the old St. Louis cemetery on Basin Street," the lady was saying. "You must see how Orleanians honor their dead. Then we will have our lunch at my favorite Creole restaurant."

The cemetery with its above-ground tombs and mausoleums was fascinating. And lunch was leisurely and as delicious as Mrs. Mayhew said it would be. But she would not let them rest for long. Their next stop was an imposing building on Bourbon Street—the French Opera House.

Mrs. Mayhew spoke about the love of music that, she said, "was woven in the city's fabric." A man at the door agreed to let them inside for a peek, and as they stood in the huge auditorium, Mrs. Mayhew described how the rows of seats could be removed for grand balls. "You should see it during Mardi Gras," she said, "when this room is filled with music and dancing and people in the most elaborate costumes. In my younger days, I quite enjoyed the fancy dress balls, and you can't imagine how handsome Mr. Mayhew was in his evening attire," she chuckled.

At last they headed back toward the Mayhews' residence. On the wide thoroughfare of Saint Charles Street, they saw all the evidence of prosperity—splendid hotels, office buildings, and theaters. Then along the residential streets, they passed many beautiful homes, some almost as grand as Viamede, and lush gardens that were truly breathtaking. Mrs. Mayhew seemed to know the history of every house and all the families who had ever dwelled there.

Reaching the Mayhews', they found Elsie waiting in the back garden, ready with cooling drinks and a listening ear. Before excusing themselves to dress for dinner, the young people excitedly told her about all they had seen and learned on their excursion.

When Elsie and Mrs. Mayhew were alone, Elsie expressed her gratitude to her old friend.

"Oh, we only scratched the surface," Mrs. Mayhew said. "The French Quarter, Saint Charles Street, and the old St. Louis cemetery. They were amazed by the tombs, as all our visitors are. I talked their poor ears off, of course," she laughed.

"Their ears all seemed intact," Elsie said, joining in the laughter. "And they clearly learned a great deal from you. I

heard Vi referring to the sidewalks as *banquettes*, just like a born Orleanian."

Mrs. Mayhew's expression changed as she said, "I think tomorrow will be even more eventful. At the mission, they will see another side of the city. It will be a powerful contrast. If my impression of your daughters and their friends is correct, our little tour today will soon pale in comparison to the wealth of love and self-sacrifice they will experience at the mission. I have never properly thanked you, dear Elsie, for introducing me to the Carpenters. They have opened my eyes again to what is possible when people walk in the footsteps of the Lord and live their faith."

CHAPTER

Days at the Mission

For you know the grace of our LORD Jesus Christ, that though he was rich, yet for your sakes he became poor....

2 CORINTHIANS 8:9

Days at the Mission

*T*he next two days of the New Orleans visit were spent at the mission. The mission's neighborhood was a far cry from the Mayhews'. There were no beautiful houses and lush gardens. Most of the dwellings were old and in bad repair, their tin roofs rusting away in the humid climate. The streets were unpaved and would turn into rivers of mud when it rained. The mission itself was in an old warehouse, a brick structure that seemed as solid as the houses around it were flimsy. The building had been recently painted, and its door was a warm red that provided the only color amid the sun-bleached surroundings.

Dinah was waiting at the door when the carriage pulled up. She called for her husband and ushered the visitors inside. It was a happy reunion, for Vi and Missy hadn't seen the Carpenters in a number of years. Elsie introduced Isa and James. Then Mr. Carpenter called for attention and took a sheet of paper from his pocket.

"Your mother has told us that you young people want to see for yourselves how our mission is run," Mr. Carpenter began. "Well, seeing is one thing and doing is another. I can just tell that you are all doers, so I made this list of chores that need doing. You can put your bonnets and purses in my office and decide among yourselves what jobs you'd like to begin with. And Mr. Keith, I have a task for you as well."

Then Dinah addressed Elsie: "I was hoping you might join me in the classroom this morning. My students are starting to arrive even now, and we provide breakfast for them. I learned a long time ago that children can't learn when their stomachs are empty."

Violet's Hidden Doubts

Elsie was very happy with her assignment, and she followed Dinah to the mission kitchen where trays of fresh-baked rolls, fruit, and milk had been prepared for Dinah's pupils. Missy wanted to help with the day's cooking, and she accompanied her mother and Dinah. Mr. Carpenter introduced Isa to Mary Johnson, a young woman whom she would assist to sort large piles of donated clothing and blankets. Vi chose to help with the little children, so Mr. Carpenter put her under the capable supervision of an older woman named Mrs. Duke. With the young ladies settled into their duties, Mr. Carpenter said to James, "You best roll up your sleeves, Mr. Keith. You and I are going out back. There's a pile of wood that needs chopping to keep that old kitchen stove hot. We serve a lot of empty stomachs here day and evening."

Mrs. Duke was a grandmotherly woman who told Vi that this was "doctor day" at the mission. A physician from one of the hospitals came in for the morning and conducted a clinic for the poor. "It's mostly mothers and children," Mrs. Duke explained. "While the mammas are seeing the doctor, we look after the little ones. I hope you like to read, Miss Violet, 'cause that's what the little ones just love. Most of them never see a book except when they come here."

She showed Vi the small collection of picture books that she kept in a closet, and Vi selected several. Then they went to the entry hall of the building. Four women were waiting for the doctor. Each had a baby on her lap, and half a dozen children played at their feet. Mrs. Duke talked with the women, writing their names on a small pad and asking about any special problems. Vi wasn't sure what to do, so she sat down on the bottom step of the hall stairs. She opened a book of fairy tales and pretended to read to herself. The children seemed to be paying no attention to her, though from the corner of her eye, Vi saw them casting shy glances in her direction. Not two minutes passed before a small hand touched her knee.

"Whatcha doin', lady?" a girl of about four asked.

"Reading a story," Vi said, smiling at the child.

"'Bout what?"

"It's about a boy and some magic beans," Vi replied. "Would you like to hear it?"

The little girl said nothing, but she sat down beside Vi on the stairway and looked at the book. Vi pointed to the drawing on the page. "See, that's the boy. His name is Jack, and that's his cow. He's supposed to sell his cow for money to buy food for himself and his poor mother. But he decides to trade the cow for some beans."

Another child had come close, a dark-eyed boy of five or so, and he said, "That's dumb. A whole cow for some beans?"

The boy slipped past the little girl and sat on the step above Vi, so he could look over her shoulder at the picture. "You gonna read that book?" he asked.

"I can read it to you, if you like," Vi said.

The girl said, "Yes, please ma'am," and scooted close to Vi. The boy said, "I guess that's okay," in a nonchalant tone, but he too moved closer.

Vi began to read and soon all the children were gathered around her, rapt in the tale of Jack and the Beanstalk. When she finished, the boy at her shoulder said, "That's a pretty good story, I think. Do you know any more?"

"Oh, I know lots of stories," Vi said. "I can read another, or I can tell you one."

"Tell one, miss," begged a curly-haired girl at her feet.

Violet's Hidden Doubts

Vi thought for a moment, then asked, "Do you all know about Jesus?"

The small heads bobbed enthusiastically, and Vi went on, "Well, when Jesus was a boy of twelve, he went with his parents to Jerusalem...."

For the next three hours, Vi read and told stories, welcoming each new child who arrived and bidding a fond farewell to them when they left with their mothers. She also talked with the little ones, just as her mother did with Danny and Rosemary, and she was delighted at how bright and curious they all were.

She remarked on this to Mrs. Duke, and the kindly lady said, "The shame is they have so few opportunities to learn. Some of them may get to go to Mrs. Carpenter's school, but nobody else cares about educating those sweet angels. The children you met today are lucky, Miss Violet. They've got mothers who do everything they can for their babies. But there's plenty who have no parents and no one to care. You see them in the streets, begging, and you see them as young as seven and eight working at jobs no self-respecting adult would take on. Sometimes they show up here, asking for a meal or a bit of clothing—boys and girls who've had all the brightness and curiosity sapped away by poverty. It's such a waste of good lives, a real tragedy. But this mission, well, it's bringing some hope into lots of lives."

Vi had many questions she wanted to ask, but Mrs. Duke had other chores to do before she left for the day. Later, Vi learned from Mr. Carpenter that Mrs. Duke was a volunteer. She helped at the mission every morning while her own grandchildren had their lessons with Dinah. Mrs. Duke and her husband, a dock worker, were raising their five grandchildren and also caring for Mr. Duke's elderly mother.

"They're good people," Mr. Carpenter said. "They don't ask anything for themselves except the chance to do what they can for others."

***

After her morning classes, Dinah paid visits to some of the older and infirm people in the neighborhood—taking food and medicines to those who could not get out on their own. James offered to accompany Dinah on her rounds, and so did Vi and Isa. As they were setting off, Vi overheard a teenaged boy gruffly expressing his opinion of inexperienced "society folk who come down here to parade their fancy clothes."

That remark and several others she heard troubled her, and on the second morning at the mission, Vi deliberately sought out the Reverend Carpenter. She found him in his tiny office behind the mission's kitchen.

"May I speak to you, Mr. Carpenter?" she asked. "I don't want to interrupt, so I can come back later."

"You're not interrupting, Miss Travilla," he replied, his deep voice as welcoming as his wide smile. "I was making some notes for my Sunday sermon, and I just finished."

He motioned her to a chair near his desk and asked, "Now, how can I help you?"

Vi took a breath and said, "I've been thinking about your mission and our being here. It means so much to us to take part in the work you're doing, but are we really helping? I mean, I heard some people yesterday say something about 'society women' and 'rich folks' and, well, it made me worry and I wanted to ask you…"

Violet's Hidden Doubts

Vi didn't complete her sentence, for in truth she wasn't quite sure what she wanted to ask.

The minister's expression grew serious. "I think I understand," he said gently. "You're afraid that people here might misread your motives and resent you because you're wealthy and they're poor."

"That's it, Mr. Carpenter," Vi said. "That's exactly it."

Mr. Carpenter leaned back in his chair and said, "It's a big question, and one I often ponder on myself. Rich and poor alike, we're all one in the eyes of the Lord, but not necessarily in each other's eyes. I imagine that yesterday and today, maybe you've been feeling the difference that money can make. And wondering why you have so much when the people you meet here have so little."

Vi's eyes widened as she said, "Last night I read again the story of the rich young man in Matthew. Jesus told him to sell his possessions and give to the poor. I'm rich by the world's standards, but I have no possessions of my own to sell. What can I do to make life better for others? How can I really help people who haven't been as blessed as I?"

Mr. Carpenter stroked his chin for several seconds. Then he said, "Miss Travilla, it's as plain as day that you want to do good, but you aren't sure how. These past two days, you've seen and heard things you've never experienced before—met people so poor they may go hungry for days or have to beg from strangers to feed their children. These are things you've known about in your head, but now they are real for you in your heart. And you want to change those things, don't you?"

Vi looked up and said, "Yes, sir, I do. I want the children to have plenty to eat and warm clothes to wear. I want them to go to school. I want their mothers not to have to work so

648

hard night and day. And I want the old people we visited yesterday to have doctors and medicine when they're sick, just as I do. But it's so unfair!"

Mr. Carpenter agreed. "Unfair, yes. But unfair because people make it that way—not God. That's one of God's challenges for us. Each of us, rich and poor, has to follow His commandment to love our neighbors as ourselves. You and your family have been blessed with material wealth. That's a fact. And there's a reason for it—God's reason. He wants you to do something with what you have, and you've got to figure out what."

Vi nodded and sighed.

"You have good examples all around you," Mr. Carpenter continued. "None better than your own mother. She and your father donated all the funds to start this mission, and they brought others into the project. Did you know that Mrs. Mayhew is one of our biggest supporters?"

Vi's expression showed her surprise, and Mr. Carpenter explained, "Mrs. Mayhew is a hard worker, though the people we help here wouldn't know it. She has a talent for convincing wealthy folks to do what's right. First thing she did for us was to convince the hospital to provide doctors for our clinic. Then she and Mr. Mayhew got some church leaders together, and the next thing you know, we've got Bibles for our services and a good piano, too. Right now, she's raising money so we can employ a nurse full time. When you get right down to it, Mrs. Mayhew and her husband aren't much different from Mrs. Duke and her husband. The Mayhews have more material wealth than the Dukes could dream of, but they've all got God in their hearts."

Mr. Carpenter went on, "I can't tell you exactly how you can best help others. Our Heavenly Father sets out different paths for each of us. But you talk with Him from your heart, and He'll show you the way. Now, don't be expecting the answers to come overnight. You've got to experience life to know how to live it. You've got to listen carefully and look inside other people, get to know them deep down, and let them help you understand what they really need."

"But what if I can't help?" Vi said.

"When you came to my door, you were worried about people taking your presence here the wrong way. The truth is, some people will do just that. They might resent you and turn away your help. And along the way, you'll meet some folks who just won't let you get close enough to help. But keep your heart open and don't get discouraged. There are as many ways to do for others as there are people who need help. Giving money is just one way, and not always the best one. You talk to the Lord and let Him guide you. He'll give you more ideas than you ever dreamed of — at least He has always done that for me."

Mr. Carpenter paused and smiled to himself. Then he said, "This mission was His idea. I'd never have thought of staying in the South, but God led me to Dinah. She told me about New Orleans and the need for people of goodwill and faith down here. Together, we talked to God, and He planted the seed of this service in our hearts."

"And do you ever get discouraged?" Vi asked.

He laughed, "About a dozen times every day. But God is always with me, telling me to go on." He rose from his chair, saying, "I get down, and He lifts me up. He never fails me."

Vi stood up quickly. "Oh, I've taken too much of your time," she apologized anxiously.

"Not at all," he said. "You're a thoughtful young lady, Miss Travilla, and I'm complimented that you wanted to

share your thoughts with me. I don't have absolute answers for you, but I can tell by your questions that you are setting out on the right track."

At that moment, Mrs. Duke looked in the open door. "There you are," she said cheerfully to Vi. "Several of the children you read to yesterday have come back, and they're begging me to find you. They want more stories."

"See that, Miss Travilla?" Mr. Carpenter said. "Opportunities to help are always looking for us."

Vi made a quick curtsey and said, "Thank you, Mr. Carpenter. Thank you so very much!" And she hurried away to her new young friends.

~~~~~~

Early in the afternoon, Elsie was able to take both the Carpenters aside to thank them for the visit.

"These two days have meant a great deal to all of us," she said. "But they have been especially meaningful for Vi. Her father's death has been so hard for her, much harder than I realized until recently. Chloe told me that a visit here would help to get Vi out of the doldrums and back to her old self again."

"If I may say so, Mrs. Travilla," Mr. Carpenter said, "I don't believe your daughter will ever be her old self. By that I mean she is growing and seeking out her way in this life. You should be prepared for her to change in ways you cannot predict."

Dinah smiled and said, "Vi has never been predictable. When she was just a little thing and I was caring for her, I was always aware of how deeply she felt things. I truly hope that being here has helped to ease her sadness, for all of you have lightened our days."

651

Violet's Hidden Doubts

"I wish we had much more time," Elsie mused. "But we must leave the city this afternoon. James will conduct the sabbath service at the plantation church, so we have to reach Viamede by tomorrow night."

"My daddy always said that a wise man tries on a hat before he buys it," Mr. Carpenter answered with a knowing smile. "I believe you want to make sure that this hat will fit the congregation at Viamede. I do hope it's a good fit because Mr. Keith's a fine Christian man with an open mind and a loving heart. He'll make a good chaplain for Viamede."

"It will be a big decision for him," Elsie said. "James came South as a visitor. To make a home here was not in his plans, and he will have to give it careful consideration."

Mr. Carpenter laughed—a deep, warm laugh—and said, "Your remark reminds me of something else my daddy used to say to me whenever I was worrying about some problem or other. He'd say that God does not always take us where we want to go, but He always leads us where we need to be. From what I now know of Mr. Keith, I'm sure that he will be led to the right choice."

Big Decisions at Viamede

*What a man desires is
unfailing love....*

PROVERBS 19:22

Big Decisions at Viamede

*T*he travelers arrived back at Viamede the next day, and on Sunday, James conducted the service for everyone on the plantation. That very evening, after meeting with the elders of the congregation, Elsie and her father asked Cousin James to join them in the library. When Elsie offered him the position of chaplain, James accepted without the slightest pause.

"I am delighted!" declared Horace. "The immediacy of your response tells me that you have already given thought to this possibility."

"I feared you might be unwilling to make a permanent move to the South," Elsie said.

"I have given it much thought and prayer," James said seriously. "Believe me, Cousin Elsie, that my answer to you may be quick, but it comes with a great deal of prayer and self-examination. I just hope I can live up to the standards set by Mr. Mason."

"But you accepted so swiftly that I was not able to tell you the terms of your service," Elsie smiled. "Let me call for coffee, and then we shall go over the details."

She walked to the door of the library, then stopped and looked at her little watch before turning back to her cousin. "By the way," she said, "Mr. Embury and several other members of the church are scheduled to arrive here in about an hour. I believe they also have an offer to discuss with you, Cousin James."

"Two congregations in one day," Horace laughed. "I hope you know what you're getting yourself into, my boy."

Violet's Hidden Doubts

By mid-June, the Masons were happily packing for their move to St. Louis, and James, though still the guest of Mr. Embury, was planning to move to Viamede.

Vi's family intended to return to Ion and The Oaks in another month. In the meantime, they settled into the leisurely ways of summer in the Deep South. Lunch was often served under the shade trees in the garden. Hammocks were strung, and the younger members of the family gathered on the lawn in the afternoons — reading, napping, or just lazing. Ice cream, they all joked, had become a necessity, and the twins could often be found on the kitchen steps, taking turns at the hard work of cranking the wooden churn that produced the chilled delicacy.

The sun hung over the flat Delta country well into the early evening, but as it finally dipped behind the treetops, the temperature fell slightly and human energies rose. Fireflies appeared, blinking and darting through the thin mist that rose from the river and inviting the people to shake off their torpor and come out and play.

"I almost hate to call them to bed," Elsie said one evening as she and Molly were sitting on the porch. The twins and Rosemary played in the garden, where candles burned in wrought iron lanterns that lined the garden paths. "They so enjoy running about after the day's heat."

"I remember running like that," Molly said in a strange tone. "I remember the feeling of summer breezes pulling at my hair as I ran and thinking that I could reach the ends of the earth if I just kept going."

Elsie said nothing at first. She had been concerned about Molly lately. After returning from New Orleans, Elsie

noticed that Molly was quieter than usual and distracted almost to absentmindedness at times. That night, Molly had eaten little and said even less at supper. Elsie had assumed the cause was the late tea Molly and Enna had enjoyed with the Emburys at their home, Magnolia Hall, where they had become frequent visitors. Now she wondered.

"Are you feeling well, Molly?" Elsie asked. "This heat can be oppressive, and some days I feel almost feverish from it."

"It is not the heat that oppresses me," Molly replied almost curtly, "nor even the mosquitoes," she added, smacking away one of the pesky creatures that had landed on her bare arm.

"Forgive me, Cousin Elsie," she said a moment later. "Maybe it is the heat that makes me short-tempered tonight." She paused, then exclaimed, "No! That's not true!"

"But what is it, dear Molly?" Elsie asked, for the emotion in her cousin's voice now gave her serious concern.

Molly drew in a deep breath, then let it out in an anguished rush. "Mr. Embury has asked me to marry him," she said, her voice breaking on the word "marry."

Elsie knew instantly not to express her pleasure at this news. She reached out and took Molly's trembling hand. In the pale light from the parlor window, Elsie could see only the outline of Molly's profile, but she instinctively felt the pain the young woman was in.

"What did you tell him?" she asked, keeping her voice low and steady.

"Nothing," Molly answered. "Rather, I told him I would have my answer tomorrow. What a coward I am! I had not the courage to deny his proposal."

"Then you do not love him?"

Violet's Hidden Doubts

"I *do* love him! And that's my tragedy! That is why I must refuse him, Elsie. He needs a real wife and a mother to his children—not a helpless invalid!"

"Does he love you?"

"Yes, I truly believe so."

"Why do you believe so?" Elsie asked.

"Because I know the look of pity. I see it often enough," Molly said with a trace of bitterness in her voice. "Yet I know the look of kindness as well, dear cousin. The kindness of real friends. When I look into Mr. Embury's eyes, I see not pity but kindness and something else that I had not expected. You'd think that I, whose life is devoted to words, could describe the look of love, but I cannot. I can only say that I see it in his eyes."

Elsie squeezed Molly's hand. "Mr. Embury does not strike me as the kind of man who would offer marriage out of sympathy."

"But that's the point, Elsie!" Molly cried. "His proposal is genuine! And what I feel for him is genuine. I *want* to be his wife, but I can't! I just can't! And I must tell him that I can't!"

Oh, Edward, what would you say to her? Elsie thought frantically. And the answer came as clearly as if he were whispering in her ear.

Elsie said with firmness, "You must make a decision, and you cannot make it if you indulge in this self-pity. God has given you a mind that is the envy of us all. You have the power to reason and pray your way through this, if you do not let yourself give way to self-indulgent emotions."

"How can you say—" Molly tried to interrupt, but Elsie would not allow protest.

"It has been a very long time since I heard you call yourself an invalid, and I do not like the sound of it," Elsie

said, amazing herself at the seeming cruelty of her words. Still she went on: "It seems clear that Mr. Embury does not want to marry out of pity. So ask yourself what he loves. A woman — a *woman*, Molly — with a brilliant talent, a generous and forgiving spirit, and true faith in the love of our Heavenly Father. You are not your handicap, but if you choose to regard yourself as less than a complete person, then it may be true that you do not deserve Mr. Embury's love and affection."

"But Elsie," Molly declared, the old strength and determination returning to her voice. "How can I take on the responsibilities for his daughters, when I am confined to this chair? He already has two children who depend on him; he does not need a third."

"Can you love? Can you listen? Can you caress a child's hair and kiss away tears? Can you teach by your example and correct when necessary? Can you raise a child to know God's love and live by His commandments? These are the things that a parent — a mother — does, dear Molly, and all of them can be accomplished from a seated position."

This last comment drew a smile from Molly. "You sound exactly like Cousin Edward," she said.

"Good!" Elsie responded with a loud sigh. "If I sound like him, then I am saying what is right. I believe he would also say that this decision is one of the most important you will make in your life. You must consider your own happiness as well as Mr. Embury's. You have for so long assumed that marriage was impossible for you that, I fear, the idea has become a truth in your mind. But is it really true?

"Think, Molly. Think of the men who came back from the War with missing limbs and broken bodies. Think of dear Charles Howard who lost his arm and Mr. Graham who lost his sight and Mr. Winslow who lost both his legs. Are they any less men for their losses? Do your Aunt Lora and Mrs. Graham and Mrs. Winslow love their husbands any less for their physical disabilities? Do their children suffer from lack of adequate fathers?

"Marriage is a union of body, mind, soul, and spirit, Molly. Frankly, if your only concern is the crippled state of your legs, then, yes, perhaps you should turn down this proposal. Mr. Embury deserves better. But I know you, and you are not one to anticipate only the worst of outcomes or to wallow in self-pity."

Softly, Molly said, "You're right, cousin. I did that once, and now I should know better. I even discussed this very thing with Vi after Cousin Edward's accident."

Gently, Elsie responded, "I would never have said what I just did if I thought you weak and self-absorbed. But we all need reminders at times to trust the better parts of our natures. You have a decision to make, and you must con-sider many factors, of which your handicap is but one. Because I love and respect you, I don't want you to look back on your choice—whatever it may be—with any regret. I want you to talk it over now with the Lord. Take it all to Him. Let Him be your sounding board, and He will help you understand the possibilities."

For a few moments, in the darkness, nothing more was said. Then Elsie heard a familiar noise—the grating of metal and wood against the stone floor of the porch as Molly maneuvered her wheeled chair.

A hand touched Elsie's arm, and Molly said, "I'm going in now. Thank you, Cousin Elsie, for being my friend and speaking honestly. Sleep well tonight, and don't worry about me. I may not be sleeping myself, for I have much to

discuss with my Lord. But thanks to you, my head is free of cobwebs. When Louis comes tomorrow morning, I will be able to speak to him with my heart and my head. Whatever my decision, I do not believe that it will be based on false and prideful assumptions."

Elsie lay her own hand atop Molly's and squeezed. "Then it will be the right decision, dearest Molly."

Molly didn't join the family at breakfast the next morning, but only Elsie guessed the reason. The others assumed simply that Molly was eating with her mother and that they would see their cousin later. In the meantime, they talked excitedly about the day's big event—Cousin James was moving in. And they were not the only ones excited by their cousin's arrival.

At breakfast, Horace received a letter that had come from Wealthy Stanhope, his charmingly eccentric and now quite elderly aunt who lived in Lansdale, Ohio. Miss Stanhope was the half-sister of Horace Dinsmore's mother and also the beloved aunt of James and all the Keith children.

Horace read the letter to the family.

I am so glad to hear that our young James will be ministering there, Aunt Wealthy wrote in her large, spidery hand. _It's high time my dear Dinsmores and Keiths become kissing cousins again. Distance has separated the two halves of my family for too long, though James will now be more distant from us but closer to you. But I am almost a hundred years away from next June, so Louisiana does not seem so far as it once did._

After reading the paragraph, Horace looked up and was not at all surprised by the looks of confusion on his grandchildren's faces.

Violet's Hidden Doubts

Chuckling, Horace said, "Your great-great-aunt is a most remarkable woman with her own distinctive style of expression."

"But what does she mean by 'a hundred years away'?" Herbert asked.

"She means that next June, she will celebrate her one hundredth birthday," Horace explained. "It has been quite some time since we last saw her," he mused, more to himself than the others. "And longer since we last visited Lansdale."

"Might we go there sometime?" Vi asked. "I've never been to Ohio. It would be exciting!"

"Perhaps we might," Horace agreed. "At least it is an idea for Rose, Elsie, and I to discuss. But we have other things to attend to now. Have you children forgotten that your Cousin James is arriving soon? Mr. Embury will be driving him over, and I expect them within the half hour. So finish your breakfast, and then we will form our welcoming committee."

The family was so busy greeting Cousin James that no one, save Elsie, noticed when Mr. Embury slipped away from the happy throng. Not many minutes later, she saw him on the veranda at the side of the house. He was pushing Molly's chair, and Elsie watched as the pair moved to a shady spot near the railing. Mr. Embury sat on a bench and bent toward Molly. With a small prayer for them both, Elsie turned away and went inside.

About an hour later, Elsie sought out Mrs. O'Flaherty and found her in the pantry. Elsie's purpose was to inform the housekeeper that the family would have their midday

meal in the dining room. It would be a larger group than usual, for James would now take a permanent place at their table. Enna, who usually ate separately with her nurse, would be there, and Mr. Embury was to be a guest.

"It's a gathering fit for an announcement, is it not?" Mrs. O'Flaherty said.

Elsie smiled. "Do you read minds?" she asked.

"No, ma'am," Mrs. O'Flaherty said, her blue eyes crinkling at their corners. "Some say we Irish have the gift of second-sight, but that is just blarney. I think we may have a talent for reading hearts, all the same. I have observed Miss Molly and Mr. Embury for some weeks now. And not many minutes ago, I saw them going into the library with Mr. Dinsmore, and the pair of them smiling from ear to ear."

"Ah," Elsie sighed knowingly. She had spoken briefly to the couple, just before their meeting with Horace, so she said, "You have read their hearts correctly, Mrs. O'Flaherty. They are engaged."

"I don't want to go putting the cart before the horse," Mrs. O'Flaherty went on, "but should we begin making plans for a wedding?"

"I believe that would be appropriate," Elsie replied. "An intimate wedding for the families. That is the couple's wish, for Molly dearly wants us here for her nuptials. Do you think we can manage all the preparations within three weeks?"

"We could manage within three days if that were the dear girl's wish," Mrs. O'Flaherty replied confidently.

"No, no. Three weeks will be adequate," Elsie laughed. "We will need that amount of time for Molly's brother to arrange his trip from Philadelphia."

"The young doctor?" Mrs. O'Flaherty asked.

Violet's Hidden Doubts

"Indeed, the young doctor," Elsie agreed. Then she suddenly took the woman's hand and shook it heartily. "The young *doctor*!" she exclaimed. Turning on her heel, Elsie gathered up her skirts and rushed away, calling back over her shoulder, "Thank you very, *very* much, Mrs. O'Flaherty!"

A few days later, a telegraph message arrived from Philadelphia. Dick Percival would reach Viamede in time to give his sister's hand in marriage. Enna and Molly were overjoyed at the prospect of Dick's arrival. He had come to Ion for Edward's funeral the previous October, but that visit with his family had been brief and steeped in sadness.

Mr. Mason and Cousin Jame happily agreed to perform the marriage service, which would take place in Viamede's formal parlor. Missy and Vi would attend Molly as bridesmaids, and Horace would stand as Mr. Embury's best man. The family and their few guests would enjoy a wedding feast in the upstairs ballroom—a room that had not known gaiety since the days when Elsie's grandparents had entertained there nearly a half-century earlier. Mrs. O'Flaherty saw to it that Viamede was polished from top to bottom. But Aunt Mamie, in much better health now, insisted on supervising the kitchen duties and making the wedding cakes herself.

Through all the hurried preparations, Molly was a marvel of patience and concern for others. She was especially solicitous of her mother and of Mr. Embury's daughters. The two little girls were invited to stay at Viamede as often as they liked, and Molly made time each day to be alone with Corinne and Maddie. Thus were the foundations of their relationship laid. As for Enna, the little girls took to her immediately and had soon christened her "Grannie Enna."

17

Growing Toward God

And we pray this in order that you may live a life worthy of the LORD...growing in the knowledge of God....

COLOSSIANS 1:10

One evening early in the week of the wedding, Molly invited Vi to join her in the garden after supper. The other girls each had something important to attend to, so it was just Molly and Vi who adjourned to a pretty little spot beside a small, bubbling fountain near the rear of the house.

"I'm going to miss you, Vi," Molly began, "more than you know."

"That's nice of you to say, but I doubt you'll have time to miss any of us," Vi replied in a teasing tone. "A new husband, new home, two sweet children, plus your writing — goodness, Molly, your days will be full to overflowing."

"That doesn't mean I won't miss you," Molly said. "I wanted us to have some private time, so I asked the others not to join us tonight."

"Oh, that explains — " Vi began.

"All those pressing duties that weighed so on Missy and Isa? Yes, it was my request," Molly continued. "I wanted us to have a chance to talk as we have so often. Do you remember when I first came to live at Ion?"

"Of course I remember. I thought you and Dick the most mature 'young' people I'd ever known. I loved to be around you, and I made a pest of myself, I'm sure."

"Not at all, dear Vi. Everyone in your family was so gracious and kind to us, but did you know that you were my favorite? You would come to my room every morning, rain or shine. You still had your baby curls then, and you would bounce about my room as if you were on springs. No matter how foul my mood, you always managed to chase it away

669

when you visited me. You were the first person, child or adult, since my accident who took no special notice of my crippled legs. You knew that I couldn't walk, and you asked me why."

"I don't remember that," Vi said.

"You asked. I explained. And that was the end of it. You weren't afraid of me, or pitying, or even sympathetic. You simply accepted me. As I began to lose my anger and struggled to think of myself as a true child of God, I looked to your example."

Molly paused for a moment, then quoted from Scripture, " 'And a little child will lead them.' Without knowing it, you led me as I learned to accept myself, limitations and all."

"That was a long time ago," Vi said softly.

"It was, but I have a feeling that you might like to know how you have influenced me."

Darkness was falling and Vi could barely see her cousin's face, but she felt Molly's hand on her wrist.

"You and I have much in common beyond kinship," Molly said. "We are different in ways that can sometimes make us uncomfortable. It's too easy for people like us to doubt ourselves. We may be tempted to think ourselves alone or to blame ourselves for things we cannot control. I'm saying this to you because I have recently been made aware, once again, of this inclination in myself."

"You said something like that before," Vi replied, "on the day of Papa's accident."

"I just wanted you to know that you aren't alone in your feelings. You'll never be alone as long as God's love lives in your heart." Molly sat back in her chair. Then she asked, "How do you feel about growing up?"

Vi's first response was a heavy sigh. She gathered her thoughts and finally said, "Confused. I want to grow up.

There are so many things that I want to do that I cannot now. Yet a part of me wants to remain as I am—to stay always at Ion with Mamma and let her guide me and be there for me. Did you ever feel that way, Molly?"

"Well, my Mamma was not an ideal parent, but yes, at times. Circumstances forced me to grow up faster than I wanted, but I fought against it. If your mother and father had not been there for me, I might still be the selfish and self-pitying child who arrived at Ion. Now, I can look back and understand myself and others so much better. I can see that Mamma always loved Dick and me. She was misguided in her goals and often thoughtless of our feelings, but she never meant to hurt us. When I was a child, everyone seemed so simple to me. There were either masters or slaves, rich or poor, young or old. But as I opened my heart to God, I learned that every life is complicated. I began to value and love other people for their differences. And I also began to see myself as a whole person—although I still have a tendency to focus too much on my handicap," Molly added, thinking of her conversation with Elsie on the night before she accepted Mr. Embury's proposal.

"I'm conscious of your chair, but I don't think of you as handicapped or disabled," Vi said.

"Because you look into my heart, dear Vi," Molly said, "and that is one of your gifts. It is a gift that you should cultivate and train—as you would a flowering vine—so that it serves others and glorifies the Giver of all gifts. What sets you apart, what you call difference, comes from the Lord, but it is up to you to make the most of it."

Vi didn't say anything, but she was grappling with the import of Molly's words.

Violet's Hidden Doubts

"Oh, dear," Molly said after several uncomfortable moments. "I must sound like a terrible old busybody telling you how to live your life."

"No, you don't! Not at all," Vi protested. "I know that I've been concentrating too much on all the sadness of the last year. What you said about little children, the way they see things in simple terms — I've been thinking that way, and it doesn't work. I want to strive to be more like my Papa. He found value in every person. He wasn't afraid of complicated problems and being responsible for himself and others."

"Your father could look back and learn," Molly said. "He could look forward and plan and dream. But he never forgot where he was. Four days from now, I will leave all of you to make my own home and family, but I have wonderful examples to guide me. When I'm unsure of myself, I can turn in my mind to Cousin Edward and his model of wisdom and compassion. I can turn to Cousin Elsie, so steadfast in faith and love. I can think of you, dear Vi, and your open heart and questioning mind. I will have each of you to guide me as I choose my own course and set the example for others. God loves me the way I am. But He wants me to continue learning from others even as I follow my heart's desire."

Vi sighed and said, "Growing up doesn't mean that we stop growing, does it? We don't stop learning?"

Molly said, "From our first to our last breath, Vi, God gives us the power to grow in faith, in hope, and in love. We change as we mature and put childish ways behind us. But think of it, Vi. Every day of our lives — even in hardships and trials — we are growing toward God. That is the real adventure, isn't it? It's the trials that help us to mature along the way."

Growing Toward God

Vi leaned forward and grabbed Molly's hand. "It is a journey," she agreed. "A great and exciting journey! Why have I been afraid to embark on it?"

"Because you're human," Molly replied. "But our Lord has shown us the way. Think about when He walked on the water and His disciples were terrified at seeing Him there. He calmed the wind and made the water smooth. 'Take courage,' he said. 'It is I. Don't be afraid.' He wants us to venture forth with courage, Vi, because He is always there to support us."

The two young women would have talked on well into the night had not Mrs. O'Flaherty come into the garden and politely reminded them of the late hour.

As Vi pushed Molly's chair back toward the house, she said, "I'll miss our talks, Molly. You said earlier that I had influenced you to accept yourself. Well, now you have returned the favor. I will confess something to you. Last month, on the day I turned fifteen, we had that lovely party. It was subdued, of course, but everyone was so happy for me and gave me such nice presents. But when I was alone that night, after my prayers with Mamma, I just cried like a baby until I finally cried myself to sleep. Yet I couldn't have said why I felt sad. Now I wish I could have that birthday over again, so that I could rejoice that I am growing up. I would be able to say, 'I'm fifteen, and I'm growing toward God. I am embarking on the greatest journey of all, and I'm not afraid.'"

"You can't have the birthday back," Molly replied, "but you always have that thought. May I share it with you? I'd like to start each new day with that thought too. Whatever the day may bring, I am growing toward God!"

Violet's Hidden Doubts

Vi considered for a moment. "If we both think it, God will hear us," she said, "and it will be as if we are praying together, won't it? Like we are together no matter how far apart we are."

Dick Percival arrived two days before the wedding, and the reunion with his mother and sister was indescribably sweet. Enna could barely allow him to leave her. But on the morning of the wedding, Elsie took her cousin for a walk in the garden.

"Do you approve of your sister's choice of husband?" she asked.

"I do," the young man said. "Their union confirms the wisdom of God's plan, doesn't it? Who would have thought that our Molly would have found her life partner in the bayous of Louisiana?"

"And what do you think of this part of the South?" Elsie asked.

"After so short an acquaintance, my thoughts are hardly worthwhile. Yet I am very happy to be back in the South. I've missed my homeland."

"But don't you intend to stay in Philadelphia?"

"That was my plan," he replied. "I could build a profitable practice and make a name for myself there. Yet what good is money and prestige if physicians do not take their knowledge to those who most need it?"

Then Dick added, "I've been giving much thought to the true meaning of a life of faith. I often turn to the words of Paul in 2 Corinthians 8: 'But just as you excel in everything — in faith, in speech, in knowledge, in complete earnestness and in

your love for us—see that you also excel in this grace of giving…. For you know the grace of our Lord Jesus Christ, that though he was rich, yet for your sakes he became poor, so that you through his poverty might become rich.' As a man, Jesus ministered to one and all, without distinction. Isn't His life the example I want to follow?"

Elsie laid her hand on his arm. "And how have you answered your own question?"

"In truth, Cousin Elsie, I've decided not to return to practice in Philadelphia. I want to be a country doctor like Dr. Barton and Cousin Art. I won't be rich. I won't be famous. But I am convinced that my happiness lies elsewhere." He laughed. "Now, I must discover where."

Elsie could have made him an offer then and there. But however much it would please her to have Dick at Viamede, she knew that it would be unfair to take advantage of the moment. She did, however, feel justified in planting one very small seed.

"There is someone I want you to meet," she said as they turned toward the house again. "An old and dear friend to Edward and me. Dr. Bayliss has seen to the health of this parish for many years, and he reminds me a good deal of Dr. Barton. He is retiring soon, and we will greatly miss his conscientious service."

"I should like to meet him," Dick said.

"You shall have your chance at the wedding," Elsie said.

They talked of other matters for the rest of their walk, but unknown to Elsie, an idea very much like her own was beginning to take shape in her young cousin's mind.

Violet's Hidden Doubts

The marriage of Miss Molly Percival and Mr. Louis Embury took place late that afternoon. Although the number of guests was small, the occasion was celebrated with enormous cheer. Except for Elsie, none of the Travillas were now expected to wear the black clothes of mourning. So Vi and Missy were attired in charming pastel frocks as they stood next to Molly, who was beautiful in her new white gown and an antique wedding veil lent to her by Mrs. Mason.

Following the ceremony, the groom carried his bride up the sweeping stairs to Viamede's ballroom. In the center of that large room, beneath the exquisite, Italian crystal chandelier purchased by Elsie's grandmother, tables had been drawn together in a U-shaped arrangement, draped in white damask cloths, and set with elegant French china, crystal, and silverware. Cut-glass bowls filled with pink and white camellias decorated the tables, alternating with silver candelabra holding white tapers. All the gallery doors into the ballroom were open to catch the evening breezes, and the candle flames flickered softly.

The two little Embury girls were seated between their father and new stepmother—comfortable cushions on their chairs raising the children up so they might see and be seen by all.

Aunt Mamie had outdone herself, and the wedding supper was superb. The guests were treated to many of the delicacies of the region including oysters and shrimp fresh from the Gulf, as well as spicy rice and vegetable dishes and an array of cool salads. Dessert included an icy orange confection made from the fruits of Viamede's grove, a variety of cakes, and Mamie's famous lace cookies.

Toasts to the bridal couple were made throughout the meal. Horace began with a prayer of thanks to God for the joys of

family. Then James offered a toast to love (which Vi thought sweet but oddly sentimental for James). Dick filled his remarks with gentle humor and expressed his special pleasure at becoming an uncle to Corinne and Maddie. Then Enna stood, and not a few eyes welled with tears as she spoke lovingly of her daughter, her son-in-law, and her new grandchildren. Her words were simple and brief, ending with a prayer of thanks to "our Savior, who must have loved weddings because He chose a wedding for His first miracle."

The party drew to its close at about nine, when Molly, Louis, their children, and Enna left Viamede for the ride to Magnolia Hall. Enna had accepted the offer to live at Magnolia Hall with the Emburys.

Dr. and Mrs. Bayliss departed soon after the Emburys, but not before receiving Dick's promise to join them for lunch the next day. Dr. Bayliss was most anxious to continue a conversation begun over the supper table with the bright young doctor from Philadelphia.

Vi had thought she would be sad to see Molly go, but in fact, her heart was nearly bursting with joy for her cousin. As the Embury carriage drove away into the night, Vi was thinking how proud her papa would be. *Papa always found his greatest pleasure in the happiness of others,* Vi told herself. *Now I understand why. When one of us is blessed, we are all blessed.*

A verse from Psalm 68 came to her mind, and she offered it as her own private toast to the newlyweds: "But may the righteous be glad and rejoice before God; may they be happy and joyful."

CHAPTER

18

Messages of Love

I will give them comfort and joy instead of sorrow.

JEREMIAH 31:13

*T*he family were to leave Viamede on the following Monday, and it was with mixed feelings that they completed their packing.

"Did you accomplish everything you needed to, Mamma?" Missy asked.

It was the afternoon after the wedding, and Missy and Vi were enjoying a rare time alone with their mother in the parlor. Dick had gone to the Bayliss home, and the twins were out on a last horseback ride over the plantation. Isa had taken Rosemary and Danny for a romp in the orange grove, and James insisted on accompanying them.

"I believe so," Elsie replied to Missy's question. "Our business enterprises are in excellent hands. Viamede has a new manager and a new chaplain."

"But we didn't find a doctor," Vi said.

"No, but I have confidence that problem may be resolved without our intervention," Elsie replied. "What's more, we have wonderful news to take home to Aunt Chloe and Joe about Dinah and her family."

Vi smiled, thinking of all that she had experienced at the mission. But then she had another, more immediate thought, and she asked, "What of Mrs. O'Flaherty? Will she have to leave Viamede now that Aunt Mamie is so much better?"

"You like Mrs. O'Flaherty very much, don't you?" Elsie asked in return.

"Oh, we do, Mamma. We all do," Vi said enthusiastically. "She's so interesting. She has told us so many things about Ireland and about Louisiana, too." A little frown came to

Vi's face as she added, "I still wish I knew more about her, though."

"Whatever Mrs. O'Flaherty's story, it is hers alone to tell," Elsie said a little firmly. "But you will be glad to know that she will stay on here for as long as she wants. Aunt Mamie will not be capable of returning to her full duties, so Mrs. O'Flaherty has agreed to remain as housekeeper while Mamie manages the kitchen and assists Cousin James to settle in."

The girls were delighted by this news. But with a sigh, Missy said, "It will be strange to return to Ion without Molly and Aunt Enna. Am I very selfish to feel sad at losing them to Mr. Embury?"

"Not at all, dearest," Elsie said. "I would wonder if you did not suffer to some extent from mixed emotions."

"We have had our share of separations this year," Vi said in a wistful tone, and her mother and sister knew that Vi was thinking of her father. For several moments, none of them spoke.

Then Elsie said, perhaps a little too brightly, "Tell me about the presents you received from Molly. She purchased something for each of you girls, but she insisted that her gifts be a secret even from me."

"We hadn't any idea that she had planned such a surprise," Missy said. "Each gift was hidden in a special place for us to find. Mine was in my stationery box." She put her hand to her throat and drew from beneath her blouse a sterling silver pendant on a delicate chain.

"See," she said, holding out the necklace. "It's a locket of the old style. It opens, and Molly left a note telling me to have Lester paint a miniature of himself to fill the frame inside. She was very specific. Lester must paint his image for me — no photograph — so that I might feel him close whenever I wear it."

Missy leaned forward so that her mother could examine the jewelry.

"What a loving gift," Elsie said, thinking of the small gold locket that she wore always. It contained a miniature of her father and the only image she had of her long-dead mother.

Vi was saying, "Molly gave Isa a book of poems by Mrs. Elizabeth Barrett Browning — *Sonnets from the Portuguese*. She'd marked one with a ribbon — 'How do I love thee? Let me count the ways' — and Isa read it out loud to us and got all dreamy. Have you noticed that Isa gets that dreamy look a lot these days? I can't think what's the matter with her."

Elsie smiled but said only, "And what did Molly leave for you, Vi?"

Vi tried to look mysterious but could not hide her dimpled smile as she said, "It's neither silver nor gold. I found it in my bedside table, in the drawer where I keep my Bible."

"A book?" Elsie asked.

"'A book yet to be written.' That's what Molly's note said," Vi replied. "It's a journal, Mamma, just like hers, but the pages are blank, of course. But not completely blank, for Molly wrote out some verses on the very first page. 'You yourselves are our letter, written on our hearts, known and read by everybody.'"

Vi hesitated, and Elsie completed the passage from Second Corinthians, saying, "You show that you are a letter from Christ, the result of our ministry, written not with ink but with the Spirit of the living God, not on tablets of stone but on tablets of human hearts.' That is a wonderful gift, pet. Do you know how Molly uses her journals?"

"She writes down things that happen and ideas for her stories," Vi said.

"That's one use," Elsie agreed. "But Molly has often said to me that her journal is also her ongoing letter to the Lord. She writes her thoughts and prayers there, and she says that writing things down can bring clarity to confusion and help her sort through her ideas. Did you not notice how frequently she retired to her room and her journal in the weeks before her engagement?"

"I did, Mamma, but I never thought of her writing to God," Vi said. She giggled and added, "Then I never thought of her marrying Mr. Embury either."

"There are many means by which we communicate with the Lord," Elsie continued. "So long as we open our hearts freely, it matters not how we speak to Him. He always hears us."

Vi's expression became serious. "I'd like to keep a journal, but I don't know where to start," she said. "I thought about describing Molly's wedding."

"That's a very good beginning," Missy said. "Write about it while the details are fresh in your memory."

"It's for you to decide, Vi dear," Elsie said, "what to write and if you wish to write at all. Molly would not want you to regard her gift as a duty. She wanted to share with each of us something that has meaning for her. I am greatly impressed by her choices, for each gift was clearly selected with personal consideration. Even in the whirlwind of her wedding preparations, Molly was thinking of us."

Vi caught her mother's use of the word "us," and she asked, "Did Molly give you a present too, Mamma?"

"She did, and it is one I shall always cherish," Elsie replied in a soft tone. "I found it tucked in my Bible. It is a

letter that your papa wrote to Molly when she and Dick first came to live at Ion nearly a decade ago. Your father wrote to ask if she would allow him to act in the role of father to her. Molly must have read it often, for its pages are worn by being unfolded and folded many times. I would like you both to hear your Papa's letter, for she asks me to share it with the family."

"Do you have it with you, Mamma?" Vi asked.

"No, pet. Molly put it in my Bible, and I think that is where it belongs. But if you like, we can go up to my room now and read it."

———

Open trunks and travel cases crowded Elsie's lovely bedroom, but after taking her Bible from the dressing table, she moved aside some clothing that lay across her favorite chair and took her seat. Missy and Vi settled comfortably on the bed as Elsie opened the Bible and carefully withdrew a yellowed envelope. Taking out the pages, she said, "It is dated in the fall of 1870," and she began to read Edward's letter.

Dear Molly,

When I first decided to write, it was because I was full of sound advice and sage words. But I have thought better. If you wish to seek my counsel on any matter, I am here for you. But you are a wise young woman, and both Elsie and I credit you with a great deal more common sense than either of us possessed at your age. I could not feel more proud of you than if you were my very own child.

Violet's Hidden Doubts

You had little chance to know your own father. May I tell you something about him? Your brother's namesake was, as a boy, what is often called "a handful" with a penchant for mischief. You have, I know, heard many stories of his youthful escapades. You have also been told, unfairly I believe, of his misdeeds. But I want to tell you about what was admirable.

Your father made mistakes but was unerringly honest in owning up to them. He was extremely intelligent and, you may be surprised to learn, a great reader, for his curiosity was unquenchable. He was profligate with money, yet he was equally generous, and his financial losses were often the result of loans to others in need. His contemporaries still speak of your father as the most loyal of friends. He was, beyond question, a man of true courage. He fought bravely in the Civil War and was unafraid to face death when it came. Most important, your father loved Enna and you and young Dick with his whole heart. Of that truth, you must never doubt.

I, like you, lost my father before I was old enough to really know him. I understand what it is like to wonder about the kind of person he was. Dear Molly, I see in you and in your brother all that was good in your father—the brave and independent spirit, the inquisitive mind and goodhearted generosity, the honesty and loyalty. He did not store up wealth for you, but from him you inherited other gifts more precious than gold.

I would never attempt to take his place, but I wish to offer you the love of a fatherly friend—as your Papa would surely have done if our roles were reversed. I have a willing ear for listening and broad shoulders to

bear weighty problems. I am tall enough so that, on occasion, I can peer above the trees to see the wide forest. Though some may dispute it, my sense of humor is rather acute, and I sense that you are a girl with considerable laughter in her heart. I am at times insightful and have a well-developed sense of justice and fairness (quite useful when negotiating spats between siblings). These qualifications will, I hope, recommend me to your service.

You would pay me a great compliment if you accept my offer. In part, I may help make up for the injustice done to you by the slanders on your father's memory. But more important is the opportunity you can give me to love and support you as your own father would have. But if surrogate parenthood is too lofty a position to seek, I will love and support you nonetheless. Like it or not, Miss Molly Percival, I intend always to be your most loyal friend and your devoted,

Cousin Edward

Elsie placed the letter on the table beside her and took up several more sheets of paper—these as white and fresh as the first letter was timeworn. "This is the rest of Molly's gift to me," Elsie said to her daughters, and she began to read aloud again.

Dearest Cousin Elsie,

I was just fourteen and recently moved to Ion when Cousin Edward wrote to me. I was still in a state of turmoil then—plagued by doubts and fears, and worst of all, self-hatred, for I had not yet learned to value myself as a child of God. I was even frightened by your

Violet's Hidden Doubts

family's Christian faith, for your lives seemed so full and mine so empty and hopeless.

I don't know what impelled Cousin Edward to write as he did, but his letter came like a spring thaw for my frozen heart. Somehow he understood that part of my suffering could be traced to my fears that I was like my father, who had always been portrayed to me as willful, self-indulgent, and irresponsible. As I later told Cousin Edward—after I accepted his offer of friendly fatherhood—one of my earliest memories is of the day we learned that my father was dead. I was very young, yet I remember Grandmother Dinsmore saying over and over, "It's for the best. He was a bad lot, a bad lot." I remember thinking that if my Papa was so bad, then I must be, too.

Cousin Edward was the first person who ever told me that my own father, for all his faults, was not a bad person. Somehow Cousin Edward knew that I needed to learn about my father if I was to begin to free myself from my terrible self-doubt. By writing forthrightly of my father and then offering his own love and support, he showed me a kind of respect that I had never experienced. Eventually, I came to regard his letter as a reminder of what it means to care for a person so much—even a person as difficult as I was then—that you are willing to look into the dark part of her and bring in light.

You will see by its tattered condition how often I have returned to Cousin Edward's letter. Now I want you to have it. When you spoke to me on the night before I accepted Louis's proposal, it was with the same uncanny understanding that Cousin Edward showed when he wrote his letter. Please share this gift with my beloved

cousins if you like, for I carry you all in my heart as I go
forward on this new path God has opened to me.

I love you,
Molly

Elsie looked up and smiled at Vi. "Your cousin added a
postscript for you, pet. She writes, 'I think Vi will especially
understand her father's letter to me. He gave me a piece of
my past so that I might grow toward my future.' Do you
take her meaning, dear?"

"Yes, Mamma," Vi said. "It is something that Molly and
I talked about."

"But, Mamma, what was it you said to Molly?" Missy
asked.

"Oh, I simply reminded her of some plain truths," Elsie
replied vaguely. "I don't remember my exact words. Yet I
can tell you that I felt as if your father were standing at my
shoulder the whole time."

Vi had picked up her father's letter and was reading it to
herself. She was about to turn to the second page when she
looked up at her mother and said, "May I borrow this for the
rest of the afternoon, Mamma? I shall be very careful with it."

"Of course, darling," Elsie replied, "but may I inquire
what you plan to do?"

Vi smiled softly, her dimple showing. "I have decided to
start my journal by copying this letter into it," she said.

"That's a nice idea," Missy said, "but wouldn't you rather
start with your own words?"

Vi looked at her sister, then her mother, and Elsie saw in
her daughter's expressive face and sparkling eyes a look so
like Edward's that she lost her breath for an instant.

"These *are* my words, in a way," Vi answered. "Molly kept
Papa's letter all these years as a reminder of him, and now she

has given it to us. If I write it out in my journal, I will have it always. I can read Papa's letter and remember what it means to love someone so much that you are willing to look into the darkness and bring in light. Isn't that what Molly said, Mamma?"

"It is, my darling," Elsie said.

"And that will remind me to do what is *really* right for others," Vi continued. "And to think —*really* think —about what people need. That's what Mr. Carpenter advised me to do. That's what Papa did, and what you do for all of us, Mamma. That's what Jesus did when He went out to teach and to heal. That's what God wants all of us to do for one another. But it's hard for me sometimes because I think too much about what *I* want and how *I* feel. Isn't it amazing that Papa understood what was hurting Molly when no one else did? And when you read his letter, Mamma, it was as if he were talking to us. So whenever I read it again, I will hear his voice as if he were still teaching me, and his words will remind me how important it is to be more understanding of others."

Vi, her face flushing with the excitement of her new insight, asked, "May I go copy this now, Mamma, before the others return? Then you can share it with them, too."

"Yes, dear, go to your work," Elsie said. And Vi hurried away, holding her father's letter before her as if it were a king's jeweled crown.

Vi was gone, but both Elsie and Missy continued to gaze at the open door as if they had just seen some startling sight that lingered on in their vision.

"My little sister is growing up," Missy said at last in a near-whisper. "I had not noticed until just now how much she has changed. She is very like Papa, isn't she?"

"Very like," Elsie replied. "Our fairy child is growing up, and I sense that she is beginning to look forward to the prospect."

"I wonder what she will do with her life," Missy said. "I have the feeling that whatever her path, it will not be predictable."

"Mr. Carpenter said that very thing to me when we were in New Orleans," Elsie replied in some surprise. "And your father often remarked that all our children must leave the nest, but Vi may have to fly farther for her happiness."

Missy thought for a moment then said, "She has Papa's spirit as well as his looks."

Elsie looked away from the door and toward her eldest child. Smiling, she said, "And you, my dear Missy, have more than your share of his wisdom."

Missy laughed happily. "I hope I have an equal portion of yours, Mamma," she said, "for then I shall be very wise indeed. Now, how may I help you?"

There were a few things left to be done, and as Missy and Elsie packed, they talked about their plans for the next day, which included church service and a final visit to the little cemetery where Elsie's mother and grandparents lay. But their conversation was interrupted when Vi danced into the room.

"Are you finished with your copying so soon?" Elsie said.

"Almost," Vi replied. "But I just had to ask you something, Mamma. What would you think if I wore my hair up? After all, I am fifteen now and as tall as you. It's time I looked my age, don't you think?"

"It is something to consider," Elsie replied, turning her head to hide her smile.

"Something to consider," Vi said gravely. She walked to her mother's mirror and looked at her reflection. She

Violet's Hidden Doubts

twisted her shoulder-length tresses into a neat chignon, a few dark wisps trailing against her long, graceful neck. She moved her head slowly from one side to the other. She was finally seeing something that she never had before — in her brown eyes, her well-shaped mouth, her straight nose and firm chin, even in the dark sleekness of her hair. She was seeing her Papa's legacy to her, visible now in her appearance, but so much more valuable for what he had left in her heart.

This business of growing up is really not so hard, she thought. *I can almost hear Papa laughing and telling me to get on with it before I am too old to leave the nest. Then he would hug my shoulder and tell me not to be afraid of what the future may bring, for my best Friend in Heaven and on earth is with my every step and will catch me if I stumble. Whatever the day may bring, I am growing toward God.*

After a few more moments of contemplation, she said in an unnaturally deep voice, "Yes, I definitely think a change of style would do me good. I will wear my hair up and perhaps try a corset on occasion."

At that, Missy burst into laughter. "You want to wear a corset?" she exclaimed. "You are a silly goose, Violet Travilla!"

Vi turned away from the mirror — her expression set like stone but her eyes sparkling with merriment. "A goose today," she said. "But who knows, dear sister, what I may become tomorrow?"

An unexpected invitation leads Vi to distant places.

What awaits her? How far must she go to help a loved one?

Violet's story continues in:

VIOLET'S AMAZING SUMMER

Book Two
of the
*A Life of Faith:
Violet Travilla* Series

A Life of Faith: Violet Travilla Series

Laylie's Daring Quest

Kersten Hamilton

Mission City Press

Franklin, Tennessee

DEDICATION

This book is dedicated to the children
of African-American saints
who laid down their lives
to bring true freedom
to anyone, black or white,
who would listen.

SETTING

$\mathscr{O}$ur story begins on an early Spring day in the mid-1830s at Meadshead, a plantation outside of Charleston, South Carolina, where Laylie Colbert lives.

CHARACTERS

∾ AT THE MEADSHEAD PLANTATION ∾

Laylie Colbert—age 7 (when the story begins), a slave.

Luke Colbert—age 13 (when the story begins), a slave.

JoMa—an elderly slave woman who cares for children whose parents have died or been sold away. Besides Laylie and Luke, the following children live in her cabin:

> **Hettie**—age 16
> **Lucindy**—age 14
> **Wim**—age 13
> **Exter**—age 4
> **Max**—age 3
> **Cicero**—age 3

Helen—a slave woman and mother of:

> **Melia**—age 6
> **George Henry**—age 10 months

Isaac—age 20, a Christian slave.

Terria — a slave who works in the kitchen.

Rozco — a slave who drives the Breandans' coach.

Andros Walsh — an elderly runaway slave who lives in the swamp.

Ruby and **Priss** — slave girls and sisters, the blacksmith's daughters.

Ronald Borse — the overseer.

Wash Hode — Borse's assistant.

Robson — a slave, Borse's driver.

Master Phil — Philip Breandan, the owner of Meadshead plantation, with his wife, **"Old Miss"** and their daughter, **"Missy Jen"** (aka **"Young Miss"**).

∽ AT ROSELANDS PLANTATION ∽

Ajax — a slave who drives the Dinsmores' coach.

Olivia — a slave who works in the laundry.

Phoebe — a slave who runs the kitchen.

Jonati — the Dinsmore children's nursemaid.

"Little John" — aka **Boston**, age 9. A slave girl and leader of the "Merry Men," a band of children including:

> **"Friar Tuck"** — age 9, a slave boy.
>
> **"Will Scarlet"** — age 8, a slave boy.
>
> **"Alan-a-Dale"** — age 8, a slave boy.
>
> **"Marion"** — age 5, Alan-a-Dale's little sister.

Mrs. Brown — the housekeeper.

Miss Worth — the governess and schoolmistress.

Master Horace — Horace Dinsmore, the owner of Roselands Plantation, and his wife **Missy Isabel**, daughter of Phil Breandan. They have 6 children, including **Arthur**, age 6, and **Lora**, age 10.

Miss Millie — Millie Keith, age 16, Horace Dinsmore's niece from Pleasant Plains, Indiana.

Charles Landreth — a young man with a romantic interest in Millie.

Mrs. Eugenia Travilla — owner of Ion Plantation.

Rachel — an older Christian slave from Ion, a neighboring plantation.

∽ ALSO APPEARING ∽

Sarah — a slave and preacher.

Cyrus Tatum — a patent medicine salesman.

Petunia Tatum — Cyrus's wife.

Mr. Blessed Bliss and his wife, **"Dearest" Bliss** — abolitionists and owners of a funeral parlor who, along with Dearest's cousin **Miz Opal** and family friend **Colonel Peabody**, help slaves escape to freedom.

Tempie Colbert — Aunt to Luke and Laylie.

CHAPTER

1

Orphans and Extras

The entire law is summed up in a single command: "Love your neighbor as yourself."

GALATIANS 5:14

Orphans and Extras

*H*ooo-hooo!

The hoot owl's call pulled Laylie awake. The wooden shutters were open, letting starlight and mosquitos into the slave cabin. The insects swarmed so thick that their hum almost drowned out JoMa's snores. Laylie sat up, looking across the tangle of sleeping children. *Orphans and extras. That's what JoMa calls them, with their parents all dead or sold away.* Laylie squinted at the darkness of the corner where her brother slept. She couldn't make him out in the shadows.

"Luke?" she whispered. There was no answer.

Laylie crawled over sleeping bodies that grumbled or swatted at her if she put a hand or knee in the wrong place.

"Luke!" She felt around in the darkness, but the shadows were empty. *Luke wouldn't leave without me. He promised he wouldn't!*

Hoo-hooo!

Haints and haunts of every kind walk in the night. That's what JoMa says. Luke goes walking too, when he wants to think.

Laylie made her way back across the sleepers and slipped past the blanket that served as a door. There were fewer mosquitos outside. Black pools of night clouds, pushed by a high wind, scudded across the stars, but the air near the ground was still. She wiggled her bare toes in the dust and peered through the trees toward Borse's house, straining for the sour smell of sweat and tobacco juice that clung on the overseer, but the night was dark and sweet.

The cabin for "orphans and extras" was the last in the row, closest to the swamp and right on the edge of the burying ground. Laylie walked toward the inky shape of the live oak tree that blotted out the stars on the eastern horizon. She slowed down when she stubbed her toe against a gravestone. *Ouch! Luke always said not to jump and skip over dead people's bones,* Laylie reminded herself. *Said it was disrespectful.*

She heard a stirring of feathers right above her.

Hoo-hooo!

"Hoo your ownself, hooty-owl!" she said. "That's my tree you're sittin' in."

"Girl, what are you doing out here?" Luke's voice was a whisper in the darkness.

"Looking for you." Laylie walked through the grave-yard to where Luke sat under the blazing stars. She sat down as close to him as she could without crawling into his lap. Luke's thirteen-year-old frame might have been nothing but ropes and bones, but it was warm. Wisps of mist were rising out of the grass over the graves, reaching toward the icy silver of the stars.

"Which one is it?" Laylie asked, looking up at the sky. "Which one is the freedom star?"

Luke pointed. "That one."

"How do you know?"

"See the drinking gourd?" Luke traced it with his finger. "It points at it. All the others change—they spin 'round with the seasons. But not that one. The North Star. That one stays put. It's gonna shine forever."

Suddenly the bright star winked out. "It didn't stay put," Laylie said.

"It did," Luke insisted. "It's hid behind a cloud is all. When that cloud moves on, it will be there shining."

"What's so good about being free?" Laylie asked after a long pause. "I like it here."

"Hush," Luke said. "I'm thinking."

"What about?"

"Promises and preacher men."

Laylie sat up. "JoMa says that new slave Isaac is a preacher man. They say he's as strong as a six-mule team!"

Luke didn't say anything more, so Laylie stretched out her legs and felt the rough stone that marked the head of her mother's grave.

"Tell me about Aunt Tempie and the man-stealers. Tell me about the rendezvous," said Laylie.

"You know that story."

"You always tell it when you've been staring at the stars." Laylie snuggled against her brother's comforting warmth.

Luke sighed.

"Mamma and Aunt Tempie was free Africans born and raised in New Orleans," he said. "One day they bought passage on a ship to New York City, where they were gonna work as nurses."

"But the captain was a man-stealer!" Laylie said. "He took their freedom papers."

"They made a plan." Luke's voice was hardly a whisper. "They were gonna fight, gonna run no matter how long it took. If they got separated, they would rendezvous in New York City, where they were headed in the first place."

"And one day," Laylie cut in, "Tempie jumped and swam. She got away . . . but Mamma didn't."

"See?" Luke said. "You don't need me to tell you that story."

"Tell me about Mamma."

"No."

"I 'member her."

"Do not," Luke said. "It's been four years, and you was just toddlin' when she passed."

Laylie's Daring Quest

"Mamma used to carry me in a sling," Laylie said. "And she sung songs to me. . . . Why don't you sing, Luke?"

A light flickered to life in the window of the overseer's cabin. The door opened, and Borse stepped out into the square of light. A stout bulldog followed him onto the porch.

"Bullseye!" Luke spat.

The dog's tattered ears and blunt face were silhouetted against the light as he sniffed the air. Laylie leaned against Luke and held her breath, but Bullseye only lifted his leg to mark the hydrangea bush at the corner of the porch. Borse stretched, raised a shotgun over his head, and fired a shot to call the slaves to wake and work before the sun was up. He turned around, stopped to scratch his armpit, and then went back inside.

"Mind JoMa," Luke said, standing up. Then he was off, loping away to check his snares in the ditches and brambles before work.

Laylie went over to the tree and jumped to reach the first branch, startling the owl. It lifted from its perch and floated off toward the swamp. Laylie shinnied up to the branch, then worked her way on up into the top of the tree. This was her own place, on top of the world. She settled down to watch the dawn. The light grew until she could see JoMa's cabin and all the cabins beyond it, all the way up to the Big House where Master Phil, Old Miss, and Missy Jen were sleeping. The other way, she could see the wall of green that marked the edge of the swamp, and far away over the field she saw Luke stopping to check a snare.

All he talks about anymore is making a strike for freedom. Every time someone tells a story about a run, Luke sits quiet, listening. "Soon as your legs are long enough, Laylie girl." That's what he says.

706

"Soon as they're long enough, we're goin'." He never even asks if I want to go. Laylie thought of the limbs and bodies she had crawled over in the night. *When will Exter's legs be long enough? Or Max's, or Cicero's? They're just babies. Wim, Hettie, and Lucindy are big and strong, already working in the fields like Luke, but JoMa's too old to make a run, and Melia . . . Melia wouldn't want to leave her mamma.*

"Well, I don't wanna go," Laylie said to the dawn breeze. "So I ain't going. That's all." The spring green leaves around her whispered their agreement. Laylie waited until people were up and moving before she scrambled back down the tree and skipped home.

By the time Laylie came into the cabin yard, Hettie was filling the kettle for JoMa, who was bent over the cooking fire, blowing it to life. Wim was teasing Lucindy. Exter had taken off his shirt and was running bare-bottom-naked, swinging it around his head as he chased Cicero and Max.

"Where you been?" Hettie asked Laylie, setting the kettle down. "You should tell somebody when you go off."

"You ain't my mamma," Laylie said. *Hettie's almost old enough to get married, so she thinks she has the right to boss others,* thought Laylie.

Hettie's lips were pursed. "Luke is missing. I expects whatever you was up to, he was too. Girl, look at your hair! It's full of sticks and straw!" She grabbed Laylie by a long, dark braid and pulled her closer. "If I had hair like that, I would keep it neat and pretty." She untwisted Laylie's braids and ran her fingers through the dark hair, combing out the tangles.

"Ouch!" Laylie said, trying to pull away, but Hettie held on tight. She wove the thick braids again and tied them.

"Here," she said, taking the yellow scarf off her own head and tying it on Laylie's. "This'll keep the sticks out, and it won't pull so much."

"Hettie," Lucindy said. "The sun's comin' up."

Hettie dashed inside and grabbed the blue head rag she'd gotten for Christmas last year. She tied it on her head as she and Lucindy walked toward the fields with Wim.

Everyone ten years old and up was moving that way. Mothers with tiny babies stopped by JoMa's cabin on their way, leaving the babies, each wrapped in a bright cotton sling. Laylie kissed each baby as she hung it, still snug in its sling, from the low branch of the yard tree. The swinging babies looked like cocoons with brown little faces, just ready to sprout wings.

"At some places," JoMa muttered, "mammas look after their own chillens. I've heard it. But not at this place. No, they brings them to JoMa, just like she don't have enough work to do . . . " As she grumbled JoMa raked six small cakes of cornmeal wrapped in corn husks out of the ashes from the previous evening's fire, one for each child big enough to walk.

"I like the babies, JoMa," Laylie said.

"I'm in no mood for back talk," JoMa said as she swatted a little bare behind as it ran past. "You put your shirt on!"

Exter ran back inside howling. Cicero and Max ran after him, howling just as loudly for no reason at all.

"Laylie!" Laylie turned to see her friend Amelia, who carried her baby brother George Henry in a cloth sling over her shoulder. He was so heavy that Amelia leaned to one side like a tree about to topple, but her mamma, Helen, was walking close by in case she did.

"You're late, Helen," JoMa said.

" 'Cause my babies are so beautiful I hate to leave them!" Helen laughed. "I'm hired out next door for laundry day, so's I have time. Don't let George Henry play with no crawlies, hear me, Amelia? I don't want him stung."

"Yes, Mamma." Melia's dimples flashed.

"Look, Laylie!" said Melia, holding up a cornhusk doll. "Mamma made her!"

Helen turned to Laylie. "Take care of Melia for me now."

"I always takes care of Melia," Laylie said, " 'cause I'm older."

"I know," Helen dimpled. "That's why I brung you —" she pulled a second cornhusk doll out of her pocket, " —this."

The doll had a yellow dress and a white bonnet and apron. The tea-dyed face was the same lovely brown as Melia's. Laylie took the little doll in her hand.

"It's the beautifulest thing I ever seen!" She wrapped her arms around Helen and squeezed.

"Say thank you, girl," JoMa said. "Didn't I teach you manners?"

"I couldn't stand bein' thanked no better," Helen said, prying herself free. "I'm going now. You girls stay close to JoMa today." Her voice grew serious. "Old Borse was moanin' and cryin' all night. We could hear him clear over to our place."

"Witches calling his name," JoMa said. She made a sign to ward off evil. "Want to drag him to Hell, but they's held back by Satan hisself, I expects, who don't want to look at him. They was walkin' last night." She spat in the dust, then squashed the spittle with her big foot. "I felt 'em pass us by."

"More likely the Zombie Man," Helen said, "come up outta the swamp."

Laylie's Daring Quest

Laylie shivered, wondering if witches or the Zombie Man had been watching her and Luke, listening to their talk.

Helen pointed her finger. "You girls better stay away from that swamp!"

"Yes, Mamma." Melia slipped her hand into Laylie's, and held her face up for her mother's kiss. Helen gave her one, and she kissed George Henry too, then started for the road.

The boys had stopped running wild and were waiting for their corncakes. Laylie got hers last, as she was the oldest. It was only two bites, but Laylie knew that JoMa made them from her own small ration of cornmeal. Other children on the place had no breakfast at all.

"Laylie," Melia whispered, so JoMa wouldn't hear, "would you moan if a witch called your name?"

A glossy black raven lit on the roof of the shack and eyed the babies hanging in the tree.

"Nope," Laylie lied. She felt around with her toes for a smooth pebble, never taking her eyes off the raven.

"JoMa says if they call your name, you hafta go. If you don't, they comes and drags you away, kicking and screaming!" said Melia.

"They didn't drag Borse," Laylie pointed out. She transferred the pebble from her toes to her hand in one smooth move and threw it at the raven. The stone struck the roof beside the bird with a *whack*! The raven exploded into outraged flight, leaving one glossy feather to flutter to the ground.

"Ain't you afraid of the Zombie Man? Mamma says he lives in the swamp with the snakes and gators," said Melia.

The raven was nearly knocked from the sky by a flock of grackles flying low and fast.

"Didn't I say it?" JoMa said, shading her eyes and looking after the birds.

"What's wrong, JoMa?" Melia asked.

"Something sent them birds up," JoMa said, shaking her head. "Laylie, bring my chair."

Laylie ducked into the cabin. Against one wall were JoMa's cot and her chair, which was actually a length of log, sawed flat on both ends. There was a shelf beside the fire pit, two cups, and a tin of rendered lard for use on cuts and burns. A soft fur cover made from the skins of rabbits Luke had caught in his snares lay on JoMa's bed.

Laylie carried the chair out of the cabin and set it by the door. JoMa had taken one of the babies down, and she sat rocking it, watching the little boys play.

"Come on," Laylie whispered, picking George Henry up. Melia followed her around the cabin and behind a woodpile where the boys couldn't see them. Laylie searched in the pile for old shingles, and when they had enough, the girls made a three-walled house for their dolls with a stick and pebble chimney. George Henry pulled it down three times until Laylie found him a shingle of his own to play with.

Laylie and Melia were just putting their dolls down to sleep when George Henry made a happy humming noise.

"George Henry!" Melia said. "What's that you got in your mouth?"

George Henry's eyes twinkled and his dimples winked. His jaws were clamped shut, but some kind of leg hung out of his mouth, waving like the arm of a drowning man. Laylie grabbed it, but only the leg came out, leaving the rest inside.

Laylie's Daring Quest

"Mmmmm." Melia pretended to take a bite of a stick. "Mmmmm-mmmm!" She offered the other end to the baby.

George Henry crowed his delight at the new game, and Laylie had her fingers in his open mouth in a flash. There was nothing there.

"He swallowed it down," she said.

"What if it stings him on the inside?" said Melia, almost in tears.

"Listen to his belly." Laylie held the baby up while Melia pressed her ear to his tummy. "Is it buzzing?"

"I don't hear nothin'," Melia said.

"Then he chewed it good enough. We best wash him out with water anyways," Laylie said, "so's it don't get stuck." She took the giggling baby, and they went back around the cabin, where she dipped a cup of water for him and held it while he drank.

" 'Bout time you two showed up!" JoMa said, pulling the pot of boiled cornmeal she'd cooked for the field hands off the fire. "They ain't come in from the fields for food yet, and every one of these babies is crying for their mamma's breast. You girls go up to the kitchen and get me some milk. I'll watch over George Henry for you." JoMa's eyes flashed to the pot of cornmeal, where a boy stood over it. "Exter! Get your finger outta that pot! That's for the field hands, and you knows it!"

She shooed him away and turned right back to Laylie and Amelia. "Tell Terria that Polly Ann ain't brought scraps for my chillen, and it's way past time. Well? What are you waitin' for?"

Melia took one last look at her brother before Laylie dragged her away. They held hands as they ran up the road past the rows of rough slave cabins, over a field, and into another small slave town, almost at the back steps of the Big House. The cabins of the house slaves and skilled laborers — woodworkers, masons, and cooks — were well built and caulked to keep the wind out. They had real stone chimneys, and some even had curtains in the windows.

Laylie and Melia didn't slow down until they reached the yard of the Big House. A black girl a few years older than Laylie was feeding chickens, tossing handfuls of cracked corn from a pan.

"Hey, Polly Ann," Melia said shyly.

Polly Ann wore a blue dress with a white apron on her lanky frame, hand-me-down brogans on her feet, and a persimmon pucker on her face. Her eyes traveled from Laylie's bare feet and legs to the long-tailed white cotton shirt that was the only clothing allowed children of field slaves.

"Y'all ain't allowed up here," Polly Ann said, sniffing like she smelled something rotten.

"JoMa sent us," Laylie said, wrinkling up her nose like she smelled something rotten too.

Polly Ann aimed her next fistful of cracked corn at the girls. It stung where it hit bare skin, and the chickens scrambled toward them, pecking at the bits that fell around their bare toes. Melia shrieked and tried to lift both feet at the same time.

"Come on," Laylie said, pulling Melia out of the yard. As soon as they were out of Polly Ann's sight, they dodged around the smokehouse and ran up to the back kitchen window. It was too high for Laylie to see in, but she could smell delicious things cooking.

"Bend over, Melia," Laylie said. "I'll climb on your back."

Melia bent over and put her hands on her knees, and Laylie scrambled up, using the wall for balance.

Laylie's Daring Quest

Inside, Terria was rolling out a piecrust. Three pies were already set on the sideboard, ready to bake. Rozco, the Breandans' coachman, was sitting in the corner peeling apples. Terria started to wipe sweat from her brow with her apron, but stopped when she saw Laylie.

"What are you doing in that window?"

"JoMa needs milk for the babies," Laylie said, reaching through the open window for a piece of piecrust. The rolling pin slammed down an inch from her fingers, and she jerked her hand back.

"Well, she can't have milk today," Terria said. "Old Miss is having company, and they want pudding."

"Just a cup?" asked Laylie. Roz winked and tossed her an apple. She stretched to catch it, but it was too high.

"Not a spoonful!" Terria said, as Laylie toppled off Melia's back.

Laylie snatched up the apple and put it in her pocket. "Bend over again, Melia."

"Ouch!" Melia said, as Laylie scrambled back up. "Why cain't I be the one to look in?"

"You're too short, that's why," Laylie said. "Now hold still."

"If there ain't enough for everybody and their uncle—" Terria was waving the rolling pin wildly, "—who do you think is gonna get it? Me, that's who!" Her eyes fell on the oak bucket of the kitchen slops beside the cookstove. "What's that doing here?"

"Polly Ann didn't take it down," Laylie said helpfully.

"Polly! Polly Ann, you lazy thing!" Terria yelled. Polly Ann came in the kitchen door, and Laylie made a face at her.

"You take this bucket down to JoMa's and hurry back."

Polly Ann picked up the bucket. Terria walked over to open the door for her. As soon as Terria's back was turned, Roz dipped a pewter cup into a pan heating on the stove. It came up dripping milk.

"What are you doing?" Terria had turned around.

Roz scooped up a spoon of molasses from a pot and dropped it, spoon and all, into the warm milk.

"You think I'm gonna marry you if you go disregardin' my instructions?" Terria asked, as he handed the cup out the window to Laylie. "Why would I marry a man like that?"

" 'Cause I'm turrible good-looking," Roz said, wrapping his arms around her and winking at Laylie over her shoulder. Laylie winked back before she slid off Melia's back, being careful not to spill the milk.

Terria managed to free herself from the good-looking Roz and leaned out the window.

"You bring back my cup and spoon when you get done!" she yelled after the girls.

Laylie stirred the molasses into the milk until there was almost none left on the spoon. Then she licked one side and let Melia lick the other. When the spoon was clean, Laylie tucked it into her pocket, and the girls shared the apple as they walked.

Polly Ann had stopped to talk to Ruby and Priss, the blacksmith's daughters. The older girls paid no attention as Laylie and Melia went by.

"Polly Ann's dress is sure pretty," Melia whispered after they'd passed. "I wish I worked at the Big House." She spread the fabric of her shirt as if it were a skirt. "I'd dress fine and eat three times a day!"

"You'd have to wear shoes," Laylie pointed out. "Most likely that's why Polly's so sour all the time."

Laylie's Daring Quest

When they walked into the cabin yard, Melia ran to George Henry and picked him up. Two of the babies had cried themselves out, and the third was hiccuping herself to sleep on JoMa's shoulder. As Laylie handed the milk to JoMa, Polly Ann finally came sashaying down the path, swinging the slop bucket. She dumped its contents—table scraps of meat, gruel, and eggs—onto a rough wooden board that Luke had left lying in the grass. The little boys gathered around and scooped up the food with their hands, eating as quickly as they could.

"Some folk feed pigs that way," JoMa said. "But it ain't no way to feed chillen, Polly Ann. You shoulda waited for me to get their bowls."

"Some pigs got better manners than *field* chillen," Polly Ann said.

JoMa would have cuffed her ear if she hadn't had milk in one hand and a baby in the other. Polly Ann knew it too, and smiled wickedly at Laylie.

"Su-weee!" she said, as she went back up the path, swinging her bucket again.

Laylie scooped up a rock, but as she turned to fling it at Polly Ann, she saw a look of horror on JoMa's face. JoMa's eyes weren't fixed on Polly Ann at all. Her eyes were fixed on Bullseye, who was ambling toward the children, an ugly look on his flat face and his eye on the pork bone in Exter's hand.

Laylie skipped the rock off the dog's back. Bullseye spun toward her, snarling, but she had another rock ready, and this one took him right over the ear. The dog tucked his tail between his legs and ran yelping down the road.

"That's right, devil dog!" JoMa yelled. "That's right, run! I'll turn your hide to shoe leather!"

The younger children had finished most of the sticky mess and were licking their fingers. Melia had scooped some into a bowl for Laylie and was eating her own, using a clam shell as a spoon. Laylie pulled Hettie's head rag off and made a show of spreading it in her lap, just like she'd seen Missy Jen do with a white napkin when she and Melia had peeked at a fancy picnic party.

Melia clapped her hands. Laylie took Terria's spoon out of her pocket, held it up to check for tarnish spots, then gripped it in her fist and scooped up a mess of the gruel. Max laughed as she put it in her mouth.

"Well, ain't you just the Queen of Sheba?" JoMa said, laughing too.

"Laylie!" Melia hissed. "Borse is coming!"

In the daylight and up close, Ronald Borse had washed-out blue eyes and permanent tobacco stains at the corners of his mouth. Bullseye cowered at his heels.

"Something happen over here?" said Borse. He spat red-brown tobacco juice on the ground. "Bullseye come running out of here. You do something to my dog, JoMa?"

Laylie stood up and moved closer to JoMa, her head down. *JoMa said never to look a white man in the eye. It makes them mad.*

"Not one thing, Master Borse," JoMa said. "Not one thing."

A trickle of blood showed red against the dirty white of Bullseye's head.

"Is that right, chillen?" JoMa said.

The children stood still, heads ducked, as Borse looked them over.

"Where'd you get that spoon?" he asked. Laylie realized that she was still gripping it in her fist. "You harboring a little

717

thief here, JoMa? That why you clobbered my dog? 'Cause he can smell thieves?"

Laylie's head came up, and she looked him in the eye. "I ain't no thief. And JoMa didn't clobber your dog—"

Laylie felt JoMa's hands on her shoulders, pulling her back.

"Forgive this chile, Master Borse," the old woman said. "You know Master Breandan is a good man. He don't allow no whippin' of chillen on this place." She pulled Laylie closer, and Laylie could feel the old woman trembling as she continued, "She'll learn manners soon enough, I expect."

"I expect," Borse said. "You'll teach her or I will, one or t'other." He turned to walk away, then stopped.

"Say," he said. "That Hettie. She was one of yours, wasn't she?"

JoMa's fingers tightened on Laylie's shoulders till it hurt, but she didn't say anything. Borse just smiled and walked away.

CHAPTER

2

A Foreign Land

There on the poplars we hung our harps,
for there our captors asked us for songs,
our tormentors demanded songs of joy;
they said, "Sing us one of the songs of
Zion!" How can we sing the songs
of the LORD while in a
foreign land?

PSALM 137:2-4

A Foreign Land

What did he mean — Hettie *was* one of yourn?" Laylie asked after Borse was gone. "Why didn't Hettie and them come in to eat?"

"Child—" there were tears in JoMa's eyes, "you was born with too much salt for this evil world. Too much fire. You've got to learn to hide it. You've got to learn."

"But what did he mean, JoMa?" Laylie asked again.

"If there's evil coming, it'll get here soon enough." JoMa said as she wiped her eyes with her apron. "Now help me feed these babies."

JoMa took the babies down one by one, and Laylie helped drip the molasses and milk into their mouths, or let them suck it from her fingers. When it was all gone, Laylie took the cup and spoon back up to the kitchen and left them on the windowsill.

"Story now, JoMa!" Cicero said as soon as Laylie got back.

"Story, story, story!" Max chanted, stomping his feet.

"She wouldn't start till you came back," Melia said to Laylie.

JoMa was busy weaving thick grasses into a basket, but she laid the work aside and picked up a stick. The little boys sat at her feet, and Laylie and Melia took their place beside them.

"This is a story from Africa," JoMa said.

Laylie shivered with delight. She loved JoMa's stories from Africa, stories about people with beautiful names, and strange animals.

"A story of Africa," JoMa said again, to make sure they understood. "My mother told it to me in her own African

721

words, and I carried it over the ocean—carried it in my heart. Now I'm telling it to you."

JoMa drew a lion in the dirt—a cat with a ruffle on his neck.

"One day there was a lion and a wolf and a fox that went huntin' together through the bushes and the brambles. They hunted all day before they caught themselves a wild donkey, a little deer, and a rabbit. They was all terrible hungry—growlin', gnashin' hungry. The lion up and says, 'Brother Wolf, you may divide the food for us today.' The wolf sniffed all that delicious food, *mmm-mmm!*

" 'I 'spect, master,' he says to the lion, 'you should eat that big old donkey. Brother Fox ain't too big. He'll be full if he eats the rabbit. I will take the little deer as my part.'

"Well! When the wicked old lion heard that, he raised up his paw and clobbered the wolf right on the head. That wolf's head cracked right open, and he died. Then the wicked lion says to the fox, 'Now, Brother Fox, how do you think we ought to divide what we caught?'

" 'Well, master,' says the fox, 'I expects that the donkey will be your dinner, the deer will be your supper, and that rabbit will be your breakfast for tomorrow morning.'

"That sure did surprise the lion, who was hopin' to clobber the fox, too. 'When did you up and learn so much wisdom?' the lion asked." JoMa looked at the children. "When did he learn it?" she asked them.

"Right about the time he heard the wolf's head crack," Laylie answered.

JoMa nodded. "That's right. That's all it took."

"But," Melia said, "the fox didn't get any food!"

"He didn't get killed neither," JoMa pointed out. "That fox—he's smart enough to know when to bark and when to

keep quiet." She looked right at Laylie when she said it. "He'll catch him a rabbit, I expects, when the lion ain't looking."

⌒⌒⌒

Laylie played foxes and rabbits with Melia and the little boys all afternoon. They were still playing when Helen came to take Melia and George Henry home.

The gunshot to release the workers from the fields did not sound until the sun touched the horizon. When it did, JoMa stood up and watched for them to come. She moaned when she saw them—Luke, Wim, and Lucindy, walking beside a giant black man who was carrying something in his arms. Laylie had never seen Isaac the preacher man before, but she was sure it must be him.

It wasn't until they passed the live oak that Laylie realized it wasn't a bundle of rags in the preacher's arms. Hettie's dress was wrapped around her just enough to keep her decent, but there was no hiding the deep lash wounds. JoMa moaned again as they came up to the cabin. She stood aside as the preacher carried Hettie into the cabin. The little boys followed along, but Laylie watched from the door with Luke, Wim, and Lucindy as the big man laid Hettie, stomach down, on JoMa's cot and knelt beside the bed.

"You boys get out," JoMa said. "I mean you, too," JoMa said to Isaac.

The big man stood up and walked past Laylie and kept on walking, right out of the cabin yard and off toward the swamp. Luke followed him out the door and then stood looking after him.

"Who did that to Hettie?" Laylie asked.

"Borse," Wim said. "He don't like her on account of she's got black blood and white blood both flowing in her veins," Wim explained. "Why do you think she's so light? Just like —"

Luke had come back. "I seen your blood, Wim," he said. "It's the same color as Hettie's, ain't it?"

"Laylie!" JoMa called from inside. "You get in here, and bring me a bucket of water when you come."

Laylie filled the bucket with water from the rain barrel and carried it inside. Lucindy had lit a grease lamp and was holding it up to shed light on the poor little body on the bed. JoMa had torn off a piece of Hettie's dress, and was using it to clean the dried blood from her body. Her back, buttocks, and upper legs were a mass of bruises and open cuts.

It made Laylie's stomach hurt to see it. She set down the bucket and eased toward the door.

"You stay, girl," JoMa said. "I said you got to learn." She dipped the rag in water, then pressed it against the crusted blood to soften it. "You stare down Borse and this is what's gonna happen to you. To *you*, child. You was born a slave, and slaves don't look white men in the eye. Learn it easy now, or learn it harder later on."

Her voice softened, "My poor Hettie." Laylie watched as JoMa worked in silence, cleaning each wound. When she was done, she took the tin of rendered lard from the shelf.

"Take some of this," JoMa said, holding the tin toward Laylie, "and work it in around the cuts. Work it in good. It'll keep them from pulling as they heal."

Laylie swallowed hard. She held the lard in one palm, just as JoMa was doing, and scooped some up on her fingertips.

The skin around the wounds was hot, as if the bruises had absorbed the fire of the sun.

JoMa's gnarled hands worked quickly, dark against Hettie's lighter skin. Laylie started to rub the grease in, then she stopped. Her hands weren't dark against Hettie's skin. They were the same color.

Why do you think she's so light? She's just like . . . Just like me. That's what Wim had been going to say.

~~~~~

"Luke," Laylie whispered in the darkness. "Did Borse whip Hettie 'cause she's mixed blood?"

"No," Luke said. JoMa had kept everybody but Wim out of the cabin so she could look after Hettie. Wim was strong enough to hold her down if she started thrashing, so he got to stay inside the cabin just in case JoMa needed help. The little boys were piled outside on a blanket with Lucindy on one side and Luke and Laylie on the other to keep them from wandering off if they woke up during the night.

"Then why'd he whip her?"

"He whipped her 'cause she was singing one of Isaac's songs."

"So Isaac was the one that came carrying Hettie?" Laylie asked.

"That was him," Luke said.

Laylie wiggled closer to him. "Then Borse don't hate Hettie 'cause of the color of her skin?"

"There ain't nothin' in Borse but hate," Luke said. "Some things he hates worse, that's all."

Laylie lay for a long time trying to figure it all out.

"Luke? What song was she singing?" asked Laylie.

"'Jesus calls you,'" said Lucindy's voice in a hoarse whisper. "She was singing 'Jesus Calls You to the Wilderness.'"

"Who's Jesus?" Laylie asked.

"Hush!" Luke said.

"But . . ." Laylie tried to protest.

Luke turned his back to her. "Only a fool talks when they could be sleepin'."

Isaac was standing by the cabin door the next morning when Laylie woke, twisting his hat in his hands. *I must have slept through the waking shot,* Laylie thought to herself, as she saw that Luke, Wim, and Lucindy were already gone. The little boys were sleeping piled together like puppies.

"Can I come in and pray for her?" Isaac asked JoMa.

"You ain't comin' in here," JoMa said. She was standing in the doorway, holding her broom like she was going to club him with it. "We don't need any of your prayin'."

"I'm gonna pray for Hettie, whether you let me in or not," Isaac said, "even if you wallop me with that broom. I . . . I would have taken those lashes on my own body if I could. I . . . wasn't there. He wouldn't have done it if I had been there."

"Well, you didn't and you wasn't," JoMa said bitterly. "And your prayin' and preachin' ways is the reason my baby is dyin'. That prayin' is white man talk, white man religion. You're a black man, and that ain't for us. Get outta here."

Isaac didn't move from the doorway. "No, ma'am," he said, and bowed his head. "Lord," his lips moved like he was struggling to find words and his eyes were squeezed shut.

He shook his head. "Before I talk to You about Hettie, I need You to clean this murderous hatred of Borse out of my heart. I've wrestled with it all night, Lord, and it won't leave me." His voice was shaking. "You know it won't. I'm asking You to take it."

Tears fell, splashing in the dust at his feet. JoMa had lowered her broom and was just watching him.

"Thank You, Lord," Isaac said at last, in a voice that was no longer shaking. "Thank You. Now I'm standing with a heart washed clean, asking You to spare Hettie's life. You sent me to preach words that bring life, not death. Raise this girl up. I'm asking You to raise her up." He shook his head again, then turned and walked away.

"Who was he talking to?" Laylie asked.

"God," JoMa said, shaking her head. "He thinks his Bible-God is listening to him."

"Why didn't you wallop him?" asked Laylie.

JoMa rubbed her temples. "Maybe I just seen enough meanness for one lifetime."

For two days, Hettie burned with fever, tossing and turning and crying in her sleep. Every morning and every night, the young preacher stopped outside, took off his hat, bowed his head, and prayed.

JoMa set Laylie to watching Hettie during daylight hours, while Melia helped take care of the babies. Laylie washed Hettie's brow with cool water and dribbled it in her mouth when she asked for a drink. On the third day, Laylie and Melia kept the little boys while JoMa went to the woods. She brought back a basketful of plants with raggedy-shaped leaves and tiny green flowers.

"Oak of Jerusalem," JoMa said. "This will take the fly-blow out, so's she can heal up."

Laylie's Daring Quest

She boiled the leaves in a kettle until the water turned dark and bitter to smell. When it had cooled, she dipped her rag in the water and squeezed it over Hettie's wounds. Hettie seemed to rest easier after that, sleeping without tossing and turning.

The fifth day, Saturday, Hettie was standing in the door, held up by Lucindy's arms, when Isaac came by in the evening. He just stood looking for the longest time. Then he smiled, and Hettie smiled back at him.

"Praise God!" he shouted, lifting his hands to the sky and throwing back his head. "Praise God!"

"Get!" JoMa said.

He went down the road, but he went whistling a song. The sound of it sent a chill down Laylie's spine.

"Luke," she whispered, "I know that song. He's whistling Mamma's song!"

"No, he ain't." Luke turned and walked away.

Laylie had to trot to keep up. "It *was* Mamma's song!" she said. "What's wrong?"

Luke stopped. "I'm scared, that's what."

"You ain't," Laylie said. "You ain't scared of nothing!"

"I am scared," Luke said. "Scared all the time, scared I ain't strong enough or smart enough to do what needs doing. JoMa told me about you whackin' Bullseye with a rock."

"Had to," Laylie said. "He would'a bit Exter."

"JoMa says you got too much salt." He shook his head. "You stay away from Borse, and you stay away from Isaac."

"Isaac's nice," Laylie said. "And—"

"And nothing! What am I gonna do with you?" he asked.

"I don't know," Laylie said sadly. She hadn't meant to make him mad. "What?" she asked.

"I'll let you know when I figure it." He started walking again.

"Luke!" she called. He stopped.

"I . . . I'll stay away from that Isaac. And I'll keep out of trouble," she promised.

"That's good," Luke said. "I expect Isaac will be the next slave sold off this place. You just keep away from him until then."

⌒⌒

It was three weeks before Hettie was able to do much. When she could walk, Laylie and Melia made her a place to sit in the shade beside their shingle dollhouse. She helped them weave mats of straw and make doll bowls from acorn caps. Laylie made a carpet for one room out of live moss, and Hettie declared it the prettiest house she had ever seen. Soon Hettie was helping with the babies and walking a bit more.

It wasn't too hard for Laylie to keep her promise about Borse and Bullseye. They never came around. But when Isaac came to speak to Hettie, it was harder. When he took Hettie walking, Melia wanted to follow them, but Laylie wouldn't go, no matter how hard Melia begged. She only peeked at them out of the corners of her eyes when they came back. Hettie was always smiling, and Laylie wished Master Phil would hurry and sell Isaac away.

One morning Helen had two baskets on her arm when she brought Melia and George Henry.

"What's in those baskets?" Laylie asked.

"Why, dewberry cobbler," Helen said, holding out a basket for Laylie to see. Laylie looked in, but it was empty.

729

Helen laughed. "Well, there'll be cobbler in it if someone will pick the berries."

"Is it that time already?" JoMa asked.

"They's ripe and sweet," Helen said. "Ready for the pickin' all along the briar bushes. I was thinking these girls might like to pick a few."

JoMa pursed her lips and looked at George Henry.

"I can help you watch the babies," Hettie said. "Let the girls go."

"It's gonna rain," JoMa said.

Helen looked up at the clouds. "I'll send them home before it does."

"Please, JoMa!" Laylie grabbed her hand. "We won't go too far from where Helen is working."

"Well," JoMa said. Laylie could tell she was hungry for the taste of fruit. "You watch out for snakes and bears."

"I'll keep an eye on things," Helen assured JoMa.

Laylie took a basket in one hand and one of Helen's hands in the other, and Melia held her mamma's other hand as they walked to the brambles above the rice fields.

"I'll be working right there if you need me," Helen said, pointing to the middle of the flooded field. "Give me some sugar, baby."

"Yes, Mamma," Melia said, turning her face up for a kiss.

Helen went down to join the other women working in the rice field.

The purple-blue dewberries grew on vines that wound themselves over and around other bushes. The berries in the sun ripened faster, and the birds had been at them already, pecking bits out of each one. Laylie reached into a bush to get a berry the birds hadn't been at, and popped it into her mouth. It was sour-sweet and delicious.

"Ouch!" Melia said, pulling her hand back. "They got stickers!"

" 'Course they do," said Laylie, taking Melia's hand and examining it. "It ain't even bleeding!" Laylie blew on it anyway to take away the sting. "You got to be more careful," she said.

Melia soon had the hang of picking the berries and avoiding the thorns. Laylie ate two berries for every one she put in the basket, but the berries were growing so thick that both baskets were soon full to overflowing.

"Meeeelia!" Helen called. "Layleeee!"

The girls carried their baskets down to the edge of the field and showed her how full they were. Helen took a berry from Melia's basket. "Mmm-mmm. When your daddy comes to visit tonight, we'll feed him cobbler till he busts! JoMa was right. It's fixin' to rain, so you girls go on back—and don't let the little boys eat all my berries, neither! Save one full basket for me."

The little boys crowded around Laylie and Melia when they came back into the yard, grabbing for handfuls of berries before JoMa shooed them away.

"Take those inside," she said, "and—"

"Why, there's Master Phil!" Hettie said, looking up from the baby she was rocking.

Mr. Breandan was riding his fine chestnut jumper, and with him were two people Laylie had never seen before: a thin man and a large, plump woman, riding horses from the Breandan stables. The little boys ran out to see them go past, but instead they rode right up to JoMa's cabin.

Mr. Breandan dismounted and looked at the children, a smile on his flushed pink face. Laylie had never seen him up close before. His nose was redder than his cheeks, but he didn't look unkind.

"Hello, JoMa!" he said cheerily. Then he pointed at Laylie. "Come here, child. What is your name?"

"Laylie, Master Phil," Laylie said, remembering to keep her eyes down.

"Look! There's another one," the woman said, pointing with her riding crop.

Melia was peeking from behind JoMa.

"Come out here," Mr. Breandan commanded. Melia came out and took Laylie's hand.

The man with Master Breandan got down off his horse.

"Master Breandan," JoMa said, "What . . . what are you doing today . . . sir?"

"The Johnsons are moving to Texas," he said, "and Royce promised his wife a new house girl before they go. They were going to buy a girl in Charleston, but I said, 'Nonsense! I have girls right here!'"

"Which one, dear?" Mr. Johnson spoke to his wife.

"The little one," Mrs. Johnson said, pointing her riding crop at Melia.

"I thought as much," Mr. Johnson said. "What's your name, girl?"

"Amelia," Melia whispered.

"Excellent choice," Master Phil said. "Her mother is a diligent and cheerful woman. I'm sure this one will be perfect for you."

"Master Breandan," JoMa said, "please let this child say good-bye to her mamma. She'll be along real soon, or we could send for her . . . please . . ."

"That would only make it more difficult." Master Phil's voice was kind, as if he were speaking to a child.

Melia screamed as the man took her arm.

"Take her to the wagon," Mr. Breandan said.

732

The other man lifted Melia off the ground.

"Let her go!" Laylie kicked his shins, and he swatted at her like she was a fly.

"Mamma!" Melia screamed. There was terror in Melia's voice now. "Mamma!"

Laylie doubled up her fists and pounded at the stranger. "Let her go! She wants her mamma!"

This time the back of Mr. Johnson's fist caught Laylie just below the eye, sending her flying. Laylie's ears were ringing, and she saw bright spots before her eyes.

"Now, now!" Mr. Breandan said. "Enough of that! They have some rudimentary sentiments, after all, and she is just a child. Best be on our way before the rain catches us."

Laylie tried to get up, but JoMa ran to her and scooped her into her arms.

"Hush, baby, hush!" she said. "She's sold away, and nothin' you can do—"

Laylie pulled herself out of JoMa's arms and ran as fast as she could to the live oak. From the top branches, she watched the wagon take Melia away. She watched Helen coming home from the fields, too late, too late, and saw JoMa touch Helen's shoulder as she spoke the words. Laylie saw Helen fall to the ground, holding George Henry and crying all the grief of the world into his little arms.

Laylie held on when the wind began to lash her, and the first fat raindrops stung her skin.

"Laylie, girl?" Luke was climbing up beside her.

"You were wrong," Laylie said. "Isaac wasn't the next slave to be sold off the place. You were wrong," she said.

"You comin' down?"

Laylie's Daring Quest

"No," Laylie said.

Luke wrapped his arms around her as the storm broke, and just held on.

CHAPTER 3

Too Much Salt

*Wisdom is supreme; therefore
get wisdom. Though it cost
all you have, get
understanding.*

PROVERBS 4:7

Too Much Salt

*L*ook at that eye!" said JoMa, shaking her head. "Mmm-mmmmm-mmm."

Lucindy pinched Laylie's chin and turned her face to catch the light of the grease lamp. JoMa had started a fire in the fire pit against the back wall. Laylie was huddled on one side of it and Luke on the other, waiting for their clothes to dry. The storm was still raging outside, doing its best to put out the flames, spitting rain down the smoke hole in the cabin ceiling.

"She walloped a white man?" Wim asked.

"Pow!" Cicero yelled, punching the air. "Pow, pow!" JoMa picked him up and tucked him under her arm.

"You have somethin' to say for yourself?" Lucindy asked, still examining Laylie's eye.

"I wished I'd had a rock," Laylie said.

"Mmmm-mmm-mmm," JoMa said again. "Too much salt, girl. That's what I'm talkin' about."

"She's gonna bring it down on us," Lucindy said. "What's gonna happen when Borse hears? Or if she acts up with him?"

"Hush," said Hettie as she put her own shawl around Laylie's shoulders.

"He'll whip somebody, that's what," Lucindy said. "Master Phil has rules about whipping chillen, so who you think it's gonna be? He'll sure take it out on somebody."

"Don't be so sure he won't whip a chile," said JoMa. "That man Borse has a gizzard where his heart oughtta be. An' he don't mind breaking rules, if he don't get caught."

Luke was rocking back and forth on his heels, while Exter and Max reenacted Laylie's battle behind him.

737

"You boys lay down!" JoMa said. Exter and Max stopped wrestling. JoMa put Cicero down with them. "Go to sleep. I don't want any more foolishness neither. You all go to sleep. Tomorrow's coming whether we have worries or not."

"Story, JoMa?" Exter asked hopefully.

"I'm all storied out," JoMa said.

Laylie lay on her mat beside Luke, her eye throbbing with each beat of her heart. Luke wasn't asleep. He had his arm over his eyes, the way he did when he was thinking. *He's figuring*, Laylie thought. *Figuring what to do about me. How to wash the salt right out of me.*

Laylie woke with the shot the next morning, but Luke was already gone. She scrambled to the door, suddenly afraid that he was gone for good, gone North without her. Then she saw Luke and JoMa standing with their heads together, whispering.

Luke looked up and saw Laylie watching.

"You be waiting for me when I come to eat," he said. "Be waiting right here. I've got to get on out to roll call."

"Luke!" Laylie ran after him, even though it made her eye hurt worse, and caught his hand. "Are we going . . . North?" She whispered the last word, even though there was no one around to hear.

Luke just shook his head.

Laylie took her breakfast corncake behind the woodpile where she could be alone. The two little dolls lay side by side in the shingle house, where they had been forgotten in the excitement of berry picking. The rain had splashed in, leaving them damp and dotted with mud. Laylie picked Melia's little blue doll up and brushed the mud away. *Who will take care of Melia now?* She couldn't stand to think of

Too Much Salt

Melia crying and all alone. Laylie chewed on her lip. *I promised Luke I wouldn't go talking to Isaac. But I never promised I wouldn't talk to his Bible-God.* She bowed her head like Isaac had done and tried to remember how he prayed.

"Lord," she whispered. "This is Laylie. I ain't never talked to You before, so maybe You don't know who I am. I figure if You helped Hettie get better on account of Isaac's asking . . . You might help Melia . . . if I asks." Laylie swallowed hard. "She's just a little girl. Somebody's got to watch over her. Please, Lord, take care of her."

It made her feel a little better, but she still sat beside the little shingle house with the dolls all morning, not wanting JoMa's fussing at her or Hettie's worried eyes watching her. When the noon shot sounded, she waited until she saw Luke and Wim before she came out of the bushes.

"Come on," Luke said to her, leaving Wim to go on alone. "You and me don't have time to eat." Laylie trotted after him to the edge of the fields, where he stopped and took down a rabbit hung up in a tree and tied it to his rope belt. She walked even closer to him as they turned toward the swamp. Luke never let her go near the swamp, not even on hot Sundays when everyone else took a shortcut through it to the bay to dig clams or swim. Luke made her walk with him up along the east road past the dunes. Wim had said it was five whole miles farther that way.

Luke wasn't taking any road this time. The trees around them wore fringed shawls of Spanish moss, and the air smelled of black-water swamp—tangy with cypress and tupelo. The pools and channels of dark water they walked past looked oily from the fallen, rotting leaves. *JoMa said witches drag people to the swamp and feed them to the Zombie Man.* The water in a pool beside them stirred.

"Luke!" Laylie said, pointing at dimpled ripples where something moved beneath the surface. "What's that?"

"I'm gonna piggyback you from here," Luke said. He grabbed her hands and swung her up on his back. Laylie wrapped her arms around his neck and her legs around his middle and tried to peer over his shoulder with her one good eye.

"Stop leaning," Luke said. "You're gonna topple us."

She held on tight as Luke jumped over roots, sometimes wading through knee-deep water, sometimes walking on spongy ground. Dark lines on the trunks of the water oak and dogwood showed that the swamp came up with the tide, hiding the spongy ground where Luke was walking.

"You smell that?" he asked.

Laylie closed her eye and sniffed. "Wood smoke?"

Luke nodded and turned upwind, following his nose. The ground rose, becoming more solid, and soon they were walking on a path. Suddenly, Luke stopped. He didn't even fuss when Laylie leaned to look over his shoulder. They were standing on the edge of a small clearing with a little hut that seemed to be woven from living branches and Spanish moss. The smoke they smelled curled up from the coals of a fire pit. Luke pulled Laylie off his back and set her on her feet.

"Hello!" he called.

Something stirred inside the mound. A shaggy, four-legged creature crawled out. Laylie gasped and backed up against Luke as it stood up, unfolding into an old black man. His skin was the color of mahogany, as wrinkled as a walnut shell, and his clothes were so old they were color-less. A cloud of white hair drifted above him. He brushed it back with one bony hand, but Laylie's eyes fixed on the other—or where it should have been. His other arm ended in a stub, the scarred end bright pink and white.

"The Zombie Man!" Laylie's voice was hardly a squeak. "Run, Luke!"

"He ain't no zombie," Luke said, but he didn't sound sure.

"Perhaps I am a pirate who has lost his hook!" The man leapt toward them waving his stump in the air.

Luke grabbed Laylie's shirt and backed up so fast he fell on his bottom, pulling Laylie down on top of him. Laylie scrambled up. The old man's shoulders were shaking. He wiped his eyes with his good hand.

"He's laughing at us," Laylie said. She planted herself between the pirate and her brother. She pointed at the stub where his right hand used to be. "Did you lose that in a pirate fight?"

He considered the stump.

"I didn't lose it at all," he said. "It was taken from me. Now what brings you to my swamp?"

"I heard of you," Luke said, "from some runaways, and JoMa."

"What did you hear?" he asked.

"Your name is Andros Walsh—"

"At your service!" The old man bowed.

". . . and you were a teacher one time," Luke went on. "Before you were a slave. JoMa says she heard of you before you crawled off to the swamp. She says you are a good man, too cobbled up to catch your own food." Luke paused. " I have a sister—" Luke pushed Laylie forward.

"I may be called the Zombie Man," the man said, raising his white eyebrows, "but I do not make a habit of eating small children. Besides, she'd hardly be two mouthfuls!"

Luke untied the rabbit from his belt and tossed it at the old man's feet.

"She is little," Luke said, "but she's real smart."

"You are suggesting a . . . barter? I teach your sister, and you provide . . . rabbits?"

"Yes," Luke said.

The shot sounded in the distance, calling the workers back to the fields.

"Stay here, Laylie, you hear me?" Luke said. "I don't want you wanderin' in the swamp." He turned and ran back the way they had come.

"Wait!" Laylie said.

"See here!" Andros called. "I didn't agree to be a nanny or a teacher!"

"I didn't ask you to, neither," said Laylie, squinting up at him through her one good eye. *He is kind of cobbled up.*

"When is he coming back for you?" asked Andros.

"I don't know," she replied.

"He is coming back, though?" The old man ran his hand through his hair. "Of course he is. What is your name?"

"Laylie. Laylie Colbert."

"I don't recall a Colbert plantation around here," the old man said.

"We're from Meadshead. It belongs to Master Phil Breandan," Laylie said. "Colbert was Mamma's name, and she gave it to us. To me and Luke. She said it was ours and nobody could take it."

Andros's eyebrows went up even higher than they had before.

"Well, Laylie Colbert," he said, "what does Master Phil think of your last name?"

"He don't know we got one. Luke said—" Laylie put her hand over her mouth.

"Your brother said not to tell a soul, am I right?" Andros asked, and Laylie nodded. "Do you know why all of the slaves on Master Phil's plantation use the name Breandan?" asked Andros. This time Laylie shook her head.

"Because if he let them have their own names—" Andros picked up the rabbit, "he would have to admit they were human beings just like himself. Dogs and horses don't have last names, do they? They are mere beasts. He believes his slaves are little better."

"You got two names," said Laylie.

"I do indeed," Andros said. "We might as well share this rabbit, Laylie Colbert. We will talk some sense into your brother when he returns."

Andros turned and walked out of the clearing. Laylie hesitated before realizing she was being left all alone, and then ran after him.

They followed a well-beaten path across the tussock to the base of a fallen cyprus tree. Andros climbed the roots like a ladder, pulling himself up on top of the trunk, and Laylie scrambled up after him. He walked along the leaning trunk, his bare feet sure on the old wood. The tree bridge carried them over dense shrubbery, then marsh, and finally over a deep channel where its branches sank into the water ten feet below, like strong arms holding them up. Here, Andros sat down and wrapped his legs around the trunk. He pulled a jackknife from his pocket, pried open the blade with his teeth, and holding the rabbit's head against the trunk with his stub, set about skinning it.

Two bubble eyes rose out of the water, and continued to rise. When Laylie realized that they belonged to an alligator the size of a canoe, she sat down carefully and held on tight. Andros finished making his cuts, stabbed the knife through the rabbit into the wood to hold it in place, then peeled the skin off, and dug the entrails out.

The gator's maw gaped open and it caught the skin and guts as Andros dropped them. The swamp echoed with the call of another bull gator, and this monster replied, its roar shaking the branch Laylie clung to.

"Noisy watchdogs," Andros said. "They keep my back door safe." He wiped his knife blade on his pants, then folded it shut. They made their way back along the trunk and down the root ladder.

"Do you know how old you are?" he asked, as he spitted the rabbit on a stick for cooking.

"Seven."

"Do you know what a teacher is?"

She shook her head.

"Do you know what a book is?"

"I've seen the Young Miss looking at them in the garden," she said. "And I seen stacks of them one time, when I carried a message to the Big House."

Andros sighed. "Do you know why your brother brought you here?"

"Because I have too much salt," Laylie said.

"Too much salt?"

"JoMa said it when I whacked Bullseye with a rock." Andros's eyebrows were making a habit of trying to crawl into his hairline.

"Master Borse's dog," Laylie explained. "He was gonna bite Exter, so I whacked him, and JoMa told Luke that he had to do something with me. After I lit into that white man who bought Melia, Lucindy said I'd bring it down on all of them. So, Luke brung me here." Laylie tried to hold back the tears at the mention of Melia, but her shiner stung with them anyway. She put her hand up to it.

"Is that how you got that lovely black eye?" Andros asked softly. "Trying to keep them from taking . . . Melia?"

"She's only six," Laylie said. Misery rose up inside her, and this time she couldn't keep it from bubbling out. "I was supposed to take care of her. Her mamma always told me to take care of her." Laylie wiped her face on her sleeve and turned away from the old man so he wouldn't see her tears.

"Ten years ago," Andros said, "I taught a black man to read and write. He wrote himself a pass and walked right past the patrollers on his way to freedom. When they found out what I had done, they dragged me out to the woodblock and they used an ax to chop off my hand."

Laylie turned to peek at the stump.

"I don't know if he made it," Andros went on. "If he did, he will never know I paid for his freedom with my hand. But he knew the risk I was taking for him."

Rabbit fat sizzled and popped as it dropped in the fire.

"You couldn't stop them from taking Melia," he said. "But you have given her a gift. Melia will always remember that you fought for her. Perhaps that memory will give her courage someday when she needs to fight for herself or for someone else."

Andros sat quietly for a long time, turning the meat on the spit.

"Slavery is evil, Laylie Colbert," he said, taking the rabbit off the fire and laying it on a rock so he could cut it in half. He gave Laylie the half still on the stick. "You 'light into it' every chance you get. Every chance!"

Laylie's Daring Quest

They ate in silence but for the crunching of bones. When Andros was finished, he dipped a pan full of water from the spring by his hut. He washed the grease from his face, then carefully scrubbed his hand and stub, rubbing them with sand and rinsing them with water until they were clean.

"Your turn," he said, dipping a clean pan of water. While Laylie washed her hands and face, Andros crawled into the hut. Laylie washed as quickly as she could, wiped her hands on her shirttail, and then peeked in after him.

The walls of the hut were decorated with bits and pieces of plants and animals. Laylie recognized the skins of copperheads and water moccasins woven through the branches of the roof, piles of clean, polished bones against one wall, and a giant sea turtle shell. She jumped back as Andros crawled out of the hovel, an oilskin package clutched to his chest.

"Your brother did not bring you here because you have too much salt," he said. "He brought you here because you have enough salt to learn." He sat on his log bench and carefully unwrapped his package. It held three thick books.

Laylie took a step back.

"Slaves ain't allowed to touch books," she said.

"Of course not," Andros said, holding up a book with a lovely green cover. Laylie took a step closer. "I have only three," Andros said. "Not a great library, but a beginning."

"Ain't you afraid to hold them?" Laylie whispered. "After they lopped off your hand?"

"They took my hand," Andros said, running his hand lovingly over the leather binding of a book. "Not my heart and my soul."

"Where'd you get 'em?" she asked.

"All kinds of people wander through my swamp. Trappers and traders, pirates and thieves. I traded a good kettle for these, to a man who could cook but could not read. I did not ask how he came to have them."

He opened one of the books, and Laylie could see pictures inside, which were even better than the ones JoMa scratched in the dirt.

"That's Robin Hood," Andros said, seeing her stare. "Fighting with Little John."

"Can I . . . touch it?" Laylie whispered.

"Be my guest," he said.

Laylie reached out one finger and touched the page. A little shock went through her, and she looked around to make sure Borse and Bullseye had not appeared in a puff of smoke. The clearing was peaceful and still.

"Here." Andros put the book in her hands. "Get acquainted with this one while I spend some time with another old friend. I have to turn the pages every now and then, let the sunshine in, or they'll get moldy."

He settled himself on the log bench with his book. Laylie sat on the ground at his feet and opened *Robin Hood*.

The book fell open to the picture she had seen before. Her swollen eye blurred the images, but she could see well enough if she kept it shut and looked with the other eye. She traced the picture with her finger, trying to tease the story out of it. When she had finished studying it, she turned the pages until she found another.

There were men with bows and arrows who wore pointed shoes on their feet. Other men wore clothes that looked like they were made out of cooking pans, and they carried knives as long as their arms. There were ladies in long dresses and tall pointed hats with flags on top. Laylie liked the pictures, but she wished JoMa was here to tell the story that went with them. She looked at every picture in the book, then she stood up and looked at the book in Andros's hands.

"There ain't no pictures!" she said.

Andros pointed at the squiggles on the page. "These marks are words. As I read them, they make pictures in my head."

"What pictures?"

"A picture of a young man named Galahad," Andros said. "He is the bravest and best young man alive, full of courage and valor!"

Laylie closed her good eye and tried to imagine him.

"I see him!" she said. "He looks like Luke!"

"Excellent!" Andros said. "Galahad is on a quest."

Laylie opened her eye. "What's a quest? Is it a horse?"

"A quest is a journey, through terrible danger, to find something you *must* have. Perhaps something that has been lost."

"Our mamma lost something," Laylie said. "She lost her freedom when a man-stealer took her. She was going to New York City with her sister, my Aunt Tempie."

"Your mother was a free woman?" Andros asked.

"Luke says it," Laylie said. "Mamma was taken, but maybe Aunt Tempie got through." Laylie paused. "What did Galahad lose?"

"Galahad is on a quest to find a special cup called the Holy Grail." Andros's voice changed as he began to read aloud.

Laylie closed her good eye and let the story make pictures in her head.

"Galahad died?" Laylie asked, pressing her hand to her middle when he finished. The stories JoMa told didn't hurt, even when wolves got clobbered.

"The hero often dies in stories of quests," Andros said, as if that made it all right.

Laylie sat quietly, thinking of Luke as Galahad lying dead, looking beautiful with his sword at his breast, all because he had gone off without her.

Andros built up his fire, adding some green leaves so the smoke would drive the mosquitos away.

"Well, Laylie girl?" said a voice.

Laylie hadn't even heard Luke come up behind her. She turned and wrapped her arms around his legs. "I thought you forgot me!"

Luke knelt beside her and pressed her hand to his heart, which was beating fast from running.

"Feel that?" he asked. Laylie nodded. "It's saying Lay-lee, Lay-lee. Could I forget you with that racket going on?"

Luke looked up at Andros. "We have a deal?"

"You understand what you are asking?" Andros asked. "If she ever tells anyone what she is learning, they will kill me, sell you . . . and who knows what would happen to her."

"Mamma said learnin' is the first step to freedom," said Luke. "She said to learn when we could. I ain't never had the chance."

Andros ran his hand through his bushy hair.

"A teacher needs only two things," he said. "Books . . . and a student." He squatted in front of Laylie. "Do you truly want to learn?"

The first step to freedom. Laylie looked up at Luke, "I want to learn." Her voice was barely a whisper.

"Then put your hand on my stump," Andros said, holding it up in front of her, "and swear that you will never tell."

Laylie's Daring Quest

Laylie bit her lip as she reached for the pink and white stump. It was hot and soft beneath her hand, but she looked straight into Andros's eyes.

"I swear." She held her hand there a second longer before she snatched it away and slipped it into Luke's.

"Finding Mamma's freedom," she said, "is our quest."

4

Dead Pigs and Live Gators

"I revealed myself to those who did not ask for me; I was found by those who did not seek me. To a nation that did not call on my name, I said, 'Here am I, here am I.'"

ISAIAH 65:1

Dead Pigs and Live Gators

*L*aylie glanced around to make sure no one was watching before she ducked into the brambles at the edge of the swamp. The early summer growth on the berry bushes was threatening to choke the path. One thick new wand smacked her in the nose. Laylie set down the basket she was carrying and pulled a red cotton string from her hair. *The colored strings Lucindy insists on tying in my hair are pretty, and sometimes very useful, too,* Laylie thought. She wrapped the thick new wand around an older branch and used the string to tie it in place, stopping once to shake her sore hands so her fingers could manage the small knot. She'd have to borrow Andros's jackknife again to trim the wands and creepers, or her path would disappear.

When she stepped out of the leafy tunnel, the bird calls and insect buzzing told her that all was well. Three years ago, when Luke first carried her to Andros's hut, these same sounds had given her the shivers. They were comforting now, the sounds of peace in the swamp. She knew each voice and the creature that made it. Andros had taught her about them, showing her how to trace out the letters of their names in a patch of smooth sand.

Even after Isaac had married Hettie and carried her away to live with him, JoMa had not let Laylie stay at the cabin during the day to help take care of the babies. Instead she wanted Laylie to continue learning from Andros. "Master don't want you learning to read," JoMa said when they were all alone. "Seems to me there's somethin' in those books they don't want you to find. Somethin' important. You find it, girl. Go and find it!"

Laylie's Daring Quest

Laylie had found wonderful stories in those books and words she couldn't speak out loud to anyone but Andros. Andros himself was better than a hundred books, full of answers to every question she asked.

Laylie stepped lightly as she drew close to the clearing. The light was dimmer here, the far trees swallowed in swamp shadow. She moved into the clearing very quietly, hoping to catch Andros sleeping. He'd jump right out of his skin when she said—

"Hello," a voice said behind her.

Laylie squeaked and almost dropped the basket.

"Andros! How'd you do that?"

"I was sitting right here, watching a lizard," Andros said innocently. "And you walked past. Where have you been for the past week?"

"Busy." Laylie held up the basket she had brought, as he climbed down from the split tree where he'd been perched. "I thought I'd come along and see if you'd starved."

Andros snorted. "The swamp is just as full of snakes and possums as it was before you came along. But you've never missed a week of school before. Put that up and wash your hands."

Laylie set the basket by the hut door. She went to the bucket, but she couldn't force herself to scoop up the sand.

"I . . . can you read to me today?" she asked.

"Read to you? I haven't read to you in a year or more." He caught her wrist and turned her palm up. The blisters across her palms had burst, leaving weeping wounds.

"I can't wash 'em off with sand," Laylie said, trying not to wince as he examined them. "Blood'll get on the books."

"They have set you to work in the fields, haven't they? Can you be ten already?"

754

"I came to tell you to get ready," said Laylie, pulling her hand away. "We can't stay much longer. If we get called to go north with the field hands Master Phil sends to Roselands at harvest, we'll make our strike for freedom from there."

"Did Luke tell you to tell me this?" he asked.

Laylie pressed her lips together.

Andros folded his arms. "I asked if Luke told you to tell me this?"

Laylie folded her arms too. "I ain't going without you, no matter what he says."

"Am not," Andros said. "You can use correct grammar here, if nowhere else."

"Am not," Laylie repeated, "going without you. You'd starve out here all alone."

"I see. How soon do the wagons leave?" Andros asked.

"They go up to help with harvest, so we've got some time. They take a supply wagon," Laylie said. "I don't have it all figured, but maybe you could hide in that."

"Hide in it?" Andros frowned. "You suppose no one will notice an ancient, one-handed black man sitting in the wagon?"

"You told me plenty of times," Laylie said. "If you can't outrun them or outfight them, you gotta outthink them. You could outthink anybody, Andros."

"Then I will start thinking about what must be done," he said. "Now, which book for your last day in Andros Walsh's school?"

"*Robin Hood*," Laylie said without hesitation. She had long since read through *Ivanhoe* and the *Roundtable Tales* as well, but the first book she had ever opened was still her favorite. Andros sat on his log chair and Laylie leaned against his knee. He read until the shadows disappeared at noon, then Laylie unpacked the cornbread and jar of black-strap molasses from the basket and divided it between them.

"If you find your aunt," he said, laying the book aside, "are you going to stay in New York City or go on to Canada?"

"No ifs about it." Laylie licked molasses off her finger-tips. "Luke says we gotta find her. She's the only family we got — she's a Colbert. We'll stay in New York."

"No child of a free woman can be a slave. That is the let-ter of the law," said Andros as he set the book aside. "But in reality, the courts are not friendly to free Africans, not even in New York City. It might be a hard thing to prove that your mamma was free."

"Have you ever been to New York City?" Laylie asked.

"No," Andros said. "But I've heard that there are schools there — African Free Schools, where black children can get an excellent education."

"I don't want any other school besides this one," Laylie said.

Andros was studying her. "What do you want to be, Laylie?" he asked. "What do you want to do with your life?"

"I want to be free," Laylie said.

The old man laughed. "Freedom isn't worth a thing if you don't do something with it. It's like having a very fine horse. Are you going to ride it somewhere, or just look at it?"

"Did you want to be a teacher?" Laylie asked as she put the empty blackstrap molasses jar back in her basket. "Is that what you did with your freedom?"

"Yes," Andros said, "it's all I ever wanted to be."

"Why?" she asked.

"Because I thought that a teacher could change the world."

"Did you change it?"

Andros looked at her for a long moment. "I hope so," he said at last. "I do hope so. Sometimes we do not get to see the results of our efforts."

"Like when you taught that man to write, but never knew if he made it to freedom?"

"Exactly like that," Andros said.

Laylie stood up and brushed the cornbread crumbs from her lap. "I'll be back next Sunday. Maybe by then I'll have figured out how to get you to the wagon, and to hide you in it."

"Sunday, then. Good-bye, Laylie Colbert," he said.

Laylie kept to the bushes as long as she could on her way home. Master Phil had done well for himself in the last three years. There were a hundred more slaves on Meadshead, twelve new cabins, and thousands of acres of land. Borse had a black driver, Robson, and a white man named Wash Hode, to help him keep the slaves in line.

It was well before dark when Laylie stepped out onto the roadway that ran from the fields to the quarters. People were drifting home, careful not to be out too late.

"Laylie!" Hettie was holding Isaac's hand. "Are you sneaking off into the bushes again? Why didn't you come to meeting?"

"She wasn't sneaking off," Isaac pointed out. "She was sneaking back. But you could come to the meeting next time, Laylie."

"I promised not to," Laylie said. Isaac and Hettie glanced at each other. Laylie had told them this a thousand times before.

Laylie's Daring Quest

"Why? Why won't Luke let you come?" Isaac asked.

Laylie shrugged. JoMa said that Isaac was the reason the rest of the slaves got whipped, what with his stirring people up so they'd sneak away for meetings and all. Before Isaac had come with his singing and praying, Borse had never checked the cabins at night. Now he came around with Hode and whipped anyone he found outside after dark.

Borse hated Isaac more than any slave on the place, but he couldn't do anything about it. Master Phil showed Isaac off like a prize stallion. When they had drinking parties up at the Big House, he would call Isaac up from the fields and have him strip off his shirt and then lift a wagon or an anvil and hold it up while the guests walked around him. After a time, Master Phil would ask how much a slave like that — black as night, strong as an ox, without mark or blemish — was worth. If Hettie was there, she would bow her head and pray while Master Phil listened to their offers, fearing that the drink or the money would go to his head and he would sell her husband away. She'd keep right on praying until after he turned every offer down.

"Laylie," Isaac said, "God's calling your name. He's calling Luke, too, to come be His child. He told me so."

"What does God sound like when he talks?" Laylie asked, walking beside them.

"Sometimes a whisper of love," Isaac said. "Sometimes a shout of gladness. And sometimes . . . sometimes He speaks to me in words, saying, 'Isaac, go do this or that.'"

"I never heard any of those things," Laylie said.

"You listen. You'll hear Him. Come to meeting next time, and bring Luke with you," Hettie said as Laylie turned toward JoMa's cabin.

Dead Pigs and Live Gators

Laylie was quiet as she sat beside Luke that night. She wanted to ask about the wagons and about carrying Andros out of the swamp, but she knew they couldn't talk of such things in the cabin. Not where the little boys might hear and repeat it. *How far is it to New York City? Andros will know. He will have drawn a map in the sand. Funny that in all the times we've talked about New York and Aunt Tempie, I didn't think to ask him how far it is or how long it will take to get there.*

⌒‿⌒

"Work faster," Wim said. "He'll be coming by, and we better have a pile done."

Laylie used her teeth to tighten the rags JoMa had wrapped around her hands. The fields were too dry for planting rice, and the river too low to irrigate. A few fat raindrops had splashed to the ground the day before, raising hopes and settling dust, but the clouds had rolled away without a downpour. Now they were clearing land, cleaning bone-dry ditches, and the machete handle was just as rough as the handle of a hoe.

Laylie stopped to wipe the sweat from her brow.

"You decided yet, Wim?" she asked.

"You're kinda small for running, ain't you?" Wim said. "If they catch us —"

"They won't," Luke said from the other side of the brush pile.

"She's too little, Luke," Wim said. "We could make it without her, but her legs ain't half long enough. Borse will be after us lickety-split, and he'll have hounds."

"I thought of it, but I ain't leavin' her," said Luke as he slashed at the dry brush. "If we strike from Roselands the night before the wagons come back here, Borse won't have any hounds, and he won't have time to chase us, neither."

"I'll go," Wim said. "If I'm on the wagon to Roselands, I'll go."

"I heard Borse is taking them wagons early," said Lucindy, who already decided she wasn't going anywhere. "On account of the droughty weather."

Laylie stopped her machete in mid-swing and started to open her mouth.

"Speak of the devil," Luke said, just as Laylie's ears picked up the dull thud of the horse's hooves on dry dust. She went back to hacking at the canes, watching from the corner of her eye as Borse rode by. He was red-faced and sweating, just sitting on his horse in the heat. Bullseye ambled beside the horse, his tongue lolling out of his mouth. The slaves worked in silence until the sound of hooves faded.

"How early?" Laylie asked, when they were alone again.

"Next week, I heard," said Lucindy.

Next week! *What if they leave before Andros is ready? Before I can figure out a plan?* The dinner shot sounded in the distance, and everyone stopped. Wim wiped his brow.

"What if you don't get called for the wagons?" asked Wim.

"Then I'll figure something out," Luke said as they started to walk home. "They say Master Phil wants to get as many off the place as he can till things start to grow. If he sends us to Roselands, they got to feed us."

"Luke," Laylie said as she took his hand and pulled him to a stop. "I got to go see Andros," she whispered. "I got to."

"You all go on, Wim," Luke said. "Laylie and me got some thinkin' to do."

Dead Pigs and Live Gators

"How are we gonna get Andros on that wagon?" Laylie asked when Wim and Lucindy had walked away.

"I don't know," he said.

"Well, Andros will," she said, pulling him toward the swamp. "He said he'd think on what to do."

Luke shook his head, but he came with her, walking across the stubble of a crop that wouldn't grow. The fields were dried up, leaving sinkholes of dark water here and there where fields of rice should have been ankle-deep in water.

"What's that smell?" Laylie wrinkled her nose.

"Something dead," Luke said. He stopped and scanned the sky. A buzzard was settling in a sweet gum tree, the only spot of shade around. "Let's go see what."

"Master Phil lost a pig," Laylie said when they got there. The carcass was bloating in the sun, three stiff legs pointing at the sky. The pigs ran free in the fields after the crops were in, eating what they could find. This year there hadn't been a crop.

"Where's its other leg?" Laylie held her nose as she walked closer.

Luke pointed at the sinkhole thirty feet away. Flies buzzed along a trail of thick black blood leading back to the water.

"Gator took it. Somebody's gonna hafta pull him outta there, or he'll eat more pig."

"Stink draws more than flies," Luke said as he saw Borse riding up on the other side of the sinkhole. He saw them standing over the carcass and swung his horse toward them.

"What you got over there?" Borse called, as Bullseye loped down to the water's edge to lap at the oily-looking liquid.

761

"It's a pig, Master Borse," Luke yelled. Suddenly, the water in front of Bullseye exploded in reptile jaws. The gator lunged so fast it seemed as though Bullseye leapt down its throat on purpose. The horse reared, but Borse reined it down, pulling his pistol from his belt.

Laylie stood with her mouth hanging open, hardly believing what she had seen. It had happened so fast that no one had time to say a word. Red blood welled in brown water, staining the surface, but there was no other sign of Bullseye. The devil dog was gone, gone into the biggest gator she had ever seen.

Borse pointed his pistol at the still waters, as if he could force the gator to release his dog, then he changed his mind and lifted the gun to point at Luke. He kicked the horse into motion, but the pistol never wavered as he came toward Laylie and Luke.

"You knew," Borse said when he reined up. "You knew there was a gator in that hole, and you didn't warn me. That dog was worth ten of you. I swear I'd kill you right now if I didn't need somebody to haul it out. Girl, run get Wash Hode. Tell him we got a gator; he'll know what to bring. And you, boy—drag that pig outta here. It's offendin' my nose."

Laylie turned and ran, her ears straining for the sound of a shot the whole way.

"Wash is up to the Big House, visiting his gal," Robson said when Laylie found him. "Why you lookin' for him?"

"Borse has got a gator in a hole," she said.

Laylie found Wash on the back porch of the Big House, sitting in a wicker rocking chair drinking lemonade.

"Gator," she managed to gasp. "Borse says you know what to bring."

"Well," he said. He belched, then smiled. "We're gonna have some fun then, ain't we?"

Laylie wished she could grab him and hurry him along, but she couldn't do a thing but wait while he finished his drink. He patted his belly, belched again, and then heaved himself up out of the wicker chair. He stopped at the toolshed for a hook-pole and a hatchet. Word had spread, told by Robson, Laylie guessed. People started coming from the kitchen and the stables. Field slaves who were eating their dinner stood up and came along when they saw the crowd moving toward the fields after Wash.

Luke was standing very still at the water's edge when they arrived, right where Bullseye had disappeared. Borse stood in the shade of the sweet gum tree, his pistol still in his hand.

"Take that pole to the boy," Borse said. Wash walked partway, then tossed the pole to Luke. He caught it with one hand. Wash tossed the hatchet, and Luke caught it with his other hand. The crowd that had followed along was buzzing with talk. Borse motioned Luke toward the water with the pistol, and everyone went quiet as he stepped in.

"Is it a big one, Laylie?" Wim asked, pushing his way through to her elbow.

Laylie nodded. Luke slapped the water, once, twice, with the end of his pole. There was a slow roiling under the surface, as if something huge had stirred and then gone still.

Luke waded farther out, watching the murky water for any ripple of movement that would show him where the reptile was. Suddenly he whirled, and in a blink he had disappeared beneath the surface.

Laylie screamed.

"Quiet!" Borse yelled, just as Luke's head broke the surface.

Luke scrambled out of the water, spitting filthy liquid. He wiped his hand across his mouth.

"Lost my step," he said. "Deeper than I thought. But he's awake, all right. Brushed right by me."

"Get back in there," Borse said, raising his gun. "I said get in there and bring him up."

Luke turned the hatchet over once, twice, hefting its weight.

"Don't think I don't know what's in your mind," Borse said. "You throw that thing at me — " the pistol turned to point at Laylie's head, " — I shoot your sister."

"I don't care, Luke," Laylie shouted. "Don't go back!"

Luke turned to the still, dark waters. The hook staff was floating. He started wading in.

"I'm gonna help," Wim said, starting forward.

"Nobody's gonna help," Borse said. "You know why not? Because I said not. And if anybody tries, I'll shoot 'em right between the eyes."

Wash grabbed Laylie's arm as she started toward her brother, gripping it until it hurt.

Luke's hand was on the handle of the hook now, and not a moment too soon, as there was a swelling in the water before him. The alligator surfaced just to look around. Luke lunged forward, catching the hook under the gator's front leg. The sharp iron cut into the animal's soft under-side, making it thrash and almost causing Luke to lose his grip on the pole.

"You got him, Luke!" Wim shouted. "Hold him now . . ." His voice faded as he saw the size of the monster. Luke dug in his feet and leaned back on his heels, the muscles in his back standing out like ropes. If he could drag the gator to land he could kill it with the hatchet. In the water he had no chance.

Laylie twisted against Wash's grip, silent tears on her face. *Luke can't hold that monster. Not by himself.*

"Lord," she said, "Isaac says you're calling Luke to be your child." She hadn't prayed since they took Melia, but the words spilled out of her now. "He can't do it if the gator eats him! Help him!"

"You think the Lord wants the likes of your brother?" Wash laughed. "You think the Almighty hears dirt people pray? I think He hears the gator, that's what I think. You just watch and see who He answers."

Laylie tried to turn her head away, but Wash twisted his hand in her hair. She caught a glimpse of someone coming across the field just as he jerked her face back around.

"Please, Lord, please!" she pleaded. "Let it be . . ."

"Hold on, Luke!" someone shouted.

Wash turned to see where the voice came from, and Laylie gave a sob of relief. It was Isaac, running across the field full tilt and furious.

"Stay back!" Borse yelled, lifting his pistol, but if Isaac heard him, he never slowed down. The pistol bucked in Borse's hand, but Isaac ran right on past, leaping the last six feet into the water. He grabbed the end of Luke's pole and gave a mighty heave. The gator heaved back, but Isaac's footing wasn't any better than Luke's. They were both being pulled deeper into the pool.

"God has a word for you, gator!" Isaac bellowed. "He . . . says . . ." he heaved on the pole again, "let . . . my . . . people . . . go!"

CHAPTER

Plans and Good-byes

Two are better than one, because they have a good return for their work: If one falls down, his friend can help him up. But pity the man who falls and has no one to help him up!

ECCLESIASTES 4:9-10

Plans and Good-byes

"Haul on my count," Luke said. "One, two, three!"

He and Isaac heaved together, gained a foot, and heaved again. The gator must have sensed it was losing the battle, because suddenly it opened its huge mouth and lunged toward them.

Isaac lost his footing and went down in the water, but Luke leapt sideways, twisting the pole with all his might, pulling the jaws away from the preacher. The gator was coming on his own now, almost faster than Luke could move. People scattered as the monster followed him up onto dry land. It stopped, twisted, and clamped its jaws shut on the offending pole, snapping it like a straw.

In that instant, Luke threw himself forward, wrapped one arm around the gator's snout to keep the jaws shut, and swung the hatchet. The gator rolled, crushing Luke underneath its back, its tail lashing and legs clawing at the sky. Then Luke was up again, and Laylie didn't know whether the blood was his or the gator's. The hatchet flashed again and again before the beast collapsed. Luke staggered to his feet, his chest heaving, blood running down his arm and dripping from his fingertips. Isaac waded out of the water and stood beside him.

"By Jove!"

Laylie hadn't seen Master Phil ride up. "Well done!" said Master Phil. "I'll have his hide for boots!" Master Phil dismounted, handed the reins to Wim, and walked as close as possible without stepping in the mud with his shiny black riding boots.

Laylie pulled out of Wash's grip and ran to Luke.

"Are you kilt?" she asked him.

"Nope," Luke replied as he flung blood from his fingertips over the water.

"You may want to tourniquet that," said Master Phil, pulling a white kerchief from his pocket and holding it out. "Luke, isn't it? Wrap it tight now, and it'll stop the bleeding. I'll send something around for you, I certainly will!"

Laylie took the handkerchief and twisted it around her brother's arm. "And Isaac! Magnificent! I saw you running and thought that something must be amiss," Master Phil went on. He turned his attention to the dead gator and Borse, who was standing over it. "Skin this creature, Ronald, and have the hide sent to be cured."

Laylie put her arm around Luke and pulled him away as Borse took his knife from its sheath. Isaac stepped close enough to catch Luke if he fell.

"Isaac," Laylie said, "I thought you was shot."

"Shot?" he felt his head. "Somethin' did buzz past my ear."

Luke was steady on his feet now, but Laylie didn't let go of him. Isaac walked close on the other side, glancing sideways at Luke now and then. People parted to let them pass. Hettie pushed her way through the crowd. She slipped her little hand into Isaac's big, muddy one, and they walked together all the way to JoMa's front door.

JoMa took one look, then she shooed the little boys away and started gathering what she needed to doctor Luke's arm.

"Wrestlin' gators!" JoMa said, shaking her head as if it had been Luke's own idea. "Well, it ain't too bad. I seen baby rash worse'n that on your behind, so I expect you'll live."

Plans and Good-byes

Wim and Lucindy arrived, and Exter, Max, and Cicero crowded close as Wim told about the battle. When he reached the part of the story where Isaac landed in the water beside Luke, he stopped.

"Why . . . why'd you come running like that, Isaac?" Luke asked.

Isaac glanced at JoMa, who was bent over Luke's arm, and then at Hettie. She smiled and nodded at him.

"I was talking with God when the Holy Spirit said, 'Get a move on. Luke needs help.' So I moved. I moved as fast as I could."

JoMa looked up at him, lips pursed, but Isaac went on, "God is calling your name, Luke. He's saying, 'Come to Jesus, come to My Son.' Me and Hettie—we pray for you all every single day, pray that you will listen to His call."

"Hush that!" JoMa said. "I don't want to hear it around here. I've been to the white man's church, been filled as full as I ever wants to be with the white man's religion." She worked as she talked, cleaning every bit of mud from Luke's arm.

"My first master, Thomas Brady, used to take a great string of us along the road, walking behind his carriage to church. When we got there we had to sit on a log with the sun beating down, while a white man preached at us. He holds up his God-Book and says, 'God's Word says you was born to be a slave, so don't kick about it. It says the Master and Missus know what's good for you. Obey them. That makes Jesus-God happy. And don't you steal from them, or you go right to Hell.' Monday morning, that old man would be whippin' us again for trying to fill our bellies when he wouldn't give us no food. Little chillen whipped to the grave. That was an evil place." She shook her head. "People sang and shouted for joy when they was sold off that place."

771

She had finished cleaning Luke's arm and was wrapping it in strips of cloth. "If slavery is what Jesus-God wants for us, then I don't want no part of Him!" She finished tying the rag around Luke's arm with a tug that made him wince.

"JoMa," said Hettie. Everyone stopped and looked at her. "I always respect what you say. You took me in as a little child and you raised me up. You told me, 'Don't forget Africa. Remember the stories. Remember the wisdom of your people, the place where we were free before man-stealers came.'"

JoMa put her fists on her hips. "Then why have you forgot?"

Isaac put his hands on his wife's shoulders and bowed his head like he did when he was talking to God, but the words weren't coming out of him.

"I haven't," Hettie said gently. "I haven't, JoMa. We had our own kings and kingdoms in Africa, and wise men and women. That's what you said. We had stories that told us the truth." JoMa pursed her lips, but Hettie went on. "Remember the story of the Tortoise and the Lizard? You told it to me, JoMa."

"Tell the story, JoMa!" Exter shouted, but JoMa didn't say anything.

"I can tell it," Hettie said. "I'm carrying this story from Africa in my heart, because you put it there, JoMa.

"When God finished all of His creating," Hettie began, "He wanted to send people a message. He looked around for a critter to carry His words, and He seen a tortoise. She was slow-moving, but wise and faithful. He called that tortoise up to Him and said, 'Go, tell the people, after they dies, they can come back to life. There is a way.'

"Now, when God said that, there was a lizard listenin'. She was faithless and stupid, but she was real fast. She ran to tell the people 'bout God's message before the tortoise arrived, so she could be more important than the tortoise. The lizard reached the people while the tortoise was still making her way.

"The lizard said, 'God say this: After death there ain't no return. There ain't no way.' People heard the lizard's message, and they figured it was true, all right, 'cause the lizard say God said it.

"Now, the tortoise was comin' fast as she could, carrying the true message from God. When she got there, the tortoise said, 'Good news, people! God says, after you die, you can return to life. There is a way!'

"But the people wouldn't listen to the true message from God 'cause they'd already heard from the lizard. They say, 'You fool tortoise, we already knows we're gonna die, and death is the end of everything.' The people had no ears for the true message from God, because of the lizard's words."

Wim, Lucindy, and Luke were looking from Hettie to JoMa, but the old woman turned her back.

"JoMa," Hettie said, and all the love in creation was in her voice, "don't you listen to the lizard. That man did not preach God's Word to you. God didn't say you was born to be a slave and God didn't want you starved and beat. He loves you as His very own chile, and He —"

JoMa shooed them away. "Go on. We don't need you around here."

Laylie was surprised to see tears in JoMa's eyes.

"You know you're always welcome at the meeting," Isaac said, looking around to include all of them. "We'll be

waiting for you, praying every day until you come." He took Hettie's hand and they walked away.

"Luke," Laylie asked, "who's the Holy Spirit?"

"Nobody," Luke said.

"Then how'd he tell Isaac you needed help? Can't we go to the meeting and—"

"No."

"But Luke, I prayed and—"

"You made a promise," said Luke. He grabbed her with his good hand and shook her hard. "You said you'd never go to Isaac's meeting. Never."

"But I did pray!" Laylie said when her teeth stopped rattling. "And God sent Isaac to help you! If you went with me . . ."

"I ain't going," Luke said. "And you won't neither. Colberts keep their word, that's all."

Master Phil did send something along for Luke, just like he said—a brown paper package. Everyone crowded around as Luke opened it and held up a fine red shirt with a double row of shiny black buttons. Luke tried it on, and Laylie thought he was the handsomest thing she'd ever seen.

"Borse sees that shirt, he'll remember why you got it. He'll remember his devil dog every time he sees it go by. Better fill it full of rocks and sink it in the swamp," JoMa said.

Luke peeled it off. "I'll think on it a while."

"If Borse don't call us to work at Roselands," Laylie said as she chopped at the weed with her hoe, "we're still making our strike, right?" She tried not to let Luke see how worried she was about him. He insisted on coming to the fields with her even though his arms were sore and blood sometimes seeped through the bandages. He could have stayed at JoMa's at least a day, but he wouldn't do it.

"Borse will call us," Luke said. "Master Phil won't be around at Roselands to stop his wicked ways. I seen him watching us. You and me. Stay close to me when we go. We won't have nobody looking after us, just each other."

So Luke seen it too, seen Borse watching us with his crazy-man eyes, thought Laylie.

"Can I take that red shirt to Andros?" Laylie asked. "He could find someone to trade it to before we go."

"Probably better to get it out of the house before Lucindy decides to wear it," Luke said.

"I'll take it Sunday," Laylie promised. "I still don't know how I'm gonna get Andros on the wagon."

Luke stopped and leaned on his hoe handle.

"We're out of time, Laylie girl," he said. "We've gotta go, no matter who's on the wagon. No matter who we have to leave."

Laylie just went on hoeing up the dry weeds. *Andros will be there. He said he would think about what must be done, and Andros can outthink anybody.*

Sunday morning, Laylie rolled up the shirt, stuffed two sweet potatoes in her pockets, and ran down the road to her shortcut through the bramble hedge. The tide was up, so she took the long way around to avoid the channels where the gators might be hunting. She moved so silently that the birds and insects didn't pause in their summer song as she passed.

"Andros!" she called, when she stepped into the clearing. "You're not watching your back door!" The swamp-song hushed at the sound of her voice.

"Andros?" Silence. There was no curl of smoke, no smell of burning wood.

Laylie ran to the door of the hut and stooped to look inside. He wasn't there. She looked around the clearing again. The ashes in the fire pit showed the clear print of raindrops, and the footprints in the sandy soil had rain spatters in them as well. *When did it rain? Five days ago, at least. Five days since there has been a fire in the pit, since someone walked here.*

Witches drag people to Hell . . .

Andros said he wasn't afraid of witches. But gators and painter cats could drag people off too. Wim told me of a man who was work-ing in the camps clearing canals, and a gator came and took him in the night. But a gator or cat would have left tracks, and there aren't any.

Laylie crawled into the hut. Andros's blanket was gone. The sea turtle shell lay in its usual spot. She lifted it. The books were missing, and in their place a single word was carved deep in the hard-packed dirt of the floor.

Freedom.

It was wobbly as all Andros's words had been, scratched with his left hand that had never learned to write well, no matter how hard he tried.

Laylie felt the tears rising up in her chest, rising up from her heart and spilling out her eyes. *Does he think he can get to New York City without me? He's too old to make it by himself. He can't even catch rabbits! Cobbled up, that's what Luke called him. Too old and cobbled up to walk to New York City. 'Then I will start thinking about what must be done' — that's what Andros had said. Hide in the swamp like a rotten skink . . . that's what he'd meant. Hide until I was gone.*

Laylie crawled out of the hut and brushed away her tears, searching the greenness for any sign of the old man.

Plans and Good-byes

There was no hint of which direction he had gone or where he might be hiding.

"I hate you, Andros!" she yelled. Carolina parakeets exploded from the trees, shocked to flight by her words. Laylie sat down on the log and cried into the red shirt until every tear was gone. Then she spread the shirt on her lap, brushed the tears and wrinkles away, folded it carefully, and put it under the turtle shell just in case he came back.

Three days later the shot didn't sound at four in the morning. The quarters were buzzing with excitement by the time the sun rose. Men and women gathered in the roadway, waiting as Borse called the names of the slaves who would travel to Roselands.

Luke's name was called, and then Laylie's. Wim stood beside them until every name was read out, but he wasn't on the list. When the men were ordered into line to be shackled, Wim just turned and walked away.

Lucindy wasn't called either, but Ruby and Priss were. "I'm gonna get me a husband at Roselands," Priss said. "A fine, tall house slave!"

Old Miss wouldn't allow her slaves to marry off the plantation. Lucindy said it was because she wanted all the children to be property of the Breandans, and none to profit the neighbors. But Roselands was owned by Old Miss's daughter Isabel and her husband, Horace Dinsmore, so it was considered family. The two plantations traded slaves back and forth, dividing the profits from the children produced between them. The slaves at Roselands held dances every year when the wagons from Meadshead came up.

Laylie's Daring Quest

Husbands and wives, who had not seen one another for a year, were reunited. Fathers saw babies they had never met, sometimes never even suspected were on the way.

Ruby, Priss, and the other girls who were going ran back to gather anything they had to dress up for parties — colored threads for their hair, pretty scarves, and shoes if they had them. Laylie stayed with the wagons and close to Luke, afraid to lose sight of him, afraid that if she saw JoMa or the little boys she would start bawling like a baby, and someone would guess she wasn't coming back.

Luke moved along with the other men and then stood patiently while the heavy iron shackle was fastened on his ankle. The blacksmith had each man put his left leg up on the anvil. He wrapped the shackle around it, then placed a rivet into the hole designed to fasten the halves of the metal cuff together, and slammed it once with his hammer, flattening the top of the rivet and fixing it in place. Then he told them to move along.

After each ten men were fitted, Wash ran a heavy chain through loops on the ankle irons, fastening the men together. It was noon before the chains were in place and the men were sitting in rows in the wagons. Borse gave the command, and they started forward. Laylie looked back. JoMa was leaning on her broom in the dirt yard. Laylie lifted her hand, but JoMa just stood looking after them.

The moment Laylie's feet hit the hard-packed dirt of the road, her heart broke open. *Every place my foot has ever touched — even Andros's clearing in the swamp — has belonged to Master Phil. Just like they say I belong to Master Phil. Now I am walking down a road that don't belong to nobody, not nobody at all. The road to freedom.*

Plans and Good-byes

They stopped for supper just at dusk, and after they'd eaten, the slaves lay on the hard ground while Borse and his men spread their blankets on the hay in the wagons. Laylie lay on her back and looked up at the stars. The drinking gourd was blazing, pointing the way to the North Star.

The same stars looking down on me are shining over JoMa and the little boys, and over Andros, and over free Africans walking on the streets of New York City. Andros said when the world spins around, they shine on Africa too — those very same stars.

Suddenly Laylie had the feeling that something more than the stars was watching her, something . . . someone bigger than the sky. *Luke said, "We have no one looking after us." But someone heard me when I prayed. Someone sent Isaac running to help Luke.*

"My name is Laylie Colbert," she whispered. "Do you know who I am?"

The Someone seemed to step closer, and suddenly Laylie was afraid. *Isaac's God is listening to me. Jesus-God heard my voice!* She jerked her blanket up over her head.

Of course Jesus-God listened to Isaac when he prayed. Isaac's good. I can feel goodness seeping out of him, hear it in his voice when he talks. Hettie's good, too.

But Laylie was suddenly very sure that she was not good, and Isaac's God knew it. He knew exactly who she was.

"Go away," she whispered.

6

Petticoats and Pantalettes

Man looks at the outward appearance, but the LORD looks at the heart.

1 SAMUEL 16:7

Petticoats and Pantalettes

hey set out just after sunup the next day, plodding along at the slow pace of the draft horses. When the women's feet grew tired, they would climb into the wagons wherever they could find space among the shackled men. Borse didn't seem to care, so long as the wagons kept moving. Luke used his elbows to push people aside to make room for Laylie when she wanted to ride.

As they drew closer to Charleston the road became a parade of people. Carriages, coaches, and wagons rattled and bounced over the ruts. White men on foot or on horseback waved or spoke to Borse as they went by. The slaves seemed to be invisible to the white travelers, but Laylie studied the travelers with interest. Many of them were poor, dressed in clothes as shabby as the ones worn by the slaves, but they had no master, no whip marks on their backs.

A group of men and women in iron collars linked together by chains passed them. One young woman had tears running down her cheeks and a baby in her arms. Two men on horseback hurried them along toward the market where they would be sold. *If Jesus-God saw me lying in the dark, didn't he see that mamma and baby too? If he could send Isaac running to help Luke, why didn't he send someone to help her?*

Laylie crawled up into the wagon. Luke's chains rattled as he made room for her.

"If you're good like Hettie says," Laylie whispered, "why don't you send somebody to break these chains and set us free?"

"What?" Luke said.

"Nothin'."

Just after sunset they passed a group of laughing young men who had stopped an elderly slave with hair as white as Andros's. One slapped his face, then shoved him to the ground.

"What are they doing?" Laylie asked.

"Patrollers having their fun," Luke said. "He's out past curfew, or he don't have a pass from his master allowing him to be walking on the road."

Laylie's stomach hurt. When she had dreamed about freedom in the top of the live oak tree, she could almost see it, just past the fields and hedges of Meadshead. Anywhere away from Borse and Wash Hode was free. But everyone out here on the road was like Borse. *How many patrollers will we have to pass to get to New York City?* she wondered.

Laylie was sitting beside Luke on the morning they turned onto the long, tree-shaded drive of Roselands. The Big House was just as fine as the one at Meadshead, with a wide veranda. A white woman was standing on it now, speaking to a man in a sharp, red riding coat and shiny black boots. She glanced at the wagon, then looked again. The woman pointed at the slaves as she spoke to the man in the red coat.

"Stop!" the man called. "Driver, stop!" The wagon stopped, and the driver looked inquiringly at Borse.

"Mr. Borse," the man said, "I trust that your journey was a pleasant one." His eyes went to the wagons of slaves. "And that everyone is in good health."

"Yes, sir, Mr. Dinsmore," Borse said in the same groveling voice he used with Master Phil.

The man in the coat must be Master Horace, the one that married Missy Isabel.

"This is my housekeeper, Mrs. Brown," Master Horace said, waving toward the woman beside him. "She is in need of a girl for the house just now, and she noticed that you have one in the wagon."

Borse looked at Laylie.

"Yes, that one," Mr. Dinsmore said, as if Borse's look had been a question. "She will work in the house for the duration of your stay."

Laylie grabbed Luke's arm, but he just shook his head and spread his hands.

"What is your name, child?" asked Mrs. Brown.

"Laylie, Missus."

"Laylie," Mrs. Brown said, "you are to come with me."

"You gotta go," Luke whispered.

Laylie scrambled out of the wagon and followed the woman up the steps and onto the veranda, looking back once before she stepped through the door. Luke lifted his hand.

Mrs. Brown walked so fast that Laylie had to trot to keep up, but that didn't keep her from gaping at everything around her. They passed glass-paned windows, and every one had curtains of the finest fabric Laylie had ever seen. *What Lucindy would give for just one length of that cloth!* There were little tables here and there along the hall, each with some pretty thing on it, a vase or little statue. Laylie caught a glimpse of chairs with curled legs and a table with lion's feet in one room as they hurried past. When they reached the back of the house, Mrs. Brown led her out the door and down the steps.

"You can't wear that to work in the house," she said, waving at Laylie's shirt. Her voice was kinder than it had seemed outside. "Olivia keeps the extra clothes. I expect she has a

dress your size. And you are going to need some shoes, as well. You've never worked in the house, have you?"

"No, Missus," Laylie said.

"I thought not. This is a great opportunity for you, if you are an honest, hard worker. If you do well, you may never have to work in the fields again."

"Yes, Missus."

"I'm glad you understand that," Mrs. Brown smiled. "Come along." The woman led her to the kitchen, and a black woman looked up from the stove as they went through. "What," she asked, pointing a spoon at Laylie, "is that dirty field child doin' in my kitchen?"

"Now, Phoebe," Mrs. Brown said. "She's too little to work in the fields. I don't know what they were thinking, sending her along. She will be working in the house."

Phoebe snorted. "Where's she gonna sleep? You gonna send her out with the field hands every night?" Laylie looked up hopefully, but Mrs. Brown shook her head.

"She can sleep in the kitchen," she said, "and tend the firebox."

"I'll show you tendin' . . ." Phoebe muttered. Laylie edged past her and hurried out the back door after Mrs. Brown. The laundry house was a short walk from the kitchen door. When they entered, they were met by a stout, middle-aged woman with a friendly smile.

"Olivia, this one needs a little fixing up," Mrs. Brown said.

Olivia winked at Laylie. "I think I can manage."

"Then I will leave her to your care," Mrs. Brown said. "Bring her to me when you have finished."

"Straight from the fields, ain't you, child?" Olivia asked. "Well, first things first, and the first thing you needs is a

bath." She showed Laylie a big washtub, already full of water.

"I scrubbed underthings in it this morning," she said. "It's still clean enough to scrub you."

Laylie looked at the milky water uncertainly.

"You've been swimmin' before, ain't 'cha?" Olivia said. Laylie nodded. "Well! Just pretend that's a pond," she said, pulling Laylie's long shirt over her head, "and hop on in." Laylie stepped into the water.

"That's not too bad, is it?" Olivia laughed. "I used rose soap on the underthings, so you're gonna smell awful good when we get done!"

After Laylie was scrubbed from head to toe, Olivia produced a stack of clothing. Laylie picked up what looked like a pair of white pants.

"House slaves wear decent underclothes," Olivia explained. "Those are pantalettes. You put 'em on, now. And this," she held up a white skirt, "is a petticoat. It goes on over the pantalettes. Decent women never shows their limbs, and they don't want to see yours, neither!"

Laylie struggled into the strange garments with a little help from Olivia.

"Now we pull the dress over your head . . ." Olivia did so as she spoke, then pulled it tight with a wide green sash. "You do have hair, don't you!" Olivia combed the tangles out of Laylie's hair, then twisted it into braids and tied them with ribbons.

"Does your mamma know what a pretty baby she made? 'Course she do," she said, not waiting for an answer. "Bet she tells you all the time!"

"Well!" she said at last. "If your feet wasn't sticking out, you'd look almost civilized! Pick up that stack of clean things, and we'll carry them in."

Laylie's Daring Quest

Laylie's skirts made a strange swish-swish sound as she walked behind Olivia up the steps to the back porch. She caught a glimpse of a little Miss in a yellow dress, started to drop her eyes, then looked again. It was her own reflection in the plate glass window!

"Here," Olivia laughed as she took the underthings from Laylie's arms. "Didn't I say you was a pretty thing?"

Laylie twirled. Her skirts spun out and she laughed, too. *What would Luke say about this?*

"Now don't be gettin' vain and glorious on me," said Olivia, handing Laylie back the stack of laundry. "We've still got work to do."

They went past the kitchen, up the back steps, through the door, and down a long carpeted hall. Olivia told her what was behind each door along the way. Then they turned and went up a back stairway.

"We've got two little Masters and four little Misses to look after at Roselands," Olivia said when they reached the nursery, "countin' the baby girl. And if their laundry ain't just right . . . ." She shook her head.

"Missy Isabel is a hard woman, but keep out of her way and you'll be fine. Specially if she's got one of her headaches. Mind your business, do your work, no matter what you see or hear. Nobody will take notice of you." They put the lacy underthings in drawers and went to find Mrs. Brown.

"Now doesn't she look pretty!" Mrs. Brown said, turning Laylie around and around as if she were a doll. "Thank you, Olivia. You may go." Olivia winked at Laylie on her way out.

"Let's get some shoes on you," said Mrs. Brown. The housekeeper sat Laylie in a chair and forced a pair of button-up boots onto her feet. "These are Miss Lora's castoffs . . ."

"Ouch," Laylie said. "They pinch, Missus!"

"Stand up," Mrs. Brown said, "and wiggle your toes."

Laylie stood up. "They won't wiggle!"

Mrs. Brown knelt and squished the toe of the boot in with her finger.

"Nonsense," she said. "You simply have to grow used to wearing them. Now —" she looked very serious, "—we are going to meet the mistress. Do you know how to curtsy?"

Laylie shook her head. Mrs. Brown showed her three times how to spread her skirt and bend her knee, and then led her down the hall to a closed door.

"Come in," a voice said. Mrs. Brown opened the door, and Laylie followed her into the room. Missy Isabel was sitting in front of a crackling fire, wrapped in a robe even though the day was warm. She looked so much like Old Miss that it made Laylie shiver.

"Is she from Meadshead?" Missy Isabel asked as Laylie curtsied.

"Yes, ma'am," Mrs. Brown said.

"Really, Mrs. Brown, you should have consulted me about this before you allowed her in the house." Missy Isabel stood and walked around her. Laylie could feel the woman's breath as she leaned in close to examine her hair. "Has she been checked for nits and lice, Mrs. Brown?"

"Olivia didn't find any vermin," Mrs. Brown assured her.

"I won't have vermin in the house." Missy Isabel sniffed, and Laylie was glad she smelled like roses. "Walk across the room, girl."

Laylie walked as well as she could in her new shoes.

"She is . . . ornamental," Missy Isabel said. "Now come here."

Laylie's Daring Quest

Laylie clomped back, and Missy Isabel grabbed her chin and pulled her mouth open to inspect her teeth.

"We are leaving for Philadelphia in a few days," she said at last. "So I will not be here to train her. But she will still be here when we return. If she has any rough edges left . . . I will smooth them."

"Yes, ma'am," said Mrs. Brown.

Laylie kept her eyes on the floor as she followed Mrs. Brown out the door.

"That went very well," Mrs. Brown assured her. "Very well indeed!"

Laylie spent the rest of the day itching in her new clothes and trying without success to wiggle her toes as she followed the housekeeper around the mansion learning her duties—cleaning ashes out of the fireplaces, carrying wood, and scouring copper pots and pans until they shone.

By the time she finished her assigned duties and helped clear the dishes from the Dinsmores' supper table, Laylie was so tired she could hardly stand up. At Meadshead, the field hands went to bed with the sun, but in the Big House at Roselands, they lit candles and lamps when the sun went down, and the slaves kept right on working. *Master Horace and Missy Isabel don't even eat their supper until the middle of the night,* thought Laylie as she carried the last stack of plates into the kitchen. She was surprised to find the house slaves sitting down at the table, piling mashed potatoes, meat, and biscuits on their plates.

"Hello," a tall black man with gray at his temples said. "Are you going to join us?"

Laylie shook her head, but he handed her his own plate full of food.

"Thank you," Laylie said.

"My name is Ajax," the man said. "I drive the Dinsmores' carriage. And you're Laylie. Phoebe has been telling us all about you." He winked. "But I heard about you from Olivia, too. She asked me to watch out for you."

Laylie nodded and sat down on the wood box, eating with her fingers while she listened to them talk.

She had learned some of the house slaves' names during the day—Jonati, the rawboned, grim woman with a loud voice, was the Dinsmore children's nurse. Annie and Sara were housemaids, and Harry, who was about Luke's age, worked in the stables when he wasn't serving as a doorman. Everyone was talking about Jonati and a Miss Worth, the governess of the little Masters and Misses, going off with Missy Isabel to Philadelphia.

After the meal was done, Phoebe poured tea and passed around a blue sugar bowl. Everyone took a lump and dropped it in their teacup. Ajax passed the bowl to Laylie, and she fished out a lump of sugar and slipped it in her pocket. If Luke came for her tonight, she'd give it to him.

Talk went on and on as the dishes were done. Finally, everyone said good night and went off to bed, leaving Laylie half asleep where she sat.

"There you are." Mrs. Brown's voice woke her. "You worked very hard today, and hard work makes for sound sleep." She handed Laylie two blankets. "You can use the horse blanket as a mat, and pull the other blanket over you. When you get up tomorrow, fold them and put them in the bottom of the table linen closet in the hall. Good night."

Laylie spread the thick wool blanket on the floor behind the stove and collapsed in exaustion.

CHAPTER

7

Toad Kissers and Merry Men

*Then Samson prayed to the LORD,
"O Sovereign LORD, remember me.
O God, please strengthen me just
once more, and let me with one
blow get revenge on the
Philistines for my
two eyes."*

JUDGES 16:28

A sharp pain jerked Laylie out of her dreams. Phoebe was standing over her, a wooden spoon raised to strike again. Laylie scrambled away from her. "The fire's gone out and the kindling box is empty," Phoebe said. "Get your lazy self up and get busy."

Laylie folded her blankets and carried them to the linen closet, and then hurried outside to chop kindling. When she had an armload, she brought it in and watched as Phoebe put small sticks and wood shavings into the stove's firebox, and coaxed them into flames. Soon the whole kitchen was warm as toast and the teakettle whistled a happy song, but it didn't improve Phoebe's mood.

The house slaves came in for a breakfast of cold biscuits that had been set aside the night before, while Phoebe sent porridge to the nursery. Then she cooked thick slices of ham, scrambled eggs, and pancakes for Master Horace. Mrs. Brown stepped into the kitchen to discuss the day's baking with Phoebe.

"Laylie," Mrs. Brown said when she had finished, "Take an ash bucket and clean the fireplace in the nursery. It was completely overlooked yesterday, and we don't want Mrs. Dinsmore to hear of such a thing two days in a row. See that a fire is laid there before you go on to the other rooms. And do not enter Mrs. Dinsmore's room until after she has risen for breakfast at ten. She is suffering from a headache this morning."

Laylie took the ash bucket and shovel and hurried to the house and toward the nursery, slowing to tiptoe past the door to Mrs. Dinsmore's room. She was reaching for the knob of the nursery door when it flew open and a little girl ran past, sobbing through a napkin pressed to her mouth. Laylie looked after her, uncertain what to do. *Mind your business, do your work, no matter what.* She shrugged and stepped into the nursery.

The rest of the Master's children were sitting at a table eating their porridge. Jonati was standing against the wall, a baby girl in her arms. When she saw the ash bucket, she waved Laylie toward the massive fireplace.

The children did not even glance up at Laylie as she went past. They were staring at a pudgy little boy with a smile on his face.

Laylie knelt by the fireplace and started to sweep up the ashes.

"Arthur, you are a *beast!*" said a voice.

Laylie leaned forward, peeking sideways at the children every time she turned to put a shovel full of ashes in the bucket.

"And Papa's going to spank you." It was the oldest girl talking.

"No, he won't," the plump boy said. "Mother won't allow it."

At that moment the nursery door opened, and Master Horace stepped in. Miss Worth was with him, holding the hand of the little girl who had run out in tears.

"Arthur," Master Horace said, "did you tell your sister that she will never marry?"

"Because of warts!" a smaller boy shouted. "Big, fat warts on her lips!"

The little girl started wailing again, louder than before.

"Is this what you told your sister?" Master Horace demanded.

"She kissed a toad, Father," Arthur said, "a big, horrid toad."

"She did not, Papa!" The oldest girl stood up. "The toad kissed her!"

Laylie put her hand over her mouth. *Mind your business, do your work, no matter what you see or hear* . . . But she could barely keep her giggles in.

"Will someone please explain?" Master Horace said.

"It's like this, Papa," the oldest girl stood up. "Arthur told Lora to close her eyes and he would give her a surprise . . . and then he held up a horrid toad and made it kiss her!"

"While her eyes were closed?" Master Horace asked.

The toad-kissing girl sobbed more loudly.

"And he says she will grow warts if she does not give him all her candy money while we are in Philadelphia. Because he has the cure, you see. For warts."

"Jonati?" Master Horace said.

"It was a toad, all right," Jonati answered. "I don't mess with no toads. I made him throw it out the window."

"No, Father, please . . ." Arthur screamed as Master Horace started toward him.

The door opened and Missy Isabel stalked into the room. Arthur ran to his mother and hid his face in her skirts, wailing loudly.

"Whatever the child has done, Horace," Isabel said, putting her hand to her head, "you must forgive him at once! He is making a horrible racket."

"He's going to beat me, Mamma!" Arthur sobbed.

"No one is going to strike you!" Missy Isabel said. "Of course not!"

"As you wish, Madam," Master Horace said. "Arthur, you may have no sweets, none at all, until we return from Philadelphia. And if you terrorize your sisters in such a manner again —"

Laylie's Daring Quest

"Horace, please!" Missy Isabel said, putting both hands to her head. "Miss Worth, take Arthur and Lora to the parlor and settle this where I can't hear it!"

"Yes, ma'am," Miss Worth said.

Laylie remembered that JoMa had said she worked in a Big House once, but she'd been glad to leave because the Master there was crazy. *Maybe Missy Isabel and her children are crazy too.* Laylie finished cleaning the fireplace, set the fire, then carried the ash bucket downstairs, careful not to spill any ashes. She had just passed Mr. Dinsmore's study when she heard Missy Isabel's voice, shouting at Mrs. Brown. Laylie dodged into the nearest room, pushing the door shut behind her.

The walls were lined from floor to ceiling with books. She set down the ash bucket and walked along the wall, just looking. *What would Andros say about this! He never told me there were this many books in the world!* Laylie stopped.

Robin Hood! Andros's book was on the shelf right in front of her. She started to reach for it, but realized her hands were covered with soot. *How could it have gotten here? He wouldn't have traded it away, not even for food.* She heard footsteps in the hall and dashed back to pick up the ash bucket. The footsteps passed, and Laylie stepped into the hall again and hurried out the back door to empty the ashes.

Mrs. Brown kept her busy for the rest of the day, but when Laylie lay down on her horse blanket that night, she couldn't sleep. She wasn't as tired as she had been the night before, and the kitchen seemed too big. It was empty of the right sounds—sounds of JoMa's snores—and full of all the wrong ones, like the scratching of mice's feet on the polished floor. Suddenly she missed Luke so hard it hurt, missed Lucindy, Wim, and the little boys, and Andros.

Toad Kissers and Merry Men

Laylie sat up. *His book is in the library! What if Luke comes for me tonight? I can't just leave it there. And with all those books on the walls, no one will notice it's gone.*

She took a candle from the table and padded barefoot up the back steps, slipping into the Big House. Shadows bobbed and leapt against the walls as she passed, and her heart pounded. Once in the library, she pulled the book from the shelf, then hurried through the dark hall. Back in the kitchen, she set the candle stub on the floor by her mat, opened the book, and started to read. She could hear the words in Andros's voice, and they washed the loneliness and fear right out of her. The kitchen was as grim as a dungeon, but if she were Robin Hood, the Merry Men would help her escape.

"Slaves aren't allowed to have books."

Laylie jumped so hard she banged her head on the stove. The plump little boy from the nursery was looking at her.

"If I tell Mamma, she'll smack you with her cowhide whip." His eyes narrowed. "But maybe I won't tell. If you get me some sweets."

"I'll get you some, Master Arthur," Laylie said, slipping the book under her blanket. "If you don't tell."

She looked around the kitchen. Phoebe's blue sugar bowl was on the shelf by the window. She pulled a chair over and took it down. "Here," she held out a sugar lump. He popped it in his mouth.

"S'good," he said, snatching the whole bowl.

"Don't eat them all," Laylie said, trying to take it back.

"Why not? They'll whip you for it, not me. You stole it right off the shelf." He shoved another in his mouth and crunched loudly. He kept right on until the bowl was empty. "Maybe I'll come back for some more tomorrow."

Laylie's Daring Quest

After he had gone, Laylie sat on her blankets, hugging Andros's book to her chest. *I'm gonna get a whipping for stealing sugar. Robin Hood never stole from the rich and gave to the rich.* She tucked the book under the covers again. *If I'm gonna get whipped, it's gonna be for stealing from the rich and giving to the poor, not for feeding sugar to a fat boy.*

Laylie looked around the kitchen, but there was nothing she could take except the pan of breakfast biscuits on the table. She wrapped them in a napkin and tied it with a long piece of string from Phoebe's scrap drawer, then slipped out the back door.

The half-moon was bright enough for Laylie to see her way down the path through the woods. The slave shacks were just on the other side of the woods, where they could not be easily seen from the Big House. *Which one is Luke in?*

The shadow of a man moved in between the shacks, and his cigar glowed as he took a draw on it.

Laylie stepped back into the woods. There was a stump there, where a giant tree had been felled with a crosscut saw, leaving a perfect wooden table. *The slave children must play here,* Laylie thought. *If I leave the biscuits, surely they will find them.* She looked around at the saplings that had sprung up from the roots of the felled tree. *If I tie the bundle of biscuits high enough, the racoons can't reach it but the children will see it.* She stood on the stump and tied the bundle of biscuits to one of the saplings as high as she could reach, and then hurried back toward the Big House.

Laylie jumped, as what she had thought was a stick moved on the hard-packed dirt in front of her, twisting into a snake. Her heart pounded until she saw the spots more clearly.

It was a rat snake, just like the ones Andros had caught in the swamp. Her hand darted down, and she caught it

behind the head, where it couldn't twist around and bite her with its tiny, sharp teeth. She held the snake carefully as she crept through the back door, then slipped out into the hall, walking shoeless and silently upstairs to the nursery.

Jonati was mumbling on her cot against the wall and the little misses were asleep. Laylie walked silently across the room to the bureau she and Olivia had filled with lacy underthings. She slid a drawer open and felt inside with her free hand. Lace. She dropped the snake in and closed the drawer quickly. Then she slipped back out into the hall and hurried down the stairs, out the back door, and all the way to the kitchen.

***

"Did you eat that sugar?" Phoebe's slap was still stinging on her cheek. The other house slaves were standing around behind the cook, and only one looked friendly.

Phoebe was ready to strike her again, but Ajax caught her arm.

"It's just sugar and biscuits," he said gently. "And I never did know anyone to have the truth beat out of them. More likely you'll beat out some lies."

"What is going on here?" Mrs. Brown had come into the kitchen.

"The sugar bowl is clean this morning," Phoebe said. "And every biscuit I cooked is missing. That child you brought in ate it all last night!"

"Stealing is a serious matter," Mrs. Brown said. "Did you eat the sugar, Laylie?"

"I—" Laylie said.

A scream from the Big House cut her off.

"My babies!" Jonati cried, pushing past Laylie. Everyone followed the shrieks through the halls, up the stairs, and to the nursery. Laylie had to wiggle through a crowd in the hall to see what was happening. Lora was standing on her bed, screaming and pointing at the open drawer.

"What is it, baby?" Jonati cried.

"Snake!" Lora said. "There's a snake in my drawer."

Jonati jumped right up with her, and started screaming as well. Mr. Dinsmore pushed his way through the crowd, and Laylie backed into a corner to watch.

"Quiet!" he bellowed, and both Jonati and Lora stopped screaming. He approached the drawer carefully, but when he saw the small snake, he reached in and pulled it out.

"It is not a poisonous variety," he said, carrying it to the window and tossing it out. "And not a variety that generally nests in ladies' bureau drawers either."

"What . . . what if it laid eggs in my petticoats, Papa?" Lora asked. "Don't snakes lay eggs?"

Jonati shrieked at the thought of hatchling snakes filling the underwear drawers.

"Please!" Master Horace said. "Stay calm! Snakes do not lay eggs in drawers. Where is Arthur?"

Arthur came forward.

"What did I tell you yesterday about terrorizing your sisters?" Master Horace said.

"But I . . . I didn't do it!" Arthur wailed, as his father turned him over his knee. Laylie slipped into the hall and leaned against the wall as she listened to Arthur's howls. *Robin Hood couldn't have done it any better!* She was sure of it.

Laylie hummed one of JoMa's songs from Africa to herself as she finished washing the dishes.

"I'm glad to see someone is cheerful," Mrs. Brown said. "You are the only one in this house in good humor, it seems." She looked at Laylie closely. "We were discussing biscuits and sugar when Lora screamed."

"I did not eat any biscuits or sugar, Missus," Laylie said. "I swear."

"Then what could possibly have happened to them?"

Laylie didn't say anything.

"You do understand that no one believes you?" Mrs. Brown shook her head. "It's fortunate for you that it is Saturday. The house slaves have Saturday afternoon off, and perhaps they will be in a more forgiving mood when they return this evening."

"Do field slaves have a day off too?" Laylie asked hopefully.

"No," Mrs. Brown said. "They only have Sundays off. However, you might meet some of the children and play this afternoon. Come back when the shot sounds."

Laylie skipped down the path to the clearing. The biscuits were gone, and the napkin was neatly folded on top of the stump, held in place by three pretty rocks. Laylie picked it up.

"I-is that her?" a boy's voice said. "Th-the one who left the biscuits? She's p-pretty."

"Maybe it is." A girl about Laylie's age came out of the bushes, followed by a group of smaller children.

"My name's Boston," the girl said. "What's yours?"

"Robin Hood," Laylie said, "and I'm looking for a band of Merry Men."

"What's that?" Boston asked.

"Outlaws," Laylie said, "who live in a hideout in the woods, and rob the rich and give to the poor."

"Th-there ain't no outlaws r-round here," the tall, bony boy said. "J-just us."

"There's one now," Laylie said as she jumped up on the stump. "I'm here to tell you the story of Robin Hood and his Merry Men."

She folded her arms the way JoMa did before she started a story, and waited until they quieted down.

"Once there was a hungry man named Much-the-Miller's Son," she began. "He was a hard worker, but the Sheriff of Nottingham and his men took all his food away. So, Much went hunting and shot him a deer. Before he could carry it home, the patrollers came along. They were just about to hang him by the neck when, shnick!—an arrow cut the rope!" The children gasped.

"It was Robin Hood, come to save him!"

Laylie sat down on the stump, and her audience sat on the grass around her.

"Now Robin wasn't afraid of nothing." They didn't even fidget as she finished the story of how Robin Hood saved the miller's son, and how Much swore loyalty to Robin and joined his outlaw band.

"Did you really do all that?" a little girl in braids asked.

"Girl!" Boston smacked the questioner in the back of the head. "That's a story. She playactin'."

"But I want to be an outlaw!" the little girl cried.

"Anyone who swears an oath never to betray the band can be an outlaw," Laylie said, standing up. The children looked at one another.

"If you want to join my Merry Men, then raise up your hands!"

Everyone's hand went up.

"Now say, 'I swear I will never betray Robin Hood or the outlaw band.' " The voices mixed in the oath, and when it was silent, Laylie reached out and laid her hand on Boston's head.

"You," she said, "will be Little John, even though you're a girl."

The boy with the stutter became Friar Tuck, and the little girl Maid Marion, because she was too small to do much anyway, and her older brother became Alan-a-Dale. Will Scarlet was a little boy who never said a word, just nodded. "We'll call this place Sherwood Forrest," said Laylie.

"W-what do we do now?" Tuck asked. "R-rob somebody?"

"Build a hideout," Laylie said, "where no one will ever find us."

Laylie settled on a spot in the woods, well hidden from both the Big House and the slave quarters. It would have been too close to the road that ran by Roselands but for a giant rock that hid it from sight. The face of the rock was thick with brambles and dotted with poison ivy.

"I-I'll take care of that ivy for you," Tuck said. By the time the sun was setting, he was scratching like a hound dog, but they had cleared enough space to start a hut, bending berry wands and weaving them together, tying them with strips of green willow bark.

A shot sounded in the distance, calling the slaves in from the fields. Calling Luke in.

"Little John," Laylie said, "I gotta go, but I need to get a message to my brother, Luke. He came on the wagons from Meadshead."

"We'll find him," Little John promised.

"Tell him I'll meet him right here tomorrow morning."

"Tomorrow's Sunday," Maid Marion said. "Mama makes us help with wash and such."

"Yeah," several voices chorused.

"You tell him where to meet me," Laylie said. "You all can come along when you're done."

CHAPTER

8

Preparing a Room

*For the word of God is living
and active. Sharper than
any double-edged sword,
. . . it judges the thoughts
and attitudes of
the heart.*

HEBREWS 4:12

Preparing a Room

When Laylie got back, she found Mrs. Brown waiting for her in the kitchen.

"Come with me," she said, leading Laylie into the hall, away from Phoebe's curious ears. "Mrs. Dinsmore was inquiring after you," she said. "Asking how your training was coming along. What was I supposed to tell her? That the house slaves all refuse to work with you? Every one of them believes you took the sugar and biscuits." As she talked, she paced down the hall and back. "And they don't want you around. Oh, Ajax and Olivia like you well enough, but you can hardly drive a coach, and we don't need any help in the laundry."

"Are you sending me to the fields?" Laylie asked hopefully.

"Of course not, child!"

Mrs. Brown stopped pacing. "I told Mrs. Dinsmore that I had decided to train you as a personal servant—a lady's maid. Come to my room tomorrow morning before sunup."

"Yes, missus," Laylie said.

That night the house slaves gathered early for supper, as the elder Dinsmores were dining at a neighboring plantation. Ajax had driven them, so to Laylie, there was not one friendly face in the kitchen. She ate quietly, perched on top of the wood box. When the sugar bowl was passed around, Laylie wasn't offered anything but dirty looks.

I don't care, Laylie thought. *They're the sheriff's men anyway.*

The meal was almost over when Friar Tuck slipped in, carrying a basket of pignuts. Poison ivy welts had risen all over his arms, but he smiled as he scratched.

Laylie's Daring Quest

"L-Luke says he'll s-s-see you tomorrow," he whispered.

Laylie pulled out the lump of sugar she had slipped into her pocket at supper the night before and put it in Friar Tuck's hand. He grinned a gap-toothed grin, hiked up his britches, and strutted away.

The next morning Laylie was standing at the foot of Mrs. Brown's bed when the woman awoke.

"Goodness, child! Your job is to look after the comfort of your mistress, not to scare her out of her wits! Well, at least you are prompt. Bring me my dressing gown." She pointed the robe out to Laylie. After she was wrapped, Mrs. Brown sat at her bureau while Laylie brushed out her long grey hair—one hundred strokes with a pig-bristle brush. Then she helped the woman dress.

"Well," Mrs. Brown said when every button was buttoned and her hair tucked into a bun. "What do you think?"

"I think," Laylie said, "if folks didn't have so many clothes to put on, they wouldn't need help."

Mrs. Brown rubbed her temples.

"When your mistress asks you what you think," she said, "you are not to tell her what you really think. You are to tell her what she wants to hear. In a case such as this, you would assure your mistress that she looks beautiful."

"But, missus," Laylie said, "didn't you say lying was wicked?"

Mrs. Brown's face turned very red. "I have had quite enough for one day. Since it is the Sabbath, you may go play until the evening shot sounds. Then you must come straight in."

"Yes, missus!" Laylie practically flew down the hall and out of the house.

Luke was sitting in front of the rock where they were building their hideout, eating pignuts and tossing shells. He

stood up just in time for Laylie to launch herself into his arms. He whirled her around before he set her on her feet and looked her over.

"Look at you!" he said. "Petticoats and button-shoes!"

"Can't run too fast in these skirts," Laylie said. "And the shoes pinch."

Luke laughed as he wiggled his own bare feet in the dust.

"Get used to it, Laylie girl. You can't go barefoot in New York City. I'll have to get me some shoes too, pretty soon!"

"Can't we go now, Luke? I don't like it at the Big House."

"We'll wait, like we planned. And you gotta stay out of trouble up there as long as it takes. Do what you're told. Don't get your temper up, and don't let them see how smart you are, neither."

Laylie shook her head.

"You ain't been in any trouble, have you?" Luke asked.

" 'Course not," Laylie said.

"What have you been up to?" he asked.

She told him about Olivia, Ajax, and the toad-kissing girl, but she didn't tell him about Andros's book wrapped up in her blankets. *Maybe I'll tell him after we're gone.*

"H-hey, Robin," Friar Tuck said as he came out of the bushes.

"They call me Robin Hood," Laylie whispered. Luke's eyebrows went up.

"I brung you somethin'." Friar Tuck held out a red head rag.

Laylie took it. It smelled so strongly of roses that it made her eyes water.

"Mamma has some water that makes things smell good like that," he said happily. "You h-hang that out the window or s-somethin' if you need me. I m-mean us."

Luke was laughing at her now, and Laylie would have slugged him if he hadn't seen it coming and got up.

She shoved the head rag in her pocket. The rest of the Merry Men arrived, and Luke sat watching as they worked on building the hideout.

The Dinsmores left for Philadelphia the next morning, taking Miss Worth and Jonati with them. Over the next weeks, Laylie learned to pull Mrs. Brown's hair up in French twists, braids, and buns, carry tea trays, and stand quietly while the woman ate, and then remove her dishes when she was done. The housekeeper showed Laylie how to settle the coals in the fireplace, then set a flatiron on a trivet over the hot embers to heat, while she sprinkled the clothes to be ironed with water. The iron was hot enough when Mrs. Brown flicked water on it and it sizzled. Then she would spread a skirt or blouse on the ironing board and press the hot, flat metal against it until steam rose and the wrinkles were flattened. Laylie learned how to use two irons. One was always heating while she worked with the other.

Laylie practiced on flour sacks — until the blisters on her fingers from grabbing the hot iron handles went down and there were no burn marks or soot smudges on the cloth — before Mrs. Brown set her to ironing real clothes.

It wasn't too hard to stay out of trouble with Arthur gone and no one speaking to her. Mrs. Brown let Laylie spend almost every afternoon in the woods with her Merry Men. The hut was soon finished, with the flat face of the boulder serving as the back wall, and saplings and branches woven together to make a roof. Little John had found a pan and two

chipped cups, and they boiled water in a fire pit, using dried strawberry leaves to make their tea. Luke spent every Sunday with them. In time, the leaves fell from the trees, but still Borse made no move to go back to Meadshead.

"He's waiting for Master Horace to come home," Luke said. "I heard him say it. We're not going to leave until then, because Master Horace has to feed us as long as we're here. That saves Master Phil the expense. Borse keeps us busy enough here, though. Clearing new land."

"Laylie! Are you listening?" Mrs. Brown caught her just before she went out the door. "You can't go play today. I received a message from Mr. Dinsmore this morning. They are in port and will be here this evening!" Laylie thought her heart would jump out of her chest. *They're back! That means...*

"They are bringing a young lady with them. Are you listening to me?" asked Mrs. Brown.

"Yes, missus," said Laylie.

"We must prepare a room."

Laylie helped Mrs. Brown freshen the linens in a guest room and set a fire to take the chill out of the air.

"Now polish the candleholders on the mantel," Mrs. Brown said. "Everything must shine!"

Laylie polished until they were almost worn away. *The wagons will have to go back to Meadshead now. Me and Luke, we're going north!*

When she couldn't find a spot of tarnish or a single fingerprint, Laylie went to the kitchen for fresh candles.

"They's at the bottom of the drive," Harry called from the door.

"Finish up, and then everyone onto the veranda!" Mrs. Brown said, clapping her hands. She caught Laylie by the arm as she went by. "Remember, you must reach out your hands and smile with joy when you greet the Master and Missus. Now run those candles to the guest room and hurry back!"

Laylie hurried to the guestroom, set the candles in their holders, and raced back to take her place on the veranda with the other house slaves, holding out her hands and smiling as the Dinsmores came up the wide steps. There was a pale, blonde girl with them.

Mr. Dinsmore stopped in front of the housekeeper. "Mrs. Brown, this young lady is my niece, Miss Millie Keith, from the state of Indiana. I commend her to your special care. Please see that she is well attended and wants for nothing that this house or plantation can supply."

"Yes, sir." Mrs. Brown curtsied. "Welcome to Roselands, Miss Keith."

"Here, Laylie!" Laylie felt a jolt at the sound of Missy Isabel's voice. She glanced at Mrs. Brown, who motioned her forward. "I appoint you Miss Millie's waiting maid, Laylie." Out of the corner of her eye, Laylie saw Mrs. Brown wince.

"You are to be always at her call," Missy Isabel went on, "and do whatever she directs."

"Yes, mistress." Laylie curtsied as Mrs. Brown had done. "Shall I show you the way to your room now, miss?" asked Laylie.

"Please," Miss Millie said.

Laylie led her to the room.

"This is a lovely room . . . Laylie? Was that your name?"

"Yes, miss."

"Do you think there is time to dress before tea?" asked Millie.

Preparing a Room

"Plenty of time," Laylie said, hoping it was what Miss Millie wanted to hear.

Harry and Ajax carried in Miss Millie's luggage, with Mrs. Brown right behind them.

Laylie stood in the corner while the housekeeper spoke to the guest.

"Laylie is young and has not had much experience in the duties of a lady's maid. I hope you will find her trustworthy and willing." The housekeeper's glance at Laylie was pointed. "Would you like to have Laylie unpack your things and arrange them in the bureau and wardrobe? Then the trunk can be put out of sight until it is wanted again."

"I could use some help," Miss Millie said, taking a key from her pocket, "but I doubt we will finish before tea."

"What does that matter?" Mrs. Brown said. "Laylie will finish while you eat. You do exactly as I showed you now, Laylie."

As the housekeeper left, Laylie set about taking the dresses out of the trunk and laying them on the bed.

"You don't have to unpack for me," Miss Millie said. She took a dress right out of Laylie's hands and laid it on the bed. "You go ahead and have your tea, too, and we'll finish before bedtime."

"We don't have tea, miss," Laylie said. "We won't have supper until the work is done, after the white folks have gone to bed."

Miss Millie's face turned pink, then pinker still. She turned away and started unbuttoning her travel dress.

"Let me help you with that dress, miss." Laylie started forward but Miss Millie backed away.

"I am good at dressing myself," she said. "It's something one learns on the frontier." She not only dressed herself, she

took down her hair, ran a brush through it, then twisted it into a knot again, as if Laylie weren't even there.

"Hello?" Miss Worth peeked in the door. "If you are ready, I'll show you the way." She saw Laylie standing in the corner and stepped into the room. "Laylie, what's wrong? What is going on here?" asked Miss Worth.

"She won't let me do anything," Laylie said.

"Then you stand and do nothing until you are given permission to speak," Miss Worth said. "You don't want a visit with Mrs. Dinsmore, do you?"

Laylie looked at her toes. "No, miss."

"And I am very sure Mrs. Brown told you to unpack this trunk."

"Yes, miss."

Miss Millie followed the older woman into the hall, and Laylie set to work unpacking the trunk, brushing the wrinkles out of dresses and hanging them in the wardrobe. Miss Millie's clothes weren't anything like Mrs. Brown's, not anything at all. Some were bright as parrot feathers—yellow, blue, and red. One pink dress had skirts that swung and swished when Laylie twirled it, and a blue one was covered with tiny spots like stars. Laylie took out a green dress with white lace at the tips of the sleeves and collar, looked quickly at the door to make sure no one was watching, then held it up in front of the mirror. *Someday I'll wear a dress like this, wear it to walk right down the street.* Footsteps passed in the hall, and Laylie quickly hung up the dress and went back to work unpacking Miss Millie's trunk and bags.

Laylie put all of the underthings away in drawers, then hesitated over a jar of sweet-smelling oil. *Mrs. Brown doesn't have anything of this sort,* thought Laylie, wondering where to put the jar, *but she does keep bottles of cologne on her dressing*

table with her hairbrush. Laylie set the jar on the bureau along with Millie's brush, hair combs, and small mirror. Then she pulled the trunk out into the hall for Ajax to take away.

The fire had burned low, and the firewood in the box would not last the evening. Laylie went out for an armload of wood. When she came back Miss Millie was in the room. Laylie stacked the firewood and put another log on the fire.

"I wasn't sure where to put that," said Laylie, pointing to the jar on the dressing table. "Is it perfume, miss?"

"It's my Aunt Wealthy's miracle cure," Miss Millie said. "Good for coughs, cuts, and burns, she says. I put it on before I get ready for bed."

"Are you getting ready for bed? Then you must want your slippers and nightclothes." This time, Miss Millie seemed happy to have her help. Laylie opened the drawers and pulled them out. "Shall I brush out your hair?"

"Yes, when I have put on my dressing gown. I will read while you are brushing," said Miss Millie.

Miss Millie sat down at her dressing table and opened a thick black book. Laylie's eyes wandered to the printed words, and Miss Millie began to read. " 'In the beginning was the Word, and the Word was with God, and the Word was God. He was with God in the beginning. Through him all things were made; without him nothing was made that has been made.' "

Miss Millie winced and Laylie realized she was brushing too hard, but the older girl just went on reading.

Laylie looked back at the page.

" 'The Word became flesh and made his dwelling among us. . . . For the Law was given through Moses; grace and truth came through Jesus Christ.' "

Jesus-God! Laylie's ears tingled.

"Do you read, Laylie?"

She jumped at the sound of Miss Millie's voice.

"No, miss!" she lied quickly. "That's for white folk. We're not allowed."

Did Miss Millie see me reading over her shoulder? I can't get in trouble. Not now.

"I read my Bible every night before I go to sleep," said Miss Millie.

"What's a Bible?" Laylie asked.

"You have never heard of a Bible?"

"I've lived all my life at Meadshead Plantation," Laylie said, going back to brushing, as if she wasn't interested at all. "Black folk don't have books there. I seen them though, in the Big House."

"The Bible is a little bit like a letter," Miss Millie said, picking up the book. "It's like a letter from Jesus to us. To me and to you. It's full of His thoughts, His plans, and what He wants us to do."

"Well, somebody ought to tell him you can get into big trouble for writing letters to black people. We're not allowed to have them."

"Can you listen while someone else reads?" asked Miss Millie.

"Nobody said I can't," Laylie said. "So I guess that means I can."

"Then I will read the Bible to you every night and morning while you do my hair." Miss Millie hesitated a moment, then flipped back through the pages to the beginning of the book.

" 'In the beginning,' " she read, " 'God created the heavens and the earth . . . .' "

Head Rags
and Horses

*In his heart a man plans
his course, but the LORD
determines his steps.*

PROVERBS 16:9

Head Rags and Horses

hen Laylie left Miss Millie's room, she was too excited to sleep. Every sound made her get up and look out the window for Luke, but when dawn pinked the horizon, he still had not come. Laylie folded up her blankets and ran to Miss Millie's room before Phoebe came into the kitchen. Embers still glowed in the fireplace. She added wood shavings and blew them to life, feeding the flames small pieces of wood until the fire was crackling again. Miss Millie was awake before the flames had caught well.

Laylie brushed Miss Millie's hair as the older girl read aloud from the Bible—a story about Adam and Eve and a snake that tricked them into disobeying God.

"I think I will go to the library now to write my letters," Miss Millie said. "And after breakfast, I will ride with Uncle Horace. Do you know where the library is?"

Laylie led her down the hall, left her at the library door, and went to find the housekeeper. She hoped that Mrs. Brown would let her go to the woods while Miss Millie went riding. But the housekeeper had other ideas.

"You will iron every piece of Miss Millie's clothing while she is gone," she said, "even if it does not appear wrinkled to you."

Laylie set to work, taking the things from the drawers first, and trying to keep from staring out the window. She was glad she had a stack of ironing to show for her morning's work when Mrs. Brown brought Missy Isabel by just before noon.

"She's coming along nicely," Mrs. Brown said. "I'm sure Miss Keith will have no complaints."

821

Laylie's Daring Quest

"Miss Keith is an ignorant girl who has never been served by a slave before," Missy Isabel said. "She wouldn't know a quality servant if she were assigned one." She looked at Laylie, and Laylie dropped her eyes. "That's why I decided not to waste one of my trained servants on her."

"Yes, ma'am," said Mrs. Brown.

❧

That night, Miss Millie read to Laylie from the Bible for a long time—a story about an evil Pharaoh who ordered Hebrew midwives to kill babies, and a baby named Moses who was saved by his sister and grew up to talk to God. *It doesn't sound like the same book the white preacher read to JoMa,* thought Laylie. *The Israelites were slaves, far away from their own land. Their masters sounded just as bad as Borse, but this Bible doesn't say, "You were born to be a slave. Pharaoh knows what's good for you. Obey him. That makes Jesus-God happy. And don't you steal from them." This Bible says God looked on those Israelite slaves and was concerned about them. He sent Moses to rescue them by using plagues and mighty miracles.*

Miss Keith was reading about the Israelite slaves making bricks out of straw when she glanced up.

"Would you like to go riding with me tomorrow?" Miss Millie asked Laylie.

"Yes, miss," replied Laylie. *Luke won't come for me during the day, and it will be better than ironing. I still have half the dresses in the closet to do.*

After breakfast the next morning, Miss Millie called for their horses to be saddled and brought up. Then she turned to Laylie. "Where is your bonnet?" she asked.

822

"Slaves don't have bonnets," Laylie said, "at least not around here." Miss Millie turned pink. "I got a head rag, though," said Laylie.

"I . . . I suppose that will do," Miss Millie said. Laylie ran for the red head rag Friar Tuck had given her, and held her breath as she tied it over her braids. It still smelled like a whole rose garden.

Millie was standing on the veranda, waiting for the horses. Harry led the first one around the corner, a lovely horse, tall and thin-legged with huge, gentle eyes, just like the one Master Phil rode.

"This is Dolly," Miss Millie said. "I will be riding her."

Laylie reached up and touched the horse's nose. It was softer than rabbit fur. Then Ajax came around the corner leading a fuzzy barrel with hooves.

"Gypsy needs a little exercise, I'm afraid," Miss Millie said.

Laylie stood very still as Gypsy stretched her neck toward her. The pony's nostrils flared, and she wiggled her rubbery lips as if she were commenting on the perfume the head rag had been soaked in.

"Behave," Ajax said, pulling Gypsy's head down. "Now, don't you be nervous," he whispered as he put his hands around Laylie's waist and lifted her into the saddle. The fat pony, her nostrils still quivering, turned her head and looked at Laylie.

"Hold the reins in this hand," said Ajax. He threaded them through her fingers. Laylie twisted her other hand into the pony's mane.

"Riding is simple," Miss Millie said. "Just do everything I do."

Dolly started walking, and the pony trotted to keep up, rattling Laylie's teeth with each step. She felt her head rag

slipping off and caught it with one hand when it reached the end of her braids. When they got to the road, Miss Millie turned her horse's head toward a distant hill and gave Dolly's flank a little nudge with her heel. Dolly stretched her long legs in a fast walk.

Laylie dug her heel into Gypsy's side. Gypsy stopped. Her ears pointed in the direction Dolly had gone. One ear slowly lay back, as if a great struggle was going on inside her shaggy head, then the other ear followed it.

"Whoa, horse!" Laylie yelled as Gypsy turned around and started plodding back toward the stable. "Not that way!" Laylie sawed on the reins, but the pony paid no attention. "Are you deaf, horse? I said, whoa!" Laylie swatted at the pony's ears with the head rag. Gypsy stopped, turned her head, and tried to snatch the rag from Laylie's hand with her teeth.

Laylie jerked her hand away, but with her head turned, the pony caught sight of Dolly's rump disappearing in the distance. She suddenly decided she did not want to be left behind after all. Her body swung sideways until it was lined up behind the head again, and then Gypsy exploded in a bone-jarring run.

Laylie held on for dear life as Gypsy flew like a hairy cannonball straight through low bushes and ditches, never slowing until she had caught up with the bigger horse.

They skidded to a stop on top of a hill with a view of the distant ocean, and it took Laylie a full minute to untangle her hand from the pony's mane. Her fingers just wouldn't obey her when she told them to let go.

Miss Millie dismounted, tied her reins to a bush, and helped Laylie down.

"Well," Miss Millie said, "do you like riding?"

Head Rags and Horses

"Yes, miss," Laylie lied, rubbing her behind.

Gypsy attacked the grass of the small clearing voraciously, her huge teeth ripping it up almost by the roots.

"We'll let Gypsy graze a bit," said Miss Millie. "She won't go off without Dolly. I'm going to sketch for a while." Miss Millie took a sketch pad and charcoal out of her saddlebag and settled down under a shade tree, with her back to Laylie and the pony.

Gypsy rolled her eyes toward Laylie. The pony caught sight of the head rag, and the whites showed around the edges of her bulbous eyes. Her nostrils quivered. Laylie backed away, toward a wind-twisted tree. *Luke said bulls will charge a red rag. Maybe that's the problem—Gypsy isn't a real pony at all, but some kind of cow, driven mad by the sight or smell of Friar Tuck's head rag.* Laylie scrambled up into the tree and tied it to a branch. *If Friar Tuck wants it back, I'll tell him where it is and he can crawl out and get it himself—when Gypsy isn't around.*

When the pony looked toward Dolly, Laylie crawled out of the tree and edged off the other way toward Miss Millie. When she was sure Gypsy wasn't going to follow her, she sat down on a rock and looked out toward the ocean.

Miss Millie set down her sketch pad and came over to stand beside Laylie. She was twisting her charcoal stick in her hand.

"Do you want to learn to read?" Miss Millie asked suddenly. "I know it's against the law. But I want to teach you if you want to learn."

"No, miss," Laylie said. *Missy Isabel is right. Miss Millie doesn't know a thing.*

Laylie's Daring Quest

Miss Millie took Laylie riding for the next two mornings. Gypsy rattled Laylie's teeth and shook her bones until she could hardly stand it, but it was still better than ironing or being sent for by Missy Isabel. On Thursday, Millie brought letters from home and read them aloud. She had so many brothers and sisters that Laylie had a hard time keeping them straight: Ru, Zillah, Adah, Cyril, Don, Fanny, and Annis. Cyril and Don reminded Laylie so much of Exter and Max that she laughed out loud.

"I have a brother," Laylie said. "His name's Luke."

"Is he on this plantation?" asked Miss Millie.

"Yes, miss. He's working in the fields," replied Laylie.

"I miss my brothers very much," Miss Millie said. "Do you get to see Luke often?"

"No, miss. He's down at the quarters. That's where field slaves stay."

Miss Millie was quiet for some time, and then she said, "I am an abolitionist. Do you know what that means?"

"No, miss," said Laylie.

"It means I do not believe in slavery," the older girl said. "I want to help you. But . . . I don't know how."

Laylie was careful not to look up. *We'll be gone any day now. Any day. And we don't need help.*

"Well," Miss Millie said at last. "I suppose we should go back. Whatever happened to the pretty red scarf you wore the first day we went riding?"

Laylie shrugged.

"Never mind," Miss Millie said. "I'll give you a proper bonnet next time."

Before their ride the next morning, Miss Millie did give Laylie a bonnet—a blue bonnet and a blue cloak as well—because there was a chilly fog rolling over the trees. "They are yours to keep," Miss Millie said. "I certainly have more than enough bonnets and more than two cloaks."

Laylie tied the bonnet on and wrapped the cloak around her. *Mine to keep! Luke will never believe it.*

She almost ran into Phoebe, who was standing in the downstairs hall. "Some people shouldn't put on airs," Phoebe said as Laylie edged past her wearing her new bonnet and cloak. " 'Cause changin' spots don't change the cat."

Gypsy thought they did, though. She didn't try to bite once, and she pranced like a show pony up the drive after Dolly. Laylie decided that she did like riding after all, better than anything but swimming in the bay.

"I'm afraid we must skip our ride today," Miss Millie said on Friday morning. "I am going to town with Mrs. Dinsmore. But Mrs. Brown said she could use your help all day today, as we are preparing for a party tonight."

Every brass candleholder and chandelier that had been polished a week before was re-polished, and floors were cleaned until they shone. Phoebe ruled the kitchen like a queen, waving her spoon-scepter over bubbling pots, and pulling pans of delicious-smelling pastries from the oven. Laylie tried to stay out of her way as much as possible, but by noon, hunger forced her to duck into the kitchen for bread and cheese.

Phoebe shook her head when she saw Laylie, and the kitchen maids whispered to one another.

"What are you waggin' your heads for?" Laylie asked, but nobody said a thing. Laylie finished her food, then went back to Miss Millie's room where the rest of the ironing waited for her. As Laylie walked down the hall, she could see the slaves looking the other way—looking away from her. *Surely Mrs. Brown would have told me if I were in trouble?* She pulled a dress out of the wardrobe.

Ting. A pebble hit the window. Little John was waving at her from the bushes in the garden. Laylie waved back and shook her head.

Ting. Little John was right outside. Her eyes were wide and scared. Laylie slid the window up.

"You better come," Little John said.

"I can't," said Laylie.

"It's Luke. He's . . . " Little John started crying. Laylie pushed the window open wide enough to crawl out onto a tree. She dropped to the ground and ran across the lawn with Little John.

"What about Luke?" Laylie asked as soon as they were in the woods.

"Borse is a bad man," Little John said. "A really, really bad man."

Laylie ran as fast as she could down the road to the quarters. There was blood on the ground under the whipping post, and something heavy had been dragged from the post into the nearest shack. Laylie almost tripped on the body when she went in the door.

Luke was stripped to the waist, lying stomach down on the dirt floor of the shack. His head was turned to face her, and his eyes were rolled back in his head, showing white slits. His back was a mass of cuts and bruises.

"Luke!" Laylie touched his face, but he did not respond. She felt her breakfast coming back up and ran outside.

"They w-whipped him and w-washed him down with s-salt water," Friar Tuck said when Laylie stopped retching.

 828

"He wouldn't let me get you sooner," Little John said.
Alan-a-Dale nodded. "He said you'd cut him down. Borse
said anyone who cut him down would get worse'n he did."

"W-we looked after him," Friar Tuck said. "G-gave him
w-water and shooed the flies."

"Our overseer came around about an hour ago and cut
him down. That's when Luke passed out," Boston went on,
"and I come for you. I never seen somebody whipped
before." She was crying again. "He didn't do anything. That
Borse just lit into him."

Laylie's eyes stung, but she wiped them angrily. *Crying
isn't going to help Luke. What can I do?* Then an idea struck her.
JoMa would put grease on him, like she did for Hettie!

"Watch over him," Laylie said with urgency. She ran all
the way to the Big House, but stopped at the edge of the
woods to catch her breath.

"Laylie," Mrs. Brown said in surprise when she came in
the door. "I thought you were busy in the dining room!"

"Miss Millie sent me on an errand," Laylie said, "before
she left. I've got to hurry." She went to Miss Millie's room
and found the jar of ointment on the dresser. She stuck it in
her pocket, then dodged past Mrs. Brown on her way back.

"Laylie girl?" Luke opened his eyes when she put the
first dab on his back.

"Does it hurt? I'm trying to be careful," Laylie said.

"Naw, it feels good. I need a drink."

Friar Tuck went for a gourd of water, while Laylie kept
working the salve into the wounds.

"This is miracle cure," Laylie said. "It's gonna make you
better fast. It can bring you back from the dead, almost."

"That's good," Luke said with great effort, " 'cause I feel
dead, almost." There were so many whip cuts on his back
that Laylie used the whole jar and could have used another.

Laylie's Daring Quest

Luke was quiet until Friar Tuck brought the water, then Luke drank the whole gourdful.

A Roselands field slave looked in the window. "Overseer's comin' up from the fields," he said to Laylie. "Better get on outta here, girl, lest you cause your brother more grief."

"Go on!" Luke's voice was harsh. "And don't come back unless I send for you, you hear?"

"But I—"

"I said get out of here!"

Laylie took the empty ointment jar and ran back up the hill to the house. Every candle and chandelier was lit, and the whole house echoed with laughter. She saw Miss Millie through a window, laughing as she played the piano.

Laylie put the empty ointment jar back on the dresser. Then she sat down on a chair, pulled her knees to her chin, and cried out every tear that was in her.

There was a comforter tucked around Laylie when she woke the next morning.

"Would you like to go riding this morning?" Miss Millie asked.

"If you like, miss," Laylie said listlessly.

"Is something wrong, Laylie?" asked Miss Millie.

"No, miss."

Miss Millie opened her Bible and began to read as Laylie picked up the hairbrush.

" 'But now, this is what the LORD says—he who created you, O Jacob, he who formed you, O Israel: "Fear not, for I have redeemed you; I have summoned you by name; you are mine. When you pass through the waters, I will be with you; and when you pass through rivers, they will not sweep over

you. When you walk through the fire, you will not be burned; the flames will not set you ablaze. For I am the LORD, your God, the Holy One of Israel, your Savior; I give Egypt for your ransom, Cush and Seba in your stead. Since you are precious and honored in my sight, and because I love you, I will give men in exchange for you, and people in exchange for your life. Do not be afraid, for I am with you.' ' "

Laylie's tear wells must have filled during the night, because they were overflowing now.

"Laylie, why are you crying?" asked Miss Millie with concern.

Laylie shook her head and ran from the room, down the halls, and outside where she could lean her head against the cool stone of the wall behind the steps. *"Don't come back unless I send for you, you hear?"* Laylie replayed Luke's words in her mind. *What if he doesn't send for me?* she thought as she savagely rubbed the tears from her eyes. *"Stay out of trouble."* *That's what he'd say.*

Laylie wiped her nose on the corner of her apron and walked to the veranda. She was standing there when Miss Millie came out to ride. They were hardly out of the drive before Miss Millie reached over and caught Gypsy's harness. "I want you to take me to the quarters," said Millie.

"You don't want to go there, miss."

"Yes, I do," Miss Millie said firmly. "You will have to tell me the way, and I will lead your horse. When I went to put on my ointment last night, I found the jar completely empty. You are the only one who could have taken it. I believe someone is hurt, and you are caring for them. If this is true, you have no reason to be afraid. I am not angry."

Laylie swallowed hard, then pointed to a footpath that led through the hedge and down toward the slave cabins.

Luke was lying in the corner when they got there. Someone had covered him with a cotton sheet.

"Luke . . . are you dead?" asked Laylie with alarm. He didn't answer, and Laylie ran to him. She could tell by the heat of his face that the fever had hold of him.

Miss Millie lifted the sheet and gasped. "He needs a doctor!" she exclaimed. She left Laylie dripping water onto Luke's dry lips.

The sunspot from the window crawled across the floor as Laylie waited. The Merry Men peeked in the door now and again, and went away without saying a word.

Luke's breathing grew ragged, and Laylie tried to shake him awake, but he wouldn't open his eyes. She could feel the life going out of him, slipping away, as the shadows deepened in the corners of the room.

"Jesus . . ." She tried to pray, but her thoughts wouldn't form into words. There was something dark and terrible pressing around her, confusing her mind.

"No, you don't!"

A form stepped through the door. "Back off, Satan! Get gone, death!" The shadows fled, and Laylie blinked up at a tiny old woman.

"I come in the mighty name of Jesus," she declared, "and you won't take this boy today!"

The woman dropped her bag and started rolling up her sleeves even as she spoke. Laylie made room for her as she knelt beside Luke. She felt his forehead, pried open his eyelids, and gazed into his eyes.

"Can you help him?" Laylie asked.

"No, child," the old woman said. "I can't. But God can." She lifted her gnarled old hands and prayed, "Father, he's beyond me, but not beyond Your help. Let Your Holy Spirit guide my hands."

CHAPTER

10

A Rescue

For the grave cannot praise you,
death cannot sing your praise;
those who go down to the pit
cannot hope for your
faithfulness.

ISAIAH 38:18

A Rescue

*M*y name is Rachel," the old woman said as she opened her black bag and took out clean cotton rags. "What's yours?"

"Laylie," Laylie's voice cracked, and she brushed tears from her face, "and this here's my brother Luke."

"Well, Laylie, you just dry those tears. This ain't no time for cryin'. We've got to fight now . . . fight for your brother's life!"

Laylie watched as the old woman ministered to Luke with poultices, prayers, and gentle hands. The flicker of life that was left in him steadied, and then grew. Miss Millie came back and stood silently in the corner, her head bowed and her lips moving in prayer. It was very late when the old woman, who said her name was Rachel, shooed Laylie and Miss Millie out of the cabin.

"I'll brush my own hair tonight," Miss Millie said as they reached the house. "You just go on to bed."

Laylie slipped quietly into the kitchen and lay down to sleep on the bare floor, too tired to even think about her blankets.

The words Miss Millie had read echoed in Laylie's mind. *"This is what the LORD says — he who created you, O Jacob, he who formed you, O Israel; "Fear not, for I have redeemed you; I have summoned you by name; you are mine."*

"Thank you for saving Luke," Laylie whispered, and then she was asleep.

When Miss Millie allowed her to go down to the quarters the next day, Laylie found Luke sleeping deeply and the old woman asleep as well, sitting in a rocking chair that someone had carried in for her. She had a book open in her lap. Laylie crept close enough to see that it was just like Miss Millie's Bible. The woman's hands were folded on the open pages, as if she'd prayed herself to sleep. Laylie was careful not to wake her. She just sat quietly, watching Luke breathe.

By evening of the second day, Luke was drinking the broth Laylie fed him with a spoon, and listening while she told him about the wild girl from Indiana who read aloud from the Bible and was so ignorant that she offered to teach a slave to read, and about the devil horses that went crazy over red head scarves.

"Horses don't care what color you wear," Luke said, wincing.

"This one does," said Laylie, folding her arms.

"I expect," Luke said, "it was the perfume. That pony thought you smelled dee-lishous. Good enough to gobble up! Did you tell your sweetie that you lost it?"

Laylie's face grew hot. "He's not my sweetie! I wouldn't even have been wearing that old rag if Miss Millie hadn't—"

"Since you're well enough to argue," Rachel said, from the corner where she'd been watching them, "I'm taking these old bones home. But if you need me, you just send someone running over to Ion for Old Rachel."

As soon as she was out the door, Luke pushed himself up. "Help me sit against that wall, so I won't fall over." Laylie helped him edge over to the wall. "Now go on back to the Big House," he said. "I don't want you here."

"Why do you keep trying to chase me off?" Laylie asked.

A Rescue

"Borse musta known we was gonna run, that's why." He lifted his hand with difficulty and wiped it across his mouth. "He whipped me to cobble me up so's we couldn't and he could take us back to Meadshead. You gotta stay at Roselands."

"But what about our quest, Luke? What about freedom?" asked Laylie.

Luke closed his eyes. "You gotta stay here, girl."

"They won't keep me," Laylie said. "They don't like me one bit. When are the wagons leaving?"

Luke shook his head. "Not as soon as I thought. They say Master Horace done left again, so Borse can drag his heels."

"Hello? Is anyone here?" Miss Millie was at the door. Luke pulled his shirt closed so he would be decent.

"Come in, miss," he said. Then he nudged Laylie. "G'wan," he said to her. "Git. I want to talk with Miss Millie."

"No." Laylie moved out of reach, just in case he was feeling better than he looked.

"You been minding me all your life," he said. "Don't you tell me 'no' now."

Laylie stood beside the door, still holding the broth and spoon, but she didn't leave.

"Stubborn as a mule! Then sit there," said Luke.

He turned to Miss Millie. "I heard what you did," he said. "You got help for me. I don't know why you done that, but now I have something else to ask, and no right to ask it."

"No, you don't!" Laylie said. *There's nothing Miss Millie can do for Luke, now that he's feeling better. We don't need her.*

"Hush," Luke said, and then turned back to Miss Millie. "Keep Laylie here at Roselands, miss. She'll be a good worker, and Meadshead is no place for that child."

The words wrapped around Laylie's heart and squeezed until it hurt. *We've always looked after each other. Always. Why would he leave me behind?*

"I won't stay," Laylie said.

"You will, if I can manage it," said Luke. *He's decided Wim's right, that's why,* Laylie thought. *Now that he's going to have to make his strike from Meadshead, he's decided Wim was right. They're going to go without me!*

"No!" Laylie threw the spoon across the room. "I hate you!"

"Laylie!" said Luke, dodging the spoon. She heard him yelp, but she didn't stop. She stomped out of the cabin, brushing the tears from her eyes, and ran through the bushes to the hideout. Friar Tuck and Maid Marion saw her leave the cabin and followed behind. Pretty soon the whole outlaw band was gathered. No one said a thing about Luke.

"Today we're gonna fight with quarterstaffs," Laylie said. *I feel like hitting something.*

"What's that?" Little John asked.

"Sticks," Laylie said. "Like broomsticks and rake handles." The Merry Men scattered to find quarterstaffs, while Laylie found a log that was just right for a bridge. When they'd found two good staffs, they spent the afternoon knocking each other off of the log.

Luke's fever peaked again late that evening, and Little John came running to tell Laylie. Miss Millie sent for Rachel again, and Laylie paced the floor until Little John brought word that the old woman had arrived. Millie refused to let Laylie go down to see her brother. "Luke needs peace and quiet," Miss Millie said. "And you need sleep."

A Rescue

Old Rachel sent word the next morning that Luke was better. Miss Millie sent Laylie out to play with the Merry Men, with strict orders to stay away from the cabin.

Laylie gathered the outlaws at the log bridge. *Miss Millie will have to pass this log on her way to see Luke, and again when she goes back to the Big House. Soon as she does, I'll cut through the woods and sneak into the cabin,* Laylie thought. *I have to talk to Luke. He can't leave me behind. He promised . . . and Colberts keep their promises!*

Laylie watched for Miss Millie as she knocked Merry Men off of the log. Miss Millie went past just after noon, carrying a basket. For the next hour, Laylie kept one eye on the path, and the other on any Merry Man who dared to challenge her.

"I-I don't wanna h-hurt you," Friar Tuck said. He was standing on one end of the log, a broomstick gripped in his hand.

"You haven't even knocked her off once," Little John said.

"Yeah!" Maid Marion laughed. "Not once!"

"But I d-don't want to—"

"Are you gonna fight or get down?" said Laylie, gripping her stick with both hands.

Tuck closed his eyes and swung his stick back and forth, but Laylie blocked it easily.

"You will not pass!" she said, just as she caught a movement out of the corner of her eye. It was Miss Millie. In the moment it took to turn and look, Tuck swung again. His staff caught Laylie on the ear, knocking her into the bushes.

"Don't hit Laylie!" Maid Marion howled.

"Laylie!" Miss Millie shrieked, and the outlaws vanished into the bushes.

"Yes, miss?" Laylie crawled out, shaking her head to clear the ringing.

"Are you hurt?"

"No, miss." She could feel the blood trickling down from the nick on her ear, and her head throbbed from Friar Tuck's blow.

"Come with me," Miss Millie said.

They stopped in the kitchen for some pepper. Then Miss Millie led her to the guest room.

Laylie noticed a small cot in the corner of Miss Millie's room, and her own blankets were on it. *Did Miss Millie put them there? She must have found Andros's book.* Laylie felt her eyes filling with tears again, and blinked hard. *We're going back. At least I could have returned Andros's book to him, if someone hadn't been snooping.*

Miss Millie didn't say anything as she sprinkled pepper on Laylie's cut ear. The blood stopped oozing.

"How did you learn that, miss?" Laylie asked.

"You learn many things on the frontier," Miss Millie said. "Especially if you have brothers like mine. And that brings me to this." She pulled down the covers on her own bed. "*Robin Hood.*"

"That's not mine, miss," Laylie said.

"That is correct," Miss Millie said. "It does not belong to you. This book belongs to Uncle Horace."

"I've never seen it before, honest, miss," Laylie said, but she felt just like she did when she was lying to Hettie, and Miss Millie had the same gentle disappointment in her eyes that Hettie did.

"Really?" Miss Millie said as she opened the book to the picture of Robin and Little John on the footbridge. The words below it read, "You shall not pass."

"Laylie, who taught you to read?" asked Miss Millie.

"No one, miss. Slaves don't know how to read."

"That is nonsense, and you know it. Some slaves can read. In fact, Miss Rachel was reading her Bible just now as she cared for your brother. Have you finished reading this book yet?"

"No, miss," said Laylie.

"My Uncle said I could borrow any books I like. I will borrow this book and allow you to read it, since you already know how."

There is still a chance. If I can keep it until I leave, I might be able to hide it in the wagon and take it home to Andros.

"But you must promise not to lie to me," Miss Millie said. "And stop calling me 'Miss Millie' while we are alone. Call me Millie. Can you do that?"

"Yes, mi—Millie," said Laylie.

"Now, we will see how good you are at telling the truth. Would you like to hold the book while we talk?"

Laylie hugged Andros's book.

"How did you learn to read?" Millie asked.

I can't tell Millie that! I promised not to tell anyone. But wouldn't Andros want me to break my promise to bring his book back? He would.

"Andros taught me," Laylie said at last, her face growing hot at the broken promise.

"Andros?"

Laylie's face grew hotter still. *Will Millie send someone looking for him?*

"He lived in the swamp when I was a little girl, eating snakes and possums. Luke caught rabbits to pay him to teach me to read . . . but Andros up and disappeared one day. Folks say he got dragged to Hell by sixteen witches, kicking and screaming all the way."

"You don't believe that, do you?" asked Millie.

Laylie's Daring Quest

Laylie saw that Millie did not. *Lucindy would have believed it.*

"If he did, he took his books with him, and his cook pot too, 'cause I went and looked. Nothing left in that hut but snake skins and possum bones."

"Did you steal sugar lumps and biscuits from the kitchen?" asked Millie.

Good. No more questions about Andros. Laylie almost wilted from relief.

"Yes, I stole them," Laylie said.

By the time they were finished, Millie knew all about Robin Hood and the Merry Men.

~

The next morning Millie came into the guest room with a box in her hands.

"I have something for your Merry Men," she said. "But you can't take it to them until the field hands go back to work after their noon meal."

"What is it?" asked Laylie.

"Chocolate," Millie said. "It's like sugar lumps, only better."

Laylie tasted one of the lumps. *It is better than sugar!* It melted in her mouth like butter. *The Merry Men will like it . . . and Luke will too, if I can just sneak it to him.*

"I thought you'd like that," Millie said. "But your friends will have to share. I don't think there are enough pieces in here for each child to have one of their own."

"They'll share. But why can't I take it to them now?" asked Laylie.

"We have other things we need to do," Millie said. "Do you know how to sew?"

"I sewed a shirt last year at Meadshead," Laylie said, her heart sinking. *It takes days and days to get stitches right. I*

don't have days to stay here . . . not unless Millie has found a way to keep me at Roselands.

Millie opened her wardrobe. "Let's see which color suits you best," she said.

Laylie touched the green silk with white lace at the collar and cuffs.

"Not that one," Millie said quickly, and Laylie pulled her hand away.

"That one is from a very special friend. Choose another," said Millie.

Laylie chose the pink dress that swished when she twirled it.

"We'll start with that one," Millie said. "I will cut it down for you, and you can help. But I want to see the quality of your needlework before you try any seams. You will work on pantalettes and petticoats first."

Laylie spent the morning pricking her fingers with needles and bleeding onto the white fabric of the pantalettes, while Millie read aloud from letters sent by her family. Laylie was sure Millie had promised Luke that she would keep her away from the slave quarters. Every time she thought about it, her stitches went wrong. *Who did Luke think was gonna watch over him?*

Laylie was ripping out a whole seam of bad stitches when Arthur came into the room. *He must have seen Millie carrying the box of chocolates*, thought Laylie. Arthur nosed around the room like a plump possum until he was next to the box.

"I was wondering what you were going to do with these." he said to Millie.

"I have already given them away, to Laylie," Millie replied.

Arthur picked up the box and opened it.

"Arthur!" Millie said. "Put that box down. If you take something that belongs to someone else, it is stealing."

"I'm not a thief," he said, looking at Laylie. "Nobody could whip *me*. And you can't steal from slaves. You just take what you want, because they don't own anything." He picked a candy from the box and opened his mouth, but Millie was across the room in a flash and took it from his hand.

"I'm going to tell Mamma," he said.

"Good. I am proud that you will confess to your mother. Stealing is a sin."

"I don't mean about the chocolate," Arthur said, giving Laylie a sly look. "I mean about the —"

"The book?" Millie asked. "Your father has given me permission to read any book in his library, and to take them to my room." She picked up the copy of *Robin Hood*. "Would you like me to read you a chapter of *Robin Hood* this after-noon?"

"No," Arthur said. "I hate that story. And slaves should-n't have chocolate." He stormed out of the room.

⌒

After the noon meal, Millie at last said they could go down to visit Luke. Old Rachel was sitting in her rocker when they came in the door.

"Hey, Luke!" Laylie said, offering him a chocolate. "I brought you something."

"You speakin' to me again?" Luke asked as he put it in his mouth. "Last I heard you hated me."

"That's enough of that kind of talk," said Old Rachel, looking from Laylie to Luke, and then including Millie. "I have all you children together here just one time, and I'm too old to waste my breath. I'm going to tell you the truth, and I don't know how many times you're going to hear it, so listen good."

"Sit down, Laylie," Luke said. "I want to hear what she has to say."

"I know you want freedom," Old Rachel said. "I have wanted it myself, many a time, with a wanting worse than hunger, worse than thirst." She looked at Laylie. "I knew the taste and feel of it when I was your age. I was born a free woman in Africa."

"Did white men catch you?" Laylie asked.

"Child, sin doesn't live under just one kind of skin. I was captured and sold by men with skins as black as mine. I was purchased and beaten by men whose skins were white. You see this?" She pointed her gnarled finger at Luke's back. "That don't come from black or white. That comes from sin in the hearts of evil men. I know. I got scars just like them on my back." She rocked for a moment before she went on. "I've been offered my freedom since then. I said no. I wanted to stay right here."

"Why?" Luke asked. "I would give anything to be free."

"You remember that Jesus I been tellin' you about? Well, Jesus faced a choice one day. He could let evil men beat Him and nail Him to a Cross. Or He could walk away. He had the power to do it. He chose to stay and die—to save me and to save you from the evil one. When I was offered my freedom, I thought about the choice He had made. I thought about the children here who needed to hear about Him. And I stayed."

"He's gonna save us from the masters?" Laylie asked. "They're evil, and I hate them."

Laylie's Daring Quest

"Then you get over that right now," Old Rachel said. "Hate is a sin, and I told you, sin is not particular about skin color. You can't tell me you never met a bad slave."

"Robson—he helps Borse," Luke said.

"And maybe you have met some good white folk now." Old Rachel looked at Millie as she spoke, and the girl flushed.

"You have a choice. You can be given to evil, like Borse or Robson, or you can be given to good, like me and Miss Millie. It don't have anything to do with the color of your skin. It has to do with your heart. It's either washed clean of sin or it's not. If it's not, then you will never be free, no matter how far you run."

"You mean becoming a Christian, like you were talking about?" asked Luke.

"That's right," Old Rachel said.

"What does it mean exactly?" Luke asked as he sat up, and Laylie edged closer to him.

"It means accepting the fact that you are a sinner," Old Rachel said. "And because of that you can't ever get to Heaven. The only way is through Jesus—by gettin' credit for His pure heart. 'Cause Jesus was the only One that never did nothin' wrong. So God—who's His Father—let Him go up on that Cross and die for all our sins—yours, mine, and everybody else's too. All you gotta do is accept that free gift. Then, one day, you'll be with Him in Heaven, where there won't be no more hurtin' or cryin' or pain, 'cause in Heaven, lambs will even lay down with lions." She paused. "So . . . are you children ready to give your lives over to Jesus?"

Laylie could see that Luke was fighting with something inside.

"No," he said at last. "I want my life to be my own."

"Your life won't ever be your own. If you don't belong to Jesus, you are a slave of sin, no matter how far you run."

"I got to think about it," Luke said.

"You do that," Old Rachel said. "We got until sundown tonight, and then I got to go home. My pass is only good until then."

Laylie listened to them talk until Millie stood to go.

"Laylie," she said, "I expect you to come back up to the Big House when Miss Rachel leaves."

"I'll see she does," Rachel said. Millie took her leave and Old Rachel talked a little longer with Luke, and then stood up and said, "Let's go, child."

Laylie followed Rachel out the door and walked with her until the path split. Laylie went almost to the kitchen before she ducked into the bushes and circled back around to the cabin. Luke was sitting with his head in his hands when she came back in.

"Sorry about that spoon," Laylie said.

"Sorry you threw it, or sorry it missed?" Luke sighed. "Girl, I thought Miss Millie told you to go up to the Big House."

Laylie shrugged. She asked, "What did she say about keeping me here? Keeping me at Roselands?"

"She didn't say, one way or the other," said Luke.

"Well, they won't keep me," Laylie said with certainty. "Mrs. Brown said they wouldn't keep a slave that lied and stole in the house."

"Have you been lying and stealing? Mamma wouldn't like that," said Luke.

"She wouldn't like you leaving me here, neither," Laylie said.

They sat quietly for a time, Luke's head in his hands.

"Are you thinking about what Old Rachel said?" Laylie asked at last.

"I've thought about it plenty," Luke said. "But I know some things. I know when you come to God, there's things you have to lay down. Things you have to forget. I've got things I won't lay down. Not ever."

"What things?" Laylie asked.

Luke shook his head. "I'm not sayin'. "

CHAPTER

11

Brothers and Sisters

*A friend loves at all times,
and a brother is born for
adversity.*

PROVERBS 17:17

Brothers and Sisters

*E*arly the next morning, Laylie came awake in complete darkness. *Something is wrong.* She pulled the heavy window curtains aside and saw the dim light of a rainy dawn. *Luke!*

She dressed quickly, grabbing the cloak that Millie had given her to keep off the rain. When she stepped out the back door she could hear the distant clang of a blacksmith's hammer, and as she drew closer, the rattle of chains. *Borse is leaving! Why hasn't anyone called for me?* Some men were standing in line, waiting for their shackles, while others were already sitting in the wagons. The Meadshead women were standing nearby in the rain. Borse sat under the eaves by the smithy.

Where's Luke?

"Don't you look pretty?" Ruby said. "Fact is, I'd look good in that." She grabbed Laylie's arm, twisted her around, and pulled the cloak away before Laylie could catch her balance. Borse looked over from his seat by the smithy and laughed.

"I want that apron," Priss said, when she saw Borse wasn't going to stop them. Ruby grabbed Laylie's arms from behind. Priss pulled Laylie's apron off, tearing one string. "Hold her, Ruby," she said. "I'll get the shoes!" Priss grabbed one of her feet, and Laylie kicked with all her might.

"Put her down!"

Laylie landed face-first in the mud. She scrambled up, kicked Ruby hard, and then punched at Priss, who jumped out of the way. Millie Keith was standing there in the rain.

Where is Luke? Laylie dodged past the older girls and ran to the cabin, leaving the cloak and apron behind.

Laylie's Daring Quest

Luke's not here! Laylie ran back to the wagons just in time to see Millie climbing into one. Laylie scrambled past her. Luke was lying in the wagon bed, his face turned away from the drizzling rain.

"I'm here, Luke!" Laylie said as she huddled down beside him, trying to keep the rain off.

"Hey, miss," he said, looking right past Laylie to Millie. Millie took off her cloak and laid it over him.

"Luke, are you able to travel?" asked Millie.

"I'm fine, miss, just fine," he said. "Laylie, you stay here with Miss Millie, like I said."

Laylie looked from one to the other. *They've arranged something between them. That's why nobody called me.*

"I won't! Don't you dare go without me!" cried Laylie.

"Laylie, girl." Luke's grin was weak. "I wouldn't never go nowhere without you, could I help it. I done made you a promise, didn't I?" He reached for her hand and pressed it against his chest.

"You feel that old heart thumping? It's saying Lay-lee, Lay-lee, Lay-lee. You think I could forget you for one minute with that racket going on in there? As long as my heart keeps thumping, as long as the wild geese fly—"

"As long as the North Star shines?" asked Laylie through her tears.

"The promise I made you stands," said Luke. He grimaced and tried to hide it with a smile.

"Luke, I . . . I'll take care of her," Millie said.

"Better get out of there, Miss," said Borse, as he rode past the wagon. Millie nodded and climbed out of the wagon. Laylie held on to Luke as the wagon started to move.

"Is Miss Millie walking along?" Luke asked. Laylie nodded. "Good," he said. "That's good." The wagons went down the long drive.

"Laylie, come on down now!" Millie called when they reached the road. Laylie ignored her. "Laylie! Do you hear me? Driver, I need to get her out!"

Suddenly the wagon stopped, and Laylie lifted her head to see what was happening. Millie was holding the lead horse by the harness.

"What's going on here?" Borse asked as he rode up on his horse.

"I want Laylie off that wagon," Millie said. "She has to go back to the house with me."

"That girl's not going anywhere," Borse said. "I told you, I'm taking them all back."

"Not this one. Mrs. Dinsmore sold her to me," said Millie.

Millie, who doesn't believe in slavery, has bought me? Laylie looked at Luke, and there was no surprise on his face, none at all.

"Is that right?" Borse tipped his hat back with the butt of his whip. "Mrs. Dinsmore didn't say a word about that to me. You got the papers?"

"Papers?" Millie looked confused.

"You buy a horse, you get papers that say you own it. You buy a slave, it's the same thing. I'm not letting her go without papers. Let me tell you a secret." He glanced at Laylie. "That little gal is gonna end up the same place as her brother—six feet deep." Laylie felt Luke tense under her hands. "And it's me that's gonna put her there."

"Let me tell you something that is not a secret, sir!" Millie stepped toward him. "My uncle would not be amused to hear you calling his favorite niece a liar! That child was sold to me by Isabel Dinsmore—papers or no papers. Now turn over my slave!"

Borse cursed.

"Mr. Dinsmore will peg your hide to the barn, boss," Robson said, "even if he has to follow you to do it. He don't allow no one to disrespect his ladies."

The overseer jumped from his horse, throwing his reins to Robson, and with one jump was in the wagon. The other slaves cowered away as he stepped over them to reach Laylie. He grabbed her arm, half-jerking it out of the socket as he lifted her into the air with one hand. The pain of it ripped a scream out of Laylie, though she tried to choke it back.

"Shut up!" Borse slapped her with his free hand, hard enough to jerk her head around. She saw Luke come up off the wagon bed, fists clenched, but Borse's own fist connected with his jaw, and Luke went down limp and still. Laylie screamed in fury this time, kicking at the overseer.

"You want her?" Borse called to Millie. "Here!"

Then the world was spinning. Laylie landed in a water-filled ditch, her mouth and nose filling with mud. She struggled to her hands and knees as Millie jumped in the ditch and splashed out to her. Millie was talking, but Laylie couldn't hear the words. All she could see was the wagon, carrying Luke away.

Millie led Laylie back to the Big House and left her shivering by the fire under the watchful eye of Mrs. Brown while she went to church with the Dinsmores.

In the next few days, Laylie got up each morning and did each chore Millie gave her without comment or complaint. Millie still read the Bible every morning and night, but Laylie wasn't listening anymore. *Millie Keith is a slave owner, just like Master Phil and Missy Isabel. She buys people, and she sets them to work.*

Brothers and Sisters

How long did it take Hettie to get well when Borse whipped her? A month. JoMa will make Luke well in a month, and then he will come for me. Laylie started counting the days.

It was a week later when Laylie carried an armload of clean wash into the room to find Millie sitting on the bed.

"Put those down and come sit with me," Millie said.

"Is something wrong?" asked Laylie.

"Yes," Millie said. "Very wrong. Uncle Horace has just returned. He had gone to meet with his solicitor in Charleston. After Luke was whipped, I asked my uncle if he would buy him, and Uncle Horace agreed to do so. However, he happened to meet Mr. Borse on the street in Charleston. He asked after Luke, and . . . that horrible Mr. Borse said . . ."

"Luke is dead," Laylie whispered. Through the stillness that settled over Laylie, hushing sounds and dimming the light, she saw Millie nod.

"He lied," Laylie said. "He said he was coming back for me."

"He didn't lie. He would have come," Millie said. She put her arms around Laylie. "Luke wanted you to be free. I will not leave you here, I promise. I'm going to take you to Indiana with me where you will be free."

Laylie could hear her own heartbeat rushing in her ears. *Wild geese fly, the North Star shines, but Luke's heart isn't beating anymore. It isn't saying Lay-lee, Lay-lee. I hope that Borse didn't whip him again. I hope that JoMa was there holding his hand. JoMa or Hettie.*

"Is what Rachel said about Heaven true? No more hurting or tears?" asked Laylie.

"Yes," Millie said.

"I lied to you about Meadshead. There's people there that believe in God. After everyone is supposed to be in

bed, you hear them singing 'Steal away to Jesus,' and then some of them walk to the swamp. That's where they meet. Do you think . . . Luke went there before he died?"

"I hope so. He listened very carefully to what Old Rachel had to say."

"But how could he go, all cobbled up and beat down like he was?" Laylie asked. She knew he couldn't have.

"Laylie . . ." Millie asked, "do you want to steal away to Jesus right now?"

"No," Laylie said. "I want Luke."

Laylie went about her duties in a fog, losing track of hours and days. *Why did God stop calling Luke's name? He saved him twice. If Luke had answered the call, would God have saved him again? What if God is mad at me for something I have done, and that's why he let Luke die?*

"Mrs. Travilla, the mistress of Ion, has sent her carriage because she would like me to visit," Millie said one day. "I think you should come, too. Perhaps a change of scenery will be good for you." Laylie only nodded and followed Millie out to the carriage.

When the carriage stopped at Ion, the driver opened the door and helped them out. A manservant let them in the front door and led them to a parlor where they were greeted by a plump woman with salt-and-pepper hair and a very sweet smile. Millie had just finished introducing the woman as Mrs. Travilla when Rachel came in carrying a tea service.

"Well!" she said when she saw Laylie. "It looks like I brought one cup too few."

Brothers and Sisters

Mrs. Travilla pulled a cord and the manservant re-appeared. She asked him to bring another cup, and when he did, Mrs. Travilla poured the tea herself, passing Rachel a cup first, then Millie and Laylie, and serving herself last.

Laylie had never seen a slave sit down to tea with her mistress.

"Laylie," Mrs. Travilla said, seeing her look, "you have met Rachel, and you know she is a slave. But what you may not know is that she is my dear older sister." Laylie looked at Rachel, who smiled.

"Oh, not my flesh and blood sister, of course," Mrs. Travilla went on. "She was born in Africa, and I was born not far from here. But we are sisters in the Lord, and a sister is a wonderful thing to have."

"Couldn't wash my hair without you," Rachel agreed. "My arms are too stiff!"

"And I couldn't have managed my home without you," Mrs. Travilla said. "My neck was too stiff!"

"Well, well," Rachel said. "Between us we manage. We do manage. Laylie, I was mighty sad to hear about your brother. Why don't you and me go for a walk and talk for a while? I had a brother, too, once upon a time."

Millie nodded, so Laylie stood up. Rachel started to rise, but only made it halfway.

"Let me help," Mrs. Travilla said, taking Rachel's arm and helping her out of the chair.

"Halls getting longer, chairs getting lower. I guess I'm getting closer to Heaven," Rachel said. She took Laylie's hand and led her through another room and out French doors into a winter garden. The air was cool and Rachel drew her shawl close around her shoulders as they walked. Dark evergreen hedges and dry yellow lawns stretched out around them.

"Tell me about Luke," the old woman said.

"Luke took me to JoMa's after Mamma died," said Laylie. All the memories that had been tumbling around inside her just started spilling out. The words kept coming and coming—big things like how Luke had taken her to Andros to keep her out of trouble, and his promise to take her to freedom, and little things like how he wasn't afraid to sit in the burying ground at night.

"Luke wasn't afraid of anything," Laylie said. "Not anything but rats." Then she laughed because that sounded so funny, but the laugh was tears when it came out. "Rachel? Did . . . did God let Luke die because he was mad at me?"

"No, child!" Rachel said. "No. Luke died because there is evil in this world, terrible evil."

A gust lifted leaves by their feet and swirled them into the air. Rachel stopped a moment and watched the leaves until they settled.

"Kimbareta was my younger brother," she said when the leaves were still. "One day he came home from hunting to find slave traders rounding up the women and children of the village. He should have run. Should have just turned and run. But he didn't. He tried to hold them off until my daddy and the other men could come. He tried to fight." She became silent, and Laylie knew Rachel was seeing her brother, just like she saw Luke.

"Kimbareta was a boy that loved Jesus. He done what Jesus done, not hesitating to lay down his life for another."

"In Africa? JoMa said that Jesus was white man's religion," Laylie said.

"I knew my Jesus long before the slave traders came." Rachel pulled her shawl closer. "Long before I ever saw a

white face. Our church had been a house of worship longer than anyone could remember. But there was plenty that didn't know God, I guess. My daddy used to go walking days and days to tell people the Good News about Jesus."

"JoMa told us stories about God sending a message to the people," Laylie said. "But she never said it was about Jesus."

"The Holy Spirit is calling out to people in every place," Rachel said. "Like Saint Paul said, 'Since the creation of the world God's invisible qualities—his eternal power and divine nature—have been clearly seen, being understood from what has been made, so that men are without excuse.'"

"Sometimes, when the stars fill up the sky," Laylie said, "I don't feel like I have any excuse. Not with them blazing down on me."

"That's right out of the Bible, child," Rachel said as she eased back against a rock wall. "King David wrote, 'The heavens declare the glory of God; the skies proclaim the work of his hands. Day after day they pour forth speech; night after night they display knowledge. There is no speech or language where their voice is not heard. Their voice goes out into all the earth, their words to the end of the world.'"

Rachel laughed at the look on Laylie's face. "God told me a long, long time ago to hide His Word in my heart. I've been hiding it ever since, like gold and jewels all piled up inside me. I first read God's Word in Portuguese. Lord, that was a long time ago. When I was first brought here, I had a time learning the language. But soon as I did, I started telling people 'bout my Jesus. I haven't stopped. Here's something you can tell JoMa if the Good Lord ever lets you see her again. The Bible says, 'The Son is the radiance of

God's glory and the exact representation of his being.' Jesus isn't a white man's God. He's the message JoMa's waiting for. God's own message to Africa, and to this sad old South, too. His people have to carry it. They have to speak the Good News until folks listen. That's the only way this broken world is going to change. The only way."

Rachel stood up, and they started back up the garden path.

"After I was brought here," Rachel said, "I was all alone, alone like you are now. God gave me Mrs. Travilla as my sister. Now that Millie girl—she's wanting to be your sister."

"She bought me," Laylie said.

Rachel stopped and looked at her. "Did you ever hear the word 'redeemed'? "

Laylie shook her head.

"Well, redeemed means someone paid a price for you, to set you free. Jesus died to redeem you from Satan, the devil. Maybe that Miss Millie paid a price to set you free. Maybe she's trying to be like Jesus."

CHAPTER

12

Plots and Plans

You prepare a table before me in the presence of my enemies. You anoint my head with oil; my cup overflows.

PSALM 23:5

Plots and Plans

ou wanna p-play quarterstaffs?" Friar Tuck asked. "You can h-hit me if it makes you f-feel better."

"It's raining too hard," Laylie said. It was the first time she had come to the hideout since they'd heard that Luke was dead.

The Merry Men were huddled together, both for warmth and to stay dry. The branches over their heads kept most of the early December drizzle out, but now and then someone would wiggle as an icy drip slipped down their spine.

"Borse is a bad man," Marion said, but Alan-a-Dale shushed her, pulling her close.

"She cries all the time now," he said. "We never seen nobody whipped before." Little John nudged him hard, and everyone looked at the dirt floor, or out the door at the rain—anywhere but at Laylie.

"Tell us a story," Alan-a-Dale said at last.

"About Robin Hood and me!" Marion said as she wiggled away from him and closer to Laylie.

"I don't feel like a story about Robin Hood," Laylie said. "I'll tell you a story from Africa instead. My JoMa carried it over the ocean in her heart." She waited until they were quiet to begin.

"When God finished all of His creating," said Laylie, "He wanted to send the people a message. He looked around for a critter to carry His words . . . ."

After Laylie finished the story, Marion asked, "Was that a true story?"

"I don't think it's true," Little John said.

"M-maybe it's t-true in Africa!" Friar Tuck said loyally.

Laylie's Daring Quest

"True is true, no matter where you are," said Laylie, standing to leave. "I'll be back tomorrow."

Laylie would have spent all day in the woods, but Millie kept her busy with needle and thread every morning. The pantalettes were soon finished.

"You have a gift, Laylie," Millie said the next morning. "It takes most little girls years of practice to make their stitches so fine and even! Now, we could work on your pink dress, or . . ."

"Or what?" asked Laylie.

"Do you know why we celebrate Christmas?" Millie asked.

Laylie shook her head.

"It's because of Jesus," Millie said. "We celebrate because God loved us so much that He sent His Son to die for us."

"Rachel read that to us from her Bible. Why would God do that? Send his boy to die?" asked Laylie.

"Why did you give biscuits to your Merry Men?" Millie asked.

"I wanted to take care of them. And nobody else would give them any."

"That's why God sent His Son. Because we needed a Savior—someone to pay the price for our sins—and no one else could send one. It was wrong of you to steal, Laylie. But when you took care of your friends, you were being a little bit like Jesus."

"I liked taking care of them."

"Would you like to give your friends some gifts for Christmas?" asked Millie.

"I don't have anything to give them," Laylie said.

Millie pulled a petticoat out of her bureau and spread it on the bed.

Plots and Plans

"We could make rag dolls. Would your friends like that?"

"Maybe the girls would," Laylie said. *That petticoat is ghost-white. Maid Marion will cry if she wakes up with a ghost-baby looking at her.* "But . . . it's the wrong color," said Laylie.

"Oh!" Millie said. "I see what you mean."

Millie begged fabric scraps from Isabel's seamstress, and Laylie found coffee-brown material for Marion's doll and a piece as shiny-dark as Little John herself for the other.

It took two days for Laylie to finish the first doll body, stuff it with cotton, and stitch it up. Millie spent the mornings sewing with Laylie, making fancy doll clothes while Laylie stitched the body of Little John's doll.

One unusually warm morning, they were able to take their sewing to the garden, and a young man stopped to talk. He stared calf-eyed at Millie every time she looked away, and pretended he hadn't when she looked back. Millie didn't notice, even when he picked up a piece of lace she dropped and tucked it in his vest pocket. He turned pink when he saw Laylie watching him.

"That's a beautiful doll," he said, as if he hadn't just swiped a piece of doll pantalette. "May I see her?"

Laylie handed over Little John's doll reluctantly, afraid he might stick it in his pocket too.

"I would think someone who could make a doll like that would be very proud," he said, handing it back.

Millie smiled at him.

"Charles Landreth," Millie said, "meet Robin Hood." She explained about the Christmas gifts for Laylie's friends. "But we don't have anything for the boys."

"Perhaps I can think of something for the boys," he said. "I've got it! Come on!"

Laylie's Daring Quest

They followed him to the kitchen where he sweet-talked Phoebe out of two tin cans. They went to the smithy next, where Charles borrowed a hammer and nail and punched holes in the cans. When each one had two holes, he strung loops of twine through them, stepped up on top of them, and holding the twine in his hands, started walking around.

Millie laughed and clapped her hands, and Charles turned pink all over again as he handed the can stilts over to Laylie.

By Christmas Eve, Laylie had both dolls finished and can stilts for each of the boys. That night she dreamed about giving the gifts to the Merry Men. They shouted and whooped in her dreams, and Luke was sitting in the hideout laughing with them all. When Laylie woke up, there were tears on her face and a box wrapped in paper and tied with a bow on the foot of her bed.

"It's for you," Millie said. "Open it."

Laylie tore the paper apart and gasped. "A cloak and cap just like Robin Hood wore!" Laylie ran her fingers across the silky fabric. *The cloak is made from the green silk of Millie's special dress.*

Millie laughed as Laylie tried on the cap and then wrapped herself up in the cloak. It was lined in warm wool, and best of all, it was big enough to hide all of the dolls and tin cans while she ran down to Sherwood Forrest.

"Y-you look pretty," Friar Tuck said first thing when Laylie arrived.

"Corncakes, Robin!" Marion shouted, holding up a sack. "We made you corncakes on account of Christmas!"

"I made you something, too," Laylie said, "on account of Christmas." She handed out her presents one by one. They

did whoop and shout, and Little John cried because her doll was so pretty. Then they ate the corncakes and drank hot raspberry tea.

That night, Millie read about God sending His Son as a present for the world. Laylie pulled the green cloak close around her as Millie read. *No one would give a slave something this fine. People don't chop up their best dress for a slave. . . . But people might do that for their own sister . . .*

Redeemed. Millie paid a price for me . . . it musta been like Rachel said. Millie was trying to be like Jesus, like how I try to be like Robin Hood. Laylie smiled. *I'm going back to Pleasant Plains with Millie Keith. I will have sisters and brothers . . . and I will be free.*

Laylie spent the rest of the Winter listening to Millie read letters from Pleasant Plains. She sewed as Millie told stories of Ru, Cyril and Don, Zillah, Adah, Fan, Annis, and Millie's Mamma and Pappa, imagining what it would be like to live with them all. Millie sewed, too, helping Laylie with tricky seams, and making her a brown apron to wear when she went to the woods to play with the Merry Men.

"Mamma will be proud of your skill with a needle," Millie said one day, as she examined the tiny stitches on the hem of Laylie's pink dress. "I'll tell her how hard you have worked. In fact, I think you should wear this dress on your first day in Pleasant Plains."

"My freedom dress!" Laylie said happily.

When they were all alone on the hill, or in Millie's room, Millie listened while Laylie read from the Bible, just as if she was already free to open any book she wanted and speak the words out loud.

Laylie's Daring Quest

Millie showed Laylie where to find stories about God walking in the fire with Shadrach, Meshach, and Abednego, closing up the mouths of hungry lions for Daniel, making soldiers blind, and sending chariots of fire to help Elisha.

As Spring deepened and their departure day drew near, every day Laylie felt lighter, like chains were falling off of her. She spent as many hours as Millie would allow running in the woods with the Merry Men. But even when it came time to tell them good-bye, she didn't say, "I'm going to freedom." She just hugged each one tight.

"Are you comin' back at harvest, Robin?" Maid Marion asked. "My daddy's coming back at harvest."

"No," Laylie said. "I'm not coming back at all." *I'm going to freedom, and I can't take them with me, or bring freedom back to them either. There is evil in this world, terrible evil, that's what Rachel said, and it's true.*

"Who's gonna tell us stories then?"

"Little John can tell them," Laylie said.

"She's not good at it," Alan-a-Dale said. Will Scarlet just nodded.

"I-I'll tell them," Friar Tuck said.

Maid Marion was so sad that Laylie could hardly stand it. Suddenly she wanted them to remember her, her and Luke.

"I'm gonna tell you one more story," Laylie said. "There was a gator in a sinkhole. My brother, Luke, was sent in after it." Laylie told the story of Luke's fight with the gator and of Isaac's help.

"Did God really send that Isaac running?" Maid Marion asked.

"Isaac says it," Laylie said.

"I'm gonna pray to God to send us a new Robin Hood," Maid Marion said.

Laylie thought about God sending Isaac to help as she walked back to the Big House, and about all the stories where God sent help to the people in the Bible. *If he can do all that, why doesn't he just crush the evil in the world? Crush it out and leave the good.*

That night Millie gave Laylie a carpetbag to pack her things in.

"Laylie!" Millie said, when she saw her tucking the book *Robin Hood* into the bag. "You can't take that book with you! It belongs to Uncle Horace. Don't worry—my brothers have one just like it, and I am sure they will let you read it. We have many other books as well."

One just like it? Laylie blinked. *So that wasn't Andros's book at all? That means Andros's book is safe in the swamp with him!* Laylie smiled as she handed the book to Millie. *In two days I'm leaving for Pleasant Plains, for freedom, and all the books I can read, and nothing can stop me.*

However, two days later, Millie announced, "We are not going directly to Pleasant Plains. Uncle Horace needs me to go with him to a plantation called Viamede. He must pick up his granddaughter Elsie there, because her guardian has died. We can't leave for Pleasant Plains until we return. Elsie is a very little girl, Laylie—just four years old, and she needs our help."

"Is Viamede north?" Laylie asked warily.

"No," Millie said slowly. "It is south, almost as far as we can go," Millie said. "I will not leave you here. You will be with me the whole way, there and back. But Laylie . . . we will be visiting with the Breandans in their house in Charleston."

Laylie curled into a very small ball, and not even her Robin Hood cloak could hide her. Millie sat on Laylie's cot

and rubbed her back while she read, "The LORD is my shepherd, I shall not be in want. . . ."

⌒⌒

"Even though I walk through the valley of the shadow of death, I will fear no evil, for you are with me; your rod and your staff, they comfort me."

Those words kept running through Laylie's mind as she stood by the carriage the next morning, but she didn't feel comforted at all. Her freedom dress was rolled tight in the bottom of her carpetbag where she could sneak her hand in and feel it if she wanted to. Millie smiled like nothing was wrong, but it was. They were about to get on a coach that would carry them south.

"I was thinking," Ajax said as he lifted a box onto the boot of the carriage, "that it gets awful lonely up on top. It's a long ways to Charleston. I was thinking I could use some company."

Laylie looked to Millie for permission before she scrambled up to the driver's seat. Ajax laced the reins through his strong fingers, and then the horses started out.

At first, they followed the same road Laylie had walked on her way to Roselands, but eventually Ajax turned the horses east.

"We'll take the ocean road," he said. "There's an inn Mr. Dinsmore likes to stay at when he travels to Meadshead."

The road soon turned south along the low, seaside dunes. When they stopped at the inn at last, Laylie jumped down and waited while Master Horace helped Millie out of the carriage.

"What a marvelous view," Millie said, walking over to the bluff's edge.

While Horace went into the inn to arrange for rooms and dinner, Laylie and Millie walked down the path to the

sea to stretch their legs. The waves were wild and the flumes of spray felt wonderful after the heat of the road. Laylie started to pull her dress off over her head so she could get in the water.

"Laylie! Put your dress back on this instant!" Millie said. "Ladies do not take off their clothes in public!"

"I'm not a lady," Laylie said. "I'm a slave. And we take 'em off to go swimming. I've got dust all over from riding on top of the coach. Look." She pulled her lips back. "Even in my teeth!"

"We will wash up later in our room," Millie said. "Just as Adah or Zillah or Fan would."

Millie picked up a stick and wrote in the damp sand. The letters were connected and had curlycues on them.

"What's that say?" Laylie asked.

"It's my name in cursive writing," Millie said. "Can you read it?"

Laylie shook her head. "It don't look much like letters in books."

"Would you like me to write your name?" asked Millie.

"No," Laylie said. "Write 'freedom.' I want to see what it looks like."

Millie took her time on the word, making it extra fancy.

"Do you remember when Old Rachel talked to you about freedom?" asked Millie.

"And Jesus," said Laylie as she walked toward the ocean, lifting her skirt to keep it from the wave that chased her back toward Millie.

"And Jesus," Millie said. "The Savior we read about in the Bible. Have you thought any more about Him?"

"You mean about being a Christian like you?" asked Laylie.

"Yes, about giving your life to Him. Remember how you said that you hoped Luke had stolen away to Jesus?"

Pain shot through Laylie's heart. *When we get to Meadshead, we'll be close, so close to Luke's grave.*

"Well, you can do that right now," Millie said. "He wants to save you."

"I thought about it some," Laylie said at last. "About Jesus and sin. Especially about sin. I'm not good like you or Rachel. Even Luke was better than me. I steal, and sometimes I lie. Lately I've been lying more than I've been stealing." She picked up a rock and threw it at the ocean. "But if I could hit Borse in the head with a rock, I surely would. That's sin, like Rachel said. Hateful sin, but I don't care. If I was God, and God was me, I wouldn't like Borse."

"God knows you hate Borse," Millie said. "He knows what's in your heart and He knows everything you have ever done. He still loves you, Laylie. Jesus died for you while you were still a sinner. That's what the Bible says. Remember, you can ask His forgiveness, and He can change your heart right now."

"If he can do all of the stuff in the Bible," Laylie said, "why's this old world such a rotten place?"

"Do you remember who Satan is?" asked Millie.

"He's the bad guy who tricked Eve," Laylie replied.

"He is the bad guy. Like . . . like wicked King John in *Robin Hood.* King John was just a pretender—he took the throne while the real king, good King Richard, was away. And he did all kinds of evil things. Well, Satan is just like that. He is a pretender who is doing evil things, and convincing men to do them, too." Millie took Laylie's hand. "When Jesus, the real King, comes back, He is going to throw that pretender in prison and lock him up forever."

"Just like King John got thrown in prison?" said Laylie.

"That's right. But until he is thrown in prison . . . the whole world is a little like Nottingham. There is an evil impostor trying to rule it. And we only have two choices. We can be on the side of the good king, or we can be on the side of the bad king. But if we are going to be on the side of the good king — on Jesus' side — then we can't serve the bad king. We can't keep on lying or stealing or hating. We have to let Jesus help us stop doing that and serve Him with all our hearts."

"I wish the good king would hurry up and come back," Laylie said, "and throw Satan in Hell, and Borse with him."

"Laylie," Millie said, "if King Jesus came back right now, which side would you be on? Would you be one of His good followers? Or would you be serving the impostor — just like Borse?"

"I —" The ocean had come up, swallowing the word Millie had written in the sand. "I want to go back now," Laylie said.

⌒

Laylie stood behind Millie as Old Miss and Master Phil came down the steps of their Charleston townhouse to greet their guests, and then Laylie followed Millie up the steps into the house. Roz, the Breandans' coachman, gave her a surprised look as she went by. As soon as Laylie stepped inside, someone touched her elbow, then pulled Laylie aside.

"Terria!" Laylie said. "What are you doing here?"

"I'm head cook and housekeeper, that's what."

The young woman motioned for Laylie to follow her. "I'll show you the rooms we set up for Miss Millie."

Laylie followed Terria up the stairs to a pretty room with a large bed and lace curtains on the windows.

Laylie's Daring Quest

"If you're servin' as her maid, you just sleep on the floor," Terria said.

Ajax brought in Millie's trunk and valise and Laylie started to unpack.

"We was all wondering where you was at," Terria said when he was gone. "Look at you! All dressed up and fancy! My, my." She shook her head. "And still as wicked as you ever was, I guess."

Millie came in just then, escorted by Old Miss herself.

"What a pretty room," Millie said. "I'm sure I will be comfortable here."

"I'll leave you to Terria's care," Old Miss said.

"This is Terria, Millie," Laylie said, when Old Miss was gone. Terria's eyes grew wide at Laylie's familiar use of Millie's first name, but Laylie ignored it. "Terria used to be in the kitchen at the Big House at Meadshead."

"And you was always stealin' food," teased Terria, cuffing Laylie's ear. "What your brother would say if he knew you was in Charleston, I don't know. He thinks you're away safe at Roselands."

"Luke?" The hairbrush Laylie had just taken from the valise clattered to the floor.

Terria folded her arms. "You got other brothers I don't know about?"

Laylie sat down suddenly and Millie knelt beside her.

"We thought Luke was dead," Millie said, putting her arm around Laylie.

"Most troublesome dead man I ever saw," Terria said. "He's run twice, but they dragged him back both times. Borse can't beat him to death, starve him to death, or work him to death, though Lord knows he's tried. Yes, ma'am. I'd say he was alive."

CHAPTER

Curtains and Trains

Now choose life, so that you . . .
may love the LORD your God,
listen to his voice, and hold
fast to him.

DEUTERONOMY 30:19–20

Curtains and Trains

"I've got to see him, Millie," said Laylie. She had spent the whole night sitting up, wondering how anyone in the world could sleep. "He's not gonna know I'm here, and we're leaving tomorrow."

"I will do everything in my power to help you see Luke," Millie said. "In fact, I will speak to Uncle Horace today while we are sightseeing. I don't have the money to buy Luke and take him with us, Laylie. But Uncle Horace offered to buy him once before. If his offer still stands, we can get Luke away from Borse at least."

But when Millie came back in the late afternoon, she had no news for Laylie.

"Be patient," Millie encouraged softly. "I don't feel I can discuss it in front of the Breandans. I must find a chance to speak to Uncle Horace alone."

"But we're leaving tomorrow!" Laylie said.

Millie only shook her head. "I will have news for you when I come back from dinner," she promised.

The sun was down by the time Millie had bathed and dressed for the evening meal. Laylie sat still as long as she could, hoping that Old Miss's dinner parties did not run as late as Missy Isabel's did. But they did. When she couldn't stand it any longer, Laylie started to pace, six steps one way, six steps another.

Six paces . . . turn. *How could Millie have been with Master Dinsmore all day and not asked about Luke?* Six paces . . . turn. The big old tree outside the window was swaying in the wind, the moon causing its shadow to move on the white lace curtains. . . . Turn. *If Luke knew I was here, he'd* . . . tap, tap, tap! *If Luke was here . . . That's not a shadow of a tree on the curtain!*

Laylie's Daring Quest

Laylie raced across the floor, threw the curtain aside, and shoved the window up.

"Luke!" she cried. He was sitting on the tree limb.

He didn't say anything, just jumped in, gathered her up, and squeezed until she squeaked.

"I thought you were dead!" she said when she could breathe again.

"A time or two," Luke's smile flashed, "I thought I was too. Whooo!" He sat down on the edge of the bed. "I've been running all day and half the night to get here. Roz said he saw you. I've been brushbustin' away from roads, trying to get here before Borse did."

"Is he coming?" Laylie shivered.

"He would if he knowed. He's been waitin'. You're not going back to Meadshead, that's all."

A loose board in the hall creaked. Luke dropped to the floor and scooted under the bed. Millie came through the door. She closed it behind her and leaned against it. Her face was pale and she looked sick.

"Luke ran," Laylie said.

"He what?" asked Millie.

"He heard I was in town from Terria's man Roz, and he ran. Borse is going to come here, Millie. I'm afraid."

"Why would you be afraid? He . . ." Her eyes went to the open window. "You can come out, Luke. I know you are here."

Luke scooted out from under the bed.

"Hey, miss!" he said.

"Does anyone else know you are here?" Millie asked.

"No, miss. I came up the tree and in the window."

"Laylie—" Millie squeezed her eyes shut. "When I talked to my uncle about Luke, I found out . . . Isabel Dinsmore lied to me. She told me she could sell you to me,

but she could not. They are going to take you back to Meadshead, and I . . . I can't stop them."

"I can," Luke said. "We gotta go now, Laylie girl. I don't know how we're gonna get out of town, but . . ."

"I know a way," said Millie, and they both turned to look at her.

"I know a way you can get far away from here in one day. Too far for Borse to follow. Uncle Dinsmore took me on a tour today and I saw a train—the Phoenix," said Millie.

"They're not going to let us on any train, miss," Luke said.

"You're not going to ask. Do you know where the train yard is?" Millie asked.

"No, miss," said Luke.

"I'll have to show you then," said Millie.

Laylie's carpetbag was too big to take, so she made a bundle of her Robin Hood cloak, stockings, an extra petticoat, and her freedom dress, wrapping them all in a brown work apron. Then she followed Luke out the window into the branches of the tree. She dropped her bundle and scrambled down after it.

"Psst!" Millie was at the window. She dropped a hatbox, and Laylie caught it just before it hit the dirt.

"What is that?" Luke asked, as Millie dropped another.

"It's a hatbox," Laylie said.

"Hats? We're making a strike for freedom. Why do we need hats?" he asked.

Millie dropped two more of the boxes and then crawled out of the window. Luke caught her as she dangled from a branch and helped her down.

"Why are we carrying these hatboxes?" Laylie asked.

"So it will look like I have been shopping," Millie said.

Laylie's Daring Quest

"Do people shop in the middle of the night?" Luke whispered as they started to walk.

Laylie shook her head. Millie must have been more worried than she seemed. They were each carrying two boxes, and Laylie could barely see the top of Millie's head bobbing along ahead of her. There were few people on the streets of Charleston at this time of night, and those that were seemed to have no interest in them.

"Where are we going?" Luke whispered, after they had been walking for some time. "We've been past this butcher shop twice!"

Suddenly Luke grabbed Laylie by her apron strings and pulled her back into an alley. Millie had stopped to speak with two young men. They both lifted their hats to Millie.

"The tall one is Charles Landreth," Laylie whispered. "He wants to be Millie's beau." The other young man left, but Charles Landreth took Millie's elbow and led her back toward the entrance to the alley.

"He better be friendly," Luke said. "This is a dead end. We ain't got nowhere to go."

Charles looked directly at Laylie and winked as they passed. Millie nodded and motioned for them to follow her.

Charles led them straight to the train. The locomotive looked like a sideways kettle on wheels, and it was separated from the passenger cars by a flatcar filled with bales of cotton. Millie started tugging at a bale.

"You can hide in here, if we can make room," she said. "No one will see you."

Luke jumped to help, and Millie let him tug at the heavy cotton bale.

"Why is there cotton on the train?" Laylie asked as Luke and Charles pulled a bale around the corner into an alley to hide it.

 880

"Occasionally," Millie said, "very, very occasionally, the locomotive blows up, sending pieces of metal flying in all directions. The cotton keeps the fragments of metal from piercing the passengers."

"We're done," said Luke. Then he picked Laylie up like she was a sack of spuds and started hauling her toward the train. Laylie saw Millie's hand go to her mouth. In all the joy and hurry, Laylie had never thought that finding Luke meant losing Millie. *I'll never see Millie again!*

"Wait, Luke!" Laylie kicked and squirmed until he put her down. "There's something I've gotta do." *Millie paid a price to take me to freedom — and if anyone ever found out that she helped us escape, she'll pay a lot more. They will throw Millie in jail and never let her out!*

Laylie ran back to Millie.

"Did . . . did something ever happen to you that was so good that you couldn't believe it really happened?" Laylie asked.

"Yes," Millie said. She reached out and touched Laylie tenderly on the face. "I think it has."

"I think something that good . . . it's got to be from King Jesus," Laylie said. "I want to be on his side. Will you show me how?" asked Laylie.

"What are you gonna do?" Luke asked.

"The Bible says, 'If you confess with your mouth, "Jesus is Lord," and believe in your heart that God raised him from the dead, you will be saved,' " said Millie. " 'For it is with your heart that you believe and are justified, and it is with your mouth that you confess and are saved.' " Tears glistened on Millie's cheeks in the moonlight. "Laylie is about to get saved."

"She don't need savin'," Luke said. "She needs to get on that train." But he didn't pick her up again.

881

Laylie's Daring Quest

"Now don't be hasty," Charles Landreth said. "The lady has gone through a great deal of trouble for you tonight. Give her a moment." Charles pulled Laylie and Millie out of sight between two railcars. "Best to try and conceal ourselves a little," he said.

"Thank you," Millie said. She took a deep breath. "Laylie, do you believe that Jesus is Lord, and that you are a sinner who needs a Savior?"

"I do, I really do," said Laylie. She was shaking inside.

"Then you need to ask Jesus to forgive your sins," Millie said.

"Jesus," Laylie prayed, closing her eyes, "forgive my evil heart. I'm tired of Satan, and I don't want anything to do with him anymore. I don't want to hate or steal or lie." *Do I have to list all my sins one by one? I'll never get through. God, you know them all.* Laylie figured the sins knew he was coming for them, too, cause she could feel them wiggling around inside her, stinging like nettles.

"Millie says you died on a Cross to take my sins away," Laylie continued, "and I want you to have them. I want you to be my King Jesus from now on, amen." There was one great sob, and Laylie gasped. *The nettles are gone!*

"Millie, it worked!" she said. "I don't want to hit Borse with a rock anymore!"

"Get in that hole," Luke said, picking her up. He sounded angry.

"Tell them about me, Millie," said Laylie as she pushed her bundle into the hole. "Tell Zillah and Adah and Fan."

"I'll tell them," Millie said. "I'll tell them to pray for you every single day. I'm going to miss you so much . . ."

Laylie wiggled back to make room for Luke. Charles muscled the last bale of cotton into place. Laylie heard their

footsteps grow faint as Millie and Charles walked away, and then there was silence, except for Luke's ragged breathing.

"Don't worry," Laylie said at last to her brother. "Borse's not going to catch us. God is helping us."

"Girl," Luke said. "If I'd have knowed Miss Millie would fill your head full of talk like that, I'd have dragged you outta that Big House myself. I never want to hear it out of you again, you understand?"

"Why?" asked Laylie.

"Because . . . because I said so, that's why. I got plenty of other things to worry about. There's a whole city out there that's gonna be lookin' for us in the morning."

"There was once a man named Elisha," Laylie said. "I read about him in the Bible. A bad guy named Aram wanted to kill him. He sent an army to capture Elisha. Elisha's servant looked outside one morning, and the whole city was surrounded by Aram's army. Elisha told him, 'Don't worry.' He prayed to God and God opened the servant's eyes. He saw the hills were full of horses and chariots of fire, all there to watch over Elisha!"

"God didn't send no chariot of fire to save us," Luke said.

"Maybe He did," Laylie said. "Maybe we're sitting on it."

"I said I don't want to hear about God no more," Luke whispered. "I thought about what Rachel said, thought about it hard, but I can't do it. I got things I can't lay down."

"What kind of things?" she asked.

"I've made two promises," Luke said. "Two. I'm gonna keep them both, and nothin's gonna stop me. Not whippings or starving or God. The first promise was to Mamma. I promised to take care of you. I'm gonna get you to freedom, girl. But the second one I made to myself. When you are safe

with Aunt Tempie, I'm going back. I'm going back to kill a man. That's the promise I made."

Luke!

"I don't want to hear any more preachin' from you. I've heard all I need from Isaac and Hettie."

If Luke kills Borse, they'll hang him by the neck!

"But we can get far away, where he can't find us . . ." said Laylie.

"Hush," Luke said. He sounded tired, more tired than she'd ever heard him sound before. "I ran all night last night, and we're gonna hafta run again. Only a fool would talk when he could be sleeping."

Laylie listened to his breathing grow deep and even. Mamma's freedom. That was their quest. Hadn't Luke whispered to her in the darkness when she was just a baby, promising they'd find it? Hadn't they talked about it a thousand times in the top branches of the live oak — talked and planned and dreamed? But somewhere in all the beating and the starving and the hurt, Luke had gotten lost. He'd forgotten the quest.

Laylie slept in fits and starts, waking completely as people started moving around the train. She could tell it was early morning by light seeping in through the crack between the bales. She squeezed past Luke so she could peer out. Two men were dragging a bale of cotton out of the alley where it had been hidden by Luke and Charles to make room for the two stowaways. The men stood over it, scratching their heads. A bell clanged twice, and a voice called, "All aboard!"

Then with a sound like a dragon rising up in its chains, the Phoenix started her run.

CHAPTER

14

Ambassadors in Chains

*Pray also for me, that whenever I
open my mouth . . . I will fearlessly
make known the mystery
of the gospel, for which I
am an ambassador
in chains.*

EPHESIANS 6:19–20

Ambassadors in Chains

$\mathcal{T}$he next stop, we take our chance," Luke said. The train had rattled through the morning and most of the afternoon, stopping now and then for fuel and water. "If we ride her to the end, there'll be all kinds of folk around," he said.

Laylie was ready when the train stopped moving. Luke pressed his feet against the bale and pushed, shoving it far enough to allow them space to wiggle out. He went headfirst. Laylie pushed her bundle out after him, and then tumbled out herself. She tried to run, but her legs had been tucked under her too long. She took one step and fell into the bed of cinders.

"Better get up," said a strange voice.

Laylie scrambled up and looked straight into the eyes of an old man. He was sitting on a rickety chair with a checkerboard spread out on a half-whisky barrel in front of him. His checkers partner must have left to tend the train. He nodded as Luke shoved the cotton back in place.

"I'd go that away, was I you," said the old man, pointing a bony finger toward the bushes on the other side of the tracks. "Lickety-split!"

Laylie took one look back along the train, where passengers were stepping down to stretch their legs, before Luke grabbed her hand and they ran, jumping the tracks and scrambling over the rocky slope until they reached the bushes. The pins and needles in her feet let up by the time they hit the bushes.

There was a rutted lane on the far side of the bushes, and they stopped to make sure no one was coming. The sun was hidden by clouds, and there was no way to tell which way was north, south, east, or west.

Laylie's Daring Quest

"Over there!" Luke pointed to a stand of trees across a wide field.

They ran again, and this time Laylie's side was hurting when they stopped. The trees were thick and the bushes dense, but another road ran right through them. This one was more traveled than the last, with a ditch cut by the side to carry the rain away.

"Horse is coming," Laylie said. They flung themselves down among the brambles, wiggling until they were in the bottom of the ditch and holding their breath as a farmer passed by on a swaybacked nag.

"We're gonna have to wait here," Luke said, "till the sun goes down."

Laylie tensed every time the clip-clop of a horse or the rattle of wagon wheels passed on the road above them. She tried not to think about how hungry she was, but the more she tried not to think about food, the more she thought about all the good things she'd had to eat at Roselands. That made her think of tea and sugar. Suddenly she was so thirsty she couldn't suck a thimbleful of spit.

"I'm thirsty," she whispered, when she couldn't stand it anymore.

"Here." Luke handed her a small, smooth pebble. "Put it under your tongue."

She did, and her mouth washed with spit. She sucked the pebble until the sun went down and the stars were spread like a map across the sky.

"This road don't run in the right direction," Luke said. "We're gonna have to make our own trail."

They had walked for an hour before they came to a stream. Laylie scooped the water up in her cupped hands, drinking until she couldn't hold any more, and then they

started out again. Once, they heard a dog barking and turned west up a long hill to avoid its yard. They kept walking until dawn washed their map from the sky, then they found a little hollow to huddle in. Laylie spread her cloak over both of them against the morning dew.

"How far do you think we came?" she asked.

"Five miles, maybe," Luke said. "We'll do better tomorrow."

Luke was still sleeping when she woke in the late afternoon. Laylie lay still, listening for the sound that had waked her—a rustling. Something was stirring in the underbrush. She would never have seen it if she hadn't been hiding in the bushes herself. Even so, it took a moment for her eyes to pick it out—a turkey hen nesting under the bushes not fifteen feet away. *Turkey eggs!* Laylie's stomach rumbled as she reached for a rock. The turkey squawked as the rock skipped on the ground and bounced off her breast, but she didn't give up the nest.

"What are you doing?" The sound had waked Luke.

"Getting us a late breakfast." Laylie grabbed a stick and started crawling through the bushes toward the nest. The turkey hen turned her head sideways, peering at Laylie with one beady eye as she approached. Laylie stood up.

"Get!" Laylie said, poking at the turkey. The hen came out of her nest like a fury of feathers, hitting Laylie right in the chest and beating at her face with powerful wings. Laylie dropped the stick and flailed her arms, trying to get rid of the bird, and finally managed to push her away. The old hen glided to a nearby branch.

Luke was laughing so hard he had to crawl to the nest. There were eight eggs. They sucked one each and then

wrapped the others in Laylie's bundle. They ate the last of the eggs two mornings later for breakfast.

On their fifth night of walking, they stumbled on a road heading north. They made better time, but there were cultivated fields on each side of the road. Somewhere close by a shot sounded.

"Almost dawn," Luke said. "That's an overseer's gun." They started looking for a place to hide, but the only thing close was a wooden footbridge that spanned a small creek choked with creeping vines. Luke pulled aside the vines so that they could crawl under and rest, but Laylie couldn't sleep, thinking about cottonmouths and spiders. They sat back-to-back, listening to the boards creak as people walked above them.

"I've had enough of roads," Luke said when it was dark enough to crawl out from under the bridge at last. "We're goin' cross-country again."

They had walked for half an hour when someone just busted out singing right in front of them. Laylie nearly jumped out of her skin, and Luke pulled her down, putting his hand over her mouth to keep her from talking.

"My Lord calls me, he calls me by the thunder;
The trumpet sounds it in my soul,
I ain't got long to stay here."

It was a woman's voice, low and strong. Suddenly other voices answered—men's and women's and children's too, rising up together.

"Steal away, steal away, steal away to Jesus!
Steal away, steal away home,
I ain't got long to stay here."

"It's a meeting, Luke! Like back home!"

"Laylie," Luke said, grabbing for her arm, "don't you—"

But she was already running through the woods.

There must have been fifty men and women in the clearing, raising their voices to the Lord in the moonlight.

"Green trees are bending, poor sinners stand trembling;
The trumpet sounds it in my soul,
I ain't got long to stay here."

No one had noticed Laylie standing in the shadows. "Steal away," Laylie whispered.

"My Lord calls me, he calls me by the lightning;
The trumpet sounds it in my soul,
I ain't got long to stay here."

Luke had come out of the trees and was standing beside her now. His face was very still, and his arms just hung at his sides.

Can't he feel the lightning and thunder inside? It made Laylie want to shout.

The people started another song now, this one joyous and fast, and they clapped their hands and shouted, stomping out a rhythm. A young man picked it up on a log drum, pounding out a heartbeat of praise, while the people sang and danced, some lifting up their arms and shouting out to God. The air quivered with joy, and Laylie thought angels must be dancing and shouting with them.

"Did you ever see anything like it?" Laylie whispered.

"Yes," Luke said, but he didn't say anything more.

"Why are you children hidin' in the shadows?" asked a man. He was standing over them. "Come on out and join the meeting!"

The drummer stopped and people turned to look as they came out into the moonlit clearing.

"Why, they's strangers," a large woman said. Luke tried to step back, but hands grabbed at them, pulling them into the center.

"Runaways," someone whispered.

"They don't look like they've eaten in days," said the woman who had led the singing. "Lindy, run and get them what we got."

"Where are you from?" the questions started, followed by, "Where're you going? And how long you been on the run?"

"Quiet!" the woman said. "You're gonna scare them to death! I'm Sarah, and you are welcome in our prayer meeting. I'm sure the Lord sent you to us, because to get north you have to cross the river, and the only way over it is a bridge in the middle of town."

Laylie looked at Luke, but Sarah leaned close.

"Don't you worry. I know a way to get you across," Sarah said.

Lindy came back with a crockery jug full of thick buttermilk and a plate of cornbread. While Luke and Laylie ate, Sarah explained that the town was on both sides of a spring-swollen river.

"After the meeting, I'll take you to a place you can sleep. And tomorrow, you're going to walk right through that town in broad daylight, and I'll tell you where you can get help on the other side," Sarah assured them.

A small lamp was lit and Sarah produced a Bible. The people quieted to hear her words.

"I'm reading to you," she said, "The words of Zechariah, the time God filled him up with the Holy Spirit when his son John the Baptist was born. He started singing God's praise, and prophesying of the comin' birth of our Lord Jesus. 'Praise be to the Lord, the God of Israel, because he has come and has redeemed his people. . . .' "

Thrill shot through Laylie at the sound of the words. Luke leaned over and whispered, "I'll be waitin' out there."

People watched as he left the meeting, but no one stopped him, and Sarah went on.

" 'He has raised up a horn of salvation for us in the house of his servant David . . . salvation from our enemies and from the hand of all who hate us — to show mercy to our fathers and to remember his holy covenant, the oath he swore to our father Abraham; to rescue us from the hand of our enemies, and to enable us to serve him without fear in holiness and righteousness before him all our days.' "

She set the Bible aside. "The Jews were some of the most hated people on earth," Sarah said. "But God never forgot them. And He ain't forgot us neither, in these times. He sees the whips."

Someone said, "Save us, Jesus!"

"He sees the chains," Sarah assured them.

"Mercy, Lord!" a woman cried out.

"And He sees a people who praise His name," Sarah proclaimed, "by the mighty power of His Spirit, a people willing to walk in holiness and righteousness before Him all our days!"

"Amen!" many voices shouted together.

"Satan thinks he can keep us from worshiping God by binding us up in slavery," said Sarah.

"He thinks wrong!" the drummer shouted.

"He thinks he got his foot on our necks!" Sarah was was pacing as she preached.

"He thinks wrong!" the people shook their heads.

"He thinks we don't know God hears our prayers!"

"He thinks wrong!" the crowd roared.

"We are hard-pressed on every side," Sarah said, her voice growing softer, "but we are not crushed. We are perplexed, but not in despair. We are persecuted, but not abandoned."

"Not abandoned," the people whispered.

"Struck down, but not destroyed. We carry around in our own bodies the death of Jesus, so that life . . . the life of Jesus may also be revealed in our bodies!"

"Give us life, Lord!"

And then the people were praying, speaking praise to God and encouragement to each other. Laylie prayed too, asking for the Holy Spirit to speak to Luke sitting alone in the dark.

Finally, the meeting started to break up, and Luke came walking back. Sarah led them through the darkness to a small cabin set alone in a field. She pushed the door open. There was a snoring lump wrapped in blankets on a cot on one side of the room.

"Don't worry," Sarah said. "Jane's only sickness is old age. She's not gonna recover from it, but you won't catch it neither. Her mind has already gone the way her body is going. She won't even know you was here. I'll send some things with the girl that comes to care for Jane tomorrow. One of them will be a pass to get you through town. It'll have Master Olivet's name on it. I can write it as well as he can himself. You have to destroy it once you reach the other side, so no one can trace it back. Follow the road north, and in two days you will come to a place where you can get some help. There's a man there named Miller, at a farm with two windows facing the road, two little windows on a big red barn. It's got a horse-and-carriage weather vane on top. If it's safe to stop, he hangs a fishnet in one window."

After Sarah was gone, Laylie said, "Luke . . . that song they were singing, 'Steal Away,' I remember that song. Not just the part I heard Isaac sing. I remember all of it, all of the words."

Luke didn't say anything.

"It was Mamma's song, wasn't it?" she asked.

"She used to sing a lot of songs," Luke said.

"She sang them for Jesus, didn't she? Mamma was a Christian. She belonged to Jesus, didn't she?"

"It got her killed," Luke said bluntly. "She was teaching at a meeting—"

"Like Sarah?" said Laylie.

Luke nodded and said, "And Borse broke it up. He said that Jesus was for white men, and that he would kill anyone he caught preaching the Bible to slaves. Mamma told Borse God sent her to preach about Jesus, so she couldn't stop. She told Borse she was gonna pray for him." Luke put his head down. "The next night Borse came knocking on the cabin door. Mamma put you in my arms. She said, 'Luke, take care of your sister now. You promise you will take care of her.'"

Laylie reached out and touched Luke's face. It was wet with tears, but he didn't bother to push her hand away.

"I said, 'Where are you goin', Mamma?'" His voice had dropped to a whisper. "She says, 'I'm going to Jesus now, baby. I love you forever.' The next day they found her floatin' in the swamp. Jesus didn't save her. Not from Borse."

Laylie put her arms around her brother and held on as sobs shook his body. She was still staring into the darkness when his breathing went steady with sleep at last.

Laylie's Daring Quest

"Jesus," Laylie whispered. "My Mamma's with You. Could You tell her . . . tell her not to worry. I'm looking after Luke now."

CHAPTER

Courage and Keys

Be joyful always; pray continually;
give thanks in all circumstances,
for this is God's will for you in
Christ Jesus.

1 THESSALONIANS 5:16-18

Courage and Keys

*B*y mid-morning, Laylie could see that Sarah had been right. There were too many yards and fences and dogs to go cross-country here, but no one gave them a second glance as they walked along the side of the road. Many other people, black and white, were on their way to or from town, carrying baskets and bundles.

In the middle of town, just before they reached the river bridge, they found the street blocked by a crowd gathered around a painted wagon.

"Buy Dr. Tatum's Miracle Elixir today, and wake up well tomorrow!" yelled a fat man standing in the wagon. He held up a brown bottle. "Dr. Tatum's heals arthritis, rheumatism—" He stopped as a cough shook him and pressed a dainty white kerchief to his lips before proceeding, "vapors, croup, and gout!"

"Doesn't seem to have helped you," an old woman said, and the crowd laughed.

"Keep walking," Luke said, pulling Laylie up onto the boardwalk. "We'll go right past." Laylie craned her neck to watch, depending on Luke to pull her along.

"Ah! Madam," the fat man bowed his bulk in the old woman's direction. "You see before you an almost perfect picture of health. Just this morning, I was on my deathbed—" The cough took him again.

"That cough sounds kinda fatal," a sheriff said to him. "We don't want your carcass left here. Move along!"

Luke stopped so suddenly that Laylie ran into him.

"You two from around here?" Two white men were blocking their way.

899

Luke mumbled something and handed the pass Sarah had written to one of them. The man glanced at it. "James Olivet," the man spat, "spoils his slaves."

Then the second man spat tobacco juice on Luke's feet. The thick, red-brown liquid splattered Laylie's skirt as well.

Laylie noticed the painted wagon going by. It was the fat man's turn to stare at her.

"Get into the street," said the second man as he shoved Luke. "Slaves don't use the boardwalk in this town."

"Yes, master," Luke said, stepping down. He held out his hand for the pass, but the man dropped it in the street. Laylie picked it up quickly, crumpling it in her hand as they hurried on, over the bridge, and out the other side of town. As soon as they were past the last houses, she tore the pass into tiny bits, scattered them under a bush, and then covered them with leaves.

That night they slept in a haystack, after drinking from a ditch and eating a little dried meat from the provisions Sarah's church had put together.

Late the next afternoon they passed the fat doctor again, selling a bottle of Miracle Elixir to a child at a crossroads. Darkness was falling, helped along by thick storm clouds. Thunder rumbled in the distance, and a few fat raindrops fell as they passed the remains of a burned-out farm.

"How far did Sarah say to Miller's barn?" Luke asked. "We ain't gonna see no fishnet or weather vane in the dark. We need some place to hole up. Come on."

They went back through the quickly dimming light to the ruined house. Two rooms were gutted and blackened, but the third still had enough of a roof to keep the rain out, and three walls to block the wind. They huddled together in the corner under the Robin Hood cape. They heard the wheels of the

painted wagon rattle past and ate the last of their dried meat before the storm broke in earnest. A tremendous bolt of lightning slashed a zigzag through the sky, and the rain poured down, but they were dry enough for sleeping.

⌒

"Laylie," Luke said. "Sit up slow."

The fat doctor from the painted wagon was standing over them. He had a shotgun pressed against Luke's chest. A towheaded boy stood beside him, his mouth hanging open.

"Now, this isn't as bad as it would appear," the fat man said. "I expect that you have run away. Fortunately for us all, I have work that needs to be done on my own place, work I am simply not fit to do."

He coughed, and then motioned for them to move outside. Laylie snatched up her bundle of clothes.

"Now, climb right into the wagon, both of you," said the man.

Luke nodded, and Laylie jumped up into the wagon. There were six short chains, each one fastened to the wagon bed on one end and a leg iron on the other end.

"I am an occasional trader in slave flesh," the man said, still pointing the shotgun at them. "And I know all the tricks, so I suggest you don't try any. Lock them up the way I showed you, Roy."

The boy scrambled into the wagon. He put a leg iron on Luke first, fastening it with a lock and key. Laylie's leg was too thin, so the fat man directed him to wrap the chain tightly around her waist and fasten it there. When they were both secure, the boy handed the keys to the fat man in return for a coin.

"Thank you for your assistance," the man said. The boy laughed and went down the road whistling.

"Do you wonder how you have been caught?" the man asked. "I didn't see you down the road, and with the rain coming and all, I thought to myself, 'If I had a little sister and needed to get her out of the rain, where would I go?' Of course I thought of this place. I gave that boy a coin to help me and he was all the help I needed. Cyrus Tatum! That's the name of the man who outthought you!"

Two miles down the road, they passed a red barn with a fishnet hanging in the window and a horse-and-carriage weather vane on the roof.

"You still trusting that Jesus of yours?" Luke whispered.

"Yes," Laylie whispered back.

"Why? He let you get locked up in chains."

"He let me get sent back to Charleston, too," Laylie said. "And I thought that was bad. But it wasn't. I would have never found you, Luke, and you wouldn't have found me, neither, if I'd gone off with Millie."

"That's not the same thing," Luke said.

Cyrus stopped at the smithy in the next town.

"Don't usually shackle kids," the smith said. "Don't have anything small enough."

"One leg will do," Mr. Tatum said. "What I want is a ball and chain—and make it a long one. She'll have to get around the house."

"I think I got a locking wrist iron about that size," the man said. Laylie lifted the hem of her skirt. Her pantalettes were stained and muddy from running through the fields, but the smithy didn't seem to mind. He fitted the wrist iron right over her clothing, locked it shut, and handed Cyrus Tatum the key.

Courage and Keys

Cyrus dropped it in his coat pocket, then grunted as he lifted the iron ball and dropped it with a thunk in the wagon bed. He motioned for Laylie to get in. It was awkward pulling the heavy chain along with one leg. She heaved herself up, then pulled the chain in hand over hand. She was rubbing her ankle when the wagon started off again.

A fortnight later, Cyrus Tatum reined his poor old horse to a stop in front of a little house on a back lane. They had been traveling southeast by Luke's reckoning—back toward Meadshead, taking their time at every town and crossing where Tatum could sell his elixir. They wouldn't leave until Cyrus had sold a bottle to everyone in town, or been thrown out by the law, whichever came first. Whenever he could hire Luke out to work shoveling out stables or pigstys for two or three days, he did, using the money to provide room and board for himself while Luke and Laylie slept chained in the wagon.

The house they stopped at this time looked more run-down than most they had been to. Luke sat in the wagon, but Laylie jumped down and stretched her legs.

The chain rattled against the wooden wagon as it snaked out behind her. The sound brought two huge black-and-tan hounds scrambling out from under the porch. They rumbled deep in their throats, and Laylie backed up against the wagon as they stalked toward her.

"Samson! Delilah!" Cyrus yelled. "Shut up!"

The hounds slunk back toward the house. Laylie looked around with more interest. *If those are Tatum's hounds, then this is his house,* thought Laylie. The shutters hung crooked

now and half the pickets on the fence were missing. The gardens around it were full of spring weeds, and the fields lay fallow, barren of crops.

"Petunia!" the fat man sang. "Come see what I have brought you!"

"Oh, Tater Pie!" The huge woman who stepped out onto the porch was as run-down and washed-out as the house. "I had no idea you were even thinking of bringing me slaves!"

"I wasn't," Cyrus said. "They're runaways."

"Runaways." She looked down at Laylie. "You seen our hounds, didn't you?" she asked. Laylie nodded. "We hire those dogs out to track runaways. There wasn't enough left of the last slave they caught to collect a reward on, though."

"I'll bring the little girl in before I get this one situated in the shed." Cyrus picked up the iron ball at the end of Laylie's chain to carry it inside.

"In the kitchen," the woman said, leading the way. The kitchen smelled of rancid fat. Cyrus put the iron down in the middle of the floor.

"How long do you expect to keep them?" the woman asked.

"Long enough to get some stumps removed," he said. "The boy's big enough for it."

"You gonna sit with him the whole time? He'll run again if you don't."

"If he was going to leave his sister," Cyrus said, "he'd have left her back where they came from. Keep her in here, and he won't go anywhere."

Petunia followed her husband out of the house, and Laylie looked around. There were stacks of dirty plates, cups, and pans on the table, and a pile of trash in the corner. Laylie's chain was just long enough to reach the doorway of the parlor.

When she leaned in and looked, she saw more piles of trash, and a hallway that must have led to the Tatums' bedroom.

Laylie watched through the window as Cyrus and his shotgun ushered Luke into a shed. Luke was carrying Laylie's bundle with him. *At least he'll have a pillow,* Laylie thought.

Petunia was angry when she learned that Laylie couldn't cook. But that night, Petunia sat like a queen in her shabby kitchen while Laylie waited on her—just as if Petunia was mistress of Roselands—with Laylie standing behind Petunia's chair, filling her cup, and taking her plate away when she had finished.

When Cyrus and Petunia went off to bed, Laylie cleaned the dishes they had used in a pan of soapy water on the stovetop, making just enough noise to reassure them she was hard at work. When she heard soft snores coming from the back of the house, she wiped her hands on her skirt and picked up the iron ball. She cradled the cold weight in her arms and staggered to the door. If she could get out to Luke, he might be able to bust the chains. She balanced the ball between her stomach and the wall, steadying it with one hand as she turned the doorknob with the other. She eased the door open. Samson was lying right outside. He came to his feet quickly, hackles rising. Laylie shut the door again. There was no way she could get past the hound—not carrying this cannonball. *If I hit him with it, Cyrus will wake up for sure.*

The Tatums hadn't given her a blanket or a mat, so Laylie curled up on the dirty floor. *Does God see my chains, like Sarah said?* Laylie wiped her eyes. *Maybe Satan thinks he can keep me from worshiping God by binding me up.*

"He thinks wrong," Laylie whispered. She pushed herself up to her knees and folded her hands the way she had seen Millie do so many times. She talked to God about

Laylie's Daring Quest

Cyrus and Petunia and their ugly hounds, and about Luke lying all alone in the shed — Luke who hated Borse so much he'd forgotten all about their Mamma's freedom.

～～～

Laylie prayed all of the time after that, praying out loud when the Tatums weren't around, or silently if they were. Sometimes she made up her own songs to Jesus, singing her prayers and praises. Petunia caught her at it one day and just stood staring before she slammed the parlor door so she couldn't hear.

Before the week was over, Laylie knew there was nothing in the kitchen that would open the lock on her anklet and nothing sharp enough to cut the chain. *Cyrus might still have the key in his coat pocket, but he never leaves the coat where I can reach it,* she thought.

Every morning, Laylie watched as Cyrus let Luke out of the shed and sent him off to work. Luke always turned and looked before he went, lifting his hand when he saw her in the window. She'd wave back, then get to work on scouring pots or boiling laundry. Cyrus and Petunia worked together, brewing elixir in a big copper washtub in the back yard. Cyrus ladled it up and Petunia held the funnel as they filled bottle after bottle with the brown liquid. They were always close enough to keep an eye on Laylie.

"We need bacon and flour, Tater Pie," Petunia said one evening as Laylie cleared the dishes. "I've used it all up, and those slaves are the reason why. They eat more than they're worth, and it's high time you collect that reward."

"Perhaps you are right," he said. Laylie heard the chair creak. "I need to order more bottles tomorrow. I will check the notices in town. Someone must be looking for them."

"Let's hope it's someone rich," Petunia said, "who wants them back real bad."

Laylie bit her lip. *Master Phil is very rich, but it will be Borse who is looking, and Borse who is waiting for us when we are taken back to Meadshead.*

After the Tatums had gone to bed, Laylie took the grease pot from the back of the stove. She sat down on the floor, took off her boot, and pulled up her pantalettes so that the cold iron was against her skin. Then she scooped up a fingerful of grease and smeared it over her ankle, packing it under the metal, then pushing the manacle down over her foot. It felt as if the bones in her foot would break. Laylie gritted her teeth and pushed as hard as she could. It wouldn't come off.

"Lock that Luke up in the shed before you go," Petunia said the next morning after Cyrus had his coffee, toast, and eggs. Petunia was wearing a dressing gown and slippers, too lazy to get dressed if they weren't going to be brewing that day. Cyrus was in his medicine show suit, with his coat draped over the back of his chair.

"I've already sent him to work. I'll be back before he knows I'm gone. I don't want to lose a day's work out of him."

Laylie clenched her fists under the soapy water where she was scrubbing Petunia's bloomers. *Even if Luke knows Cyrus is gone, he can't come for me. Samson and Delilah will be waiting on the porch.*

"Don't you sleep all day while I'm gone," Cyrus said to his wife. "There's plenty you could do around here."

Petunia glared at him.

"I have a headache," she said.

"Try some elixir," Cyrus laughed.

"Don't try to sell it to me," she said. "I know what's in it. And don't stop at the saloon, neither. I want you back here by noon." She glanced at Laylie. "You know I don't like to be left alone when we have them on the place."

"I'd think a sizable woman like yourself would have no fear," Cyrus said.

Petunia stood up, her rosebud mouth hanging open.

"Sizable?!" She slapped her napkin down and stomped from the room.

Cyrus put his coffee cup down. "Aw, Petunia!" he called after her. "You know I didn't mean it! Come on back and give me a good-bye kiss!"

"No!"

He scooted his chair back, got up, and went after her.

"Petunia, baby, I meant respectable, not sizable. That's what I meant to say . . ."

Laylie stood frozen for just a second after he left the room. His coat was hanging on the back of his chair. *Has he ever taken the key out of his pocket?* She jumped across the room, remembering at the last minute to dry her hands on her skirt.

Cyrus's pocket was full of dirty kerchiefs, and Laylie grimaced as she rooted through them. Her fingers felt something hard in the bottom of the pocket. She had it out and was standing at the washtub holding the key under the water when Cyrus came back into the room.

"Don't you give Petunia any trouble today," Cyrus said, picking up his coat. "She's got a sizable *and* respectable headache. So you be quiet. And don't you open up the back door. I'm leaving Samson and Delilah on the porch, and I won't be here to call them off if they set on you."

If God has given me the key, just like that, Laylie thought, *it must be time to go.*

908

Laylie waited at the window until she saw Cyrus ride away, then she unlocked the ankle iron and took it off. Her ankle was still slick with grease from the night before. The hounds would love that when they were coming after her. *The hounds. How can I get past them?*

"If you can't outrun them or outfight them, you must outthink them." That's what Andros used to say. She left the key on the floor, grabbed the grease pot and a spoon, and headed for the door. Samson and Delilah were sprawled on the back porch. Delilah lifted her head as Laylie came out the door.

"I'm not goin' anywhere," Laylie said. "Just painting the wall." She took a spoonful of grease and smeared it along the wall, holding her breath as Samson came close enough to lick at it. Soon Delilah's tongue was busy, too. Laylie spread the grease as far and as thin as she could, emptying the whole pot. Then she set the pot down and walked slowly toward the shed. The dogs were too busy licking the wall to notice.

She pushed the shed door open. There were chains in the corner where they shackled Luke each night, and her travel bundle was there as well. He'd been using it for a pillow and her cloak as a blanket.

Laylie wrapped the bundle up in the cloak, and slipped out the door. The hounds didn't even look up as she dodged behind the woodpile and started for the fields.

Luke had dropped his shovel when he saw her coming, and he met her halfway through the field.

"Cyrus has gone to town," Laylie said. "They're turning us in for the reward."

"How much time do you expect we have?" Luke asked.

"Petunia probably knows I'm gone already," Laylie said, as he took her bundle from her and tied it to his belt. "She won't come looking on her own. She'll wait for Cyrus to get home, him and his horse. When he comes after us, he'll have the hounds."

"We'll figure that out when we come to it," said Luke, starting out. "We might find a creek to throw 'em off the scent."

They kept up a steady pace all afternoon, and Laylie was beginning to hope that Cyrus wouldn't come at all. Then the wind shifted and Laylie heard the distant bay of a hound.

"They're still far off," Luke said. "Far off. But I want you to run now. Try to keep up with me."

He set off at a lope and Laylie did her best, running until her side cramped.

"Run through it," Luke said. "Keep going." He was running barefoot over the sticks and rocks, but he was still having to hold himself back to wait for her.

Arooooooooo. The hounds were closer now. Each breath felt like fire in Laylie's lungs.

"I can't . . ." she had to suck in air to finish, "run no further, Luke."

"You got to. Come on."

Laylie leaned against a tree to keep from falling over.

"I can't. You go on. You can make it without me."

Luke's fist clenched as he looked back the way they had come.

"No," he said, and the next thing she knew he had thrown her over his shoulder.

"Put me down!" she said.

"Shut up," Luke said. "I don't have breath to waste." He started to run.

Arooooooooo. When Laylie lifted her head to look back she saw blood in Luke's tracks. A few more moments and the hounds noticed it too. There was a fierce edge to their cry, a savage, killing sound. Luke must have heard it too, because he put on speed, running full out through the trees.

Courage and Keys

Lord Jesus, Laylie prayed, *a man can't outrun hounds and horses!*

Nobody had told Luke that. He just stretched out and started eating up the miles, the bay of the hounds always behind him but never getting closer. He ran until Laylie thought she was going to pass out from the pain of hanging upside down, or vomit from the thud of his shoulder slamming into her stomach.

Suddenly Luke stumbled, and when he caught his balance, he was limping. Ten more steps, and he was running again, but not as fast. The hounds were gaining now, and they knew it by the heat of the trail. They were close enough for Laylie to hear their yips and snarls of excitement, when Luke turned and headed uphill. Laylie lifted her head. Black and tan flashes showed through the trees. The dogs were closing the distance with every leap.

Luke stopped at last, dropping Laylie against a wall of rock. It was taller than the treetops and went off on each side as far as she could see.

"Climb!" Luke gasped, grabbing her again and lifting her up as high as he could. Laylie found handholds and scrambled with her boots until the toes caught, then pulled herself up.

"Faster, girl!" Luke was right behind her. Samson broke through the bushes below them, leaping and snapping just short of Luke's feet. Delilah raced from the brush and launched herself up, twisting and frothing in her frustration. Laylie closed her eyes and pressed her face against the stone. Her legs started shaking so hard she thought she was going to fall off the cliff.

You're almost there. The words spoke in her head, but they weren't her own.

"Holy Spirit?" Laylie said. "Is that You?" *Is He speaking to me like He did to Isaac?* Laylie wondered in amazement.

Laylie's Daring Quest

Be strong, the voice said, and the shaking in her legs stopped. *Be strong and courageous. It's time to bring Luke home.*

Laylie started climbing again, faster than before, handhold by handhold up the rock.

"Get down here!"

Cyrus had caught up with his hounds. A pistol cracked and rock shards stung Laylie's arm, but by the time he could reload she was over the top. Luke came right after her. He grabbed a rock the size of his head and pushed it over the edge. A dog screamed in pain and kept screaming until the pistol cracked again.

"That one won't be runnin' no more slaves," Luke said. "Let's go."

They walked, too tired to do anything else, and kept on walking even after the sun went down. They found a creek and followed it downstream, splashing through the cold water until Laylie's feet went numb.

Finally, Luke crawled up out of the stream and collapsed. Laylie untied her bundle from his belt and spread the cloak over him before she fell asleep.

"Luke," Laylie said and shook him. "Wake up. We need to be going." Luke stood up and sat right back down again. The soles of his feet looked like slabs of raw liver. Laylie took her extra petticoat and tore the edge with her teeth until she could rip it into strips. She wrapped his feet tight.

"How's that feel?" she asked.

"Fine," Luke said, but she knew by his limp he was lying.

"Luke," Laylie said, as she helped him along, "the Holy Spirit talked to me while we were on that cliff, just like He talked to Isaac that time. He said—"

Luke shoved her hand away.

912

"I don't want to hear no more about your chariots of fire," he said. "That train carried us to nothing but trouble. And that God of yours let you spend a month chained up."

"We're out of there now," Laylie pointed out. "And maybe God did have a reason, like when He sent me to Charleston."

"I said I don't want to hear any more of your preachin', " Luke said. "Not one more word. You think you can tell me something I don't know, but you can't. You think your preachin' is gonna keep me from goin' back, but it's not!"

Laylie shivered. It was almost like Luke's hatred of Borse was lashing out at her. "I am goin' back," Luke's fists were clenched. "I'm gonna kill Borse. And you can't stop me. If you ever preach at me again, I swear. . . . you'll be no sister of mine! Now come on."

Not his sister? Laylie followed behind him in miserable silence. *Luke couldn't just throw me away. Could he?*

The sun was hidden behind a thick ceiling of clouds, so they followed the stream, now and then catching crawdads under the shadows of the bank, eating every soft bit they could swallow and spitting out the shells.

Once, they crept past a farmhouse in the dark. Luke stopped when he heard the cluck of chickens.

"They don't got a dog," he said, "or it would be barking already. You could sneak in there and get us some eggs. I can't run fast enough if they should come."

"I thought you said Mamma wouldn't like it if I stole stuff," Laylie said.

"And I thought you wanted to be like Robin Hood, stealin' from the rich and givin' to the poor. You can't get much poorer than we are now."

"I don't want to be like Robin Hood. I want to be like Jesus."

Luke groaned.

"I bet Jesus was never as hungry as I am now," he said.

"He was too," Laylie said. "I read it in Millie's Bible. He went without eating for forty days, and when Satan tempted Him to do wrong and make some bread to eat, He didn't do it."

"Well, Robin Hood was never hungry," Luke said. "He probably never missed a meal! And don't make me tell you again about that preachin'."

"I'm not preachin'," Laylie said. "I'm just telling you what's what. I'm not gonna steal." Her stomach grumbled as they went on past.

The stream finally emptied onto a wide, lonely beach, and they turned north. They walked only a few miles a day. Whenever they found a bay with telltale holes in the sand, they stayed as long as they could, digging clams and smashing them open with rocks to get the meat.

Holy Spirit, Laylie prayed silently as she used the last of her clean cloth to change Luke's crusted bandages, *I know You talked to me on that rock. I'm doing my best, but . . . I don't know how to bring him home. I don't know what to do. I need help.*

Luke's feet weren't getting any better. They would have to stop and rest for them to heal up, and there was no place to rest. There wasn't anything to do but keep going, so Laylie walked close to her brother so that he could lean on her when his feet hurt too bad.

Two days later, Luke lay down to rest in the shade of a drift log, and Laylie sat beside him, wondering if she would get him up. The narrow beach they were on would disappear when the tide came in. Laylie studied the sandy dunes behind them. There was a faint path all the way up to a twisted tree standing on a hill.

Laylie stood up.

A tattered red rag dangled from its branches.

CHAPTER

16

Blissful Blessings

You are the light of the world. A city on a hill cannot be hidden. Neither do people light a lamp and put it under a bowl. Instead they put it on its stand, and it gives light to everyone in the house.

MATTHEW 5:14-15

know where we are!" said Laylie.

"What are you talkin' about?" Luke said.

"I tied that red rag up there," she pointed at the tree, "the first time I rode Gypsy. We're near Roselands!" She pulled him to his feet.

"Where do you think you're going?" he asked.

"To get some food," Laylie said. "The Merry Men know us, and—"

And if Millie is still there, she might have fresh bandages and medicine for Luke's feet, she thought. But Laylie knew better than to say it. *Luke will never go if he knows I'm looking for Millie.*

"We can't go up there!" Luke stopped in his tracks. "People know us. They know we belong at Meadshead. How long do you think it would take Borse to come fetch us? This is the worst place we could be, girl. We're goin' right on by."

"Then you're goin' without me." Laylie dropped his hand and kept walking. "I'm hungry."

Luke swore, but then he hobbled after her. Laylie stayed close to him as they made their way up the trail. It was Friar Tuck's head rag all right, hanging right where she'd left it.

It had taken fat little Gypsy a long time to trot from the Big House to that hilltop, and Laylie wished she had the little beast now. She'd put Luke on Gypsy and make him ride, even if the pony rattled his teeth out. As it was, they stopped so often to let Luke rest it was nearly dark by the time they reached the hideout.

"R-Robin?" Friar Tuck's voice was so loud it made her jump.

"Shhh!" Laylie said.

The boy's mouth dropped open. He looked from Laylie to Luke. Then he turned and ran.

"Told you we shouldn't have come here," Luke groaned. "Who do you think he's runnin' for? Someone who's gonna turn us over to the law, that's who."

Luke had crawled into the hideout and collapsed.

Friar Tuck came back, but he didn't have the law with him. He had Little John. Each of them was carrying a bowl of cornmeal mush.

"S-see, Little John?" Friar Tuck said. "s-she looks real s-skinny." He held out one of the bowls. "You h-hungry, Robin?"

Laylie took the bowl, careful not to spill a drop as she crawled back to Luke. Little John and Friar Tuck followed her inside and watched as the hungry runaways scooped up the mush with their fingers.

"They're starvin' all right," Friar Tuck said. "We're gonna hafta get 'em more."

"They're not playing," Little John said. "They're on the run."

Friar Tuck just nodded.

"You can't tell nobody we're here," Laylie said, looking up from the bowl.

"We can't get you any more food until tomorrow morning," Little John said. "We gotta be in our cabin before curfew."

Laylie crawled out of the hut with them.

"Is Millie still at Roselands?" she whispered.

"She's here," Little John said. "I seen her in the garden."

"I need to talk to her," Laylie said.

"What are you whispering about out there?" Luke called.

"Nothing," Laylie said, crawling back inside.

Friar Tuck and Alan-a-Dale brought corncakes the next morning, as many as Laylie and Luke could eat.

"It's our breakfast," Alan-a-Dale said. "We all saved it, after Friar Tuck told us you was hungry."

Laylie crawled out of the hut and almost bumped into Millie's knees.

"Laylie!" Millie gathered her up in her arms. "What on earth are you doing back at Roselands? And where is Luke?"

"Right here, miss."

Millie followed Laylie into the hut, where Luke sat leaning against the stone wall.

"What happened?" Millie asked when she saw his feet.

"Got caught," Luke said. " 'Bout eight nights after we left the train."

Millie untied one end of the rag on his foot and started to peel it off.

"Ouch! Those rags are stuck on, miss. I told Laylie not to come here," Luke frowned. "People here know us. It's the worst place we can be. But I couldn't move fast enough to stop her, so I had to come along."

"Luke is right, Laylie," Millie said. She looked worried. "They are hunting you, of course."

"Can you help Luke's feet, Millie?" Laylie asked.

"I'll go for Rachel," Millie said. She gathered Laylie in her arms again. "Praise God you came when you did! I haven't been back long myself, and I may be leaving any day. I so wanted to see you again, to know that you were

919

safe." Millie set Laylie on her feet. "I . . . I'll come again if I can. But if I can't . . . my prayers will be with you always, little sister. Don't forget me, because I will never forget you."

Laylie hugged her hard, until Millie pulled herself away.

"Luke needs Rachel," Millie said, "and they will be looking for me soon. Heaven help us if cousin Arthur decides to track me into the woods!"

It was late that afternoon, and all the Merry Men had assembled before Old Rachel arrived.

"Well, well," she said. "If it ain't Lazarus come right out of his tomb! Every time I think these old eyes have seen their last miracle, the Lord goes and shows me another one! Let's get these grave clothes off." She started to peel the crusted cloth from Luke's feet, and he moaned.

"Somebody get me a stick," she said.

Maid Marion scurried out of the hideout and brought back a sturdy stick, then squatted with her elbows on her knees and her hands on top of her head, watching every move Old Rachel made.

"Here," said Rachel, giving the stick to Luke. "I've got to doctor those feet or the gangrene will take 'em. If the pain hurts too bad, bite down on it. I don't want to hear a sound come past it. There's a road not too far on the other side of this rock. Last thing we need is for someone to hear you moaning and crying and to come see who it is."

Luke bit down hard as she peeled the cloth, layer by layer, off his wounded feet. He was shaking by the time she took a jar of ointment from her black bag and started

gently working the grease into his feet, but he never made a sound.

"That's that," she said at last. "We're gonna let the air on 'em tonight, and I'll bandage 'em again tomorrow."

"We ain't gonna be here tomorrow," Luke said.

Old Rachel sat back on her heels and looked at him.

"That's too bad. I sent Miss Millie to fetch some friends of mine, the Blisses. They're the kind of friends you need right 'bout now. I expect if you stay put, help will come along. 'Course you can go hobblin' off into the dark if you want to. Have you decided to answer the call of God yet? Because it's beyond all reason that you are sitting here now. Beyond all reason!"

Luke shook his head.

"Now, what possible thickheaded reason could you have? Miss Millie told me your sister came to the Lord."

Luke shook his head again.

"Well, you think about it," Old Rachel said. "Laylie, you bring my bag."

Laylie carried it out, then helped Rachel stand up. The old woman sighed and stretched her back.

"I'm getting too old for this kind of thing," said Rachel.

"Are you the new Robin Hood?" asked Maid Marion, who was staring at Old Rachel with her huge brown eyes. "Laylie can't be anymore. She's gotta run. Friar Tuck says so."

Rachel considered the little girl.

"What is a Robin Hood?" Rachel asked.

"We're the outlaws," Marion explained, "and—"

"She means Merry Men," said Alan-a-Dale, pulling Marion back.

"And R-Robin Hood t-tells us stories," Friar Tuck said. "Mostly."

"And brings us biscuits," Marion said, shaking off her brother's hand and glaring at him. The evening shot sounded, calling the Merry Men home, and Rachel shook her head as they scattered.

"A Robin Hood!" Rachel said. "I never heard of such a thing. Where do they get these ideas? Eugenia is going to send the carriage down the road sometime soon, so I don't have to dodge the patrollers on the way home."

It took Laylie a moment to figure out that Eugenia must be Mrs. Travilla. Rachel stretched her back again and grimaced up at the sky. "I am too old for this. When are You gonna give me rest, Lord?"

Laylie walked with Rachel to the edge of the bushes, where they could listen for the carriage wheels.

"Have you been praying for that brother of yours and telling him about Jesus?" Rachel asked.

"I pray," Laylie said. "But Luke don't listen when I talk."

"You sure he's not listening?" asked Rachel.

"He says I'm just a kid, and I can't tell him anything he doesn't know."

"Luke said that? Now, listen here. The Word of God has power, no matter who is preaching it. Paul wrote a letter to a young man some people thought was too young to preach. His name was Timothy. Paul told him, 'All Scripture is God-breathed and is useful for teaching, rebuking, correcting and training in righteousness, so that the man of God may be thoroughly equipped for every good work.' That works for women too. You just speak the Scripture to Luke. He'll hear something he don't know, all right!"

"I don't know very much," Laylie said slowly. "Just a few verses that Millie taught me. I...I don't think I can do it." *You'll be no sister of mine. That's what Luke said, Lord. He's all I got in this world!*

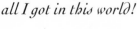 

"Can't do it?" Rachel said. "Hmmm. God gave me a Scripture for you just now, while you were talkin'. " The old woman set her bag down and took her Bible out and held it up to the light. "Either the light is failing or my eyes are."

"I'll read it for you," offered Laylie.

"That's right! You've been to school," Rachel said. "It's right here." She pointed.

" 'You are the salt of the earth,' " Laylie read. " 'But if the salt loses its saltiness, how can it be made salty again? It is no longer good for anything, except to be thrown out and trampled by men.' "

Horse hooves sounded on the road, and someone was whistling a tune.

"That's the carriage," said Rachel, taking her Bible back. "Don't lose your salt, girl. Luke needs to hear God's Word."

It was late the next afternoon when Rachel appeared again, carrying her black bag in one hand and a covered basket in the other.

"What's in there?" Little John asked.

"Biscuits," Rachel said, "and blackberry jam and sweet butter." She left the Merry Men eating while she bandaged Luke's feet. When she was finished, the Merry Men gathered around her expectantly.

"Have you ever heard the story," Rachel asked, "of two folks called Adam and Eve, who lived in a place called Eden?"

"Where's Eden?" Little John asked. "Is it in Africa?"

"I don't know for certain," Rachel said. "But it might have been. It surely might have been . . ."

Rachel stayed at the hideout that night long after the Merry Men had gone; she was waiting for her friends, the Blisses.

"They sent word they would be here," she said. "They're bringing a wagon. I thought I'd stay and say hello. I don't want you children to be frightened of them when they come. The Blisses are God's own people, but He does have some peculiar friends."

"What's peculiar about them?" Luke asked, but Rachel just shook her head.

"God made all different kinds of people," she said, "and the Blisses are about as different as they come. Everything about them is odd, but their hearts belong to the Lord. You can trust them." Rachel turned to Laylie. "Now, tell me about your swamp school. I've thought of that many times since the day we talked."

It took Laylie some time to describe Andros. From his three cherished books to his sacrificed hand, every story reminded her of another, and every one of them made Laylie smile.

"A man like that," Rachel said, "with a love of books and all that learnin' in his head, hidin' in a swamp." She shook her head. "This old world ain't right. It wasn't meant to be that way. Well, you were lucky to know him, child. He gave you the keys. All that's left for me to do is give you the treasure box." She held out her Bible.

"She can't have that," Luke said quickly. "If they catch her with a book—"

"If they catch her," Rachel said, "it's not going to cause any more trouble than she's already got."

"But . . ." Laylie said, taking the book, "don't you need it?"

"I expect Eugenia and me can share, for the time I got left."

"She can read to me while I make biscuits for your Merry Men," Rachel added.

"Rachel?" a deep voice called.

"He's here. Now don't be frightened," Rachel said, then more loudly, "Over here, Blessed!"

A man came walking through the trees, his black suit and tall hat part of the darkness itself, and his face long and pale in the starlight. He took off his hat and knelt beside Luke.

"Young man," he said, holding out a thin white hand, "how do you do? My name is Blessed Bliss."

Luke shook Mr. Bliss's hand.

"I'm Luke, and this here's my sister, Laylie," he said.

"Pleased to meet you, Luke," Mr. Bliss said in a voice that sounded like his best friend had just died. "I am the owner of Blessed Bliss's Funeral Parlor. Perhaps Rachel has conveyed to you my deep abhorrence of the peculiar institution we call slavery."

"She said you'd help us," Laylie said.

"Precisely so. In the wagon yonder," he pointed a long, bony finger, "is a coffin. I am going to put you in it, both of you. We will travel by wagon to my home in India Bay. There we will spend the night, and tomorrow you will be on your way, aboard a sailing ship. Are you willing to go with me?"

"Yes," Luke said.

"He can't walk, Blessed," Rachel said. "And you'll have to drop me at Ion too, or I'll have to dodge the patrollers, and I'm too old for that."

"Of course," Blessed Bliss said. He scooped Luke up and slung him over his shoulder. When they got to the wagon, he set Luke down and opened the coffin's lid.

"Now I want to assure you," he said as he helped Luke in, "that this is the first time this coffin has been used. Some people can be very sensitive about these things. I have fixed the lid so that it does not quite close. I don't think that you will suffocate."

Laylie crawled in beside Luke, Mr. Bliss closed the lid, and soon they were moving. After a while, the wagon stopped once and Laylie heard Rachel call good-bye, and then they were moving again.

"It ain't too bad," Luke said to Laylie. "It's like travelling in a bed. Don't breathe so hard. You're using up the air."

Laylie tried not to, but barely enough air seeped in for both of them. Time passed slowly. Then the wagon finally stopped and the coffin was lifted, carried, and set down again. The lid was opened, and Laylie gulped in fresh air.

"They didn't have enough air, Blessed. We're going to have to fix that," a woman said as she helped Laylie out.

"It will take some adjustment, of course," Mr. Bliss said. "Most of my clients don't need air."

"Miss Laylie, Mr. Luke," he went on, "may I present my wife, Mrs. Dearest Bliss?" Dearest was a round little woman dressed in black funeral clothes and a small black cap with a black net veil, and she had rings on every one of her plump, pink fingers.

"This is our dear friend, Colonel Peabody," Blessed said, pointing to a little man whose white mustachio was twisted into two curls. The Colonel bowed. Then Blessed gave the final introduction. "And this is my sister-in-law, Miz Opal."

Blissful Blessings

It was Miz Opal who had helped Laylie out of the coffin, and she looked as normal as any middle-aged woman could be.

"I have made arrangements for three to sail on the *Valiant*," Miz Opal said. "My home is in New York. I was planning on staying some weeks longer here with my sister, but clearly the Lord has other plans. The captain has been informed that the Colonel and I will be escorting my niece," she smiled at Laylie, "and the body of my dear sister-in-law."

"That's you!" the Colonel said, slapping Luke's shoulder. "The body! Many ship's captains read the papers, and they would be happy to return you for the reward. But I have devised a plan . . ."

"He read about it in a women's weekly," Dearest whispered loudly. "Smuggling mummies, you see."

The Colonel glared at her.

"That was the merest inspiration. I have refined the idea, addressed the details—"

"You will have to dress as a bereaved orphan," Dearest told Laylie. "Fortunately we have everything you will need. We hire children to play orphans now and then, if the dearly departed have no children of their own. An orphan's sobbing makes the funeral seem more homey, don't you think?"

Laylie backed up against Luke, clutching Rachel's Bible to her chest.

"Now, Dearest," Miz Opal said, "try not to be theatrical. You are frightening the child." All four of the strange people stopped talking and looked at Luke and Laylie, as if waiting for them to say something.

"Won't the folks around here think it's strange, you going off with a coffin and a dead relation that never came to visit in the first place?" Luke asked.

927

"We are the Blisses," Dearest said, waving her plump fingers. "Our neighbors are not surprised by anything we do."

Miz Opal served the children soup and bread while Blessed and the Colonel set to work on the coffin, drilling air holes in the bottom and attaching small wooden legs so that it rested two inches above the floor. The satin lining on the inside was snipped away to allow air to flow in. Four dime-sized holes were drilled in the lid, and an ornately lettered brass plate fitted over them in such a way that it could be lifted off.

"Now, step in," the Colonel said, "and let's see how it fits."

Luke stepped into the box, and Dearest started humming a funeral dirge.

The Colonel cleared his throat.

"Sorry," Dearest said.

Luke lay down, and Mr. Bliss lowered the lid and lifted off the brass plate.

"Can you hear me?" he asked.

"Yes," said Luke.

"And do you have enough air?" asked Mr. Bliss.

"I can feel it flowin' by," Luke said.

"Wonderful!" Mr. Bliss exclaimed.

Blessed opened the lid and helped him out, while the Colonel started filling bottles with water.

"You will need to have some in there with you," he said.

"What if someone opens the coffin?" Laylie asked.

"Oh, my poor deceased sister-in-law died from a terribly contagious disease," Blessed explained. "No one will dare open it."

"How long will I be in the box?" asked Luke.

"It takes eight days for a fast ship with fair weather to reach Philadelphia," the Colonel said. "It seems like a long time, but I can tell you of a time I was pinned down by a sandstorm in the Sahara for ten —"

"Perhaps later, Colonel," Miz Opal said. "We must get an early start tomorrow. Come along, dear."

Miz Opal showed Laylie to a room where a tub of warm water, a towel, and a night shirt waited for her.

"Your brother can take the second bath," she said. When Laylie was clean, she followed the woman to a tiny room that had a bed with real pillows and sheets.

After Miz Opal had gone, Laylie pulled the sheet up to her nose. "Thank You, King Jesus!" she prayed.

Millie had read to her about mighty cherubim and seraphim, and even angels with eyeballs all over their bodies. Laylie wouldn't have been surprised at all to wake up and find a whole crowd of them sitting in the Blisses' parlor, sipping tea with Dearest.

CHAPTER

A Whale Tale

*Let your conversation be always
full of grace, seasoned with salt,
so that you may know how to
answer everyone.*

COLOSSIANS 4:6

A Whale Tale

"If all goes according to plan," the Colonel said, as Laylie tucked another bottle of water into the lining of the coffin where it wouldn't spill or rattle, "Luke will be able to come out once a day, and we will be able to provide him with fresh water bottles and food. If it does not go well . . ." he handed Luke a hard salami, "save this, in case of emergency. There are three extra bottles of water as well. What have we forgotten?" He started pacing, twirling the ends of his mustache as he went.

"We haven't forgotten anything," Blessed said. "Not one thing." He had worked all night, fitting a hidden lock on the coffin lid so that grave robbers couldn't open it to steal the jewelry they hoped was inside.

"Your sister will be a member of the Catholic Church," Blessed said.

"Catholic's pray for their departed loved ones, you see," Dearest said, fluttering her rings. "That will be the little girl's excuse for visiting the coffin. We've sewn cunning little pockets in her skirt where she can carry your bottles of water and food!"

The Colonel stopped pacing suddenly. "Do you think we should include a paddle?"

"What for?" Luke asked.

"In case the ship sinks," the Colonel explained. "You could paddle your coffin like a canoe."

"If the ship sinks, we will simply have to trust in God," Miz Opal said calmly. "Are we ready, Blessed? We haven't much time."

Blessed nodded. "Time to get in, son."

Laylie's Daring Quest

Luke climbed into the coffin and lay down. Blessed reached in and straightened Luke's collar, brushing a wrinkle from his shirt.

"Rest in peace," he said. Suddenly a smile stretched his somber face out of shape. "And may everyone I tuck in have as good a chance of a joyful resurrection as you do, young man."

The coffin was loaded on a cart, and Laylie, dressed in orphan's black, walked beside it down to the sea. The docks were busy already as ships prepared to leave with the tide.

The Captain summoned four sailors to help carry the coffin up the gangplank. Laylie, her veil down and gloves on her hands, stood holding Miz Opal's hand as it was lowered into the hold.

"What did your sister-in-law die of?" the Captain asked as the coffin disappeared.

"Hydrophobia," the Colonel said. "She went frothing mad, growling and snapping at the last." Miz Opal gave him an alarmed look, but he went on. "We are watching the little girl carefully, I assure you, sir. The moment she starts to foam or bite —"

"Colonel!" Miz Opal said quickly, but the sailors were already backing away.

"Perhaps it would be best if you retired to your cabin," the Captain said.

"I believe it would," Miz Opal said, leading Laylie away. Their cabin was a small room with two bunks for sleeping. The Colonel's room was next door, and they shared a small sitting room with a table and chairs.

"I'm afraid you will have to wear the veil whenever you leave these rooms," Miz Opal said to Laylie when

they were safe behind the locked door. "Would you like to sew perhaps? I usually bring sewing to keep my hands busy."

"Thank you," Laylie said. "I think I will read for a while."

"Good," Miz Opal said. "I must go find the Colonel before he causes any more trouble. Hydrophobia indeed! The man is incorrigible."

Laylie locked the door behind her, then curled up on her cot and opened Rachel's Bible. She thumbed through the pages for a moment, then stopped to read.

"The word is near you; it is in your mouth and in your heart... If you confess with your mouth, 'Jesus is Lord,' and believe in your heart that God raised him from the dead, you will be saved."

Laylie sat up. *It's the verse Millie quoted to me when I gave my life to King Jesus!*

"For it is with your heart that you believe and are justified, and it is with your mouth that you confess and are saved."

"I'm tryin' to trust in You, Lord," Laylie said. "But if Luke don't get free from Satan's chains before we reach New York City, he's going back for sure. Luke always does what he says he'll do. He's gonna kill Borse."

"... faith comes from hearing the message, and the message is heard through the word of Christ."

That's just what Rachel said! The Word of God has power, no matter who is preaching it.

Laylie jumped at the sound of a knock. She put her veil down before she opened the door, but it was only Miz Opal and the Colonel.

"I thought my idea was inspired," the Colonel was saying as he came into the sitting room. "No one will come near the child now."

"But *frothing*, Colonel!" said Miz Opal.

Laylie's Daring Quest

Laylie staggered as the ship started to move. "Can we go check on Luke?" she asked.

"Not yet, dear," Miz Opal said. "Try not to worry. He is safe in the coffin for now."

"We have been asked to dine at the Captain's table tonight," the Colonel said. "I declined for you both, of course. But I will attend and arrange for you to go below."

"No more wild stories," Miz Opal said firmly.

"Of course not," said the Colonel, twisting the ends of his mustache. "At least, no more than absolutely necessary."

Miz Opal opened the basket the Colonel had carried in for her and produced a plate of cookies. "We have been in such a rush, we haven't had a chance to get properly acquainted," she said to Laylie.

"I'd love to hear of your journey thus far," the Colonel said.

Laylie put the first two cookies in her pocket for Luke, then ate the rest as she told them about Meadshead and Borse, Millie, and the great train escape.

"You escaped on the Phoenix? Fantastic!" the Colonel said, delighted. "I couldn't have planned it better myself."

"And your Aunt Tempie?" Miz Opal looked worried. "You have no idea whether she ever made it to New York City?"

Laylie shook her head.

"You certainly have courage, Laylie," Miz Opal said. "Coming all this way."

"JoMa called it salt," Laylie said.

Miz Opal laughed. "I see her point," she said with a smile. Miz Opal took a stack of brightly colored quilt squares from her sewing basket. "I'm starting a new quilt," she said. "Would you like to help?"

A Whale Tale

Laylie helped her with the colorful squares all day, while the Colonel told stories.

When a steward brought the ladies their evening meal, the Colonel excused himself and went to dine with the Captain.

Laylie and Miz Opal saved every scrap of food that wouldn't spoil for Luke, and ate the rest.

"The Captain was reluctant," the Colonel said when he returned. "I'm afraid . . ." he glanced at Miz Opal and winced. "I'm afraid I had to tell him that the child has a fragile mind, and we fear for her sanity if she is not allowed to visit the coffin to pray."

Miz Opal squeezed her eyes shut, but the Colonel was very pleased with himself.

"Starting tomorrow," he said, "he will allow Laylie to go down once a day and stay a suitable time for prayer, as long as I accompany her."

"The salt of the earth," Laylie whispered. "The salt of the earth." *I'm not gonna lose my saltiness just when Luke needs me. Just because he said I wouldn't be his sister anymore.* She had filled two empty water bottles to replace the water Luke had surely drunk. He had been in the coffin a day and a night already.

"Is she ready?" the Colonel asked, leaning his head through the doorway.

"Yes," Miz Opal said.

Laylie smoothed her skirts to make sure there were no telltale bulges where the food and water were hidden; then she lowered her veil and picked up her Bible.

The sailors watched them as they passed. One crossed himself, but most turned their eyes away.

Laylie's Daring Quest

"Carefully now!" the Colonel said when they reached the hatch. "This ladder wasn't made for ladies in skirts. I'll be right behind you with the lantern."

The morning was bright, but the inside of the hold of the ship was as dark as the belly of a beast. When the Colonel held up the lantern, Laylie could see the bare wood planks and the curved ribs of the hull. They creaked with the weight of the water outside.

The ship-beast had swallowed boxes, crates, and trunks, so many that there was hardly room to walk down the narrow aisle between them all. Cargo nets stretched over some of the belongings like thick spiderwebs, holding them in place.

Luke's coffin was mid-ship, wedged between one of Miz Opal's travel trunks and three barrels of molasses. Laylie kept watch on the ladder while the Colonel hung the lantern, then turned the key and opened the lid.

Luke scrambled out, but the Colonel put his finger to his lips and motioned toward the open hatch. Luke nodded. They could all hear the murmur of voices on the deck above. Luke stretched, then jogged in place while Laylie took his empty water bottles and replaced them with full ones.

Laylie was putting the last bottle in the coffin when she saw feet coming down the ladder. "Psst!" she said, quickly pulling down her veil. Luke ducked behind a box as the Colonel closed the coffin lid.

Laylie folded her hands and bowed her head.

" 'Even though I walk through the valley of the shadow of death,' " she recited, " 'I will fear no evil, for you are with me.' " The Colonel put his hand consolingly on her shoulder. Laylie peeked at the sailor through her lashes and her

veil. He was staring at them with frank curiosity. He picked up a small cask, carried it to the ladder, then started up. But when he had gone halfway, he craned his neck around for one last look, and his foot missed the rung. Both feet went off the ladder, and his chin connected with a thunk on the wooden rung as he went down. He cursed but did not drop the cask.

"Do you mind, sir!" the Colonel said sternly. "There is a young lady present!"

"Powlogize, ma'am," he said, "Ah bit maw towng." He climbed back up the ladder more carefully this time.

"You've got to get back in," the Colonel said quietly as soon as the sailor was gone. Luke grimaced, but he looked more cheerful when Laylie handed him the food.

"Courage, young man," the Colonel said. "Remember, you're on the road to freedom!" He closed the lid. Laylie climbed up on the coffin with her back to the hatch so she could lift her veil. *Courage, Laylie!* she said to herself as she took off the brass plate.

"Can you hear me?" she asked softly.

"Yes," Luke said.

"Do you want me to read to you?"

"You can do anything you want," Luke said, "so long as you don't go away."

Laylie opened the Bible confidently. *Luke's gotta hear the Word . . . he's got to listen.*

" 'The southernmost towns of the tribe of Judah in the Negev toward the boundary of Edom were: Kabzeel, Eder, Jagur, Kinah . . .' "

"What?" Luke said.

Laylie felt a tickle of panic. She flipped quickly through the pages. Psalm 116. She remembered Millie reading that

to her. " 'The cords of death entangled me,'" she tried again, " 'the anguish of the grave came upon me; I was overcome by trouble and sorrow. Then I called on the name of the LORD: 'O LORD, save me. . . .' "

"I know what you're doing," Luke said when she finished the psalm. "And I guess I'll listen."

Laylie almost melted with relief.

"But it ain't gonna do any good," Luke said. "I've been preached at before."

"Hey!" a voice called from the hatchway, "Cap'n says he wants you outta there now."

"We had best go quickly," the Colonel said. "We don't want to stretch the Captain's goodwill."

Laylie spent the rest of the day trying to figure out what to read next. She decided on the book of Luke. *If there was a book in the Bible named after me, I'd listen to it*, she thought.

The next morning they went down early. The night watch and day watch both ate breakfast at the same time, and the Colonel felt that it might give Luke a little more time out of his box while the sailors were eating.

"You might have half an hour," the Colonel said. "I do not think that the Captain gives his crew sufficient time for healthful chewing. A person should chew each bite one hundred times, at least."

They did have more time, and Luke spent it stretching, swinging his arms, doing pushups in the narrow aisle, and even chinning himself up on beams. When they heard voices above them, the Colonel motioned him back into the coffin. Luke groaned as he lay back down.

The Colonel settled himself on Miz Opal's trunk, and Laylie sat on the coffin with her back to the hatch again and started to read. She could hear sailors coming and

going behind her. Whenever one came down the ladder, the Colonel would tap the coffin with his boot toe to let Luke know to keep quiet.

Laylie tried to ignore the men and just focus on the words, but it was hard when they came close and stopped to listen.

"Nothing is as comforting as Scripture, eh?" the Colonel always said if a sailor lingered too long.

When Laylie and the Colonel were called up onto the deck, three sailors were standing close to the hatch. As Laylie started toward them, one backed away. His heel caught on a rope, and he fell backwards.

"Allow me," the Colonel said, extending a hand.

"No," the man scrambled back, still looking at Laylie. "No thanks. You just take her away."

By the third morning of reading Luke and the other Gospels, Laylie had grown so accustomed to the sailors' comings and goings that the sights and sounds of the hold had disappeared, replaced by the pictures that the words made in her mind. Judas, when he sold Jesus for silver, looked just like Robson, shifty and sly. And when they had stripped the Lord and beaten Him, Laylie could see His poor back—cut and bleeding just like Luke's had been—as they nailed Him to the post and raised Him up for everyone to see.

" 'Father,' " Laylie read, " 'Forgive them, for they do not know what they are doing.' "

"I don't want to hear no more," Luke said.

"There isn't time for more, anyway," said the Colonel, helping Laylie off the coffin. He fit the brass plate in place.

That night Laylie dreamed that she was standing by the side of Luke's coffin crying, with him dead inside instead of

just hiding. And then the dream changed, and it was Jesus crying, but it wasn't Luke in the coffin at all. It was Borse.

"Why would You cry for Borse, King Jesus?" Laylie asked in her dream.

"Because no one else will," Jesus said. *"Forgive him."*

"He killed my Mamma," Laylie whispered. "And he almost killed Luke."

"But if you do not forgive men their sins, your Father will not forgive your sins," Jesus replied.

Laylie came awake with the words still sounding in her head. The moon was peeking in the portal. "I want to be like You, Jesus," she prayed. "Help me forgive like You do."

"Laylie?" Luke said when he came out of the coffin the next morning. "I don't want no more stories like that. It's giving me dreams."

"What kind of dreams?" Laylie asked.

"The kind I don't want to have no more of, that's what kind," said Luke.

"Why not try the Old Testament," the Colonel said, when Luke was settled in once more. "There's a story about a ship and a whale." He turned the pages in Laylie's Bible to the Book of Jonah: " 'The word of the LORD came to Jonah son of Amittai. "Go to the great city of Nineveh and preach against it, because its wickedness has come up before me," ' " read the Colonel before handing the Bible back to Laylie.

Laylie read the story of the wicked city repenting before God and how He forgave them. One sailor came down to

listen. He was muttering to himself as he left, but Laylie kept right on reading. It wasn't a long story, and when she finished, something slammed against the inside of the coffin.

"I knew it!" Luke bellowed.

"Hush," Laylie said quickly. "What if somebody hears you?"

"I knew it!" Luke whispered. "I suppose you're forgivin' everybody now, too. You tell me this. Can you forgive Borse?"

"I . . . I couldn't have without Jesus' help," Laylie said. "He'll help you too, Luke, if you ask Him."

"I'm goin' back," Luke said. But Laylie noticed that this time he didn't sound angry. He sounded afraid.

There was a small group of sailors standing at the top of the ladder again when Laylie came out.

"Jonah," someone said. It was the sailor who had bitten his tongue.

"She's readin' it against us, that's what," another said. Laylie glanced at him in surprise. He had a black eye, bruised nose, and a very unhappy look on his face.

That afternoon, the Captain himself came to Miz Opal's little parlor. Laylie ducked into the sleeping room when he knocked, but she could hear every word.

"I'm very sorry, Madam," he said, "but the little girl will have to stay in your rooms. The men have voiced a complaint. It seems they are afraid of her."

CHAPTER

18

A Rendezvous

"In my distress I called to the
LORD, and he answered me.
From the depths of the grave
I called for help, and you
listened to my cry."

JONAH 2:2

A Rendezvous

ut why?" Miz Opal said. "She is just a small child!"

The Captain cleared his throat in embarrassment. "They think the child is a Jonah," he said.

"A Jonah?" Miz Opal sounded a little puzzled.

"Sailors call a person who brings bad luck to a ship a 'Jonah,'" the Colonel explained.

"There have been a series of unfortunate accidents," the Captain said, his voice almost apologetic. "Trips and falls, lines snapping in men's faces, and the like. They feel she is to blame."

"But that's ridiculous!" said Miz Opal.

"Nonetheless, she is confined to quarters. We are only two days out of port. It won't be too long."

"Two days!" Laylie said, when the Captain had gone. "Luke can't stay in that box for two days!"

"This all comes from not paying attention," the Colonel said. "I knew of the superstitions about the Book of Jonah. I should never have suggested you read it."

"This all comes," Miz Opal said firmly, "of telling ridiculous stories of hydrophobia and insanity to superstitious people!"

The Colonel sank into a chair, looking completely thunderstruck. "It *is* my fault," he said.

"I'm sorry for being harsh," Miz Opal said, seeing the look on his face. "You could not have anticipated this—and you did provide him with extra water, in case of an emergency."

"And a hard salami," the Colonel said, brightening. "I hope he remembers what I told him about chewing his food."

Laylie's Daring Quest

They arrived in Philadelphia on the morning of the second day that Laylie had been confined to the cabin. The coffin had already been lifted from the hold when the Captain allowed her on deck. Sailors stared as Laylie followed the coffin down the gangplank.

"Gone mad, poor little thing," one whispered, "but not frothing."

Laylie felt mad—mad with worry about Luke. Even the Colonel looked pale and nervous as he hired a cart and two men to carry the coffin.

"We're going to the home of a dear friend," Miz Opal whispered. "We'll have Luke out of there very soon."

Mr. Pearson, Miz Opal's friend, was an old Quaker man with twinkling blue eyes that turned first to the coffin, and then to Laylie. "You are welcome in my home, friends," he said.

The cart driver and his men helped haul the coffin inside and left it in the parlor. When the door was shut behind them, the Colonel leapt to the coffin, inserted the key, and turned it. Hinges creaked as he opened the lid. The smell made Miz Opal lift a hanky to her nose, but Luke was moving. He raised his arm up to keep the light from his eyes.

"I'm going back," he said, and Laylie's heart sank. She'd done her best, but it hadn't been good enough.

"Let me help you out," said the Colonel, offering Luke a hand.

"I'm not gettin' out until I'm ready," Luke said. Miz Opal and the Colonel exchanged worried glances. Laylie helped Luke sit up.

A Rendezvous

"God was talkin' to me," Luke said, "the whole time I was in the coffin. The first day in that box I saw Isaac standing in a field, looking right at me. And I heard a voice say, 'Stop draggin' your heels, Luke. Isaac needs your help.' I said I couldn't help Isaac, 'cause I had a something else to do . . . an evil thing." Luke shook his head and looked right at Laylie. "Then you read to me about Jesus coming for sinners . . . not for righteous men. And I dreamed that God said, 'Go back to the South and preach against it, because its wickedness has come up before me.' "

The old Quaker gentleman stepped forward and laid his hand on Luke's shoulder.

"We are all called to speak against evil, son," he said. "Come on out of there."

But Luke still shook his head.

"I thought I could thunder and shout against the evil of slavery. I thought I could, until you read about Jonah preaching to them Nin — Ninev — "

"Ninevites," said the Colonel.

Luke went on. "To them Ninevites. They turned from their sins and God forgave them. What if I preached and men like Borse repented? I told God he had the wrong man. I told him no soul on earth could forgive Borse, and he couldn't expect it."

Luke turned back to Laylie. "But you said you did, and when you said it, I knew Mamma had too, 'cause . . ." Luke paused and then sighed, " 'cause you sounded just like her." He burst into sobs and buried his face in his hands.

"I'm believing with my heart," Luke said, "and I'm confessing with my mouth, and I'm leaving my sins in this box when I get out. Won't somebody help me pray?"

Laylie's Daring Quest

With tears on her cheeks, Laylie put her arms around her brother as he gave his life to King Jesus. Then with the Colonel's help, Luke stepped out of the coffin at last. He was weak as water and smelled real bad, but his face was shining.

"It's Mamma's freedom, Luke!" Laylie said. "You finally made it to Mamma's freedom!"

The box where Luke had left his sins was buried, along with the clothes he'd worn, in the Quaker cemetery, and Laylie's orphan clothes were packed away, to be returned to Bliss's Funeral Parlor. Mr. Pearson's Quaker friends found them clothes for their journey, and carpetbags as well. Laylie borrowed a wash tub and scrubbed her travel dress and her brown apron clean. The Robin Hood cloak was hopelessly stained by mud and rain and salt water spray, but she cleaned it as best she could.

On the ship from Philadelphia to New York, Luke traveled as the Colonel's manservant, and they spent hours walking on the deck or talking in the larger parlor of the Colonel's room.

"You're sure the Lord is calling you back?" Miz Opal said one day when a summer rain kept them inside.

"I'm sure," Luke said. "I'm goin' back just as soon as I know Laylie is safe."

"You ain't leavin' me," Laylie said without looking up from her stitching. Her brown apron had proved to be just the color she needed for a doll's body.

Luke sighed. "What are you making?"

"A doll for Millie," Laylie said. "I'm going to send it to her to help her remember me."

"Don't worry," he said. "You're not only hard to forget, you're impossible to get rid of."

"In any campaign," the Colonel said, "it pays to have a plan, to train yourself for battle, as it were. I believe it was Saint Peter who said, 'Train yourself to be godly. For physical training is of some value, but godliness has value for all things, holding promise for both the present life and the life to come.'"

"That was the Apostle Paul," Miz Opal said, looking up from her own sewing, "writing to Timothy. But I believe the Colonel is giving you wise counsel. Paul also advised Timothy to choose leaders who had been given time to grow in the Lord, however much time that takes." She snipped a thread. "You need to be prepared, and you are both welcome to stay with me until you're ready, or until you have found your aunt. And even after, if you would like."

Laylie spread the Robin Hood cloak on the floor, searching for a patch that was not too stained. She finally decided on a section and started to cut.

"Laylie mentioned that your mother was a Christian," Miz Opal said. "I would love to know more about her."

"She took care of widows and orphans," Luke said. Laylie laid down her scissors to listen. "She helped anyone who needed help, and she preached God's Word to anyone who would listen. She didn't have a Bible. All she had was the Scriptures she knew before the man-stealers took her. She said that God helped her remember them." A look of wonder came over his face. "I remember one. I remember a Scripture she taught me when Laylie was a baby. 'Choose for yourselves this day whom you will serve. . . . But as for me and my household, we will serve the LORD.'"

"It's Joshua 24:15!" Miz Opal said.

Laylie's Daring Quest

Laylie found the verse in her Bible and helped Luke read the words one by one.

Laylie checked her reflection in the mirror — pink dress, carried all the way from Roselands, bonnet, button-up boots, and bows on the ends of her braids. Luke stood behind her, looking solemn and uncomfortable in his new suit.

"The coach is waiting," he said, picking up the two red roses he had clipped from Miz Opal's garden.

Miz Opal followed them down the steps to the street.

"You both look lovely," she said as they climbed into the coach. "Are you sure you don't want me to go with you?"

Luke shook his head and gripped the flowers more tightly as he settled in the seat.

It had taken the Colonel a month of inquiries to find Tempie Colbert. When he found her at last, it wasn't in the neatly kept tenement houses, or even the busy streets around Five Points. Laylie blinked back tears as the carriage stopped in front of the iron gates of Greenwood Cemetery. Aunt Tempie's grave was near the back wall. The small plot was almost lost amongst the broken and discarded pieces of marble dumped there, but it was neatly trimmed and someone had planted flowers around the headstone.

Laylie knelt and traced the words carved in the headstone: Tempie Colbert, 1799-1834, a servant of God.

"She was a Christian," Luke said. "Just like Mamma."

"She was a Colbert," Laylie said. "I guess it runs strong in this family."

"Aunt Tempie," Luke said, "Mamma told me she was sorry she couldn't keep the rendezvous. She wanted to real bad, but . . . there was things she had to do."

A Rendezvous

Luke's lips were pressed together, like he was trying to keep his sorrow from spilling out.

Laylie stood up and opened Rachel's Bible to the verse she had marked the night before. "Mamma, I know you're not here, but Luke said no one had ever read over your grave, so we're gonna do it now." Laylie had spent hours searching through the Bible for just the right words, and when she found them at last, they were on a page worn by Rachel's fingers and stained by Rachel's tears.

"We found your freedom, Mamma," Laylie said. "It's the kind Rachel had, and Isaac and Hettie, too. Freedom in Jesus." She swallowed the lump that rose in her throat, and started to read.

" 'I consider everything a loss compared to the surpassing greatness of knowing Christ Jesus my Lord, for whose sake I have lost all things,' " Her voice was a whisper at first, but it grew stronger as she read, as strong as Sarah's had been. " 'I consider them rubbish, that I may gain Christ and be found in him. I want to know Christ and the power of his resurrection and the fellowship of sharing in his sufferings, becoming like him in his death, and so, somehow, to attain to the resurrection from the dead.' "

Luke wasn't pressing his lips together anymore. Tears were spilling down his cheeks.

"I love you forever, Mamma," he said, and laid the second rose down.

"You remember when we were leaving Meadshead with the wagons?" Laylie asked, after Luke had wiped his eyes. "We passed slaves with chains on their necks being hurried along to market."

"I remember," Luke said.

"There was a mamma with a little-bitty baby. I asked God why He didn't send someone to help her, to break the

chains and set her free." Laylie shook her head. "Now I know that God *did* send someone to break the chains. He sent Jesus. And then God sent Mamma to tell people about Him. Now . . . He's sending us, ain't He?"

"I'm willing," Luke said. "Whenever He says go."

"God gave us freedom," Laylie said, "but freedom ain't worth a thing if you don't do something with it. That's what Andros told me."

Luke sucked in a great breath, like he was drawing in freedom itself—freedom, forgiveness, and the very love of God. "And do you know what you're gonna do with all of this freedom, little sister?" he laughed.

"Yes," Laylie said, slipping her hand into his. "I'm gonna change the world."

AFTERWORD

∾ How We Know What Slavery Was Like ∾

It is hard for anyone living in America today to imagine what life as a slave would have been like. Much of what we do know about slavery we have learned from the testimonies of men, women, and children who were held as slaves.

In the three decades preceding the Civil War, thousands of slave narratives—firsthand accounts of what it was like to live in slavery—were published by abolitionists (people who called for slavery to be stopped). The stories were so horrific that many people in the North did not believe that they were true. Pro-slavery writers in both the North and South wrote books and articles claiming that slaves were happy and content, and in a better situation than the free black people in the North. They created a mythical South in which docile slaves lived in harmony with kind, benevolent masters.

Runaway slaves and free blacks published books and papers of their own to refute the claims of the pro-slavery writers. They fought slavery with the spoken word, preaching from pulpits and speaking at town halls. When they were not allowed to enroll in law schools because of their race, they educated themselves in order to fight slavery in the courts of law.

Forty years after the Civil War, the picture of the kindly southern plantation owner was rising again in popular books, entertainment, and educational circles. But there were still many people who had lived under harsh and brutal slavery and could deny the claims. Black scholars such as Carter G. Woodson, who created the *Journal of Negro History*, started conducting detailed, careful research to document the reality of slave life.

Historians also realized that the last generation who had been born and lived as slaves was dying. Between 1920 and 1930 several small collections of ex-slave narratives were made. Finally, between 1936 and 1939, writers from The Federal Writer's Project were sent to interview ex-slaves. They collected 2,300 narratives. These accounts, along with one thousand non-narrative resources, such as newspaper advertisements of slave auctions, bills of sale, and state laws pertaining to slavery, were sent for permanent storage in the Library of Congress in 1941.

∾ THE CHRISTIAN HERITAGE OF AFRICAN-AMERICANS ∾

The continent of Africa was touched by the Gospel of Jesus Christ long ago. The New Testament of the Bible tells us that a disciple named Philip converted an Ethiopian eunuch, who was the treasurer of Candace, Queen of Ethiopia, to Christianity (Acts 8:26-40). Whether by this disciple's preaching or the witness of later missionaries, Christianity took root in Africa. Today, the oldest Christian church in the world is in Africa — the Coptic Christian Church in Egypt. The ancient kingdom of Aksum (in present-day Ethiopia) officially adopted Christianity in the fourth century. From Aksum, Christianity spread through much of North Africa. Early church leaders such as Origen (circa 185-254), Anthony (circa 250–355), and Augustine (circa 354-430) came from North Africa. However, Africa is a huge land mass, and Christianity did not reach the west coast of the continent for almost 1,500 years.

Afterword

∽ KINGDOM OF THE KONGO ∽

In 1484, Diego Cam, a Portuguese explorer, traveled down the coast of Africa. Diego Cam invited several Kongolese men to return to Portugal with him. The following year they returned to their own country, having learned Portuguese and something about Christianity. The Manikongo (ruler of the Kingdom of the Kongo) was intrigued by what they told him. He asked for Catholic missionaries to be sent to the Kingdom of the Kongo so that he could learn more about this religion. They arrived in 1491.

Many Kongolese accepted Christ, including the Manikongo's son Mbemba Nzinga, who became the next king. During his reign, Christianity spread throughout the kingdom.

Unfortunately, missionaries were not the only ones to come to Africa from Portugal. Slave traders came as well. Over the next 300 years, millions of people living along Africa's west coast, educated and uneducated alike, Christian, Muslim, and pagan, were "harvested" by brutal slave traders—some African and some European—and sold into slavery in the Americas and the Caribbean.

∽ CHRISTIANITY AND AFRICAN-AMERICANS ∽

In the 1700s, Christianity was at a low ebb in Europe and the Americas. In the northern colonies, the generations that followed the Pilgrims and the Puritans had not continued in the faith of their fathers. The spiritual condition of people in the southern colonies, which had been colonized with an eye toward profit rather than religious freedom, was no better. In both the North and the South, many people understood

Laylie's Daring Quest

Christianity as nothing more than being listed on the membership roll of a church. In this atmosphere, slavery flourished and grew.

However, starting in the 1730s and continuing for the next forty years, something new began to happen—first in England, Scotland, and Germany, but quickly jumping the ocean to the Americas. Preachers from many denominations, filled with the Holy Spirit, started calling people to repent and live in relationship with and accountability to God. Evangelists such as Gilbert Tennent, Jonathan Edwards, and George Whitefield preached that all people, black and white, were equally sinful and in need of Jesus to save them. In fact, all men were slaves—slaves to sin until they were "born again" by the Spirit of God. The First Great Awakening had begun, and the seeds that would eventually put an end to slavery were sown.

Although the early white evangelists did not directly attack the institution of slavery, they did call slave owners into account for their behavior. In 1740, George Whitefield (though he was a slave owner himself) published a pamphlet warning slave holders that "God has a quarrel with you" for treating slaves "as bad or worse than brutes." He said, "If slaves got the upper hand . . . the judgment would be just!"

Phrases such as "If slaves got the upper hand . . . the judgment would be just" sent chills down the spines of slave owners. They were far outnumbered by their slaves, which they considered "human chattel," and depended on the slaves' ignorance and the overseers' brutality to keep their slaves in line. Christians condemned brutality and started schools where African-Americans could learn to read Scripture.

Afterword

Many years later, Frederick Douglass, a slave who had escaped to freedom in 1838, described in his book *The Life and Times of Frederick Douglass* the common attitude of masters toward slaves who were learning to read. He asked his young mistress, who had never owned slaves, to teach him to read the Bible.

"My mistress seemed almost as proud of my progress as if I had been her own child, and supposing that her husband would be as well pleased, she made no secret of what she was doing for me."

Instead of being pleased, her husband told her to stop at once, as it was dangerous to teach a slave to read. He said, "For if you give a [slave] an inch he will take an ell. Learning will spoil the best [slave] in the world. If he learns to read the Bible it will forever unfit him to be a slave. He should know nothing but the will of his master, and learn to obey it. As to himself, learning will do him no good, but a great deal of harm, making him disconsolate and unhappy. If you teach him how to read, he'll want to know how to write, and this accomplished, he'll be running away with himself."

Douglass's mistress did stop teaching him, but he learned something of great importance from her husband's speech: "Knowledge unfits a child to be a slave." So Douglass set about teaching himself to read and then to write, and did in fact "run away with himself," becoming a respected Christian scholar, writer, and speaker in the fight against slavery.

∞ THE FIRE OF REVIVAL ∞

From the very dawn of the First Great Awakening on the American continent, God raised up African-American evangelists, both men and women. Some could read and write, but many could not. We know of them mainly through the writings and journals of people such as Edmund Botsford, a white Baptist minister in South Carolina, who in 1790 wrote about black missionaries going to the plantations to preach to the slaves.

Slaves were not the only ones catching the fire of revival. Some slave owners embraced Christ and encouraged their slaves to do so as well. Some even freed their slaves. However, more slave owners responded to this threat to their way of life with hostility. They were afraid that if the slaves were allowed to have their own preachers and read the Bible for themselves, they, the white owners, would lose control of them. This would mean the loss of their livelihood, as well as the money that had been paid for the slaves themselves.

Some plantation owners, unwilling to free their slaves yet wanting to appear godly, paid white preachers to present a watered-down religion to the slaves. In *Voices from Slavery — 100 Authentic Slave Narratives*, Lucretia Alexander describes this practice: "The [slaves] didn't go to the church building. The [white] preacher came to preach to them in their quarters. He'd just say, 'Serve your masters. Don't steal your master's turkey. Don't steal your master's chicken. Don't steal your master's hogs. Don't steal your master's meat. Do whatsoever your master tell you to do.' Same old thing, all the time. My father would have church in dwelling houses, and they had to whisper... that would be when they wanted a real meetin' with some real preachin'.... They used to sing their songs in a whisper and pray in a whisper. There was a prayer meeting house to house once or twice — once or twice a week."

Afterword

Some Christian slaves were not only denied the right to attend church, they were beaten and even killed for refusing to stop preaching the Good News of Christ. But persecution could not stop the black evangelists. John Thompson, who was a slave in Maryland during the early 1800s, wrote that as soon as news of a new spiritual birth ". . . got among the slaves, it spread from plantation to plantation, until it reached ours, where there were but few who did not experience religion." (*Slave Religion: "The Invisible Institution" in the Antebellum South* by Albert J. Raboteau, New York: Oxford University Press, 1978.)

By 1822 slave owners had greatly increased their persecution of black Christians, passing laws against separate assemblies of blacks, against black literacy, and even against blacks being evangelists and preachers. In 1831 North Carolina passed an ordinance forbidding either slaves or free blacks from acting "in any manner to officiate as a preacher or teacher in any prayer meeting." By 1855 events such as the arrest of Daniel Payne—a black preacher who had traveled to St. Louis, Missouri—for the crime of entering the state "to preach the gospel" had become common.

Christian slaves were forced to meet in secret, much like the persecuted early church. They met together to worship and praise in "hush arbors" in the woods, and in slave cabins. The forms of praise and worship practiced by these African-Americans at their secret church meetings—the use of drums and dancing, oral traditions of memorization and storytelling—were deeply rooted in their African cultures and traditions. They seemed odd to those of a more sedate European tradition. There were, however, some instances when the prayer and preaching of slaves brought their masters into the Kingdom of God.

From these meetings a special kind of worship song emerged—the spiritual. Many spirituals spoke of God's love for His people and their love for Him. Some spirituals, like "Steal Away to Jesus," could have double meanings—people might be called to literally run away to secret worship meetings in the woods, or it could be a call to steal away North to freedom. Still others were songs of protest.

∾ THE UNDERGROUND RAILROAD ∾

Today, we refer to the routes that the fugitive slaves took to freedom as the "Underground Railroad." Although the name conjures up pictures of an efficient organization with many people all working together to move passengers, the "Underground Railroad" is only a symbolic term. People of faith and strong conviction—Quakers, Methodists, and Baptists, black and white abolitionists, African-American slaves, and American Indians—helped runaway slaves escape, often risking their own lives to gain freedom for others. In some areas these abolitionists were organized, but in other areas they were not. News of houses or farms where a slave could find help spread among the slaves by word of mouth, but only a few ever found help escaping in this way.

The 1998 Underground Railroad Theme Study published by the National Park Service estimates that about 100,000 persons successfully escaped slavery between 1790 and 1860. In 1860 there were 4 million people living in slavery. The writers of the National Park service report estimated that in that year only 1,500 people made it to freedom along the Underground Railroad. There is no record of how many

Afterword

slaves tried to escape but were captured, dragged back and whipped, or even killed in the attempt.

∾ THE END OF SLAVERY IN THE UNITED STATES ∾

On April 12, 1861, nearly a hundred years after the seeds of freedom were planted in the Great Awakening, the American Civil War began. Almost two years later, on January 1, 1863, President Abraham Lincoln issued the Emancipation Proclamation, freeing the slaves.

Finally, on December 18, 1865, Congress ratified the 13th Amendment to the Constitution, abolishing slavery in the United States.

A LIFE OF FAITH®

Girls Club

An Imaginative New Approach to Faith Education

*I*magine…an easy way to gather the young girls in your community for fun, fellowship, and faith-inspiring lessons that will further their personal relationship with our Lord, Jesus Christ. Now you can, simply by hosting an A Life of Faith Girls Club.

This popular Girls Club was created to teach girls to live a *lifestyle* of faith.

Through the captivating, Christ-centered, historical fiction stories of Elsie Dinsmore, Millie Keith, Violet Travilla, and Laylie Colbert, each Club member will come to understand God's love for her, and will learn how to deal with timeless issues all girls face, such as bearing rejection, resisting temptation, overcoming fear, forgiving when it hurts, standing up for what's right, etc. The fun-filled Club meetings include skits and dramas, application-oriented discussion, themed crafts and snacks, fellowship and prayer. What's more, the Club has everything from official membership cards to a Club Motto and original Theme Song!

For more info about our Girls Clubs, call or log on to:
www.alifeoffaith.com • **1-800-840-2641**

— ABOUT THE AUTHOR —

$\mathcal{M}$artha Finley was born on April 26, 1828, in Chillicothe, Ohio. Her mother died when Martha was quite young, and James Finley, her father, soon remarried. Martha's stepmother, Mary Finley, was a kind and caring woman who always nurtured Martha's desire to learn and supported her ambition to become a writer.

James Finley, a doctor and devout Christian, moved his family to South Bend, Indiana in the mid-1830s. It was a large family: Martha had three older sisters and a younger brother who were eventually joined by two half-sisters and a half-brother. The Finley's were of Scotch-Irish heritage, with deep roots in the Presbyterian Church. Martha's grandfather, Samuel Finley, served in the Revolutionary War and the War of 1812 and was a personal friend of President George Washington. A great-uncle, also named Samuel Finley, had served as president of Princeton Theological Seminary in New Jersey.

Martha was well educated for a girl of her times and spent a year at a boarding school in Philadelphia. After her father's death in 1851, she began her teaching career in Indiana. She later lived with an elder sister in New York City, where Martha continued teaching and began writing stories for Sunday school children. She then joined her widowed stepmother in Philadelphia, where her early stories were first published by the Presbyterian Publication Board. She lived and taught for two years at a private academy in Phoenixville, Pennsylvania—until the school was closed in 1860, just before the outbreak of the War Between the States.

Determined to become a full-time writer, Martha returned to Philadelphia. Even though she sold several stories (some written under the pen name of "Martha Farquharson"), her first efforts at novel-writing were not successful. But during a period

967

of recuperation from a fall, she crafted the basics of a book that would make her one of the country's best known and most beloved novelists.

Three years after Martha began writing Elsie Dinsmore, the story of the lonely little Southern girl was accepted by the New York firm of Dodd Mead. The publishers divided the original manuscript into two complete books; they also honored Martha's request that pansies (flowers, Martha explained, that symbolized "thoughts of you") be printed on the books' covers. Released in 1868, Elsie Dinsmore became the publisher's bestselling book that year, launching a series that sold millions of copies at home and abroad. The Elsie stories eventually expanded to twenty-eight volumes and included the lives of Elsie's children and grandchildren.

The stories of Mildred Keith, Elsie's second cousin, were released as a follow-up to the Elsie books. The Mildred books are considered to be partly autobiographical. Like the fictional Mildred, Martha's family moved to Indiana in the mid-1830s in hopes of a brighter future on the expanding western frontier. Also like Millie, Martha was one of eight children. Her experiences surely provided the setting and likely many of the characters for her Mildred Keith books. In a foreword to one of the books, Miss Finley specifically mentions that the Keith family's journey to Indiana and the sickly season that they faced there, were events from her own childhood.

Miss Finley published her final Elsie novel in 1905. Four years later, she died less than three months before her eighty-second birthday. She is buried in Elkton, Maryland, where she lived for more than thirty years in the house she built with proceeds from her writing career. Her large estate, carefully managed by her youngest brother, Charles, was left to family members and charities.

Martha Finley never married, never had children of her own, but she was a remarkable woman who lived a quiet life of creativity and Christian charity. She died at age 81, having written many novels, stories, and books for children and adults. Her life on earth ended in 1909, but her legacy lives on in the wonderful stories of faith and family that are at the heart of all her work.

— ABOUT THE AUTHOR —

*K*ersten Hamilton was born in High Rolls, New Mexico, in 1958. By her sixth birthday, she knew what she wanted to be when she grew up — a writer. She had a very exciting childhood, which included tracking caribou and arctic wolves across her family's homestead in Alaska, catching tiny tree frogs in the swamps and rain forests of the Pacific Northwest, and chasing dust devils and rattlesnakes across the high desert of New Mexico. All of her many adventures fueled her creative imagination and story-telling ability.

Before she settled down to have children, Kersten worked as a ranch hand, a wood cutter, a lumberjack, a census taker, a wrangler for wilderness guides, and an archeological surveyor. When her children grew up and went off on their own adventures, she began writing full time.

A prolific children's writer, Kersten is known for her fast-paced, dramatic storylines. She is the author of 24 books for children and middle-graders, numerous Christian school curriculum, audio tapes and musicals, and more than 40 periodical publications. She has been a Sunday school teacher and youth leader for many years, and works with the house church movement in her home town of Albuquerque, New Mexico.

In 1999 Mission City Press employed Kersten to write a series of novels based on characters created by Martha Finley, resulting in the *A Life of Faith: Millie Keith* Series, which has captured the hearts of today's readers. Kersten created many memorable secondary characters in the Millie Keith series, including a slave girl named Laylie Colbert. Kersten's development of the Laylie character was so compelling that Mission City Press commissioned Kersten to develop a stand-alone, special edition novel about her life — *Laylie's Daring Quest.*

Kersten's unique and exciting literary contributions continue the legacy of life-changing Christian storytelling that Mission City Press is proud to present.